Domestic Annals of Scotland

Vol. I

Anatiposi

Robert Chambers

Domestic Annals of Scotland

Vol. I

Reprint of the original, first published in 1859.

1st Edition 2023 | ISBN: 978-3-38230-714-1

Anatiposi Verlag is an imprint of Outlook Verlagsgesellschaft mbH.

Verlag (Publisher): Outlook Verlag GmbH, Zeilweg 44, 60439 Frankfurt, Deutschland
Vertretungsberechtigt (Authorized to represent): E. Roepke, Zeilweg 44, 60439 Frankfurt, Deutschland
Druck (Print): Books on Demand GmbH, In de Tarpen 42, 22848 Norderstedt, Deutschland

DOMESTIC

ANNALS OF SCOTLAND.

DOMESTIC
ANNALS OF SCOTLAND

From the Reformation to the Revolution.

By ROBERT CHAMBERS,
F.R.S.E., F.S.A.Sc., &c.

SECOND EDITION.

VOLUME I.

Bannatyne House, Strathmore.

W. & R. CHAMBERS, EDINBURGH AND LONDON.

MDCCCLIX.

PREFACE TO THE FIRST EDITION.

It has occurred to me that a chronicle of domestic matters in Scotland from the Reformation downwards—the period during which we see a progress towards the present state of things in our country—would be an interesting and instructive book. History has in a great measure confined itself to political transactions and personages, and usually says little of the people, their daily concerns, and the external accidents which immediately affect their comfort. This I have always thought was much to be regretted, and a general tendency to the same view has been manifested of late years. I have therefore resolved to make an effort, in regard to my own country, to detail her DOMESTIC ANNALS—the series of occurrences beneath the region of history, the effects of passion, superstition, and ignorance in the people, the extraordinary natural events which disturbed their tranquillity, the calamities which affected their wellbeing, the traits of false political economy by which that wellbeing was checked, and generally those things which enable us to see how our forefathers thought, felt, and suffered, and how, on the whole, ordinary life looked in their days.

Nor are these details, broken up and disjointed as they often are, without a useful bearing on certain generalisations of importance, or devoid of instruction for our own comparatively enlightened age. A good end is obviously served by enumerating, for example, all the famines and all the pestilences that have beset the country; for when this is done, it becomes evident that famine and pestilence have been connected in the way of cause and effect. For the astronomer, the meteorologist, and the naturalist, many of the accounts of comets, meteors, and extraordinary natural productions here given, must have some value.[1] To the political economist, it may be of service to see the accounts here drawn from contemporary records of the productiveness and failure of many seasons, and of the varying proportions of

[1] 'A man of science as well as of philosophic mind would employ himself well in examining those accounts of prodigies in the early annalists and chroniclers, which of late years have been regarded as only worthy of contempt.'—SOUTHEY—*Omniana*, i. 266.

bad seasons to good throughout considerable spaces of time. As for the numberless narratives and anecdotes illustrative of the mistaken zeal, the irregular passions, the deplorable superstitions, and erroneous ideas and ways in general, of our ancestors, they furnish beyond doubt a rich pabulum for the student of human nature; nor may they be without some practical utility amongst us, since many of the same errors continue in a reduced style to exist, and it may help to extinguish them all the sooner, that we are enabled here to look upon them in their most exaggerated and startling form, and as essentially the products and accompaniments of ignorance and barbarism.

It will probably be matter of regret that this work consists of a series of articles generally brief and but little connected with each other, producing on the whole a desultory effect. Might not the materials have been fused into one continuous narration? I am very sensible how desirable this was for literary effect; but I am at the same time assured that, in such a mode of presenting the series of occurrences, there would have been a constant temptation to generalise on narrow and insufficient grounds—to make singular and exceptional incidents pass as characteristic beyond the just degree in which they really are so—namely, as matters just possible in the course of the national life of the period to which they refer. It seemed to me the most honest plan, to present them detachedly under their respective dates, thus allowing each to tell its own story, and have its own proper weight with the reader, and no more, in completing the general picture.

As one means of conveying 'the body of each age, its form and pressure,' the language of the original contemporary narrators is given, wherever it was sufficiently intelligible and concise. Thus each age in a manner tells its own story. It has not been deemed necessary, however, to retain antiquated modes of orthography, beyond what is required to indicate the old pronunciation, nor have I scrupled occasionally to omit useless clauses of sentences, when that seemed conducive to making the narration more readable. This procedure will not be quite approved of by the rigid antiquary; but it will be for the benefit of the bulk of ordinary readers.

In general, the events of political history are presented here in only a brief narrative, such as seemed necessary for connection. But I have introduced a few notices of these events where there was a contemporary narration either characteristic in its style, or involving particulars which might be deemed illustrative of the general feeling of the time.

EDINBURGH, *January* 25, 1858.

CONTENTS OF VOL. I.

Illustrations.

VOL. I.

INDEX

TO SUCH

BOOKS AND AUTHORITIES AS, FROM THEIR MORE FREQUENT OCCURRENCE, ARE QUOTED IN AN ABRIDGED FORM.

D. O.—Diurnal of Remarkable Occurrents in Scotland, 1513–1575. (Maitland Club.) 4to. 1833

Cal.—History of the Kirk of Scotland. By Mr David Calderwood. (Wodrow Society.) 8 vols. 1842

Pit.—Criminal Trials in Scotland, from 1488 to 1624, with Historical Notes and Illustrations. By Robert Pitcairn, Esq. 3 vols. 4to. Edin. 1833

Knox.—History of the Reformation in Scotland. By John Knox. From MS. Edited by David Laing. 2 vols. (Wodrow Society.) Edin. 1846

C. F.—Chronicle of Fortingall [a composition of the sixteenth century, preserved in the charter-chest of the Marquis of Breadalbane, and printed in the same volume with the Black Book of Taymouth, Edinburgh, 4to. 1855]

P. C. R.—Privy Council Record, MS. in General Register House, Edinburgh.

Mar.—Annales of Scotland from the year 1513 to the year 1591. By George Marioreybanks, burges of Edinburghe. From MS. 8vo. 1814

Bir.—Diary of Robert Birrel, burges of Edinburghe, from 1532 to 1605. Dalyell's Fragments of Scottish History. From MS. 4to. Edin. 1798

E. C. R.—Edinburgh Council Record, MS. in Council Chamber, Edinburgh.

H. K. J.—Historie of King James the Sext. 4to. Edin. 1825

C. C. R.—Canongate Council Record [extracts printed in Maitland Club Miscellany, vol. ii.]

Ban.—Journal of the Transactions in Scotland, 1570, 1571, 1572, 1573. By Richard Bannatyne, Secretary to John Knox. From MS. 8vo. Edin. 1806

Ken.—Historical Account of the Name of Kennedy. From MS. With Notes by Robert Pitcairn. 4to. 1830

Ja. Mel.—Autobiography and Diary of Mr James Melville, 1556–1610. From MS. Edited by Robert Pitcairn. (Wodrow Society.) 8vo. 1842

Bal.—Annales of Scotland, 1057–1603. By Sir James Balfour. From MS. 4 vols. 8vo. Edin. 1824

Spot.—History of the Church of Scotland. By the Right Rev. John Spottiswoode, Archbishop of St Andrews. 3 vols. 8vo. 1847

Howes.—Chronicle of England. By Edmond Howes. Fol. 1615

H. of G.—History of the House of Douglas. By Mr David Hume of Godscroft. 2 vols. 1748

Jo. R. B. Hist.—Historia Rerum Britannicarum, &c. Auctore Roberto Johnstono. Fol. Amstel. 1655

R. G. K. E.—Register of the General Kirk of Edinburgh, 1574–1575. Maitland Club Miscellany, vol. i.

B. U. K.—Booke of the Universall Kirk of Scotland. (Bannatyne Club.) 3 vols. 4to. Edin. 1839–40

Chr. Aber.—Chronicle of Aberdeen, 1491–1595. (Spalding Club Miscellany.)

Hist. Acc. Fam. Innes.—Historicall Account of the Origine and Succession of the Family of Innes, &c. From orig. MS. Edin. 1820

M. of S.—*Mem. Som.*—The Memorie of the Somervilles, &c. 2 vols. 8vo. 1815

Moy.—Memoirs of the Affairs of Scotland, 1577–1603. By David Moysie. From MS. (Maitland Club.) 4to. 1830

Moy. R.—Idem, Ruddiman's edition. 12mo. 1755

Ab. C. R.—Extracts from the Council Register of the Burgh of Aberdeen, 1570–1625. (Spalding Club.) 1848

Row.—Row's History of the Kirk of Scotland. (Wodrow Society.) 1842

Pa. And.—History of Scotland. By Patrick Anderson. MS. Advocates' Library.

M. of G.—Memorabilia of the City of Glasgow, selected from the Minute-books of the Burgh. Glasgow, printed for private circulation. 1835

C. K. Sc.—Chronicle of the Kings of Scotland. From MS. (Maitland Club.) 1830

Jo. Hist.—Johnston's History of Scotland. MS. Advocates' Library.

Chron. Perth.—The Chronicle of Perth, &c., from 1210 to 1668. (Maitland Club.) 4to. Edin. 1831

G. H. S.—Genealogical History of the Earldom of Sutherland. By Sir Robert Gordon, Bart. Fol. Edin. 1813

Stag. State.—The Staggering State of Scots Statesmen from 1550 to 1650. By Sir John Scot of Scotstarvet. From MS. 12mo. Edin. 1754

S. A.—Acts of Parliament made by King James I., and his Royal Successors. 3 vols. 1682

Acts of the Parliament of Scotland. 11 vols. fol.

P. K. S. R.—Perth Kirk-Session Records. Spottiswoode Club Miscellany.

A. K. S. R.—Aberdeen Kirk-Session Records. (Spalding Club.) Aber. 1846

A. P. R.—Aberdeen Presbytery Records. (Spalding Club.) Aber. 1846

M. S. P.—State Papers, &c., of Thomas Earl of Melrose. (Abbotsford Club.) 2 vols. 4to. Edin. 1837

An. Scot.—Analecta Scotica: Collections illustrative of the Civil, Ecclesiastical, and Literary History of Scotland. Edited by James Maidment. 2 vols. Edin. 1834–38

R. P. L.—Selections from the Registers of the Presbytery of Lanark, 1623–1709. 4to. Edin. 1839

Foun. Hist. Ob.—Historical Observes, &c. By Sir John Lauder of Fountainhall. 4to. Edin. 1840

Foun. Dec.—Fountainhall's Decisions of the Court of Session. 2 vols. fol. Edin. 1759

Fount.—Historical Notices of Scottish Affairs, from the MSS. of Sir John Lauder of Fountainhall. 2 vols. 4to. Edin. 1848

W. A.—Analecta, or Materials for a History of Remarkable Providences, &c. By the Rev. Robert Wodrow. 4 vols. (Maitland Club.) Edin. 1842

Stev. Hist. C. of Scot.—History of the Church of Scotland. By Andrew Stevenson, writer in Edinburgh. 2d ed. Edin. 1844

B. A.—Book of Adjournal. MS. Advocates' Library.

Gillies.—Historical Collections relating to Remarkable Periods of the Success of the Gospel, &c. By John Gillies. 2 vols. Glas. 1754

Spal.—Memorials of the Troubles in Scotland and England, A.D. 1624–A.D. 1645. By John Spalding. 2 vols. 4to. (Spalding Club.) Aber. 1850

Ab. Re.—A Little yet True Rehearsal of Several Passages of Affairs that did occur from the year 1633 till this present year 1655. Collected by a friend of Dr Alexander's at Aberdeen. Sir Lewis Stewart's Collections. MS. Advocates' Library.

Pa. Gordon.—A Short Abridgment of Britanes Distemper, from the year of God 1639 to 1649. By Patrick Gordon of Ruthven. (Spalding Club.) 1844

Carlyle.—Oliver Cromwell's Letters and Speeches, with Elucidations by Thomas Carlyle. 2 vols. 1845

Lam.—Diary of Mr John Lamont of Newton, 1649–1671. Edin. 1830

C. P. H.—Collections by a Private Hand at Edinburgh, 1650–1661. Stevenson, Edin. 1832

Nic.—Diary of Public Transactions and other Occurrences, chiefly in Scotland. By John Nicoll. 4to. Edin. 1836

R. C. E.—Register of the Committee of Estates. MS. General Register House, Edinburgh.

Spreull.—Some Remarkable Passages of the Lord's Providence towards Mr John Spreull, Town-clerk of Glasgow, 1635–1664. Stevenson, Edin. 1832

Law.—Memorials; or Memorable Things, &c., from 1638 to 1684. By the Rev. Robert Law. From MS. Edin. 1818

Bail.—Letters and Journals of Robert Baillie, A.M., Principal of the University of Glasgow. From MS. 3 vols. Edin. 1841

Kir.—Secret and True History of the Church of Scotland, from the Restoration to the year 1678. By the Rev. James Kirkton. 4to. Edin. 1817

Pat. Walker.—Biographia Presbyteriana. [Lives of Alexander Peden, &c., by Patrick Walker.] 2 vols. Edin. 1827

Edinburgh Castle, *restored* as in 1573.

DOMESTIC

ANNALS OF SCOTLAND.

INTRODUCTORY.

Our attention lights, a few years after the middle of the sixteenth century, on a little independent kingdom in the northern part of the British island—a tract of country now thought romantic and beautiful, then hard-favoured and sterile, chiefly mountainous, penetrated by deep inlets of the sea, and suffering under a climate not so objectionable on account of cold as humidity. It contains a scattered population of probably seven hundred thousand:—the Scots—thought to be a very ancient nation, descended from a daughter of Pharaoh, king of Egypt, and living under a monarchy believed to have originated about the time that Alexander conquered India. A very poor, rude country it is, as it well might be in that age, and seeing that it lay so far to the north and so much out of the highway of civilisation. No well-formed roads in it—no posts for letters or for travelling. A printing-press in the head town, Edinburgh, but not another anywhere. A regular localised court of law had not yet existed in it thirty years. No stated means of education, excepting a few grammar-schools in the principal towns, and three small universities. Society consisted mainly of a large agricultural class, half enslaved to the lords of the soil: above all, obliged to follow them in war. Other industrial pursuits to be found only in the burghs, the chief of which were Edinburgh, Glasgow, Stirling, Perth, Dundee, and Aberdeen.

In reality, though it was not known then, the bulk of the people of Scotland were a branch of the great Teutonic race which possesses Germany and some other countries in the north-west of Europe. Precisely the same people they were with the bulk of the English, and speaking essentially the same language, though for ages they had been almost incessantly at war with that richer and more advanced community. As England, however, was neighboured by Wales, with a Celtic people, so did Scotland contain in its northern and more mountainous districts a Celtic people also, rude, poor, proud, and of fiery temper, but brave and possessed of virtues of their own, somewhat like the Circassians of our own day. These Highland clansmen—whom the English of that time contemptuously called *Redshanks,* with reference to their naked hirsute limbs—were the relics of a greater nation, who once occupied all Scotland, and of whose blood some portion was mingled with that of the Scots of the Lowlands, producing a certain fervour of character—'*perfervidum ingenium Scotorum*'—which is not found in purely Teutonic natures. The monarchy had originated with them early in the sixth century of the Christian era, and had gradually absorbed the rest of Scotland, even while its original subjects were hemmed more and more within the hilly north. But, by the marriages of female heirs, this thorn-encircled crown had come, in the fourteenth century, into a family of Norman-English extraction, bearing the name of Stuart.

The present monarch was 'our Sovereign Lady Mary,' a young and beautiful woman, married to Francis II. of France. She had been carried thither in a troublous time during her childhood, and in her absence, a regent's sceptre was swayed by her mother, a princess of the House of Guise. Up to that time, Scotland, like most of the rest of Europe, was observant of the Catholic religion, and under vows of obedience to the pope of Rome. But the reforming ideas of Luther and Melancthon, of Zuinglius and Calvin, at length came to it, and surprising were the effects thereof. As by some magical evolution, the great mass of the people instantaneously threw off all regard to the authority of the pope, with all their old habits of worship, professing instead a reverence for the simple letter of Scripture, as interpreted to them by the reforming preachers. Indignant at having been so long blinded by the Catholic priesthood—whose sloth and luxury likewise disgusted them—they attacked the churches and monasteries, destroyed the altars and images—did not altogether spare even the buildings, alleging that rooks were best banished by pulling down their nests: in short, made a very complete practical reformation through all the more important provinces. This was done by the populace, with the countenance and help of a party of the nobility and gentry; and the regent, Mary de Guise, who was firm in the old faith, in vain strove to stem the torrent. Obtaining troops from France, she did indeed maintain for a time a resistance to the reforming lords and their adherents. But they, again, were supported by some troops from Elizabeth of England, whose interest it was to protestantise Scotland; and so the Reformation got the ascendency. Mary the Regent sunk into the grave, just about the time that her faith came to its final and decisive ruin within her daughter's dominions.

This change may be considered as having been completed in August 1560, when an irregular parliament, or assembly of the Estates of the kingdom, abolished the jurisdiction of the pope, proscribed the mass under the severest penalties, and approved of a Confession of Faith resembling the articles which had been established in England by Edward VI. The chief feature of the new system was, that each parish should have its own pastor, elected by the people, or at least a reader to read the Scriptures and common prayers. While thus essentially presbyterian, there was a trace of episcopal arrangements in the appointment of ten *superintendents* (one of whom, however, was a layman), whose duty it should be to go about and see that the ordinary clergy did their duty. The great bulk of the possessions and revenues of the old church fell into the hands of the nobles, or remained with nominal bishops, abbots, and other dignitaries, who continued formally to occupy their ancient places in parliament, while the presbyterian clergy were insufficient in number, and in general very poorly supported.

'Lo here,' then, 'a nation born in one day; yea, moulded into one congregation, and sealed as a fountain with a solemn oath and covenant!' So exclaims a clerical writer a hundred years later; and we, who live two hundred years still further onward, may well echo the words. But a little while ago, there were priests, with vestments of ancient and gorgeous form, saying mass in churches, which were the only elegant structures in the country. The name of the pope was a word to bow at. Confession was one of the duties of life. Barefooted friars wandered about in the enjoyment of universal reverence. Any gentleman going out with his sovereign on a military expedition, would have been thought liable to every evil under the sun, and altogether a scandalous person, if he did not beforehand obtain pardon for his sins from the Grayfriars, and leave in their hands his most valuable possessions, including the very titles of his estate, which he might hope to get back if he survived; but otherwise, he well knew all would go to the enriching of these same friars, who were under vows to live in perpetual poverty.[1] The king himself sought for his highest religious comfort in pilgrimising to St Duthac's shrine in Ross-shire, or to the chapel of our Lady of Loretto, at Musselburgh. The

[1] De Fratribus Minoribus nulla est quæstio, professi siquidem simulatam paupertatem, nulla prædia, nullos fundos habent; sed sub prætextu pietatis ex interceptis testamentis, et stultæ pietatis zelo, ditissimi facti sunt: quod ex eventu, post infelicem pugnam de Flodden, compertum est: nam qui eo pugnaturi proficiscebantur, nisi confessione facta remissionem a Fratribus Minoribus impetrassent, omnia mala ominabantur. Interea omnem pecuniam, monumenta, et si quid pretiosum alioqui habebant, eorum fidei committebant, sperantes, se mortuis, illos ea quæ credebantur omnia fide integra posteris suis restituros: at illi, eorum qui in prælio occubuerunt, nec fidem reposcere poterant, bona in fundi comparatione, et ecclesiæ et monasterii exstructione ad sui ordinis homines convertebant: nec aliter accidit in acie Pinquini.—*Craig*, *Jus Feudale*, lib. i.

bishop of Aberdeen felt a solacement in the hour of death, in the trust that his bowels would be buried, as he requested, in the Black-friars Monastery in Edinburgh.[1] So lately as 1547, the Scotch, fighting with the English at Pinkie, called out reproachful names to them, on the score of their having deserted the ancient faith. But here is now Scotland also converted, and that as it were in a day, from all those old reverences and observances, and taken possession of by a totally new set of ideas. *The Bible in the vulgar tongue has been suddenly laid open to them.* Their minds, earnest and reflecting, though unenlightened, have been impressed beyond description by the tale of miraculous history which it unfolds, and the deeply touching scheme for effecting the salvation of man which the theologian constructs from it. They feel as if they had got hold of something of priceless value, and in comparison with which all the forms and rites of medieval Christianity are as dust and rubbish. The *Evangel*, the *True Religion*, as they earnestly called it, is henceforth all in all with this poor and homely, but resolute people. Nothing inconsistent therewith can be listened to for a moment. Scarcely can a dissentient be permitted to live in the country. The state, too, must maintain this system, and this system alone, or it is no state for them. Above all, the errors of Popery must be unsparingly put down. The mass is idolatry: God, in his Book, says that idolatry is a sin to be visited with the severest judgments; therefore, if you wish to avoid judgments, you must extinguish the mass. Even modified forms and rituals which have been preserved by English Protestantism, as calculated to raise or favour a spirit of devotion, and maintain a decency in worship, are here regarded as but the rags of Rome, and spurned with nearly the same vehemence as the mass itself. Scotland will have nothing but a preacher to expound, and say a prayer. That, with the Bible in the hands of the people, is enough for her. No hierarchy does she require to maintain order in the church. Let the ministers meet in local courts and in General Assembly, and settle everything by equal votes. Bishops and archbishops are a popish breed, who must, if possible, be kept at a distance.

Even one who may now take more charitable and lenient views can scarcely fail to sympathise with, yea, admire, this little out-of-the-way nation, in seeing it dictate and do thus against the might of an ancient institution of such imposing dimensions as the Romish Church. And to do it, too, in the teeth of their own ruling power, such as it was. And all so effectually, that from that hour to this, Rome, in all her back-surgings upon the ground she lost in the sixteenth century, was never able to put Scottish Protestantism once in the slightest danger. Undoubtedly, if there be merit in a faithful contending for what is felt to be all-important truth, it was a worthy thing, and one that shewed there was some

[1] *Registrum Episcopatus Aberdonensis*, ii., 309, 310.

good metal in the constitution of the Scottish mind. It could not surprise one that a people who acted thus, should also prove to be a valiant and constant people under physical difficulties; that they should make wonderful results out of a poor soil and climate; that they should do some considerable things in the science of thinking and in letters; and, above all, stand well to their own opinions and ways, and to the maintenance of their political liberties and national independence, frown, threaten, and drive at them who might.

It was so—*and yet*—for every picture of noble humanity has its reverse—it is forced upon us that the Scots were, at this very time, a fearfully rude and ignorant people. As usual, they were so without having the least consciousness of it: their greatest author of that age, George Buchanan, speaks in perfect earnest of the *refinement* of his own time, in comparison with the barbarism of former days.[1] But, whatever the age might be relatively to past ages, it was rude in itself. The Scotland of that day was ruder than the England of that day, ruder than many other European states. Few persons could read or write. Few knew aught beyond their daily calling. Men carried weapons, and were apt to use them on light occasion. The lords, and the rich generally, exercised enormous oppression upon the poor. The government was a faction of nobles, as against all the rest. When a man had a suit at law, he felt he had no chance without using 'influence.' Was he to be tried for an offence?—his friends considered themselves bound to muster in arms round the court to see that he got fair-play; that is, to get him off unharmed if they could. Men were accustomed to violence in all forms, as to their daily bread. The house of a man of consideration was a kind of castle: at the least, it was a tall narrow tower, with a grated door and a wall of defence. No one in those days had any general conceptions regarding the processes of nature. They saw the grass grow and their bullocks feed, and thought no more of it. Any extraordinary natural event, as an eclipse of the sun or an earthquake, still more a comet, affected them as an immediate expression of a frowning Providence. The great diseases, such as pestilence, which arose in consequence of their uncleanly habits and the wide-spread famines from which they often suffered, appeared to them as divine chastisements; not perhaps for the sins of those who suffered—which would have been comparatively reasonable—but probably for the sins of a ruler who did not suffer at all. The ruling class knew no more of a just public economy than the poor. Through absurd attempts to raise the value of

[1] As often as I turn my eyes to the niceness and elegance of our own times, the ancient manners of our forefathers appear sober and venerable, but withal rough and horrid.—*Buchanan: De Jure Regni, as quoted by Dugald Stewart in Preliminary Dissertation, Encyclopædia Britannica.*

coin by statute, the Scotch pound had fallen to a fraction of its original worth. By ridiculous endeavours to control markets, and adjust exportation and importation, mercantile freedom was paralysed, and penury and scarcity among the poor greatly increased. The good plant of Knowledge not being yet cultivated, its weed-precursor, Superstition, largely prevailed. Bearded men believed that a few muttered words could take away and give back the milk of their cattle. An archbishop expected to be cured of a deadly ailment by a charm pronounced by an ignorant country-woman. The forty-six men who met as the first General Assembly, and drew from the Scriptures the Confession of Faith which they handed down as stereotyped truth to after-generations, were every one of them not more fully persuaded of the soundness of any of the doctrines of that Confession, than they were of the reality of sorcery, and felt themselves not more truly called upon by the Bible to repress idolatry than to punish witches. They were good men, earnest, and meaning well to God and man; but they were men of the sixteenth century, ignorant, and rough in many of their ways.

While, then, we shall see great occasion to admire the hardy valour with which this people achieved their deliverance from bondage, we must also be prepared for finding them full of vehement intolerance towards all challenge of their own dogmas and all adherence to alien forms of faith. We shall find them utterly incapable of imagining a conscientious dissent, much less of allowing for and respecting it. We must be prepared to see them—while repudiating one set of superstitious incrustations upon the original simple gospel—working it out on their own part in creeds, plats, covenants, and church institutions generally, full of mere human logic and device, but yet assumed to be as true as if a divine voice had spoken and framed them, breathing war and persecution towards all other systems, and practically operating as a tyranny only somewhat less formidable than that which had been put away.

REIGN OF MARY: 1561-1565.

The regent, Mary de Guise, having died in June 1560, while her daughter Mary, the nominally reigning queen, was still in France, the management of affairs fell into the hands of the body of nobles, styled Lords of the Congregation, who had struggled for the establishment of the Protestant faith. The chief of these was Lord James Stuart, an illegitimate son of James V., and brother of the queen—the man of by far the greatest sagacity and energy of his age and country, and a most earnest votary of the new religion.

Becoming a widow in December 1560, by the death of her husband, Francis II., Mary no longer had any tie binding her to France, and consequently she resolved on returning to her own dominions. When she arrived in Edinburgh, in August 1561, she found the Protestant religion so firmly established, and so universally accepted by the people—there being only some secluded districts where Catholicism still prevailed—that, so far from having a chance of restoring her kingdom to Rome, as she, 'an unpersuaded princess,' might have wished to do, it was with the greatest difficulty that she could be allowed to have the mass performed in a private room in her palace. The people regarded her beautiful face with affection; and, as she allowed her brother, Lord James, and other Protestant nobles to act for her, her government was far from unpopular.

Mary's conduct towards the Protestant cause appeared as that of one who submits to what cannot be resisted. Before she had been fifteen months in the country, she accompanied her brother (whom she created Earl of Moray) on an expedition to the north, where she broke the power of the Gordon family, who boasted they could restore the Catholic faith in three counties. What is still more remarkable, she dealt with the patrimony of the church, accepting part of the spoils for the use of the state. It is believed, nevertheless, that she designed ultimately to act in concert with the Catholic powers of the continent for the restoration of the old religion in Scotland. One obvious motive for keeping on fair terms with Protestantism for the present, lay in her hopes of succeeding to the English crown, in the event of the death of Elizabeth, whose next heir she was.

A custom, dating far back in Catholic times, prevailed in Edin- 1561.
burgh in unchecked luxuriance down almost to the time of the Reformation. It consisted in a set of unruly dramatic games, called

1561. *Robin Hood*, the *Abbot of Unreason*, and the *Queen of May*, which were enacted every year in the floral month just mentioned. The interest felt by the populace in these whimsical merry-makings was intense. At the approach of May, they assembled and chose some respectable individuals of their number, very grave and reverend citizens perhaps, to act the parts of Robin Hood and Little John, of the Lord of Inobedience, or the Abbot of Unreason, and 'make sports and jocosities'[1] for them. If the chosen actors felt it inconsistent with their tastes, gravity, or engagements, to don a fantastic dress, caper and dance, and incite their neighbours to do the like, they could only be excused on paying a fine. On the appointed day, always a Sunday or holiday, the people assembled in their best attire and in military array, and marched in blithe procession to some neighbouring field, where the fitting preparations had been made for their amusement. Robin Hood and Little John robbed bishops, fought with pinners, and contended in archery among themselves, as they had done in reality two centuries before.[2] The Abbot of Unreason kicked up his heels and played antics like a modern pantaloon. The popular relish for all this was such as can scarcely now be credited. 'A learned prelate [Latimer] preaching before Edward VI., observes, that he once came to a town upon a holiday, and gave information on the evening before of his design to preach. But next day when he came to the church, he found the door locked. He tarried half an hour ere the key could be found, and instead of a willing audience, some one told him: "This is a busy day with us; we cannot hear you. It is Robin Hood's day. The parish are gone abroad to gather for Robin Hood. I pray you let [hinder] them not." I was fain (says the bishop) to give place to Robin Hood. I thought my rochet should have been regarded, though I were not; but it would not serve. It was fain to give place to Robin Hood's men.'[3]

Such were the Robin Hood plays of Catholic and unthinking times. By and by, when the Reformation approached, they were found to be disorderly and discreditable, and an act of parliament was passed against them.[4] Still, while the upper and more serious

[1] This phrase occurs in an order of the provost of Edinburgh (Earl of Arran), dated 1518, excusing Francis Bothwell from taking the part of Little John.—*Napier's Life of Napier of Merchiston*, p. 53.

[2] See the Rev. Joseph Hunter's tract, *The Ballad Hero Robin Hood*, 1852; making it at length tolerably certain that the outlaw lived in the reign of Edward II, and for a short time held office in that king's household.

[3] Arnot's *History of Edinburgh*.

[4] Scots Acts, 1555.

classes frowned, the common sort of people loved the sport too much to resign it without a struggle. It came to be one of the first difficulties of the men who had carried through the Reformation, how to wrestle the people out of their love of the May-games. 1561.

In April 1561, one George Durie was chosen in Edinburgh as Robin Hood and Lord of Inobedience, and on Sunday the 12th of May, he and a great number of other persons came riotously into the city, with an ensign and arms in their hands, in disregard of both the act of parliament and an act of the town-council. Notwithstanding an effort of the magistrates to turn them back, they passed to the Castle Hill, and thence returned at their own pleasure. For this offence a cordiner's servant, named James Gillon, was condemned to be hanged on the 21st of July.

'When the time of the poor man's hanging approachit, and that the [hangman] was coming to the gibbet with the ladder, upon which the said cordiner should have been hangit, the craftsmen's childer[1] and servants past to armour; and first they housit Alexander Guthrie and the provost and bailies in the said Alexander's writing booth, and syne came down again to the Cross, and dang down the gibbet, and brake it in pieces, and thereafter passed to the Tolbooth, whilk was then steekit [shut]; and when they could not apprehend the keys thereof, they brought fore-hammers and dang up the same Tolbooth door perforce, the provost, bailies, and others looking thereupon; and when the said door was broken up, ane part of them past in the same, and not allenarly [only] brought the same condemnit cordiner forth of the said Tolbooth, but also all the remanent persons being thereintill; and this done they past down the Hie Gait [High Street], to have past forth at the Nether Bow, whilk was then steekit, and because they could not get furth thereat, they past up the Hie Gait again; and in the meantime the provost, bailies, and their assisters being in the writing-booth of Alexander Guthrie, past to the Tolbooth; and in their passing up the said gait, they being in the Tolbooth, as said is, shot forth at the said servants ane dag, and hurt ane servant of the craftsmen's. That being done, there was naething but tak and slay; that is, the ane part shooting forth and casting stanes, the other part shooting hagbuts in again; and sae the craftsmen's servants held them [conducted themselves] continually fra three hours afternoon while [till] aucht at even, and never ane man of the town steirit to defend their provost and JULY 21.

[1] Persons in the employment of the craftsmen; journeymen.

1561. bailies. And then they sent to the masters of the craftsmen to cause them, gif they might, to stay the said servants; wha purposed to stay the same, but they could not come to pass, but the servants said they wald have ane revenge for the man whilk was hurt. And thereafter the provost sent ane messenger to the constable of the Castle to come to stay the matter, wha came; and he with the masters of the craftsmen treated on this manner, that the provost

An Edinburgh Hammerman, 1555.[1]

and bailies should discharge all manner of actions whilk they had against the said craftschilder in ony time bygane, and charged all their masters to receive them in service as they did of before, and promittit never to pursue them in time to come for the same. And this being done and proclaimit, they skaled [disbanded], and the provost and bailies came furth of the Tolbooth.'—*D. O.*

This was altogether an unprotestant movement, though springing only from a thoughtless love of sport. We may see in the

[1] From a sculpture on the Magdalen Chapel, Cowgate, Edinburgh.

attack on the Tolbooth a foreshadow of the doings of the Porteous mob in a later age. It appears that the magistrates, though reformers, were unpopular; hence the neutrality of the citizens, who, when solicited to interfere for the defence of the city-rulers, went to their four hours penny,[1] and returned for answer: 'They will be magistrates alone; let them rule the multitude alone.'—*Cal.* Thirteen persons were afterwards 'fylit' by an assize for refusing to help the magistrates.—*Pit.* 1561.

On its being known that Queen Mary was about to arrive in Scotland from France, there was a great flocking of the upper class of people from all parts of the country to Edinburgh, 'as it were to a common spectacle.'

The queen arrived with her two vessels in Leith Road, at seven in the morning of a dull autumn-day. She was accompanied by her three uncles of the House of Guise—the Duc d'Aumale, the Grand Prior, and the Marquis d'Elbeuf; besides Monsieur d'Amville, son of the constable of France, her four gentlewomen, called the *Maries*, and many persons of inferior note. To pursue the narrative of one who looked on the scene with an evil eye: 'The very face of heaven, the time of her arrival, did manifestly speak what comfort was brought unto this country with her; to wit, sorrow, dolour, darkness, and all impiety; for in the memory of man, that day of the year, was never seen a more dolorous face of the heaven, than was at her arrival, which two days after did so continue; for beside the surface weet and corruption of the air, the mist was so thick and so dark, that scarce might any man espy ane other the length of twa butts. The sun was not seen to shine two days before nor two days after. That forewarning gave God unto us; but, alas, the most part were blind. AUG. 19.

'At the sound of the cannons which the galleys shot, the multitude being advertised, happy was he and she that first might have presence of the queen. . . . . [At ten hours her hieness landed upon the shore of Leith.] Because the palace of Holyroodhouse was not thoroughly put in order . . . . she remained [in Andrew Lamb's house] in Leith till towards the evening, and then repaired thither. In the way betwixt Leith and the Abbey, met her the rebels of the crafts . . . . that had violated the authority of the magistrates and had besieged the provost; but because she was

[1] Refreshment at 4 o'clock afternoon. Latterly, the term has been applied to tea-drinking.

1561. sufficiently instructed that all they did was done in despite of the religion, they were easily appardoned. Fires of joy were set forth all night, and a company of the most honest, with instruments of music, and with musicians, gave their salutations at her chalmer window. The melody, as she alleged, liked her weel; and she willed the same to be continued some nichts after.'—*Knox*.

The magistrates of Edinburgh, although all of them zealous for the reformed religion, resolved to give their young sovereign a gallant reception, taxing the community for the expenses. It was likewise thought good that, 'for the honour and pleasure of our sovereign, ane banquet sould be made upon Sunday next, to the princes, our said sovereign's kinsmen.'

Sep. 2. The queen 'made her entres in the burgh of Edinburgh in this manner. Her hieness departed of Holyroodhouse, and rade by the Lang Gate[1] on the north side of the burgh, unto the time she came to the Castle, where was ane yett [gate] made to her, at the whilk she, accompanied by the maist part of the nobility of Scotland, came in and rade up the castle-bank to the Castle, and dined therein.

'When she had dined at twelve hours, her hieness came furth of the Castle . . . . , at whilk departing the artillery shot vehemently. Thereafter, when she was ridand down the Castle Hill, there met her hieness ane convoy of the young men of the burgh, to the number of fifty or thereby, their bodies and thies covered with yellow taffetas, their arms and legs frae the knee down bare, coloured with black, in manner of Moors; upon their heads black hats, and on their faces black visors; in their mouths rings garnished with untellable precious stanes; about their necks, legs, and arms, infinite of chains of gold: together with saxteen of the maist honest men of the town, clad in velvet gowns and velvet bonnets, bearand and gangand about the pall under whilk her hieness rade; whilk pall was of fine purpour velvet, lined with red taffetas, fringed with gold and silk. After them was ane cart with certain bairns, together with ane coffer wherein was the cupboard and propine [gift] whilk should be propinit to her hieness. When her grace came forward to the Butter Tron, the nobility and convoy precedand, there was ane port made of timber in maist honourable manner, coloured with fine colours, hung with sundry arms; upon whilk port was singand certain bairns in the maist heavenly wise; under the whilk port there was ane cloud opening with four leaves, in the whilk was put

[1] A road in the line of the present Princes Street.

ane bonnie bairn. When the queen's hieness was coming through the said port, the cloud openit, and the bairn descended down as it had been ane angel, and deliverit to her hieness the keys of the town, together with ane Bible and ane Psalm-buik coverit with fine purpour velvet.[1] After the said bairn had spoken some small speeches, he delivered also to her hieness three writings, the tenour whereof is uncertain. That being done, the bairn ascended in the cloud, and the said cloud steekit. 1561.

'Thereafter the queen's grace came down to the Tolbooth, at the whilk was . . . . twa scaffats, ane aboon, and ane under that. Upon the under was situate ane fair virgin called Fortune, under the whilk was three fair virgins, all clad in maist precious attirement, called , Justice, and Policy. And after ane little speech made there, the queen's grace came to the Cross, where there was standand four fair virgins, clad in the maist heavenly claithing, and frae the whilk Cross the wine ran out at the spouts in great abundance. There was the noise of people casting the glasses with wine.

'This being done, our lady came to the Salt Tron, where there was some speakers; and after ane little speech, they burnt upon the scaffat made at the said Tron the manner of ane sacrifice. Sae that being done, she departed to the Nether Bow, where there was ane other scaffat made, having ane dragon in the same, with some speeches; and after the dragon was burnt, and the queen's grace heard ane psalm sung, her hieness passed to the abbey of Holyrood-house, with the said convoy and nobilities. There the bairns whilk was in the cart with the propine made some speech concerning the putting away of the mass, and thereafter sang ane psalm. And this being done, the . . . . honest men remained in her outer chalmer, and desired her grace to receive the said cupboard, whilk was double over-gilt; the price thereof was 2000 merks; wha received the same and thankit them thereof. And sae the honest men and convoy come to Edinburgh.'—*D. O.*

The Sunday banquet to the queen's uncles duly took place in the cardinal's lodging in Blackfriars' Wynd. The entire expenses on the occasion of this royal reception were 4000 merks.

Before the queen had been settled for many weeks in her capital, Oct. 2.

[1] Knox says she frowned here, and gave the books to Arther Erskine, the captain of her guard, 'the maist pestilent papist within the realm.'

1561. the new-born zeal of the people against the old religion found vent in a way that shewed in how little danger she was of being spoilt by complaisance on the part of her subjects. The provost of Edinburgh, Archibald Douglas, with the bailies and council, 'causit ane proclamation to be proclaimit at the Cross of Edinburgh, commanding and charging all and sundry monks, friars, priests, and all others papists and profane persons, to pass furth of Edinburgh within twenty-four hours, under the pain of burning of disobeyers upon the cheek and harling of them through the town upon ane cart. At the whilk proclamation, the queen's grace was very commovit.'—*D. O.* She had, after all, sufficient influence to cause the provost and bailies to be degraded from their offices for this act of zeal.

The autumn of this year, the weather was 'richt guid and fair.' In the winter quarter, the weather was still fair, and there was 'peace and rest in all Scotland.'—*C. F.*

Dec. 16. William Guild was convicted, notwithstanding his being a minor and of weak mind, of 'the thiftous stealing and taking forth of the purse of Elizabeth Danielstone, the spouse of Niel Laing, hinging upon her apron . . . . she being upon the High Street, standing at the krame of William Speir . . . . in communing with him, the time of the putting of ane string to ane penner and inkhorn, whilk she had coft [bought] fra the said kramer, of ane signet of gold, ane other signet of gold set with ane cornelian, ane gold ring set with ane great sapphire, ane other gold ring with ane sapphire formit like ane heart, ane gold ring set with ane turquois, ane small double gold ring set with ane diamond and ane ruby, ane auld angel-noble, and ane cusset ducat.'—*Pit.* This account of the contents of Mrs Laing's purse, in connection with the decorations of the fifty young citizens who convoyed the queen in her procession through the city, raises unexpected ideas as to the means and taste of the middle classes in 1561.

Dec. 24. Mr William Balfour, indweller in Leith, was convicted of breaking the queen's proclamation for the protection of the reformed religion. One of his acts—'He, accompanied with certain wicked persons . . . . upon set purpose, came to the parish kirk of Edinburgh, callit Sanct Giles Kirk, where John Cairns was examining the common people of the burgh, before the last communion . . . . and the said John, demanding of ane poor woman, "Gif she had ony hope of salvation by her awn good works," he, the said Mr William, in despiteful manner and with thrawn countenance, having naething to do in that kirk but to trouble the said examination, said to the said John thir words: "Thou demands of that woman the thing whilk thou nor nane of thy opinion allows or keeps." And, after gentle admonition made to him by the said John, he said to him alsae thir words: "Thou art ane very knave, and thy doctrine is very false, as all your doctrine and teaching is." And therewith laid his hand upon his weapons, and provoking battle; doing therethrough purposely that was in him to have raisit tumult amang the inhabitants of this burgh.'—*Pit.* 1561.

1561-2. JAN. 1.

Alexander Scott, a poet of that time, sometimes called the Scottish Anacreon, because he sung so much of love, sent *Ane New Year Gift* to the queen, in the form of a poetical address in twenty-eight stanzas. 'Welcome, illustrate lady, and our queen!' it begins. 'This year sall richt and reason rule the rod'—'this year sall be of peace, tranquillity, and rest!' says the sanguine bard, speaking from his wishes rather than a contemplation of known facts. He calls on Mary to found on the four cardinal virtues, to cleave to Christ, and be the 'protectrice of the puir.' 'Stanch all strife'—'the pulling down of policy reprove.'

'At Cross gar cry by open proclamation,
Under great pains, that neither he nor she
Of haly writ have ony disputation,
But letterit men or learnit clerks thereto;
For limmer lads and little lasses low
Will argue baith with bishops, priests, and frier;
To danton this thou has eneuch to do,
God give thee grace against this guid new year!'

Mary would probably feel the force of the seventh line of this stanza.

With commendable prudence, seeing he was addressing a papist queen, honest Alexander says:

'With mess nor matins noways will I mell,
To judge them justly passes my ingine;
They guide nocht ill that governs weel themsel.'

Yet he deems himself at liberty to remark—doubtless suspecting that Mary would not be much displeased—that instead of old idols has now come in another called *Covetice,* under whose auspices, certain persons, while

'Singing Sanct David's psalter on their books,'

1561-2. are found

> 'Rugging and ryving up kirk rents like rooks.'

'Protestants,' he goes on to say,

> 'takes the friers' antetume,[1]
> Ready receivers, but to render nocht.'

On this Lord Hailes remarks: 'The reformed clergy expected that the tithes would be applied to charitable uses, to the advancement of learning and the maintenance of the ministry. But the nobility, when they themselves had become the exactors, saw nothing rigorous in the payment of tithes, and derided those *devout imaginations*.'[2]

In one verse of his poem, Scott makes pointed allusion to certain prophecies which seemed to assign a brilliant future to Mary:

> 'If saws be sooth to shaw thy celsitude,
> What bairn should brook all Britain by the sea,
> The prophecy expressly does conclude
> The French wife of the Bruce's blood should be:
> Thou art by line from him the ninth degree,
> And was King Francis' perty maik and peer;
> So by descent the same should spring of thee,
> By grace of God against this good new year.'

The poet here undoubtedly had in view a prediction which occurs in a rude metrical tract printed at Edinburgh by Robert Waldegrave in 1603, under the title, 'The Whole Prophesies of Scotland, England, and somepart of France and Denmark, prophesied by mervellous Merling, Beid, Bertlingtoun, Thomas Rymour, Waldhave, &c., all according in one.'[3] These so-called prophecies are unintelligible rhapsodies about lions, dragons, foumarts, conflicts of knights, of armies, and of navies—how there should be fighting on a moor beside a cross, till by the multitude of slain the crow should not find where the cross stood—how the dead shall rise, 'and that shall be wonder'—how

> 'When the man in the moon is most in his might,
> Then shall Dunbarton turn up that is down,
> And the mouth of Arran both at one time,
> And the lord with the lucken hand his life shall he lose—'

and much more of the like kind.

From the style of the verse, which is in general alliterative, as

[1] Anti-tune, antiphone, or response.

[2] *Notes to Ancient Scottish Poems from the Bannatyne Manuscript*, 1770.

[3] From a unique copy of this tract a reprint was given by Mr John Robertson to the Bannatyne Club, 1833.

well as some of the allusions, it may be surmised that these 1561-2.
prophecies were written in the minority of James V., on the basis of obscure popular sayings attributed to Merlin, Rymour, and other early sages. The special passage which Alexander Scott refers to was in Rymour's prophecies, but also given in a slightly different form in those of Bertlingtoun:

'A French wife shall bear the son,
Shall rule all Britain to the sea,
That of the Bruce's blood shall come,
As near as to the ninth degree.'

There can be no doubt that it is applicable to Queen Mary, who was a French wife, and in the ninth degree of descent from Bruce; and did we know for certain that it formed a part of the prophecies made up in the minority of her father, it would be remarkable. But the probability is, that the verse was a recent addition to the old rhymes, a mere conjecture formed in the view of the possibility and the hope that a child of Mary would succeed to the English crown at the close of Elizabeth's life. What makes the allusion of Scott chiefly worthy of notice, is the knowledge it gives us of the public mind being then possessed by such soothsayings. It certainly was so, to a degree and with effects beyond what we now may readily imagine.[1]

While Scotland was noted in the eyes of foreigners as a barren land—Shakspeare comparing it for nakedness to the palm of the hand[2]—its own people were fain to believe and eager to boast that it was rich in minerals. In 1511, 1512, and 1513, James IV. had gold-mines worked on Crawford Muir, in the upper ward of Lanarkshire—a peculiarly sterile tract, scarcely any part of which is less than a thousand feet above the sea. In the royal accounts for those years, there are payments to Sir James Pettigrew, who seems to have been chief of the enterprise, to Simon Northberge, the master-finer, Andrew Ireland, the finer, and Gerald Essemer, a Dutchman, the melter of the mine. Under the same king, in 1512, a lead-mine was wrought at Wanlock-head, on the other side of the same group of hills in Dumfriesshire. The operations, probably interrupted by the disaster of Flodden, were resumed in 1526, under James V., who gave a company of Germans a grant of the mines of Scotland for forty-three years. Leslie tells us that these Germans,

[1] See under October 1570; also April 5, 1603.
[2] *Comedy of Errors*, Act III. sc. 2.

1561-2. with the characteristic perseverance of their countrymen, toiled laboriously at gold-digging for many months in the surface alluvia of the moor, and obtained a considerable amount of gold, but not enough, we suspect, to remunerate the labour: otherwise the work would surely have been continued.

We shall find that the search for the precious metals in the mountainous district at the head of the vales of the Clyde and Nith, did not now finally cease, but that it never proved remunerative work. On the other hand, the lead-mines of the district have for centuries, and down to the present day, borne a conspicuous place in the economy of Scotland. It must be interesting to see the traces of the first efforts to get at

> 'the wealth
> Hopetoun's high mountains fill.'

JAN. 23. John Acheson, master-cunyer, and John Aslowan, burgess of Edinburgh, now completed an arrangement with Queen Mary, by virtue of which they had licence to work the lead-mines of Glengoner and Wanlock-head, and carry as much as twenty thousand stone-weight of the ore to Flanders, or other foreign countries, for which they bound themselves to deliver at the queen's cunyie-house before the 1st of August next, forty-five ounces of fine silver for every thousand stone-weight of the ore, 'extending in the hale to nine hundred unces of utter fine silver.'

Acheson and Aslowan were continuing to work these mines in August 1565, when the queen and her husband, King Henry, granted a licence to John, Earl of Athole, 'to win forty thousand trone stane wecht, counting six score stanes for ilk hundred, of lead ore, and mair, gif the same may guidly be won, within the nether lead hole of Glengoner and Wanlock.' The earl agreed to pay to their majesties in requital fifty ounces of fine silver for every thousand stone-weight of the ore.—*P. C. R.*

How the enterprise of Acheson and Aslowan ultimately succeeded does not appear. We suspect that, to some extent, it prospered, as the name Sloane, which seems the same as Aslowan, continued to flourish at Wanlock-head so late as the days of Burns.

A similar licence, on similar terms, was granted by the king and queen to James Carmichael, Master James Lindsay, and Andrew Stevenson, burgesses of Edinburgh, referring, however, to any part of the realm save 'the mine and werk of Glengoner and Wanlock.'

FEB. 8. The Lord James, newly created Earl of Mar (subsequently of

Moray), 'was married upon Annas Keith, daughter to William Earl Marischal, in the kirk of Sanct Geil in Edinburgh, with sic solemnity as the like has not been seen before; the hale nobility of this realm being there present, and convoyit them down to Holyroodhouse, where the banquet was made, and the queen's grace thereat.' The *solemnity* was of a kind which seems rather frisky for so zealous an upholder of the presbyterian cause. 'At even, after great and divers balling, and casting of fire-balls, fire-spears, and running with horses,' the queen created sundry knights. Next day, 'at even, the queen's grace and the remaining lords came up in ane honourable manner frae the palace of Holyrood-house to the Cardinal's lodging in the Blackfrier Wynd, whilk was preparit and hung maist honourably; and there her hieness suppit, and the rest with her. After supper, the honest young men in the town [the youths of the upper classes] came with ane convoy to her, and other some came with merschance, well accouterit in maskery, and thereafter departit to the said palace.'—*D. O.* 1561-2.

There was 'meikle snaw in all parts; mony deer and roes slain.' —*C. F.* FEB.

1562. APR.

The queen was at St Andrews, inquiring into a conspiracy of which the Duke of Chatelherault and the Earl of Bothwell had been accused by the Duke's son, the Earl of Arran. In the midst of the affair, Arran proved to be 'phrenetick.' On the 4th of May, 'my Lords Arran, Bothwell, and the Commendator of Kilwinning came fra St Andrews to the burgh of Edinburgh in this manner; that is to say, my Lord Arran was convoyit in the queen's grace's *coach*, because of the phrenesy aforesaid, and the Earl of Bothwell and my Lord Commendator of Kilwinning rade, convoyit with twenty-four horsemen, whereof was principal Captain Stewart, captain of the queen's guard.'—*D. O.*

This is not the first notice of a travelling vehicle that occurs in our national domestic history. Several payments in connection with a chariot belonging to the late Queen Mary de Guise, so early as 1538, occur in the lord-treasurer's books.[1] It is not, however, likely that either the chariot of the one queen or the coach of the other was a wheeled vehicle, as, if we may trust to an authority

[1] In July 1538, there is an entry in the treasurer's books, of 14s. 'to Alexander Naper for mending of the Queen's sadill and her *cheriot*, in Sanct Androis.' In January 1541–2, there is another: 'To mend the Quenis cheriot vi¼ elnis blak velvet, £16, 17s. 6d.' Besides something for cramosie, satin, and fringes.

1562. about to be quoted, such a convenience was as yet unknown even in England.

'In the year 1564, Guilliam Boonen, a Dutchman, became the queen's coachman, and was the first that brought the use of coaches into England. And after a while, divers great ladies, with as great jealousy of the queen's displeasure, made them coaches, and rid in them up and down the countries, to the great admiration of all the beholders; but then, by little and little, they grew usual among the nobility and others of sort, and within twenty years became a great trade of coachmaking.

'And about that time began long waggons to come in use, such as now come to London from Canterbury, Norwich, Ipswich, Gloucester, &c., with passengers and commodities. Lastly, even at this time (1605) began the ordinary use of carouches.'—*Howes's Chronicle.*

The author of the *Memorie of the Somervilles*—who, however, lived in the reign of Charles II., and probably wrote from tradition only—says that the Regent Morton used a coach, which was the *second* introduced into Scotland, the *first* being one which Alexander Lord Seaton brought from France, when Queen Mary returned from that country. It is to be remarked that the Lord Seaton of that day was George, not Alexander; and it is evident that Mary did not use a coach on her landing, or at her ceremonial entry into Edinburgh.

To turn for a moment to one of the remoter and wilder parts of the country—John Mackenzie of Kintail 'was a great courtier with Queen Mary. He feued much of the lands of Brae Ross. When the queen sent her servants to know the condition of the gentry of Ross, they came to his house of Killin; but before their coming he had gotten intelligence that it was to find out the condition of the gentry of Ross that they were coming; whilk made him cause his servants to put ane great fire of fresh arn [alder] wood when they came, to make a great reek; also he caused kill a great bull in their presence; whilk was put altogether into ane kettle to their supper. When the supper came, there were a half-dozen great dogs present, to sup the broth of the bull, whilk put all the house through-other with their tulyie. When they ended the supper, ilk ane lay where they were. The gentlemen thought they had gotten purgatory on earth, and came away as soon as it was day; but when they came to the houses of Balnagowan, and Foulis, and Milton, they were feasted like princes.

'When they went back to the queen, she asked who were the ablest men they saw in Ross. They answered: "They were all able men, except that man that was her majesty's great courtier, Mackenzie—that he did both eat and lie with his dogs." "Truly," said the queen, "it were a pity of his poverty—he is the best man of them all." Then the queen did call for all the gentry of Ross to take their land in feu, when Mackenzie got the cheap feu, and more for his thousand merks than any of the rest got for five.'[1] 1562.

This day commenced a famous disputation between John Knox and Quintin Kennedy, abbot of Crossraguel, concerning the doctrines of popery. Kennedy was uncle to the Earl of Cassillis, a young Protestant noble, and the greatest man in the west of Scotland. The birth and ecclesiastical rank of the abbot made him an important person in his province, and he possessed both zeal for the ancient religion and talents to set it in its fairest light. Early in September, John Knox, coming into Ayrshire for certain objects connected with the Protestant cause, found that Abbot Kennedy had set forth, in the church of Kirkoswald, articles in support of the Catholic faith, which he was willing to defend. The fiery reformer immediately resolved to take up the challenge; and after a tedious correspondence between the two regarding the place, time, and number to be present, they met in the house of the provost of the collegiate church of Maybole, under the sanction of the Earl of Cassillis, and with forty persons on each side. The conference commenced at eight in the morning, being opened by John Knox with a prayer, which Kennedy admitted to be 'weel said.' SEP. 28.

We can imagine the forty supporters of Kennedy full of joyful anticipation as to the defeat which their champion was to give the unpolite heretic Knox, and the company of the latter not less hopeful regarding the triumph which he was to achieve over the luxurious abbot. Acts of parliament had done their best to put down the old church, and still it had some obstinate adherents; but now comes the valiant reformer, with pure argument from Scripture, to sweep one of these recusants off the face of the earth, and leave the rest without an excuse for their obstinacy. Now are the mass, purgatory, worship of saints, and other popish doctrines, to be finally put down. If such were the anticipations, they were doomed to a sad disappointment. The

[1] History of the Family of Mackenzie, MS. in possession of J. W. Mackenzie, Esq., W.S., Edinburgh.

1562. disputation proved to be the very type of all similar wranglings which have since taken place between the two parties.

It will scarcely be believed, but there is only too little reason why it should not, that three days were consumed by these redoubted controversialists in debating one question. The warrant of the abbot for considering the mass as a sacrifice was the priesthood and oblation of Melchizedek. 'The Psalmist,' said he, 'and als the apostle St Paul affirms our Saviour to be ane priest for ever according to the order of Melchizedek, wha made oblation and sacrifice of bread and wine unto God, as the Scripture plainly teacheth us. . . . . Read all the evangel wha pleases, he sall find in no place of the evangel where our Saviour uses the priesthood of Melchizedek, declaring himself to be ane priest after the order of Melchizedek, but in the Latter Supper, where he made oblation of his precious body and blude under the form of bread and wine prefigurate by the oblation of Melchizedek: then are we compelled to affirm that our Saviour made oblation of his body and blude in the Latter Supper, or else he was not ane priest according to the order of Melchizedek, which is express against the Scripture.'

To this Knox answered that Scripture gives no warrant for supposing that Melchizedek offered bread and wine unto Abraham, and therefore the abbot's warrant fails. The abbot called on him to prove that Melchizedek did not do so. Knox protested that he was not bound to prove a negative. 'For what, then,' says Kennedy, 'did Melchizedek bring out the bread and wine?' Knox said, that though he was not bound to answer this question, yet he believed the bread and wine were brought out to refresh Abraham and his men. In barren wranglings on this point were nearly the whole three days spent; and, for anything we can see, the disputation might have been still further protracted, but for an opportune circumstance. Strange to say—looking at what Maybole now is—it broke down under the burden of eighty strangers in three days! They had to disperse for lack of provisions.[1]

Nov. There raged at this time in Edinburgh a disease called the *New Acquaintance*. The queen and most of her courtiers had it; it

[1] A tract containing the disputation was printed by Lekprivik in 1563, and has been republished, Edinburgh, George Ramsay & Co., 1812. Dr M'Crie, in his *Life of John Knox*, gives an ample abstract of this curious pamphlet.

spared neither lord nor lady, French nor English. 'It is a pain in their heads that have it, and a soreness in their stomachs, with a great cough; it remaineth with some longer, with others shorter time, as it findeth apt bodies for the nature of the disease.'[1] Most probably, this disorder was the same as that now recognised as the influenza. 1562.

1563. May 19.

Sir John Arthur, a priest, was indicted for baptising and marrying several persons 'in the auld and abominable papist manner.' Here and there, the old church had still some adherents who preferred such ministrations to any other. It appears that Hugh and David Kennedy came with two hundred followers, 'boden in effeir of weir;' that is, with jacks, spears, guns, and other weapons; to the parish kirk of Kirkoswald and the college kirk of Maybole, and there ministered and abused 'the sacraments of haly kirk, otherwise and after ane other manner nor by public and general order of this realm.' The archbishop of St Andrews in like manner came, with a number of friends, to the Abbey Kirk of Paisley, 'and openly, publicly, and plainly took auricular confession of the said persons, in the said kirk, town, kirk-yard, chalmers, barns, middings, and killogies thereof.'—*Pit.* 'After great debate, reasoning, and communication had in the council by the Protestants, wha was bent even to the death against the said archbishop and others kirkmen, the archbishop passed to the Tolbooth, and became in the queen's will; and sae the queen's grace commandit him to pass to the Castle of Edinburgh induring her will, to appease the furiosity foresaid.'—*D. O.* The other offenders also made submission, and were assigned to various places of confinement. William Semple of Thirdpart and Michael Nasmyth of Posso afterwards gave caution to the extent of £3000 for the future good behaviour of the archbishop.—*Pit.*

June 4.

In the parliament now sitting, some noticeable acts were passed. One decreed that 'nae person carry forth of this realm ony gold or silver, under pain of escheating of the same and of all the remainder of their moveable guids,' merchants going abroad to carry only as much as they strictly require for their travelling expenses. Another enacted, that 'nae person take upon hand to use ony manner of witchcrafts, sorcery, or necromancy, nor give themselves

[1] Randolph to Cecil, Edin. Nov. 30, 1562. Chalmers's *Life of Queen Mary.*

1563. furth to have ony sic craft or knowledge thereof, there-through abusing the people;' also, that 'nae person seek ony help, response, or consultation at ony sic users or abusers of witchcrafts . . . . under the pain of death.' This is the statute under which all the subsequent witch-trials took place.

A third statute, reciting that much coal is now carried forth of the realm, often as mere ballast for ships, causing 'a maist exorbitant dearth and scantiness of fuel,' forbade further exportations of the article, under strong penalties. In those early days, coal was only dug in places where it cropped out or could be got with little trouble. As yet, no special mechanical arrangements for excavating it had come into use. The comparatively small quantity of the mineral used in Edinburgh—for there peat was the reigning fuel—was brought from Tranent, nine miles off, in *creels* on horses' backs. The above enactment probably referred to some partial and temporary failure of the small supply then required. It never occurred to our simple ancestors, that to export a native produce, such as coal, and get money in return, was tending to enrich the country, and in all circumstances deserved encouragement instead of prohibition.

JULY 2. Henry Sinclair, Bishop of Ross and President of the Court of Session—'a cunning and lettered man as there was,' remarkable for his 'singular intelligence in theology and likewise in the laws,' according to the *Diurnal of Occurrents*—'ane perfect hypocrite and conjured enemy to Christ Jesus,' according to John Knox—left Scotland for Paris, 'to get remede of ane confirmed stane.' This would imply that there was not then in our island a person qualified to perform the operation of lithotomy. The reverend father was lithotomised by Laurentius, a celebrated surgeon; but, fevering after the operation, he died in January 1564–5: in the words of Knox, 'God strake him according to his deservings.'

At the same time there were not wanting amongst us pretenders to the surgical art. In this very month, Robert Henderson attracted the favourable notice of the town-council of Edinburgh by performing sundry wonderful cures—namely, healing a man whose hands had been cut off, a man and woman who had been run through the body with swords by the French, and a woman understood to have been suffocated, and who had lain two days in her grave. The council ordered Robert twenty merks as a reward.[1]

[1] Edin. Council Register, apud Maitland.

Two gentlemen became sureties in Edinburgh for Marion Carruthers, co-heiress of Mousewald, in Dumfriesshire, 'that she shall not marry ane chief traitor nor other broken man of the country,' under pain of £1000 (*Pit*)—a large sum to stake upon a young lady's will. 1563. Sep. 13.

This was a year of dearth throughout Scotland; wheat being six pounds the boll, oats fifty shillings, a draught-ox twenty merks, and a wedder thirty shillings. 'All things apperteining to the sustentation of man in triple and more exceeded their accustomed prices.' Knox, who notes these facts, remarks that the famine was most severe in the north, where the queen had travelled in the preceding autumn: many died there. 'So did God, according to the threatening of his law, punish the idolatry of our wicked queen, and our ingratitude, that suffered her to defile the land with that abomination again [the mass]. . . . . The riotous feasting used in court and country wherever that wicked woman repaired, provoked God to strike the staff of breid, and to give his malediction upon the fruits of the earth.'

It was of the frame of the reformer's ideas, that a judgment would be sent upon the poor for the errors of their ruler, and that this judgment would be intensified in a particular district merely because the ruler had given it her personal presence. He failed to observe, or threw aside, the fact, that the same famine prevailed in England, where a queen entirely agreeable to him and his friends was now reigning, and certainly indulging in not a few banquetings. Theories of this kind sometimes prove to be two-edged swords, that will strike either way. It might have been replied to him: 'Accepting your theory that nations, besides suffering from the simple misgovernment of their rulers, are punished for their personal offences, what shall we say of the Protestant Elizabeth, whose people now suffer not merely under famine, as the Scotch are doing, but are visited by a dreadful pestilence besides,[1] from which Scotland is exempt?'

'God from heaven, and upon the face of the earth, gave declaration that he was offended at the iniquity that was committed within 1563-4. Jan. 20.

[1] In England, the spring of 1562 had been marked by excessive rains, and the harvest was consequently bad. Towards the end of the year, plague broke out in the crowded and harassed population of Havre, in France, then undergoing a siege, and from the garrison it was imparted to England, which had been prepared for its reception by the famine. There it prevailed throughout the whole year 1563, carrying off 20,000 persons in London alone. 'The poor citizens,' says Stowe, 'were this year plagued with a threefold plague—pestilence,

1563-4. this realm; for, upon the 20th day of January, there fell weet in great abundance, whilk in the falling freezit so vehemently, that the earth was but ane sheet of ice. The fowls both great and small freezit, and micht not flie: mony died, and some were taken and laid beside the fire, that their feathers might resolve. And in that same month, the sea stood still, as was clearly observed, and neither ebbed nor flowed the space of twenty-four hours.'—*Knox.*

In the ensuing month meteorological signs even more alarming to the great reformer took place. There were seen in the firma-

FEB. 15 and 18. ment, says he, 'battles arrayit, spears and other weapons, and as it had been the joining of two armies. Thir things were not only observed, but also spoken and constantly affirmed by men of judgment and credit.' Nevertheless, he adds, 'the queen and our court made merry.'

The reformer considered these appearances as declarations of divine wrath against the iniquity of the land, and he is evidently solicitous to establish them upon good evidence. There can be no difficulty in admitting the facts he refers to. The debate must be as to what the facts were. Most probably they were resolvable into a simple example of the *aurora borealis.*

The crimes of unruly passion and of superstition predominated in this age; but those of dexterous selfishness were not unknown.

FEB. Thomas Peebles, goldsmith in Edinburgh, was convicted of forging coin-stamps and uttering false coin—namely, *Testons, Half-testons, Non-sunts,* and *Lions* or *Hardheads.* It appeared that he had given some of his false hardheads to a poor woman as the price of a burden of coal. With this money she came to the market to buy some necessary articles, and was instantly challenged for passing false coin. 'The said Thomas being named by her to be her warrant, and deliverer of the said false coin to her, David Symmer and other bailies of the burgh of Edinburgh come with her to the said Thomas's chalmer, to search him for trial of the verity. He held the door of his said chalmer close upon him, and wald not suffer them to enter, while [till] they brake up the door thereof upon him, and entered perforce therein; and the said Thomas, being inquired if he had given the said poor woman the said lions, for the price of her coals, confessit the same; and his

dearth of money, and dearth of victuals; the misery whereof were too long here to write. No doubt the poor remember it.' On account of the plague at Michaelmas, no term was kept, and there was *no lord-mayor's dinner!* The plague spread into Germany, where it was estimated to have carried off 300,000 persons.

chalmer being searched, there was divers of the said irons, as well sunken and unsunken, together with the said false testons, &c., funden in the same, and confessit to be made and graven by him and his colleagues.' Thomas was condemned to be hanged, and to have his property escheat to the queen.—*Pit.* 1563-4.

In consequence of the slaughter of the Laird of Cessford, in an encounter with the Laird of Buccleuch, at Melrose, in 1526, a feud had ever since raged between their respective dependents, the Kerrs and Scotts. In 1529, there had been an effort to put an end to this broil by an engagement between Walter Kerr of Cessford, Andrew Kerr of Ferniehirst, Mark Kerr of Dolphinston, George Kerr, tutor of Cessford, and Andrew Kerr of Primsideloch, for themselves and kin on the one part, and Walter Scott of Branxholm, knight, with sundry other gentlemen of his clan on the other side, whereby the latter became bound to perform the four pilgrimages of Scotland—that is, to the churches of Melrose, Dundee, Scone, and Paisley—as a reparation for the slaughter. Bad blood being nevertheless kept up, Sir Walter Scott of Branxholm, Laird of Buccleuch, was slain on the streets of Edinburgh by Cessford, in 1552.[1] MAR. 22.

At the date now under attention, a meeting of the heads of the two houses took place in Edinburgh, and a contract was drawn up, setting forth certain terms of agreement, and arranging that, 'for the mair sure removing, stanching, and away-putting of all inimity, hatrent, and grudge standing and conceivit betwin the said parties, through the unhappy slaughter of the umwhile Sir Walter Scott of Branksome, knight, and for the better continuance of amity, favour, and friendship, amangs them in time coming, the said Sir Walter Kerr of Cessford sall, upon the 23 day of March instant, come to the perish kirk of Edinburgh, now commonly callit Sanct Giles's Kirk, and there, before noon, in sight of the people present for the time, reverently upon his knees ask God mercy of the slaughter aforesaid, and sic like ask forgiveness of the same fra the said Laird of Buccleuch and his friends whilk sall happen to be present; and thereafter promise, in the name and fear of God, that he and his friends sall truly keep their part of this present contract, and sall stand true friends to the said Laird of Buccleuch and his friends in all time coming: the whilk the said Laird of Buccleuch sall reverently accept and receive, and promise, in the fear of God, to remit his grudge,

[1] See notes to Scott's *Lay of the Last Minstrel.*

1563-4. and never remember the same.' A subsequent part of the agreement was, that the son of Cessford should marry a sister of Buccleuch, and Sir Andrew Ker of Fawdonside another sister, both without portion.[1]

This singular meeting would of course take place, but with what effect may well be doubted. It appears that the feud which had begun in 1526 still remained in force in 1596, 'when both chieftains paraded the streets of Edinburgh with their followers, and it was expected their first meeting would decide their quarrel.'[2]

MAR. 24. At a time when the most prominent events were clan-quarrels and the rough doings connected with the trampling out of an old religion, it is pleasant to trace even speculative attempts to enlarge the material resources and advance the primary interests of the country.

At the date noted, the queen granted to John Stewart of Tarlair,[3] and William Stewart his son, licence to win all kinds of metallic ores from the country between Tay and Orkney, on the condition of paying one stone of ore for every ten won; and this arrangement to last for nine years, during the first two of which their work was to be free, 'in respect of their invention and great charges made, and to be made, in outreeking of the same.' In the event of their finding any gold and silver where none were ever found before, they had the same licence, with only this condition, that the product was to be brought to her majesty's cunyie-house, 'the unce of gold for ten pund, and the unce of utter fine silver for 24s.' It was too early for such an enterprise, and we hear no more of it in the hands of the two Stewarts of Tarlair.

1564. MARCH. John Knox, at the age of fifty-eight, entered into the state of wedlock for the second time, by marrying Margaret Stewart, daughter of Lord Ochiltree. She proved a good wife to the old man, and survived him. The circumstance of a young woman of rank, with royal blood in her veins—for such was the case—accepting an elderly husband so far below her degree, did not fail to excite remark; and John's papist enemies could not account for it otherwise than by a supposition of the black art having been employed. The affair is thus adverted to by the reformer's shameless enemy, Nicol Burne: 'A little after he

[1] This curious contract is printed entire in Pitcairn, iii. 390.

[2] Scott's notes, *ut supra*.

[3] There is a place called Tarlair near Banff.

did pursue to have alliance with the honourable house of Ochiltree, of the king's majesty's awn bluid. Riding there with ane great court [cortège], on ane trim gelding, nocht like ane prophet or ane auld decrepit priest, as he was, but like as he had been ane of the bluid royal, with his bands of taffeta fastenit with golden rings and precious stanes: and, as is plainly reportit in the country, by sorcery and witchcraft, [he] did sae allure that puir gentlewoman, that she could not live without him; whilk appears to be of great probability, she being ane damsel of noble bluid, and he ane auld decrepit creature of maist base degree, sae that sic ane noble house could not have degenerate sae far, except John Knox had interposed the power of his master the devil, wha, as he transfigures himself sometimes as ane angel of licht, sae he causit John Knox appear ane of the maist noble and lusty men that could be found in the warld.'[1] 1564.

'. . . . the Lord Fleming married the Lord Ross's eldest daughter, wha was heretrix both of Ross and Halket; and the banquet was made in the park of Holyroodhouse, under Arthur's Seat, at the end of the loch, where great triumphs was made, the queen's grace being present, and the king of Swethland's ambassador being then in Scotland, with many other nobles.'—*Mar*. MAY 17.

In the romantic valley between Arthur's Seat and Salisbury Crags, there is still traceable a dam by which the natural drainage had been confined, so as to form a lake. It was probably at the end of that sheet of water that the banquet was set forth for Lord and Lady Fleming's wedding. The incident is so pleasantly picturesque, and associates Mary so agreeably with one of her subjects, that it is gratifying to reflect on Lord Fleming proving a steady friend to the queen throughout her subsequent troubles. He stoutly maintained Dumbarton Castle in her favour against the Regents, and against Elizabeth's general, Sir William Drury; nor was it taken from him except by stratagem.[2]

At the beginning of this month, Queen Mary paid a visit of pleasure to the Highlands of Perthshire, where the Earl of Athole was her entertainer. It is understood that Glen Tilt AUG.

[1] Nicol Burne's Disputation, p. 143.

[2] While Drury lay before the castle, Lord Fleming entered into a hostile correspondence with Sir George Carey, one of Elizabeth's officers. This is given in *Holinshed's Chronicle*.

1564. was the scene of a grand hunt, in the characteristic style of the country, at which the queen was present, and of which an account has been preserved to us by a scholarly personage who was in the royal train. 'In the year 1563,' says he (mistaking the year), 'the Earl of Athole, a prince of the blood-royal, had, with much trouble and vast expense, a hunting-match for the entertainment of our most illustrious and most gracious queen. Our people call this a royal hunting. I was then,' says William Barclay, 'a young man, and was present on the occasion. Two thousand Highlanders, of wild Scotch, as you call them here, were employed to drive to the hunting-ground all the deer from the woods and hills of Athole, Badenoch, Mar, Murray, and the counties about. As these Highlanders use a light dress, and are very swift of foot, they went up and down so nimbly that in less than two months' time they brought together 2000 red deer, besides roes and fallow-deer. The queen, the great men, and others, were in a glen when all the deer were brought before them. Believe me, the whole body of them moved forward in something like battle order. This sight still strikes me, and ever will, for they had a leader whom they followed close wherever he moved. This leader was a very fine stag, with a very high head. The sight delighted the queen very much; but she soon had occasion for fear, upon the earl's (who had been accustomed to such sights) addressing her thus: "Do you observe that stag who is foremost of the herd? There is danger from that stag; for if either fear or rage should force him from the ridge of that hill, let every one look to himself, for none of us will be out of the way of harm; for the rest will follow this one, and having thrown us under foot, they will open a passage to this hill behind us." What happened a moment after confirmed this opinion; for the queen ordered one of the best dogs to be let loose upon a wolf;[1] this the dog pursues, the leading stag was frightened, he flies by the same way he had come there, the rest rush after him, and break out where the thickest body of the Highlanders was. They had nothing for it but to throw themselves flat on the heath, and to allow the deer to pass over them. It was told the queen that several of the Highlanders had been wounded, and that two or three had been killed outright; and the whole body had got off, had not the Highlanders, by their

[1] Mr Pennant, from whom the above translation is borrowed, says, by a strange mistake, 'on one of the deer.'

skill in hunting, fallen upon a stratagem to cut off the rear from the main body. It was of those that had been separated that the queen's dogs, and those of the nobility, made slaughter. There were killed that day 360 deer, with five wolves and some roes.'[1] 1564.

The queen, in the course of her excursion, is believed to have taken an interest in the native music of the Highlands, in which, as in Ireland, the harp bore a distinguished part. It is even reported that a kind of competition amongst the native harpers took place in her presence, at which she adjudged the victory to Beatrix Gardyn, of Banchory, Aberdeenshire. Certain it is, that the Robertsons of Lude possessed a harp of antique form, which

Queen Mary's Harp.

family tradition represented as having come to them through a descendant of Beatrix Gardyn, who had married a Robertson of

[1] William Barclay, *De Regno et Regali Potestate adversus Monarchomachos.* Parisiis, 1600. This author was a native of Aberdeenshire, but finally settled at Angers, in France, as Professor of Civil Law in the University there. He died in 1604.

Bishop Geddes, in introducing this extract from Barclay's forgotten work to the notice of the Society of the Antiquaries of Scotland (1782), remarks that a still more grand entertainment of the same kind was given in 1529 to King James V., his mother, Queen Margaret, and the pope's legate, by the then Earl of Athole, and that an account of the affair has been preserved in Lindsay of Pitscottie's *History of Scotland.* The venerable bishop adds: 'Need I take notice that the hunting described by Barclay bears some resemblance to the *batidas* of the present king of Spain, where several huntsmen form a line and drive the deer through a narrow pass, at one side of which the king, with some attendants, has his post, in a green hut of boughs, and slaughters the poor animals as they come out almost as fast as charged guns can be put into his hand and he fire them. These are things sufficiently known; and the same manner of stag-hunting is practised in Italy, Germany, and other parts of Europe.'[1]

[1] *Archæologia Scotica*, ii. 111.

1564. Lude; and the same authority regarded this harp with veneration, as having been the prize conferred on the fair Beatrix by Queen Mary, for her superior excellence as a performer on the instrument.[1] Queen Mary's harp, as it is called, is now in the possession of Mr Stewart of Dalguise.[2] It is a small instrument compared with the modern harp, being fitted for twenty-eight strings, the longest extending twenty-four inches, the shortest two and a half. There had once been gems set in it, and also, it is supposed, a portrait of the queen. It was strung anew and played upon in 1806.

This summer there was 'guid cheap of victuals in all parts. The year afore, the boll of meal gave five merk, and this summer it was 18s. There ye may see the grace of God.'—*C. F.*

OCT. '. . . . William Smibert, being callit before the kirk [session of the Canongate] why he sufferit his bairn to be unbaptised, answers: "No, I have my bairn baptised, and that in the queen's grace's chapel," because, as he allegit, the kirk refusit him; and being requirit wha was witness unto the child, answers: "I will show no man at this time." For the whilk, James Wilkie, bailie, assistant with the kirk, commands the said William to be halden in ward until he declare wha was his witness, that the kirk may be assurit the bairn to be baptisit, and by wham.'—*Kirk-session Rec. of Canongate.*

1564-5. JAN. The queen making a progress in Fife caused so much banqueting as to produce a scarcity of wild-fowl: 'partridges were sold for a crown a-piece.'—*Knox.*

1565. APR. 1. The communion was administered in Edinburgh, and as it was near Easter, the few remaining Catholics met at mass. The reformed clergy were on the alert, and seized the priest, Sir James Carvet, as he was coming from the house where he had officiated. Knox tells us with what an absurd degree of leniency the offender was treated. They 'conveyed him,' says he, 'together with the master of the house, and one or two more of the assistants, to the Tolbooth, and immediately revested him with all his garments upon him, and so carried him to the Market Cross, where they set him on high, binding the chalice in his hand, and himself tied fast to

[1] Gunn's *Historical Enquiry respecting the Harp in the Highlands.* 1807.
[2] Agnes Strickland's *Life of Queen Mary.*

the said Cross, where he tarried the space of one hour; during which time *the boys served him with his Easter eggs.* 1565.

'The next day, Carvet with his assistants were accused and convinced by an assize, according to the act of parliament; and, albeit for the same offence he deserved death, yet, for all punishment, he was set upon the Market Cross for the space of three or four hours, the hangman standing by and keeping him, [while] the boys and others were busy with eggs-casting.'

The queen sent an angry letter to the magistrates about this business; from which 'may be perceived how grievously the queen's majesty would have been offended if the mess-monger had been handled according to his demerit'—that is, hanged.—*Knox.*

A discovery of antique remains was made at Inveresk, near Musselburgh, revealing the long-forgotten fact of the Romans once having had a settlement on that fine spot. Randolph, the English resident at Mary's court, communicated some account of the discovery to the Earl of Bedford. 'April 7, For certain there is found a cave beside Musselburgh, standing upon a number of pillars, made of tile-stones curiously wrought, signifying great antiquity, and strange monuments found in the same. This cometh to my knowledge, besides the common report, by th' assurance of Alexander Clerk, who was there to see it, which I will myself do within three or four days, and write unto your lordship the more certainty thereof, for I will leave nothing of it unseen.' 'April 18, The cave found beside Musselburgh, seemeth to be some monument of the Romans, by a stone which was found, with these words graven upon him, APPOLLONI GRANNO Q. L. SABINIANUS PROC. AUG. Divers short pillars set upright upon the ground, covered with tile-stones, large and thick, torning into divers angles, and certain places like unto chynes [chimneys] to avoid smoke. This is all I can gather thereof.'[1] APR.

The reader will be amused at the difficulty which Randolph seems to have felt in visiting a spot scarcely six miles from Edinburgh. He will, however, be equally gratified to know that the queen herself became interested in the preservation of the remains found on this occasion. Her treasurer's accounts contain an entry of twelvepence, paid to 'ane boy passand of Edinburgh, with ane charge of the queen's grace, direct to the bailies of Musselburgh, charging them to tak diligent heed and attendance, that the

[1] *Archæologia Scotica*, ii. 287.

1565. monument of grit antiquity, new fundin, be nocht demolishit nor broken down.'

The monument here spoken of was, in reality, an altar dedicated to Apollo Grannicus, the Long-haired Apollo, by Sabinianus, proconsul of Augustus, while the cave with pillars was the hypocaust or heating-chamber of a bath, connected with a villa, of which further remains were discovered in January 1783. The spot where the antiquities were discovered in 1565 is occupied by the lawn in front of Inveresk House. Camden reports the following as an accurate copy of the inscription, made by Sir Peter Young, preceptor to King James VI.—'APPOLLINI GRANNO Q. LUSIUS SABINIANUS PROC. AUG. VSSLVM.'—which is thus extended and translated by the ingenious Robert Stuart in his *Caledonia Romana* (1845): 'Appollini Grannico Quintus Lusius Sabinianus Proconsul Augusti, votum susceptum solvit lubens volens merito;' that is, 'To Appollo Granicus, Quintus Lusius Sabinianus, the Proconsul of Augustus [dedicates this], a self-imposed vow, cheerfully performed.'

Napier alludes to the Inveresk altar in his Commentary on the Apocalypse, and it appears to have attracted the attention of Ben Jonson, when he was in Scotland in 1618. We last hear of it from Sir Robert Sibbald, who died in 1711. In Gordon's *Itinerarium*, published a few years later, it is not noticed; wherefore it may be conjectured that this interesting relic of antiquity was lost sight of or destroyed about the beginning of the eighteenth century.

REIGN OF MARY: 1565-1567.

In July 1565, Mary married her youthful cousin, Henry Lord Darnley, son of the Earl of Lennox. This was a match not without its politic aspect, as things stood at that time, for, by accepting Darnley as her husband, the Scottish queen took a rival out of her way to the English throne, and added his pretensions to her own. As Darnley, however, was a Catholic, the union was disrelished by Queen Elizabeth, as well as by all the leaders of the Protestant interest in Scotland. A still greater objection to it lay in the weak and childish character of the young king.

Moray and his friends were thrown by the event into a rebellion; which, however, quickly ended in his defeat and exile. The queen then ruled for some time with the assistance of her husband and of her Italian secretary, David Riccio. In such circumstances, it was unavoidable that the confidence of her Protestant people should abate. Darnley soon proved to be little worth the sacrifice she had made for his sake. By a freak of youthful folly, prompted by jealousy of Riccio's influence, he associated in a conspiracy with the banished Moray and his associates, for putting the Italian away from the queen; thinking he might then bear undivided sway. Riccio was assassinated at Holyroodhouse, in the queen's presence (March 9, 1566), and the Protestant lords immediately returned. The horrible outrage took a strong hold of Mary's feelings, and was allowed too much to sway her subsequent actions. She seemed, however, to be reconciled to her husband; and not long after, her son, who afterwards became James VI., was born (June 19, 1566).

The childishness and low habits of Darnley completely unfitted him to become an adviser and help to the queen; he proved, on the contrary, a source of great trouble and vexation. Indignant as she was at Moray, Morton, and other Protestant lords who had been concerned in the Riccio assassination, she was little inclined to lean upon them as before. As the only remaining resource, she began to give her confidence to the Earl of Bothwell and the Earl of Huntly, two nobles of great power, but whose administration could not bring her so much popularity. Bothwell was a man of coarse character, fully as much disposed as any man in that age to gain his ambitious ends by violence. As early as March 1561-2, he had formed a plan for seizing the queen's person, and carrying her to the castle of Dumbarton, that he and the Duke of Chatelherault might enjoy the government between them. He had since then been restored to favour; but, so far from the queen having ever appeared to regard him as a lover, she had, so lately as February 1565-6, promoted and sanctioned his marriage to a friend of her own, a sister of the Earl of Huntly. He seems now to have thought that an opportunity was presented for his acquiring a mastery in Scotland. He caused the wretched Darnley to be murdered at his lodging in the Kirk of Field, near Edinburgh (March 12, 1567). Being suspected and accused of this act, he submitted to a trial, but was able to overbear justice, and to maintain his place in the queen's councils.

Mary, consequently, suffered in reputation, though whether she was aware of Bothwell's guilt is to this day a matter of doubt; much less is it certain that she had, as has been suspected, a guilty knowledge of her husband's death.

Having procured the countenance of some of the nobility to his plans, Bothwell seized the queen at the river Almond (April 24), and conducted her to his castle of Dunbar, where he kept her a prisoner, as was generally believed, by her own consent. His wife being hastily divorced, he married the queen (May 15), and thus seemed to have fully attained the object of his ambition; but the Protestant leaders rose in arms, took the queen away from him, and drove him into banishment. Mary, as one suspected of horrible crimes, was imprisoned in Lochleven Castle (June 17), and forced to sign a deed of abdication in favour of her infant son, who was consequently crowned as James VI., with the Earl of Moray as regent during his minority (July 29).

'Ane guid summer and har'est.'—*C. F.*

1565. Aug. 6. The queen and her husband were obliged, immediately after their marriage, to set about the suppression of a rebellion. The measure they adopted for raising troops was according to the custom and rule of the Scottish government. 'There was ane proclamation at the Mercat Cross of Edinburgh, commanding all and sundry earls, lords, barons, freeholders, gentlemen, and substantious yeomen, to address them with fifteen days victuals, to pass and convoy the king and queen to the parts of Fife, under the pain of tinsel [loss] of life, lands, and guids; and also commanding all and sundry the inhabitants of the burgh of Edinburgh, betwixt sixteen and sixty, to address them in the same manner, under the pains aforesaid.'—*D. O.* On the 22d of the month, this order was extended to 'all our sovereign's lieges.'

This feudal mode of raising an army was felt as a serious burden, particularly in the larger towns, where industry had attained, of course, the highest organisation. For the Rothschilds of Edinburgh, such as they were, there was another trouble. The mode of raising money adopted by Henry and Mary was not quite what would suit the views of modern men of that class. Sept. 27, 1565. 'Our soveranes causit certain of the principals of Edinburgh to come to them to Halyrudehouse, and after their coming, some of free will, and some brought agains their will, our soverane lady made ane orison to them, desiring them to lend her certain sowms of money, whilk they refusit to do; and therefore they were commandit to *remain in ward within the auld tower* wherein my lord of Murray lodgit, wherein they remainit.' Ultimately, the two difficulties were in a manner solved by each other. On the 6th of October, the above-mentioned notables of the city 'agreeit with our soveranes in this manner, to lend their majesties ten thousand merks, upon the superiority of Leith, under reversion . . . . . and alse to give their highnesses ane thousand pounds, *to suffer the haill town to remain at hame.*'

For some time after, the criminal records abound in cases of persons 'delatit for abiding from the queen's host.' On such occasions, some are found excusing themselves on account of sickness or personal infirmity; others plead their having sent substitutes. When no excuse could be made, fines are imposed. On the whole, it appears to have been a public burden of no light character, and during the reign of Mary, and the subsequent regencies, it was, owing to the great troubles of the country, of frequent occurrence.

'Great herships and oppression in mony parts of Scotland, in Strathearn, in Lennox, in Glenalmond, in Breadalbin; baith slaughter and oppression being made in sundry other parts by the Earl of Argyle and M'Gregor and their accomplices. Siclike in Strathardle, mony men slain by the men of Athole and the Stuarts of Lorn.'—*C. F.*

The town-council of Edinburgh were accustomed annually, at Nov. this time, to bestow upon their chief a bullock, which was called *The Provost's Ox*, twelve pounds Scots being allowed for the purpose of buying the best that was to be had. They also now gave him a tun of wine, and twelve ells of velvet to make him a gown, as an acknowledgment of special services he had done to the city.—*City Register, apud Maitland.*

'. . . . it was ordainit by the ministers, exhorters, and readers 1565-6. Mar. 2. of this realm, that they should begin ane public abstinence fra that day aucht hours afternoon, whilk was Saturday, unto Sunday at five hours at even, and then to take but bread and drink, and that

1565-6. in ane sober manner, during the whilk time the people to be occupiet in prayers and hearing the word of God; and as meikle to be done the next Sunday thereafter, for to pray to the eternal God that he wald saften and pacify his angry wrath whilk appearandly is come upon us for our sins, and specially that God wald inform, mollify, and make soft the hearts of our sovereigns towards our nobility whilk are now banished in England. . . .'—*D. O.*

These nobles were meanwhile arranging very active measures by the arm of flesh to bring about the desired change. Before the second fast had taken place, Riccio lay cold with his fifty-six wounds in the ante-chamber of Holyrood, the palace was in the hands of Morton, and the exiled lords had returned to Edinburgh.

1566. June. Paul Methven, originally a baker in Dundee, afterwards minister of Jedburgh, for an immorality of a gross kind, was excommunicated by the General Assembly in 1563. He was from the first penitent, offering to submit to any punishment which the church might impose for his offence, 'even if it were to lose any member of his body.' After two or three years of troubles and buffetings to and fro, he succeeded in inducing the Assembly to look mildly on his case. 'It was ordainit that he present himself personally before the Assembly, and, being entrit, [he] prostrate[d] himself before the whole brethren with weeping and howling, and, being commandit to rise, might not express farther his request, being, as appeared, so sore troublit with anguish of heart.' The penance imposed gives a striking idea of the discipline of these Calvinistic fathers: 'The said Paul upon the twa preaching-days betwixt the Sundays, sall come to the kirk door of Edinburgh when the second bell rings, clad in sackcloth, bareheaded and barefooted, and there remain while [until] he be brought in to the sermon, and placed in the public spectacle above the people. . . . . in the next Sunday after sall declare signs of his inward repentance to the people, humbly requiring the kirk's forgiveness; whilk done, he sall be clad in his awn apparel, and received in the society of the kirk as ane lively member thereof.'

June 19. A prince, who subsequently became James VI., was born to the queen in Edinburgh Castle, within that small irregularly shaped room, of about eight feet each way, which is still to be seen in the angle of the old palace. The wet-nurse of the royal babe was a certain Lady Reres, whose name occurs unpleasantly in the subsequent history of Mary. At the same time, the Countess of Athole, who was believed to have magical gifts, was brought to bed in the Castle. In a conversation which took place five years after, at Fallside in Fife, between one Andrew Lundie and John Knox, the former related that, 'when the queen was lying in *gisson* of the king, the Lady Athole, lying there likewise, baith within the Castle of Edinburgh, he came there for some business, and callit for the Lady Reres, whom he fand in her chalmer, lying bedfast, and, he asking of her disease, she answerit that she was never so troubled with no bairn that ever she bare, for the Lady Athole had casten all the pyne of her childbirth upon her.' [1] 1566.

It was a prevalent belief of that age that the pains of parturition could be transferred by supernatural art, and not merely to another woman, but to a man or to one of the lower animals. Amongst the charges against an enchantress of the upper ranks called Eupham M'Calyean, twenty-five years after this time, is one to the effect, that, for relief of her pain at the time of the birth of her two sons, she had had a bored stone laid under her pillow, and enchanted powder rolled up in her hair—likewise 'your guidman's sark tane aff him, and laid womplit under your bed-feet; the whilk being practisit, your sickness was casten aff you unnaturally, upon ane dog, whilk ran away and was never seen again.' [2]

'The Earl of Bedford, accompanied with forty horsemen, Englishmen, come as ambassador frae the queen's majesty of England, to nominate ane woman in Scotland, to be *cummer* to our sovereigns, to the baptising of our prince, their son, to the burgh of Edinburgh, and was lodgit in my lord duke's lodging at the Kirk of Field. In his coming in Edinburgh, he was honourably convoyit by the gentlemen of Lothian, but for the maist part by them of the Religion, because the said earl favourit the same greatumly. The said earl brought ane font, frae the queen's grace of England, of twa stane wecht, to be presentit to our sovereigns, in the whilk their son and our prince should be baptisit; the same was of fine gold. And he brought ane ring with ane stane, to be delivered to the said woman wha should occupy the place of the queen's grace of England in the time of the said baptising.'—*D. O.* Dec. 10.

[1] Richard Bannatyne's *Memorials*, p. 238.

[2] Dalyell's *Darker Superstitions of Scotland*, p. 130.

1566. Dec. 17. The young prince was baptised at Stirling Castle, and named Charles James. The preparations in apparel and decorations were magnificent beyond everything of the kind hitherto known. 'The said prince was borne out of his chalmer to the chapel by the French ambassador, my Lady of Argyle, *cummer* for the Queen of England by commission, and Monsieur La Croc for the Duke of Savoy. All the barons and gentlemen bore prickets of wax, wha stood in rank on ilk side, frae the prince's chalmer door to the said chapel. Next the French ambassador, ane great serge of wax by the Earl of Athole, the salt-vat by the Earl of Eglintoun, the cude by the Lord Semple, the basin and laver by the Lord Ross; and at the chapel door, the prince was receivit by my Lord Sanct Androis, wha was *executor officii in pontificalibus,* with staff, mitre, cross, and the rest. Collaterals to him were the Bishops of Dunkeld [and] Dumblane, with their rochets and hoods; and also assistit with rochets and hoods the Bishop of Ross, the Prior of Whithorn, and sundry others with serpclaiths and hoods, and the hale college of the chapel royal, with their habits and u[p]maist copes[?]. The prince was baptisit in the said fount, and thir solemnities endit by near five hours afternoon, with singing and playing on organs.' —*D. O.*

It appears that at these festivities the skeleton was not wanting. 'There was sitting in the entry of the Castle a poor man asking alms, having a young child upon his knee, whose head was so great [hydrocephalus?] that the body of the child could scarce bear it up. A certain gentleman perceiving it, could scarce refrain from tears, for fear of the evils he judged to be portended.'—*Knox.*

1566-7. Feb. 10. '. . . . At twa hours in the morning, there come certain traitors to the provost's house [in the Kirk of Field], wherein was our sovereign's husband Henry, and ane servant of his, callit William Taylor, lying in their naked beds; and there privily with wrang keys openit the doors, and come in upon the said prince, and there without mercy worried him and his said servant in their beds; and thereafter took him and his servant furth of that house, and cuist him naked in ane yard beside the Thief Raw, and syne come to the house again, and blew the house in the air, sae that there remainit not ane stane upon ane other, undestroyit. . . . . At five hours, the said prince and his servant was found lying dead in the said yard, and was ta'en into ane house in the Kirk of Field, and laid while [till] they were buriet.'—*D. O.*

Buchanan relates two 'prodigies' which happened in connection with the death of Darnley. 'One John Lundin, a gentleman of Fife, having long been sick of a fever, the day before the king was killed, about noon, raised himself a little in his bed, and, as if he had been astonished, cried out to those that stood by him, with a loud voice, "to go help the king, for the parricides were just then murdering him;" and a while after he called out with a mournful tone, "Now it is too late to help him; he is already murdered;" and he himself lived not long after he had uttered these words.' The other circumstance occurred just at the time the murder happened. 'Three of the familiar friends of the Earl of Athole, the king's cousin, men of reputation for valour and estate, had their lodgings not far from the king's. When they were asleep about midnight, there was a certain man seemed to come to Dugald Stewart, who lay next the wall, and to draw his hand gently over his beard and cheek, so as to awake him, saying, "Arise, they are offering violence to you." He presently awaked, and was considering the apparition within himself, when another of them cries out presently in the same bed, "Who kicks me?" Dugald answered, "Perhaps it is a cat, which used to walk about in the night;" upon which the third, who was not yet awake, rose presently out of his bed, and stood upon the floor, demanding "who it was that had given him a box on the ear?" As soon as he had spoken, a person seemed to go out of the house by the door, and that not without some noise. Whilst they were descanting on what they had heard and seen, the noise of the blowing up of the king's house put them into a very terrible consternation.' 1566-7.

'. . . . whilk was Sanct Mark's even, our sovereign lady, riding frae Stirling (whereto she passed a little before to visie her son) to Edinburgh, James Earl of Bothwell, accompaniet with seven or aucht hundred men and friends, whom he causit believe that he would ride upon the thieves of Liddesdale, met our sovereign lady betwixt Kirkliston and Edinburgh, at ane place called the *Briggis*, accompaniet with ane few number, and there took her person, [which he conducted] to the castle of Dunbar. The rumour of the ravishing of her majesty coming to the provost of Edinburgh, incontinent the common bell rang, and the inhabitants ran to armour and weapons, the ports was steekit, [and] the artillery of the Castle shot.'—*D. O.* 1567. APR. 24.

The place indicated was well chosen for the purpose, being in an angle of ground enclosed by the Almond River and the Gogar

1567. Burn, which meet here; so that the queen and her little party could not have fled except at considerable risk. The post-road from Linlithgow to Edinburgh still passes by the spot, immediately after crossing the river Almond by the Boat-house Bridge.[1] Thus characterised, it is perhaps of all places on the road from Linlithgow to Edinburgh, that which Bothwell might be expected to choose if he had been in no collusion with the queen, and anxious to take her at advantage.

May 11. The queen had time at this remarkable crisis of her history—when just about to be married to Bothwell—to grant a letter to 'the cunning men of the occupation and craft of chirurgeons,' freeing them from the duty of attending hosts and wappenshaws, and also from that of 'passing upon inquests and assizes,' in order that they might have 'the greater occasion to study the perfection of the said craft, to the uttermost of their ingynes [abilities].'[2]

There is a common belief that surgeons and butchers are exempt from serving on juries, on account of the assumed effect of their profession in making them reckless as to destruction of life. Perhaps the notion has in part taken its rise in this exemption from service for the surgeons, though it appears to have been granted on more honourable consideration.

[1] Walter Goodall and Miss Agnes Strickland have been misled by the description of the place in Bothwell's Act of Forfeiture—'*ad pontes, vulgo vocatos foulbriggs*'—into the belief that the queen was seized at the suburb of Edinburgh formerly called Foulbriggs, and now Fountain Bridge. In reality, the expression in the Act, rightly translated, applies to the place indicated in the *Diurnal of Occurrents*—'at the Briggs, commonly called Foulbriggs,' the syllable *foul* being presumably a vulgar casual addition which the ancient marshy condition of the place rendered appropriate. All the other contemporary writers place the scene of the seizure at the Almond—Buchanan, Birrel, and Herries—while Sir James Melville, who was one of the party seized, says 'betwixt Linlithgow and Edinburgh'—an expression he could scarcely have used if the fact had happened close to the city. In *Ane Chronicle of the Kings of Scotland*, printed by the Maitland Club, and apparently contemporary, *the brig of Awmont* is the locality assigned. But the most powerful evidence on the subject, and what sets the matter at rest, is a Remission under the Privy Seal, of date October 1, 1567, to Andrew Redpath, for his being concerned in 'besetting the queen's way . . . . *near the water of Awmond*, and for taking and ravishing her,' &c. It may be remarked that there is no evidence of the suburb alluded to by Miss Strickland having been called Foulbriggs, or having existed at all, at that time, while we have proof of the existence of a place on the Almond Water, under the name of the *Briggs*, long before this time. In the Register of the Privy Seal is 'ane lettre maid to Robert Hamilton in Briggis, makand him capitane and kepar of the place and palace of Linlithgow,' &c. 1543, Aug. 22.

[2] Privy Seal Register.

REGENCY OF MORAY: 1567-1570.

Mary remained a prisoner in Lochleven Castle for ten months, while Moray, as Regent, maintained a good understanding with England, and did much to enforce internal peace and order. At length (May 1568), the unhappy Queen made her escape, and threw herself into the arms of the powerful family of Hamilton, who had continued unreconciled to the new government. They raised for her a considerable body of retainers, and for a few days she seemed to have a chance of recovering her authority; but her army was overthrown at Langside by the Regent, and she had then no resource but to pass into England, and ask refuge with Queen Elizabeth. By her she was received with a show of civility, but was in reality treated as a prisoner, and even subjected to the indignity of a kind of trial, where her brother Moray acted as her accuser. The proofs brought forward for her guilt were such as not to allow of any judgment being passed against her by Elizabeth, and it cannot be said that they have secured a decidedly unfavourable verdict from posterity. The series of circumstances is, no doubt, calculated to excite suspicion; yet they are not incompatible with the theory, that she was trained into them by others; and it must be admitted that one who had previously lived so blamelessly —rejecting the suit of Bothwell when they were both free persons— and who afterwards made so noble an appearance when adjudged to a cruel death for offences of which she was innocent, was not the kind of person likely to have assisted in murdering a husband, or to have deliberately united herself to one whom she believed to be his murderer.

Under a protestant Regent, with the friendship and aid of Elizabeth, whose interest it was to keep popery out of the whole island, Scotland might have enjoyed some years of tranquillity. Moray, whatever opinion may be entertained of his conduct towards his sister, proved a vigorous and just ruler, insomuch as to gain the title of the *Good Regent;* but he was early cut off in his course, falling a victim to private revenge at Linlithgow (January 23, 1569–70).

The long-enduring system of predatory warfare carried on by the borderers against England rendered them a lawless set at all times; but in the present state of the government, they were unusually troublesome. 'In all this time,' says the *Diurnal of Occurrents,* 'frae the queen's grace' putting in captivity to this time, the 1567. Oct.

1567. thieves of Liddesdale made great herslip on the poor labourers of the ground, and that through wanting of justice; for the realm was sae divided in sundry factions and conspirations, that there was nae authority obeyed, nor nae justice execute.'—*D. O.*

Sir Richard Maitland of Lethington gives us a lively description of these men and their practices:

'Of Liddesdale the common thieves
Sae pertly steals now and reaves,
That nane may keep
Horse, nolt, or sheep,
For their mischieves.

They plainly through the country rides,
I trow the meikle De'il them guids,
Where they onset,
Ay in their gait,
There is nae yett,
Nor door, them bides.

Thae thieves that steals and turses[1] hame
Ilk ane of them has ane to-name,[2]
Will of the Laws,
Hab of the Shaws;
To mak bare wa's,
They think nae shame.

They spulyie puir men of their packs,
They leave them nought on bed nor balks,[3]
Baith hen and cock,
With reel and rock,
The *Laird's Jock*
All with him taks.

They leave not spendle, spoon, nor spit,
Bed, bolster, blanket, sark, nor sheet;
John of the Park
Rypes[4] kist and ark;
For all sic wark
He is right meet.

He is weel-kenned, *Jock of the Syde,*
A greater thief did never ride.
He never tires
For to break byres;
O'er muir and mires,
O'er guid ane guide. . . .

[1] Carries. [2] Nickname. [3] Garret. [4] Searches.

Of stouth[1] though now they come good speed, 1567.
That nother of God nor men has dread,
Yet or[2] I die,
Some shall them see
Hing on a tree,
While[3] they be dead.'[4]

If it was at this time, as is likely, that Sir Richard wrote these verses, he might well calculate on the vigour of the Regent while prophesying sad days for the Border men.

'. . . . there was ane proclamation [October 10], to meet the Regent in Peebles upon the 8 of November next, for the repressing of the thieves in Annandale and Eskdale; but my Lord Regent thinking they wald get advertisement, he prevented the day, and came over the water secretly, and lodged in Dalkeith; this upon the 19 day [October]; and upon the morrow he departed towards Hawick, where he came both secretly and suddenly, and there took thirty-four thieves, whom he partly caused hang and partly drown; five he let free upon caution; and upon the 2nd day of November, he brought other ten with him to Edinburgh, and there put them in irons.'—*Bir.*

We have some trace of these men in the Lord Treasurer's accounts as inmates of the Tolbooth of Edinburgh. On the 30th of November, thirty-two pounds are paid to Andro Lindsay, keeper of that prison, for the furnishing of meat and drink to Robert Elliot, alias *Clement's Hob,* and Archy Elliot, called *Archy Kene.* On the same day, twenty-three pounds four shillings are disbursed for a month's board in the same black hotel, for 'Robert Elliot, called *Mirk Hob;* Gavin Elliot, called *Gawin of Ramsiegill;* Martin Elliot, called *Martin of Heuchous;* Robert Elliot, son to *Elder Will;* Robert Elliot, called the *Vicar's Rob;* Robert Elliot, called *Hob of Thorlieshope;* Dandy Grosar, called *Richardtoncleucht;* and Robert Grosar, called *Son to Cockston.*'

In an act of the Privy Council, 6th November 1567, it is alleged that the thieves of Liddesdale, and other parts of the Scottish Border, have been in the habit, for some time past, of taking sundry persons prisoners, and giving them up upon ransom—exactly the conduct of the present banditti of the Apennines. It is also averred that many persons are content to pay 'black-mail' to these thieves, and sit under their protection, 'permittand them to reif, herry, and oppress their neighbours in their sicht, without contradiction or stop.' Such practices were now forbidden

[1] Thievery. [2] Ere. [3] Till. [4] *Ancient Scottish Poems,* 2 vols. 1786.

1567. under severe penalties; and it was enjoined that 'when ony companies of thieves or broken men comes ower the swires within the in-country,' all dwelling in the bounds shall 'incontinent cry on hie, raise the fray, and follow them, as weel in their in-passing as out-passing,' in order to recover the property which may have been stolen.

Walter Scott of Harden, a famous Border chief, was this year married to Mary Scott of Dryhope, commonly called the *Flower of Yarrow*. The pair had six sons, from five of whom descended the families of Harden (which became extinct); Highchesters, now represented by Lord Polwarth, Raeburn (from which came Sir Walter Scott of Abbotsford), Wool, and Synton; and six daughters, all of whom were married to gentlemen of figure, and all had issue.

It is a curious consideration to the many descendants of Walter Scott of Harden, that his marriage-contract is signed by a notary, because none of the parties could write their names. The father-in-law, Scott of Dryhope, bound himself to find Harden in horse meat and man's meat, at his own house, for a year and day; and five barons engaged that he should remove at the expiration of that period, without attempting to continue in possession by force.

Harden was a man of parts and sagacity, and living to about the year 1629, was popularly remembered for many a day thereafter under the name of 'Auld Watt.' One of his descendants relates the following anecdote of him:—'His sixth son was slain at a fray, in a hunting-match, by Scott of Gilmanscleuch. His brothers flew to arms; but the old laird secured them in the dungeon of his tower, hurried to Edinburgh, stated the crime, and obtained a gift of the lands of the offenders from the crown. He returned to Harden with equal speed, released his sons, and shewed them the charter. "To horse, lads!" cried the savage warrior, "and let us take possession! The lands of Gilmanscleuch are well worth a dead son."'[1]

Oct. 30. Bessie Tailiefeir, in the Canongate, Edinburgh, having slandered Bailie Thomas Hunter by saying 'he had in his house ane false stoup [measure],' which was found not to be true, she was sentenced to be *brankit* and set on the Cross for an hour.[2]

The punishment of branking, which was a customary one for scolds, slanderers, and other offenders of a secondary class,

[1] *Border Minstrelsy*, i. 157.
[2] Burgh Record of Canongate, *Maitland Club Mis.*, ii. 303.

consisted in having the head enclosed in an iron frame, from which projected a kind of spike, so as to enter the mouth and prevent speech. 1567.

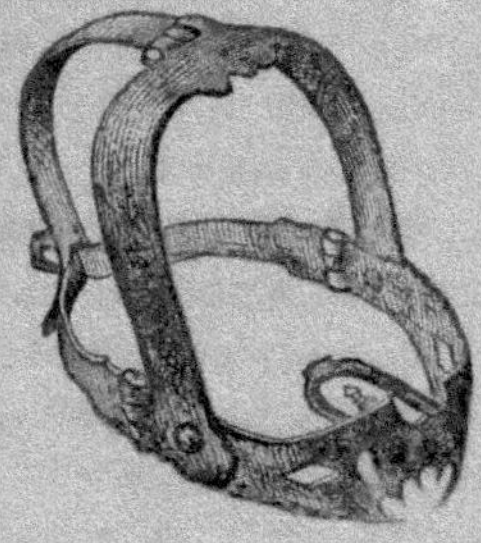

The Branks.

Charles Sandeman, cook, on being made a member of the guild of Edinburgh, came under an obligation that, from that time forth, 'he sall not be seen upon the causey,' like other cooks, carrying meat to sell in common houses, but cause his servants pass with the same; and 'he sall hald his tavern on the Hie Gait . . . . . and behave himself honestly in all time coming, under pain of escheat of his wines.'—*E. C. R.* Nov. 20.

'. . . At 2 afternoon, the Laird of Airth and the Laird of Wemyss met upon the Hie Gait of Edinburgh; and they and their followers faught a very bluidy skirmish, where there was many hurt on both sides with shot of pistol.'—*Bir.* Apparently in consequence of this affair, there was, on the 27th, 'a strait proclamation,' discharging the wearing of culverins, dags, pistolets, or 'sic other firewerks,' with injunctions that any one contravening should be seized and subjected to summary trial, 'as gif they had committit recent slauchters.'—*P. C. R.* Nov. 24.

This is the first of a series of street-fights by which the Hie Gait of Edinburgh was reddened during the reign of James VI., and which scarcely came to an end till his English reign was far advanced. It is worthy of note that *sword and buckler* were at this time the ordinary gear of gallant men in England—a comparatively harmless furnishing; but we see that small firearms were used in Scotland.

An act of parliament was passed to prevent horses being exported, it being found that so many had lately been taken to Bordeaux Dec. 15.

1567. and other places abroad, as to cause 'great skaith' by the raising of prices at home.

There has been a feeling of rivalry between Perth and Dundee from time immemorial, and it probably will never cease while both towns exist. At a parliament now held by the Regent Moray, the representatives of each burgh strove for the next place after Edinburgh in that equestrian procession which used to be called the *Riding of the Estates.* A tumult consequently arose upon the street, and it was with difficulty that this was stilled. Birrel relates how the Regent was 'much troubled to compose those two turbulent towns of Perth and Dundee,' and that 'it was like to make a very great deal of business, had not the same been mediate for the present by some discreet men who dealt in the matter.' Due investigation was afterwards made (January 9, 1567–8), that it might be ascertained 'in whais default the said tumult happenit.' It was found that 'James Wedderburn and George Mitchell, burgesses of Dundee, and William Rysie, bearer of the handsenyie [ensign] thereof,' were no wise culpable; and they were accordingly allowed to depart.

DEC. 27. Alexander Blair younger of Balthayock, and George Drummond of Blair, gave surety before the Privy Council for Alexander Blair of Freirton, near Perth, 'that Jonet Kincraigie, spouse to the said Alexander, sall be harmless and skaithless of him and all that he may let, in time coming, under the pain of five hundred merks; and als that he sall resave the said Jonet in house, and treat, sustene, and entertene her honestly as becomes ane honest man to do to his wife, in time coming;' besides paying to her children by a former husband their 'bairn's part of geir.'—*P. C. R.*

DEC. 31. 'Robert Jack, merchant and burgess of Dundee, was hangit and quarterit for false coin called *Hardheads,* whilk he had brought out of Flanders.'—*Bir.* 'Fals lyons callit hardheades, plakis, balbeis,[1] and other fals money,' is the description given in another record, *literatim.*

The hardhead was originally a French coin, denominated in Guienne *hardie,* and identical with the liard. It was of debased copper, and usually of the value of three-halfpence Scotch; but further debasement was oftener than once resorted to by Scottish

[1] Babees, halfpence, from *bas billon,* a low piece of money.

rulers as a means of raising a little revenue. Knox, in 1559, complains that 'daily there were such numbers of *lions* (alias called *hardheads*) prented, that the baseness thereof made all things exceeding dear.' So also the Regent Morton increased his unpopularity by diminishing the value of hardheads from three halfpence to a penny, and the plack-piece from fourpence to twopence.[1] 1567.

Robert Jack had probably made a sort of mercantile speculation in bringing in a debased foreign *hardhead*. The importance attached to his crime is indicated by the payment (January 28, 1567-8) of £33, 6s. 8d. to George Monro of Dalcartie, for 'expenses made by him upon six horsemen and four footmen for the sure convoying of Robert Jack, being apprehended in Ross for false cunyie.'

1567-8. Jan. 5.

It may somewhat modify the views generally taken of the destruction of relics of the ancient religion under the Protestant governments succeeding the Reformation, that John Lockhart of Bar was denounced rebel at this time for conveying John Macbrair forth of the castle of Hamilton, and 'for down-casting of images in the kirk of Ayr and other places.'[2]

About the same time, the Regent learned that the lead upon the cathedrals of Aberdeen and Elgin was in the course of being piecemeal taken away. Thinking it as well that some public good should be obtained from this material, the Privy Council ordered (February 7, 1567-8) that the whole be taken down and sold for the support of the army now required to reduce the king's rebels to obedience.

Jan. 17.

'A play made by Robert Semple,' was 'played before the Lord Regent and diverse others of the nobility.'—*Bir*. There have been several conjectures as to this play and its author, with little satisfactory result. It was probably a very simple representation of some historical scene or transaction, such as we can imagine the life of the execrable Bothwell to have gratefully furnished before such a company. Semple appears to have been in such a rank of life as not to be above ordinary pecuniary rewards for his services, as on the 12th of February there is an entry in the treasurer's books of £66, 13s. 4d. 'to Robert Semple.' He was a fruitful, but dull writer, being the author of *The Regentis Trajedie*, 1570; *The Bishopis Lyfe and Testament*, 1571; *My*

[1] Hume's *Hist. House of Douglas*.
[2] Privy Seal Register.

1567-8. *Lord Methvenis Trajedie*, 1572; and *The Siege of the Castle of Edinburgh*, 1573: besides various poems preserved in the Bannatyne Manuscript.

FEB. 24. Seeing that 'in the spring of the year all kinds of flesh decays and grows out of season, and that it is convenient for the commonweal that they be sparit during that time, to the end that they may be mair plenteous and better cheap the rest of the year,' the Privy Council forbade the use of flesh of any kind during 'Lentern.' Fleshers, hostelers, cooks, and taverners, were forbidden to slay any animals for use during that season hereafter, under pain of confiscation of their movable goods.—*P. C. R.* This order was kept up in the same terms for many years, a forced economy preserving a rule formerly based on a religious principle.

MAR. 4. The Regent granted a licence to Cornelius De Vois, a Dutchman, for nineteen years, to search for gold and silver in any part of Scotland, 'break the ground, mak sinks and pots therein, and to put labourers thereto,' as he might think expedient, with assurance of full protection from the government, paying in requital for every hundred ounces of gold or silver which could be purified by washing, eight ounces, and for every hundred of the same which required the more expensive process of a purification by fire, four ounces.—*P. C. R.*

Stephen Atkinson, who speculated in the gold-mines of Scotland a generation later, gives us[1] some account of Cornelius De Vois, whom he calls a German lapidary, and who, he says, had come to Scotland with recommendations from Queen Elizabeth. According to this somewhat foolish writer, 'Cornelius went to view the said mountains in Clydesdale and Nydesdale, upon which mountains he got a small taste of small gold. This was a whetstone to sharpen his knife upon; and this natural gold tasted so sweet as the honeycomb in his mouth. And then he consulted with his friends at Edinburgh, and by his persuasions provoked them to adventure with him, shewing them at first the natural gold, which he called the temptable gold, or alluring gold. It was in sterns, and some like unto birds' eyes and eggs: he compared it unto a woman's eye, which entiseth her lover into her bosom.' Cornelius was not inferior to his class in speculative extravagance. He found in his golden dreams a solution for the question regarding the poor. He

[1] *Discoverie and Historie of the Gold Mynes in Scotland.* Written in 1619. Bannatyne Club, 1825.

saw Scotland and England 'both oppressed with poor people which beg from door to door for want of employment, and no man looketh to it.' But all these people were to find good and profitable employment if his projects were adopted. We are not accustomed to consider our countrymen inferior in energy and enterprise to the Germans. Yet Cornelius stated, that if he had been able to shew in his own country such indications of mineral wealth as he had found in Scotland, 'then the whole country would confederate, and not rest till young and old that were able be set to work thereat, and to discover this treasure-house from whence this gold descended; and the people, from ten years old till ten times ten years old, should work thereat: no charges whatsoever should be spared, till mountains and mosses were turned into valleys and dales, but this treasure-house should be discovered.' 1567 8.

It appears that Cornelius so far prevailed on the Scots to 'confederate,' that they raised a stock of £5000 Scots, equal to about £416 sterling, and worked the mines under royal privileges. According to Atkinson, this adventurer 'had sixscore men at work in valleys and dales. He employed both lads and lasses, idle men and women, which before went a-begging. He profited by their work, and they lived well and contented.' They sought for the valuable metal by washing the detritus in the bottoms of the valleys, receiving from their employer a mark sterling for every ounce they realised. So long after as 1619, one John Gibson survived in the village of Crawford to relate how he had gathered gold in these valleys in pieces 'like birds' eyes and birds' eggs,' the best being found, he said, in Glengaber Water, in Ettrick, which he sold for 6s. 8d. sterling per ounce to the Earl of Morton. Cornelius, within the space of thirty days, sent to the cunyie-house in Edinburgh as much as eight pound-weight of gold, a quantity which would now bring £450 sterling.

What ultimately came of Cornelius's adventure does not appear. He vanishes notelessly from the field. We are told by Atkinson that the adventure was subsequently taken up by one Abraham Grey, a Dutchman heretofore resident in England, commonly called *Greybeard*, from his having a beard which reached to his girdle. He hired country-people at 4d. a day, to wash the detritus of the valleys around Wanlock-head for gold; and it is added, that enough was found to make 'a very fair deep basin of natural gold,' which was presented by the Regent Morton to the French king, filled with gold pieces, also the production of Scotland.

The same valleys were afterwards searched for gold by an

1567-8. Englishman named George Bowes, who also sunk shafts in the rock, but probably with limited success, as has hitherto been experienced in ninety-nine out of every hundred instances, according to Sir Roderick Murchison.

In consequence of an extremely dry summer, the yield of grain and herbage in 1567 was exceedingly defective. The ensuing winter being unusually severe, there was a sad failure of the means of supporting the domestic animals. A stone of hay came to be sold in Derbyshire at fivepence,[1] which seems to have been regarded as a starvation price. There was a general mortality among the sheep and horses. In Scotland, the opening of 1568 was marked by scarcity and all its attendant evils. 'There was,' says a contemporary chronicler, 'exceeding dearth of corns, in respect of the penury thereof in the land, and that beforehand a great quantity thereof was transported to other kingdoms: for remeed whereof inhibitions were made sae far out of season, that nae victual should be transported furth of the country under the pain of confiscation, even then when there was no more left either to satisfy the indigent people, or to plenish the ordinar mercats of the country as appertenit.'—*H. K. J.*

During his short administration, the Regent Moray gave a large portion of his time and attention to the repression of lawless people. Justice was executed in no sparing manner. March 8, 1567–8, 'the Regent went to Glasgow, and there held ane justice-aire, where there was execute about the number of *twenty-eight persons* for divers crimes.' July 1568, he 'rade to St Andrews, and causit drown a man callit Alexander Macker and six more, for piracy.' Sep. 13, 'the Lord Regent rade to the fair to Jedburgh, to apprehend the thieves; but they being advertised of his coming, came not to the fair; sae he was frustrate of his intention, excepting three thieves whilk he took, and caused hang within the town there.'—*Bir.* April 1569, the Regent made a raid to the Border against the thieves, accompanied by a party of English. 'But the thieves keepit themselves in sic manner, that the Regent gat nane thereof, nor did little other thing, except he brint and reft the places of Mangerton and Whithope, with divers other houses belonging to the said thieves.'—*D. O.*

In the same month, a number of the most considerable

[1] *Holinshed's Chronicle.*

persons in the southern counties entered into a bond at Kelso, agreeing to be obedient subjects to the Regent Earl of Moray, and to do all in their power for the putting down of the thieves of Liddesdale, Ewesdale, Eskdale, and Annandale, especially those of the names Armstrong, Elliot, Nickson, Croser [Grozart?], Little, Bateson, Thomson, Irving, Bell, Johnston, Glendoning, Routledge, Henderson, and Scott; not resetting or intercommuning with them, their wives, bairns, tenants, and servants, or suffering any meat or drink to be carried to them, 'where we may let;' also, if, 'in case of the resistance or pursuit of any of the said thieves, it sall happen to ony of them to be slain or brint, or ony of us and our friends to be harmit by them, we sall ever esteem the quarrel and deadly feid equal to us all, and sall never agree with the said thieves but together, with ane consent and advice.'[1] 1567-8.

Axel Wiffirt, servant of the king of Denmark, was licensed to levy 2000 men of war in Scotland, and to convey them away armed as culviriners on foot, 'as they best can provide them,' being to serve the Danish monarch in his wars.[2] 1568. JULY 13.

'Touran Murray, brother-german to the Laird of Tullibardine, was shot and slain out of the place of Auchtertyre, in Stratherne, by one Wood [Mad] Andrew Murray and his confederates, who kept the said place certain days, and slew some six persons more, yet made escape at that present.'—*Bir.* JULY 15.

'Ane called James Dalgliesh, merchant, brought the pest in[to] Edinburgh.'—*D. O.* SEP. 8.

According to custom in Edinburgh, when this dire visitor made his appearance, the families which proved to be infected were compelled to remove, with all their goods and furniture, out to the Burgh-moor, where they lodged in wretched huts hastily erected for their accommodation. They were allowed to be visited by their friends, in company with an officer, after eleven in the forenoon; any one going earlier was liable to be punished with death—as were those who concealed the pest in their houses. Their clothes were meanwhile purified by boiling in a large caldron erected in the open air, and their houses were 'clengit' by the proper officers. All these regulations were under the care of two citizens selected

[1] The original, preserved in the General Register House, is printed at length in Pitcairn, iii. 394.

[2] Privy Seal Register.

1568. for the purpose, and called *Bailies of the Muir;* for each of whom, as for the cleansers and bearers of the dead, a gown of gray was made, with a white St Andrew's cross before and behind, to distinguish them from other people. Another arrangement of the day was, 'that there be made twa close biers, with four feet, coloured over with black, and [ane] white cross with ane bell to be hung upon the side of the said bier, whilk sall mak warning to the people.'[1]

The public policy was directed rather to the preservation of the untainted, than to the recovery of the sick. In other words, selfishness ruled the day. The inhumanity towards the humbler classes was dreadful. Well might *Maister Gilbert Skeyne, Doctour in Medicine,* remark in his little tract on the pest, now printed in Edinburgh: 'Every ane is become sae detestable to other (whilk is to be lamentit), and specially the puir in the sight of the rich, as gif they were not equal with them touching their creation, but rather without saul or spirit, as beasts degenerate fra mankind.'[2] This worthy mediciner tells us, indeed, that he was partly moved to publish his book by 'secand the puir in Christ inlaik [perish] without assistance of support in body, all men detestand aspection, speech, or communication with them.'

Dr Skeyne's treatise, which consists of only forty-six very small pages, gives us an idea of the views of the learned of those days regarding the pest. He describes it as 'ane feverable infection, maist cruel, and sundry ways strikand down mony in haste.' It proceeds, in his opinion, from a corruption of the air, 'whilk has strength and wickedness above all natural putrefaction,' and which he traces immediately to the wrath of the just God at the sins of mankind. There are, however, inferior causes, as stagnant waters, corrupting animal matters and filth, the eating of unwholesome meat and decaying fruits, and the drinking of corrupt water. Extraordinary humidity in the atmosphere is also dwelt upon as a powerful cause, especially when it follows in autumn after a hot summer. 'Great dearth of victual, whereby men are constrained to eat evil and corrupt meats,' he sets down as a cause much less notable. He does not forget to advert to the suspicious intermeddling of comets and shooting-stars. 'Nae pest,' he says, 'continually endures mair than three years;' and he remarks how 'we daily see the puir mair subject to sic calamity nor the potent.'

Dr Skeyne's regimen for the pest regards both its prevention and

[1] Council Register, quoted in *Maitland's History of Edinburgh,* p. 32.
[2] *Ane Breve Descriptioun of the Pest,* &c. 1568.

its cure, and involves an immense variety of curious recipes and 1568. rules of treatment, expressed partly in Latin and partly in English. He ends by calling his readers to observe—'As there is diversity of time, country, age, and consuetude to be observit in time of ministration of ony medicine preservative or curative, even sae there is divers kinds of pest, whilk may be easily knawn and divided by weel-learnit physicians, whase counsel in time of sic danger of life is baith profitable and necessar, in respect that in this pestilential disease every ane is mair blind nor the moudiewort in sic things as concerns their awn health.'

There has been preserved a curious letter which Adam Bothwell, bishop of Orkney, addressed in this time of plague to his brother-in-law, Sir Archibald Napier of Merchiston, regarding the dangers in which the latter was placed by the nearness of his house to the bivouac of the infected on the Burgh-moor.[1] It opens with an allusion to Sir Archibald's present position as a friend of Queen Mary in trouble with the Regent:

'RICHT HONOURABLE SIR AND BROTHER—I heard, the day, the rigorous answer and refuse that ye gat, whereof I was not weel apayit. But always I pray you, as ye are set amids twa great inconvenients, travel to eschew them baith. The ane is maist evident—to wit, the remaining in your awn place where ye are; for by the number of sick folk that gaes out of the town, the muir is [li]able to be overspread; and it cannot be but, through the nearness of your place and the indigence of them that are put out, they sall continually repair about your room, and through their conversation infect some of your servants, whereby they sall precipitate yourself and your children in maist extreme danger. And as I see ye have foreseen the same for the young folk, whaise bluid is in maist peril to be infectit first, and therefore purposes to send them away to Menteith, where I wald wiss at God that ye war yourself, without offence of authority, or of your band, sae that your house get nae skaith. But yet, sir, there is ane mid way whilk ye suld not omit, whilk is to withdraw you frae that side of the town to some house upon the north side of the samen; whereof ye may have in borrowing, when ye sall have to do—to wit, the Gray Crook, Innerleith's self, Wairdie, or sic other places as ye could choose within ane mile; whereinto I wald suppose ye wald be in less danger than in Merchanston. And close up your houses,

[1] Mr M. Napier's Notes to Spottiswoode's History, Spot. Club edition.

1568. your granges, your barns, and all, and suffer nae man come therein, while [till] it please God to put ane stay to this great plague; and in the meantime, make you to live upon your penny, or on sic thing as comes to you out of Lennox or Menteith;[1] whilk gif ye do not, I see ye will ruin yourself; and howbeit I escape in this voyage,[2] I will never look to see you again, whilk were some mair regret to me than I will expreme by writing. Always [I] beseeks you, as ye love your awn weal, the weal of your house, and us your friends that wald you weel, to tak sure order in this behalf; and, howbeit your evil favourers wald cast you away, yet ye tak better keep on yourself, and mak not them to rejoice, and us your friends to mourn baith at ance. Whilk God forbid, and for his goodness, preserve you and your posterity from sic skaith, and maintein you in [his] holy keeping for ever. Of Edinburgh, the 21st day of September 1568, by your brother at power,

'THE BISHOP OF ORKNEY.'

The bishop speaks with unmistakable friendship for his brother-in-law; but what he says and what he does not say of the miserables of the Burgh-moor, tends much to confirm Dr Skeyne's remarks on the absence of Christian kindness among the upper classes towards the afflicted poor on this occasion.

This pestilence, lasting till February, is said to have carried off 2500 persons in Edinburgh, which could not be much less than a tenth of the population. From the double cause of the pest and the absence of the Regent in England, there were 'nae diets of Justiciary halden frae the hinderend of August to the second day of March.'[3] Such of the inhabitants of the Canongate as were affected had to go out and live in huts on the Hill (by which is probably meant Salisbury Crags), and there stay till they were 'clengit.' A collection of money was made among the other inhabitants for their support.[4]

The distresses of pestilence were preceded and attended by those of a famine, which suffered a great and sudden abatement in the month of August 1569, perhaps in consequence of favourable appearances in the crop then about to be gathered. At least, we are informed by the *Diurnal of Occurrents*, that on that day, in the forenoon, 'the boll of ait meal was sauld for 3*l.* 12*s.*, the boll

[1] Where Napier had other estates.

[2] The bishop was about to go to York, to attend the investigation respecting the queen.

[3] Justiciary Records, MS., Adv. Lib., quoted by Mr Mark Napier.

[4] Burgh Records of Canongate, *Mait. Club Mis.*, ii. 313.

of wheat for 4*l.* 10*s.*, and the boll of beare for 3*l.*; but ere twa 1568.
afternoon upon the same day, the boll of ait meal was sauld for 40*s.*, 38*s.*, and 36*s.*, the boll of wheat for 50*s.*, and the beare for 33*s.*'—*D. O.*[1]

Little doubt is now entertained that the exanthematous disease called long ago the Pest, and now the Plague, and which has happily been unknown in the British Islands for two centuries, was the consequence of miasma arising from crowded and filthy living, acting on bodies predisposed by deficient aliment and other causes, and that at a certain stage it assumed a contagious character. It will be found throughout the present work that the malady generally, though not invariably, followed dearth and famine—a generalisation harmonising with the observations of Professor Alison as to the connection between destitution and typhus fever, and supporting the views of those who hold that it is for the interest of the community that all its members have a sufficiency of the necessaries of life. The pest was not the only epidemic which afflicted our ancestors in consequence of erroneous living and misery endured by great multitudes of people. There was one called the *land-ill* or *wame-ill*, which seems to have been of the nature of cholera. In an early chronicle quoted below,[2] is the following striking notice of this kind of malady in connection with famine as occurring in 1439:—'The samen time there was in Scotland a great dearth, for the boll of wheat was at 40*s.*, and the boll of ait meal 30*s.*; and verily the dearth was sae great that there died a passing [number of] people for hunger. And als the land-ill, the wame-ill, was so violent, that there died mae that year than ever there died, owther in pestilence, or yet in ony other sickness in Scotland. And that samen year the pestilence came in Scotland, and began at Dumfries, and it was callit the *Pestilence but Mercy*, for there took it nane that ever recoverit, but they died within twenty-four hours.'

At the time when the pest broke out in Edinburgh, there lived in
the city a young man of the middle class, bearing the name of Oct.
George Bannatyne, who was somewhat addicted to the vain and unprofitable art of poesy. He was acquainted with the writings of his predecessors, Dunbar, Douglas, Henryson, Montgomery, Scott, and others, through the manuscripts to which alone they had as yet

[1] The pest was severe in London in autumn 1569, whether by communication from Scotland does not appear.

[2] Ane Addicioun of Scottis Cornicklis and Deidis, printed from an original manuscript by Thomas Thomson, Esq.

1568. been committed. It was not then the custom to print literary productions unless for some reason external to their literary character, and these poems, therefore, were existing in the same peril of not being preserved to posterity as the works of Ennius in the days of

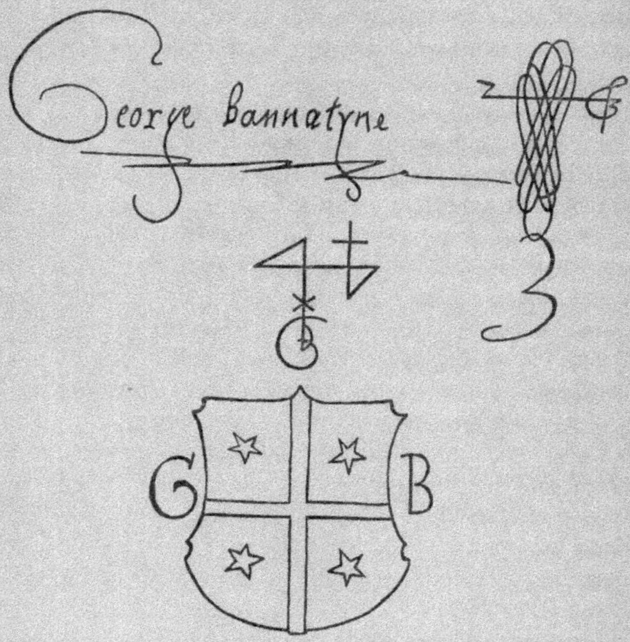

George Bannatyne's Arms and Initials.

Augustus. In all probability, the greater part of them, if not nearly the whole, would have been lost, but for an accidental circumstance connected with the plague now raging.

In that terrible time, when hundreds were dying in the city, and apprehensions for their own safety engrossed every mind, the young man George Bannatyne passed into retirement, and for three months devoted himself to the task of transcribing the fugitive productions of the Scottish muse into a fair volume. His retreat is supposed to have been the old manor-house of Newtyle, near the village of Meigle in Strathmore, and nothing could be more likely, as this was the country-house of his father, who seems to have been a prosperous lawyer in Edinburgh. In the short space of time mentioned, George had copied in a good hand, from the mutilated and obscure manuscripts he possessed, three hundred and seventy-two poems, covering no less than eight hundred folio pages; a labour by which he has secured the eternal gratitude of his countrymen, and established for himself a fame granted to but few for their own compositions. The volume—celebrated as the BANNATYNE MANUSCRIPT—still exists, under the greatest veneration, in the Advocates' Library, Edinburgh, after yielding from its ample stores the materials of Ramsay's, Hailes's, and other printed selections.[1] 1568

In this time of dearth and pestilence, the council of the Canongate providently ordained that 'the fourpenny loaf be weel baken and dried, gude and sufficient stuff, and keep the measures and *paik* of twenty-two ounces;' 'that nae browsters nor ony tapsters sell ony dearer ale nor 6d. the pint;' and 'that nae venters of wine buy nae new wine dearer than that they may sell the same commonly to all our sovereign's lieges for 16d. the pint.' Nov. 18.

They also ordained (January 10, 1568–9), that 'nae maner of person inhabiter within this burgh, venters of wine, hosters, or tapsters of ale, nor others whatsomever, thole or permit ony maner of persons to drink, keep company at table in common taverners' houses, upon Sunday, the time of preaching, under the pain of forty shillings, to be upta'en of the man and wife wha aucht the said taverners' houses sae oft as they fails, but favour.'[2]

It is evident from this injunction, that the keeping of public-houses open on Sundays, at times different from those during which there was public worship, was not then forbidden.

In presence of the magistrates of the Canongate, Edinburgh, 'William Heriot, younger, baxter, became, out of his awn free motive will, cautioner for George Heriot, that the said George sall remove furth of this burgh and freedom thereof, within the space of fifteen days next, and nae be fund thereintill, in case the said George associate not himself to the religion of Christ's kirk, and satisfie the kirk in making of repentance, as effeirs.'—*C. C. R.* 1568-9. Jan. 10.

This was a part of the process of completing the Reformation.

'. . . . the Regent made progress first to Stirling, where four priests of Dumblane were condemnit to the death, for saying of mess against the act of parliament; but he remittit their lives, and causit them to be bund to the mercat cross with their vestments 1569. May.

[1] *Memorials of George Bannatyne.* Edited by Sir Walter Scott. Bannatyne Club-book, 1829.

[2] Extracts from Canongate Council Register, *Maitland Club Miscellany*, ii. 314.

1569. and chalices in derision, where the people cast eggs and other villanie at their faces, by the space of ane hour; and thereafter their vestments and chalices were burnt to ashes. From that he passed to Sanctandrois, where a notable sorcerer called Nic Neville was condemnit to the death and brunt; and a Frenchman callit
Aug. 16. Paris, wha was ane of the devisers of the king's death, was hangit in Sanctandrois, and with him William Stewart, Lyon King of Arms, for divers points of witchcraft and necromancy.'—*H. K. J.*

The *Diurnal of Occurrents* relates the Regent's proceedings against the powers of the other world in this journey in a style equally cool and laconic. 'In my Lord Regent's passing to the north, he causit burn certain witches in Sanctandrois, and in returning he causit burn ane other company of witches in Dundee.'

Sep. The Regent once more set out on an expedition against the Border thieves, attended by a hundred men of war. In the words of a poetical panegyrist:

'. . . having established all thing in this sort,
To Liddesdale again he did resort.
Through Ewesdale, Esdale, and all the dales rade he,
And also lay three nichts in Cannobie,
Where nae prince lay thir hunder years before;
Nae thief durst stir, they did him fear so sore;
And that they should nae mair their theft allege,
Threescore and twelve he brought of them in pledge,
Syne warded them, whilk made the rest keep order,
Than *might the rash buss keep kye on the Border.*'[1]

It is said that no former ruler had ever so thoroughly awed the Border men. On his return to Edinburgh in November, he distributed the hostages among certain barons of the realm.

This, however, was the last of Moray's expeditions against the thieves. He was approaching the end of his career, doomed by party hatred in conjunction with private malice.

1569-70. Jan. 23. 'The Earl of Moray, the Good Regent, was slain in Linlithgow by James Hamilton of Bothwell-haugh, who shot the said Regent with a gun out at ane window, and presently thereafter fled out at the back, and leapt on a very good horse, which the Hamiltons had ready waiting for him; and, being followed speedily, after that spur and wand had failed him, he drew forth his dagger, and struck his horse behind; whilk causit the horse to leap a very broad stank; by whilk means he escaped.'—*Bir.*

[1] *Ane Trajedie in forme of ane Diallog betwix Honour, Gude Fame, and the Authour heirof, in ane Trance.* Lekprevik, 1570.

REGENCIES OF LENNOX AND MAR: 1570-1572.

The death of the Regent Moray proved a great blow to the infant king's party, for there was no man of equal mark and energy to take his place. The friends of the exiled queen raised their heads again, and in a force which might well give the ruling party some anxiety. Seeing the imminence of the danger, Elizabeth yielded to the wishes of Mary's enemies, and sent an army under the Earl of Sussex into Scotland in April, who 'burnt, herrit, and destroyit sae mickle of the Merse and Teviotdale as they might be masters of, asseizit the castle of Farniehirst, and demolishit the same, and thereafter past to Hawick and to Branksholm, and burnt and herrit the same,' thus punishing the Scotts, Kerrs, and others who had lately made a hostile incursion in Mary's behalf into England. Towards the end of the month, they besieged and took Hume Castle. A similar army under Sir William Drury entered Scotland in the ensuing month, and committed the like havock in Lanarkshire, so as to disable the queen's friends of the house of Hamilton. The sufferings thus occasioned in certain districts were dreadful, and the principal sufferers were the poor. In Hume Castle, when taken by Sussex, 'was the hale guids and gear perteining to the hale tenants of my Lord Hume, wherethrough the saids puir tenants were allutterly herrit.' The devastation at Hamilton was 'in sic sort and maner as the like in this realm has not been heard before.' And when the English troops came thence to Linlithgow on their return, 'they herrit all the Monkland, the Lord Fleming's bounds, my Lord Livingstone's bounds, together with all their puir tenants and friends, in sic maner that nae heart can think thereon but the same must be dolorous.'—*D. O.* Yet this was but a foretaste of the woes which a disputed succession was now for three years to lay upon the land.

At the dictation of Elizabeth—for the Protestant lords in Scotland were wholly subservient to her—Matthew, Earl of Lennox, paternal grandfather of the young king, was elected Regent (July 17, 1570). The real ruling spirit was the Earl of Morton, who lost no time in proceeding against some friends of Queen Mary in the north. Taking the town of Brechin, which had been held for her, he caused thirty-one of the garrison to be mercilessly put to death. 'The deaths of thir persons were greatomly bewailit by mony.' At the same time, the Earl of Sussex made an inroad into Dumfriesshire, cast down many houses of Mary's friends, 'burnt certain houses in the town of Dumfries, and reft and spulyit all that they micht get.' Three considerable districts in Scotland were this summer reduced to a desert.

The Gordon power in the north, that of the Hamiltons and Argyle in the west, and the Border chiefs, formed the great centres of Mary's party, which altogether was so strong, that it must have triumphed but for the backing which the other party received from England. As matters stood, the king's friends were able to maintain themselves in possession of the country at large, holding Stirling as the seat of government, while Kirkaldy of Grange, governor of the Castle of Edinburgh, unexpectedly went over to the queen's side, as did Maitland of Lethington, and some others lately arrayed against her. Edinburgh and its castle consequently became a centre of operations for that party. Then commenced an intestine war, at first consisting of mutual devastations on each other's lands, but soon assuming a sanguinary character. It is not consistent with our design to relate it in detail; but a few characteristic proceedings are given in the chronicle, usually in the simple and pathetic language of the time.

Lennox being killed in a surprise at Stirling (September 3, 1571), the Earl of Mar was chosen to the vacant regency. Under him the war advanced with even increased ferocity, until it came to be a rule that no quarter should be given on either side. In little more than a twelvemonth, this gentle-natured noble sunk under the burden of government; 'the maist cause of his deid was that he lovit peace, and could not have the same.'—*D. O.* The Earl of Morton, the ablest man of the whole party since Moray, but merciless and greedy in the extreme, succeeded, with the full approbation of the Mistress of the Protestant party of Scotland.

1570. May. Lord Fleming being a conspicuous leader on the queen's side, and captain of Dumbarton Castle, his lands in the counties of Lanark and Dumbarton were amongst those which fell under the vengeance of the ruling party. As one of the enormities perpetrated by the Earl of Lennox and his men on Lord Fleming's estates—'they have slain and destroyit the deer of his forest of Cumbernauld, and the white kye and bulls of the said forest, to the great destruction of policy and hinder of the commonweal. For that kind of kye and bulls has been keepit thir mony years in the said forest, and the like was not maintenit in ony other parts of the Isle of Albion, as is weel knawn.'[1]

The 'white kye and bulls' here spoken of are believed to have been a remnant of the original wild cattle of the Caledonian forest. Boece describes them as white, with lion-like manes, fierce, untamable, and shunning human society—so misanthropical, indeed, that

[1] Dalyell's *Illustrations of Scottish History*, p. 521.

they would eat nothing which the hand of man had touched. He, like the writer quoted above, says that none of them were left but only in Cumbernauld. Leslie, however, tells us that they also existed in the parks of Stirling and Kincardine. Latterly, there have been herds of the same oxen (but perhaps imported) in the Duke of Hamilton's park of Cadzow, in Lanarkshire; in the Duke of Buccleuch and Queensberry's at Drumlanrig; and in Lord Tankerville's park at Chillingham, in Northumberland. 1570.

Perhaps the severities of the English army on this occasion were only what her Scottish allies would themselves have practised against their opponents. What follows, however, seems to have gone a little beyond the bounds of partisan vengeance, while it not less illustrates the sacrifice of national dignity at which the enemies of Mary were content to purchase the aid of the English queen.

Sir William Drury, returning with the English army from the devastation of the Duke of Chatelherault's country in Lanarkshire, resolved to destroy the town of Linlithgow, in retribution for its having proved a harbour for the enemies of Elizabeth and of her ally the young Scottish king. It seemed but right that the scene of the murder of Moray should thus suffer. He therefore called the provost of the burgh before him, and announced his intention, saying, however, that he would allow time for the carrying away of any women in childbed or impotent people, and also conceding that a place should be appointed, to which the goods belonging to the citizens should be brought for preservation. MAY 29.

'The time being come for this execution, the Earl of Morton, that still accompanied the English general, offered himself as an intercessor to entreat and sue for a pardon, bringing afore the general a multitude of wailing people, whose mournful and most piteous cries was lamentable and very importunate.'

Drury insisted that justice demanded an example being made of Linlithgow; but 'the people of all sorts so pressed about him, and made such pitiful cries and sorrowful noise, with children sucking of their mothers' breasts, that he, taking ruth of their miserable estates, at this their lamentable suit, especially at the great instance of the Earl of Morton, *who came bareheaded to speak for them*, the general was content to save the town and people therein.' He took assurance from them, however, that the chief inhabitants should follow his camp to Berwick, and there wait the clemency of the queen of England.—*Holinshed.*

1570. July 4. '. . . . at 10 hours at night, there was ane earthquake in the city of Glasgow, and lastit but ane short space; but it causit the inhabitants of the said city to be in great terror and fear.'—*D. O.*

'In this time there was ane monstrous fish seen in Loch Fyne, having great een in the head thereof, and at some times wald stand aboon the water as high as the mast of a ship; and the said [creature] had upon the head thereof [twa crowns, ane] aboon little, and the downmaist crown meikle; whilk was reportit by wise men, that the same was ane sign and taiken of ane sudden alteration within this realm.'—*D. O.*

The low intelligence of the age is seen in nothing more conspicuously than in the numerous tales of animals alleged to have been seen, with peculiarities impossible in nature, and believed to be ominous of public calamity. The appearance of a similar animal in another of the Argyleshire lochs in 1510 is noted by Hector Boece, on the information of Duncan Campbell, a noble knight. This 'terrible beast' was 'of the bigness of a greyhound, and footed like a gander. Issuing out of the water early in the morning about midsummer,' he 'did very easily and without any force or straining of himself overthrow huge oaks with his tail, and therewith killed outright three men that hunted him with three strokes of his said tail, the rest of them saving themselves in trees thereabouts, whilst the aforesaid monster returned to the water. Those that are given to the observation of rare and uncouth sights, believe that this beast is never seen but against some great trouble and mischief to come upon the realm of Scotland.'[1]

In Holinshed's *Chronicle* (1577), the Firth of Forth is said occasionally to contain 'sundry fishes of a monstrous shape, with cowls hanging over their heads like unto monks, and in the rest resembling the body of man. They shew themselves above the water to the navel, howbeit they never appear but against some great pestilence of men or murrain of cattle; wherefore their only sight doth breed great terror to the Scottish nation, who are very great observers of uncouth signs and tokens.'

On the whole, it is most likely that some species of the *cetacea* or *phocidæ* was concerned in giving rise to these tales of sea-monsters.

Sir William Sinclair of Roslin, who was living at this time, thus

[1] Harrison's translation, *apud* Holinshed.

notes the appearance of an extraordinary animal in the year 1500: 1570.
'Hutcheon Frizell in Glenconie, the best and maist in estimation of the Lord Lovat's kin, he and ane servand with him, being at the hunting on ane hie land amang very rank heather, twa arrow-draught frae him he heard like the call of ane ratch approaching near and near, while [till] at the last he saw it, and shot at it ane dead straik with ane arrow; where it lap and welterit up and down ane spear length of breadth and length. The heather and bent being mair nor ane foot of height, it being in the deid-thraw, brint all to the eird [earth], as it had been muirburn. It was mair nor twa eln of length, as great as the coist of ane man, without feet, having ane mickle fin on ilk side, with ane tail and ane terrible head. His great deer-dogs wald not come near it. It had great speed. They callit it ane dragon.'[1]

He commemorates a sea-animal not less wonderful, which was thrown upon the coast of Northumberland in 1544. 'At the sea-side at Bamburgh, there was nae kind of fish ta'en by the space of twa year; but the sea made ane great routing and horrible noise, which was by [beside] custom and use. So it chancit, at the hie spring [tide], that ane terrible beast was casten in dead, of the quantity [bulk] of ane man. Nae man could devise ane thing mair terrible, with horns on the head of it, red een, with misshapen face, with lucken [webbed] hands and feet, and ane great rumple hinging to the eird. It consumit and stinkit sae, that in short time nae man nor beast might come near it; but all the country about saw it before, and sundry took great fear and dreadour for the sicht of it a lang space after. It was callit a Sea-devil. Witness the Laird of Mow.'[2]

'The summer right guid, and all victuals guid cheap; the August right fair and guid weather.'—*C. F.*

An extraordinary act of Gilbert, Earl of Cassillis, sometimes called King of Carrick, on account of the great power which he possessed in that district. Sep. 1.

The revenues of the abbey of Crossraguel, in Carrick, had been

[1] *Extracta e Chronicis Scocie.* Edin. 1842.

[2] Sir William Sinclair, who records these curious particulars, was Lord Justice-general of Scotland, and altogether an estimable person. According to Father Hay: 'He gathered a great many manuscripts, which had been taken by the rabble out of our monasteries in the time of the Reformation.'—*Genealogy of the Sinclairs of Roslin*, edited by James Maidment, Esq. 1835. See something further about him under June 1623.

1570. bestowed upon Master Allan Stewart. The earl had got a feu of the abbey from a predecessor of Stewart, but it never was confirmed. After some fruitless endeavours to obtain a confirmation from Stewart, the earl inveigled him to the castle of Dunure, a strong fortalice situated on a rocky part of the coast overlooking the Atlantic.

Here the Commendator was honourably entertained—'gif a prisoner can think ony entertainment pleasing. But after that certain days were spent, and that the earl could not obtain the feus of Crossraguel according to his awn appetite, he determined to prove gif a collation could work that which neither dinner nor supper could do of a long time. And so the said Master was carried to a secret chalmer [according to Stewart's own account, to a house called the *Black Voute* (Vault) of Dunure; there is something horribly suitable in the name]. With him passit the honourable earl, his worshipful brother, and sic as was appointed to be servants at that banquet. In the chalmer there was a great iron chimney, under it a fire; other great provision was not seen. The first course was: "My lord abbot (said the earl), it will please you confess here, that with your awn consent ye remain in my company, because ye dare not commit you to the hands of others." The abbot answered: "Wald ye, my lord, that I should make a manifest leasing for your pleasure? The truth is, my lord, it is against my will that I am here; neither yet have I ony pleasure in your company." "But ye sall remain with me at this time," said the earl. "I am not able to resist your will and pleasure," said the abbot, "in this place." "Ye maun then obey me," said the earl. And with that were presented unto him certain letters to subscrive, amongst which there was a five-year tack [lease] and a nineteen-year tack, and a charter of feu of all the lands of Crossraguel, with all the clauses necessar for the earl to haste him to hell! For gif adultery, sacrilege, oppression, barbarous cruelty, and theft heaped upon theft, deserve hell, the great King of Carrick can no more escape hell, for ever, nor the imprudent abbot escaped the fire for a season, as follows.

'After that the earl espied repugnance, and that he could not come to his purpose by fair means, he commandit his cooks to prepare the banquet. And so first they flayit the sheep, that is, they took off the abbot's claithes, even to his skin; and next they band him to the chimney, his legs to the one end and his arms to the other; and so they began to beet the fire, sometimes to his buttocks, sometimes to his legs, sometimes to his shoulders and arms. And that the roast should not burn, but that it might roast in sop, they spared not flamming with oil. (Lord, look thou to sic cruelty!) And, that the crying of the miserable man sould not be heard, they closed his mouth. . . . . In that torment they held the poor man, while that ofttimes he cried "for God's sake to dispatch him; he had as meikle gold in his awn purse as wald buy powder eneugh to shorten his pain." 1570.

'The famous King of Carrick and his cooks, perceiving the roast to be eneugh, commandit it to be tane from the fire, and the earl himself began the grace in this manner: "*Benedicite, Jesus, Maria!* you are the most obstinate man that ever I saw! Gif I had known that ye had been so stubborn, I wold not for a thousand crowns handled you so. I never did so to man, before you." '—*Ban.*

The abbot's own account, in the complaint which he afterwards rendered to the privy-council, is different, in as far as it describes him as now yielding to the earl's desire, in order to save his life and free himself from the pain he was suffering. He also says that he at this time subscribed the papers presented by the earl, though, it would appear, in an incomplete manner. He goes on—'which being done, the earl causit the tormentors of me sweir upon ane bible never to reveal ane word of this my unmerciful handling to ony person or persons.

'Yet he, not being satisfied with their proceedings, came again upon the 7 day of the month, bringing with him the same charter and tack, which he compellit me to subscrive, and required me to ratify and approve the same before notar and witnesses; which alluterly I refused. And therefore he, as of before, band me, and put me to the same manner of tormenting, and I said, notwithstanding, "he should first get my life ere ever I agreed to his desire;" and being in so great pain as I trust never man was in, with his life, I cried: "Fye upon you! will ye ding whingers in me, and put me out of this world! Or else put a barrel of powder under me, rather nor be demeaned in this unmerciful manner!" The earl hearing me cry, bade his servant, Alexander Richard, put ane serviette [towel] in my throat, which he obeyed; the same being performed at 11 hours at night; wha then seeing that I was in danger of my life, my flesh consumed and burnt to the bones, and that I wald not condescend to their purpose, I was releivit of that pain; wherethrough I will never be able nor well in my life time.'

The abbot was relieved from Dunure by the Laird of Bargeny, an enemy of Cassillis. The government was too weak and in too much trouble to avenge his cause against the earl, who thenceforth

1570. continued to draw the revenues of Crossraguel. But 'my lord gave the abbot some money to live upon, whilk contentit him all his days.'—*Hist. Ken.*

Sep. 7. Robert Hepburn, second son of the Laird of Waughton, was a partisan of the queen. Travelling to visit his friends in Lothian, he was betrayed by a companion to the knowledge of a party of the king's friends, consisting of the Lairds of Applegarth and Carmichael, who consequently made an attempt to lay hold of him as he was passing Bathgate. 'He, being alone with ane boy, fled, and they chasit him continually fra the said place while he come to the castle of Edinburgh, wherein he was resavit with great difficulty; for when the said Robert was passand in at the castle-yett, his adversaries were at Patrick Edgar his house-end. Ane thing to be wonderit at that he could escape the hands of the said persons, considering their multitude and [their being] as weel horsit as he was; and he being riding upon ane brown naig, could never have space to change off the same upon his led horse, but continually rade while he come to the castle foresaid; but his pursuers not only changit horse, but also did cast from them saddles and other gear, to mak licht for pursuing of him.'[1]—*D. O.*

Oct. 4. John Kello, minister of Spott, in Haddingtonshire, was executed in Edinburgh for the murder of his wife. The confession of this wretched man shews that he was tempted to the horrible act by a desire to marry more advantageously, his circumstances being somewhat straitened. He deliberated on the design for forty days; tried poison, which failed; then accomplished it by strangulation. His confession admits the amiable character of the victim; nay, he tells that, 'in the verie death, she could not believe I bure her onie evil will, but was glad, as she then said, to depart, gif her death could do me either vantage or pleasure.'[2] According to a contemporary recital, 'he stranglit her in her awn chamber, and thereafter closit the ordinar door that was within the house for his awn passage, and sae finely seemit to colour that purpose after he had done it, that immediately he passed to the kirk, and in the presence of the people made sermon as if he had done nae sic thing. And when he was returnit hame, he brought some neighbours into his house to vissie his wife, and callit at the ordinar

[1] The distance from Bathgate to Edinburgh is eighteen miles.

[2] *Bannatyne's Journal*, 46.

door, but nae answer was made. Then he passed to another back 1570.
passage with the neighbours, and that was fund open, and she hinging stranglit at the roof of the house. Then, with admiration, he cryit, as though he had knawn naething of the purpose, and they for pity in like manner cryit out. But, in [the] end, finding himself prickit with the judgments of God, of the grievous punishment wherewith transgressors have been plagued in time bygane, he thought gude to communicate his fact to ane of his brether in office, wha then was schoolmaster at Dunbar.'—*H. K. J.*

To resume his own confession: 'Mr Andrew Simson, minister of Dunbar, did so lively rype furth the inward cogitations of my heart, and discover my mind so plainly, that I persuaded myself God spak in him . . . . he remembered me of ane dream which in my great sickness did apparently present the self. "Brother," said he, "I do remember when I visited you in time of your sickness, ye did expose to me this vision, that ye were carried by ane great man before the face of ane terrible judge, and to escape his fury, ye did precipitate yourself in ane deep river, when his angels and messengers did follow you with two-edged swords, and sae when they struck at you, ye did decline and jouk in the water, while in the end, by ane way unknown to you, ye did escape. This vision I do interpret, that ye are the author yourself of this cruel murder then conceived in your heart, and ye were carried before the terrible judgments of God in your awn conscience, which now stands in God's presence to accuse you; the messengers of God is the justice of the country before the which ye sall be presented; the water wherein ye stood is that vain hypocrisy of your awn, and feigned blasphemy of God's name, whereby ye purpose to colour your impiety; your deliverance sall be spiritual." . . . . At this time did God move my heart to acknowledge the horror of my awn offence, and how far Sathan had obteinit victory ower me.'—*Ban. J.* 'Briefly, by his awn confession, being clearly convict, he was condemnit to be hangit, and his body to be casten in the fire and brynt to ashes, and so to die without any burial. And thus he departit this life, with an extreme penitent and contrite heart, baith for this and all other his offences in general, to the great gude example and comfort of all beholders.'—*H. K. J.*

In those days, while as yet there were not only no newspapers, OCT.
but no ready means of conveying letters, true intelligence made its way slowly, and the most ridiculous rumours obtained circulation. For example, on John Knox being at this time struck with

1570. apoplexy, 'a bruit [report] went through Scotland and England, that he was become the most deformed creature that ever was seen; that his face was turned awry to his neck; and that he would never preach or speak again.' In the ensuing year, while the venerable reformer lived at St Andrews, it was rumoured, and very generally believed as a serious truth, that he had been banished from the town, 'because in his yard he had raised some sancts, among whom came up the devil with horns; which, when his servant, Richard Bannatyne, saw, he ran wood, and so died.' It is stated that Lady Hume and some others thronged round the postman of St Andrews, with anxious inquiries whether it was true that Knox was banished from St Andrews, and that Bannatyne had run mad in consequence of seeing the devil raised.[1]

At this time, the witches of Athole are spoken of as noted personages. In the late and present civil dissensions they sided with the unfortunate queen, having probably too much Highland feeling to dissent from the great man of the district, the Earl of Athole, who was one of her majesty's warmest friends. About the time indicated, a present was sent to Mary, supposed to be from this uncanny portion of her late subjects. It was 'a pretty hart horn, not exceeding in quantity the palm of a man's hand, covered with gold, and artificially wrought. In the head of it were curiously engraven the arms of Scotland; in the nether part of it a throne, and a gentlewoman sitting in the same, in a robe-royal, with a crown upon her head. Under her feet was a rose environed with a thistle. Under that were two lions, the one bigger, the other lesser. The bigger lion held his paw upon the face of the other, as his lord and commander. Beneath all were written these words:

> "Fall what may fall,
> The lion shall be lord of all."'

This was evidently designed to convey a hope and wish that Mary should erelong, in spite of all contrarious circumstances, be in possession of England as well as of her native dominions.[2] In the

[1] *Calderwood*, iii. 20, 167, and *note*.

[2] The couplet almost verbatim occurs in the prophecies of Bertlingtoun, in R. Waldegrave's brochure, already quoted (under Jan. 1, 1561-2):

> 'However it happen for to fall,
> The Lyon shall be lord of all.'

same spirit was a rhymed prophecy which, at the same time, came 1570.
into circulation, but which was quickly falsified:

'The howlet shall lead the bear to his bane,
The queen of England shall die the twelfth year of her reign;
The court of England that is so wanton,
Shall shortly be brought to confusion.'—*Cal.*

A sad picture of civil war is presented by the so-called *Harrying of Bothwell Moor.* 'Captain Andrew Cunningham and Captain Thomas Crawford, accompanied with certain men of weir, departit of Glasgow, and passed in the night to Bothwell Moor, where they reft and spulyit all the inhabitants and tenants thereof; and because the Hamiltons was gathering to rescue the said guids, they fearit to return again to the said town of Glasgow, but came to Edinburgh with the same. They brought to the said burgh of Edinburgh 400 kye and oxen, 600 sheep, and 60 mares and staigs [colts]; this done, they passed to my Lord Regent, he being in Dalkeith, and knew his mind, whither they should take ane composition from the poor tenants, awners of the same, or not; but the matter was sae unmercifully handled, that the said guids were proclaimit by sound of drum and trumpet, to be sauld [to] whatsomever persons wald buy the same. . . . . To hear the lamentable crying of the said poor tenants, for the unmerciful robbery and oppression committit upon the said persons by the men of weir, it wald made ane stane-heartit man to greit and bewail. But cry what they wald cry, and lament as they pleasit, there was nane that obtainit comfort at their unmerciful hands; for when the said poor creatures made their complaint to the Regent, he wald not hear them, while [till] the oppression was cryit out upon by John Craig, minister. And then the Regent and lords of secret council ordainit that ane half of the guids be renderit again to the said poor tenants; but ere this time, the men of weir had sparfilit the best of them, and then the poor tenants were constrainit either to take again the ane half of the warst of the said guids that were left behind, or else they wald not have gotten naething.'—*D. O.* Nov. 12.

'. . . . there was ane day of law betwixt the Hoppringles and Elliots in Edinburgh, wherein the ane party set upon the other, and, had not the town of Edinburgh redd [separated] them, there had been great slauchter done the said day.'—*D. O.* Dec. 7.

1570. Dec. 9. 'Patrick Moscrop, son to John Moscrop, advocate, and Eupham M'Calyean, only apparent heir to Mr Thomas M'Calyean, ane of the senators of the College of Justice, were married in the said Thomas M'Calyean's house within Edinburgh, but nocht by permission of the kirk, and that for fear of tumult to be made by Archibald Ruthven, brother to William Lord Ruthven, wha allegit he had the first promise of her. . . . This order of marriage endured in ane manner ane slander to the kirk of God.'[1]—*D. O.*

1570-1. Jan. 15. From this day till the 22d March, 'great frost, that nae plews gaed while aucht days; and men might pass and repass on the ice of Lyon the 3d day of March.' February 22, after noon, 'there came ane great storm, and snaw and hail and wind, that nae man nor beast might take up their heads, nor gang, nor ride, and mony beasts, and mony men and women, were perished in sundry parts, and all kind of victuals right dear, and that because nae mills might grind for the frost.'—*C. F.*

1571. Mar. A General Assembly sitting in Edinburgh issued an order that adulterers, murderers, and others guilty of heinous offences, who might desire to be received back into Christian fellowship, should first appear penitently before their respective ministers, and then present themselves in linen clothes, bareheaded and barefooted, before the synod of their district. It was presently found, however, that divers of these penitents were too far distant from the meeting-places of the synods, and others were in such poverty, or *under such terror of enemies*, that they could not, or durst not travel through the country.

This fact verifies to us a passage in a contemporary historian: 'The haill realm of Scotland was sae divided in factions, that it was hard for any peaceable man as he rade out the hie way, to profess himself openly, either to be a favourer of the king or queen. All the people were casten sae lowss, and were become of sic dissolute minds and actions, that nane was in account but he that could either kill or rieve his neighbour.'—*H. K. J.*

Incidents characteristic of such a time abound in the contemporary diarists. 'March 27, David Lawtie, writer to the signet [in Edinburgh] was invaded by Thomas Douglas, and the maist part of his fore-finger strucken fra him.'—*D. O.* October 30, 'There was ane combat betwixt Campbell on the king's part, and ane

[1] Eupham M'Calyean subsequently attained still higher notoriety in the character of a witch. See under Dec. 26, 1590.

Smith, a lieutenant or servant within Edinburgh. Campbell strack him twice through the body without blood drawn upon himself, except a scrape upon the thumb.'—*Ban.* 1571.

The castle of Dumbarton being taken by surprise, great joy was experienced by the king's party on finding John Hamilton, archbishop of St Andrews, among the prisoners. The primate, a zealous adherent of the ancient faith, and partisan of the queen, was suspected of various crimes against the Protestant cause; so no mercy was to be expected for him. Then was seen the remarkable spectacle of the head of the church in Scotland—he whom Jerome Cardan travelled from London to Scotland only to cure of some trifling ailments—dragged with but little ceremony to a scaffold and put to a dog's death—a victim of the frightful passions excited by civil war. In answer to a dittay which George Buchanan assisted in bringing against him at Stirling, he denied everything but a foreknowledge of and participation in the death of Moray, 'of whilk he repentit, and askit God mercy. Being further accusit gif ony of his surname or friends were upon the counsel thereof, he answerit that he wold accuse nae man at that time but himself. As touching his religion,' says this chronicler, 'I reasonit with him, and could find naething but that he was ane papist, and exhortit sic as were near hand upon the scaffold to abide at the Catholic faith—sae he termed the papistry. In the castle, he desirit some papist priest to whom he micht confess him, and of whom he micht resave consolation [absolution] of his sins, according to the order of the kirk (as he spak); and sae he continuit to the death in the papistry, as he livit. As the bell struck at six hours at even, he was hangit at the mercat-cross of Stirling, upon ane gibbet, on whilk was written thir twa verses following: APR. 7.

> "Cresce diu, felix arbor, semperque vireto
> Frondibus, ut nobis talia poma feras." '—*D. O.*

At this time, Mr William Collace was first regent in St Leonard's College, St Andrews; he 'had the estimation of being the maist solid and learnit in Aristotle's philosophy.' James Melville gives an interesting picture of this learned person, to whose class he came at fifteen years of age, so ill prepared for understanding the language (Latin) in which the prelections took place, that 'I did naething,' says Melville, 'but bursted and grat at his lessons, and was of mind to have gone home again, were [it] not the loving care of that

1571. man comforted me; [he] took me in his awn chalmer, causit me to lie with himself, and every night teached me in private till I was acquainted with the matter. Then he gave us ane compend of his awn of philosophy and the parts thereof . . . whilk I thought I understood better. About the whilk time my father, coming to the town, begoud to examine me, and, finding some beginning, was exceeding rejoiced, and uttered sweeter affection to me than ever before. He enterteinit my regent very heartily in his lodging, and gave him great thanks; he sent me to him, after he had taken leave, with twa pieces of gold in a napkin; but the gentleman was sae honest and loving, that he wald have none of his gold, but with austere countenance sent me back with it; nay, never wald receive gold or silver all the time of my course.'

Melville mentions having frequent opportunities at this time of seeing and hearing John Knox, who had taken refuge in St Andrews, while Edinburgh was possessed by the queen's party. 'Mr Knox wald some time come in and repose him in our college yard, and call us scholars unto him and bless us, and exhort us to knaw God and his wark in our country, and stand by the gude cause, and follow the guid example of our masters.'

'I saw him every day of his doctrine go hooly and fair [softly and fairly] with a furring of matricks about his neck, a staff in ane hand, and guid godly Richard Ballanden, his servant, halding up the other oxter [armpit] from the abbey to the parish kirk, and by the said Richard and another servant, lifted up to the pulpit, whaur he behovit to lean at his first entry, but ere he had done with his sermon, he was sae active and vigorous, that he was like to ding that pulpit in blads [knock the pulpit in splinters], and flie out of it.'

He adds: 'This year, in the month of July, Mr John Davidson, ane of our regents, made a play at the marriage of Mr John Colvin, whilk I saw playit in Mr Knox's presence, wherein, according to Mr Knox's doctrine, the castle of Edinburgh was besieged, taken, and the captain, with ane or twa with him, hangit in effigy.'

This dramatic performance represented an unfulfilled prophecy of the reformer. When Kirkaldy of Grange, after many years of zealous service in the reforming cause, declared for the Queen, and held out Edinburgh Castle against the Regent, Knox, who had loved him much, was deeply grieved. He felt, however, no doubt as to the ultimate triumph of his own cause against all such opposition, and it was perhaps no great venture for so acute a person to utter the

prediction that, notwithstanding the trust which Kirkaldy put in 1571.
that powerful fortress, it should yet run like a sand-glass; it should spew out the captain with shame; he should not come out at the gate, but over the walls. Mr Robert Hamilton, minister of St Andrews, asking his warrant for this vaticination, he said: 'God is my warrant, and ye shall see it.' 'As the other was scarcely satisfied,' says James Melville, 'the next sermon from the pulpit, he repeats the threatenings, and adds thereto: "Thou that will not believe my warrant, shall see it with thy e'es that day, and shall say: 'What have I to do here?'" This sermon the said Mr Robert's servant wrote. . . . '—*Ja. Mel.*

This year 'great weirs in the north land betwixt the Gordons and Forbeses, and the Forbeses put till the warst, and mony slain of them, and towns wasted and burnt.'—*C. F.*

Adam Gordon, brother of the Earl of Huntly, was a leader in these broils, and of some avail in supporting the queen's cause. He stained his name by a frightful act of cruelty. The house of Towie, belonging to Alexander Forbes, was maintained by his lady against Gordon. On his sending to demand its surrender, the brave dame answered that she could not give it up without direction from her husband. Gordon then set fire to it, and burnt the heroic woman, her children and servants—twenty-seven persons in all!

The queen's party, after holding a parliament in Edinburgh, July.
where they affected formally to re-establish her government, sent a pursuivant to Jedburgh, 'to proclaim the new erected authority,' probably thinking that the man would be safe in the performance of his duty at that town through the favour of Kerr of Ferniehirst, their fellow-partisan. They little reckoned on the spirit of the Border burghers. 'He was suffered to read his letters till he came to this point, that the lords assembled in Edinburgh had found all the proceedings against the queen null, and that all men should obey her only. Then the provost caused the pursuivant to come down from the cross, and *eat his letters*. Thereafter, [he] caused loose down his points, and gave him his wages —— with a bridle; and threatened that if ever he came again, he should lose his life. Ferniehirst threatened the town: but they gave him the defiance.'—*Cal.*

A few months after, Ferniehirst and Buccleuch mustered a great multitude of the Border thieves, and came to take vengeance

1571. on the burghers of Jedburgh. The town, assisted by Kerr of Cessford, stood to its defence; and when Lord Ruthven came with a party of horse to aid them, they were able to beat back the assailants, many of whom fell into their hands.

Aug. 1. 'There was ane sow farried in William Davidson's house, flesher in Edinburgh, of thirteen gryces [pigs], of the whilk there was ane a monster. It had the gruntle [snout] in the heich of the heid, and under that it had twa een, ane nose and mouth, ane brow, ane cheek, ane tongue, and lugs like to the similitude of man in all sorts; the remanent thereof was like ane other gryce without hair. This portendit some mischief to this burgh.'—*D. O.*

Aug. The Earl of Argyle, Robert Lord Boyd, and some other nobles, lately friends of the queen, were now brought over to the king's side, after sundry meetings and discussions with the Regent. 'The greedy and insatiable appetite of benefices was the maist cause thereof, for there was nane that was brought under the king's obedience but for reward either given or promised. Als he [the Earl of Argyle] was greatumly persuadit hereto by Lord Boyd, wha persuadit the kirk to part the said earl and his wife, and [the earl] to marry his [Lord Boyd's] daughter, wha was married upon the young laird of Cunninghamheid of before.'—*D. O.*

After these particulars, it is instructive to read the epitaph inscribed on Lord Boyd's tomb in the Laigh Kirk (Burns's Laigh Kirk) of Kilmarnock:

'Heir lyis y[t] godlie, noble, wyis Lord Boyd,
Quha kirk and king and commonweil decoird,
Quhilk war (quhill they yis jowell all injoyd)
Defendit, counsaild, governd, by that lord.' &c.

Aug. 28. The Regent Lennox held a parliament at Stirling, where he made an oration to the nobility. The king, five years old, was present, and, while his grandfather was speaking, he looked up and espied a hole in the roof, occasioned by 'the lack of some sclates.' At the conclusion of the harangue, the child remarked: 'I think there is ane hole in this parliament.'

'In effect, his majesty's words came true; for the same month, about the end of the parliament (September 3), there came to Striviling in the night, ere the nobility or town knew, the Earl of Huntly, the queen's lieutenant, Claud Hamilton, with the Lairds

of Buccleuch and Ferniehirst, who, ere day brake, had possessed 1571.
themselves of the town, crying "God and the Queen!" so that those that were for the King and his Regent could not, for the multitude of enemies, come to a head. Wherever they could see any that belonged to the Regent, him they killed without mercy. The Regent being taken prisoner by the Laird of Buccleuch, and horsed behind him, ane wicked fellow lift up his jack, and shot him through the body with a pistol. . . . . [On a counter-surprise, the queen's party] departed the town immediately. The Earl of Mar was declared Regent, and concluded the parliament. This was the hole which the young king did see in the parliament, although he meant nothing less.'—*Bal.*

Robert Lord Boyd entered this day into a bond of *manred* with Nov. 10.
William Fairly, brother of David Fairly of that Ilk. Manred, properly, is a service of allegiance; but in Scotland it had come, in the course of time, to be an agreement, sometimes between a great man and a less, sometimes between two or more equally great men, to stand by each other in all contingencies of war and law, excepting only (and perhaps it was but a hypocritical exception) where the king's majesty and his commands were concerned. It was an arrangement dictated by the exigencies of a rude time, when law was but partial and uncertain in its actings, and natural feeling often called for something being done, whether the law would or no. As something not very consonant with good government, or even such attempts at the same as might be made in those days, manred had been denounced by a statute so long ago as 1457, when it was enacted 'that nae man dwelling within burgh be fund in manrent, nor ride in rout in feir of weir with nae man, but with the king or his officers, or with the lord of the burgh.' But acts of parliament were voices crying in the wilderness in Scotland, and manred still continued to have its place in the economy of life in this age.

On this occasion, William Fairly binds and obliges himself to be 'man and subject servant' to Lord Boyd and his heirs, 'aefaldly and truly to serve them upon their retinue and expenses in household and out of household, as best sall please them in all their affairs, and as weel in defence as pursuit, with whom or against whom it sall happen them to have action and ado,' the king excepted. He is likewise to help them with his good counsel, 'and sall never hear nor know their hurt, damage, nor skaith, in ony sort, but sall diligently sift out the same, and mak true declaration thereof.'

1571. The consideration for all this service is the possession of 'the thretty-shilling land of auld extent of Byrehill.'

This was but the first of a long series of similar engagements which Lord Boyd formed down to his death in 1589.[1] For a forty-shilling land, the Laird of Fergushill becomes bound, October 26, 1572, in the same way as William Fairly, and to take part with the said lord and his heirs, in all their actions, quarrels, questions, and debates. The Laird of Lochrig, the Laird of Rowallan, Andrew Macfarlane of Arroquhar, and the Laird of Camstroddan, all in succession put themselves in this relation to his lordship. In March 1575, the Laird of Blair engaged with his friends, tenants, and servants, to 'ride, gang, and assist with the said lord, in all kind of leeful conventions.' It was with such satellites that a great man of that age, if to be tried on any criminal charge, appeared at the place of law, professedly that he might be sure of fair-play, but in reality with the effect of overbearing justice. It was with such assistants that two or three lords were sometimes enabled to take possession of the government, and for a time rule all at their pleasure. Amongst the most curious things in the early history of the reformed religion, are the occasions when it was manifestly indebted for its progress to associations of this irregular kind.

DEC. 24. About this time, there was apprehended 'one that keepit ane hostelry at Brechin, who before, at divers times, had murdered sundry that came to lodge with him, the wife being also as busy as the man with a mell [mallet], to fell their guests sleeping in their beds.'—*Ban.*

1571-2. JAN. Among numberless skirmishes, surprises, and barbarous ravagings which marked the struggle between the friends of the queen and those of the infant king, was an affair of several parts or acts in this and the ensuing month. Lord Maxwell being contracted in marriage to a sister of the Earl of Angus, the lady's relation, the Earl of Morton, proposed to give a banquet on the occasion at Dalkeith Castle. The wine required at the feast was to be brought in carts from Leith, together with some venison and a quantity of silver plate. Kirkaldy and his friends in the castle hearing of this, sent out a party of horse, which surprised Morton's servants, and took as spoil the materials of the proposed banquet. Morton who, it was said, smarted more from the loss of the plate than the

[1] The whole series is printed in *Abbotsford Miscellany*, p. 5.

killing of a few of his servants in the struggle, immediately sent 1571-2. a party to requite Kirkaldy's attack by laying waste his estate in Fife. Kirkaldy, again, repaid these attentions by sending a party FEB. 8. a few nights after to set fire to the town of Dalkeith. On this occasion, he killed ten of Morton's people, and took nine prisoners. 'In their return [they] perceived fifty-sax horses from Dalkeith to Leith, passing laded with ale; they brake the barrels, and made prey of the horses, and brought into Edinburgh many kye and oxen forth of that lordship for supply of their scant and hunger.'—*H. K. J.* 'These three scuffles went all under one name, and were ever after called *Lord Maxwell's Handfasting.*' [1]

The condition of the ordinary places of worship in this time of 1572. MAR. civil war is sketched in the *Lamentation of Lady Scotland*, printed by Lekprevik in 1572.

> 'The rooms appointit people to consider,
> To hear God's word, where they suld pray together,
> Are now convertit in sheep-cots and faulds,
> Or else are fallen, because nane them uphalds.
> The parish kirks, I ween, they sae misguide,
> That nane for wind and rain therein may bide:
> Therefore nae pleasure tak they of the temple,
> Nor yet to come where nocht is to contemple,
> But craws and dows, cryand and makand beir,
> That nane throuchly the minister may hear.
> But feathers, filth, and dung does lie abroad,
> Where folk should sit to hear the word of God;
> Whilk is occasion to the adversaries,
> To mock and scorn sic things before your eyes.
> Thus to disdain the house of orison,
> Does mak folk cauld to their devotion;
> And als they do disdain to hear God's word,
> Thinking the same to be ane jesting bourd;
> They go to labour, drinking, or to play,
> And not to you,[2] upon the Sabbath day.'

The civil war told nowhere with more severity than on Edinburgh, which was the scene of the principal transactions. The bringing of victuals or coal to the city was forbidden by the beleaguering troops under pain of death, and the penalty was exacted in many instances. The consequence was 'great penury and scant of vivres,

[1] Crawford's *Memoirs*, 215.

[2] The Lady Scotland is understood to address 'the richt honorable and godly learnit gentleman, the Laird of Dun, minister of God's word.'

1572. sae that all was at ane exceeding dearth.'—*D. O.* In May, oatmeal was nine shillings of the native money per peck; eleven ounces of wheaten bread cost 8d., 'and baps of nine [ounces] for 12d.' It was found necessary to demolish some houses for the sake of the wood, to be used as fuel. At the commencement of a truce on the 22d of July, the meal had risen to twelve shillings, the boll of wheat to ten pounds, and a carcass of beef to sixteen pounds. On that day, 'after noon, the victuals whilk was keepit to ane dearth was brought to Leith and sauld, the meal for five shillings the peck, . . . and [sae] very mickle bread baken, that it that was sauld for sixteen pennies was sauld for six pennies. Thanks to God.' During the scarcity, ale not being to be had, a drink of vinegar and water was substituted.—*D. O.* 'Nochttheless,' if we are to believe the same chronicle, 'the remainers therein [that is, in Edinburgh] abade patiently and were of good comfort, and usit all pleasures whilk were wont to be usit in the month of May in auld times, viz., Robin Hood and Little John.'

Apr. 16. From the day here noted to the 8th of June, the war between the queen's party in Edinburgh and the king's beyond the city was conducted on the principle of *No quarter*. All who were taken on either side were presently put to death. The common belief was, that this frightful system originated with Morton, who conceived that by such severity the war would sooner cease. In the end, both parties, 'wearied of execution daily made, were content to cease from such rigour, and use fair wars, as in former times.'—*Spot.*

Apr. 21. '. . . . there was ane minister [named Robert Waugh] hangit in Leith (and borne to the gibbet, because he was birsit[1] with the boots[2]). The principal cause was that he said to the Earl of Morton, that he defended ane unjust cause, and that he wald repent when nae time was to repent. And when he was required by whom he was commanded to say the same, he answered and said: "By the haly spreit."'—*D. O.*

In the same year, Mr Andrew Douglas, minister of Dunglass, was first tortured, and then hanged, for publicly rebuking Morton on account of his living with the widow of Captain Cullen.

July 19. Another characteristic incident of the time, but of a somewhat mysterious character, occurred in a southern burgh. James Tweedie, burgess of Peebles, John Wightman, Martin Hay, and John Bower there, and Thomas Johnston, son to Thomas Johnston

[1] Bruised. [2] He 'wes extremelie pynit in the beitis lang of befoir.'—*D. O.*

of Craigieburn, were tried for being concerned in 'the cruel slaughter of the umwhile John Dickison of Winkston; committit within the town of Peebles on the 1st of Julii instant.' They were acquitted. The fact is only worth mentioning here, to afford an opportunity of illustrating the long perseverance of tradition in certain favouring circumstances. In his youth, which was passed in the town referred to, the author distinctly remembers hearing an aged person speak of how Provost Dickison was long ago 'stickit' at the back of the Dean's Well in the High Street. The event was then 240 years past. 1572.

'The Earl of Mar, Regent, ended his life, about three hours in the morning. It was constantly affirmed, that about the time of his death, the trough of the water of Montrose, where it runneth through his lands, was dry, the water running nevertheless above [higher up]. At the same time, a violent wind drave a great number of sheep from the links of Montrose into the sea.'—*Cal.* Oct. 29.

Some events of the kind did certainly occur about the time of the Regent's death; but, contrary to all rule in such matters, they came after that event, if we are to believe another historian, who places them under November, and describes them as follows:

'In this mean time was ane great ferly in Montrose. By the space of six hours, the water thereof was dry in the sea, and during the whilk space the people past within the said sea, and got sundry fishes. . . . . After the whilk space, the people on the sands perceiving the water as ane popill pitt, frae the whilk they fled to land, and syne it was sea again suddenly, and never nane perishit hereinto. Also there was ane hill callit , whilk burnt by the said space; men riding by the way, the manes and coils of their horses burnt, the wands of their hands burnt; poor men passing on the way, the staves in their hands burnt, and when they wald dight [wipe] off the fire thereof, it wald entres again.'—*D. O.*

REGENCY OF MORTON: 1572-1578.

The Earl of Morton had no sooner assumed the reins of government, than his vigorous talents began to be felt. The chief strength of Mary's friends was in Edinburgh Castle, held for her by Kirkaldy of Grange. All the means at the Regent's command proving insufficient to reduce this fortress, he obtained from England an army of 1500 men, commanded by Sir William Drury, and provided with artillery. The castle stood a siege of three weeks, and was then obliged to yield (May 29, 1573). With mean vindictiveness, Morton sent the gallant Kirkaldy to the gallows. Maitland of Lethington might have shared the same fate, if it had not been anticipated either by a natural death or suicide. The other chiefs of the queen's party were spared. After this event, the friends of Mary could no longer make an appearance anywhere in her favour. The new government remained triumphant, and peace was restored to a bleeding and exhausted country.

Morton was, on the whole, a serviceable, though not a just or clement ruler. It was his policy, arising from his love of money, to punish his adversaries rather by fines than bloodshed. All the persons of note who had befriended the queen, he caused to give security for their future behaviour. The smallest offence forfeited the pledge, and the cautioners were then mulcted without mercy. Under this ruling passion, he tampered with the coin, sold justice, and cheated the church of its revenues. It was supposed that he had concealed large treasures in his castle of Dalkeith; but we have no certain account of their ever being found, and probably the popular notions on the subject were exaggerated.

Under Morton, a slight move was made towards the establishment of a kind of episcopacy in the church, though the persons he appointed to the sees were mere creatures who consented to be receivers of the revenues on his account. The general feeling of the people continued to be decidedly in favour of the simple presbyterian polity, and the Regent's interference with the purity of that system was one cause of his loss of popularity, and of his subsequent ruin. While the recognised champion of the Protestant interest in Scotland, and, as such, the *protégé* of Elizabeth, he disliked the presbyterian clergy. He not only refused to countenance by his presence any of their assemblies, but 'threatened some of the most zealous with hanging, alleging that otherwise there could be no peace or order in the country.'[1] The noted efforts of

[1] *Calderwood*, iii. 393.

King James to bring the church into a prelatic conformity with England, had in reality an exemplar in the doings of the Regent Morton.

Meanwhile the young king was reared in great seclusion in Stirling Castle, under the care of the celebrated scholar George Buchanan. His acquirements, at a very early age, were such as to raise great hopes of his future rule. Killegrew, the English ambassador, reports having heard him, at eight years of age, translate the Bible, *ad aperturam libri*, from Latin into French, and from French into English, 'so well as few men could have added anything to his translation.' But, in reality, his character was a strange mixture of cleverness and weakness, of wit and folly. His greatest deficiency was in a courageous will to pursue the ends of justice. He could clearly enough apprehend the disease, and speak and write about it plausibly; but he could do little towards its cure, because he shrank from all strong measures except against poor and inferior people, and those who had wounded his own pettier feelings.

The regency of Morton came to a premature conclusion in consequence of a combination raised against him by the Earls of Athole and Argyle; and James became nominally the acting ruler (March 1578), ere he had completed his twelfth year.

'. . . . in the morning, was seen a star northward, very bright and clear, in the constellation of Cassiopeia, at the back of her chair; which, with three chief fixed stars of the said constellation, made a geometrical figure lozenge-wise, of the learned men called *rhombus*. This star, at the first appearing, seemed bigger than Jupiter, and not much less than Venus when she seemeth greatest . . . . the said star never changed his[1] place . . . . and so continued (by little and little appearing less) the space of sixteen months; at what time it was so small, that rather thought, by exercise of oft viewing, might imagine the place, than any eye could judge the presence of the same.'—*Holinshed.* 1572. Nov. 18.

This was the celebrated *Star of Tycho*, so called because Tycho Brahé made it the subject of observation. The Danish astronomer is known to have first observed it a few days before the date assigned by Holinshed—namely, on the 11th of November, while taking an evening walk in the fields. From the suddenness of its appearance, and its very great brightness, he suspected that his sense was deceived, and was only convinced he saw truly when he found some

[1] The word *its* did not then exist, and writers were forced to use either *his* or *her* instead.

1572. peasants gazing at the imposing stranger with as much astonishment as himself. It has been regarded as an example of a class of stars which move in periods between remote and comparatively near points in space; and as there was a similar object seen in 945 and 1264, it was supposed that the period of this star was somewhat over 300 years. But 'the period of 300 years, which Goodriche conjectured, has been reduced by Kiell and Pigot to 150 years.'[1]

The Star of Tycho, during the time it was visible, 'suffered several very remarkable changes. On a sudden it became so brilliant, that it surpassed in brightness even Venus and Mercury, and was visible on the meridian in the daytime. Its light then began to diminish, till it disappeared sixteen months after it had been first seen.'[2]

1572-3. 'This year, a great and sharp frost almost continually lasted from before the feast of All Saints, till after the feast of Epiphany of our Lord, with sometimes great and deep snows, and sometimes rains, which freezed as fast as the same fell to the ground, wherethrough at Wrotham, in Kent, and many other places, the arms and boughs of trees, being overcharged with ice, broke off and fell from the stocks . . . . also the wind continued north and east till after the Ascension Day, with sharp frosts and snows, whereby followed a late spring.'—*Stowe.*

1573. Apr. 3. The gipsies, who are usually said to have wandered into Europe from the East in the beginning of the fifteenth century, are not heard of in Scotland before 1540, when a writ of the Privy Seal was passed in favour of 'John Faw, Lord and Earl of Little Egypt,' enabling him to rule his company in conformity with the laws of his pretended country. First accepted as noble refugees, possessing a semi-religious character, they were in time discovered to be mere rogues and vagabonds. It was now declared in the Privy Council, that 'the commonweal of this realm was greatumly damnifiet and harmit through certain vagabond, idle, and counterfeit people of divers nations, falsely named Egyptians, living on stowth and other unlawful means.' These people were commanded to settle to fixed habitations and honest industry; otherwise it should be competent to seize and throw them into the nearest prison, when, if they could not give caution for a due obedience to this edict, they were 'to be scourgit throughout the town or

[1] Humboldt's *Cosmos.* [2] Brewster's *Encyclopædia.*

parish, and sae to be imprisonit and scourgit fra parish to parish, while [till] they be utterly renderit furth of this realm.'—*P. C. R.* 1573.

Little more than three years onward (August 27, 1576), it was declared that this act had 'wantit execution'—a very common misfortune to acts of council in those days; and it was found that 'the said idle vagabonds has continuit in their wicked and mischievous manner of living, committing murders, theft, and abusing the simple and ignorant people with sorcery and divination.' Men in authority were now enjoined to stricter courses with these wanderers, on pain of being held as their accomplices.

An English force having come to help the Regent in winning Edinburgh Castle, the operations of the siege commenced by the fixing up of twenty 'great pieces' at four several places around the ancient fortress. 'They shot so hard continually, that the second day they had beat down wholly three towers. The Laird of Grange . . . . would not give over, but shot at them continually, both with great shot and small; so that there was a very great slaughter amongst the English cannoneers, sundry of them having their legs and arms torn from their bodies in the air by the violence of the great shot. At last, the Regent continuing his siege so close and hard—the captain being forced by the defendants for lack of victuals—rendered the same, after a great many of them were slain [May 29].'—*Bir.* MAY 2.

Mr Robert Hamilton, minister of St Andrews, was in Edinburgh at this time, along with the servant who had written down John Knox's prediction regarding the fate of Kirkaldy (see under 1571). According to James Melville, 'they gaed up to the Castle-hill, and saw the forewark of the castle all demolished, and running like a sandy brae; they saw the men of weir all set in order. The captain, with a little staff in his hand, taken down over the walls upon the ladders, and Mr Robert, troubled with the thrang of the people, says: "Go, what have I ado here?" In going away, the servant remembers his master of the sermon, and the words, wha was compelled to glorify God, and say he was a true prophet.'

'William Kirkaldy of Grange, knight, sometime captain of the Castle of Edinburgh, and James Mosman, goldsmith, were harlit in twa carts backward, frae the Abbey to the Cross of Edinburgh, where they, with Mr James [Kirkaldy] and James Cockie, were AUG. 3.

1573. hangit,' 'for keeping of the said castle against the king and his regent.'—*D. O. Bir.*

Such was the dismal end of one who had undoubtedly been a most valiant soldier, though, it must be added, an unsteady politician, and too much a follower of private ends in public affairs. His concern in the assassination of Cardinal Beaton also detracts somewhat from the sympathy which would naturally be felt for him on this occasion. James Melville relates some curious particulars regarding his latter days and his execution:

When John Knox was on his death-bed in Edinburgh, November 1572, the situation of Kirkaldy and his friends in the castle had become critical. Mr David Lindsay, minister of Leith, came to visit the reformer, and asked how he did. 'He answerit: "Weel, brother, I thank God; I have desired all this day to have you, that I may send you yet to yon man in the castle, whom ye ken I have loved sae dearly. Go, I pray you, tell him that I have sent you to him yet ance to warn and bid him, in the name of God, leave that evil cause, and give ower that castle: gif not, he shall be brought down ower the walls with shame, and hing against the sun: sae God has assured me." Mr David, howbeit he thought the message hard, and the threatening over particular, yet obeyed, and passed to the castle; and meeting with Sir Robert Melville walking on the wall, tauld him, wha was, as he thought, meikle movit with the matter. Thereafter [he] communed with the captain, whom he thought also somewhat moved; but he passed from him into the Secretar Lethington, with whom, when he had conferred a while, he came out to Mr David again, and said to him: "Go, tell Mr Knox he is but ane . . . . prophet." Mr David, returning, tauld Mr Knox he had discharged the commission faithfully, but that it was not weel accepted of after the captain had conferrit with the secretar. "Weel (says Mr Knox) I have been earnest with my God anent the twa men; for the ane [Kirkaldy] I am sorry that so should befall him; yet God assures me there is mercy for his saul: for that other [the Secretary Lethington], I have nae warrant that ever he shall be weel."'

The castle surrendered, and Kirkaldy fell into the power of the Regent Morton. He offered all he possessed for his life. But the reformer's prophecy was to be fulfilled, and how far it served to fulfil itself, we may surmise from what Morton wrote to the English agent. 'Considering,' he says, 'what has been, and daily is, *spoken by the preachers, that God's plague will not cease while the land be purged of blood*, and having regard that such as are interested by the death of their friends, the destruction of their houses, and away taking of their goods, could not be satisfied by any offer made to me in particular . . . . I deliberated to let justice proceed.'[1] 1573.

Mr David Lindsay, who had gone with Kirkaldy's fruitless offer, 'the morn by nine hours comes again to the captain, the Laird of Grange [who was now confined under a guard in a house in the High Street], and taking him to a fore-stair of the lodging apart, resolves him it behoved him to suffer. "O, then, Mr David (says he), for our auld friendship, and for Christ's sake, leave me not." So he remains with him, wha, passing up and down a while, came to a shot [a hole fitted with a sliding panel in the wooden front of the house], and seeing the day fair, the sun clear, and a scaffold preparing at the Cross, he falls in a great study [reverie], and alters countenance and colour; whilk, when Mr David perceived, he came to him and asked what he was doing. "Faith, Mr David (says he), I perceive weel now that Mr Knox was the true servant of God, and his threatening is to be accomplished."' Lindsay mentioned the assurance which Knox had had regarding the ultimate salvation of the unfortunate man; which gave him much comfort and renewed courage; 'sae that he dined moderately, and thereafter took Mr David apart for his strengthening to suffer that death, and in [the] end beseeks him not to leave him, but to convoy him to the place of execution. "And take heed (says he), I hope in God, after I shall be thought past, to give you a taiken of the assurance of that mercy to my saul, according to the speaking of that man of God."

'Sae, about three hours afternoon, he was brought out, and Mr David with him, and about four, the sun being wast about the northward nook of the steeple, he was put aff the ladder, and his face first fell to the east, but within a little while, turned about to the west, and there remained against the sun; at whilk time Mr David, ever present, says he marked him, when all thought he was away [dead], to lift up his hands that were bund before him, and lay them down again saftly; whilk moved him with exclamation to glorify God before all the people.'

On the destruction of the queen's party, 'the burgesses and craftsmen wha remainit the time of the cummers [troubles] in Edinburgh, behovit to compone for their life, and the least that any man payit was twenty merks, and they that had nocht to pay Aug.

[1] Tytler, vii. 388.

1573. were continuit to the third day of the aire, with fifteen days' warning, to be halden within the sheriffdom. This composition should have been equally distributed betwixt the Regent and the burgesses that had their houses destroyit; but the Regent causit bring the haill to the Castle of Edinburgh, and wald not part with ane penny; for the whilk causes the burgesses stayit and wald not pursue nane hereafter, by occasion they were nocht the better, and also therethrough obteinit the indignation of their neighbours. God of his grace grant the poor consolation, for they thole great trouble!'

Afterwards—'the burgesses and craftsmen and others wha remainit in the town in the time of the cummers, were chargit that they, on their awn expenses, might mak black gray gowns, with the whilk they stood at the kirk door ane hour before the preaching . . . ., whilk gowns were decernit to be dealt to the poor.' —*D. O.*

Aug. 25. During the late troubles, the Border-men had been in a great measure left to pursue their own courses unmolested. Now that the civil war was ended, Morton was able to turn his attention in that direction. At this date, he proceeded from Dalkeith with a host of 4000 men to Peebles, where he was met by the Earl of Argyle with a hundred horse and an equal number of 'carriage-men;' and the party then went to Jedburgh against 'the thieves.' 'Some thieves came in and gave band for the rest, and some pledges were delivered to the Regent for good order; but or [ere] they wald obey, their corns and houses were destroyed, with great spulyie of their goods.' The Regent returned in a few days to Dalkeith. 'Notwithstanding of this raid, the haill thieves convenit, and harried the country, following ay on the host.' A second and more vigorous expedition of the same kind having then been resolved on, 'seven score or thereby of the thieves come to the Regent, and pledges for the rest, wha was put in prison, some in the Castle of Edinburgh, some in the Tolbooth thereof, and some in the north land.'—*D. O.*

1573-81. The burgh records of Glasgow from 1573 to 1581, of which liberal excerpts have been published by the Maitland Club,[1] throw much light on manners and the state of society, and also on the burgal or municipal customs. Glasgow was then a little town,

[1] Under the care of John Smith, youngest, the secretary of the Club. 1832.

undistinguished from any other of its size, excepting in its university and a small commerce, chiefly of a coasting description. We see in these records all the common affairs of a petty town, but with the rough character proper to an age of ignorance and ill-regulated feeling. 1573-81.

The quarrels, flytings (scoldings), and acts of personal violence form by far the most conspicuous entries in these records. Men strike women, women clapperclaw each other, and even the dignitaries of the town are assailed on the street and in their council-house. Whingers (that is, swords) and pistols are frequently used in these conflicts, and sometimes with dire effects. As examples—

April 9, 1574.—'Alexander Curry and Marion Smith, spouses, are found in the wrang for troublance done by them to Margaret Hunter, in casting down of two pair of sheets, tramping them in the gutter, and striking of the said Margaret.' Surety is given that Alexander and Marion shall in future abstain from striking each other; and 'gif they flyte, to be *brankit*'—that is, invested with the kind of iron bridle, with a tongue retroverted into the mouth, of which a description has already been given. (See under Oct. 30, 1567.)

April 23.—William Wilson is found in the wrong for blooding of Richard Wardrope on the head. Richard and Andrew Wardrope are at the same time found in the wrong as the occasion thereof; and John and Andrew Wardrope, for hurting and wounding of the said William Wilson, to the great effusion of his blood in the Gallowgate on the morning thereafter. So also, Richard and John Wardrope are declared guilty of 'onsetting and invading of the said William with drawn swords and pistols in the mercat, on Shere Thursday last.' Shere Thursday,[1] otherwise called Maundy Thursday, is the day before Good Friday.

One common species of case is an attack of one female upon another, 'striking of her, scarting of her, and dinging her to the erd' [earth]; in one instance, 'shooting of her down in her awn fire.' Injurious words often accompany or provoke these violent acts. Bartilmo Lawteth strikes 'ane poor wife' to the effusion of her blood. Ninian Swan strikes Marion Simpson with 'ane tangs' [pair of tongs], and knocks her down—she, however, having previously spit in his face. 'Andrew Heriot is [November 8, 1575] fund in the wrang and amerciament of court for troublance

[1] So called 'for that in old Fathers' days the people would that day shear their heads and clip their beards, and so make them honest against Easter Day.'—Authority quoted in Brand's *Pop. Antiquities*, by Ellis.

1573-81. done to David Morison, in striking of him with his neive in Master Henry Gibson's writing-chamber, on the haffet [side of the head], and also for the hitting of him on the face with his neive upon the Hie Gait, and making him baith blae and bloody therewith.'

George Elphinstone of Blythswood, one of the bailies, suffered a violent attack in the council-house (August 24, 1574) from Robert Pirry, a tailor, who wounded him with his whinger, striking one of the officers at the same time. For this, Pirry lost his freedom as a burgess. Six years afterwards, the same magistrate was assaulted on the street by George Herbertson, 'saying how durst he be sae pert to deal ony wines without his advice;' after which he threatened the bailie with his whinger. Immediately thereafter, Herbertson assailed the magistrate in the Tolbooth, 'giving him many injurious words, sic as knave, skaybell, matteyne, and loon, and that he was gentiller nor he, having his hand on his whinger, rugging it halflings in and out, and that he cared him not, nor the land that he had nowther.'

In June 1589, Thomas Miln, chirurgeon, was brought before the magistrates for slanderous speeches against them, and for applying to the town itself an epithet which now, at least, appears strangely inapplicable—the Hungry Town of Glasgow. He was sentenced to appear at the Cross and openly confess his fault.

Much light is thrown on the character of the age by the magistrates ordering 'every booth-halder [shopkeeper] to have in readiness within the booth ane halbert, jack, and steel bonnet, for eschewing of sic inconveniences as may happen, conform to the auld statute made thereanent.'

The streets of the town appear to have been kept much in the same state in which we now find those of neglected country villages, yet not without efforts towards a better order of things. The ordinances for good order may be said to prove the disorder. It is statute (1574) 'that there be nae middings laid upon the fore-gate [front street], nor yet in the Green, and that nae fleshers toom their uschawis upon the fore-gate, and that nae stanes or timber lie on the gate langer nor year and day.' In 1577, this statute is renewed in nearly the same words, shewing that it was but imperfectly obeyed; and next year there is a simple order 'that the haill middings be removed off the Hie Gait, and that nane scrape on the Hie Gait.'

The town, according to a common custom, had its 'minstrels,' by which is inferred simply musicians—probably a couple of bagpipers. In 1579, there is an entry of ten shillings 'to the minstrels, for their expenses to Hamilton siege.' This was a siege in which popular affections would probably be engaged at Glasgow, as its object was to destroy the last vestige of the queen's interest in Scotland. At the Whitsunday court 1574, the minstrels are continued until 'the Summerhill,' by which was meant a court annually held at a place so called, when the marches of the town's property were subjected to review. There, accordingly, on Sunday the 20th June, Archibald Bordland and Robert Duncan are 'admittit to be menstrals to the town for this instant year, and to have frae ilk freeman allenarly, but meat, twa shillings money at the least, with mair at the giver's pleasure.' 1573-81.

In the treasurer's accounts, we are struck by the many considerable presents, chiefly of wine, given by the town to noblemen possessing influence over its fortunes. We find, amongst frequent propines of wine to the Earl of Argyle, as much as seventeen gallons given at once. Two hogsheads are given to Lord Boyd, six quarts to the lord provost, two quarts to the parson of Glasgow, and so forth. At the town's banquets, aquavitæ figures on several occasions, a quart being charged twenty-four shillings.

Several allusions are made in these records to the 'knocks'—that is, clocks—set up for the public conveniency. An old one is repaired, and James Scott gets a sum 'for labour done by him in colouring of the knock, moon, and horologe, and other common work of the town.' References are made to several trades not known in our age by the same names, as a *lorimer*, the maker of the ironwork in horse-furniture; a *snap-maker*, by which is to be understood a maker of firelocks, then called *snap-hances;* a *ladleman;* a tabroner, meaning a drummer; &c. In 1577, the magistrates grant a pension of ten marks to Alexander Hay, chirurgeon, to encourage him to remain in Glasgow, 'in readiness for serving of the town by his craft and art.' This gentleman would bleed the citizens in exigencies of their health, and shave them daily.

The editor of these records remarks on the treasurer's accounts, that the revenue is fully stated, and the whole expenditure minutely detailed. 'It is true,' he says, 'the magistrates and "divers honest men" occasionally treat themselves to a dejeune; but this is after the completion of some public business, tending to the honour and profit of the commonweal. Indeed, the class of

1573-81. disbursements which, strictly speaking, are the least legal, the most rigid corrector of abuses could not well object to. We allude to the numerous benevolences bestowed upon poor scholars to buy them a suit of clothes, or books, to enable them to prosecute their studies; the sums voted to shipwrecked mariners, to ruined merchants who had lost their horses by some untoward accident, or to the widows and children of those burgesses whom unforeseen difficulties had plunged into absolute want. Not a little of the public funds is sometimes devoted to ransom unfortunate burgesses from captivity among the Turks, while considerable sums are expended in providing medical aid for those afflicted with physical infirmities, or who have met with severe bodily injuries. . . . . Much curious matter may be elicited regarding the sports and pastimes of the people. The diverse disbursements for foot-balls are not unworthy of notice. We also meet with payments made to a piper called *Ryall Dayis*, and to "a fule with a treen sword," as well as to certain young men of the town, for their playing—probably bearing a part in some mask or public pageant. The care bestowed on the decorement of the town's minstrels is evinced in the entry of the purchase of blue cloth to make two coats for them, with as much "cramosie" as would serve for containing the town's arms thereon. Nevertheless, though this care was shewn for the recognised minstrels of the burgh, the profession had thus early fallen into disrepute; for in the ordinance anent the pest [in 1574], "pipers, fiddlers, and minstrels," are unceremoniously classed together as vagabonds, and threatened with severe penalties, should they venture into the city in contravention of the act.'

In those days, the citizens of Glasgow kept each his cow, which was fed, under the care of a town's herdsman, in a common beyond the walls, as is the case with small burghs like Lauder and Peebles at the present day. In March 1589, John Templeton and John Hair were appointed herds for the year to come, John Templeton for 'the nolt and guids aboon the Cross,' and John Hair for 'the nolt and guids beneath the Cross and the rest of the nether parts of the town.'

1574. Apr. 11. A strange tragedy took place at the Cross of Edinburgh. Robert Drummond, sometimes called *Doctor Handie*, who had been a great seeker and apprehender of papists, had been punished for adultery by exposure in the church and banishment from the city. Out of favour on account of his services against popery, he was pardoned and brought back; but being again found guilty of the same offence, he was condemned to exposure in the stocks at the Cross, along with the companion of his crime; after which he was to be burnt in the cheek. While undergoing this punishment, 'there being great science (?) of people about them, and the Doctor Handie being in ane great furie, said: "What wonder ye? I sall give you more occasion to wonder." So, suddenly, he took his awn knife, wha strake himself three or four times fornent the heart, with the whilk he departit. This done, the magistrates causit harl him in ane cart through the town, and the bloody knife borne behind in his hand; and on the morn harlit in the same manner to the gallows on the Burgh-muir, where he was buried.'—*D. O.* 1574.

The Regent had passed an act, very agreeable to the people, to prevent the transporting of grain out of the country. There were, however, certain merchants who found it not difficult, by means of bribes, to obtain from him a licence enabling them to break the law. One of these was Robert Gourlay, originally a servant of the Duke of Chatelherault,[1] but now a rich merchant in Edinburgh—at least so we may reasonably infer from the grandeur of his house, not long ago existing. Robert was driving a good trade in this way, when the kirk, of which he was an elder, interfered to put an end to what it regarded as an unrighteous traffic. He was pronounced by the General Assembly to be guilty of a high offence in transporting victual out of the realm, and was sentenced to appear in the *marriage-place* in the church, and publicly confess his offence, clad in a gown of his own, which should thereafter be given to the poor. He obstinately refused to submit. The Regent came forward as his friend, and told the minister, Mr James Lowson: 'I gave him licence, and it pertaineth not to you to judge of that matter.'[2] But it was all in vain. A week after, Robert was glad not only to go through the prescribed penance, but to crave forgiveness of the kirk for his temporary disobedience.[3] MAY.

The press was not likely to be a friend to the Regent, and the JULY 29.

[1] 'Robert Gurlay, the duke's servant,' is the last in the list of persons forfeited by the parliament of James VI., August 1571.

[2] Calderwood.

[3] Register of the General Kirk of Edinburgh, *Maitland Club Mis.*, i. 101.

1574. Regent, therefore, was not a friend to the press. At this date he induced the Privy Council to issue an edict that 'nane tak upon hand to emprent or sell whatsoever book, ballet, or other werk,' without its being examined and licensed, under pain of death, and confiscation of goods.—*P. C. R.*

Sep. 3. The town-council of Edinburgh agreed with a Frenchman that he should set up a school in the city, to teach his own language, for which he should be entitled to charge each child twenty-five shillings yearly, besides enjoying a salary of twenty pounds during the council's pleasure.—*City Register, apud Maitland.*

'The summer right evil weather, and dear; the boll of malt five merk and half merk, and the boll of meal four merk and three merk. Evil August; wind and rain. The harvest evil weather that ever was seen; continual weet.'—*C. F.*

Consequently, in autumn and winter, 'there was ane great dearth in Scotland of all kinds of victuals.'—*D. O.* 'About Lammas, wheat was sold at London for three shillings the bushel; but shortly after it was raised to four shillings, five shillings, six shillings, and before Christmas to a noble and seven shillings, which so continued long after. Beef was sold for twenty pence and two-and-twenty pence the stone, and all other flesh and white meats at an excessive price; all kind of salt fish very dear, as five herrings twopence. Yet great plenty of fresh fish, and oft times the same very cheap. . . . All this dearth notwithstanding (thanks be given to God) there was no want of anything to him that wanted not money.'—*Howes.*

Oct. 14. 'The pest came to Leith by ane passenger wha came out of England, and sundry died thereof before it was known.' On the 24th, it entered Edinburgh, 'brought in by ane dochter of Malvis Curll out of Kirkaldy.' The Court of Session abstained from sitting in consequence. 'My Lord Regent's grace skalit his house and men of weir, and was but six in household; I know not whether for fear of the pest or for sparing of expenses.'—*D. O.*

In December, the kirk-session of Edinburgh, 'foreseeing the great apparent plague and scourge of pest, hinging universally upon the haill realm,' and considering that 'the only ordinary means appointed by God in his holy word, whereby the said apparent scourge may be removed, is ane public fast and humiliation,' did accordingly appoint such a fast, to last for eight days, with sermon and prayers every day, and the people's 'food to be breid and drink with all kind of sobriety.'[1] 1574.

We do not hear of the pest proving very deadly in Scotland on this occasion.

This Christmas-day, the minister and reader of Dumfries having refused to teach or read, 'the town . . . . brought a reader of their own, with tabret and whistle, and caused him read the prayers.' This extraordinary exercise they maintained during all the days of Yule. It was complained of at the subsequent General Assembly, and referred to the Regent.—*Cal.* Dec. 25.

In this year died David Home of Wedderburn, a gentleman of good account in Berwickshire, and father of the David Home of Godscroft, to whom Scottish literature owes the *History of the House of Douglas*. The son has left us a portraiture of the father, which, even when we make a good allowance for filial partiality, must be held as shewing that society was not then without estimable members. 'He died in the fiftieth year of his age, of a consumption, being the first (as is said) of his family who had died a natural death—all the rest having lost their lives in defence of their country. 1574.

'He was a man remarkable for piety and probity, ingenuity [candour], and integrity; neither was he altogether illiterate, being well versed in the Latin tongue. . . . He had the Psalms, and particularly some short sentences of them, always in his mouth; such as: "It is better to trust in the Lord than in the princes of the earth:" "Our hope ought to be placed in God alone." He particularly delighted in the 146th psalm, and sung it whilst he played on the harp with the most sincere and unaffected devotion. He was strictly just, utterly detesting all manner of fraud. I remember, when a conversation happened among some friends about prudence and fraud, his son George happened to say, that it was not unlawful to do a good action, and for a good end, although it might be brought about by indirect methods, and that this was sometimes necessary. "What," says he, "George, do you call ane indirect way? It is but fraud and deceit covered under a specious name, and never to be admitted or practised by a good man." He himself always acted on this principle, and was so strictly just, and so little desirous of what was his neighbour's,

[1] Reg. of Gen. Kirk of Edinburgh, *Maitland Club Mis.*, i. 111.

1571. that, in the time of the civil wars, when Alexander, his chief, was forfeit for his defection from the queen's party, he might have had his whole patrimony, and also the abbacy of Coldingham, but refused both the one and the other. When Patrick Lindsay desired that he would ask something from the governor [Morton], as he was sure whatever he asked would be granted, he refused to ask anything, saying that he was content with his own. When Lindsay insisted, says he: "Since you will have it so, I will ask something; but you must first assure me I will not be refused." Then Lindsay swore to him that he should have whatever he desired. "Let me have, then," says he, "the abbacy of Haddington." "That you cannot get," says Lindsay, "as I received it myself some time ago. But ask something seriously; for if you do not get a share of our enemies' estates, our party will never put sufficient trust in you." To this David answered: "If I never can give proofs of my fidelity otherwise than in that manner, I will never give any, let him doubt of it who may. I have hitherto lived content with my own, and will live so, nor do I want any more."

'David was a man of that temper, that he never was willing to offer any injury, nor to take notice of one when offered. His uncle George Douglas sometimes stayed at Wedderburn. He still kept up a secret grudge at Alexander of Home on account of that controversy they had had about Cockburnspath. Alexander happened to be at this time at Manderston, which is within half a mile of Wedderburn. Alexander of Manderston, with a great number of attendants, goes out with him to hunt; and as he was a turbulent man, and much given to ostentation, under the pretext of seeking game, he ranges through all Wedderburn's fields. This was intended as an affront to George Douglas, and to shew him what trouble he occasioned to his nephew David.

'George had resolved to bear the thing patiently, and to dissemble; but David, knowing their intention, and not bearing that any affront should be put upon his uncle, mounts his horse, and orders his servants to do the like, and, taking George along with him, he presses hard upon the heels of Alexander, who was then going home, and follows him to the very doors of his own house of Manderston, and hunted about the whins and broom at the back of the garden, till evening forced him to return home.[1]

At this time was the conspiracy or Black Band formed against

[1] As this conduct was such as might lead to a collision between the parties, it is not easy to see how it illustrates the author's proposition of Wedderburn's pacific temper.

him, which he bore patiently, and at the same time wisely repulsed. 1571. I know not upon what account some gentlemen of the Merse entered into this conspiracy; it is certain it was for no misdemeanour of his, nor did they pretend any. Alexander of Manderston was the contriver of the whole. It was a thing openly known, for in the meetings of the judges on the Borders about mutual restitutions, the one [party] stood on this side, and the other on that, like opposite armies. . . . . One day, when both parties were returning home, and among the rest Manderston, some of Wedderburn's followers, flushed with indignation, advised him no longer to bear the arrogance of the confederates. He, on the other hand, refused to stain his hands in blood, saying that Manderston was furious and insolent in his youth, but would grow wiser when he was old, and acknowledge his fault.'

John Stuart, the titular abbot of Coldingham, a natural son of James V., was importuned to join the Black Band, but had too much regard for Wedderburn to do so. While he was absent in the north with his brother the Regent Moray, his wife, who had a spite at Wedderburn, made a strange kind of demonstration against him. She 'ordered the men of her faction to be present on a certain day, and to bring along with them wains, carts, and other things fit for carrying off the corns, all of which was carefully done. But Wedderburn with his friends having gathered together about 500 horse, hastens to the fields, and dissipates the scattered troops before they could unite themselves into one, breaks the wagons, looses the horses, and drives them away. On this they all betake themselves to flight, together with Stuart's wife (she was called Hepburn, and a sister of old Bothwell). A few received some strokes; none were wounded; but so great was the terror struck into them all, that they all sought hiding-places in their flight. Some hid themselves among the furze or broom; others under the banks of the river; some in the fields of corn, and all either in one place or other. One John Edington (commonly called the Liar, as he was always the messenger of strange news, which was commonly false) hid himself in the ambry of a poor old woman, from which he was dislodged, to the great diversion of his enemies and his own great terror. When their fear a little subsided, and it appeared that none were hurt, the affair appeared so ridiculous both to themselves and others, that Hepburn (as she was a woman of a pretty good genius and poetically inclined) described the whole in some verses. Nor was there ever anything afterwards attempted by the confederates.'

1574. David is described as being swift of foot, and fond of foot-races. Horse-racing was also one of his amusements. 'He collected a number of the swiftest horses both from the north of Scotland and from England, by the assistance of one Graeme, recommended to him by his brother-in-law, Lochinvar. He generally had eight or more of that kind, so that the prize was seldom won by any but those of his family. . . . He was so great a master of the art of riding, that he would often be beat to-day, and within eight days lay a double wager on the same horses, and come off conqueror. . . . . He went frequently from home to his diversion, sometimes to Haddington, and sometimes to Peebles, the one of which is eighteen, and the other twenty-four miles distant, and sometimes stayed there for several days with numerous attendants, regardless of expense, as being too mean and sordid a care, and below the dignity of one of his rank.

'Being educated in affluence, he delighted in fencing, hunting, riding, throwing the javelin, managing horses, and likewise in cards and dice. Yet he was sufficiently careful of his affairs without doors. Those of a more domestic nature he committed to the care of his wife, and when he had none, to his servants; so that he neither increased nor diminished his patrimony.'

The writer, in the true spirit of his age, cites Wedderburn's love of the house of Home as '*not the least of his virtues.*' The chief was prejudiced against him, but 'he bore it patiently, and never failed giving him all due honour.' At length, Lord Home being taken prisoner by Morton at the close of the queen's wars, and put into Leith Fort, Wedderburn went to see him, and acted so much as his friend as to obtain his release and secure his love.

David's first wife, of the Johnstons of Elphinston, in Haddingtonshire, was a paragon of benevolence. She not only supplied the poor bountifully, but often gave large help to superior people who had fallen back in the world. She would give the clothes of her own children to clothe the naked and friendless. Yet, such was her good management, that she left at her death 3000 merks in gold—'a great sum in those days.' 'Everything in the family had a splendid appearance; and this she affected in compliance to her husband's temper. As she was herself, so she instructed her children in the fear of God, and in everything that was good and commendable. To sum up her whole character, she obtained from all the appellation of the Good Lady Wedderburn.'

David 'was of a beautiful and manly make. His complexion (for a man) was rather too fair. He had yellow hair, and an aquiline nose; his stature rather inclining to tall, his countenance comely and majestic, claiming at the same time both love and reverence. He much affected elegance in his dress, but not extravagance. He was very fond of his children, and seldom ceased to dance them in his arms. . . . These are the parents who make me rejoice in my birth. These are the parents who are an honour to their posterity. To live and die like them, loving and beloved by all, is my great and only ambition.'[1] 1574.

'In the meantime, there was ane great dearth in Scotland of all kind of victuals.'—*D. O.* 1574-5. FEB.

In the course of the late civil war, Lords John and Claud Hamilton came to an inn to apprehend old Carmichael and the Laird of Westerhall. The house being beset and set on fire, the two gentlemen surrendered, on condition that their lives should be spared; but after they came forth, and were disarmed, Westerhall was slain, and Carmichael carried away a prisoner. MAR. 7.

Westerhall being a dependent of the house of Angus, his death added largely to the resentment already felt by the Regent towards the Hamiltons. Love, however, which so often raises wrath, here came in to smooth it. There was a certain widowed Countess of Cassillis, whom Lord John knew and loved; and, as she was a cousin of the Regent, it became necessary to effect a reconciliation with him before a match could be effected. As one step towards this object—for doubtless there would be others, and particularly one involving a money-payment to the griping Morton—Lord John, now the actual head of the princely house of Hamilton, agreed, along with his brother, to perform a ceremony of expiation for the death of Westerhall. The Earl of Angus, head of the house of Douglas, being placed in the inner court of Holyrood Palace, Lords John and Claud walked across barefooted and bareheaded, and falling down on their knees before the earl, held up to him each a naked sword by the point, implying that they put their lives in his power, trusting solely to his generosity for their not being immediately slain. Soon after this strange scene, Lord John wedded Lady Cassillis.

This seems, after all, to have been but a partial and temporary restoration of the Hamiltons to court favour. There were many

[1] From a copy in the editor's possession of a manuscript long preserved in Broomhouse, Berwickshire.

1574-5. who could not forget or forgive their concern in the slaughter of the Regents Moray and Lennox. Douglas of Lochleven, uterine brother of Moray, was irreconcilably bitter against them. 'Twice he set upon the Lord Hamilton, as he was coming from Aberbrothick, and chased him so that he was constrained to return to Aberbrothick again. Another time, as he was coming through Fife, he made him flee to Dairsie, which he beset and lay about it till the Regent sent to him and commanded him to desist.'—*H. of G.*

MAR. 8. Though copies of the English Bible had found their way into Scotland, and been of great service in promoting and establishing the reformed doctrines, there was as yet no abundance of copies, nor had any edition been printed within the kingdom. There was, however, a burgess of Edinburgh named Thomas Bassendyne, who for some years had had a small printing-office there. He was probably too poor a man to undertake the printing of a thick quarto, the form in which the Bible was then usually presented; but he took into association with himself a man of better connection and means, named Alexander Arbuthnot, also an Edinburgh burgess; and now it was deemed possible that an edition of the Scriptures might be brought out within the realm of Scotland. The government, under the Regent Morton, gave a favourable ear to the project, and it was further encouraged by the bishops, superintendents, and other leading men of the kirk.

On the day noted, the Privy Council, seeing that 'the charge and hazard of the wark will be great and sumptuous,' decreed that each parish in the kingdom should advance £5 as a contribution, to be collected under the care of the said officers of the church, £4, 13s. 4d. of this sum being considered as the price of a copy of the impression, to be afterwards delivered, 'weel and sufficiently bund in paste or timmer,' and the remaining 6s. 8d. as the expense of collecting the money. The money was to be handed to Alexander Arbuthnot before the 1st of July next.

Arbuthnot and Bassendyne, on their parts, bound themselves to execute the work under certain penalties, and respectable men came forward as their sureties. Those who stood for Arbuthnot were David Guthrie of Kincaldrum, William Guthrie of Halkerton, William Rynd of Carse, and James Arnot of Lentusche—all Forfarshire gentlemen, be it remarked—a fact arguing that Arbuthnot himself was of the same district. The exact arrangements of Arbuthnot and Bassendyne between themselves do not at this time appear; but we find that Bassendyne engaged in

Flanders one 'Salomon Kerknett of Magdeburg' to come and act as 'composer' at 49s. of weekly wages, and sought the aid of Mr George Young, servant of the abbot of Dunfermline, as corrector of the press. Having 'guid characters and prenting irons,' it was to be expected that the work, great and sumptuous as it was, would go quickly and pleasantly on. This hope, however, was not to be realised. (See under July 18, 1576.)—*P. C. R.* 1574-5.

Among the evils of these times, was one which the present generation knows nothing of but from history. Owing to the constant exporting of good coin, and the importing of bad, the circulating medium of the country was in a wretched state. There seems to have been a regular system for coining base placks and lions (otherwise called *hardheads*) in the Low Countries, to be introduced by merchants into Scotland. The Regent, in a proclamation, described the abundance of debased money as the chief cause of the present dearth, the possessors of grain being thus induced to withhold it from market. For this reason, according to his own account, proceeding upon an act of the convention now sitting, he ordained the old coin to be brought to the cunyie-house, where it would be 'clippit, and put in ane close lockit coffer upon the count and inventar of the quantity receivit frae every person;' and meanwhile the lately issued genuine placks and lions were to have currency at twopence and a penny apiece respectively—that is, at denominations above their value. Any one hereafter possessing the false coin, was to be punished as an out-putter of false money. MAR.

'Every day after this proclamation, induring the convention, the poor veriit and banned the Regent and haill lords openly in their presence, whenever they passed or repassed frae the Abbey, whilk was heavy and lamentable to hear.'—*D. O.*

The Regent, while thus an oppressor of his people by attempting to enhance the value of the coin, was engaged in several sumptuous undertakings. He was restoring the Castle of Edinburgh at a vast expense, and also erecting a new mint—putting over its door, by the way, a prayer which he had at this time much need to use—

BE MERCYFULL TO ME, O GOD.

His own personal extravagances were not less remarkable. He erected at Dalkeith a magnificent palace, richly adorned with tapestries and pictures, and fitter for a king than a subject. Here

1574-5. he lived in an appropriate style. All this he did at the expense of his enemies. He kept a fool named Patrick Bonny, who, seeing him one day pestered by a concourse of beggars, advised him to have them all burnt in one fire. 'What an impious idea!' said the Regent. 'Not at all,' replied the jester; 'if the whole of these poor people were consumed, you would soon make more poor people out of the rich.'—*Jo. R. B. Hist.*

1575. MAR. 30. 'There was ane calf calfit at Roslin, with ane heid, four een, three lugs [ears], ane in the middle, and ane on ilk side, twa mouths.'[1]—*Sinclair of Roslin's MS. additions to Extracta ex Chronicis Scotie.*

JUNE. A number of French Protestants having at this time taken refuge in London in great poverty, there was a collection in Edinburgh for their benefit, one person being commissioned to go 'through the Lords of Session, advocates, and scribes,' and another 'to pass to the deacons and crafts,' in order to gather their respective contributions.—*R. G. K. E.*

AUG. The General Assembly declared its mind regarding the dress fit for clergymen and their wives. 'We think all kind of broidering unseemly; all begares[2] of velvet, in gown, hose, or coat, and all superfluous and vain cutting out, steeking with silks, all kind of costly sewing on passments[3]. . . . . all kind of costly sewing, or variant hues in sarks; all kind of light and variant hues in clothing, as red, blue, yellow, and such like, which declare the lightness of the mind; all wearing of rings, bracelets, buttons of silver, gold, or other metal; all kinds of superfluity of cloth in making of hose; all using of plaids in the kirk by readers or ministers, namely in the time of their ministry, or using of their office; all kind of gowning, cutting, doubletting, or breeks of velvet, satin, taffeta, or such like; all silk hats, and hats of divers and light colours.' It was recommended to the clergy, that 'their whole habit be of grave colour, as black, russet, sad gray, or sad brown; or serges, worset, chamlet, grogram, lytes worset, or such like. . . . And their wives to be subject to the same order.'

It is rather curious that any such sumptuary regulations should

[1] 'There was presented to the Queen Regent (1558), by Robert Ormiston, a calf having two heads, whereat she scripped [mocked], and said: "It was but a common thing."'—*Knox.*

[2] Coloured stripes sewed on a garment.

[3] Fringes or trimmings.

have been required for the Presbyterian ministers, or even their helpmates, as, according to all accounts, their incomes for the first forty years after the Reformation were wretchedly narrow and irregular. The thirds of the old benefices assigned to them by Queen Mary's act were far from being well paid. In the pathetic words of a memorial they presented to Mary in 1562, 'most of them led a beggar's life.' They were as ill off under the grasping Morton as at any other time. The proceedings of the General Assembly of 1576 reveal that some were compelled to eke out their miserable stipends by selling ale to their flocks. The question was then formally put: 'Whether a minister or reader may tap ale, beer, or wine, and keep an open tavern?' to which it was answered: 'Ane minister or reader that taps ale or beer or wine, and keeps ane open tavern, sould be exhorted by the commissioners to keep decorum.'—*B. U. K.* 1575.

Towards the end of this year, the Regent Morton was at Dumfries, holding justice-courts for the punishment of the Borderers. 'Many were punished by their purses rather than their lives. Many gentlemen of England came thither to behald the Regent's court, where there was great provocation made for the running of horses. By chance my Lord Hamilton had there a horse sae weel bridled and sae speedy, that although he was of a meaner stature than other horses that essayit their speed, he overran them all a great way upon Solway Sands, whereby he obtained great praise both of England and Scotland at that time.'—*H. K. J.*

It was found that in Meggotland, Eskdale-muir, and other parts near the Border, 'where our sovereign lord's progenitors were wont to have their chief pastime of hunting,' the deer were now slain with guns, not only by Scotsmen, but by Englishmen whom Scotsmen smuggled in across the Border, and this often at forbidden times; all which was 'against the commonweal and policy of the realm.' The Privy Council accordingly took measures to put a stop to these practices.—*P. C. R.* 1576. MAR. 27.

'The first day of May, 1576 years, was sae evil, the wind and weet at the west-north-west, with great showers of snaw and sleet, that the like was nocht seen by them that was living, in mony years afore, sae evil.'—*Chr. Aber.* MAY 1.

The Earl of Huntly died in a sudden and mysterious manner MAY.

1576. at Strathbogie Castle. Having fallen down in a fit while playing at football, he was carried to bed, where he foamed at the mouth and nostrils, struggled with his hands, and stared wildly, as if he would have spoken, but could never command but one word—'Look, look, look.' He also vomited a good deal of blood. After four hours' illness, he expired.

'The Earl of Huntly being dead thus on Saturday at even, Adam [Gordon, his brother] immediately causit bear but [out, outward] the dead corpse to the chalmer of dais [room of state], and causit bear into the chalmer where he had lain, the whole coffers, boxes, or lettrens [desks], that the earl himself had in handling, and had ony gear in keeping in; sic as writs, gold, silver, or golden work, whereof the keys were in ane lettren. The key of that lettren was at his awn bag, whilk Adam took and openit that, and took out the rest of the keys, and made ane inventory upon all the gear he fand within that coffer, or at least on the maist part and special part of that that was within; and when he had ta'en out sic money as to make his awn expenses south, he lockit all the coffers again, and thereafter lockit the chalmer door, and put up the key, and causit lock the outer chalmer door where the dead corpse lay. After they had set candles in the chalmer to burn, and gave the key of that chalmer door to John Hamilton, wha was man having greatest care within that place and credit of the Earl of Huntly in his time—this done, with sic other directions made for waiting on the place, Adam made him ready, and took the post south at 12 hours on the night, as I believe. . . . . At ten hours or thereby before noon, on the morn after the earl was dead, there was in ane chalmer together, callit the leather chalmer, ... fourteen or sixteen men lamenting the death that was so suddenly fallen, every man for his part rehearsing the skaith [damage] that was to come by that death to them. Amangst the whilk there was ane westland man standing upright [with] his back at the fire, wha said the cause was not so hard to nane as [it] was to him, for he was newlings come out of Lochinvar, for some evil turn that he had done that he might not brook his awn country for . . . . he falls flat down on his face to the ground dead. The men pullit him up, cuist up door and window, and gave him air; there could appear no life in him, except he was hot.' After lying several hours in the fit, 'he recovered with great sobbing and working with his hands, feet, and body, and he cried, "Cauld, cauld."' This lasted till next morning, when he recovered thoroughly.

'On the morn . . . . Tyesday next after the earl's death, John

Hamilton was gone up to the gallery of the new wark [building] to bring down spicery or some other gear for the kitchen, and had with him ane Mr James Spittal, and ane other man of the place, whose name I have forgotten. . . . . This John Hamilton opened ane coffer, taking out something that he needit; he says: "I am very sick," and with that he falls down, crying, "Cauld, cauld." The other twa took him quickly up, cast up the window, and had him up and down the house. At length he said he was very sick; he wald have been in ane bed. Mr James Spittal convoyit him down the stair. When he was there down, he remembered that he had forgotten ane coffer open behind him; he turned again and the said Mr James with him, and when they had come again, they found the third man that was with them fallen dead ower the coffer, and he on his wambe lying ower the coffer. John Hamilton might make no help, by reason he himself was evil at ease. Mr James Spittal ran down, and brought up twa or three other men, and carried him down the stair, and up and down the close, but could find no life in him. At length they laid him in ane bed, where within ane while he recovered, with sighing and sobbing, wrestling with hands, feet, and body, and ever as he got ony words betwixt the swooning, he cried, "Cauld, cauld;" and this lasted twelve or thirteen hours, and I trow langer, if he was sae weel waited on as the lave [rest], as he was not, but gave him leave to work him alane, because he was ane simple poor man. All these wrought as the Earl of Huntly did in his dead passions, except they vomited not, nor fumed at the mouth and nostrils. 1576.

'Upon that Tyesday after the deid [death], ane surgeoner of Aberdeen, callit William Urquhart, came to Strathbogie and bowelled the dead corpse, which, after the bowelling, was ta'en out of the chalmer and had into the chapel, where it remaineth to the burial. John Hamilton receivit the key of the chalmer door again when the dead corpse was ta'en out. On Wednesday next after the deid, Patrick Gordon, the earl's brother, was sitting on ane form next to that chalmer door where that the dead corpse was bowelled; he hears ane great noise and din in that chalmer, whether it was of speech, of graning, or rumbling, I cannot tell. There was sixteen or twenty men in the hall with him; he gars call for John Hamilton, and asks gif there was onybody in that chalmer; the other said: "Nay." He bade him hearken what he heard at the door, wha heard as he did. Then the key was brought him. He commandit John Hamilton to gang in, wha refused; he skipped in himself; John Hamilton followed ane step or twa,

1576. and came with speed again to the door for fear. Patrick passed to the inner side of the chalmer, and heard the like noise as he did when he was thereout, but yet could see nothing, for it was even, at the wayganging of the daylight. He came back gain very affrayedly, and out at the door, and show[ed] so mony as bidden in the hall what he had heard, wha assayit to pass to the chalmer, to know what was there; but nane enterit ower the threshold; all came back for fear. This pastime lasted them more nor ane hour. Candles were brought, the chalmer vissied [examined]; nothing there. As soon as they came to the door again, the noise was as great as of before, the candles burning there ben [within]; they said to me that knows it, there is not sae meikle a quick thing as a mouse may enter within that chalmer, the doors and windows [being] steekit, it is so close all about. Judge ye how ghaists and gyre-carlins come in among them. They were ane hour or twa at this bickering, while ane man of the place comes in among them, and said to Patrick: "Fye, for gif he was not tentie [careful], the bruit [report] wald pass through the country that the Earl of Huntly had risen again." Then Patrick called them that had heard it, and commandit that nae sic word should be spoken.'—*Ban.*

JULY 18. The work of printing the Bible, undertaken by Arbuthnot and Bassendyne in March of the year preceding, had proved a heavier undertaking than they expected, and had met with 'impediments.' They now therefore came with their sureties before the Privy Council, and pleaded for nine months further time to complete the work, obliging themselves, in case of failure, to return the money which had been contributed by the various parishes. This grace was extended to them.

On the 5th January 1576-7, the work of the Bible was still in hand, and we have then a complaint made to the Regent by 'Salomon Kerknett of Magdeburg, composer of wark of the Bible,' to the effect that Thomas Bassendyne had refused since the 23d of December by past, to pay him the weekly wages of 49s., agreed upon between them when he was engaged in Flanders. The Regent, finding the complaint just, ordered Bassendyne to pay Kerknett his arrears, and continue paying him at the same rate till the work should be finished.

Six days later, a more serious complaint was made against Bassendyne—namely, by Alexander Arbuthnot, that he would not deliver to Alexander, as he had contracted to do, the printing-house and the Bible, so far as printed, 'wherethrough the wark lies idle, to

the great hurt of the commonweal of the realm.' The Regent, 1576.
having heard parties, and being ripely advised by the Lords of the Council, ordered that Bassendyne should deliver the printing-house and Bible to Alexander Arbuthnot before the end of the month.—*P. C. R.*

Such were the difficulties which stood in the way of the first edition of the Bible printed in Scotland.

It was found necessary to issue an edict to the gold-seekers in Crawford-muir, Roberton, and Henderland, forbidding them to continue selling their gold to merchants for exportation, but to bring all, as was legally due, to the king's cunyie-house, to be sold there at the accustomed prices, for the use of the state.—*P. C. R.*

'The whilk summer was right guid weather; but there was weir betwixt my Lord of Argyle and my Lord Athole, and great spoliation made by the men of Lochaber on puir men. God see till that.'

'All June, July, and August right evil weather. . . . . Nae aits shorn in Fortirgall the 23 day of September. . . . . All October evil weather; mickle corn unshorn and unled.'—*C. F.*

The trial of Elizabeth or Bessie Dunlop of Lyne, in Ayrshire, for Nov. 8.
the alleged crime of witchcraft. Bessie was a married woman, apparently in middle life, and her only offence was giving information, as from a supernatural source, regarding articles which had been stolen, and for the cure of diseases. 'She herself had nae kind of art nor science sae to do;' she obtained her information, when she required it, from 'ane Tom Reid, wha died at Pinkie,' that is, at the battle fought there twenty-nine years before. Her intercourse with a deceased person seems to have given herself little surprise, and she spoke of it with much coolness.

Being asked, 'what kind of man this Tom Reid was, [she] declairit, he was ane honest, weel, elderly man, gray-beardit, and had ane gray coat with Lombard sleeves of the auld fashion; ane pair of gray breeks and white shanks [stockings], gartenit aboon the knee; ane black bonnet on his head, close behind and plain before; with silken laces drawn through the lips thereof; and ane white wand in his hand. Being interrogat how and in what manner of place the said Tom Reid came to her, [she] answerit, as she was ganging betwixt her awn house and the yard of Monkcastle, driving her kye to the pasture, and making heavy sair dule with herself, greeting very fast for her cow that was dead, her husband

1576. and child that were lying sick in the land-ill, and she new risen out of gissan [child-bed], the said Tom met her by the way, halsit her [took her round the neck, saluting her], and said: "Gude day, Bessie;" and she said: "God speed you, gudeman." "Sancta Maria," said he, "Bessie, why makes thou sae great dule and sair greeting for ony warldly thing?" She answerit: "Alas, have I not cause to make great dule? for our gear is traikit [dwindled away], and my husband is on the point of deid, and ane baby of my awn will not live, and myself at ane weak point; have I not gude cause, then, to have ane sair heart?" But Tom said: "Bessie, thou hast crabbit [irritated] God, and askit something you should not have done; and therefore I counsel thee to mend to him, for I tell thee thy bairn shall die, and the sick cow, ere you come hame; thy twa sheep shall die too; but thy husband shall mend, and be as haill and feir as ever he was." And then was I something blyther, frae he tauld me that my gudeman wald mend. Then Tom Reid went away from me in through the yard of Monkcastle; and I thought he gaed in at ane narrower hole of the dyke nor ony eardly man could have gane through; and sae I was something fleyit [frightened].' . . . . The third time that Tom and Bessie met, 'he appeared to her as she was ganging betwixt her awn house and the Thorn of Damustarnock, where he tarriet ane gude while with her, and speerit [inquired] at her, "Gif she wald not trow in him?" She said: "She wald trow in onybody did her gude." And Tom promisit her baith gear, horses, and kye, and other graith, gif she wald deny her christendom and the faith she took at the font-stane. Whereunto she answerit: "That gif she should be riven at horse-tails, she should never do that," but promisit to be leal and true to him in ony thing she could do.

'. . . . The feird [fourth] time, he appearit in her awn house to her, about the 12 hour of the day, where there was sitting three tailors and her awn gudeman . . . . he took her apron and led her to the door with him, and she followit, and gaed up with him to the kiln-end, where he forbade her to speak or fear ony thing she heard or saw . . . . when they had gane ane little piece forward, she saw twelve persons, aucht women and four men: the men were clad in gentlemen's claithing, and the women had all plaids round about them, and were very seemly-like to see. And Tom was with them. Demandit if she knew any of them, answerit: "Nane, except Tom." Demandit what they said to her, answerit: They bade her sit down, and said, "Welcome, Bessie; will thou go with us?" But she answerit not, because Tom had forbidden her.

And further declairit, that she knew not what purpose they had 1576. amongst them; only she saw their lips move; and within a short space, they partit all away; and ane hideous ugly sough of wind followit them; and she lay sick till Tom came back again frae them. . . . Being demandit gif she speerit at Tom what persons they were, answerit: "That they were the gude wights that winnit in the court of Elfame, wha came there to desire her to go with them." And further, Tom desirit her to do the same; wha answerit: "She saw nae profit to gang thae kind of gaits [to go such ways], unless she kend wherefore." Tom said: "Sees thou not me, baith meat-worth, claith-worth, and gude eneuch like in person? and [he] should make her far better nor ever she was." She answerit: "That she dwelt with her awn husband and bairns, and could not leave them." And sae Tom began to be very crabbit with her, and said: "Gif sae she thought, she wald get little gude of him."'

Bessie from time to time consulted her ghostly friend about cases of sickness for which her skill was required. 'Tom gave out of his awn hand, ane thing like the root of ane beet, and bade her either seethe or make ane saw [salve] of it, or else dry it, and make powder of it, and give it to sick persons, and they should mend. . . . . She mendit John Jack's bairn, and Wilson's of the town, and her gudeman's sister's cow. . . . . The Lady Johnston, elder, sent to her ane servant to help ane young gentlewoman, her doughter, now married on the young Laird of Stanley, and I thereupon askit counsel of Tom. He said to me, "that her sickness was ane cauld blude that gaed about her heart, that causit her to dwalm [faint]" . . . . and Tom bade her take ane part of ginger, clows, anniseeds, liquorice, and some stark [strong] ale, and seethe them together, and share it, and put it in ane vessel, and take ane little quantity of it in ane mutchkin can, and some white suckar casten amang it; take and drink thereof ilk day, in the morning; gang ane while after, before meat; and she wald be haill. . . . . Demandit what she gat for her doing, declairit "ane peck of meal and some cheese." . . . . Interrogate, gif she could tell of ony thing that was away, or ony thing that was to come, [she] answerit, that she could do naething of herself, but as Tom tauld her . . . . mony folks in the country [came to her] to get wit of gear stolen frae them. . . . The Lady Thirdpart in the barony of Renfrew sent to her and speerit at her, wha was it that had stolen frae her twa horns of gold, and ane crown of the sun, out of her purse? And after she had spoken with Tom, within twenty days, she sent her word wha had them; and she gat them again. . . . . Being demandit of William Kyle, burgess in

1576. Irvine, as he was coming out of Dumbarton, wha was the stealer of Hugh Scott's cloak, ane burgess of the same town? Tom answerit: 'That the cloak wald not be gotten, because it was ta'en away by Mally Boyd, dweller in the same town, and was put out of the fashion of ane cloak in[to] ane kirtle," ' &c.

Bessie, being asked how she knew that her visitor was Tom Reid who had died at Pinkie, answered: 'That she never knew him when he was in life, but that she should not doubt that it was he bade her gang to Tom Reid his son, now officer in his place to the Laird of Blair, and to certain others his kinsmen and friends there, whom he named, and bade them restore certain goods and mend other offences that they had done. . . . . Interrogate gif Tom, at his awn hand, had sent her to ony person to shaw them things to come, declarit that he sent her to nae creature in middle-eard but to William Blair of the Strand, and his eldest dochter, wha was contractit and shortly to be married with   Crawford, young Laird of Baidland, and declare unto them, "That gif she married that man she should either die ane shameful death, slay herself, or gae red-wod [mad];" whereby the said marriage was stayit, and the laird foresaid married her youngest sister.'

Bessie denied any further advances on Tom's part than his taking her once by the apron, and asking her to go with him to Elfame, that is, Fairyland. He used to come chiefly to her at noon. She had seen him walking among the people in the kirk-yard of Dalry; also once in the High Street of Edinburgh, on a market-day, where he laughed to her. Having once ridden with her husband to Leith to bring home meal—'ganging afield to tether her horse at Restalrig Loch, there came ane company of riders bye, that made sic ane din as heaven and eard had gane together; and incontinent they rade into the loch, with mony hideous rumble. Tom tauld it was the gude wights that were riding in middle-eard.'

Being found guilty of the sorcery and other evil arts laid to her charge, Bessie Dunlop was consigned to the flames.—*Pit.*

The modern student of insanity can have no difficulty with this case: it is simply one of hallucination, the consequence of diseased conditions.

1576? The family of Innes of that Ilk, seated in their fine old castle on the coast of Moray, near Elgin, was one of prime importance in the country. The present laird, Alexander, 'though gallant, had something of particularity in his temper, was proud and positive in his deportment, and had his lawsuits with several of his friends; amongst the rest with Innes of Peithock, which had brought them both to Edinburgh in the year 1576, as I take it; where the laird having met his kinsman at the Cross, fell in words with him for daring to give him a citation, and in choler either stabbed the gentleman with a dagger, or pistolled him (for it is variously reported). When he had done, his stomach would not let him fly, but he walked up and down upon the spot, as if he had done nothing that could be quarrelled (his friend's life being but a thing that he could dispose of without being bound to account for it to any other); and there stayed until the Earl of Morton, who was Regent, sent a guard and carried him away to the Castle. 1576?

'When he found truly the danger of his circumstances, and that his proud rash action behoved to cost him his life, he was then free to redeem that at any rate; and made an agreement for a remission with the Regent, at the price of the barony of Kilmalemnock, which this day extends to twenty-four thousand merks rent yearly.

'The evening after the agreement was made, and writ given, being merry with his friends at a collation, and talking anent the dearness of the ransom the Regent had made him pay for his life, he vaunted that, had he his foot once loose, he would fain see what Earl of Morton durst come and possess his lands; which being told to the Regent that night, he resolved to play sure game with him; and therefore, though what he spoke was in drink, the very next day he put the sentence in execution against him by causing his head to be struck off in the Castle, and then possessed the estate.' —*Hist. Acc. Fam. Innes.*

This is a traditionary tale, perhaps true in the main facts; but there is reason to believe that it is to some extent misreported. On the 8th of January 1575–6, Robert Innes, of Innermarky, and James Adamson, burgess of Edinburgh, gave security to the extent of a thousand pounds, that Alexander Innes of that Ilk, being relieved from ward in Edinburgh Castle, should not go beyond the bounds of the town.

On the 18th of February, this surety was discharged by the Regent in council, in order that the laird might 'do his utter and exact diligence for apprehending of John Innes in Garmouth, callit the *Sweet Man*; Thomas Innes, callit the *Little*; John Adam, callit *Meat and Rest*; and John Innes, callit the *Noble*; and bringing them before the justice to be punished for the slauchter of umwhile David Mawer of the Loch;' which duty he had undertaken to perform before the 1st of August next, under pain of a thousand pounds.—*P. C. R.*

1576? It is of course not impossible that after these events the laird was treated in the manner described by the family memoirs.

1576-7. Feb. 14. The Regent, seeing the present abundance of corns in the country, and considering how in bypast times of dearth the people of Scotland had 'received large help and support of victuals out of the easter seas, France, Flanders, and England,' thought it proper that 'the like favour and guid neighbourheid, charity and amity, should be extendit towards the people of the said countries in this present year, when it has pleasit God to visie them with the like dearth and scarcity.' This was the more proper, in as far as 'the farmers sould be greatly interested, gif they were constrainit to sell their corns at the low prices now current,' seeing that their expenses were now as great as when in other times they were getting double prices. For these and other good reasons (whereof probably not the least was a good douceur from a few corn-merchants, such as Robert Gourlay), the Regent was pleased to arrange for a short suspension of the act of parliament forbidding the export of corn out of the country, taking on himself the power of licensing that operation to a certain modified extent. —*P. C. R.*

1577. 'That April, right evil weather; and the May, mickle weet and rain; and June, right evil, weet and wind; and the beir seed right late in all places, while after Sanct Colm's Day [9th June].'—*C. F.*

Nov. 13. 'This year, in the winter, appeared a terrible comet, the stern [star, forming the head] whereof was very great, and proceeding from it towards the east a long tail, in appearance of an ell and a half, like to a besom or scourge made of wands all fiery. It raise nightly in the south-west, not above a degree and a half ascending above the horizon, and continued about a sax weeks or twa month, and piece and piece wore away. The greatest *effects* whereof that out of our country we heard, was a great and mighty battle in Barbaria in Afric, wherein three kings were slain, with a huge multitude of people. And within the country the chasing away of the Hamiltons, &c.'—*Ja. Mel.*

The notices of comets given by our old historical writers and diarists have no scientific value. They are only worthy of notice, as shewing the views entertained regarding comets by

the people of an early and unenlightened age. The real nature 1577.
of these strangers of the sky is not yet ascertained; but we have at least come to know some of the laws by which they are governed; above all, we know the great fact, that they are obedient to law. To our ancestors, they appeared in a very different light—as menacing messengers, sent for special reasons, 'importing change of times and states.' Some of the views expressed regarding them are sufficiently remarkable to be worthy of preservation.

The comet of 1577 was a very noted one, seen over Europe and Asia, also in Peru, and well observed by Tycho Brahé. Its tail, according to the description of the Danish astronomer, extended over 22 degrees. Such was the real space described by James Melville as an ell and a half! This comet passed its perihelion on the 26th of October in the year mentioned, and was visible, as we see, for a considerable portion of the winter. The date here given for its first appearance in Scotland is from the *Aberdeen Chronicle*.

The most noted comet at this time recent, was one called in Scotland the *Fiery Besom*, which has been set down at various dates by English and Scottish historians, but was undoubtedly identical with that so well known in the history of astronomy as having appeared in 1556. John Knox tells us that it presented itself during the winter which he spent in Scotland before his last return to France—a time when the doctrines of the Reformation stood in the most perilous circumstances in both England and Scotland, and men's minds were consequently in a state of great excitement. Sir James Balfour speaks of it as having portended change not only in government, but in religion, and Knox takes care to note—'*Soon after*, Christian, king of Denmark, died, and war raise betwixt Scotland and England, &c.' Modern astronomers believe this comet to be the same with one which alarmed Europe in 1264, and Professor Hind is predicting that it must speedily revisit our skies, at the very time when these sheets are passing through the press. It is a curious consideration, that a heavenly body which left the confines of our sphere on its stated journey when Cranmer stood at the stake in Oxford, should next come amongst us when we are busy with such an affair (for example) as the laying of the electric telegraph across the Atlantic.

'The Lord Somerville had often importuned the Lords of Dec. 18.
Session for a hearing in the Inner House [of a cause respecting

1577. lands, in which he was engaged against his relation, Somerville of Cambusnethan], but was still postponed by the moyen [means] and interest of the Laird of Cambusnethan and the Lady. At length he was advised to use this policy, by one who knew the temper and avarice of Morton, then Regent. This gentleman's advice was, that the Lord Somerville should have his advocates in readiness, and his process in form, against the next day; timely in the morning, that he might not be prevented by other solicitors, he should wait upon the Regent in his own bed-chamber, and inform him that his business was already fully debated and concluded; that only Cambusnethan had given in a petition of new, craving that his business might be heard again *in presentiâ*, before their decerniture, which hitherto, notwithstanding of his bill, he had hindered himself; therefore his desire should be that his royal highness[1] should be pleased to call his action against Cambusnethan, that so long had been depending before them. And, whatever answer he should receive from the Regent, he desired my Lord Somerville not to be much concerned; but upon his taking leave, he should draw out his purse, and make as though he intended to give the waiting-servants some money, and thereupon slip down his purse with the gold therein, upon the table, and thereafter make quickly down stairs, without taking notice of any cry that might come after him. The Lord Somerville punctually obeyed this gentleman's direction and advice in all points; for, having advised his business the night before with his advocates, and commanded his agents to have all his papers together against the morrow, for he hoped to bring his business to a close, being prepared, timely the next morning with his principal advocate he was with the Regent, and informed him fully of his affair; he gave a sign to his advocate to remove, as though he had something to speak to the Regent in private; when he observed his advocate to be gone, he takes his leave of the Regent, there being by good-fortune none in the room but themselves, two of the Regent's pages, and the door-keeper within. It being the custom for noblemen and gentlemen at that time always to keep their money in purses, this the Lord Somerville draws out, as it were to take out a piece of money to give to the door-keeper, and leaves it negligently upon the table. He went quickly down

[1] This seems too high a phrase of compliment for the Regent Morton. *His Grace* was the ordinary phrase, according to Sir James Melville.

stairs, and took no notice of the Regent's still crying after him: 1577.
"My lord, you have forgot your purse," but went on still, until he came the length of the outer porch, now the Duke of Hamilton's lodging, when a gentleman that attended the Regent came up, and told him that it was the Regent's earnest desire that his lordship would be pleased to return and breakfast with him; which accordingly the Lord Somerville did, knowing weel that his project had taken effect.

'About ten o'clock, the Regent went to the house, which was the same which is now the Tolbooth Church, in coach. There was none with him but the Lord Boyd and the Lord Somerville. This was the second coach that came to Scotland, the first being brought by Alexander Lord Seaton, when Queen Mary came from France. Cambusnethan, by accident, as the coach passed, was standing at Niddry's Wynd head, and having inquired who was in it with the Regent, he was answered: "None but the Lord Somerville and the Lord Boyd;" upon which he struck his breast, and said: "This day my cause is lost;" and indeed it proved so; for about eleven hours, the 18th day of December 1577, this action was called and debated until twelve most contentiously by the advocates upon both sides. . . . . After the debate was closed, the interlocutor passed in my Lord Somerville's favours. . . . . Thus ended that expensive plea betwixt the houses of Cowthally and Cambusnethan, after seven or eight years' debate, and these lands of Lothian [Drum, Gilmerton, and Goodtrees] returned again to the Lords Somerville, when they had been fourscore years complete in the possession of the family of Cambusnethan.'—*M. of S.*

Although this story was transcribed from family tradition a century after the alleged occurrence, there is too much reason in the monstrous avarice of Morton to believe it near the truth.

The commencement of the lawsuit between Lord Somerville and his cousin forms an equally curious tale. The Laird of Cambusnethan had a second wife, exceedingly ambitious of the advancement of her own children. First and second alike had been favourites of King James V., and women of great beauty. To promote a match for her son with Lord Somerville's second daughter, Lady Cambusnethan brought a package of family papers to Cowthally, intending to shew that the young man would inherit a large portion of his father's property—namely, the Mid-Lothian estates. It happened that Mr John Maitland, younger brother of Secretary Lethington, was then living in retirement with his kinsman, Lord Somerville; and, the papers being put into his hands, he soon

1577. discovered that the lands destined for the young man were recoverable by his lordship. He took a duplicate of one important document, and then the whole were returned to Lady Cambusnethan, who by and by took her leave with a fair answer from Lord Somerville, though in reality he only felt disgust at a proposal which aimed at a severe injury to the heir of her husband's house.

Lord Somerville and Maitland took the pleasure of hunting that afternoon. 'During their sport, Mr Maitland takes occasion to inquire at his cousin, if his lordship's predecessors had ever any interest in Mid-Lothian, and if he knew how they parted with the same. He answered they had; and to the best of his knowledge, the house of Cambusnethan had these among many other lands they received from his great-grandfather, Lord John, who, upon the account of his son of the second marriage, went near to have ruined his family, by reason of the great fortune he left to the son of that marriage. By this answer, Mr Maitland understood that his cousin Lord James was altogether ignorant of the way and manner of the conveyance of Drum, Gilmerton, and Goodtrees from his family to that of Cambusnethan, and therefore, in a drolling way, he asked his cousin what he would bestow upon that person that should put him in a way to recover these lands. My Lord, smiling, said: "Cousin, the bargain should soon be made, if once I saw the man that made the offer." Whereupon Mr Maitland pulling out the paper, which was the double of King James the Fourth's gift, delivers it to my lord, saying: "There it is that will effectuate and do that business; and seeing I am the man that has made the discovery, I crave no more but your lordship's white gelding." Hearing this discourse, and having read the note, Lord Somerville immediately lights from his horse, and taking his cousin all in his arms—"Here is not only my gelding, but take this, which in these troublesome times I have still kept upon me, not knowing what might befall, having, as was my duty, sided and taken part with that just interest of my princes which has had but bad success in the world." That which the Lord Somerville gave with the gelding to his cousin was a purse sewed by his mother, Dame Janet Maitland, with silk and silver, containing twenty old pieces of gold; and, indeed, it could not be better bestowed than upon her nephew, a brave gentleman, whose great abilities and personal worth afterward brought him to be the principal officer of state in Scotland.'

The crop of this year must have failed to a lamentable extent, as, immediately after harvest, we hear of 'exorbitant dearth of

victual and penury thereof,' and the ensuing year was, according 1577.
to a contemporary diarist, marked by 'ane great dearth of all kinds of victuals, through all Scotland, that the like was not seen in man's days afore.' According to the latter authority, 'the meal was sauld for sax shillings the peck, the ale for tenpence the pint, the wine for the best cheap forty pence the pint; fish and flesh was scant and dear.'—*Aber. Chron.*

In November 1577 two boat-loads of *beir* were about to sail from Aberdeen harbour for Leith, when the town-council arrested them, and ordained the victual to be sold to the inhabitants of Aberdeen at 'competent prices.'[1]

According to the usual policy in such cases, the government (April 14, 1578) issued a proclamation commanding the possessors of grain to thrash it out before the 10th of June, under pain of escheating, and that no person should keep more victual than was sufficient to serve him and his family a quarter of a year, the rest to be brought to the market within twenty days. It was also ordered, that no grain should be taken forth of the kingdom, but 'strangers bringing in victual should be favourably enterteened and thankfully paid.'—*Cal.* This proclamation, being entirely accordant with the prejudices of the masses, was 'mickle commendit.'—*Moy.*

Following the usual rule, the scarcity of 1577 was attended by an epidemic disease. At least, so we think may be inferred from an entry in Marjorebanks's *Annals*, under 1580:

'There was twa years before this time ane great universal sickness through the maist part of Scotland: uncertain what sickness it was, for the doctors could not tell, for there was no remede for it; and the commons called it *Cowdothe.*'

There was an ancient feud between the families of Glammis 1577-8. Mar. 17
and Crawford, but as the present lords were on the same side in politics, it was felt by both as inexpedient that any hostility should take place between them. Moreover, it would have been highly indecent of Lord Glammis, who was chancellor of the kingdom, to allow any demonstration of rancour to come from his side. Nevertheless, a fatal collision took place between these two nobles.

About the dusk of a spring day, Lord Glammis was coming down from Stirling Castle to his own house in the town, attended as usual

[1] Aberdeen Council Register, *Spal. Cl. Mis.* i. 30.

1577-8. by some of his friends and followers, when, in a narrow lane, he encountered the Earl of Crawford similarly attended. The two nobles bade their respective followers give way to the other; and the order was obeyed by all except the two last, who either wilfully or by accident jostled each other, and then immediately drew their swords and fell a-fighting. A skirmish then took place between the two parties, in the course of which Lord Glammis, whose stature made him overtop the company, was shot through the head with a pistol, and many were hurt on both sides.

'Lord Glammis was a learned, godly, and wise man. He sent to Beza when the work of policy was in hands, and craved his judgment in some questions of policy; whereupon Beza wrote the book *De Triplici Episopatu*, Of the threefold bishopric, divine, human, and devilish, and his answers to his questions. Mr Andrew Melville made this epigram upon him after his death:

> Tu Leo magne jaces inglorius: ergo, manebunt
> Qualia fata canes? qualia fata sues?
>
> Since lowly lies thou, noble lyon fine,
> What sall betide, behind? the dogs and swine?—*Cal.*

The respective friends of Glammis and Crawford fell into active hostilities after this event, and Crawford was seized and thrown into prison. Being really free from blame, and befriended by many of the nobility, he was soon liberated, to the great joy of his own people. The general joy diffused by this event exasperated Thomas Lyon, a nephew of the deceased chancellor, insomuch that 'Crawford all his life was glad to stand in a soldier's posture.'—*Jo. Hist.*

Godscroft relates that the slaughter of Lord Glammis, which was committed at five in the afternoon in Stirling, was 'reported punctually and perfectly in Edinburgh at six, being twenty-four [Scotch] miles distant.' He perhaps means to insinuate that the deed was premeditated. Under November 1585 will be found another instance of miraculous-looking quickness in the communication of intelligence.

1578. June 13. A *Band of Friendship*—a sort of modification of the old bonds of manred—was formed by the Earl of Eglintoun, the Earl of Glencairn, Lord Boyd, the respective eldest sons of these nobles, Sir Matthew Campbell of Loudon, and Wallace of Craigie, for the repressing of diverse troubles in the country, and with a view to their greater efficiency in the king's service. They bound themselves, upon their faith and honours, 'the holy evangel touched, to tak true, faithful, plain, and aefald part all together, as weel by way of law as deed, pursuit as defence, ... in all actions, causes, quarrels, controversies, and debates, movit or to be movit by or against us . . . . against whatsomever person or persons, the king's majesty alane excepted.' It was also concluded 'that all castles, houses, strengths perteining to us sall be ready and patent to ilk ane of us, as the occasion may require.' Then came a remarkable clause—'Gif it sall happen, as God forbid, ony different, slaughter, bluid, or other inconvenient, to fall out amangs us, our friends, servants, or dependers, the same, of whatsomever wecht or quality it sall be of, sall be remitted to the decision and judgment of the remanent of us, wha sall have power to judge and decern thereintill, whase sentence and decreet baith the parties sall bide at, fulfil, and observe without reclamation, and sall be as valid and effectual in all respects, and have as full execution, as the same had been given and pronounced after cognition in the cause, by the Lords of Session, Justice-general of Scotland, or ony other judge ordinar within this realm.'[1] 1578.

In the parliament held at this time, Lord Home was restored from the forfeiture passed against his father in consequence of his adherence to the queen's party. David Home of Godscroft represents this as being mainly brought about by the intervention of Sir George Home of Wedderburn with the Earl of Morton; and according to Godscroft's narration, it was against the will and judgment of Morton that Wedderburn's end was gained. The affair stands out in strong illustration of the principle of clanship and kindred as affecting even Lowland bosoms in that age. Morton freely told Wedderburn that 'he thought it not his best course; "For," said he, "you never got any good of that house, and if it were once taken out of the way, you are next—and it may be you will get small thanks for your pains." JULY.

'Sir George answered, that "the Lord Home *was his chief*, and he could not see his house ruined. If they were unkind, that would be their own fault. This he thought himself bound to do. And, for his own part, whatsoever their carriage were to him, he would do his duty to them. *If his chief should turn him out at the fore door, he would come in again at the back door.*"

[1] *Abbotsford Miscellany*, 45.

1578. "Well," says Morton, "if you be so minded, it shall be so. I can do no more but tell you my opinion." And so [he] consented to do it.'[1]

Sir George Home of Wedderburn was son and successor of the Merse gentleman described under 1574, and a sketch of him, drawn by the perhaps partial hand of his brother, David of Godscroft, is well worthy of preservation. He was now twenty-eight years of age; he had been trained to pious habits by his parents, and completed his education at the Regent's court, in company with the young Earl of Angus. He knew Latin and French thoroughly, had studied logic, and acquired such an extensive knowledge of geography, that, 'though he had never been out of his own country, he could dispute with any one who had travelled in France or elsewhere. He learned the use of the triangle in measuring heights, without any teaching, or ever having read of it; so that he may be said to have invented it.

'He was diligent in reading the sacred Scriptures, and not to little purpose. He was assiduous in settling controverted points, and at table, or over a bottle, he either asked other people's opinions, or freely gave his own. . . . . He did read a great deal when his public and private business allowed him. He likewise wrote meditations upon the Revelations, the soul, love of God, &c. He also gave some application to law, and even to physic. . . . As to his body, he was well-proportioned; his countenance was lovely and modest, and his limbs handsome and of great strength. He was polite and unaffected in his manners. He sung after the manner of the court. He likewise sang Psaltery to his own playing on the harp. He also sometimes danced. He was very keen for hare-hunting, and delighted much in hawks, particularly that kind that have a small body and large wings, called *marlins*. With these he caught both partridges and muirfowl. He was so much given to diversion that he built a hunting-house, which he called *Handaxewood*, in the hills of Lammermuir, in which he might divert himself in the night-time. He first delighted most in those hawks called *falcons*; but, wearying of them, he took to the other kind, called *tercels*, which he used even in his old age.

'He rode skilfully, and sometimes applied himself to the breaking of the fiercest horses. He was skilful in the bow beyond most men of his time. He was able to endure cold, hunger, thirst, fatigue, and watching. . . . . He was moderate both in his eating

[1] *Hist. of the House of Douglas*, ii. 260.

and drinking, which was in those days scarce any praise, temperance being then frequent, though it is now very rare.' 1578.

Being, while at court in his youth, stinted of money by a step-mother, he had to avoid cards and dice, and restrict himself to tennis. He was forced by the same cause to restrain the affection he began to feel for the sister of Angus, who, by and by, was married to Lord Maxwell, 'not at all agreeable to her own inclination, but by the express command of the Regent, who would not neglect this opportunity.' Having succeeded to his estate, 'his first care was to restore his family to its ancient splendour and fulness, from which it had fallen by the sordidness of his step-mother. Therefore he always went with a great number of attendants, kept a great family, about eighteen horsemen, each of whom had two horses. He was likewise attended by his vassals in Kimmerghame, which was a village at no great distance. They were about twelve in number, and had generally been made use of by his predecessors in services of this kind. They never took greater care of their fields than of their horses, and never ceased accustoming and perfecting themselves in the use of arms. They seldom employed themselves in the country work, and never made use of their horses for that purpose, and they were so swift and beautiful that they might even have contended with those of their master's domestics. They were always ready at command on every emergency to be led or sent where he pleased. Thus, he was always guarded with twenty or thirty horsemen, all brave and warlike, in order that he might be more respected. Nor was he mistaken in his opinion; it procured him such great fame and authority both with his friends and others, it so much checked his rivals, that they all yielded to him in the beginning, nor ever dared to oppose any of his attempts.

'Nor did he acquire less glory in the care he took of his sisters, which was crowned with success. The remembrance of the best of mothers, their own goodness and beauty, procured them his love. Chance assisted the care he had, advantageously to dispose of Isobel, the eldest. John Haldane of Gleneagles, who having come to the Earl of Morton, who was then governor, to transact and agree with him about the ward and marriage of his lands, Morton answered he had given all right he had to it to Isobel, Wedderburn's sister, and he might go and take her and it together. There were, along with Haldane, his uncles, Richard and Robert, and David Erskine, abbot of Dryburgh. They, without delay, come to Wedderburn, where they see, converse

1578. with, and please the young lady, who had before been known to them by report only; they treat and agree with the brother, and the marriage-day is set. He had resolved that she should be dismissed as honourably as possible. For that purpose, there was a most splendid apparatus and entertainment, which was made up by the bride's direction, and it greatly added to the fame of her prudence, as few had ever seen so grand and genteel a marriage-feast, and all who were present never failed to give it the greatest commendations.'

SEP. 11. An attempt was made by proclamation to raise the value of the coin, thirty-shilling pieces being ordained to pass for 32s. 8d., and twenty, ten, and five shilling pieces in proportion, refusal of the coin at the exalted rates being threatened with capital punishment. 'This was altogether mislikit by the common people, and specially by the inhabitants of Edinburgh.'—*Moy.*

1578-9. FEB. 21. 'The whilk day, the lords of secret council has thought meet and expedient that the king's majesty sould not write to the lords of his hienes' council and session, in furtherance or hindrance of ony particular persons' actions and causes in time coming, but suffer them to proceed and do justice in all actions privilegit to be decidit by them, as they sall answer to God and his hienes thereupon.'—*P. C. R.*

James was now twelve and a half years old, but nominally in possession of the government. We see that his influence was already sought by individuals, to affect the course of the chief civil tribunal of the country. It will appear a characteristic circumstance, and there are many others to corroborate its general purport. Yet it is but right to remark, as the general impression produced by a perusal of the Privy Council Record, that the decisions given there on matters of right between individuals are, on the whole, marked by an appearance of fairness and impartiality. Oppression from high quarters is frequently denounced; and there are numberless instances of a humane and forbearing spirit towards poor and unfortunate people.

1579. 'The magistrates of [Glasgow], by the earnest dealing of Mr Andrew Melville and other ministers, had condescended to demolish the cathedral, and build with the materials thereof some little churches in other parts, for the ease of the citizens. Divers reasons were given for it—such as, the resort of superstitious people to do their devotion in that place; the huge vastness of the church, and that the voice of a preacher could not be heard by the multitudes that convened to sermon; the more commodious service of the people; and the removing of that idolatrous monument (so they called it) which was of all the cathedrals in the country only left unruined, and in a possibility to be repaired. To do this work, a number of quarriers, masons, and other workmen, was conduced, and the day assigned when it should take beginning. Intimation being made thereof, and the workmen by sound of a drum warned to go unto their work, the crafts of the city in a tumult took arms, swearing with many oaths, that he who did cast down the first stone should be buried under it. Neither could they be pacified till the workmen were discharged by the magistrates. A complaint was hereupon made, and the principals cited before the council for insurrection: where the king, not as then thirteen years of age, taking the protection of the crafts, did allow [sanction] the opposition they had made, and inhibited the ministers (for they were the complainers) to meddle any more in that business, saying, "That too many churches had already been destroyed, and that he would not tolerate more abuses in that kind."'—*Spot.* 1579.

John Stewart, Earl of Athole, was one of the more respectable of the Scottish nobility of this age. To Queen Mary—whom he had entertained at a hunt in Glen Tilt in 1564—he proved a faithful friend,[1] till her fatal marriage with Bothwell, when, although a Catholic, he joined those who crowned her son as king. During the regencies, he lived in dignified retirement, till called upon to make an effort to rescue the young king from the thraldom in which he was held by Morton. A temporary fall of Morton in 1577 left Athole chancellor of the kingdom. APR.

He now came to Stirling, to assist in accommodating some quarrels of the friends of the Mar family regarding the custody of the young king and the government of Stirling Castle. 'Matters being seemingly adjusted, the old Countess of Mar, or the Earl of Morton, in her name, invited the chancellor to an entertainment. While they were drinking hard, somebody conveyed a deadly poison into the chancellor's glass.' April 16th, 'the chancellor passed forth of Stirling to Kincardine,[2] very sick and ill at ease,

[1] The wife of the earl—Margaret Fleming, relict of the Master of Montrose and the Master of Erskine—was believed to have the powers of incantation. See under June 19, 1566.

[2] The seat of the Earl of Montrose, on the skirts of the Ochil Hills.

1579. and upon the 24th day deceased there.' His friends, thinking he had got foul play, sent to Edinburgh for surgeons to open the body; and though these men of skill declared upon oath that they found no trace of poison or mark of violence done to the deceased, the widow and eldest son entered a protest that this should not prejudge the criminal process which they intended before the Justice-general. 'Some blamed the old Countess of Mar for it; others suspected the Earl of Morton at the bottom of it.' Both suspicions were probably groundless; it may even be doubted if the earl was poisoned at all. When under sentence of death some years after, Morton solemnly denied the crime imputed to him, and said in no circumstances would he have injured a hair of Athole's head.

'Upon the sevent of July, the corpse of the Earl of Athole being convoyit to Dunblane, was carried forth thereof the direct way to Dunfermline, where they remained that night. Upon the morn, they passed forth to Edinburgh, where a great number of friends were convenit to the burial. Upon the tenth day, [the body of the earl] was honourably convoyit with his friends from Haliroodhouse to St Giles' Kirk, where he was buried on the east side of the altar on the south side of the church.' Owing to the general belief as to the mode of the earl's death, his funeral brought forth strong marks of public feeling.[1] It appears that, before it took place, there was a rumour that the relatives of the deceased designed that it should be attended with sundry superstitious rites, as 'a white cross in the *mortclaith*, lang gowns with stroups, and torches.' A deputation from the General Assembly came to inquire, and were asked to satisfy themselves by inspecting the preparations. 'The kirk thought the cross and the stroups superstitious and ethnic-like, and desirit them to remove the same.' It was accordingly arranged to cover the cross with black velvet and to remove the stroups.—*B. U. K.*

MAY. There was at this time a collection of money in Aberdeen and other parts of Scotland, for the support and relief of the 'Scottismen prisoners in Argier in Affrik, and other parts within the Turk's bounds.' One Andro Cook engaged himself to dispose of this money as intended, and to deliver the surplus, 'gif ony,' to the royal treasurer, to be used as his majesty might think fit.—*Ab. C. R., P. C. R.*

[1] Crawford's *Officers of State.* Moysie's *Memoirs.*

This collection did not go on briskly, or come to any important effect. On the 26th of October 1583, nothing had been done beyond the collecting of £562, exclusive of what had been bestowed in expenses. Cook was dead, but his son had this sum in his hands, and was desirous of rendering it up under proper authority. It was found, however, that the unhappy captives at Algiers were removed from all earthly hardships, so that it was desirable to devote the money to some other object. By the king it was ordained in council that the sum resting with Cook's son should be paid to the procurators of David Hume, shipper in Leith, who was now lying captive at Bordeaux. 1579.

'Twa poets of Edinburgh, remarking some of his [the Earl of Morton's] sinistrous dealing, did publish the same to the people by a famous libel written against him; and Morton, hearing of this, causit the men to be brought to Stirling, where they were convict for slandering ane of the king's councillors, and were there baith hangit. The names of the men were William Turnbull, schoolmaster in Edinburgh, and William Scott, notar. They were baith weel beloved of the common people for their common offices.'—*H. K. J.* 'Which was thought a precedent, never one being hanged for the like before; and in the meantime, at the scattering of the people, there were ten or twelve despiteful letters and infamous libels in prose, found, as if they had been lost among the people, tending to the reproach of the Earl of Morton and his predecessors.' —*Moy. R.* Aug. 12.

At the fall of Morton, less than two years after, when he was taken prisoner and conducted to Edinburgh Castle—'as he passed the Butter Tron, a woman who had her husband put to death at Stirling for a ballad entitled *Daff and dow nothing*,[1] sitting down on her bare knees, poured out many imprecations upon him.'—*Cal.*

During the night following this day, 'there blew sic ane tempest at the herring drave of Dunbar, that threescore fisher-boats and three hundred men perished.'—*Moy.* Aug. 17.

[1] As much as to say, 'Sport, and be at your ease.'

REIGN OF JAMES VI.: 1578-1585.

Very soon after Morton had demitted the regency, he partly recovered his power, and this he continued for some time to exercise. The young king remained in Stirling Castle, under considerable restraint. With a view to acquire some control over him, as the only means of resisting the English or Protestant interest, his mother and French grand-uncles sent to his court a young gentleman of engaging manners, in whom they had confidence. This was Esme Stuart, usually called Monsieur d'Aubigné, a member of the Lennox family, being nephew of the late Regent, but who had been brought up in France. It was believed that he carried with him forty thousand pieces of gold, to be employed in winning favour with the Scottish nobility. 'He was,' says a contemporary, 'a man of comely proportion, civil behaviour, red-beardit, honest in conversation, weel likit of by the king and a part of his nobility at the first.'[1] To aid him in his purpose, he brought with him one called Monsieur Mombirneau, 'a merry fellow, able in body and quick in spirit.'[2] The young king readily opened his heart to this pleasant relative, who took care to accommodate himself to his tastes, and to assist, above all, in making his time pass agreeably. About the same time, another but more distant relative, James Stuart, of the Ochiltree family, a captain in the royal guard, began to acquire favour with the king. This was altogether a less worthy person than D'Aubigné, being arrogant, domineering, and vicious. D'Aubigné, however, being a Catholic, and suspected of designs in favour of popery, was perhaps the least liked of the two.

It was in September 1579, when little more than thirteen years of age, that James was for the first time so far liberated from the control of Morton and other councillors, as to be able to leave his castle of Stirling. Accompanied by D'Aubigné, then newly arrived, he made a formal visit to Edinburgh, where the citizens gave him a most affectionate reception.

This was a more important crisis of British history than is generally supposed. It was now that a commencement was made of that struggle for authority which we see going on through the remainder of this and the whole of the ensuing century. James had been reared as the creature of the zealous Presbyterian party. When he began to judge for himself, and to become conversant with minds beyond the range of his earlier associations, his affections led him to prefer those who had been his mother's friends, and he soon came to believe that they and such as they were likely

[1] Moysie. [2] Calderwood.

to be his own warmest supporters. What was most important of all, he found that the Presbyterian clergy, while professing respect for him as the chief-magistrate of the land, and disposed to obey him in civil matters, claimed to be, in things ecclesiastical, not merely independent of him, but his superiors. Restricting the idea of the church to those 'exercising the spiritual function among the congregations of them that profess the truth,' they asserted that it had 'a certain power granted by God,' having 'ground in the word of God,' and 'to be put into execution by them unto whom the government of the kirk by lawful calling is committed.' And, 'as the ministers and others of the ecclesiastical state are subject to the magistrate civil, so aucht the person of the magistrate to be subject to the kirk spiritually and in ecclesiastical government.' In their view, as far as his own religious and moral practice was concerned, King James was only a parishioner of the Canongate. On the other hand, when one of their order interfered with politics in his sermon, he was only liable to be challenged by his presbytery. The claim was presented by men of whose disinterestedness there can be no more doubt than of their religious zeal; that it might have worked satisfactorily if it had ever found a monarch who would cordially accept and submit to it, cannot be denied, for we have had no experience on the subject, the final settlement of the Scotch church at the Revolution having left it in a doubtful state. The compromise which was attained at the end of a century-long struggle, was unattainable in the days of King James. The pretension only set him upon looking up scriptural texts too, texts which could be interpreted as setting the royal authority equally above human challenge; and such were not difficult to be found. Hence arose the celebrated doctrine of the divine right of kings—a sort of antithesis to a doctrine which would have made kings in one important respect the subjects of a set of church-courts. And so commenced that unfortunate course of things in our national history, which has presented this king as in constant antagonism to the ecclesiastical forms and order of worship preferred by the great bulk of his people, as seeking by all arts to thrust hated systems upon them, and as founding a policy which, becoming a deadly and obstinate struggle with his descendants, alternately gave us anarchy and despotism, till it ended in the total overthrow of the main line of the House of Stuart. Such were the natural fruits of the earnestness, beautiful but terrible, with which men then seized and worked out principles which they found, or thought they found, in the Bible—arguing on the religion of peace and good-will to men, with swords in their hands, and laws as cruel as swords, till a sense of the inconsequentiality of such reasoning for any good at length came over most of them with the sickening effect of a wind from a field of battle, and disposed them to rest content with the sulky mutual protest in which they have since lived.

Notwithstanding a strenuous opposition from Elizabeth and the

Presbyterian clergy, D'Aubigné, whom James made Earl, and finally Duke of Lennox, succeeded in greatly advancing the French interest. It was in vain that the ministers railed at him as a papist: he coolly came before them and abjured popery. A confession of faith, condemning the pope and all his pretensions and works, was brought forward: James and his councillors, including the Earl of Lennox, unhesitatingly signed it (January 28, 1580-1). Morton, who alone possessed the personal character that could effectually stand for the English interest and the kirk, had, by his cruel and avaricious conduct, lost the support of all classes, the clergy included. It was even found possible to effect the ruin of this great man. On the last of December 1580, the adventurer Stuart came into the council-chamber, and, falling on his knees, accused the ex-Regent of being concerned in the murder of his majesty's father. To the general surprise, he fell without a struggle, and after a few months' confinement, he perished on the scaffold (June 2, 1581).

Under Lennox and Stuart—the latter now created Earl of Arran—a movement was made for bringing an episcopate into the church. Arran is said to have put the idea of absolute power into the king's mind, and a French alliance was threatened. The clergy, in general assembly, shewed their usual courage in protesting against the court proceedings. The conduct of their moderator, Andrew Melville, was specially remarkable. When he and his fellow-commissioners came before the council with their *grieves*, Arran, according to a contemporary narration, 'begins to threaten, with thrawn brow and boasting language. "What!" says he, "wha dar subscryve thir treasonable articles?" Mr Andrew answers: "We dar, and will subscryve them, and give our lives in the cause!" And withal starts to, and taks the pen fra the clerk and subscryves, and calls to the rest of his brethren with courageous speeches; wha all cam and subscryvit.' Such were the men who faced the king in behalf of an independent rule for the kirk of Scotland.

At length there was a reaction against the dominion of the two court favourites. A combination of nobles of the ultra-Protestant party—the Earl of Gowrie, the Earl of Mar, Lord Glammis, and others, laid a gentle compulsion on the young king while he was staying at Ruthven House near Perth (August 1582), and his councillors Lennox and Arran were debarred from his presence. After this event, known in our history as the *Raid of Ruthven*, the king remained under the control of his new councillors for a year, during which a pure Presbyterianism was again encouraged, and the English alliance was cultivated. The Duke of Lennox was forced to withdraw to France, where, to the great grief of the king, he soon after contracted a sickness, and died.

Regaining his liberty by stratagem, James once more put himself under the guidance of the profligate but energetic Arran. A modified episcopate was established in the church, under a subordination to the state, and a restraint was imposed on the tongues of the clergy in the pulpit. The Earl of Gowrie was brought to the block. Several ministers, including Melville, had to take refuge in England. But the general tendency of things in Scotland was inconsistent with the rule of a man possessing the genius of Arran. Elizabeth, too, deemed it best for her interests that others should have the control of Scottish affairs. Accordingly, a new and more formidable combination was formed. Joined by Lord John Hamilton, the head of the long proscribed house of Hamilton, and by Lord Maxwell, whom Arran had offended, they advanced with an army of 5000 men to Stirling, then the seat of the court. Arran, unable to resist, fled, and was allowed to fall into obscurity. The king with great placidity put himself into the hands of his new councillors (November 1585). This *coup d'état* was followed by the restoration of the Hamilton family to its titles and estates.

The young king having now assumed the government, and being about to make his first visit to Edinburgh, the magistrates and citizens were anxious to give him an honourable reception. There was immediately a great bustle regarding the preparation of a silver cupboard and other pieces of plate to be presented to him, as well as the getting of dresses suitable to be worn by the chief men at the royal entry. There was even a deputation to the High School, 'to vesie the maister of the Hie Schule tragedies to be made by the bairns, and to report;' besides another 'to speak the Frenchman for his opinion in device of the triumph.' 1579.

All merchants stented to above ten pounds were enjoined to have 'everilk ane of them ane goune of fine black camlet of silk of serge, barrit with velvet, effeiring his substance.' All stented to sixteen pounds, 'to have their gounes of the like stuff, the breists thereof linit with velvet, and begairit with coits of velvet, damas, or sattin.' The thirteen city-officers were to have each a livery composed of three ells of English *stemming* to be hose, six quarters of Rouen canvas to be doublets, with 13s. 4d. for passments, and a black hat with a white string.

Another preparative was an edict, that all manner of persons having *cruives* for swine under their stairs or in common vennels, 'and sic like as has middings and fulyie collectit, or has tar barrels on the Hie Street, as also ony redd[1] stanes or timber on the said Hie Street or common vennels, remove the same.' Pioneers, too,

[1] Arranged—not lying as rubbish.

1579. 'to shool in the muck outwith the West Port.' The inhabitants to hang their stairs with tapestry and arras wark.[1] The Privy Council, on their part, proclaimed penalties against all who should come with firearms, or any other armour than their swords and whingers.

SEP. 30. The boy-king came from Stirling attended by about two thousand men on horseback, and his reception in the city was quaintly magnificent. 'At the West Port he was receivit by the magistrates under a pompous pall of purple velvet. That port presentit unto him the wisdom of Solomon, as it is written in the thrid chapter of the first book of Kings; that is to say, King Solomon was representit with the twa women that contendit for the young child. This done, they presented unto the king, the sword for the one hand, and the sceptre for the other. And as he made further progress within the town, in the street that ascends to the Castle there is an ancient port [the West Bow], at the whilk there hang a curious globe that openit artificially as the king came by, wherein was a young boy that descendit craftily, presenting the keys of the town to his majesty, that were all made of fine massy silver; and these were presently receivit by ane of his honourable council at his awn command. During this space, Dame Music and her scholars exercisit her art with great melody. Then in his descent [along the High Street], as he came fornent the house of Justice, there shew themselves unto him four gallant vertuous ladies; to wit, Peace, Justice, Plenty, and Policie; and either of them had ane oration to his majesty. Thereafter, as he came toward the chief collegiate kirk, there Dame Religion shew herself, desiring his presence, whilk he then obeyit by entering the kirk; where the chief preacher for that time made a notable exhortation unto him for the embracing of religion and all her cardinal vertues, and of all other moral vertues. Thereafter he came forth, and made progress to the Mercat Cross, where he beheld Bacchus with his magnifick liberality and plenty distributing of his liquor to all passengers and beholders, in sic appearance as was pleasant to see. A little beneath is a mercat place of salt, whereupon was paintit the genealogy of the kings of Scotland, and a number of trumpets sounding melodiously, and crying with loud voice, *Welfare to the King!* At the east port was erectit the conjunction of the planets, as they were in their degrees and places the time of his majesty's happy nativity, and the same vively representit by the assistance of King Ptolemy. And withal the haill streets were spread with flowers, and the fore-

[1] *Documents Relative to Royal Receptions*, 4to. Edinburgh, 1822.

houses of the streets, by the whilk the king passit, were all hung 1579.
with magnifick tapestry, with paintit histories and with the effigies of noble men and women. And thus he passed out of the town of Edinburgh, to his palace of Halyroodhouse.'—*H. K. J.*

The Estates passed an act against 'strang and idle beggars,' and Oct. 20.
'sic as make themselves fules and are bards;' likewise against 'the idle people calling themselves Egyptians, or any other that feigns them to have knowledge of charming, prophecy, or other abused sciences, whereby they persuade the people that they can tell their weirds, deaths, and fortunes, and sic other fantastical imaginations.' The act condemns all sorts of vagrant idle people, including 'minstrels, sangsters, and tale-tellers, not avowed in special service by some of the lords of parliament or great burghs,' and 'vagabond scholars of the universities of St Andrews, Glasgow, and Aberdeen.' The same act made some provision for the genuine poor, enjoining them all to repair to their native parishes and there live in almshouses: a very nice arrangement for them, it must be owned; only there were not any almshouses for them to live in.

Two poets hanged in August, and an act of parliament against bards and minstrels in October; truly, it seems to have been sore times for the tuneful tribe!

By this time, Arbuthnot's edition of the Bible was completed and in circulation. The gratification of the clergy on seeing such a product of the native press, found eloquent expression in an address of the General Assembly to the king (June 1579), when they took occasion to praise the printer as 'a man who hath taken great pains and travel worthy to be remembered;' and told how there should henceforth be a copy in every parish kirk, to be called the Common Book of the Kirk, 'as the most meet ornament for such a place.' 'Oh what difference,' exclaimed these devout men, 'between thir days of light, when almost in every private house the book of God's law is read and understood in our vulgar language, and the age of darkness, when scarcely in a whole city, without the cloisters of monks and friers, could the book of God once be found, and that in a strange tongue of Latin, not good, but mixed with barbarity, used and read by few, and almost understood and exponed by none.' All worldly wealth seemed vain and poor compared with this fountain of spiritual comfort. 'We ought,' they said, 'with most thankful hearts to praise and extol the infinite goodness of

1579. God, who hath accounted us worthy to whom He should open such an heavenly treasure.'—*B. U. K.*

Nov. 10. In that unmistrusting reliance on force for religious objects which marked the age, it was enacted in parliament, that each householder worth three hundred merks of yearly rent, and all substantious yeomen and burgesses esteemed as worth five hundred pounds in land and goods, should have a Bible and psalm-book in the vulgar tongue, under the penalty of ten pounds. A few months later (June 16, 1580), one John Williamson was commissioned under the privy seal to visit and search every house in the realm, 'and to require the sicht of their Bible and psalm-buke, gif they ony have, to be marked with their awn name, for eschewing of fraudful dealing in that behalf.'[1]

The zeal of the clergy, their self-denying poverty, their resoluteness in advancing their views of church polity against court influence, have all been touched upon. Little more than six hundred in number—for hundreds of the parishes had no minister—they were indefatigable in their efforts to moralise the rude mass of the community; although it was, by their own account, such as might have appeared hopeless to other men; there being now, as they said, an 'universal corruption in the whole realm,' 'great coldness and slackness' even in the professors of religion, and a 'daily increase of all kinds of fearful sins and enormities, as incest, adulteries, murders, . . . cursed sacrilege, ungodly sedition and division, . . . with all manner of disorders and ungodly living.'[2]

The picture which James Melville gives of the four ministers of Edinburgh, then living in one house—where the Parliament House now stands—is very interesting: 'God glorified himself notably,' says he, 'with that ministry of Edinburgh in these days. The men had knawledge, uprightness, and zeal; they dwelt very commodiously together, as in a college, with a wonderful concert in variety of gifts; all strake on ae string, and soundit a harmony. John Durie was of small literature, but had seen and marked the great warks of God in the first Reformation, and been a doer baith with tongue and hand. He had been a diligent hearer of Mr Knox, and observer of all his ways. He conceivit the best grounds of matters weel, and could utter them fairly, fully, and fearfully, with a mighty spreit, voice, and action. The special gift I marked in him was haliness, and a daily and nightly careful, continual walking with

[1] *Maitland Club Miscellany*, ii. 19. [2] General Assembly, April 1578.

God in meditation and prayer. *He was a very gude fallow,* and took delight, as his special comfort, to have his table and house filled with the best men. These he wald gladly hear, with them confer and talk, professing he was but a book-bearer, and wald fain learn of them; and getting the ground and light of knawledge in any guid point, then wald he rejoice in God, praise and pray thereupon, and urge it with sae clear and forcible exhortation in assemblies and pulpit, that he was esteemed a very furthersome instrument. There lodgit in his house at all these assemblies in Edinburgh for common, Mr Andrew Melville, Mr Thomas Smeaton, Mr Alexander Arbuthnot, three of the learnedest in Europe; Mr James Melville, my uncle, Mr James Balfour, David Ferguson, David Home, ministers; with some zealous, godly barons and gentlemen. In time of meals was reasoning upon guid purposes, namely matters in hand; thereafter earnest and lang prayer; thereafter a chapter read, and every man about [in turn] gave his note and observation thereof; sae that, gif all had been set down in write, I have heard the learnedest and best in judgment say, they wald not have wished a fuller and better commentary nor [than] sometimes wald fall out in that exercise. Thereafter was sung a psalm; after the whilk was conference and deliberation upon the purposes in hand; and at night before going to bed, earnest and zealous prayer according to the estate and success of matters. And oft times, yea almost daily, all the college was together in ane or other of their houses, &c.' 1579.

The picture which the same writer gives of his uncle Andrew is full of fine touches. Andrew was principal of the theological college (St Mary's) at St Andrews; deeply learned, logical, not arrogant for himself, but possessed of all that disinterestedness and integrity which form the peculiar glory of Knox's character; to crown all, strenuous and fearless in the advocacy of his views of religion and church-discipline. James describes him as remarkable for patience and equal temper, where others were hot. Yet—'this I ever marked to be Mr Andrew's manner: Being sure of a truth in reasoning, he wald be extreme hot, and suffer nae man to bear away the contrair, but with reason, words, and gesture, he wald carry it away, caring for nae person, how great soever they were, namely in matters of religion. And in all companies at table and otherways, as he understood and took up the necessity of the persons and matter in hand to require, he wald *freely and bauldly hald their ears fu' of the truth;* and, take it as they wald, he wald not cease nor keep silence; yea, and not only anes or twice, but at all

1579. occasions, till he fand them better instructed, and set to go forward in the good purpose.'

His 'heroic courage and stoutness' in advancing his own views, and resisting persons of authority set upon establishing what he thought error, was equally remarkable. For example—'The Regent [Morton], seeing he could not divert him by benefits and offers, calls for him ae day indirectly, and after lang discoursing upon the quietness of the country, peace of the kirk, and advancement of the king's majesty's estate, he breaks in upon sic as were disturbers thereof by their conceits and ower-sea dreams, imitation of Geneva discipline and laws; and after some reasoning and grounds of God's word alledgit, whilk irritat the Regent, he breaks out in choler and boasting [threatening]: "There will never be quietness in this country till half a dozen of you be hangit or banishit the country." "Tush, sir," says Mr Andrew, "I have been ready to give my life where it was not half sae weel wared [spent], at the pleasure of my God. I lived out of your country ten years as weel as in it. Let God be glorified, it will not lie in your power to hang or exile his truth."'

1580. Apr. John Innes, of that Ilk, being childless, entered, in March 1577, into a mutual bond of *tailyie* with his nearest relation, Alexander Innes, of Cromy, conveying to him his whole estate, failing heirs-male of his body, and taking the like disposition from Cromy of his estate. There was a richer branch of the family represented by Robert Innes, of Innermarky, who pined to see the poorer preferred in this manner. So loud were his expressions of displeasure, that 'Cromy, who was the gallantest man of his name, found himself obliged to make the proffer of meeting him single in arms, and, laying the tailyie upon the grass, see if he durst take it up—in one word, to pass from all other pretensions, and let the best fellow have it.'

This silenced Innermarky, but did not extinguish his discontent. He began to work upon the feelings of the Laird of Innes, representing how Cromy already took all upon himself, even the name of Laird, leaving him no better than a masterless dog—as contemptible, indeed, as a beggar—a condition from which there could be no relief but by putting the usurper out of the way. This he himself offered to do with his own hand, if the laird would concur with him: it was an unpleasant business, but he would undertake it, rather than see his chief made a slave. By these practices, the weak laird was brought to give his consent to the slaughter of an innocent gentleman, his nearest relation, and whom 1580. he had not long before regarded with so much good-will as to admit him to a participation of his whole fortune.

'There wanted nothing but a conveniency for putting their purpose in execution, which did offer itself in the month of April 1580. At which time Alexander, being called upon some business to Aberdeen, was obliged to stay longer there than he intended, by reason that his only son Robert, a youth of sixteen years of age, had fallen sick at the college, and his father could not leave the place till he saw what became of him. He had transported him out of the Old Town, and had brought him to his own lodgings in the New Town. He had also sent several of his servants home from time to time, to let his lady know the reason of his stay.

'By means of these servants, it came to be known perfectly at Kinnairdy in what circumstances Alexander was at Aberdeen, where he was lodged, and how he was attended, which invited Innermarky to take the occasion. Wherefore, getting a considerable number of assistants with him, he and Laird John ride to Aberdeen; they enter the town upon the night, and about midnight came to Alexander's lodging.

'The outer gate of the close they found open, but all the rest of the doors shut. They were afraid to break up the doors by violence, lest the noise might alarm the neighbourhood; but choiced rather to raise such a cry in the close as might oblige those who were within to open the doors and see what it might be.

'The feuds at that time betwixt the families of Gordon and Forbes were not extinguished; therefore they raised a cry as if it had been upon some outfall among these people, crying, "*Help a Gordon—a Gordon!*" which is the gathering-word of the friends of that family. Alexander, being deeply interested in the Gordons, at the noise of the cry started from his bed, took his sword in hand, and opening a back-door that led to the court below, stepped down three or four steps, and cried to know what was the matter. Innermarky, who by his word knew him, and by his white shirt discerned him perfectly, cocks his gun, and shoots him through the body. In an instant, as many as could get about him fell upon him, and butchered him barbarously.

'Innermarky, perceiving, in the meantime, that Laird John stood by, as either relenting or terrified, held the bloody dagger to his throat, that he had newly taken out of the murdered body, swearing dreadfully that he would serve him in the same way if he

1580. did not as he did, and so compelled him to draw his dagger, and stab it up to the hilt in the body of his nearest relation, and the bravest that bore his name. After his example, all that were there behoved to do the like, that all might be alike guilty. Yea, in prosecution of this, it has been told me, that Mr John Innes, afterwards of Coxton, being a youth then at school, was raised out of bed, and compelled by Innermarky to stab a dagger into the dead body, that the more might be under the same condemnation —a very crafty cruelty.

'The next thing looked after was the destruction of the sick youth Robert, who had lain that night in a bed by his father, but, upon the noise of what was done, had scrambled from it, and by the help of one John of Colorcasons, or rather of some of the people of the house, had got out at an unfrequented back-door into the garden, and from that into a neighbour's house, where he had shelter, the Lord in his providence preserving him for the executing of vengeance upon these murderers for the blood of his father.

'Then Innermarky took the dead man's signet-ring, and sent it to his wife, as from her husband, by a servant whom he had purchased to that purpose, ordering her to send him such a particular box, which contained the bond of tailyie and all that had followed thereupon betwixt him and Laird John, whom, the servant said, he had left with his master at Aberdeen, and that, for dispatch, he had sent his best horse with him, and had not taken leisure to write, but sent the ring.

'Though it troubled the woman much to receive so blind a message, yet her husband's ring, his own servant, and his horse, prevailed so with her, together with the man's importunity to be gone, that she delivered to him what he sought, and let him go.

'There happened to be then about the house a youth related to the family, who was curious to go the length of Aberdeen, and see the young laird who had been sick, and to whom he was much addicted. This youth had gone to the stable, to intercede with the servant that he might carry him behind him; and in his discourse had found the man under great restraint and confusion of mind, sometimes saying he was to go no further than Kinnairdy (which indeed was the truth), and at other times that he behoved to be immediately at Aberdeen. This brought him to jalouse [suspect], though he knew not what; but further knowledge he behoved to have, and therefore he stepped out a little beyond the entry, watching the servant's coming, and in the by-going suddenly leaped

on behind him, or have a satisfying reason why he refused him. 1580.
The contest became such betwixt them, that the servant drew his dirk to rid him of the youth's trouble, which the other wrung out of his hands, and downright killed him with it, and brought back the box, with the writs and horse, to the house of Innes (or Cromy, I know not which).

'As the lady is in a confusion for what had fallen out, there comes another of the servants from Aberdeen, who gave an account of the slaughter, so that she behoved to conclude a special hand of Providence to have been in the first passage. Her next course was to secure her husband's writs the best she could, and fly to her friends for shelter, by whose means she was brought with all speed to the king, before whom she made her complaint.'

The son of the murdered man was taken under the care of the Earl of Huntly, who was his relation; but so little apprehension was there of a prosecution for the murder, that Innermarky, five weeks after the event, obtained from his chief a disposition of the estate in his own favour. Two or three years after, however, the young Laird of Cromy came north with a commission for the avenging of his father's murder, and the Laird of Innes and Innermarky were both obliged to go into hiding. For a time, the latter skulked in the hills, but, wearying of that, he got a retreat constructed for himself in the house of Edinglassie, where he afterwards found shelter. Here young Cromy surprised him in September 1584. The same young man who had killed his servant was the first to enter his Patmos, for which venturesome act he was all his life after called *Craig-in-peril*. Innermarky's head was cut off, and, it is said, afterwards taken by Cromy's widow to Edinburgh, and cast at the king's feet. The Innermarky branch being thus set aside, young Cromy succeeded in due time as Laird of Innes.—*Hist. Acc. Fam. Innes.*

'. . . . being Saturday, betwixt three o'clock afternoon and JUNE 25.
Sunday's night thereafter, there blew such a vehement tempest of wind, that it was thought to be the cause that a great many of the inhabitants of Edinburgh contracted a strange sickness, which was called *Kindness*. It fell out in the court, as well as sundry parts of the country, so that some people who were corpulent and aged deceased very suddenly. It continued with every one that took it three days at least.'—*Moy. R.*

The king being at St Andrews, on a progress with the Regent JULY.

1580. Morton, the gentlemen of the country had a *guise* or *fence* to play before him. 'The play was to be acted in the New Abbey.[1] While the people is gazing and longing for the play, Skipper Lindsay, a phrenitic man, stepped into the place which was kept void till the players came, and paceth up and down in sight of the people with great gravity, his hands on his side, and looking loftily. He had a manly countenance, but was all rough with hair. He had great tufts of hair upon his brows, and also a great tuft upon the neb of his nose. At the first sight, the people laughed loud; but when he began to speak he procured attention, as if it had been to a preacher. He discoursed with great force of spirit, and mighty voice, exhorting men of all ranks and degrees to hear him, and take example by him. He declared how wicked and riotous he had been, what he had done and conquest [acquired] by sea, how he had spended and abased himself on land, and what God had justly brought upon him for the same. He had wit, he had riches, he had strength and ability of body, he had fame and estimation above all others of his trade and rank; but all was vanity that made him misken his God. But God would not be miskenned by the highest. Turning himself to the boss [empty] window, where the king and Aubigné was above, and Morton standing beneath, gnapping upon his staff, he applied to him in special, as was marvellous in the ears of the hearers; so that many were astonished and some moved to tears, beholding and hearkening to the man. Among other things, he warned the earl, not obscurely, that his judgment was drawing near and his doom in dressing. And in very deed at the same time was his death contrived. The contrivers would have expected a discovery, if they had not known the man to be phrenitic and bereft of his wit. The earl was so moved and touched at the heart, that, during the time of the play, he never changed the gravity of his countenance, for all the sports of the play.'—*Cal.*

Sep. 9. One Arnold Bronkhorst, a Fleming, had found his way into Scotland, as one of a group of adventurers who were disposed to make a new effort for the successful working of the gold-mines of Lanarkshire. The account we have of the party is obscure and traditional.[2] One Nicolas Hilliard, goldsmith in London, and

[1] A house called the *Novum Hospitium*, in the Priory Park. It has long been demolished, excepting only the court-gate.

[2] *Atkinson's Discoverie of Gold Mynes in Scotland.*

miniature-painter to Queen Elizabeth, is said to have belonged to it, and to have brought Bronkhorst as his servant or assistant. The story is, that, being disappointed of a patent for the mines from the Regent Morton, Bronkhorst was glad at last to remain about the Scottish court as portrait-painter to the king. He certainly did serve the king in that capacity, as we have an account of his paid at this date, to the amount of £64, for three specimens of his art —namely, 'Ane portrait of his majesty fra the belt upward,' 'ane other portrait of Maister George Buchanan,' and 'ane portrait of his majesty full length,' besides a gift of a hundred merks, 'as ane gratitude for his repairing to this country.' A twelvemonth later, King James constituted him his own painter for his lifetime, 'with all fees, duties, and casualties, usit and wont.'[1] 1580.

In the midst of the strange phantasmagoria of rudeness and murderous violence on the one hand, and exalted religious zeal on the other, which now passes before us, we find that industrious men were prosecuting useful merchandise at home and abroad, but under painful risks imposed by the general neglect of the laws of health. Witness the following little episode. John Downie's ship, the *William*, on her return with a cargo from Danskein [Dantzig], enters the Firth of Forth. Seven merchants of Edinburgh, and some from other towns, are in this vessel, returning from foreign parts, where they have been upon their lawful business. All are doubtless full of pleasant anticipations of the home-scenes which they expect to greet them as soon as they once more set foot on their native soil. Alas! the pest breaks out in the vessel, and sundry of these poor citizens are swept off. The captain dare not approach the shore, but must wait the orders which the authorities may send him. There is immediately a meeting of the Privy Council, at which an order goes forth that the survivors in John Downie's ship shall land on the uninhabited island called St Colm's Inch in the Firth of Forth, and there remain till 'cleansed,' on pain of death, and no one to traffic with them under the same penalty. SEP. 20.

The chief chapter of this sad story, so characteristic of the time, is told in few words by Moysie: 'There were forty persons in the ship, whereof the most part died.'

On the 27th of November we have a pendant to the tale of the plague-ship. Downie the skipper is dead, leaving a widow and

[1] *Trans. Ant. Soc. Scot.* iii. 312.

1580. eleven children. James Scott and David Duff, mariners, are also dead, the former leaving a widow and seven children. Several of the passengers are also dead, while the others are pining on the lonely islands of Inchkeith and Inch Garvie. The ship, with its cargo unbroken, is riding at St Colm's Inch, and beginning to leak, so that much property is threatened with destruction. In these circumstances, the Privy Council, on petition, enacted that orders should be taken, as far as consistent with the public safety, for the preservation of the vessel.

Oct. Lord Ruthven and Lord Oliphant were at feud, in consequence of a dispute about teinds. The former, on his return from Kincardine, where he had been attending the Earl of Mar's marriage, passed near Lord Oliphant's seat of Dupplin, near Perth. This was construed by Oliphant into a bravado on the part of Ruthven. His son, the Master of Oliphant, accordingly came forth with a train of armed followers, and rode hastily after Lord Ruthven. The foremost of Ruthven's party, taking a panic, fled in disorder, notwithstanding their master's call to them to stay. He was then obliged to fly also; but his kinsman, Alexander Stewart, of the house of Traquair, stayed to try to pacify the Oliphant party. He was shot with a harquebuss by one who did not know who he was, to the great grief of the Master.

Lord Ruthven prosecuted the Master for this outrage. The Earl of Morton, out of regard to Douglas of Lochleven, whose son-in-law Oliphant was, gave his influence on that side, and thus incurred some odium, which probably helped to bring about his destruction soon after.—*Cal.*

Oct. 20. In a General Assembly held at Edinburgh, an order was issued to execute the acts of the kirk upon *apostates*, and let them be punished as *adulterers*; 'perticularly that the Laird of Dun execute this act upon the Master of Gray, an apostate now returned to Scotland. It being reported to the king that the Master of Gray his house did shake and rock in the night as with an earthquake, and the king [then fourteen years old] interrogating David Fergusson [minister of Dunfermline], "What he thought it could mean that that house alone should shake and totter?" he answered: "Sir, why should not the devil rock his awn bairns?"'[1]

An earthquake, noted in Howes's *Chronicle* as having been

[1] Row's *History of the Kirk of Scotland.*

experienced in Kent at midnight of the 1st of May this year, was 1580. probably the cause of the rocking felt at the Master of Gray's house. In Kent it made 'the people to rise out of their beds and run to the churches, where they called upon God by earnest prayers to be merciful to them.'

George Auchinleck of Balmanno had been one of the confidants of the Regent in the days of his power. It being well known that he had influence in bringing about the decision of lawsuits, the highest nobility were glad at that time to pay court to him. As an illustration of the nature of his position—Coming one day from the Regent's house at Dalkeith to Edinburgh, and walking up the High Street, he met one Captain Nesbit, with whom he had some slight quarrel, and drawing his sword, instantly thrust him through the body, so that he was left for dead. So far from seeking concealment after this violence, Auchinleck held straight on to the Tolbooth, where the Court of Session sat, as though he had done no wrong; after which he coolly made his way back to the Regent's court at Dalkeith. It does not appear that he was in any way punished for stabbing Nesbit.

On another occasion, as Auchinleck stood within the bar of the Tolbooth, an old man of unprosperous appearance made his way through the crowd, asking permission to speak with him. When Auchinleck turned to ask what he wanted, the old man said: 'I am Oliver Sinclair!' and without another word, turned and went away. It was the quondam favourite of James V., now a poor and dejected gentleman, albeit connected by near ties with some of the greatest men in the country. Men talked much of this proceeding of Sinclair: it seemed to them equivalent to his saying: 'Be not too proud of your interest at court. I was once as you are; you may fall to be as I am.'—*H. of G.*

The prediction was now verified, for, Morton being now out of power and in danger of his life, Auchinleck no longer had influence at council or in court. He, moreover, stood in no small personal danger from his many enemies. As he was walking on the High Dec. 12. Street of Edinburgh, he was beset at a passage near St Giles's Church by William Bickerton of Casch, and four other gentlemen, who assailed him with bended pistols, by one of which he was shot through the body, after which he was left for dead. This was thought to be done in revenge for an attack by him upon Archibald, the brother of William Bickerton. The assailants were all found guilty of the slaughterous attempt, but without the aggravation of

1580. its being done within three-quarters of a mile of the king's person, seeing that 'the king's majesty was furth at the hunting, the time of the committing thereof.'—*Pit.*

Auchinleck survived this accident, and we find him in the ensuing March in the hands of the Earl of Arran, and put to the torture, in order to extort from him a confession of certain crimes with which he was charged, but which he denied. He took a part in the affair of the Raid of Ruthven in August 1582. When the Earl of Arran on that occasion, hearing of the king's being secluded in Ruthven House, came to try if he could gain access to him, 'the Earl of Gowrie met him at the gate, and had straightway killed him, if George Auchinleck had not held his hand as he was about to have pulled out his dagger to have stabbed him.'—*H. of G.*

1580-1. JAN. 28. A Confession of Faith was this day subscribed by the king, his household and courtiers, including Lennox, and many of the nobility and other persons, professing 'the religion now revealed to the world by the preaching of the blessed evangel,' and solemnly abjuring all the doctrines and practices of the Romish Church.[1]

JAN. 29. This day, Sunday, there were gay doings in the boy-king's court of Holyrood, namely, running at the ring, justing, and such-like pastimes, besides sailing about in boats and galleys at Leith.—*Cal.*

The reader must not be too much surprised at this occurring the day after the signing of a solemn confession of the Protestant faith. The truth seems to have been this: the signers signed under the pressure of a party they had some interest for the moment in gratifying or blinding, and the accepters of the document were content with the fact of the signing, without regard to the too probable hypocrisy under which it took place. It is not uncommon for professions to be only a symptom of the reality of the opposite of what is professed.

1581. MAR. 11. The ex-Regent now lay a hopeless prisoner in Dumbarton Castle, chiefly occupied, we are told, in reading the Bible, which, though he had forced the people to buy it under a penalty, he had hitherto much neglected himself. One of his servants, named George Fleck, 'was apprehended in Alexander Lawson's house [in Edinburgh], together with the said Alexander, not without their own consents, as was alleged, to reveal where the Earl of Morton's

[1] The original of this document, commonly called the *King's Confession*, is preserved in the Advocates' Library.

treasure lay. The bruit [rumour] went—when the boots were presented to George Fleck, that he revealed a part of the treasure to be lying in Dalkeith yard, under the ground; a part in Aberdour, under a braid stone before the gate; a part in Leith. Certain it is, he [the earl] was the wealthiest subject that had been in Scotland for many years.'—*Cal.* 1581.

Sir James Melville tells us that, long before the trial of Morton, his gold and silver were transported by his natural son, James Douglas, and one of his servants called John Macmoran. 'It was first carried in barrels, and afterwards hid in some secret parts; part was given to be kept by some who were looked upon as his friends, who made ill account of it again; so that the most part thereof lighted in bad hands, and himself was so destitute of money, that when he went through the street to the Tolbooth to undergo his assize, he was compelled to borrow twenty shillings to distribute to the poor, who asked alms of him for God's sake.'

In May, he 'was brought to Edinburgh, and kept in Robin Gourlay's house,[1] with a band of men of weir.' James Melville says: 'The very day of his putting to assize, I happened to be in Edinburgh, and heard and saw the notablest example, baith of God's judgment and mercy that, to my knowledge, ever fell out in my time. For in that Tolbooth, where oftentimes, during his government, he had wrested and thrawn judgment, partly for gain, whereto he was given, and partly for particular favour, was his judgment overthrown; and he wha, above any Scotsman, had maist gear, friendship, and cliental,[2] had nane to speak a word for him that day; but, the greatest part of the assizers being his knawn unfriends, he was condemned to be headit on a scaffold, and that head, whilk was sae witty in warldly affairs and policy, and had commanded with sic authority and dignity within that town and judgment-seat, to be set upon a prick upon the hichest stane of the gable of the Tolbooth that is towards the public street.'

Morton was condemned for being 'airt and part'[3] concerned in the murder of Darnley. He was more clearly an actor in the cruel slaughter of Riccio. After doing his best to insnare Mary into a marriage with Bothwell, he had headed a rebellion against her on hypocritical pretences. The extortions he had practised during

[1] See under May 1574. [2] Fr. *clientèle*, dependents.

[3] This Scotch law-phrase has become familiar in England, under the form of 'art and part,' and is not in general correctly understood. The first word is not art, but *airt*, meaning direction, implying that the accused was believed to have counselled and guided the actual perpetrators of the crime.

1581. his regency, in order to enrich himself, shewed an equally sordid and cruel character. Throughout all the time of his government, he had outraged decency by the grossness of his private life. Yet 'he had great comfort that he died a Christian, in the true and sincere profession of religion, whilk he cravit all the faithful to follow, and abide thereat to the death.'—*Moy.* 'He keepit the same countenance, gesture, and short sententious form of language upon the scaffold, whilk he usit in his princely government. He spake, led about and urgit by the commanders at the four nooks of the scaffold; but after that ance he had very fectfully[1] and gravely uttered, at guid length, that whilk he had to speak, there-

The Maiden.

after almaist he altered not thir words: "It is for my sins that God has justly brought me to this place; for gif I had served my God as truly as I did my king, I had not come here. But as for that I am condemned for by men, I am innocent, as God knows. Pray for me." . . . . I [am] content to have recordit the wark of God, whilk I saw with my ees and heard with my ears.'—*Ja. Mel.*

[1] Powerfully.

'After all was done, he went without fear and laid his neck upon 1581. the block, crying continually: "Lord Jesus, receive my spirit," till the axe of the Maiden—which he himself had caused make after the pattern which he had seen at Halifax in Yorkshire—falling upon his neck, put an end to his life and that note together. His body was carried to the Tolbooth, and buried secretly in the night in the Greyfriars. His head was affixed on the gate of the city.'—*H. of G.*

The Maiden, which still exists in the Museum of the Society of the Antiquaries of Scotland, is an instrument of the same nature as the guillotine, a loaded knife running in an upright frame, and descending upon a cross-beam, on which the neck of the culprit is laid. It is not unlikely that the ex-Regent introduced the Maiden; but another allegation, which asserts him to have been the first to suffer by it, is untrue.

At the death of Morton, the common people were much occupied in discussing a prophecy that the Bleeding Heart should fall by the Mouth of Arran. Morton, as a Douglas, bore the Bleeding Heart in his coat-armorial. Captain Stuart having been made Earl of Arran between the time of the accusation and the execution, here, said they, is the prediction realised, though what the Mouth of Arran meant it would have puzzled them to tell. It was probably to this unintelligible stanza in the prophecies of Merling that they referred:

> In the mouth of Arran an selcouth[1] shall fall,
> Two bloody harts shall be taken with a false train,
> And derfly dung down without any dome,
> Ireland, Orkney, and other lands many,
> For the death of those two great dule shall make.[2]

Morton may be taken as an example of a class of public men in that rude and turbulent time, who were to all appearance earnest Christians of the reforming and evangelical stamp, and nevertheless allowed themselves a licence in every wickedness, even to treachery and murder, whenever they had a selfish object in view, or, more strangely still, when the interests of religion, in their view of the matter, called on them so to act.

Nothing is more remarkable in the history of this period than the coincidence of wicked or equivocal actions and pious professions in the same person. Adam Bothwell, Bishop of Orkney, who performed the marriage-ceremony of Mary and Bothwell, and

[1] A strange thing.

[2] See under Jan. 1, 1561-2.

1581. afterwards in the basest manner took active part against her—who was in constant trouble with the General Assembly on account of his shortcomings—writes letters full of expressions of Christian piety and resignation. He is constantly 'saying with godly Job, gif we have receivit guid out of the hand of the Lord, why should we not alsae receive evil—giving him maist hearty thanks therefore, attesting our godly and stedfast faith in him, whilk is maist evident in time of probane.' Sir John Bellenden, justice-clerk, who had a share in the murder of Signor David, and who, on receiving a gift of Hamilton of Bothwell-haugh's estate of Woodhouselee from the Regent Moray, turned Hamilton's wife out of doors, so as to cause her to run mad—this vile man, in his will, speaks of 'my saul, wha baith sall meet my Maister with joy and comfort, to hear that comfortable voice that he has promisit to resotat [resuscitate], saying, Come unto me thou as ane of my elect.'[1]

JUNE 11. An entry in the Lord Treasurer's books reveals the mood of the gay king and his courtiers, nine days after the bloody end of Morton. It is Sunday, and James is residing with the Duke of Lennox at Dalkeith Castle. He attends the parish church within the town, and, after service, returns, with *two pipers playing before him.*[2]

It was, however, only four days after the death of Morton, and while his blood was still fresh upon the streets, that the man who had brought him to the block passed through the gay scenes of a marriage. Captain Stuart—for Scottish history can scarcely be induced to recognise him as Earl of Arran—had formed a shameful connection with a lady of high birth and rank now figuring at the Scottish court. Born Elizabeth Stewart, as daughter of the Earl of Athole, she had first been wife of Lord Lovat—then, after his death, wife of the Earl of March, brother of the Regent Lennox. Her intrigue with Captain James, her divorce of the Earl of March on alleged reasons which history would blush to mention, her quick-following marriage to Arran while in a condition which would have given her husband a plea of divorce against herself, and this occurring so close to the time when Arran had shed the blood of his great enemy, form a series of events sufficient to mark the character of the court into which the young king had emerged

[1] For the above illustrations of his remark, the author is indebted to Mr Mark Napier's curious notes to the edition of Spottiswoode's History published by the Spottiswoode Club.

[2] 'Item, to ane pyper and ane young boy his sone that playit in Dalkeytht upon Sonday the xj day of Junii, fra the kirk to the castell befoir his Hienes . . . . xxs.'

from the strictness of Presbyterian rule. When the lady brought 1581.
her husband a son in the subsequent January,[1] the king was invited to the baptism, and we only learn that he was prevented from attending in consequence of a temporary quarrel which had by that time taken place between Lennox and Arran.

A contemporary writer, speaking of the countess, calls her 'the maistresse of all vice and villany,' and says she 'infectit the air in his Hieness' audience.' He accuses her of controlling the course of justice, and alleges that she 'caused sundrie to be hanged that wanted their compositions, saying: What had they been doing all their days, that had not so much as five punds to buy them from the gallows?'—*Cal.*

The Presbyterian clergy regarded the frivolity of Lennox and Mombirneau, their foreign vices and oaths, joined to the coarser native profligacy of Arran and his lady, as forming a bad school for the young king. A love of amusement and buffoonery he certainly contracted from this source; but it is remarkable that he was not drawn into any gross vice by the bad example set before him.

At this time, upwards of twenty years after the Reformation, Nov.
it was still found that 'the dregs of idolatry' existed in sundry parts of the realm, 'by using of pilgrimage to some chapels, wells, crosses . . . ., as also by observing of the festival-days of the sancts, sometime namit their patrons; in setting furth of bane-fires, [and] singing of carols within and about kirks at certain seasons of the year.' An act of parliament was now passed, condemning these practices, and imposing heavy fines on those guilty of them; failing which, the transgressors to endure a month's imprisonment upon bread and water.

The archbishopric of Glasgow being vacant, Mr Robert 1582. June.

[1] A note-worthy anecdote of this lady is stated in Anderson's *History of the Family of Fraser*. On the death of her first husband, the tutorship of her infant son, Lord Lovat, became a matter of contention between the child's grand-uncle, Fraser of Struie, and his uncle Thomas; and it seemed likely there would be a fight between their various partisans. In these circumstances, a clerical gentleman of the clan, Donald Fraser Dhu, entreated the widow to interfere, and ask Struie to retire. She gave an evasive reply, remarking that whatever might befall, 'not a drop of Stewart blood would be spilt.' The mediator then drew his dirk, and told her ladyship with a fierce oath, that *her* blood would be the first that would be spilt, if she did not do as he requested. She then complied, and Thomas, the child's uncle, was accordingly elected as tutor.

1582. Montgomery accepted it from the king, on an understanding with the king's favourite, the Duke of Lennox, as to the income. The church excommunicated him. In Edinburgh, 'he was openly onbeset [waylaid] by lasses and rascals of the town, and hued out by flinging of stones at him, out at the Kirk of Field port, and narrowly escaped with his life.'—*Moy.*

SEP. 4. One consequence of the *coup d'état* at Ruthven was the return of John Durie from the banishment into which he had gone in May, to resume his ministry in Edinburgh. The affair makes a fine historic picture.

'As he is coming from Leith to Edinburgh, there met him at the Gallow Green two hundred men of the inhabitants of Edinburgh. Their number still increased till he came within the Nether Bow. There they began [with bare heads and loud voices] to sing the 124th psalm—"Now Israel may say, and that truly," &c., in four parts [till heaven and earth resounded]. They came up the street to the Great Kirk, singing thus all the way, to the number of two thousand. They were much moved themselves, and so were the beholders. The Duke [of Lennox, who was lodged in the High Street, and looked out and saw], was astonished and more affrayed at that sight than at anything that ever he had seen before in Scotland, and rave his beard for anger. After exhortation made in the reader's place by Mr James Lowson, to thankfulness, and the singing of a psalm, they dissolved with great joy.'—*Cal.*

SEP. 5. Another consequence of the change at court was, that the Duke of Lennox was forced to leave the kingdom. The Presbyterian historians relate the manner of his departure with evident relish. 'The duke departed out of the town, after noon, accompanied with the provost, bailies, and five hundred men. . . . . He rode towards Glasgow, accompanied by the Lord Maxwell, the Master of Livingstone, the Master of Eglintoun, Ferniehirst, and sundry other gentlemen.'[1] . . . . He 'remained in Dunbarton at the West Sea, where, or [ere] he gat passage, he was put to as hard a diet as he caused the Earl of Morton to use there; yea, even to the other extremity that he had used at court; for, whereas his kitchen was sae sumptuous that lumps of butter was cast in the fire when it soked [grew dull], and twa or three crowns waired upon a stock of kale dressing, he was fain to eat of a meagre guse, scoudered with beare strae.'[2]

[1] Calderwood. [2] Melville's Diary.

Died in Edinburgh, George Buchanan, at the age of seventy-eight, immediately after concluding his *History of Scotland*. His high literary accomplishments, especially his exquisite Latin composition, have made his name permanently famous. His personal character was not without its shades, yet it stands forth amidst the rough scenes of that time as something, on the whole, venerable. Sir James Melville, in noting that, while acting as one of the king's preceptors, he kept the young monarch in great awe, goes on to speak of him as 'a stoic philosopher,' who did not act in that capacity with any view to his worldly interests. 'A man of notable endowments for his learning and knowledge in Latin poesy,' says this mild contemporary, 'much honoured in other countries, pleasant in conversation, rehearsing at all occasions moralities short and instructive, whereof he had abundance, inventing where he wanted. He was also religious, but was easily abused, and so facile, that he was led by every company that he haunted, which made him factious in his old days, for he spoke and wrote as those who were about him informed him; for he was become careless, following in many things the vulgar opinion; for he was naturally popular, and extremely revengeful against any man who had offended him, which was his greatest fault. For he did write despiteful invectives against the Earl of Monteith, for some particulars that were between him and the Laird of Buchanan. He became the Earl of Morton's great enemy, for that a nag of his chanced to be taken from his servant during the civil troubles, and was bought by the Regent, who had no will to part with the said horse, he was so sure-footed and so easy, that albeit Mr George had ofttimes required him again, he could not get him. And, therefore, though he had been the Regent's great friend before, he became his mortal enemy, and from that time forth spoke evil of him in all places, and at all occasions.' 1582. SEP. 28.

A little while before Buchanan's death, while his history was passing through the press of Alexander Arbuthnot in Edinburgh, the Rev. James Melville, accompanied by his uncle Andrew, came from St Andrews 'anes-errand'—that is, on set purpose—to see him and his work. 'When we came to his chalmer,' says Melville, 'we fand him sitting in his chair, teaching his young man that servit in his chalmer, to spell, a, b, ab; e, b, eb; &c. After salutation, Mr Andrew says: "I see, sir, ye are not idle." "Better this," quoth he, "nor stealing sheep, or sitting idle, whilk is as ill." Thereafter he shew[ed] us the Epistle Dedicatory to the King; the whilk when Mr Andrew had read he tauld him it was obscure in

1582. some places, and wanted certain words to perfite the sentence. Says he: "I may do nae mair for thinking on another matter." "What is that?" says Mr Andrew. "To die," quoth he; "but I leave that and mony mae things for you to help."

'We went from him to the printer's wark-house, whom we fand at the end of the 17 buik of his chronicle, at a place whilk we thought very hard for the time, whilk might be an occasion of staying the haill wark, anent the burial of Davie.[1] Thereafter, staying the printer from proceeding, we came to Mr George again, and fand him bedfast by [contrary to] his custom; and asking him how he did—"Even going the way of weelfare," says he. Mr Thomas, his cousin, shews him the hardness of that part of his story, [and] that the king might be offended with it, and it might stay all the wark. "Tell me, man," says he, "gif I have tauld the truth?" "Yes," says Mr Thomas, "sir, I think sae." "I will bide his feid, and all his kin's then," quoth he: "pray, pray to God for me, and let Him direct all."'

The sternness of Scottish prejudices here reaches the heroic.

With its eight centuries of fable in the front, and its glaring partisanship in the latter part, we cannot now attach much importance to Buchanan's history. Yet in respect of its literary character, it contains some truly felicitous touches, as where he describes the surface of Galloway in four words—'*in modicos colles tumet;*' or the remarkable sea-board of Fife in two—'*oppidulis præcingitur.*' Expressions like these shew the master of literary art.

DEC. 10. The king's new councillors of course felt that hard measure had been dealt to the ex-Regent. At this date, 'the Earl of Morton's head was taken down off the prick which is upon the high gavell of the Tolbooth, with the king's licence, at the eleventh hour of the day; was laid in a fine cloth, convoyed honourably, and laid in the kist where his body was buried. The Laird of Carmichael carried it, shedding tears abundantly by the way.'—*Cal.*

1582-3. While the king was in the hands of the Ruthven conspirators, two gentlemen came as ambassadors from France to see what could

[1] He states that David Riccio was buried by the queen in the royal vault, 'almost in the arms of Magdalene Valois,' and thence draws a shameful inference against the chastity of Mary. To dedicate to the young king a book in which he endeavoured to prove his mother an adulteress, and the murderer of her husband, gives a strange idea of the sense of that age regarding the rules of good taste, to say nothing more.

be done for him, and were of course treated with little civility by the royal councillors. The second, M. de Menainville, must have been the less acceptable to them, if it was true which was alleged, that he had been one of the chief devisers of the league in Picardy against the Protestants. With some difficulty, De Menainville made his way into the royal presence at Holyroodhouse. 'After some words spoken to the king, he craved that he might be used as an ambassador; that, as he had the use of meat and drink for his body, so he might have food for his soul, meaning the mass, otherwise he would not stay to suffer his most Christian prince's authority and ambassage to be violated. The king rounded [whispered] and prayed him to be sober in that point, and all would be weel.' It was not likely that the concession which had been sternly refused to Queen Mary would, at such a time, be granted to him. The king, with much ado, prevailed upon the magistracy of Edinburgh to give the other ambassador, the Sieur de la Motte Fenelon, a banquet on the eve of his departure. The kirk-session opposed the entertainment; and when they found they could not prevent it, they did the next best—held a solemn fast, with preachings and psalm-singing, during the whole time of the feast—namely, from betwixt nine and ten in the morning till two in the afternoon. The ministers called the banquet a holding fellowship with 'the murderers of the sancts of God.'—*Cal.*

1582-3. JAN. 23. FEB. 4.

De Menainville remained for some time after. 'Upon Thursday the 28th of March, commonly called Skyre Thursday, [he] called into his lodging thirteen poor men, and washed their feet according to the popish manner, whereat the people was greatly offended.'—*Cal.*

1583. MAR. 28.

All previous efforts at the finding of metals in the country having failed, a contract was now entered into between the king and one Eustachius Roche, described as a Fleming and mediciner, whereby the latter was to be allowed to break ground anywhere in search of those natural treasures, and to use timber from any of the royal forests in furthering of the work, without molestation from any one, during twenty-one years, on the sole condition that he should deliver for his majesty's use, for every hundred ounces of gold found, seven ounces; and for the like weight of all other metals—as silver, copper, tin, or lead—ten ounces for every hundred found, and sell the remainder of the gold for the use of the state at £22 per ounce of utter fine gold, and of the silver at 50s. the ounce.—*P. C. R.*

AUG. 23.

1583. We light upon Eustachius again on the 3d of December 1585, and he is then in no pleasant plight with his mines. Assisted by a number of Englishmen, he had done his best to fulfil his share of the contract, but 'as yet he has made little or nae profit of his travel, partly by reason of the trouble of this contagious sickness, but specially in the default of his partners and John Scolloce their factor,' who would not fulfil either their duty to his majesty or their engagements to himself. Through these causes, 'the haill wark has been greatly hinderit.' He had Scolloce warded in Edinburgh; but he, 'by his majesty's special command, is latten to liberty, without ony trial taken.' At the same time, the king's treasurer 'has causit arreist the leid ore whilk the complener has presently in Leith, and whilk was won in the mines of Glengoner Water and Winlock.' This was the greater hardship, as it was the part he had to set aside for the Earl of Arran, in virtue of a contract for the protection of his lordship's rights to certain lead-mines. The Lords were merciful to the poor adventurer, and ordered the arrestment to be discharged.—*P. C. R.*

He rises once more before us in a new capacity under September 4, 1588.

Sep. 10. The king having now escaped from his Ruthven councillors and fallen once more under the influence of the Earl of Arran, Sir Francis Walsingham came as Elizabeth's ambassador to express her concern about these movements, and see what could be done towards opposite effects. Coming to a king with an unwelcome message has never been a pleasant duty; but it must have been particularly disagreeable on this occasion, if it be true, as is alleged by a Presbyterian historian, that Arran—who, says he, within a few days after his return to court, 'began to look braid'—hounded out a low woman, called *Kate the witch*, to assail the ambassador with vile speeches as he passed to and from the king's presence. She was, it is alleged, hired by Arran 'for a new plaid and six pounds in money, not only to rail against the ministry [clergy], his majesty's most assured and ancient nobility, and lovers of the amity [English alliance], but also set in the entry of the king's palace, to revile her majesty's ambassador at Edinburgh, St Andrews, Falkland, Perth, and everywhere, to the great grief of all good men, and dishonour of the king and country.' It is further stated, that, being imprisoned 'for a fashion,' large allowance was made for her entertainment, and she was relieved as soon as Walsingham had departed.—*Cal.*

While the kirk was beginning to feel the consequences of the king's emancipation from the Ruthven lords, it sustained an assault, though of a very petty character, from a different quarter. Robert Brown, a Cambridge student, had three years before attracted attention in Norfolk by his novel and startling ideas regarding ecclesiastical matters. The Bishop of Norwich imprisoned him, with the usual non-success as far as the correction of opinion was concerned. He had then taken refuge at Middleburgh, and there given forth his notions to the world in the form of a pamphlet. Now he was come to Scotland, perhaps thinking it a pity that a people should be in trouble between the contending claims of Prelacy and Presbytery, when he could shew them that both systems were wrong. Landing at Dundee, where, it is said, he received some encouragement, he advanced by St Andrews to Edinburgh, and there took up his quarters 'in the head of the Canongate,' along with four or five English followers, who were accompanied by their wives and children. The people—who, for the most part, were passionately attached to the simple fabric of their national church, and dreamt of no rivalship or enmity to it except in episcopacy—how they must have felt at the novel sight of a group of men who, in declaring against bishops, also found fault with sessions and synods, with indeed all ecclesiastical action whatever, considering each congregation independent in itself, and no member of it less entitled to pray and preach than the pastor! 1583.4. Jan. 9.

Brown, whose self-confidence in asserting his peculiar doctrines was very great, did not rest four days in Edinburgh before he had presented himself to the general kirk-session for a wrangle. We are told by a Presbyterian historian—he 'made shew, in an arrogant manner, that he would maintain that witnesses at baptism was not a thing indifferent, but simply evil. But he failed in the probation.' A week after, 'in conference with some of the presbytery, he alleged that the whole discipline of Scotland was amiss; that he and his company were not subject to it, and therefore he would appeal from the kirk to the magistrate.' Considering how the clergy stood with the court, this must have been a most offensive threat; the more so that the court had already shewn some symptoms of favour to Brown, in order to 'molest the kirk.' 'It was thought good that Mr James Lowson and Mr John Davidson should gather out of his book such opinions as they suspected or perceived him to err in, and get them ready, to pose him and his followers thereupon, that thereafter the king might be informed.' A week later, Brown and

1583-4. his 'complices' came before the presbytery, to answer the articles prepared against him. We only further learn that he left Edinburgh, 'malcontent, because his opinions were not embraced, and that he was committed to ward a night or two till they were tried' (*Cal.*), a form of religious disputation highly characteristic of the age. Brown afterwards, when founding his sect of Independents in England, published a volume containing various invectives against the Scottish kirk and its leaders, of which Dr Bancroft took advantage in preaching against presbytery (9th February 1589), while probably ready to consign their author to the pains which the Bishop of Peterborough actually meted out to him by excommunication.

1584. Thomas Vautrollier, a French Protestant, who had come to England early in Elizabeth's reign, migrated about this time to Edinburgh, where he set up a printing-press. From his office proceeded this year a small volume of poems, composed by the young king, under the title of *The Essayes of a Prentise in the Divine Art of Poesie;* to which was added a prose treatise embracing the 'rules and cautels for Scottish poesie:' a volume of which it may be enough to say, that it betrays a laudable love of literature in the royal author, joined to some power of literary expression. Vautrollier does not appear to have met with sufficient encouragement to induce him to remain in Edinburgh, as he soon after returned to London.

JULY. At the end of this month, the pest was brought into Scotland at Wester Wemyss, a small port in Fife—'where many departed.' —*Moy.*

King James tells us in his *Basilicon Doron,* that 'the pest always smites the sickarest such as flies it furthest and apprehends deepliest the peril thereof.' See his own conduct on this occasion. About the end of September, while he was hunting at Ruthven, 'word came that there were five or six houses in Perth affected with the plague, where his majesty's servants were for the time. Whereupon, his majesty *departed the same night,* with a very small train to Tullibardine, and next day to Stirling, leaving his whole household servants enclosed in the place of Ruthven, with express command to them not to follow, nor remove forth of the same, until they saw what became of them upon the suspicion.'—*Moy. R.*

The pest on this occasion remained in Perth for several months, working great destruction. It was ordained by the kirk-session, May 24, 1585, that 'hereafter during the time of the plague, no

banquets should be at marriages, and no persons should resort to 1584.
bridals under pain of ten pounds . . . . forty pounds to be paid by them that call more than four on the side to the banquet, or bridal, during the pest.'

In the ensuing February, under an apprehension about the arrival of the pestilence in their city, the town-council of Edinburgh adopted a highly rational sanitary measure, ordering the ashes, dust, and dirt of their streets to be put up to auction. We do not learn that any one undertook to pay for the privilege of cleaning the streets of the capital, and Maitland remarks in his history, that many years elapsed before the movement was renewed, not to say carried into effect.

'. . . a baxter's boy, called Robert Henderson—no doubt by the DEC. 2.
instigation of Satan—desperately put some powder and a candle in his father's heather-stack, standing in a close opposite to the Tron of Edinburgh [the public weighing-machine], and burnt the same, with his father's house, which lay next adjacent, to the imminent hazard of burning the whole town. For which, being apprehended most marvellously, after his escaping out of the town, he was on the next day burnt quick at the Cross, as an example.'—*Moy. R.*

1585. APR. 7.
John Lord Maxwell was at this time the most powerful man in the south-west province of Scotland. He possessed Caerlaverock Castle and many fair estates. The next man in the district was the chief of the clan Johnston, usually called Johnston of that Ilk, or the Laird of Johnston. The jealousy in which these great lords of the land usually stood of each other chanced at this time to be inflamed into hostilities, and Maxwell took such an attitude towards the profligate government of the Earl of Arran, as to cause himself to be denounced as a rebel. According to the common practice, the court gave a commission to Johnston to proceed against Lord Maxwell, only helping him with two companies of hired troops under the command of Captains Cranstoun and Lammie.

This proved an unfortunate movement for the house of Johnston. The two hired bands were cut to pieces on Crawford Moor[1] by

[1] On this occasion Captain Lammie was killed. Sir Walter Scott, in relating the incident in the *Border Minstrelsy*, expresses a hope that he was 'the same miscreant who, in the day of Queen Mary's distress, "his ensign being of white taffety, had painted on it the cruel murder of King Henry, and laid down before her majesty, at what time she presented herself as prisoner to the Lords."—*Birrel's Diary.*' It was very probably so, as we find that he then,

1585. Robert Maxwell, natural brother to the earl. The same bold man proceeded to Johnston's castle of Lochwood, and at the date noted set fire to it, jestingly remarking that he would give Lady Johnston light 'to set her hood.' Johnston himself sustained a defeat at the hands of the Maxwells, was made prisoner by them, and died of a broken heart.

This was only the beginning of a protracted feud between the Maxwells and Johnstons, which cost each family, as will be seen, the destruction of two of its chiefs.

APR. 30. John Livingstone of Belstane[1] complained to the Council of an assault which had been made upon him on the 3d of the preceding February by sundry persons, whose motive in so assailing him does not appear. The affair is most characteristic—indeed, a type of numberless other lawless proceedings of the time. John quietly leaves his house before sunrise, meaning no harm to any one, and expecting none to himself. He walks out, as he says, under God's peace and the king's, when suddenly he is beset by about forty people who had him at feud, 'all bodin in feir of weir;' namely, armed with jacks, steel-bonnets, spears, lance-staffs, bows, hagbuts, pistolets, and other invasive weapons forbidden by the laws. At the head of them was William, Master of Yester—a denounced rebel on account of his slaughter of the Laird of Westerhall's servant—Alexander Jardine, younger of Applegarth; his servants, Stephen Jardine and Matthew Moffat in Woodend, James Borthwick of Colela, John Lauder of Hartpool, Michael Hunter of Polmood, John Hoppringle in Peebles, James Hoppringle of the same place, William Brenarde [Burnett?] of the Barns, John Cockburn of Glen, and Colin Langton of Earlshaugh, were among the company, evidently all of them men of some figure and importance. Having come for the purpose of attacking Livingstone, they no sooner saw him than they set upon him, with discharge of their firearms, to deprive him of his life. He narrowly escaped, and ran back to his house, which they immediately environed in the most furious manner, firing in

as well as now, was a hired soldier of the government. As his painted ensign makes rather a conspicuous appearance in Scottish history, it may be not unworthy of notice that the following entry occurs in the Lord Treasurer's books, under March 18, 1567–8, nine months after the incident in question: 'To Captain Andro Lambie for his expenses passand of Glasgow to Edinburgh to uplift certain men of weir, and to mak ane *Handsenyie* of white taffety, £25.' He was then acting for the Regent Moray. It seems probable that, having spoiled his ensign by the picture of the king's murder, he was now gratified with a new one at the expense of his employer.

[1] In the parish of Carluke, Lanarkshire.

at the windows and through every other aperture, for a space of three hours. A 'bullon' pierced his hat. As they departed, they met his wife and daughter, whom they abused shamefully. In short, it seems altogether to have been an affair of the most barbarous and violent kind. The offenders were all denounced rebels. 1585.

The pest, which had commenced in Perth in the previous September, was believed to be now brought thence by a servant-woman to the Fishmarket in Edinburgh (*Moy.*), where it 'was first knawn to be in Simon Mercerbanks's house.' (*Bir.*) From accident or otherwise, the king acted on this occasion exactly as he had done at Perth, when the plague first declared itself there. On the very day when the disease appeared in Edinburgh, he left the city, and 'rode to Dirleton[1] to a sumptuous banquet prepared by the Earl of Arran.' (*Cal.*) The pest continued in the capital till the subsequent January, sometimes carrying off twenty-four people in a single night. 'The haill people whilk was able to flee, fled out of the town: nevertheless there died of people which were not able to flee, fourteen hundred and some odd.' (*Bir.*) It was at St Andrews in August, 'and continued till upwards of four hundred people died, and the place was left almost desolate.' (*Moy.*) Dunse is cited as a place where this pestilence 'raged extremely.' (*Mar.*) In Perth, between 24th September 1584, and August 1585, when it ceased, it carried off fourteen hundred and twenty-seven persons, young and old, or thereby. (*Chron. Perth.*) This could not be less than a sixth of the entire population. MAY 7.

June 23, 1585, on account of the pest being in Edinburgh, the business of the cunyie-house was ordered to be transported to Dundee, and the coining of gold, silver, and alloyed money to go on there as it had hitherto done in Edinburgh. On the alloyed pennies, OPPIDUM DUNDEE was to be substituted for OPPIDUM EDINBURGI. The Exchequer was also removed to Falkland, and the Court of Session to Stirling. On the 21st of October, the pest being now in Dundee, the coining was ordered to be removed to Perth, and the name of that burgh to be substituted in the circumscription.—*P. C. R.*

The severity of this pestilence excited the rage of the people against the Earl of Arran and his lady, the then ruling power of the country, to whose infamous life, and to the banishment

[1] He remained at this fine old castle twelve days, attended by Arran, Sir Robert Melville, Secretary Maitland, Ferniehirst, Colonel Stuart, and the Master of Gray; and regaled with 'the play of Robin Hood.' 'After the banquet was ended, Arran fell deadly sick.'—*Cal.*

1585. of the Protestant leaders, the evil was attributed. In the course of the summer, the air being 'perpetually nebulous,' and the growing crop 'universally corrupted,'[1] the popular feeling was further excited in the same direction, and the general cry was that the Lord would not stay his hand till the banished lords were brought home again. These lords actually did draw nearer to the Border, under the encouragement which the plague thus afforded them (*Ja. Mel.*), and by reason that the citizens of Edinburgh were not now able to come forward and act, in blind obedience to court-orders, as they were wont.

The revolution effected by the ultra Protestant party at Stirling (November 2, 1585), was followed by a stoppage of the pestilence, 'not by degrees or piecemeal, but in a instant, as it were; so that never any after that hour was known to have been infected, nor any of such as were infected before, to have died. The lane, also, in Stirling by which they [the banished lords] entered, was wholly infected; yet no man [of their party] was known to have been tainted with it, or to have received any hurt: nay, the men of Annandale did rob and ransack the pest-lodges which were in the field about Stirling, and carried away the clothes of the infected, but were never known to have been touched therewith themselves, or any others that got or wore the clothes. They also that were in the lodges, returned to their houses, and conversed with their neighbours in the town, who received them without fear, suspicion, or reproof, and no harm did ensue upon it. As for Edinburgh, before the 1st of February, within three months it was so well peopled and filled again with inhabitants, as none could perceive by the number that any had died out of it.' This change—'nothing can be alleged to have brought it to pass but the very finger of God. Let mankind advert and admire it; and whosoever shall go about to bereave God of his glory by laying it upon fortune, may his chance be such as his perverseness deserveth!'—*H. of G.*

The assumed immunity of the Border thieves is extremely amusing. Being here engaged in the right cause, it mattered not that they committed the monstrous inhumanity of plundering the sick and cheating the heirs of the dead.

James Melville remarks the same connection of circumstances, but places the improvement of the public health a month later. From the meeting of the parliament in December, under the

[1] *History of King James VI.*

auspices of the king's new advisers, 'the pest abated, and began to be strangely and remarkably withdrawn by the merciful hand of God, sae that Edinburgh was frequented again that winter; and at the entry of the spring, all the towns, almost desolate before, repeopled—St Andrews among the rest.' 1585.

Melville relates a remarkable anecdote of this pestilence, under November, when he had occasion to return from banishment at Berwick, and to proceed through Edinburgh on his way to attend a General Assembly at Linlithgow. 'On the morn, we made haste, and, coming to Losterrick [Restalrig], disjuned, and about eleven hours, came riding in at the Water-gate, up through the Canongate, and rade in at the Nether Bow, through the great street of Edinburgh, to the West Port, *in all whilk way we saw not three persons*, sae that I miskenned Edinburgh, and almost forgot that I had ever seen sic a town.'

'The news of the taking of Stirling was at the court of England and in London within aught and forty hours; for it being done on Tuesday in the morning, on the Thursday thereafter Mr Bowes tauld us, and on the Friday it was common in the mouths of all London.'—*Ja. Mel.* Nov. 2.

Under March 17, 1578, is another instance of extraordinary quickness in the communication of intelligence from Stirling to Edinburgh. In that case, we might suppose that the event only fulfilled a previous design. Such could scarcely be the case here. Sir John G. Dalyell remarks, that 'rumours subsequently verified are undoubtedly sometimes in circulation. The author recollects very well that the result of the battle of Trafalgar, or of Corunna, was currently reported in the city of Edinburgh, previous to any certain intelligence known to have been received of the fact through what was esteemed the speediest channel: nor, on subsequently computing the intervals, could satisfactory conjectures be formed how it had arrived.'[1] It may be remembered by many that, in the war in Afghanistan in 1842–3, the natives were remarked often to be possessed of intelligence of events occurring at a distance, long before any information had come to the British through recognised channels. The author just quoted expresses his opinion that, in such cases, there has merely been an anticipation on probable grounds of an event which was subsequently ascertained to have happened.

[1] *Darker Superstitions of Scotland*, p. 484.

REIGN OF JAMES VI.: 1585-1590.

THESE years were chiefly marked by the struggles of the more zealous clergy to replace the church upon a purely Presbyterian basis, and to maintain their assumed independence of the civil power. The king found his power encroached on, upon the one hand, by nobles richer, and having a greater command of followers, than himself; on the other, by divines who repudiated all subjection to civil authority in matters ecclesiastical, and yet arrogated powers which greatly concerned the secular rights and liberties of the people. While the reaction in his youthful mind against these besetting troubles inspired him with visionary ideas of the true rights of a monarch, the dissimulation practised at his court by the astute emissaries of Elizabeth, the restraints imposed on his liberty and natural sentiments by the more zealous Protestant party while he was under their rule, and the tricks he was tempted to have recourse to in order to recover his freedom, and obtain some share of real power, gave him, before he was twenty, such a tutoring in craft, as marked his character during the remainder of life. A more manly and resolute person would have either broken bravely through such a complication of troubles or perished in the attempt. With the help of a good-natured pliancy, James floated on. He was of a timid disposition, greatly disrelishing the sight of weapons, and along with this temper he exhibited much good-nature. Trembling at the outrageous dispositions of his nobles, and constitutionally a lover of peace, he exerted himself to conciliate offenders, and by persuasion to make them cease to break the laws, when a vigorous procedure against them in courts of justice would have been required. For the sake of his hopes of the English succession, if not from his own convictions—which, however, are not to be doubted—he maintained the Protestant cause. At the same time, seeing that the Catholics were friends of monarchy, and might have something to say in the English succession, he desired, if possible, to avoid offending them past forgiveness. Even the ultra-zealous Presbyterian clergy, who came to remonstrate with him, in his own palace, on his public acts or his private foibles, he could treat with such pleasantry as often disarmed them, when a more strenuous policy might have failed.

In February 1586-7, the unfortunate Mary was beheaded in Fotheringay Castle, a victim to the necessities of the Protestant cause.

In 1588, when this cause was threatened with destruction by the Spanish Armada, King James and his people manifested the greatest zeal in preparing for the defence of their part of the island. They entered into a Covenant or bond, in which they made solemn profession of the Protestant faith, and avowed their resolution to oppose Popery by every means in their power. After this danger had blown over, a new alarm was excited by the discovery of a conspiracy amongst the three leading Catholic nobles of Scotland, Huntly, Errol, and Crawford, to aid in introducing a Spanish army, through Scotland, for the conquest of the British island. These nobles having broken out in rebellion, in concert with a Protestant noble of irregular character, Stuart, Earl of Bothwell, the king led an army against them, and succeeded in reducing them to obedience (April 1589). Huntly, Crawford, Errol, and Bothwell were all convicted of treason; but the king shrank from inflicting a punishment which was certain to damage his prospects with a large party in England. They were liberated after only a few months' imprisonment.

In the latter part of 1589, James effected his marriage with the Princess Anne of Denmark. His young bride being detained in Norway for the winter, in consequence of a storm, he sailed for that country (October 22), and solemnised his nuptials at Upslo (now Christiania). In May 1590, the royal pair arrived amidst great rejoicings at Leith. The first year of the king's married life was strangely disturbed by a series of trials for the imaginary crime of witchcraft, in which the character of the age is strongly marked.

The Earl of Eglintoun, 'a young nobleman of a fair and large stature' (*Moy.*), was murdered by Cunningham of Robertland. 1586. APR. 18.

Montgomery and Cunningham were the Montague and Capulet of Ayrshire in the sixteenth century. The feud had sprung up nearly a hundred years before the above date, in consequence of the Earl of Glencairn disputing the title of the Earl of Eglintoun to the bailiery of the district of Cunningham. There had been attempts at a stanching of the feud, and even a marriage had been proposed by way of fixing the parties in amity; but at a time when peace had nearly been effected, enmity was renewed in consequence of a Montgomery killing a Cunningham in self-defence.

'The Cunninghams, being grieved hereat, made presently a vow that they should be avenged upon the fattest of the Montgomeries (for these were their words) for that fact. This vow was sae acceptable to them all, that a band was concludit, subscrivit with the chiefest of their hands, to slay the young Earl [of Eglintoun] by whatsoever mean could be devisit, and that whasoever wald

1586. take the turn in hand, and perform it, he sould not only be sustenit upon the common expenses of the rest, but sould also be maintenit and defendit by them all from danger and skaith. At last ane Cunningham of Robertland took the enterprise in hand, whilk he accomplished in this manner:

'Twa year before his treasonable attempt, he insinuate himself in familiarity and all dutiful service to the said young earl, whereby he movit him to take pleasure without ony suspicion, till he conqueist [acquired] sic favour at his hand, that neither the gold, money, horses, armour, clothes, counsel, or voyage was hid from him, that this same Robertland was made sae participant of them all, even as though they had been his awn; and besides all this, the confidence and favour that the earl shew unto him was sae great, that he preferrit him to be his awn bed-fellow. Hereat Lord Hugo, auld Earl of Eglintoun, took great suspicion, and therefore admonist his son in a fatherly manner to beware of sic society, whilk, without all doubt, wald turn to his skaith; for he knew weel the nature of these Cunninghams to be subtle and false, and therefore willit him to give them nae traist, but to avoid their company altogether, even as he lovit his awn life or wald deserve his fatherly blessing. To this counsel the son gave little regard; but that was to his pains; and the domestic enemy was sae crafty indeed, that he wald attempt naething during the life of the father for many respects. But within short time thereafter [the father died June 1585], as the noble earl was passing a short way in pastime, accompanied with a very few of his household servants, and evil horsit himself, Robertland, accompanied with sixty armed men, came running furiously against him on horseback; and the earl, fearing the thing that followit, spurrit his horse to have fled away. His servants all fled another way, and he was left alone. The horsemen ran all upon him, and unmercifully killed him with shots of guns and strokes of swords.

'The complaint of this odious murder being made to the king, he causit the malefactors to be chargit to a trial. But they all fled beyond sea. Robertland, wha was the first to make the invasion, passed to Denmark, where he remainit at court till the king came to Queen Anne. And because nane of the rest could be apprehendit, the king ordainit their houses to be renderit to the earl's brother, to be usit at his arbitrament, either to be demolishit or otherwise; and he swore the great aith, that he sould never pardon any of them that had committit that odious murder. Yet, how soon his majesty was arrivit in Denmark, his pardon was demandit of the queen for the first petition, and the same was obtenit, and he was receivit in grace there in presence of them all. Thereafter he came hame in the queen's company, and remains as ane of her majesty's master stablers.'—*H. K. J.* 1586.

MAY. The persecution of the Protestants in France at this time drove a vast number to England, where great sacrifices were made for their due entertainment. Scotland, with comparatively limited means, but perhaps warmer feeling, also made collections of money for the distressed people. According to James Melville, 'all the Protestants in France were chargit off France within sic a day, under pain of life, lands, gudes, and gear; sae that the number of banished in England were sae great, and the poor of them sae many, that they were compelled to seek relief of us for the same . . . . in the poor bounds I had under charge at the first beginning of my ministry, we gathered about five hunder merks for that effect. . . . . The sum of the haill collection whilk the French kirks gat, extended but till about ten thousand merks.' A considerable number of the exiles, including Pierre du Moulin, the minister of Paris, came to Edinburgh, where the magistrates gave them the common hall of the university for their worship, along with a stated allowance of money for support of their clergy. It cannot be doubted that the sight of these poor French exiles would deepen the feeling of dread and antipathy towards popery and papists, which was already strongly rooted in Scotland.

MAY 26. A singular collusive trial took place this day, for the purpose of clearing Mr Archibald Douglas, parson of Glasgow, of his concern in the murder of Darnley. He had been in exile or in hiding ever since, except during the regency of Morton, whose cousin he was. But now it was thought he might prove useful in advancing the king's prospects in England; so, with the most barefaced contempt for the very forms of justice, he was tried by a packed jury, and acquitted.

It is difficult to say to what extent the king was personally concerned in absolving one of his father's murderers. Perhaps he was not over-squeamish about murders of old date. On this point an anecdote may be quoted, though it stands somewhat under question on the score of authority. 'When Bothwell-haugh returned from France, whither he had fled upon the murder of the Regent, it is reported that he fell down at the king's feet, told who he was, and implored pardon. On which the king said,

1586. raising him up: "Pardon you, man; pardon you, man! Blest be he that got you! for had you not shot that fellow, I had never been king."'[1]

JUNE 3. Sundry persons of the name of Burne, dwelling in the middle march of Scotland, had appointed a day of combat with several persons residing in the opposite country within England, 'upon some light purpose unknown to his majesty, and without licence cravit of his majesty or of his dearest sister [Elizabeth] or of her officers, as aucht to be in sic case.' It was much to be feared that amongst the many persons assembled, a very small accident might be sufficient to rekindle old feuds, and that thus serious evils would arise. The Council, therefore, forbade all assembling at the place and day appointed, under pain of treason.—*P. C. R.*

JULY. While the southern and more populous parts of Scotland were, as we see, sufficiently barbarous, the Highland districts were as the comparative, and the Hebrides as the superlative degree in the same quality. The king, in the first edition of his *Basilicon Doron*, tells his son to think no more of the Islanders than as 'wolves and wild boars.' Probably, when the reader has perused the following narrative, he will think the epithet not unjustly applied, although his majesty afterwards dropped it in reprinting his book. The tale is of a commotion betwixt Angus M'Connel, Lord of Kintyre, and Maclean, Lord of Islay. 'This Angus had to his wife the sister of Maclean, and although they were brether-in-law, yet the ane was always in sic suspicion with the other, that of either side there was sae little traist, that almaist sendle [seldom] or never did they meet in amity, like unto the common sort of people, but rather as barbares upon their awn guard, or by their messengers. True it is that thir Islandish men are of nature very proud, suspicious, avaritious, full of deceit and evil intention [each] against his neighbour, by what way so ever he may circumvent him. Besides all this, they are sae cruel in taking of revenge, that neither have they regard to person, age, time, or cause; sae are they generally all sae far addicted to their awn tyrannical opinions, that in all respects they exceed in cruelty the maist barbarous people that ever has been sin' the beginning of the warld; ane example whereof ye sall hear in this history following:

'Angus M'Connel, understanding, by divers reports, the gude

[1] Note in *Maitland Club Miscellany*, iv. 123.

behaviour of Maclean to be sae famous, that almaist he was recommended and praised by the haill neutral people of these parts above himself; whilk engendered sic rancour in his heart that he pretermitted nae invention how he might destroy the said Maclean. At last he devised to draw on a familiarity amang them, and inveited himself to be banqueted by Maclean; and that the rather, that Maclean should be the readier to come over to his isle with him the mair gladly, either being required, or upon set purpose, as best should please him. And when Angus had sent advertisement to Maclean, that he was to come and make gude cheer, and to be merry with him certain days, Maclean was very glad thereof, and answered to the messenger: "My brother shall be welcome," said he, "come when he list." The messenger answered, it wald be to-morrow. So when Angus arrived in effect, he was richt cheerfully welcomed by his brother-in-law, wha remained there by the space of five or sax days. And when it was perceived that Maclean's provision was almaist spent, Angus thought it then time to remove. Indeed, the custom of that people is sae given to gluttony and drinking without all measure, that as ane is inveited to another, they never sinder sae lang as the vivers do last. In end, Angus says: "Because I have made the first obedience unto you, it will please you come over to my isle, that ye may receive as gude treatment with me as I have done with you." Maclean answered that he durst not adventure to come to him for mistrust; and Angus said: "God forbid that ever I should intend or pretend any evil against you; but yet, to remove all doubt and suspicion frae your mind, I will give you twa pledges, whilk shall be sent unto you with diligence; to wit, my eldest son and my awn only brother-german: these twa may be keepit here by your friends till ye come safely back again." Maclean, hearing this offer, whilk appeared unto him void of all suspicion, and so decreeted to pass with him to Kintyre; and further to testify that baith he simply believed all to be true, and that upon hope of gude friendship to continue, he thought expedient to retein ae only pledge, and that was Angus's brother, and wald carry with him his awn nevoy, the son of Angus. Whether he did this to save himself frae suspicion of danger, as apparently of the event he did it, or gif he brought him back again upon liberal favour, I will not dispute; because I have tauld you afore the perfect nature and qualities of these islands people; yet, because Maclean's education was civil, and brought up in the gude lawis and manners of Scotland from his youth, it may be that he has

1586.

1586. had double consideration, ane by kind, and another by art of honest dissimulation.

'To conclude, to Kintyre he came, accompanied with forty-five men of his kinsfolk and stout servants, in the month of July 1586; where, at the first arrival, they were made welcome with all humanity, and were sumptuously banqueted all that day. But Angus in that meantime had premonished all his friends and weel-willers within his isle of Kintyre to be at his house that same night at nine of the clock, and neither to come sooner nor later; for he had concluded with himself to kill them all the very first night of their arrival, fearing that gif he should delay any langer time, it might be that either he sould alter his malicious intention, or else that Maclean wald send for some greater forces of men for his awn defence. Thus he concealed his intent still, till baith he fand the time commodious and the very place proper; and Maclean being lodged with all his men within a lang house, that was something distant frae other housing, took to bed with him that night his nevoy, the pledge afore-spoken. But within ane hour thereafter, when Angus had assembled his men to the number of twa hundred, he placed them all in order about the house where Maclean then lay. Thereafter he came himself and called at the door upon Maclean, offering to him his reposing drink, whilk was forgotten to be given to him before he went to bed. Maclean answered, that he desired nae drink for that time. "Although so be," said the other, "it is my will that thou arise and come forth to receive it." Then began Maclean to suspect the falset, and so arase with his nevoy betwixt his shoulders, thinking that gif present killing was intended against him, he should save himself sae lang as he could by the boy; and the boy, perceiving his father with a naked sword, and a number of his men in like manner about, cried with a loud voice, mercy to his uncle for God's sake; whilk was granted, and immediately Maclean was removed to a secret chalmer till the morrow. Then cried Angus to the remanent that were within; sae mony as wald have their lives to be safe, they should come forth, twa only excepted, whilk he nominate; sae that obedience was made by all the rest, and these twa only, fearing the danger, refused to come forth. Angus, seeing that, commanded incontinent to put fire to the house, whilk was immediately performed; and thus were the twa men cruelly and unmercifully burnt to the death. These twa were very near kinsmen to Maclean, and of the eldest of his clan, renowned baith for counsel and manheid. The rest that were prisoners of the haill number afore-tauld, were ilk

ane beheaded the days following, ane for ilk day, till the haill 1586.
number was ended; yea, and that in Maclean's awn sight, being constrained thereunto, with a dolorous advertisement to prepare himself for the like tragical end howsoon they should all be killed. And when the day came that Maclean should have been brought forth, miserably to have made his tragical end, like unto the rest, it pleased Angus to lowp upon his horse, and to come forth for joy and contentment of mind, even to see and behald the tyrannical fact with his awn eyes. But it pleased God, wha mercifully deals with all men, and disappoints the decrees of the wicked, to disappoint his intent for that day also, for he was not sae soon on horseback, but the horse stumbled, and Angus fell off him, and brake his leg, and so was carried hame.'—*H. K. J.*

The personages of this well-told tale were properly designated Angus Macdonald of Islay, and Lachlan Maclean of Dowart; the latter is described by Mr Tytler as 'an island Amadis of colossal strength and stature,' 'by no means illiterate,' 'and possessing, by the vigour of his natural talents, a commanding influence over the rude and fierce islesmen.' Angus of Islay was step-son to the Irish Earl of Tyrone, and much mixed up with the troubled politics of the north of Ireland in that age. There was an old feud regarding land between Angus and his brother-in-law Maclean. In 1585, it received fresh excitement from an outrage on the laws of hospitality committed by Maclean's people upon the retinue of Donald Mor of Sleat, when that chief chanced to take shelter from a storm in the isle of Jura. Angus of Islay, having gone to visit Maclean soon after, was seized and imprisoned along with his followers; and he was not liberated till he had agreed to renounce the disputed lands. Such, in reality, was the nature of the visit which the annalist has described as prompted by deceit on the part of Angus. With one of the two hostages exacted from Angus on this occasion, Maclean soon after went to Islay to see after the recovered lands; with strange simplicity, he complied with an invitation of Angus to visit him at his house of Mullintrea, though not till he had received repeated protestations that no harm was intended to him. Here it was that the barbarous circumstances related by our annalist took place.[1]

By the intervention of a royal message, and the interference of the acting head of the clan Campbell, Angus rendered up Maclean, 'on receiving a promise of pardon for his crimes, and on eight

[1] *Gregory's History of the Western Highlands and Isles*, p. 234.

1586. hostages of rank being placed in his hands by Maclean, for the performance of certain conditions which the latter was forced to subscribe. To complete this singular picture of barbarism, Lachlan was no sooner free, than he ravaged Islay with fire and sword; in requital of which, Angus ravaged the isles of Mull and Tiree, killing every human inhabitant and every beast that fell into his hands.

The various clans siding with their respective friends in this contest, it became the cause of a general war throughout the islands and West Highlands, which lasted some time, notwithstanding every effort of the government to put it down.

Oct. 8. The Master of Yester, whom we have just seen as a peace-breaker, comes once more before the Council as a turbulent and wicked person. Sir John Stewart of Traquair, and his brother James Stewart of Shillinglaw, lieutenant of his majesty's guard, appear as complainers, setting forth, in the first place, how it is well known of Sir John Stewart, that 'having his dwelling-place on the south side of Tweed, in a room[1] subject to the invasions and thieves of the broken men of the Borders, and lying betwixt them and sundry his majesty's true lieges, whom commonly they herry and oppress, how at all times himself, his brother, his friends and neighbours assisting him, dwelling betwixt the burgh of Peebles and Gaithopeburn, resistit the stouthreif and oppressions of the said thieves and broken men, to the comfort and relief of mony true men, in whilk course they intend, God willing, to continue to their lives end.' Of late, however, so proceeds the complaint, 'they have been, and is greatumly hindered therein, by reason that William, Master of Yester, by the causing, direction, at least owersicht and tolerance, of William Lord Hay of Yester, his father, sheriff of Peebles and provost of the burgh of Peebles (wha, by the laws of this realm . . . . aucht to mak his said son answerable,' but had 'placit him in the principal house and strength of Neidpath,' though he has been a denounced rebel for nearly the space of a year 'for his inobedience to underlie the laws,' till within the last few days that he obtained relaxation) . . . . had in the meantime 'not only usurpit and taken upon him the charge of the sheriffship of Peebles, and provostry of the burgh thereof, but ane absolute command to proclaim and hald wappinshawings at times nawise appointit by his hieness'

[1] Estate—piece of ground.

direction, to banish and give up kindness to all persons in burgh or land where he pleases, to tak up men's gear under pretence of unlaws fra wappinshawings or other unnecessar causes, never being lawfully callit nor convenit; . . . . and forder, it is weel knawn to sundry of the lords of Secret Council, that the said Master socht the life of the said James Stewart, and dayly shores and boasts[1] to slay him, and all others of his kin, friends, allies, assisters, and partakers.' On the petition of the complainers, the Council heard parties, the peccant Master appearing for himself, and in excuse for his father, who was sick and unable to travel. And the end of the matter was, that the case was remitted to the judgment of the Court of Session, to be decided by them as they might think proper. Meanwhile, the Master was enjoined to cease molesting the Stewarts and their friends and dependents between this and the 8th of January next.—*P. C. R.* 1586.

On the 29th April 1587, it is stated that the king had dealt between these hostile parties, and arranged *letters of affirmance* between them, in order to secure peace for the future; but the Master of Yester had refused to subscribe. For this he is threatened with being denounced rebel, or, as the ordinary phrase was, being put to the horn.[2] On the 12th May, the king ordered him to enter in ward north of the Tay, and there remain till liberated; and a few weeks later, on this order not being complied with, the Master was denounced rebel, and all forbidden to assist or receive him.—*P. C. R.*

In a memoir of the Hays of Tweeddale, composed by a member of the family a century later, the character and objects of the parties in this dispute are precisely reversed. The Master of Yester—whose nickname, it seems, was *Wood-sword*—is described as a great upholder of the laws against thieves, while the Stewarts of Traquair were the reverse. The passage is worth transcribing, as an example of the favourable views of which a man's actions are always more or less susceptible in the eyes of friends, especially after the lapse of a few years.

'In his time, the Borders being much infested with broken men and thieving, this lord, who always rode accompanied with twenty-four horsemen and as many footmen armed, did take

[1] Threatens.

[2] A horn had originally, or perhaps was still used, in proclaiming a man rebel; hence the term, horning, or being put to the horn.

1586. and hanged a great [many] of them. He was at feud with the house of Traquair for seconding the thieves, in pursuit of whom he received a wound in the face. King James the Sixth being desirous to have this feud taken away, as all others of the country, and he refusing, was committed to the Castle of Edinburgh, out of which he made his escape, and immediately made ane new inroad against the thieves, of whom he killed a great many, in a place called from thence the *Bloody Haugh*, near Riskin-hope, in Rodonna; whereupon King James was pleased to make a hunting journey, and came to the house of Neidpath, whither the king called Traquair, with his two sons, who made to Lord Yester acknowledgment for the wrong they had done him, and then peace was made by the king.[1] This was witnessed by one William Geddes, who was my lord's butler, and lived till the year 1632.'—*Genealogy of the Hays of Tweeddale, by Father R. A. Hay.*

1586-7. FEB. A few days before the death of Queen Mary in Fotheringay Castle, the king, her son, 'to manifest his natural affection towards his dearest mother, whose preservation he always earnestly wished, required the ministers to pray for her, at all preachings and common prayers, after the following form: "The Lord illuminate and enlighten her spirit, that she may attain to the knowledge of his truth, for the safety of soul and body, and preserve her from the present peril."

'Some of the ministry agreed to that form of prayer, thinking it very lawful, since it was his majesty's pleasure; but some of them, especially the ministers of Edinburgh, refused to pray but as they were moved by the spirit.'

'On the 3d of February [five days before Mary's execution], the king appointed Patrick, Archbishop of St Andrews, a man evil thought of by the ministry and others, to preach in the kirk of Edinburgh, and resolved to attend the preaching himself.[2] When the day came, Mr John Coupar, one of the ministers of Edinburgh, accompanied with the rest of the brethren, came in

[1] October . . . 1587, 'his majesty raid with ane host to Peebles, for order-taking with the broken men, and returnit the tent day.'—*Moysie's Memoirs.*

[2] It is understood that this was the place of worship formed out of the choir or eastern portion of the church of St Giles. Opposite to the pulpit, which was attached to the first pillar from the east end, was the royal gallery or loft, also attached to a pillar. Thus the king and the minister were sufficiently near each other for the colloquies in which they occasionally indulged. See Wilson's *Memorials of Edinburgh.*

and prevented the bishop, by taking place in the pulpit before his coming into the kirk; and as the said John was beginning the prayer, the king's majesty commanded him to stop: whereupon he gave a knock on the pulpit, using an exclamation in these terms: "This day shall bear witness against you in the day of the Lord. Wo be to thee, O Edinburgh! for the last of thy plagues shall be worse than the first!" After having uttered these words, he passed down from the pulpit, and, together with the whole wives in the kirk, removed out of the same.'—*Moy. R.* 1586-7.

Another account says: 'The Bishop of St Andrews went up, and, after the English form, began to beck in a low courtesy to the king; whereas the custom of this kirk was first to salute God, to do God's work, and then, after sermon and divine worship, to give reverence and make courtesy particularly to the king. But soon after the bishop was entered into the pulpit, all the people in the kirk gave a shout and loud cry, so as nothing could be heard, and almost all ran out of the kirk, especially the women. . . . . This carriage of the people made the king rise up and cry: "What devil ails the people, that they may not tarry to hear a man preach!"'—*Row.*

The archbishop 'preached a sermon concerning prayer for princes, whereby he convinced the whole people who remained in the kirk, that the desire of the king's majesty to pray for his mother was most honourable and reasonable.'—*Moy. R.*

It gives a striking idea of the difficulty attending the transmission of intelligence in those days—in connection, it must be owned, in this instance, with the deceitful and stealthy conduct of Elizabeth—that Mary had been upwards of a fortnight dead before her son King James was fully apprised of the fact in Edinburgh. On the 15th, he received a message from Kerr of Cessford, the warden of the Borders, informing him that the English warden had just communicated to him this sad intelligence. Not believing it on this authority, the king went to hunt at Calder, but at the same time sent his secretary to Berwick to make inquiry. This gentleman returned on the 23d, with certain information of Mary's death. 'This put his majesty into a very great displeasure and grief, so that he went to bed that night without supper; and on the morrow, by seven o'clock, went to Dalkeith, there to remain solitary.'—*Moy. R.*

'Certain it is that King James, her only son, was not a little moved to hear such unparalleled and uncouth news, who loved his dearest mother with the greatest piety that could be seen in a son.

1586-7. [He] took exceeding grief to heart, not without deep displeasure for the same; and much lamented and mourned for her many days.'—*Pa. And.*

Many years after, when he had mounted the English throne, King James told Sir James Harrington, that his mother's death had been foreseen in Scotland, 'being, as he said, "spoken of in secret by those whose power of [second] sight presented to them a bloody head dancing in the air." He did remark much on this gift, and said he had sought out of certain books a sure way to attain knowledge of future chances.'[1]

Attention was strongly fixed at this time on the confidence manifested by such as were of the Catholic religion, chiefly gentry, in entertaining Jesuits and seminary priests, who performed mass in their houses, and even took possession of some of the ruinous parish churches, doing what in them lay to seduce the people back to the old faith. We are told, for instance, that Lord Maxwell openly caused mass to be sung in the abbey-church of Lincluden, near Dumfries, on three successive days at Christmas 1586. Pasch and Yule began again to be kept by the common sort of people, and saints' wells were much resorted to for the cure of diseases. The General Assembly declared it to be 'ane exceeding great grief to all such as have any spunk of the love of God and his kirk,' to see the land thus polluted with 'idolatry' and 'pusionable doctrine.' They considered the evil as chiefly owing to the laxity of the state in the repression of papistry, and the positive encouragement which it rendered in some instances to papists. At the same time, the reformed religion was in miserable condition, many of the parish kirks being ruinous and destitute of pastors, while the pastors that did anywhere exist were defrauded of their revenues, starved, and sometimes greatly abused in their very persons by the papist gentle-folks. A great defection was seriously apprehended as now imminent, unless some change should take place in the king's counsels and conduct. He was pathetically exhorted to execute the laws against both the priests and their entertainers. It was demanded, in particular, that all papist noblemen should be 'presently exiled the country,' while certain of the priests should be sent away by the first ships, with certification that

[1] Harrington's *Nugæ Antiquæ*, by Park. 2 vols. 1804. Vol. i., p. 369.

on their daring to return they should be hanged without further process. 1586-7.

According to the same General Assembly, the moral condition of the country was awful, 'ugly heaps of all kinds of sin lying in every nook and part' of it—no spot but what was overwhelmed as by 'a spate' [inundation], 'with abusing of the blessed name of God, with swearing, perjury, and lies, with profaning of the Sabbath-day with mercats, gluttony, drunkenness, fighting, playing, dancing, &c., with rebelling against magistrates and the laws of the country, with blood touching blood, with incest, fornication, adulteries, and sacrilege, theft and oppression, with false witness[ing], and finally with all kinds of impiety and wrong.' The poor at the same time 'vaiging [wandering] in great troops and companies through the country, without either law or religion.'—*B. U. K.*

The French poet, Guillaume Sallust, Sieur du Bartas, paid a visit to Scotland. For any eminent literary man of either England or France to travel north of the Tweed, was as yet a rarity and a marvel. The king, however, had contracted an admiration of Du Bartas, and translated some of his poetry; and now a royal invitation had brought him to Holyrood. It would be curious to learn what were the sentiments of the polite Frenchman on coming in contact with James's circle at the palace, or seeing the rude state of the people generally throughout the country. 1587. MAY.

We learn that 'he was received according to his worthiness, entertained honourably, and liberally propined'—that is, favoured with presents. At the end of June, the king made an excursion to St Andrews, taking the French poet along with him, that he might see the principal seat of learning in Scotland. We have some curious particulars of the visit from the Dutch pencil of James Melville. St Mary's College, the principal theological seminary of the country, was now presided over by the faithful Presbyterian Andrew Melville, the man of most marked talent and energy in the Scotch church after the days of Knox. In the Castle lived, in much reduced state, the nominal archbishop, Patrick Adamson, a man of fine literary talents, but weak in character, and, upon the whole, not a credit to Scottish Episcopacy. James admired and patronised Adamson; but he had a trembling faith in the powerful wit and inflexible courage and integrity of Melville. The king, 'coming first without any warning to

1587. the new college [St Mary's], he calls for Mr Andrew, saying he was come with that gentleman to have a lesson. Mr Andrew answers, "that he had teached his ordinar that day in the forenoon." "That is all ane," says the king; "I maun have a lesson, and be here within an hour for that effect." And indeed, within less than an hour, his majesty was in the school, and the haill university convenit with him, before whom Mr Andrew extempore entreated maist clearly and mightily of the right government of Christ, and in effect refuted the haill acts of parliament made against the discipline thereof, to the great instruction and comfort of his auditory, except the king alane, wha was very angry all that night.'

On the morrow, 'the bishop had baith a prepared lesson and feast made for the king. His lesson was a tighted-up abridgment of all he had teached the year bypast—namely, anent the corrupt grounds whilk he had put in the king's head contrary to the true discipline. To the whilk lesson Mr Andrew went contrair to his custom, and with his awn pen marked all his false grounds and reasons; and without further [preparation] causit ring his bell at twa afternoon the same day, whereof the king hearing, he sent to Mr Andrew, desiring him to be moderate and have regard to his presence, otherwise he wald discharge him. He answerit courageously, that his majesty's ear and tender breast was piteously and dangerously filled with errors and untruths by that wicked man, the whilk he could not suffer to pass, and brook a life [and yet remain alive]; otherwise, except the stopping of the breath of God's mouth and prejudging of his truth, he should behave himself maist moderately and reverently to his majesty in all respects. The king sent again to him and me, desiring it should be sae, and shawing that he wald have his four hours [a light meal at four o'clock] in the college, and drink with Mr Andrew. Sae, coming to that lesson with the bishop, wha requested the king for leave to make answer instantly in case anything were spoken against his doctrine. But there Mr Andrew, making him [affecting] as though he had naething to do but with the papist, brings out their warks, and reads out of them all the bishop's grounds and reasons. The whilk, when he had at length and maist clearly shawn to be plain papistry, then he sets against the same with all his mean [power], and with immutable force of reasoning, from clear grounds of Scripture, with a mighty parrhesie and flood of eloquence, he dings them sae down, that the bishop was dashed and strucken as dumb as the stock he sat upon. After

the lesson, the king, in his mother-tongue, made some distingoes, 1587.
and discoursit a while thereon, and gave certain injunctions to the university for reverencing and obeying of his bishop; wha fra that day furth began to tire of his teaching, and to fall mair and mair in disgrace and confusion. The king, with Monsieur du Bartas, came to the college-hall, where I causit prepare and have in readiness a banquet of wet and dry confections, with all sorts of wine, whereat his majesty campit very merrily a gude while, and thereafter went to his horse. But Monsieur du Bartas tarried behind, and conferrit with my uncle and me a whole hour, and syne followed after the king; wha inquiring of him that night, as ane tauld me, "What was his judgment of the twa he had heard in St Andrews?" he answerit the king, "that they were baith learned men, but the bishop's were cunned [conned] and prepared matters, and Mr Andrew had a great ready store of all kind of learning within him; and, by [besides] that, Mr Andrew's spreit and courage was far above the other." The whilk judgment the king approved.'

The Sieur du Bartas was 'dismissed in the harvest, to his majesty's great praise, sae lang as the French tongue is used and understood in the world.'—*Ja. Mel.*

The small merchant-craft of Scotland was much troubled with pirates, chiefly of the English nation. James Melville gives a lively account of an affair with an English piratical vessel, which took place in connection with the Fife port where he served as pastor.

'At my first coming to Anstruther there fell out a heavy accident, whilk vexit my mind mickle at first, but drew me mickle nearer my God, and teached me what it was to have a care of a flock. Ane of our crears,[1] returning from England, was beset by an English pirate, pill[ag]ed, and a very guid honest man of Anstruther slain therein. The whilk loon[2] coming pertly to the very road of Pittenweem, spulyied a ship lying therein, and misused the men thereof. This wrang could not be suffered by our men, lest they should be made a common prey to sic limmers.[3] Therefore, purchasing a commission, they riggit out a proper fly-boat, and every man encouraging another, made almaist the haill honest and best men in all the town to go in her to the sea. This was a great vexation and grief to my heart, to see

[1] A light bark with one mast. [2] Rascal. [3] Worthless fellows.

1587. at my first entry the best part of my flock ventured upon a pack of pirates, whereof the smallest member of the meanest was mair in valour[1] than a shipful of them. And yet I durst not stay some [un]less nor I stayed all, and all I durst not, baith for the dangerous preparative, and the friends of the honest man wha was slain, and of them that were abusit, wha were many, in sic sort as the matter concerned the haill. But my God knaws what a sair heart they left behind when they parted out of my sight, or rather what a heart they carried with them, leaving a bouk[2] behind. I neither ate, drank, nor sleepit, but by constraint of nature, my thought and care always being upon them, and commending them to God, till aucht or ten days were endit, and they in sight returning, with all guid tokens of joy, flags, streamers, and ensignie displayed, whom with great joy we receivit, and went together to the kirk, and praised God.

'The captain, for the time, a godly, wise, and stout man, recounted to me truly their haill proceeding. That they, meeting with their admiral, a great ship of St Andrews, weel riggit out by the burghs, being fine of sail, went before her all the way, and made every ship they forgathered with, of whatsomever nation, to strike and do homage to the king of Scotland, shawing them for what cause they were riggit forth, and inquiring of knaves and pirates. At last, they meet with a proud stiff Englishman, wha refuses to do reverence; therefore the captain, thinking it was a loon, commands to give them his *nose-piece*,[3] the whilk delashit[4] lights on the tie of the Englishman's mainsail, and down it comes; then he yields, being but a merchant. But there was the merciful providence of God, in staying a great piece of the Englishman, lying out her stern in readiness to be shot, whilk, if it had lighted amang our folks, being many in little room, without fence, wald have cruelly demeaned them all. But God, directing that first shot, preserved them. From them they approached to the shore at Suffolk, and finds by Providence the loon [rogue], wha had newlins taken a crear of our awn town, and was spulying her. Howsoon they spy ane coming warlike, the loons leave their prize, and run their ship on land, our fly-boat after, and almaist was on land with them; yet, staying hard by, they delash their ordnance at the loons, and a number going a-land, pursues and takes a half-dozen of them, and puts them aboard in their boat. The gentlemen of the

[1] Value.
[2] A bulk, a corpse.
[3] A gun in the poop of the ship.
[4] Discharged.

country and towns beside, hearing the noise of shooting, gathers with haste, supposing the Spanyard had landed, and apprehending a number of the loons in our men's hands, desirit to knaw the matter. The whilk when the justices of peace understood, and saw the king of Scotland's arms, with twa gallant ships in warlike manner, yielded and gave reverence thereto, suffering our folks to take with them their prisoners and pirate's ship, whilk they brought with them, with half-a-dozen of the loons; whereof twa were hangit on our pier-end, the rest in St Andrews; with nae hurt at all to any of our folks, wha ever since syne have been free from English pirates. All praise to God for ever. Amen.' 1587.

King James at this time attempted what Dr Robertson, with somewhat too much complaisance, calls a work worthy of a king. Many of his nobility were at feud with each other on account of past grievances. For example, Glammis bore deadly hatred against the Earl of Crawford, in consequence of the killing of his father by some of Crawford's people at Stirling in 1578. With the Earl of Angus, whose piety and love of the clergy induced James to call him *the Ministers' King*, it was sufficient ground of hostility against the Earl of Montrose that he had sat as chancellor on the jury which adjudged Morton to the Maiden. The Earls of Huntly and Marischal had some mutual grudge of their own, perhaps little intelligible to southern men. So it was with others. The nobility being now assembled at a convention, James, who never could check outrages amongst them by the sword of justice, did what a good-natured weak man could to induce them to be reconciled to each other, and call it peace when there was no peace. Assembling them all at a banquet in Holyrood on a Sunday, he drank to them thrice, and solemnly called on them to maintain concord, threatening to be an enemy to him who should first disobey the injunction. Next day, after supper, then an early meal, and after 'many scolls' had been drunk to each other, he made them all march in procession 'in their doublets' up the Canongate, two and two, holding by each other's hands, and each pair being a couple of reconciled enemies. He himself went in front, with Lord Hamilton on his right hand, and the Lord Chancellor Maitland on the left; next after, the Duke of Lennox and Lord Claud Hamilton; then Angus and Montrose, Huntly and Marischal, Crawford and the Master of Glammis. Coming to the Tolbooth, his majesty ordered all the prisoners for debt to be released. Thence he advanced to the picturesque

May 15.

1587. old market-cross, covered with tapestry for the occasion, and where the magistrates had set out a long table well furnished with bread, wine, and sweetmeats. Amidst the blare of trumpets and the boom of cannon, the young monarch publicly drank to his nobles, wishing them peace and happiness, and made them all drink to each other. The people, long accustomed to sights of bloody contention, looked on with unspeakable joy, danced, broke into songs of mirth, and brought out all imaginable musical instruments to give additional, albeit discordant expression, to their happiness. All acknowledged that no such sight had ever been seen in Edinburgh. In the general transport, the gloomy gibbet, usually kept standing there in readiness, was cast down, as if it could never again be needed. Sweetmeats, and glasses from which toasts had been drunk, flew about both from the table of the feast and from the responsive parties on the *fore-stairs*. When all was done, the king and nobles returned in the same form as they had come.—*Moy. Bir. Cal. H. K. J.*

Healing measures like these were not nearly so good as they seemed. In less than two months, we find six or seven of the nobles quarrelling about priority of voting, and Lord Home passing a challenge to Lord Fleming—'wha were not sufferit to fecht, albeit they were baith weel willing.'

King James had a sincere antipathy to deadly feuds and quarrels, because he loved peace and good-humour; but timidity, want of strong will, and partly, perhaps, his very *bonhomie*, prevented him from taking those severe measures with offenders which alone could effectually repress such practices. He desired to correct men by proclamations, or at the most 'hornings;' and when one gentleman had literally killed his neighbour in a casual rencontre, the king was satisfied if he could induce the son or other relations of the deceased to meet the guilty person, make up matters for a sum of money, shake hands, and agree there should be no more of it. He liked to be personally busy in effecting reconciliations, and at length came to use what he considered as compulsory measures for bringing the parties to his presence, that he might see to their renewing friendship. Thus, on the 22d November 1599, an edict of council was sent to James Hoppringle of Galashiels, and George Hoppringle of Blindlee, commanding them to come and submit the quarrel standing between them to the arbitrament of friends, on pain of being charged with rebellion. On the 12th of January ensuing, James Tweedie of Drumelzier and William Veitch of Dawick were charged, under like pains, to come and subscribe letters of assurance, for 'the feid and inimitie standing betwixt them.'—*P. C. R.* 1587.

In consequence of a bad crop in 1586, there was 'great scant and dearth' this year, 'and great death of people for hunger.'—*H. K. J.*

Elizabeth issued a proclamation regarding scarcity, 2d January 1586–7. She speaks of 'foreseeing the general dearth of corn and other victuals, partly through the unseasonableness of the year past, whereby want hath grown more in some countries than in others, but most of all, generally, through the uncharitable greediness of great corn-masters, &c.' This was the invariable cry on all occasions of dearth. All would be well if only those possessing grain would not reserve it in hope of higher prices. No one ever dreamed of that benefit which the modern political economist sees in the reservings of the corn-merchant—namely, an equalising of consumption over the whole period of the scarcity, as contrasted with the over-free use of the victual at first, and increased scarcity afterwards. Perhaps there was, after all, some grounds for the wrath at forestallers, for in former days, as we well know, there was less means of obtaining information regarding the extent of the failure of a crop than there is now, and those gentlemen, accordingly, were rather speculators on a possible, than on an ascertained case. They would hence appear as men aiming at the making of a scarcity where there was perhaps no great occasion for it. What offence greater, the poor public would naturally say, than that of deliberately trying to starve us!

King James had lately sent Vans of Barnbarroch, and his own ex-preceptor, Peter Young, as ambassadors to Denmark, to negotiate a match with the daughter of Frederick II. He now (June 14, 1587) wrote to those gentlemen, ordering them to see to certain Scotch ships which had gone to Dantzic for grain, designing to carry it to other foreign ports for a profit: he demands that they shall not be passed by the *tollender* at Elsinore, till the skippers enter into an obligation to bring the grain to Scotland, 'for the relief of the puir and supply of the dearth and scarcity.'[1] How would a modern corn-merchant feel if his vessels were now stopped at the Sound with such a demand as this!

[1] *Maitland Club Miscellany*, i. 276.

1587. SEP. Patrick Hamilton, brother of the Laird of Preston, and captain of Brodick Castle in Arran, was denounced rebel for not appearing before the king and Council, to answer a complaint of Abacuck Bisset, writer to the Signet in Edinburgh. It appears that Patrick, accompanied by two nephews, had attacked Mr Bisset in St Giles's Kirk in Edinburgh, during the sitting of parliament, with a sword, and cut off 'the haill fingers of his left hand.'

This Abacuck Bisset was clerk to Sir John Skene, Lord Clerk Register. He compiled a treatise entitled *The Rolment of Courtis, contenand the Auldest Lawis, Actis, Statutis, Constitutionis, and Antiquities of His Majesties Native and maist Ancient Realme of Scotland, as ane Frie Kingdome, &c.*

We have hitherto heard the name of Queen Mary chiefly in connection with tragic matters: verily a name of tears. For once we find her connected with a piece of pleasantry, and it was in association with the author of the *Rolment of Courtis.* The father of this worthy writer was caterer to the queen. One day, as she was passing to mass, he acquainted her with his having a child to be baptised, and desired her to assign the infant its name. She said she would open the Bible in the chapel, and whatever name she cast up, that should be given to the child. The name cast up was that of the prophet Habakkuk, which, in the form of Abacuck, was accordingly conferred on the future writer.

Abacuck Bisset's *Rolment of Courtis* exists in manuscript in the Advocates' Library, only a portion of it, containing *A Short Form of Process* for civil cases, having been printed. It was composed in the old age of the author, after the commencement of the reign of Charles I., and seems to have been designed for immediate publication, as it is prefaced with sundry of those complimentary verses with which authors used to gratify each other in days while as yet reviews were not. One set of these, by Mr Alexander Craig of Rose Craig, and which appears in his *Poetical Exercises* (Raban, Aberdeen, 1623), is not without some feeling:

'Twixt *was* and *is* how various are the odds!
What one man doth another doth undo;
One consecrates religious works to gods,
Another leaves sad wrecks and ruins new.
This book doth shew that such and such things were,
But would to God that it could say, They are!

'When I perceive the south, north, east, and west, 1587.
And mark, alas! each monument amiss,
Then I confer times present with the past,
I read what was, but cannot tell what is:
I praise thy book with wonder, but am sorry
To read old ruins in a recent story.'

Abacuck himself appears to have had a turn for verse, and in this form he gives his poetical friends notice of the contents of his book, that they may address him regarding it. After a great deal of very dry prose matters about decreets, suspensions, exceptions, &c., he either makes or quotes the following:

CERTAIN AULD RULES CONTEINED IN THE ANCIENT REGISTER OF SCOTLAND ANENT THE MEITHIS AND MERCHES OF LAND.

All landis, wherever they be
In Scotland partis, has merches three,
Headroom, water, and montis borde,
As eldren men has made record.
Your headroom to the hill direct,
Frae your haugh tilled in effect.
Betwixt twa glenis ane montis borde,
Divides thae glenis, I sall stand for 't.
Water comand frae ane glen head,
Divides that glen, and stanches feid.
Thortrom[1] burnis in montis hie
Sall stop nae headroom, though they be.

The meaning of all this is, that ancient custom in Scotland recognised three natural divisions or boundaries for land—1. Headroom, the termination of a piece of territory on the summit of the slope of the adjacent hill; 2. The line of hills between two glens; 3. The river passing through a glen. A water crossing the headroom on the summit of the mountains made no difference.[2]

[1] Transverse.

[2] It is to be feared that Abacuck was a person of a litigious and troublesome temper. A complaint was made against him before the Privy Council by Kenneth M'Kenzie of Kintail, to the effect that Bisset had purchased letters to force Kenneth to produce a clansman named Rory M'Allister M'Kenzie, alleged to be at the horn for default in a civil cause. It was alleged that, knowing that on the case being called, he (Kenneth) could shew many good arguments for exonerating himself of this responsibility, Bisset had delayed the calling, in hopes of being able to do it when Kenneth should not be at hand to make his own defence. The matter being brought fully before the Lords in the presence of parties, it was decreed that Kenneth should be absolved from the duty implied in Bisset's letters.—*P. C. R.*

In July 1608, Abacuck was involved in a still worse-looking affair. He was charged before the Privy Council with having prosecuted Mr William Reid, of Aberdeen, in a malicious manner at law, from no cause but that of 'some little eleist' fallen out between him and Andrew Reid, brother of William, in which the said William had no interest. He had also

1587. 'The pest brake up in harvest in Leith, by opening up of some old kists, and in Edinburgh about the 4th of November. It continued in these two towns this winter till Candlemass.'—*Cal.*

This pest 'strake a great terror in Edinburgh and all the coast-side,' says James Melville. He adds: 'By occasion thereof, we began the exercise of daily doctrine and prayers in our kirk, whilk continues to this day with great profit and comfort, baith of the teachers and hearers.' The kirk-session of Perth appointed a fast 'with great humiliation' for eight days. In those days, there was scarcely any other recognised method of averting pestilence. The same simple diarist tells us: 'This winter the king was occupied in commenting of the Apocalypse, and in setting out of sermons thereupon against the Papists and Spaniards: and yet, by a piece of great oversight, the Papists practised never more busily in this land, and made greater preparation for receiving the Spaniards nor [than] that year.'

In October 1588, the town-council of Glasgow was in great apprehension of a visit of the pest, as it was then in Paisley. They made arrangements for guarding the ports to prevent the entrance of people from the infected district.—*M. of G.*

1587-8. FEB. Mr James Gordon, a Jesuit, uncle to the Earl of Huntly, being now in Edinburgh, 'his majesty took purpose to convene some of the ministry of Edinburgh within his own chamber in Holyrood-house, and to send for the said Mr James; who coming before his majesty, his highness declared the cause for which he had sent for him, which was, that as he understood him to be a learned man, come into this country on purpose to persuade the people to embrace the popish religion, he would therefore shew him that his majesty was himself disposed to use some reasoning with him on religion. Whereunto Mr James objected, and said that he desired not to reason with his majesty, but would reason with any other. [James was now only twenty-one.] The king's majesty, answering, offered and promised to lay his crown and royalty aside, and to reason with him as if he were a private man. And so his majesty began and laid down some grounds of religion, which he still observed and reasoned upon for the space of four or five hours. Some things were yielded to by Mr James, and others denied. . . . . The said Mr James was kept in a chamber in Holyrood-

traduced William Hay in regard to the propriety of his marriage, though it was well known to be 'an honest and famous marriage.' The Council found the charge just, and commanded Abacuck's proceedings to be stopped.

house five or six days, and then appointed to pass to Seaton, till he was ready to depart off the country.'—*Moy. R.* 1587-8.

Alison Peirson, in Byrchill, was tried for witchcraft. The verdict recites a number of strange and incoherent charges which had been proved against her, but whose entire tenor only shews that she was a sickly nervous woman, who took her own dreams and fancies for realities. According to her own account, she had learned unlawful arts from her cousin, Mr William Simpson, son of one who had been the king's smith at Stirling, and who had acquired his skill from a big Egyptian, by whom he had been carried away in his childhood and kept for twelve years. Being in her own youth afflicted with loss of power in one of her sides, she had applied to Mr William in Lothian, and he had not only cured her, but taught her by charms to be a healer of disease herself. Since then, she had haunted the company of the queen of Elfame, but had not seen her for the last seven years. At one time she had many good friends in Elfame; but they were all dead now. Sometimes she would be in her bed quite well, but could not tell where or in what state she might be next day. Lying down sick in Grangemuir, near Anstruther, she had seen a man in green clothes, whom she asked to help her: he went away at that time, but appeared afterwards with a multitude of people, when 'she sanit her [blessed herself] and prayit, and passed with them further nor she could tell; and saw with them piping, and merriness, and gude cheer, and was carried to Lothian, and saw wine-puncheons with tasses [cups] with them.' 'Ofttimes they wald come and sit beside her, and promised that she should never want gif she wald be faithful and keep promises, but, gif she wald speak and tell of them and their doings, they sould martyr her.' For the last sixteen years, Alison had been frequenting St Andrews as a practitioner in unlawful methods of healing; and where among her patients had been no less a person than the titular Archbishop Adamson—a fact of which his enemies did not fail to take advantage in pasquinading him. For the healing of his grace, Simpson had bidden her 'make ane saw [salve] and rub it on his cheeks, his craig, his breast, stomach, and sides, and siclike gave her directions to use the ewe-milk, or waidrave [probably woodroof], with the herbs, claret wine; and with some other things she gave him ane sodden fowl; and that she made ane quart at ance, whilk he drank at twa draughts, twa sundry diets.' Poor Alison was convicted and burnt.—*Pit.* 1588. May 28.

1588. July 21. At the very time when the Spanish Armada was at sea on its way to England, a Catholic pair of high rank, much though secretly interested in favour of that enterprise, were wedded at Holyrood. The bridegroom was the young Earl of Huntly, and the bride Henrietta Stuart, eldest daughter of the late Duke of Lennox. The affair was conducted with 'great triumph, mirth, and pastime;' but some of the other circumstances were of a more remarkable nature. The Presbyterian clergy, in a paroxysm of apprehension about the Armada, took up the strange position of refusing to allow the marriage to be performed by any clergyman capable of shewing his face in the country, unless the earl should first sign the Confession of Faith—that is, abjure his religion. Huntly was induced to profess an inclination to comply, but professed to stickle at some of the Protestant doctrines. The king, on the other hand, who felt as the father of the bride, and knew that Huntly was in reality his friend, favoured and facilitated the match. To the great chagrin of the Presbyterian clergy, the ceremony was at length performed by Patrick Adamson, archbishop of St Andrews—who, however, was afterwards brought to their feet as an abject penitent, declaring, among other things, 'I married the Earl of Huntly contrair the kirk's command, without the confession of his faith, and profession of the sincere doctrine of the Word; I repent, and craves God pardon.'[1] The writer of Adamson's life in the *Biographia Britannica* has characterised this as 'one of the completest instances of ecclesiastical folly and bigotry recorded in history.' Perhaps if this biographer had been a Scottish Protestant of 1588, he would not have thought so; but the affair may at least somewhat abate our surprise that the Earl of Huntly was found next year in arms against the Protestant interest.[2]

July 30. Sir William Stuart of Monkton, a younger brother of the ill-famed ex-chancellor, 'Captain James,' and said to be 'in qualities and behaviour naething different' from that personage, had for some years had place at the king's court, serving the government in various capacities. Only a few weeks before this date, he had conducted an expedition by which the Castle of Lochmaben was taken from the rebellious Maxwells. The captain and five of the garrison had been hung up on the green before the gate,

[1] *Melville's Diary*, 291.

[2] The conduct of the clergy on this occasion is defended, but in rather subdued terms, by Dr M'Crie, *Life of Andrew Melville*, i. 395.

notwithstanding a promise of their lives, alleged to have been given. Stuart was rewarded with large spoil; and on his return to Edinburgh, with Lord Maxwell as a prisoner, he was allowed to have the custody of that nobleman. 1588.

Doubtless the blood of the upstart was somewhat heated by so rich a triumph. Meeting the unruly Earl of Bothwell a few days after in the king's chamber, he fell into a dispute with him—the lie was given, and the altercation closed with a ribald exclamation on his part, followed by a threat on the other. Nothing more occurred till nearly three weeks after, when Sir William Stuart, coming down the High Street with a party of his minions, met Bothwell, accompanied by a younger brother of the Master of Gray, whom Stuart had lately delated for his betrayal of the king's interest in his ambassage for the saving of Queen Mary's life. A collision between two such parties was unavoidable. In the general fight, Stuart killed a servant of Bothwell, but thereby lost his sword. He fled into the Blackfriars' Wynd, pursued by the vengeful Bothwell, who, as Stuart stood defenceless against a wall, 'strake him in at the back and out at the belly, and killed him.'—*Bir. Cal. H. K. J.*

We are assured by a contemporary writer, that the slaughter of Sir William Stuart was 'to the comfort of mony of the people, wha allegit that God did the same for his betraying of Mr David Maxwell and his company in Lochmaben, but specially the Lord Maxwell, wha was his prisoner in John Gourlay's house.'—*C. K. Sc.* Bothwell only deemed it necessary for a few days to keep out of the way. By and by, on the king's return from a visit to Fife, he reappeared in court as usual, 'uncallit, unpursuit, unpunist for this fact.'

It is curious to find the General Assembly sitting down exactly a week after this street-conflict, and proceeding quietly with its usual work of choosing a moderator, arranging about provision for the ministers, and denouncing the papists, just as it would have done at any time nearer our own gentler day.

Great excitement prevailed throughout all Scotland, in apprehension of invasion by the Spanish Armada. There was not wanting a party prepared to co-operate with the Spaniards, if they had landed in Scotland. In this exigency, the king was compelled to forget his anger at Elizabeth on account of the recent death of his mother; he made all possible preparation for resistance, and when Sir Robert Sidney, the English ambassador, told him that if the Aug.

1588. Spaniard took England, the king might expect no greater kindness at his hand, James 'merrily answered: "That he looked for no other benefit of the Spaniard in that case, than that which Polyphemus promised to Ulysses—namely, to devour him after all his fellows were devoured."'—*Spot.*

'Terrible was the fear,' says James Melville, 'piercing were the preachings, earnest, zealous, and fervent were the prayers, sounding were the sichs and sobs, and abounding was the tears at that fast and General Assembly keepit at Edinburgh, when the news were credibly tauld, sometimes of their landing at Dunbar, sometimes at St Andrews, and in Tay, and now and then at Aberdeen and Cromarty Firth. And in very deed, as we knew certainly soon after, the Lord of armies, wha rides upon the wings of the winds, the keeper of his awn Israel, was in the meantime convoying that monstrous navy about our coasts, and directing their hulks and galiots to the islands, rocks, and sands, whereupon he had destinat their wrack and destruction. For within twa or three month thereafter, early in the morning, ane of our bailies came to my bedside, saying (but not with fray): "I have to tell you news, sir. There is arrivit within our harbour [Anstruther, on the coast of Fife] this morning a ship full of Spaniards, but not to give mercy but to ask." And sae shaws me that the commanders had landed, and he had commandit them to their ship again, till the magistrates of the town had advisit, and the Spaniards had humbly obeyit; therefore desirit me to rise and hear their petition with them. Up I got with diligence, and assembling the honest men of the town, came to the tolbooth; and after consultation taken to hear them, and what answer to make, there presents us a very reverend man of big stature, and grave and stout countenance, gray-haired, and very humble-like, wha, after meikle and very low courtesy, bowing down with his face near the ground, and touching my shoe with his hand, began his harangue in the Spanish tongue, whereof I understood the substance, and being about to answer in Latin, he having only a young man with him to be his interpreter, began and tauld ower again to us in gude English. The sum was, that King Philip, his master, had riggit out a navy and army to land in England for just causes to be avengit of many intolerable wrangs whilk he had receivit of that nation; but God for their sins had been against them, and, by storm of weather, had driven the navy by the coast of England, and him, with a certain [number] of captains, being the general of twenty hulks, upon an isle in Scotland, callit

the Fair Isle, where they made shipwreck, and where sae mony as 1588.
had escapit the merciless sea, had mair nor sax or seven weeks sufferit great hunger and cauld, till, conducting that bark out of Orkney, they were come hither as to their special friends and confederates to kiss the king's majesty's hand of Scotland (and therewith becket [bowed] even to the yird), and to find relief and comfort thereby to himself, these gentlemen captains, and the poor souldiers, whase condition was for the present maist miserable and pitiful.

'I answerit this meikle in sum: "That, howbeit neither our friendship, whilk could not be great, seeing their king and they were friends to the greatest enemy of Christ, the pope of Rome, and our king and we defied him, nor yet their cause against our neighbours and special friends of England could procure any benefit at our hands for their relief and comfort; nevertheless, they should know by experience that we were men, and sae moved by humane compassion, and Christians of better religion nor they, whilk should kythe in the fruits and effect plain contrair to theirs. For, whereas our people, resorting amang them in peaceable and lawful affairs of merchandise, were violently taken and cast in prison, their gudes and gear confiscat, and their bodies committit to the cruel flaming fire for the cause of religion, they should find naething amang us but Christian pity and warks of mercy and alms, leaving to God to work in their hearts concerning religion as it pleasit him." This being truly reported again to him by his trunshman, with great reverence he gave thanks, and said he could not make answer for their kirk and the laws and order thereof, only for himself that there were divers Scotsmen wha knew him, and to whom he had shewn courtesy and favour at Calais, and, as he supposit, some of this same town of Anstruther. Sae [I] shew him that the bailies granted him licence with the captains to go to their lodging for their refreshment, but to nane of their men to land till the ower-lord of their town was advertised, and understand the king's majesty's mind anent them. Thus, with great courtesy, he departed.

'That night, the lord being advertised, came, and on the morn, accompanied with a gude number of the gentlemen of the country round about, gave the said general and the captains presence, and after the same speeches, in effect as before, receivit them in his house, and entertained them humanely, and sufferit the souldiers to come a-land, and lie all together, to the number of thretteen score, for the maist part young beardless men, silly [weak], trauchled [worn-out], and hungred, to the whilk a day or two

1588. kail, pottage, and fish was given. . . . . The names of the commanders were Jan Gomez de Medina, general of twenty hulks, Capitan Patricio, Capitan de Legoretto, Capitan de Luffera, Capitan Mauritio, and Signor Serrano.

'Verily, all the while my heart melted within me for desire of thankfulness to God, when I remembered the prideful and cruel nature of thae people, and how they wald have usit us in case they had landit with their forces amang us; and als, the wonderful work of God's mercy and justice in making us see them, the chief commanders of them, make sic courtesy to poor seamen, and their souldiers so abjectly to beg alms at our doors and in our streets.

'In the meantime they knew not of the wrack of the rest, but supposed that the rest of the army was safely returned, till ae day I gat in St Andrews in print the wrack of the galiots in particular, with the names of the principal men, and how they were usit in Ireland and our Highlands, in Wales, and other parts of England; the whilk when I recordit to Jan Gomez, by particular and special names, O then he cried out for grief, bursted and grat. This Jan Gomez shewed great kindness to a ship of our town, whilk he fand arrestit in Calais at his hame-coming, rade to court for her, and made great roose [praise] of Scotland to his king, took the honest men to his house, and enquirit for the laird of Anstruther, for the minister, and his host; and sent hame many commendations. But we thanked God in our hearts, that we had seen them amang us in that form.'

This is on the whole a pleasing anecdote. One cannot, however, but wish that the worthy James had not commenced his speech with a taunt at the religion of the Spaniards, and that he had had the magnanimity on such an occasion to forget any injuries formerly inflicted by that nation upon his.

The shipwrecked Spaniards were not everywhere so well treated. The kirk-session of Perth, May 18, 1589, ordered the keepers of the town-gates to exclude *Spaniards and other idle vagabonds and beggars,* and commanded that all such persons now in the town should immediately leave it.

'In the beginning of October [1588], one of these great ships was drove in at the Mull of Kintyre, in which there were five hundred men or thereby; she carried threescore brass cannon in her, besides others, and great store of gold and silver. She was soon after suddenly blown up by powder, and two or three hundred men in her, which happened by some of their own people.'—*Moy. R.*

Another of the vessels, having found its way into the Firth of Clyde, sank in ten fathom water on a sandy bottom, near Portincross Castle in Ayrshire. Tradition affirms that some of the crew in this case reached the land. A local newspaper, in October 1855, recorded the recent death of Archibald Revie, at Lower Boydstone, Ardrossan, at an advanced age—a descendant of one of the Spanish sailors saved from the Spanish ship at Portincross in 1588, and who 'retained many of the peculiarities of his race.' In 1740, a number of pieces of brass and iron ordnance were recovered from this wreck by means of a diving-machine; and one of the latter still lies on the beach beside the old castle, bearing faint traces of the Spanish crown and arms near the breech.[1] 1588.

The Earl of Bothwell having been drawn into the designs of the popish lords—though led only by a common hatred of the Chancellor Maitland—raised a company of men, under pretence of an expedition for the pacification of the remote isle of Lewis. Under favour of a royal warrant, he demanded a subsidy of five thousand merks from the city of Edinburgh. Meeting a refusal, he said he should 'cause the carles disgorge him a thousand crowns in spite of their hearts.' There was some resolution in these gentle burghers. When Bothwell impudently carried off one of their number, named James Nicol, to Crichton Castle, as a means of extorting money from him, they 'threatened to pull Bothwell out of Crichton by the ears, and make his house equal with the ground.' On their complaint to the king, 'Bothwell, fearing the king and the town of Edinburgh, set James Nicol at liberty, and so gained nothing but shame and discredit to himself.'—*Cal.* SEP.

Though Eustachius Roche is still described as tacksman-general of the mines, it is to be suspected that that adventure was seen to be unproductive, as we find him now entering upon a new contract with the king for a wholly different object. He proposed to make a superior kind of salt by a cheap process, assigning the profits to the king, excepting only a tenth for himself and his heirs, 'unsubject to confiscation for ony offence or crime.' He assured the king that this project would add a hundred thousand merks yearly to his revenue. The king on his part gave him the exclusive right to make salt in the proposed new way, with certain other privileges.—*P. C. R.* SEP. 4.

[1] *Statistical Acc. of Scot.* ed. 1845, v. 258.

1589. June 3. A Bond of Association was entered into by Sir Walter Scott of Branxholm and fifty of the most important men of his kin and clan, which throws an important light on the customs of the age. A later and more notable Sir Walter Scott says of this bond—which he had seen in the possession of his cousin, William Scott, Esq. of Raeburn—that 'it is calculated to secure against any clansman taking any "room" or possession over the head of another of the name. Any one who was accused of having done so, bound himself to stand by the award of five men, to be mutually chosen, bearing the name of Scott. Even if the chief should encroach upon the possessions of any inferior person of the name, he declares he will submit the cause, in like manner, to four persons of the name of Scott; which shews an independence on the part of the clansmen which I was not prepared for. The bond . . . . seems to have been calculated to prevent kinsmen from going to law with each other, and to secure a species of justice within the clan, to the advancement of the "guid and godlie purposes" of their chief.'—*Pit.*

June. 'In this time, [the Laird of] Easter Wemyss took up 1500 waged men for the king of Navarre, now allegit king of France.' —*Moy.*

July. A sad accident befell in the family of Lord Somerville, at Drum, near Edinburgh.

'The Lord Somerville having come from Cowthally early in the morning, in regard the weather was hot, he had ridden hard to be at the Drum by ten o'clock, which having done, he laid him down to rest. The servant, with his two sons, William, Master of Somerville, and John his brother, went with the horses to ane shot of land, called the Pretty Shot, directly opposite to the front of the house, where there was some meadow-ground for grazing the horses, and willows to shadow themselves from the heat. They had not long continued in this place, when the Master of Somerville, after some little rest, awaking from his sleep, and finding his pistols that lay hard by him wet with dew, he began to rub and dry them, when unhappily one of them went off the ratch [lock], being lying on his knee and the muzzle turned sideways. The ball struck his brother John directly in the head, and killed him outright, so that his sorrowful brother never had one word from him, albeit he begged it with many tears. A lamentable case, and much to be pitied, two brave young gentlemen so nearly related, and dearly

loving one another, who besides their being brethren by birth, were 1589.
entirely so in affection, communicating all their affairs and designs one to the other, wherein they were never known to differ in the least . . . .

'The father, hearing the shot, leapt from his [bed] (being then in the chamber of dais), to the south light, and seeing his son and servants all in a cluster, called aloud to know the matter; but receiving no answer, he suspected some mischief, and thereupon flew hastily down the stair, and went directly to the place where they were, which the gentlemen observing, they advised the Master to take him to his horse, until his father's passion and fury should be over, which at length, upon their earnest entreaty, he did, taking his direct way for Smeaton, where his lady-mother then lived by Smeaton Ford. The father, being come upon the place, first hears the lamentation of the servants, and then sees the sad spectacle of his son all bloody and breathless, with his head laid upon a cloak, whereon he falls himself, and cries aloud: "My son, my son, dead or alive? dead or alive?" embracing him all the time, which he continued for some space, and thereby giving opportunity for his eldest son to escape. At length, finding no motion in his dear son, all in a fury he arises and cries aloud: "Where is that murderer? who has done the deed?" Staring wildly about, missing the Master, he cries out: "Oh, heavens, and is it he? Must I be bereft of two sons in one day? Yes, it must be so, and he shall have no other judge nor executioner but myself and these hands." And with that immediately mounts his horse, commanding two of his servants to attend him, making protestation in the meantime that they should both go to the grave together. But God was more merciful, for by this time the Master was past Smeaton Ford, and before his father came that length, he was at Fallside House, out of all danger. . . . . Coming now a little to himself, he [the father] began much to condemn this unwarrantable attempt of his, upon second thoughts. Before he came back, the sad object of his sorrow was removed to the place of Drum, and the corpse decently handled by the ladies of Edmonston, Woolmet, and Sheriff-hall, near neighbours, for in less than ane hour the report went over all the country. Yea, before the king rose from dinner he had notice of it, being then in Holyroodhouse, with the circumstance of the father's following the other son with intention to kill him; for which the king, within three days thereafter (the Lord Somerville coming to wait upon his majesty), reproved him by saying "he was a madman; that having lost one son by so sudden an accident,

1589. should needs wilfully destroy another himself, in whom, as he was certainly informed, there was neither malice nor design, but a great misfortune, occasioned by unwary handling of the pistol, which should have rather been a matter of regret and sorrow to him that the like had happened in his family, than that he should have sought after revenge. Therefore he commanded him to send for his eldest son, and be reconciled to him, for he knew he was a sober youth, and the very thoughts of his misfortune would afflict him enough, albeit he were not discountenanced by him."'

The unhappy principal in this tragedy was in reality an amiable young man, insomuch as to be called the Good Master of Somerville. 'I have heard it reported that Sir James Bannatyne of Newhall, one of the senators of the College of Justice, asserted there was not a properer youth trod the streets of Edinburgh, nor one of whom there was greater expectation, than William, Master of Somerville; but when God designs the ruin of a family, all supports are removed, that the fall may be the more sudden, as happened in this young nobleman's case, who after he had contracted in the latter end of February, and should have been married in April 1591, that very month he took a fever, which kept him long, and so weakened his body that he never recovered, but continued under a languishing sickness for more than ten months. It was supposed the thoughts of his own great misfortune in killing of his brother, the disagreement of his parents . . . . hastened his death. He died at Cowthally in the month of January 1592. . . . . A devote gentleman, William Inglis of East Shiel, as the corpse passed the outer gate, struck upon his breast, and cried out to the hearing of many: "This day the head is as clean taken off the house of Cowthally, as you would strike off the head of a syboe!"[1] And indeed it proved so.'

Aug. 30. The king, now hourly expecting the arrival of his Danish bride, is found writing pressing letters to all persons of substance who bore him any good will, for contributions of means towards the proper outset of the court on the occasion. From the Laird of Barnbarroch, he entreated 'sic quantity of fat beef and mutton on foot, wild-fowls and venison, or other stuff meet for this purpose, as possibly ye may provide and furnish of your awn or by your moyen.'[2]

On the 2d of September, he wrote to Boswell of Balmouto

[1] A leek (Fr. *cibolle*). [2] *Maitland Club Mis.*, i. 278.

a pressing, pleading letter for the loan of a thousand merks, stating that he had been disappointed of money by any more regular course, on account of its 'scarcity in thir quarters,' and expressing his assurance that he, the laird, would 'rather hurt yourself very far than see the dishonour of your prince and native country.'[1] 1589.

The storm which impeded the Princess Anne's voyage from Denmark to Scotland was also felt very severely in our country, and a passage-boat between Burntisland and Leith was lost, with an interesting person on board. This was Lady Melville of Garvock, born Jane Kennedy, who had been one of the maids of Queen Mary, had attended her on the scaffold at Fotheringay, and bound the embroidered handkerchief upon her eyes. Jane had subsequently married Sir Andrew Melville, master of household to King James, who, desiring her presence at the reception of his queen, because she was 'discreet and grave,' caused her to take this fatal voyage. 'She, being willing to mak diligence, wald not stay for the storm, to sail the ferry; when the vehement storm drave a ship upon the said boat, and drownit the gentlewoman, and all the persons except twa.'—*Mel.* SEP.

The king, hearing of the detention of his bride by stormy weather, resolved to go to Denmark to bring her home. He sent, 'directing Robert Jameson, burgess of Air, to bring his ship whilk was callit the JAMES, to the road of Leith, she being ane gallant ship, weel appointit with ordnance, her sails being coverit with red taffeta, and her claiths red scarlet.'[2] On the day noted, he set sail in this vessel, with other five ships in company, and after outriding a gale for some time in the Firth of Forth, proceeded on his course with fair winds. Landing on the 28th at Flaikray, in Norway, he, after some days' rest, commenced a difficult land-journey to Upslo—now Christiania—where the princess had taken up her residence for the winter. 'Immediately at his coming (November 19), [he] passed quietly with buits and all, to her hieness . . . . he minded to give her a kiss after the Scots fashion, whilk she refusit, as not being the fashion of her country. Marry, after a few words spoken privily betwixt his majesty and her, there passed familiarity and kisses.'[3] They were married four days after at Upslo, and spent the remainder of the winter in Denmark. OCT. 22.

[1] See the entire letter in *Blackwood's Magazine*, ii. 313.

[2] *Chronicle Kings of Scotland.*

[3] *Moysie's Memoirs.*

1589-90. Feb. 4. Hitherto, many of the articles of domestic use now largely manufactured in our country, had been introduced by merchants from abroad. Paper, glass, tanned leather, and soap were of this number. The present reign is the era of the first attempts at a native manufacture of all these articles, as will be fully seen in the following pages.

It was while James was absent on his matrimonial visit to Denmark, that a native manufacture of paper was first spoken of. Peter Groot Heres, a German, and sundry unnamed persons associated with him, proposed to set up this art in Scotland, under favour of certain encouragements which they demanded from the government. On what river they meant to plant their work, does not appear. We only find that the Lords of Council were willing to promote the object, calculating that thus would paper be made cheaper than hitherto, and also that by and by the natives would be enabled to become paper-makers themselves.

They granted to Peter and his co-partners liberty to carry on the manufacture of paper in Scotland for nine years, without competition, personally free from the duties of watching, warding, and tax-paying, and 'under his majesty's special protection, maintenance, defence, and sure safeguard.' The only condition imposed was, that they should begin their work before the ensuing 1st of August, and carry it on constantly during the time for which the privilege was granted; otherwise the licence should be of none effect.—*P. C. R.*

Feb. 8. It is with unexpected pleasure that we find another matter betokening the progress of literature and intelligence only four days after the licence for paper-making. Andro Hart then carried on the business of a bookseller in Edinburgh, and his name appears on so many interesting title-pages, that he is really a notable man of the time. He and John Norton, Englishman, now send a petition to the Privy Council, setting forth 'what hurt the lieges of this realm susteint through the scarcity of buiks and volumes of all sorts,' and to what exorbitant prices those had risen which were brought from England. They, 'upon an earnest zeal to the propagation and incress of vertue and letters within this realm, had, two years ago, enterprisit the hame-bringing of volumes and buiks furth of Almane and Germanie, fra the whilk parts the maist part of the best volumes in England are brought, and in this trade have sae behavit themselves that this town is furnist with better buiks and volumes nor it was at ony time heretofore, and the said volumes sauld by them in this country are als guid cheap as they are to be sauld in London or ony other part of England, to the great ease and commodity of all estates of persons within this realm.' Behold, however, John Gourlay, the customer (that is, farmer of customs), had laid hands upon the books which Hart and Norton were importing, and demanded that they should pay a duty—a demand altogether unprecedented. 'Upon the like complaint made by Thomas Vautrollier, printer, he obteint ane decreet discharging the provost and bailies of this burgh and their customer fra all asking of ony customs for ony buiks sauld or to be sauld by him.' The present petitioners only demanded to be so treated likewise. It is gratifying to find that the lords unhesitatingly granted the prayer of the two booksellers, so that the books they imported from Germany would thenceforth be duty-free.—*P. C. R.* 1589-90.

In the early part of this year, 'the wicked clan Gregor, so lang continuing in blood, slaughters, herships, manifest reifs, and stouths,' fell under notice for a frightful outrage. The king had his forest of Glenartney, in Perthshire, under the care of one Drummond, usually called Drummond-*ernoch,* on account of his having spent part of his life in Ireland. His neighbours, the Macgregors, taking mortal offence at this man, for some cause probably connected with their own misdeeds, fell upon him one day, while he was collecting venison against the return of the king from Denmark with his new-wed spouse. They barbarously cut off the forester's head, which they carried off with them, wrapped in the corner of a plaid. Soon after, passing the house of Ardvorlich, the lady of which was sister of the murdered man, they entered in peaceful fashion, and were regaled with bread and cheese. While the lady was absent, looking after better entertainment, they placed Drummond-ernoch's ghastly head on the table, and put a piece of bread and cheese in the mouth, telling him in mockery to eat it, as many a similar morsel he had formerly eaten in that house. The lady, returning, and seeing the frightful object, in which she recognised her brother's features, fled from the house in a state of distraction, and was recovered to her home and sanity with great difficulty. 1590.

This part of the story rests on tradition; but the subsequent procedure of the murderers comes to us on historical authority. The bloody head being brought to the chief of Macgregor in Balquhidder, he and the whole clan assembled in the parish kirk, and the head being then presented, all present laid their hands

1590. upon it in succession, avowing that the homicide had been done under their counsel and with their sanction, and swearing to defend the actual committers of the fact with all their power![1]

These proceedings being reported to the Privy Council, a commission was granted (February 4, 1590) to the Earl of Huntly, and certain other nobles and gentlemen, to search for the culprits, and, if they should flee, to pursue them with fire and sword. What success attended this edict does not appear.

In spring, while the king was absent in Norway, a General Assembly was held in Edinburgh, and it being found that the country was surprisingly free of all *steerage* from either papists or evil-doers, the brethren praised God for the same, and agreed that there should be fasting and moderate diet observed every day till the king's return. 'The whilk custom, being found very meet for the exercise of the Sabbath, was keepit in Edinburgh, in the houses of the godly, continually thereafter. Sae that, sparing their gross and sumptuous dinners, they usit nocht but a dish of broth, or some little recreation, till night; and that whilk was spared was bestowed on the poor.'[2] Such seems to have been the origin of a custom which many travellers remark in Scotland in the seventeenth century, of having only a lunch instead of dinner on Sunday. Our diarist makes, however, only a faint allusion in the phrase 'till night,' to what the same travellers remark, that there was always a hearty supper in the evenings, amply making up for the half-fast of the day, and at which human nature found vent occasionally in a little good-humour and merriment.

MAY 1. 'The king and queen, with sundry of the nobility and blood-royal of Denmark, accompanied with sixty gentlemen—being seven great ships—convoyed by the grace of God through ane great mist by the navy of England—arrivit in the firth of Leith at two afternoon, and came by boats to Leith, to the great comfort of this nation, being on the shore of na little number.' The royal party was 'receivit by the Duke of Lennox, Earls Bothwell and Mar, with great din, and ordnance from Edinburgh Castle, and on the south and east ferries, as by the ships. The king took the queen by the hand, and led her up ane trance, whilk was made for that effect, covered with tapestry and claith of gold, whereon they passed,

[1] Act of Privy Council, Notes to Waverley Novels (*Legend of Montrose*).

[2] James Melville's *Diary*.

that their feet should not touch the bare earth: where Mr James Elphinston, ane of the Lords of Session, made ane orison in French, to the praise of God for their prosperous voyage. 1590.

'The queen being placed in her lodging in Thomas Lindsay's, the king [there] took all the noblemen of Denmark by the hand, every ane after ane other. And thereafter the king passed to the kirk, where the Lord Hamilton and Lord Fleming met her grace and convoyit them. Mr Patrick Galloway made the sermon. . . . . His majesty passed to the lodging, where they all remained while [till] the sixth day of the same month, [when] they passed, afternoon, at four hours or thereby, to the Abbey of Holyroodhouse, the king's grace and noblemen on horse, and the queen's grace in ane *dame's coach,* drawn with aught great cussers of her awn, richly reparrit with claith of gold, silver, and purpour velvet; [and] the town of Edinburgh, Canongate, and Leith, in feir of weir, to the number of 1600 footmen. At the inner yett of the said abbey, the horsemen lichtit, [and] the king took the queen by the hand, and passed through the inner close to the great hall, and through the rest of the chalmers, which were richly hung with claith of gold and silver, and tapestry of silk: the said palace was newly repaired.'—*Jo. Hist.*

'There came with the king and queen's majesty, Callipier, the admiral of Denmark, Peter Monk, the captain of Elsinburgh, Stephen Brahe, Braid Ransome Maugaret, Nicolaus Theophilus, doctor of laws, and Henry Goodlister, captain of Bocastle, as principal and of the council of Denmark; William Vanderwant, who was appointed to wait upon her majesty, with sundry other gentlemen to the number of thirty or thereby, all in gold chains of good fashion. The number of the haill train was two hundred and twenty-three persons, who were all entertained by the king and noblemen of Scotland, and banquetted daily. They were twelve hundred merks every day for their furnishing, during the time of their remaining.'—*Moy.*[1] MAY.

The young queen, who had been crowned on the 16th, made her ceremonial entry into Edinburgh by the West Port, sitting in her chariot, which was drawn by eight splendidly caparisoned horses. She was attended by thirty-six Danes on horseback, each accompanied by some Scottish lord or knight. The citizens gave her welcome 'with great triumph and joy, pageants being erected in every place, adorned with all things befitting. Young boys with MAY 19.

[1] In this article, both editions of Moysie are used.

1590. artificial wings did fly towards her, and presented two silver keys of the city'[1]—'as use is, under a veil.' The Castle fired repeatedly in honour of the day, and forty-two young men of the town, dressed in white taffeta and cloth of silver, with gold chains, and disguised as Moors, danced before her along the streets. When she came to the Over Bow,[2] 'Mr Hercules Rollock, master of the Grammar School, made his orison. Thereafter [she] came to a scaffold at the Butter Tron,[3] whilk was plenished with the fairest young women of the town, fitly apparelled, with organs playing and musicians singing; where ane bairn made ane Latin orison. At the Tolbooth was younkers on ane scaffold, in women's claithing, representing Peace, Plenty, Policy, Justice, Liberality, and Temperance [who likewise made her an oration]. Thereafter, [they] passed to the kirk, where Mr Robert Bruce, minister, made the sermon.'[4] At the Cross, to which the party next came, there was 'a covered table, whereon stood cups of gold and silver full of wine, with the goddess of corn and wine sitting thereat, and the corn in heaps by her, who, in Latin, cried that there should be plenty thereof in her time; and upon the side of the Cross sat the god Bacchus upon a puncheon of wine, winking, and casting it by cups full upon the people, besides other of the townsmen, that cast apples and nuts among them; and the Cross itself ran claret wine upon the causey for the loyalty of that day.'[5]

'All curious pastimes and conceits
  Could be imaginat by man,
Was to be seen on Edinburgh gaits,
  Frae time that bravity began:
Ye micht have heard on every street
Trim melody and music sweet.

* * * *

'Organs and regals[6] there did carp,
  With their gay glittering golden strings;
There was the hautboy and the harp,
  Playing maist sweet and pleasant springs:
And some on lutes did play and sing,
Of instruments the only king.

[1] Birrel's *Diary*.

[2] Latterly called the West Bow.

[3] A public weighing-machine at the head of the West Bow.

[4] Johnston's *Hist. Scot.* MS.

[5] From the reprint of a rare contemporary tract, in *Papers relative to the Marriage of James VI.* (Bannatyne Club), 1828.

[6] Regals, or rigols, an ancient musical instrument, composed of a series of reeded tubes

'Viols and virginals were here, 1590.
With gitterns maist jucundious;
Trumpets and timbrels made great beir,
With instruments melodious:
The seistar and the sumphion,
With clarche, pipe, and clarion.'[1]

The variety of instruments here specified as in use in Edinburgh in 1590, will probably excite surprise.

From the Cross the queen proceeded to the Salt Tron, 'where was represented the king's grace' genealogy in the form of a tree, from the Bruce till himself . . . . ane bairn at the root of the tree made ane orison in Latin describing the haill bairns and branches. And syne [they] come to the Nether Bow, where the seven planets were, and gave the weird [fortune] in Latin. All their reasons was to the thanking of God and loving of the king and queen's grace, and spoken in Latin because the queen understood na Scots.'[2]

This evening, being a Sunday, the Danish nobles and gentlemen who had convoyed the queen to Scotland, received a formal entertainment from the magistrates of Edinburgh. A handsome alcoved room, which still exists, in the house of the Master of the Mint, in the Cowgate, was appropriated for the purpose. The style of the banquet seems to have been more remarkable for abundance than for elegance. There was simply bread and meat, with four boins of beer, four gang of ale, and four puncheons of wine. The house, however, was hung with tapestry; and the tables were decorated with chandlers and flowers. We hear, too, of napery, of 'twa dozen great vessels,' and of 'cupbuirds, and men to keep them.' The furnishing of all these articles was distributed among the city dignitaries, apparently with some reference to their respective professions.[3] MAY 23.

It forms an amusing commentary on the late grand proceedings of King James, when we find him now trying to squeeze voluntary JUNE 3.

resting on a bellows, which the player worked with his left hand. See Dalyell's *Musical Memoirs of Scotland*, 1849, p. 117.

One is at a loss to understand how the poet thought of expressing his admiration of the strings of the organ and regals.

[1] Burel's *Description of the Queen's Entry*, &c., 1590, in Watson's *Collection of Scottish Poetry*, 1712.

[2] Johnston's *Hist. Scot.* MS.

[3] Edin. Council Record.

1590. contributions out of his courtiers and richer subjects generally, for the purpose of getting the expenses paid. Under the date marginally noted, he entreats the Laird of Barnbarroch to send immediately the remaining half of his subscription of two hundred pounds to Alexander Lawson, 'for the relief of him and sic others as had the charge and oversicht of their houses, that, in default thereof, they be not troubled by the furnishers, wha, being for the maist part puir folks, shores [threatens] daily to use the rigour and extremity of the law against them.'[1] There is a similar letter written in October to the Laird of Caldwell, to quicken him in sending, what had formerly been asked, 'according to the custom observit of auld by our maist noble progenitors;' namely, 'ane hackney for transporting of the ladies accompanying the queen our bedfellow.' 'In doing whereof,' he goes on to say, 'ye will do us richt acceptable pleasure, to be rememberit in any your adoes, where we may give you proof of our remembrance of your guid will accordingly. Otherwise, upon the information we have receivit of sic as ye have, we will cause the readiest ye have to be ta'en by our authority and brought in till us.'[2]

After reading these curious missives, it is not difficult to believe in the existence of a third, which unfortunately has escaped print, in which James addresses his cousin the Earl of Mar, beseeching the loan of '*the* pair of silken hose,' in order to grace his royal person at the reception of the Spanish ambassador!

JUNE. In this month commenced a feud which for many years disturbed the peace of the upper part of the valley of the Tweed. The fact in which it took its rise was the slaughter of Patrick Veitch, son of William Veitch of Dawick (now New Posso), by or through James Tweedie of Drumelzier, Adam Tweedie of Dreva, William Tweedie of the Wrae, John Crichton of Quarter, Andrew Crichton in Cardon, and Thomas Porteous of Glenkirk. These persons were in prison in Edinburgh for the fact in July of this year; but the case was deferred to the *aire* of Peebles. Meanwhile, on the 20th of the month just mentioned, two relatives of the slain youth—James Veitch, younger, of North Synton, and Andrew Veitch, brother of the Laird of Tourhope—set upon John Tweedie, tutor of Drumelzier and burgess of Edinburgh, as he walked the streets

[1] *Maitland Club Misc.*, i. 280.

[2] The entire letter is printed in *Blackwood's Magazine*, ii. 628, and in the *Caldwell Papers*.

of the capital, and killed him. Thus were the alleged murderers punished through a near relative, probably uncle, of the principal party. Six days after, the two Veitches were delated for the fact, and we find Veitch of Dawick taking their part in true Scottish style, by joining in surety for their appearance at trial to the extent of ten thousand merks. After some further procedure, the king was pleased to interfere with an order for the liberation of the Veitches; whereupon a Presbyterian historian cuttingly remarks: 'He had soon forgot his promises made in the Great Kirk.'[1] 1590.

It would appear that, within a short space of time, the Tweedies of Drumelzier took revenge to a considerable extent on the Veitches: in particular they effected the slaughter of James Geddes of Glenhegden, who seems to have been brother-in-law to a principal gentleman of that family. The recital of James Geddes's death in the Privy Council Record, affords by its minuteness a curious insight into the manner of a daylight street-murder of that time. 'James,' it is stated, 'being in Edinburgh the space of aught days together, haunting and repairing to and fra openly and publicly, met almaist daily with the Laird [of Drumelzier] upon the Hie Street. The said laird, fearing to set upon him, albeit James was ever single and alane, had espies and moyeners [retainers] lying await for him about his lodging and other parts where he repairit. Upon the 29th day of December [1592], James being in the Cowgate, at David Lindsay's buith, shoeing his horse, being altogether careless of his awn surety, seeing there was naething intendit again him by the said laird divers times of before when they met upon the Hie Gait; the said laird, being advertised by his espies and moyeners, divided his haill friends and servants in twa companies, and directit John and Robert Tweedie, his brothers-german,[2] Patrick Porteous of Hawkshaw, John Crichton of Quarter, Charles Tweedie, household servant to the said James, and Hob Jardine, to Cow's Close, being directly opposite to David Lindsay's buith, and he himself, being accompanied with John and Adam Tweedie, sons to the Guidman of Dreva, passed to the Kirk Wynd, a little bewest the said buith, to await that the said James sould not have escaped; and baith the companies, being convenit at the foot of the said close, finding the said James standing at the buith door with his back to them, they rushit out of the said close, and with shots of pistolets slew him behind his back.'

[1] Calderwood.

[2] 'Wha were lately pardonit by his majesty for slaughter of the Laird of Dawick's son.'

1590. The guilty parties were summoned, and, not appearing, were denounced as rebels.

In June 1593, we find James Tweedie of Drumelzier released from Edinburgh Castle, under surety that he should presently enter himself in ward in the sheriffdom of Fife. We next hear of the two belligerent parties in January 1600, when they were commanded to come and subscribe letters of assurance 'for the feid and inimitie standing betwixt them.' The king seems to have been content with the consideration that they had now done pretty full justice upon each other, and it was therefore unnecessary for him to trouble himself any further in the matter. It was probably with some surprise that, many years after, while residing in England, he heard that these two Tweeddale clans continued to keep up their feud. (See under March 1611.)

July 22. Two extraordinary trials took place, affording the most striking illustrations of the vices and superstitions of the time.

The family of Monro of Foulis, in Ross-shire, which still flourishes, was even then one of great antiquity, being represented by the seventeenth baron in succession. Holding possessions on the borders of the Highlands, it hovered between the characters of the Celtic chief and the Lowland gentleman. Ross of Balnagowan was a rich neighbour of similar character. The *Lady Foulis* of the year 1576—to use her common appellation—was Catherine Ross of the latter family, the second wife of her husband. She had a son named George; but the succession was barred to him by two sons of the previous marriage of her husband, Robert and Hector.

Her husband and his eldest son were dead when, at the above date, she and Hector, then representative of the family, were tried separately for sundry offences, Hector being, strange to say, the private pursuer against his step-mother, although he had immediately after to take his own place at the bar as a criminal. The dittay against the lady set forth a series of attempts at serious crime, partly prosecuted by natural means, and partly by superstitious practices. It appeared that she desired to put her eldest step-son out of the way, not, as might have been supposed, to favour the succession of her own offspring, but that her brother, George Ross of Balnagowan, might be free to marry Robert Monro's wife; to which end she also took steps for the removal of the wife of George Ross. It appears that she was not only prompted to, but assisted in her attempts by George Ross himself, although no judicial notice was taken of his criminality. Catherine Ross, described as daughter of Sir David Ross of Balnagowan, was also concerned. Having formed her design some time in the year 1576, Lady Foulis opened negotiations with various wretched persons in her neighbourhood, who practised witchcraft; and first with one named William M'Gillivray, whom she feed with a present of linen cloth, and afterwards with sums of money. One Agnes Roy, a notorious witch, was sent by her to secure the services of a particularly potent sorceress, named Marion M'Kean M'Alister, or more commonly *Lasky Loncart*, who was brought to Foulis, and lodged with Christian Ross Malcomson, that she might assist with her diabolic arts. Christian, too, was sent to Dingwall, to bring John M'Nillan, who appears to have been a wizard of note. Another, named Thomas M'Kean M'Allan M'Endrick, was taken into counsel; besides whom there were a few subordinate instruments. Some of the horrible crew being assembled at Canorth, images of the young Laird of Foulis and the young Lady Balnagowan were formed of butter, set up and shot at by Lasky Loncart with an *elf-arrow;* that is, one of those flint arrow-heads which are occasionally found, and believed by the ignorant to be fairy weapons, while in reality they are relics of our savage ancestors. The shot was repeated eight times, but without hitting the images; so this was regarded as a failure. On another day, images of clay were set up, and shot at twelve times, yet equally without effect. Linen cloth had been provided, wherewith to have swathed the images in the event of their being hit; after which they would have been interred under the bridge-end of the stank of Foulis. The object of all these proceedings was of course to produce the destruction of the persons represented by the images. This plan being ineffectual, Lady Foulis and her brother are described as soon after holding a meeting in a kiln at Drimnin, to arrange about further procedure. The result was a resolution to try the more direct means of poison with both the obnoxious persons. A stoup of poisoned ale was prepared and set aside, but was nearly all lost by a leak in the vessel. Lady Foulis then procured from Lasky Loncart a pipkin of ranker poison, which she sent to young Monro by her nurse on purpose to have destroyed him. It fell by the way and broke, when the nurse tasting the liquor, was immediately killed by it. It was said that 'the place where the pig [pipkin] brake, the gerse that grew upon the samen was so heich bye [beyond] the nature of other gerse, that neither cow nor sheep ever previt [tasted] thereof yet; whilk is manifest

1590.

1590. and notorious to the haill country of Ross.' Lady Foulis is accused of afterwards making renewed attempts, not merely to poison young Monro, but many of his relations, particularly those who stood in the way of her own son's succession. There seems, however, to have been no success in this quarter. Matters turned out better with the innocent young Lady Balnagowan. Regarding her, Lady Foulis is represented as thus expressing herself, that 'she would do, by all kind of means, wherever it might be had, of God in heaven or the devil in hell, for the destruction and down-putting of Marjory Campbell.' By corrupting a cook, Lady Foulis contrived that some rat-poison should be administered to her victim in a dish of kid's kidneys. Catherine Niven, who had brought this poison, 'scunnerit [revolted] with it sae meikle, that she said it was the sairest and maist cruel sight that ever she saw, seeing the vomit and vexation that was on the young Lady Balnagowan and her company.' By vomiting, death seems to have been evaded, but the lady contracted in consequence what is described at the trial as an incurable illness.

Not long after these events, they became the subject of judicial investigation, and Christian Ross and Thomas M'Kean were apprehended, brought to trial, convicted, and burnt, November 1577. It is alleged that, a few days before they suffered, Lady Foulis came into their presence, and referring to the common reports against her, accusing her of sorcery and poisoning, declared herself ready to abide a trial; when, there being no one present to accuse her, she asked instruments to that effect; after which, mounting a horse which had been kept ready, she rode away to Caithness, and remained there three-quarters of a year. By the intercession of the Earl of Caithness, she was then taken back by her husband; and there seems to have been no further notice taken of her case for several years. At length, in 1589, her husband being dead, his successor, Robert Monro, purchased a commission for the trial of certain witches and sorcerers, aiming evidently at retribution upon his wicked step-mother. According to the dittay: 'Before any publication thereof, and ere he might have convenient time to put the same in execution, in respect of the troubles that occurred in the north, thou, knawing thyself guilty, and fearing to bide the trial of ane assize, fand the moyen [found the means] to purchase ane suspension of the said commission; and causit insert in the said suspension, not only thy awn name, and sic others as was specified in the said commission, but also certain others who were not spoken of . . . . whilk, gif thou had been ane honest woman, and willing to abide trial, thou wald never have causit suspension of ony sic commission, but wald rather have fortherit the same.' In the same year, Robert Monro died, under what circumstances does not appear, leaving the succession to his brother Hector, who now appeared as nominal prosecutor of his mother-in-law. 1590.

In the circumstances under which the trial took place, the jury being a packed one of humble dependents on the Foulis family, a conviction was not to be expected. Lady Foulis was 'pronounced to be innocent and quit of the haill points of the dittay; whereupon she asked instruments.'

The dittay against Hector Monro of Foulis sets forth sundry affairs of necromancy, in which he was alleged to have been concerned along with reputed sorcerers. He had, in August 1588, communed with three notorious witches for the recovery of his elder brother, the then young laird. For this purpose, they 'pollit the hair of Robert Monro, and plet the nails of his fingers and taes;' seeking by these devilish means to have cured him of his sickness. Meeting no success, they told him he had been too late in sending for them. He, for fear of his father, conveyed them away under silence of night.

Having himself taken sickness in the ensuing January, while lying at a house in Alness, he had Marion M'Ingarroch, a notorious witch, brought to him for the purpose of obtaining the benefit of her skill. 'She, after her coming to you,' says the dittay, 'gave you three drinks of water forth of three stanes, whilk she had; and, after lang consultation had with her, she declarit that there was nae remede for you to recover your health, without the principal man of your blude should suffer death for you.' Having pitched upon his half-brother George, he sent for him from the hunting, and, as a means of working his destruction, gave his left hand into George's right hand, taking care at the same time not to be the first to speak. 'That night, at ane after midnight, the said witch, with certain of her complices, passed forth of the house where ye lay, and took with them spades, and passed to ane piece of earth, lying betwixt twa sundry superiors' lands . . . . and made ane grave of your length, and took up the ower [upper] part thereof, and laid it aside; the said earth being near the sea-flood. And, this being done, she came hame, and convenit certain of your familiars, that knew thir secrets, and informit them what should be every ane's part, in taking of you forth to be eardit in the foresaid grave, for your relief and to the death of your brother George.

1590. Whase [that is, the accused's] answer was, that gif George should depart suddenly, the bruit [report] wald rise, and all thir lives wald be in danger; and therefore willit her to delay the said George's death ane space; and she took in hand to warrant him unto the 17th day of April next thereafter. And after thir plats, laid by the said witch, she and certain of your servants . . . . pat you in ane pair of blankets, and carried you forth to the said grave. And they were all commanded to be dumb and never to speak ane word, unto the time that she and your foster-mother should first speak with her master, the devil. And being brought forth, [you] was laid in the said grave; and the green earth which was cuttit, was laid aboon, and halden down with staves, the said witch being beside you. . . . Christian Neill, your foster-mother, was commanded to run the breadth of nine rigs, and in her hand Neill younger, Hector Leith's son. And, how soon Christian had run the breadth of the nine rigs, she came again to the grave, and inquirit at the said witch, "Whilk was her choice?" Wha answered and said, that Mr Hector was her choice to live, and your brother George to die for you. And this form was used thrice that night; and thereafter ye was carried hame, all the company being dumb, and was put in your bed.'

Contrary to what one would expect of an invalid exposed in this manner on a January night, Hector Monro recovered. His brother George took ill in April 1590, and lingered to the beginning of July, when he died. No doubt being entertained that his mortal illness was caused by witchcraft, his mother, the subject of the preceding trial, appears to have immediately commenced a prosecution against Hector, now laird; and the result was a trial following immediately that in which he had appeared as prosecutor against her. This trial had the same issue as the other, the jury being composed in a similar manner.—*Pit.*

AUG. 18. Bessie Roy, nurse in the family of Lesly of Balquhain, was tried for sundry points of witchcraft, leading to the death of several persons. One minor offence, particularly insisted on in this woman's case, was her being 'a common away-taker of women's milk.' It was alleged that, while living in the family of William King at Barra, she had bewitched away the milk of a poor woman named Bessie Steel, who came seeking alms. 'Sitting down by the fire,' says the dittay, 'to give her bairn souk [suck], thou being ane nourice thyself, and perceiving the poor woman to have mair abundance of milk than thou had; and seeing that the goodwife, thy hussie [housewife], should have deteinit the poor woman and given her the bairn to foster; thou, by thy devilish incantations and witchcraft, abstracted and took away her milk. And immediately after the poor woman was past out of the house, she perceived her milk to be taken away, came again to the said house, and compleinit to the goodwife, that the nurse had taken away her milk, and said: "Gif she were not restorit to her milk, she should divulgate the same through the country, and shaw how ye had used her." And thou, fearing thy devilish craft to be revealed, said to the poor woman: "Gif I have thy milk, come sic a night to me to this house, and ask it for God's sake, and thou sall have it." Likeas the poor woman, being glad to receive her milk again, came that same night as thou appointed her, and lay in the house beside ye all night; and about the mids of the night, thou cried upon her and wakened her, and bade her receive her milk; and incontinent she wakened, and her paps sprang out full of milk, and remained with her thereafter.' 1590.

Bessie was pronounced innocent by the jury.—*Pit.*

The great Highland family now represented by the Marquis of Breadalbane had at this time for its head Sir Duncan Campbell of Glenurchy, ordinarily called *Donacha Dhu nan Curich* (Black Duncan of the Cowl), a man of considerable force of character, and, for his time, large means, who died at an advanced age in 1631. He was distinguished for building, planting, and *improving;* had the taste to hire artists to decorate his house; and, some years after this time, was one of the most prominent patrons of the Scottish Vandyke, George Jameson.

The household books of this great Celtic chief exhibit his style of life about the time here noted. His rents were principally paid in kind, and the corn, cattle, and poultry thus supplied by the tenantry went directly to the support of the laird and his household. 'In 1590, the family spent their time between Balloch and Finlarig. The oatmeal consumed was 364 bolls; the malt, 207 bolls (deducting a small quantity of *struck* barley used in the kitchen). They used 90 beeves ("neats," "stirks," or "fed oxen"), more than two-thirds consumed fresh; 20 swine; 200 sheep; 424 salmon, far the greater portion being from the western rivers; 15,000 herrings; 30 dozen of hard fish; 1805 "heads" of cheese, new and old, weighing 325 stone; 49 stones of butter; 26 dozen loaves of wheaten bread; of wheat flour, $3\frac{1}{4}$ bolls. The wine brought from Dundee was claret and white wine, old and

1590. new, in no very large quantities. [The malt furnished abundance of ale of three kinds—ostler ale, household ale, and best ale, serving, doubtless, for the different grades of persons in the family.] Of spices and sweet-meats, we find only notice on one occasion of small quantities of saffron, mace, ginger, pepper, "raises of cure," plumdamas, and *one* sugar-loaf.'[1]

While the Laird of Glenurchy thus kept house in Strathtay, Lord Lovat supported a *ménage* not greatly different in Inverness-shire. The weekly expenditure of provisions in his house included seven bolls of malt, seven bolls of meal, and one of flour. Each year seventy beeves were consumed, besides venison, fish, poultry, kid, lamb, veal, and all sorts of feathered game in profusion. His lordship imported wines, sugars, and spices from France, in return for the salmon produced by his rivers. He was celebrated for a liberal hospitality; and when he died in 1631, five thousand armed followers and friends attended his funeral, for all of whom there would be entertainment provided.[2]

The rude abundance shewn in these two establishments, taken in connection with the account presently to be given of the outward state of the Marquis of Huntly,[3] the reports afforded by the Water Poet of the hospitalities he experienced in the braes of Aberdeenshire and Morayshire,[4] and other particulars involved in our chronicle, ought somewhat to modify the prevalent notions as to the poverty of the Celtic part of Scotland in this age. There was, indeed, no manufacturing industry worth speaking of; but the natural wealth of the country, the cattle, the wild animals, and the grain, seem to have furnished the people with no inconsiderable share of the comforts of life. It will be found, too, that the mansions of Glenurchy and Huntly, a few years after this date, exhibited elegant architecture and decoration.

OCT. The rich temporalities of the Abbey of Deir, in Aberdeenshire, had been held since the Reformation by one who was no friend to the Reformed clergy—Robert Keith, second son of William, fourth Earl Marischal. In 1587, they had been erected into a temporal lordship, under the name of the Lordship of Altrie, in their possessor's favour, to descend, after his death, to his nephew, George Earl Marischal. There was one malcontent with this

[1] Mr C. Innes's preface to *Black Book of Taymouth*, xxv.

[2] Anderson's *Hist. of the Frasers*, p. 102.

[3] See onward, under May 1600. [4] See onward, under August 1618.

arrangement—Robert Keith of Benholm, brother of the earl—probably because he had concluded in his own mind that the abbey-lands formed a more appropriate estate for a cadet than for the chief of the family, the latter being already a rich man. It would appear, however, that the earl was understood to have requited the king for the gift by the splendid style in which he conducted his ambassage to Denmark, when negotiating the royal marriage. 1590.

At the present date, Robert Keith made an attempt to take forcible possession of the abbey—an act which would have been rash and dangerous at any ordinary time, but might look feasible enough in an age so full of violences of all kinds as the present. We learn that he kept the abbey for six weeks, at the end of which he was driven out by an armed company brought against him by the Earl Marischal. Then retiring to the castle of Fedderat, he stood a siege of three days, which ended in his coming to a truce with his brother, upon what terms does not appear.

The abbacy was well worthy of a struggle, as in 1565 it comprehended a rental of £572, 8s. 6d., with thirteen and a half bolls of wheat, fourteen chalders and ten bolls of beir, and sixty-three chalders nine bolls of meal. The revenue of the earldom to which this became an addition on the death of Lord Altrie in 1593, has been stated at an amount for which there may be some difficulty in obtaining credence—namely, 270,000 merks. Lord Marischal could enter Scotland at Berwick, and travel in the leisurely style of those days through the country to John o' Groat's House, and never need to take a meal or a night's rest off his own lands. That he used his wealth generously, no one can deny, when it is remembered that he bestowed part of it in founding the Marischal College in Aberdeen. Yet, in the eyes of the common people, a weird hung over him. It was thought he did ill to stain his hands with the plunder of the old Cistercian monastery on the banks of the Ugie.

'This Earl George, his first wife, daughter to the Lord Home, being a woman of a high spirit and of a tender conscience, forbids her husband to have such a consuming moth in his house as was the sacrilegious meddling with the abbacy of Deir. But fourteen score chalders of meal and beir was a sore tentation; and he could not weel endure the rendering back of such a morsel. Upon his absolute refusal of her demand, she had this vision . . . . she saw a great number of religious men, in their habit, come forth of that abbey to the strong craig of Dunnottar, which is the principal residence of that family. She also saw them set themselves round about the rock, to get it down and demolish it, having no

1590. instruments but only penknives; wherewith they foolishly (as it seemed to her) began to pick at the craig. She smiled to see them intend so fruitless an enterprise, and went to call her husband, to scoff and jeer them out of it. When she had fand him, and brought him to see these silly monks at their foolish work, behold! the whole craig, with all his strong and stately buildings, was by their penknives undermined and fallen in the sea, so as there remained nothing but the rack of their rich furniture and stuff floating on the waves of a raging and tempestuous sea.'[1]

The earl is believed to have mocked the popular notions and his wife's foreboding dream, by inscribing on a tower he built at Deir, and likewise on the wall of his new college, the defying legend:

THAY. HAIF. SAID: QUHAT. SAY. THAY: LAT. THAME. SAY.

The greatness of the Keith Marischal family probably seemed to him as firmly set as the old Castle of Dunnottar itself on its conglomerate basis beside the sea. When the above story was put down in writing, sixty years had elapsed, and the narrator could not but remark the reduction which the civil war and usurpation of Cromwell had by that time wrought upon the once enormous wealth of the house of Keith Marischal. What would he have felt, could he have known that in sixty years from his time, the family would be out of lands and titles, exiles from their native country; or that in sixty more, there would not be a male descendant of the Earls Marischal in existence, of cadency later than the fifteenth century, while the ancient fortress of Dunnottar would stand roofless and grass-grown, and, except for the melancholy interest of the passing visitor, might as well be crumbled beneath the waves that beat upon the subjacent cliffs!

DEC. 26. A series of extraordinary trials for witchcraft and other crimes commenced at this date.

One David Seaton, dwelling in Tranent, suspected his servant-maid, Geilie Duncan, of a supernatural power of curing sickness, and, having subjected her to the torture of the pilniewinks (a screw for the fingers), soon extorted from her, not only a confession that the devil had given her the power of a witch, but information inculpating a number of persons in the like criminality. Among these were John Fian (*alias* Cunningham), schoolmaster at Prestonpans; Agnes Sampson, a midwife at Keith; Barbara Napier, the wife of a citizen of Edinburgh; and Eupham M'Calyean, a lady

[1] *Britain's Distemper*, by Patrick Gordon, Spald. Club.

of rank, daughter of a deceased judge of the Court of Session. The confessions of these persons, for the most part wrung from them by torture, form a strange jumble of possible and impossible, of horrible and ludicrous things; nor are they even devoid of historical importance, seeing that they involved the honour of the Earl of Bothwell, who was thus apparently led into those troubles from which he never got free, and by which the peace of the king and his kingdom was for some years seriously compromised. 1590.

Fian, who was a young man, confessed to some wicked arts which he had practised for obtaining the love of a young woman of his neighbourhood. There was nothing in them or their effects but what is easily reconcilable with natural fact, even to the striking of a rival with a sort of madness, under which, when brought into the king's chamber, where Fian was under examination, he fell a-bounding and capering with an energy which it required many persons to restrain, and this for an hour together, at the end of which he declared that he had been in a sound sleep. But Fian also admitted, though only under torture, his having had conferences with the devil; he had attended various meetings of witches with the Enemy of Man, some of which took place in North Berwick Kirk, and on these occasions he had acted as registrar or clerk of proceedings. He had also been one of a party of witches which went off from Prestonpans one night to a ship at sea, which they sunk by their incantations. He had chased a cat at Tranent, with the design of throwing it into the sea, in order to raise storms for the destruction of shipping; and in this chase it was alleged that he was borne above the ground, and had leaped a wall, the head of which he could not, but for witchcraft, have touched with his hand. Out of many facts laid to his charge at his trial, there is one which modern science has no difficulty in explaining upon natural principles—'Passing to Tranent on horseback, and ane man with him, [he] by his devilish craft, raisit up four candles upon the horse's twa lugs [ears], and ane other candle upon the staff whilk the man had in his hand, and gave sic licht as gif it had been daylicht; like as the said candles returnit with the said man at his hame-coming, and causit him fall dead at the entry within the house.'

After his first examination and confession, Fian was put into a separate room, where he quickly came to a state of penitence, renounced the devil and his works, and professed to have returned to God. Next day he told his keepers that he had had a vision of the devil, who, finding him a determined rebel against his authority, said: 'Once ere thou die thou shalt be mine;' after which he

1590. broke a white wand which he held in his hand, and vanished. Fian soon after contrived to escape from prison, but was retaken and brought back, when, being found to deny his former confession, the king expressed his belief that he must have entered into a new compact with the Prince of Darkness. His person was searched for marks, but in vain; and he was then subjected to tortures of the direst kind, with a view to bringing him back to his confession. The nails of the poor wretch were torn away with pincers; needles were thrust up to the heads in his fingers, and his legs were crushed in the boots till 'the blood and marrow spouted forth.' He resisted all, and thus only impressed the king and others with the conviction that the devil had entered into his heart. He was then arraigned, condemned, and burned.

The trials of three of the women inculpated took place in the course of a few ensuing months—that of Agnes Sampson on the 27th of January 1591. At the previous examinations, the king presided, manifesting a deep interest in the declarations of the prisoners, as if he read therein the materials of a new branch of science; and, indeed, there can be little doubt that what he now learned formed the groundwork of his subsequent work on *Demonology*.

The cases were the more remarkable on account of the apparent character and station of the culprits. Sampson was a grave, matron-like woman, who gave composed, pertinent answers to all that was put to her; while Napier and M'Calyean belonged to the upper class of society. Sampson's dittay consists of no fewer than fifty-three articles, each charging some distinct form or act of sorcery, most of them cures or attempts to cure, or else prophecies of events which actually came to pass, all being done with the assistance of her familiar, the devil. The various articles, numerous as they are, must have been founded on the confessions previously drawn from the accused by means of the inhuman torture of a rope twisted round the head, which she is said to have endured for an hour unmoved. It was alleged that for her cures she uttered incantations in rhyme; but these appear to have had nothing devilish in them, one being merely a rough version of the Apostles' Creed, while another runs as follows:

'All kinds of ills that ever may be,
In Christ's name I conjure ye;
I conjure ye baith mair and less,
With all the vertues of the Mess;
And richt sae, by the nailis sae,
That nailit Jesus and nae mae;

And richt sae, by the samen blude, 1590.
That reekit o'er the ruthful rood:
Furth of the flesh and of the bane,
And in the erd and in the stane,
I conjure ye in God's name!'

In two or three cases, one is reminded of the doctrines of modern mesmerism. Being called to see a sick boy at Prestonpans, she only *graipit him*—that is, felt him over—and he was healed. Some cattle she had cured by going up between them in their stalls, 'straking their backs and wames [stroking their backs and bellies], and saying *Ave Maria* oft ower.' The thirty-fifth count charges her with 'curing Robert Kerse in Dalkeith, wha was heavily tormented with witchcraft and disease laid on him by ane westland warlock, when he was in Dumfries; whilk sickness she took upon herself, and keepit with great groaning and torment till the morn; on whilk time there was ane great din heard in the house; whilk sickness she cast off herself in the close, to the effect ane cat or dog might have gotten the same; and, notwithstanding, the same was laid upon Alexander Douglas in Dalkeith, wha dwined and departed therewith, and the said Robert Kerse was made hale.'

A curious affair is related as taking place at a gentleman's house near Edinburgh. 'When she was sent for to heal the auld Lady Edmestone, when she lay sick, before the said Agnes departit she tauld to the gentlewomen that she should tell them that night whether the lady wald heal or nocht; and appointit them to be in the garden after supper, betwix five and sax at even. She passit to the garden to devise upon her prayer, on what time she chargit the devil, calling him *Elva,* to come and speak to her; wha came in ower the dyke, in likeness of ane dog, and came sae near her, that she was afraid, and chargit him "on the law that he lived on," to come nae nearer, but to answer her; and she demandit "whether the lady wald live or not." He said: "Her days were gane." When he demandit: "Gif the gentlewomen her dochters, where they were?" And she said: "That the gentlewomen said, that they were to be there." He answerit: "Ane of them sould be in peril, and that he sould have ane of them." She answerit: "It sould not be sae;" and sae [he] departit frae her yowling. Frae this time till after supper, he remainit in the wall [well]. When the gentlewomen came in, the dog came out of the wall, and appearit to them; whereat they were affrayit. In the meantime, ane of the said gentlewomen, the Lady Torsonce, ran to the wall,

1590. being forcit and drawn by the devil, wha wald have drownit her, were not the said Agnes and the rest of the gentlewomen gat ane grip of her, and with all their forces drew her back again, whilk made them all affrayit. The dog passit away thereafter with ane yowl. Then she said to the gentlewomen that she could not help the lady, in respect that her prayer stoppit, and that she was sorry for it. . . . .'

On Sampson's trial, some of the transactions first revealed in Fian's case came out in greater detail, particularly the night-meeting of the sorcerers of the district with their grisly master at North Berwick Kirk. What follows was the woman's own confession before the king: 'The devil, in man's likeness, met her going out in the fields from her awn house in Keith, betwix five and sax at even, being her alane, and commandit her to be at North Berwick Kirk the next nicht. She passit there on horseback, convoyit by her good-son, called John Couper, and lichtit at the kirk-yard: a little before she came to it, about eleven hours at even, they dancit alangs the kirk-yard. Geilie Duncan playit to them on ane trump. John Fian, missalit [masked], led all the rest; the said Agnes and her daughter followit next; besides thir, wee [little] Kate Gray, George Mowat's wife, Robert Grierson, Catherine Duncan, Bessie Wright, Isobel Gylour, John Ramsay's wife, Annie Richardson, Jonet Gaw, Nicol Murray's wife tailor, Christian Carrington *alias* Lukit, Maisie Aitchison, Marion Paterson, Alexander Whitelaw, Marion Nicholson, Marion Bailie, Jonet Nicholson, John Graymeal, Isobel Lauder, Helen White, Margaret Thomson, Marion Shiel, Helen Lauder, Archy Hennel's wife, Duncan Buchanan, Marion Congleton, Bessie Gullan, Bessie Brown the smith's wife, Thomas Burnhill and his wife, Gilbert M'Gill, John M'Gill, Catherine M'Gill, with the rest of their complices, above ane hundred persons, whereof there was sax men, and all the rest women. The women first made their homage, and next the men. The men were turned nine times withershins about [contrary to the direction of the sun], and the women sax times.' Another account, from Sampson's confessions, states that the witches took hands and danced a reel to Geilie Duncan's music, singing in one voice:

'Cummer, go ye before; cummer, go ye;
Gif ye will not go before, cummer, let me.'

Geilie Duncan, being sent for, came and played the very tune over again, upon a Jew's harp, before the king.

To proceed with the narrative as given in the dittay: 'John Fian

blew up the doors, and blew in the lichts, whilk were like meikle 1590.
black candles sticking round about the pulpit. The devil start up himself in the pulpit, like ane meikle black man, and callit every man by his name, and every ane answerit: "Here, Master."

The Devil preaching to the Witches—From a contemporary print.

Robert Grierson being namit, they ran all hirdy-girdy, and were angry; for it was promisit, that he should be callit "Robert the Comptroller, *alias* Rob the Rower," for expreming of his name. The first thing he demandit was, "Gif they [had] keepit all promise and been guid servants?" and "What they had done since the last time they had convenit?" On his command, they openit up the graves, twa within and ane without the kirk, and took off the joints of their fingers, taes, and knees, and partit them amang them; and the said Agnes Sampson gat for her part ane winding-sheet and twa joints, whilk she tint negligently. The devil commandit them to keep the joints upon them, while [till] they were dry, and then to make ane powder of them, to do evil withal. Then he commandit them to keep his commandments, whilk were to do all the evil they could.' The devil then ordered them to perform an act of homage towards himself, which does not admit of description, but which may be said to have been at least one

1590. degree more humiliating than the kissing of the papal great toe. In the account of the confessions, it is stated that he inveighed against the king, and, being asked why he had such a hatred to him, answered: 'By reason the king is the greatest enemy he hath in the world.' According to the dittay, the devil 'had on him ane gown and ane hat, whilk were baith black; and they that were assembled, part stood and part sat. John Fian was ever nearest the devil, at his left elbock; Graymeal keepit the door.'

Mrs Sampson was adjudged to be taken to the Castle-hill, and there strangled at a stake, and her body burned to ashes.

Barbara Napier was tried, May 8, 1591, on charges similar to those preferred against Sampson: she was found guilty of a few of the less important articles, but acquitted of being at the North Berwick convention and other more grave charges; nevertheless, she was condemned to death. The king was highly incensed at the partial acquittal, and came in person to court to preside at a trial of the jurors for wilful error, when they contrived to avert his wrath by throwing themselves on his mercy. After all, Napier had execution delayed on account of pregnancy, and in the end was set at liberty. Of the royal leniency on this occasion, the clergy did not fail to take note. It will be found that they twitted the king with it some time after.

At Sampson's trial, the only charge against her in which the safety of the king was involved, was the helping to raise a storm to stop the coming of the queen to Scotland. But now, on the trial of Napier, more serious charges were preferred. It was alleged that at Lammas last there had been a witch-meeting at Aitchison's Haven, and in the midst of it was the devil, 'in likeness of ane black man.' 'Agnes Sampson proponit the destruction of his hieness' person, saying to the devil: "We have ane turn to do, and we wald be at it if we could, and therefore help us to it." The devil answerit, "he sould do what he could, but it wald be lang to, because it wald be thorterit [thwarted];" and he promisit to her and them ane picture of wax, and ordenit her and them to hing, roast, and drop ane taid [toad], and to lay the drops of the taid, mixed with strong wash, ane adder-skin, and the thing in the forehead of ane new foalit foal, in his hieness' way, where it micht drop upon his hieness' head or his body, for his hieness' destruction. . . . Agnes Sampson was appointit to mak the picture [of the king], and to give it to the devil to be enchantit, whilk she made indeed, and gave it to him; and he promisit to give it to the said Barbara [Napier] and to Effie M'Calyean, at the next meeting, to be roastit. . . . There was ane appointit to seek some of his hieness' linen claiths, to do the turn with.' At the North Berwick meeting on All-hallow even, 'Robert Grierson said thir words: "Where is the thing ye promisit?" meaning the picture of wax devisit for roasting and undoing his hieness' person, whilk Agnes Sampson gave him. . . . He answerit: "It sould be gotten at next meeting.". . . . Barbara and Effie M'Calyean gat then ane promise of the devil, that his hieness' picture sould be gotten to them twa, and that right soon.' It is highly noteworthy that none of these particulars appear either in the indictments against Fian and Sampson, or in the accounts of their confessions which came out about the time of their trials. 1590.

The trial of Eupham M'Calyean commenced on the 9th of June. She was taxed with many acts of sorcery of a common kind—such as this: 'Consulting and seeking help at Anny Sampson, ane notorious witch, for relief of your pain in the time of the birth of your twa sons, and receiving frae her to that effect ane bored stane, to be laid under the bowster, put under your head, enchanted moulds [earth] and powder put in ane piece paper, to be usit and rowit in your hair; and at the time of your drowis [throes], your guidman's sark to be presently ta'en off him and laid wimplit round your bed feet. The whilk being practisit by you . . . . your sickness was casten off you, unnaturally, in the birth of your first son, upon ane dog, whilk ran away and never was seen again: and in the birth of your last son, the same practice was usit, and your natural and kindly pain unnaturally casten off you upon the wanton cat in the house; whilk likewise was never seen thereafter.' It was also alleged of Eupham, that, eighteen years before, she had 'consulted with Jonet Cunningham in the Canongate-head, *alias* callit Lady Bothwell, ane auld indytit witch of the finest champ, for poisoning of Joseph Douglas of Pumfrastown, and that by ane potion of composit water whilk she send her servant John Tweedale for, to be brought up to Barbara Towers's house in ane chopin stoup.' What was more to the purpose, she was accused of her concern in the affair of the waxen picture, and of having conspired to raise a storm for stopping or drowning the queen on her way from Denmark. After a trial of three days, a verdict was returned against her on the chief points, and this unfortunate lady was condemned to be burned alive at a stake on the Castle-hill.

Throughout all the proceedings connected with these trials, as far as they have been preserved, there is no appearance of any

1590. imputation against the Earl of Bothwell; but Spottiswoode affirms that Sampson, in her confessions, had attributed to him the guilt of suggesting the picture device, adding that the devil, finding his plans of no avail against the king, said: 'Il est un homme de Dieu.' It also appears that James discovered further matter against Bothwell, in the course of examining the wizard Richard Graham.[1] The turbulent lord was therefore committed to ward, from which he broke out only three days before the death of M'Calyean, June 22d. He was now forfaulted on a former sentence, and henceforth became a broken man, though one still able to create no small trouble to his sovereign.

A review of these circumstances leaves a strange feeling on the mind, as if we were reading that which was deficient in some of the most necessary elements of human action. It is difficult to see to what extent the so-called wizards and witches were deluders and deluded. Was there any basis in fact for the affair at North Berwick Kirk, confessed to by two or three of the culprits, though, it may be remarked, with varying circumstances? Was Geilie Duncan's dance-tune truly repeated before the king? Or were these matters of mere hallucination? Did these women really aim at doing harm to any one, or were they only lunatics? The story reads the more inexplicably when we see so many names as of simple villagers involved in it, and find a king and all his court and clergy viewing it in a serious light.

This year was marked by 'a plague amang the bestial.'—*Chron. Perth.*

[1] Tytler's *History*, quoting letters in the State-paper Office.

REIGN OF JAMES VI.: 1591-1603.

In this period we see a continuation of the struggles of the clergy for the independence of the kirk, and those of the king for a supremacy over it; the merciless measures for repressing the Catholic faith, and the desperate practices of the Catholics for relief; the weak rule of the king in all administrative matters; and the efforts of ambitious courtiers to gain an ascendency in his councils. The first transactions of any note were those arising from the condemnation and forfeiture of Stuart, Earl of Bothwell, an illegitimate cousin of the king, and nephew by his mother to the noted Hepburn, Earl of Bothwell, the murderer of Darnley. Conceiving himself to be simply a victim of the jealousy of the Chancellor Maitland, this vivacious noble was indisposed to submit to his doom; he thought, if he could reach the king's ear, he might regain lost power and place. His consequent intrusions by night into the palace, and appearances at the head of armed parties in the field, form a strange chapter in the history of the period.

Our chronicle gives details of an unfortunate collision between the houses of Huntly and Moray, which resulted in the barbarous slaughter of the latter nobleman. The loss of public esteem which the king and the chancellor sustained through their suspected concern in this affair, and through the undoubted lenity which was shewn to the Earl of Huntly, reduced the government to such a degree of weakness, that it became necessary to give way somewhat to the demands of the clergy. To obtain their support, the episcopal arrangements of 1584 were in a great measure done away with (June 1592), and James himself passed a glowing eulogium on the Presbyterian system.

Towards the end of this year, new troubles arose, in consequence of the discovery of a treasonable correspondence between the Catholic nobles, Huntly, Errol, and Angus, with the king of Spain. These chiefs, finding themselves harassed beyond endurance by the now triumphant Presbyterians, who would allow them no freedom for the exercise of their religion, resorted to the desperate step of seeking assistance from a foreign and a Catholic sovereign. Under the urgency of Elizabeth and the kirk, James proceeded with vigour against these nobles, whose force he easily dispelled, and whom he prosecuted to forfeiture, but without meaning to effect their entire destruction. As a set-off to this procedure, he demanded that Elizabeth should cease to harbour and support his enemy the Earl of Bothwell. The English queen answered this with all smoothness, but in secret conspired with certain persons in Scotland for re-instating Bothwell in power. The unruly earl obtained by this means a temporary mastery over James (July, August 1593). The king, having contrived by craft and some share of resolution to emancipate himself, once more resumed his authority. In February 1593-4, while the queen lay in confinement after her first child, James mustered some forces, and met the Bothwell faction in the field. The rebels were overthrown, and Bothwell fell into a low and despicable state.

The general lawlessness of the country at this period, and the frightful atrocities which were almost daily committed, make some appearance in the chronicle. Amidst the universal broils, the Presbyterian clergy formed a virtuous element, zealous for an improvement of manners and the advance of the 'evangel,' but equally so in using means to force their own convictions upon others, and often interfering with matters which did not properly fall within their province. The rashness of the synod of Fife in excommunicating the papist lords (September 1593), and the freedom of speech which the members used in discussing and railing at the king's slackness regarding the putting down of popery, gave James great disgust. He spoke sharply of their 'proud enterprises,' and declared he should re-erect the estate of bishops, for the purpose of correcting the insolence of the Presbyterian clergy, and suppressing the liberties which they were abusing.

The Catholic lords, being driven to extremities, collected their vassals and appeared in the field. A royal host under the youthful Earl of Argyle was sent to meet them, and in a bloody fight which took place at Glenlivet on the 3d of October 1594, they gained a victory. This, however, only made it necessary for the king to proceed in person with a larger host against them. He spent many weeks in the north, destroying their castles and harassing their vassalage, yet in his heart was far from coming up to that standard of severity against the ancient faith which would have conciliated the Presbyterian ministers. After a little time, the papist nobles yielded to pass into exile. The Earl of Bothwell, finding his case desperate, also left his native country, and, as it proved, for ever. He died in obscurity abroad.

A singular riot in Edinburgh in December 1596, of which an account is given in the chronicle, led to a reaction in favour of the king against the ultra-zealous Presbyterians. James was enabled to acquire considerable influence in the church-courts, to obtain seats in parliament for certain ministers, as representing the ancient bishops, and to secure a peaceable restoration for the popish lords. His brightening prospects of the English succession added to his power within Scotland, and the latter years of his Scottish reign were marked by comparatively few events of importance.

The most remarkable was the mysterious Gowrie Conspiracy (August 5, 1600). The young Earl of Gowrie and his brother

Alexander Ruthven, sons of the Gowrie who suffered in 1584, appeared to have formed a plan to entrap the king, and by the possession of his person, to work out some project for placing themselves at the head of affairs. James was induced to visit their house at Perth by a tempting story about a man who knew of a concealed treasure. After dinner, he was conducted by Alexander Ruthven into a solitary room at the end of a long gallery, and put into the hands of an armed man. At the same time a false alarm was given to his attendants, that he had left the house, and was riding homeward. While they were hurrying to their horses in the court-yard, the king had a struggle with Ruthven, who first attempted to bind, and then to poniard him. With great difficulty, and not without the exercise of considerable presence of mind, he succeeded in giving an alarm to his attendants; one of whom, named John Ramsay, rushed to his rescue, and slew the two brothers on the spot. The death of the conspirators, and the very folly of their alleged plot, caused the tale of the king's preservation to be received at the time, by a few persons, as an obscure and doubtful matter; and in this light it is still regarded by some; but a dispassionate estimate of probabilities will, we think, make the affair appear as a true, though foolish scheme of two hot-headed young men, animated partly by ambition, and partly by a feeling of revenge. Their bodies were dealt with as those of traitors on the same day (November 19) on which the king's second son, afterwards Charles I., first saw the light.

The imbecility of the king amidst his rude and quarrelsome 1590-1. JAN. 7.
courtiers, is strongly marked by several occurrences of this particular time. The Presbyterian historian tells us that, on the day noted on the margin, as his majesty was coming down the High Street from the Tolbooth, where he had been attending the administration of justice, his two chief friends, the Duke of Lennox and Lord Home, meeting the Laird of Logie, pulled out their swords and assaulted him. The quarrel was that Logie, a valet of the royal chamber, had refused to 'ish' at the duke's order, till he was put out by force; whereupon he had given the duke foul words. While the two nobles set upon the valet, 'the king fled into a close-head, and incontinent retired to a skinner's booth, where it is said . . . . fear.' Six days after, King James was sitting in the Tolbooth, hearing the case of the Laird of Craigmillar, who was suing a divorce against his wife, when the Earl of Bothwell forcibly took away one of the most important witnesses, carried him to

1590-1. Crichton Castle, and there threatened him with the gallows. It seemed 'as if there had been no king in Israel.'—*Cal.*

1591. During this age of general violence, the rights of women were, as a matter of course, little respected. Abductions, both under the impulse of passion and from motives of cupidity, were frequent. The young Duke of Lennox, the cousin and favourite of the king, had contracted a violent attachment to Lady Sophia Ruthven, one of the numerous children left by the unfortunate Earl of Gowrie at his death in 1584. At the order of the king, the young lady was secluded from the duke's resort at Easter Wemyss in Fife. The
Apr. 19. duke, crossing the Firth, took the Lady Sophia out of the house where she lived, and 'carried her away on his awn horse all the night, and on the morn married the said gentlewoman, contrair the ordinance of the kirk; whereat the king was greatly commoved.'[1] —*Jo. Hist.*

In June 1593, an abduction, of which Plutus was the prompting deity, took place under extraordinary circumstances. A young lady, daughter and apparent heir of John Carnegie, had become an object of attention to James Gray, brother of that dexterous *diplomat* the Master of Gray, whose treachery has made him so noted a figure at this period of Scottish history. She had already been once in the hands of her disinterested lover, but rendered back to her father, at the command of the Council. She and her father were now living in the strong house of Robert Gourlay, the merchant, in Edinburgh, when a new and successful effort was made.

On a Sunday, being the 10th of June, Lord Home, who was one of the king's chief courtiers, came to the High Street with an armed party, designed to repress any attempt at rescue. Thus favoured, Gray and his immediate accomplices took the young lady out of her home, and, dragging her down a narrow alley to the North Loch, crossed over with her to the other side, where ten or twelve men were ready to receive her. 'They set her upon a man's

[1] This lady did not long enjoy the position of a duchess. She died on the 11th of May 1592, and was 'buried in the Trinity College, in the east end thereof, very solemnly.'—*Jo. Hist.* When the Trinity College Church was taken down, that its site might form part of a railway station, the remains of a female, believed to be those of the royal foundress, Mary de Gueldres, were found in a side-aisle, and duly re-interred in the royal sepulchre at Holyrood. Afterwards, the remains of another female, who had apparently been buried under circumstances of distinction, were found in the east end of the church, and suspected by some to be the remains of the queen. The probability is, that these latter remains were those of the youthful Sophia Ruthven, Duchess of Lennox.

saddle, and conveyed her away, her hair hanging about her face.' 1591.
The ravisher was 'a gentleman of the king's bed-chamber!'

The magistrates of Edinburgh went to Holyrood on Tuesday to complain of this outrage. 'The king desired to know if they could complean of any that was about him. In the meantime, my Lord Home, who was chief author of the riot, was standing by. They answered nothing, because they expected for no justice.'—*Cal.*

On the 6th of September 1594, Margaret Hay, a girl of only fourteen years, was forcibly taken from her mother's house at Shiplaw, Peeblesshire, by Thomas Hay, brother of Hay of Smithfield, John and Thomas Govan, brothers, and 'Willie Hay callit the Bastard.' She was rescued by Cockburn of Skirling, who refused to give her up. The end of the matter does not appear. —*P. C. R.*

Birrel notes, under 14th August 1595, how Christian Johnston, a widow, was carried off from Edinburgh by Patrick Aikenhead. 'The town was put in ane great fray by the ringing of the common bell,' and 'the said Christian was followit and brought back.' On the 27th of November 1600, a number of persons were denounced and intercommuned for taking away the daughter of George Carkettle, burgess of Edinburgh, 'furth of his awn house of Monkrig, where she was for the time [living] with her mother in peaceable and quiet manner.' It afterwards appeared that the chief guilty party was Robert Hepburn of Alderston, in East Lothian.—*P. C. R.*

About two miles to the south-west of Edinburgh, on the slope of the Craig-Lockhart Hill, there is a mansion called Craig House of the period of James VI., and which in that time belonged to a branch of the old family of Kincaid. On the 17th of December 1600, John Kincaid of Craig House, attended by a party of friends and servants, all 'bodin in feir of weir, with swords, secrets, and other weapons,' came to the village of Water of Leith, also closely adjacent to Edinburgh, and there attacked the house of Bailie John Johnston, 'where Isobel Hutcheon, widow, was in sober, quiet, and peaceable manner for the time, dreading nae evil, harm, injury, or pursuit of ony persons, but to have lived under God's peace and our sovereign lord's.' Kincaid 'violently and forcibly brak up the doors of the said dwelling-house, entered therein, and pat violent hands on the said Isobel's person, took her captive, reft, ravished, and took her away with him to his place of Craig House; where he deteined her, while [till] his majesty being upon the fields, accompanied with John,

1591. Earl of Mar, Sir John Ramsay, and divers others, hearing of the committing of sic ane horrible fact, directed the said John, Earl of Mar, Sir John Ramsay, and divers others his hieness' servants, to follow him, and relieve her furth of his hands. Wha having come to his place of Craig House, and requiring for her relief, he refusit to grant the same, while [till] they menaced to bring his majesty about his said house and raise fire therein; and sae compellit him to relieve her.'

Kincaid underwent trial for this outrage, January 13, 1601, and his doom was ordered by the king to be a fine of 2500 merks, payable 'to us and our treasurer'—'as also he sall deliver to us and our treasurer *his brown horse*.'—*Pit.*

APR. 30. 'John Dickson, younger of Belchester, being apprehended, ta'en, and brought to Edinburgh, was put to the knawledge of ane assize for the slaughter of his awn natural father [in July 1588], and also for the lying for the said offence at the process of excommunication. [Being convicted, he was] brought to the scaffold, and at the Cross broken on ane rack, [and] worried—where he lay all that night, and on the morn [was] carried to the gallows of the Burgh-moor, where the rack was set up, and the corpse laid thereupon.'—*Jo. Hist.*

JUNE 6. In the midst of the proceedings regarding the witches, two ministers of Edinburgh broke out against the king in their sermons for his feeble administration of justice. One spoke of the universal contempt of his subjects; the other said he did not seem to have any power over even a witch-wife, meaning Barbara Napier. James sent for them two days after, at the Tolbooth, where he often sat beside the judges of the session. He remonstrated with them for the freedom they had used, but could not bring them to acknowledge any fault. In the conversation which ensued, they argued with the king about their respective powers. An apostle said: 'We shall judge the angels;' and Christ had said: 'Ye shall sit upon twelve thrones and judge.' Here was sufficient warrant for the parish ministers of Scotland lording it over the head of the state. After all, they protested they loved him, and he parted with them in good-humour.

On the ensuing 8th of December, a highly characteristic scene took place at Holyrood—three of the ministers 'visiting' the royal family as censors, 'to try what negligence was in pastors, and abuses in the family.' They went again upon Friday the 10th, when the king himself was present. They urged the king to have 1591. the Scriptures read at dinner and supper, and 'willed that new elders could be chosen and the comptroller left out.' A week after, one of them, Mr John Davidson, called in a private capacity at the palace to admonish the king about his failures in the exercise of king-craft, particularly in appointing bad men to offices, and pardoning great criminals. 'The king answered, he found not concurrence in inferior magistrates . . . . there were diverse officers claimed their places by heritage. As for known pardons, he would answer for every one he gave by law and reason. As for unknown, such was the multitude of his businesses, that some about him deceived him by importunity, and got stolen subscriptions, from which kind of dealing he thought no flesh in his place could always be free. Further, he saw not where to make choice of fit officers, for when any man's particular cometh in question, then their partiality may be seen.'—*Cal.*

On this day are entered in the records of the Privy Council two Oct. 28. complaints which illustrate in a remarkable manner the state of society at that time. First, James Lord Ogilvie of Airly, ancestor of the Earls of Airly, complains that, while he was living quietly in the protection of the law, and dreading harm from no man, the Earl of Argyle, without any provocation from him, hounded out a set of broken Highlandmen to the number of about five hundred, to attack him, and spoil his lands. He had 'retired in sober and quiet manner, to dwell and make his residence in Glen Isla,' when, on the 21st of August, they entered the district under silence of night, 'with sic force and violence, that the said lord, lying far from his friends, was not able to resist them, but with great difficulty and short advertisement, he, his wife and bairns, escaped.' The invading party are described as having slain all the people they could lay their hands on, eighteen or twenty in number; besides, they 'spulyit and away-took ane grit number of nolt, sheep, and plenishing [furniture], to the utter wreck and undoing of the haill poor inhabitants of the country.' Having at the command of the king retired, they still hovered on the neighbouring hills, and some weeks after made a new attack upon Glen Isla, as well as Glen Clova, slaying three or four persons, and taking away much spoil; 'sae that the poor men dwelling in Glen Clova, Glen Isla, and other parts adjacent to the Month, wha are not able to make resistance, are sae oppressed by the broken men and sorners hounded out by the Earl of Argyle and his friends,

1591. and maintainit and reset by them, that neither by his majesty's protection, nor assurance of the party, can their lives and gudes be in surety.'

This seems very mysterious, till we read the second entry, which is a complaint that, on the 16th of August bypast (five days previous to the above incident), Leighton of Usan and sundry of the Ogilvies, to the number of about threescore persons, had, at the instigation of Lord Ogilvie, gone with jacks, spears, harquebuses, and other weapons, and attacked Robert Campbell in Millhorn, William of Soutarhouse, Thomas Campbell of Keithock, and John Campbell of Muirton, whom they had mercilessly slain. How this outrage had been provoked, does not appear; but there can be no doubt that the invasion of Lord Ogilvie's privacy in Glen Isla was a consequence of this earlier and similar incident.

The frightful cutaneous disease of leprosy prevailed in Scotland, as in most other European countries, from an early age. There was a hospital for the reception of its victims at Kingcase, near Ayr, believed to have existed from the reign of King Robert I. At Glasgow, such an establishment was planted by the Lady of Lochow, daughter of Robert, Duke of Albany, and in 1584 it had six inmates. In a solitary spot between Old and New Aberdeen, there was a leper-house, but rather poorly endowed, for in this year King James is found granting the inmates a right to one peat out of every load of peats sold in the town, in consideration that their rents were 'unable to sustene them in meat and fire, wherethrough they live very miserably.'[1] There were a few other such refuges of hopeless misery throughout the land.

In a sheltered spot called Greenside, near the northern skirts of the Calton Hill, a small monastery of Carmelite Friars had had a brief existence before the Reformation. On its desolate site, a merchant-burgess of Edinburgh, John Robertson by name (whom we soon after find in the office of bailie), now erected a small house for the reception of lepers, led thereto, it is stated, by a sense of gratitude to God for a signal deliverance vouchsafed to him. The town-council concurred in his object, and undertook

[1] May 19, 1591, the town-council of Aberdeen made arrangements for the support of one Robert Abell, who was 'visited with leprosy, and thereby unable to win his living or frequent honest men's society.' He was placed in the house here described.—*Ab. C. R.* In 1612, the magistrates made the like provision for Agnes Jameson, spouse to Patrick Jack, 'vexed and diseased with the sickness of leprosy,' although she was not born and bred in the burgh.

the oversight and direction of the establishment. A committee of their number, in conjunction with a minister of the city, and John Robertson himself, drew up rules for the house, and arranged the means of its support. Five men afflicted with leprosy, and two women, the wives of two of these men, but not themselves lepers, were admitted, each leper being allowed four shillings Scots money —equal to 4d. sterling—weekly, and also having a privilege of begging under certain restrictions. They were on no account to go about for alms, or to stir from the house at all, or to admit any visitor, under penalty of death, and, to shew how earnest was the spirit of this rule, a gibbet was erected at the gable of the hospital, ready for the instant execution of any transgressor. From sunset to sunrise, their door was to be kept fast locked, under the same penalty. Each patient was to take his turn of sitting at the door 'with ane clapper,' to attract the attention of people passing between Edinburgh and Leith, and to beg from them for the general benefit. The rest were meanwhile to stay within doors. The two wives, Isobel Barear and Jonet Gatt, were to be allowed to go to market, to purchase *vivres* for the lepers and for themselves, but not to call anywhere else in town, under penalty of death. A person was appointed to read prayers to the inmates each Sunday, and a weekly oversight was confided to the Masters of Trinity Hospital. It serves curiously to realise the whole arrangement to our minds, that this hospital still exists, though the leper-house seems to have been extinct since the middle of the seventeenth century.[1] 1591. Nov. 21.

We have under this date a curious specimen of the administration of justice under King James. Letters are raised at the instance of 'Helen Henderson, spouse of William Murray elder of Romanno; Margaret Tweedie, spouse of John Murray younger of Romanno; and —— Nisbet, spouse of William Murray, *third* Laird of Romanno, with the puir tenants, cotters, and labourers of the ground of the lands of Romanno, lying within the sheriffdom of Peebles:' stating that these three lairds, with sundry other persons, had been denounced at the horn for their concern in the slaughter of John Hamilton of Coitquott[2] and his son; and, on the complaint of the widow and children of the said John, with Dec. 10.

[1] Edin. Council Record. See Professor Simpson's curious Notices of Leprosy in Scotland, *Edin. Med. and Surg. Journal*, No. 149.

[2] Now La Mancha.

1591. a false report that the Lairds of Romanno were fortifying their tower of Romanno, there to defend themselves against the powers of the law, 'his majesty appointit the same to be keepit by four persons, allowing them monthly the sum of twenty merks . . . . to be payit out of the living of Romanno,' and caused letters to be directed to the complainers, charging them with this payment. The three ladies appeal against this order, on the ground that they had not been previously heard in their own cause. Had they been so, they could have shewn reasons to the contrary—'the house of Romanno was never keepit agains his hieness, but the same, as alsae the country, is left by the said rebels, and that immediately after committing the fact (gif in their awn defence and by procurement of other persons God knaws and time will try), and therefore needit nae sic keepers, it being bot ane auld and ruinous touir, not meet for nae man to keep or hazard his life into, and, besides this, the said Helen Henderson, Margaret Tweedie, and —— Nisbet, are infeft in conjunct fee and liferent in the haill lands of Romanno, whilk is bot a puir ten-pund land, in effect barren of the self, and subject to the incursion and stouthreif of the broken men and thieves of baith the borders, and, as is mair nor notour, will not sustene the said complenars nor their families, they having nae manner of thing else whereupon to live.' The ladies further pointed out the hardship of punishing the innocent for the guilty, and pleaded how they had already made a great composition with the representatives of the slaughtered persons. Nevertheless, on parties being heard before the Council, the letters complained of were found to be legal and proper, and so the garrison imposed on the old tower would remain for the meantime a burden on the estate.—*P. C. R.*

On the ensuing 17th of March, Jonas Hamilton of Coitquott gave surety by sundry of his friends, under large sums, that 'Margaret Tweedie, relict of John Murray of Romanno, her tenants and servants, sall be harmless and skaithless.'

The garrison consisted of this Jonas; William, his brother; William Hamilton in Cranston; and William Brown in Bordland. It appears that the Murrays had held the house in contempt of a summons from John Blainslie, 'Bute pursuivant,' and had been thrust out with their families by force. The widow Margaret, with feminine tenacity of purpose, obtained a letter under the king's signet for dispossessing the Hamilton garrison; and now this was reclaimed against. Parties being heard in presence, his majesty affirmed the order for the surrender of the house to the

widow, on condition that she should give security that it should 1591.
not prove a refuge for her outlawed relatives.—*P. C. R.*

During this troublous period of the king's reign, the book of the Privy Council becomes a kind of review of the nobility and gentry of Scotland, as they severally appear to give caution for one another as to the maintenance of the peace, or are cited or denounced for its infraction. As an example of a kind of entry which occurs several times at every meeting, John Murray of Dec. 22. Blackbarony becomes 'actit and obleist as cautioner or surety for William Burnett of the Barns [both in Peeblesshire], that he sall compeir personally before the king's majesty and Lords of Secret Council, at Halyrudhouse, or where it sall happen to be for the time, the 29 day of December instant, and answer to sic things as sall be inquirit of him, touching sic deidly feid as he has interest in, and that he sall underly sic order as his hieness and the said lords sall demene to him thereanent, under the pain of ane thousand merks.'—*P. C. R.*

The Earl of Bothwell seems to have been little distressed by his forfeiture. According to his own ideas, he was only suffering from the malice of a successful enemy, the Chancellor Maitland. All that he aimed at was a change of administration in his own favour. How to bring it about? In our days, such a discharged favourite would bide his time, in hopes that some new turn of affairs or a gust of popular favour through the House of Commons would bring him into favour again. In Scotland, at the close of the sixteenth century, the needful first step was to obtain, by whatever means, possession of the king's person. Now then commenced a series of remarkable assaults on King James by his turbulent cousin.

Having secured some favour among the royal attendants, he Dec. 27. came to Holyroodhouse at night, with his friends the Lairds of Spott and Nisbet, Mr Archibald Douglas, a natural son of the Regent Morton, Mr John Colville, and others, to the amount of forty or fifty. They 'enterit in at a stable-door beside the east gable of the Traitor's Tower, whilk was called the Duke's Stable, within the whilk there was a trap and ane entress privily made. Having enterit therein, they first bereft the porter of the keys, and then passed to the chancellor's chalmer-door; they dang up the same. He, being foreseen by the cry of ane boy that there was ane tumult of men in the close, withdrew himself and

1591. some others within his inner chalmer, whilk has ane narrow entress, at whilk the conspirators strake with fore-hammers and shot pistolets. There was some shots of muskets shot out again [by which] some of them were hurt; [so they] for fear to be trappit, passed to the queen's chalmer-door, whilk they brak up.'

'In the meantime, the haill noblemen and gentlemen of his majesty's house raise, who thought to have taken the Earl Bothwell and his complices. The earl fled; yet he returned at the south side of the abbey, where the said earl and his complices slew his majesty's master-stabler, named William Shaw, and ane with him, named Mr Peter Shaw. But the king's folk took eight of Bothwell's faction, and on the morrow hanged them all without ane assize, betwixt the Girth Cross and the Abbey-gate.' —*Moy. Bir.*

Dec. 28. 'The king's majesty came to Sanct Geill's Kirk, and there made ane oration anent the fray made by Bothwell and William Shaw's slaughter, his master-stabler.'—*Bir.*

1591-2. Feb. 7. The slaughter of the Bonny Earl of Moray at Dunnibrissle stands prominent amongst the tragic events of the time. It was much more a piece of clan warfare than is generally allowed by Scottish historians. Moray had connected himself with a number of gentlemen and heads of clans in the north, who had combined against the Earl of Huntly. In the latter part of 1590, there were in that district of Scotland musterings, marchings, and fightings, too obscure to make an appearance in general history, but enough to keep three counties in a state resembling civil war. Huntly, who acted as lord-lieutenant of the north, and thus had a colour of law on his side, pursued the Mackintoshes and Grants, who befriended the Earl of Moray, as rebels, both against himself, who was their feudal superior, and against the king. In a reconnoitring expedition which he made at Darnaway Castle, the Earl of Moray's house, one of his gentlemen was unfortunately killed by a musket-shot, discharged by a servant from the battlements—an injury which the feelings of the day made it a virtue to revenge.

By the intervention of Lord Ochiltree, Moray came south to his house of Dunnibrissle, in Fife, with a view to a reconciliation with Huntly. The northern chief was also at court; but his thoughts were not turned on peace. In consequence of Moray having befriended the turbulent Bothwell, the king and Chancellor

Maitland were wrought upon to grant a commission to Huntly for the capture of that nobleman, not dreaming, as we may charitably hope, of the cruel tragedy which was to ensue. Perhaps neither did Huntly meditate anything beyond taking Moray, and having him subjected to trial. 1591 2

Mustering forty friends on horseback, he set out with them, as to a race at Leith; but, having thus lulled suspicion, he quickly turned away, and crossed the Forth at the Queensferry. At a late hour on a winter night, the Earl of Moray heard his lonely house surrounded by the hostile Gordons, and received a summons to surrender. He had no friend with him but one—Dunbar, sheriff of Moray—and a few servants; yet he determined to make resistance. The Gordons then gathered corn from the neighbouring farms, and piling it against the door, set it on fire. To pursue the quaint recitals of the day: 'The Earl of Moray, being within, wissed not whether to come out and be slain, or be burned quick; yet, after avisement, this Dunbar says to my Lord of Moray: "I will go out at the gate before your lordship, and I am sure the people will charge on me, thinking me to be your lordship; sae, it being mirk under night, ye shall come out after me, and look if that ye can fend [provide] for yourself." In the meantime, this Dunbar came forth, and ran desperately amang the Earl of Huntly's folks, and they all ran upon him and presently slew him. During this broil with Dunbar, the Earl of Moray came running out at the gate of Dunnibrissle, which stands beside the sea, and there sat down amang the rocks. But, unfortunately, the said lord's knapscull tippet, whereon was a silk string, had taken fire, which betrayed him to his enemies in the darkness of the night, himself not knowing the same. They came down on him on a sudden, and there most cruelly, without mercy, murdered him.' —*Bir. Moy.*

Next morning, Edinburgh was full of mourning and lamentation for this sad event. That the victim was a Protestant and son-in-law of the Good Regent, while the Earl of Huntly was notedly the head of the popish party in Scotland, was chiefly remembered by them. The conflict of interests in the north, the death of John Gordon at Darnaway, and the possibility of Huntly having been far from meditating slaughter, were little known or reflected on. The sympathies of the king, on the other hand, were with Huntly; nor, had it been otherwise, would his majesty have found it an easy task to bring to justice a grandee who had recently come forth against the Protestant interest with ten thousand men at his back.

1591-2. 'The king went forth to the hunting that morning; and hunting about Inverleith and Wardie, he saw the fire, which had not yet died out; but nothing moved with the matter.'—*Cal.* It was generally believed that both he and the Chancellor Maitland had not been unwilling that Huntly should do this deed. 'The king sent for five or six of the ministers, made an harangue to them, wherein he did what he could to clear himself, and desired them to clear his part before the people. They desired him to clear himself with earnest pursuing of Huntly with fire and sword. The king alleged his part to be like David's when Abner was slain by Joab.'—*Cal.* It nevertheless appears, from the records of Privy Council, that James, on the 8th of February, being the day after the murder, retracted from Huntly his commission of lieutenancy.

FEB. 9. '—— the Earl of Moray's mother, accompanied with her friends, brought over her son's and the sheriff of Moray's dead corpse, in litters, to Leith, to be brought from thence to be buried in the aile of the Great Kirk of Edinburgh, in the Good Regent's tomb, and, as some report, to be made first a spectacle to the people at the Cross of Edinburgh; but they were stayed by command from the king. Captain [John] Gordon [a brother of the Laird of Gicht], was left for dead at Dunnibrissle; his hat, his purse, his gold, his weapons were taken by one of his own company; his shanks [stockings] were pulled off. He was taken in by the Earl of Moray's mother, and cherished with meat, drink, and clothing. A rare example! She brought him over with her son's corpse to seek justice. The earl's mother caused draw her son's picture, as he was demained, and presented it to the king in a fine *laine* cloth, with lamentations, and earnest suit for justice. But little regard was had to the matter. Of the three bullets she found in the bowelling of the body of her son, she presented one to the king, another to . . . ., the third she reserved to herself, and said: "I sall not part with this till it be bestowed on him that hindereth justice."'[1]—*Cal.*

One of the king's friends, Lord Spynie, hearing that Captain Gordon had been brought to Leith, got a warrant from the king to bring him to Edinburgh Castle, 'to have eschewit the present trial of law;' but Lord Ochiltree, being informed of this, took horse with about forty friends and servants in arms, and went forth

[1] It will be found that the body of the Bonny Earl remained above ground for six years, probably with a view to keeping up the popular indignation against his murderers. (See under February 16, 1597-8.)

after the king, who, even at this dismal moment, could not restrain his inordinate propensity to hunting. Lord Ochiltree 'came upon the king on the north side of Corstorphine Craigs, where his majesty was taking a drink. [He] lichtit and stayit his horse at the hill foot, and came to his majesty and show[ed] him . . . . how far this murder touched his highness, whereof he besought him maist humbly to consider. . . . . Upon Lord Ochiltree his earnest desire, his majesty granted him a warrant to present Captain Gordon and his man to the trial of ane assize that same day; whilk with all diligence the said lord did perform, and the said captain was beheadit, and his man hanged. The captain condemned the fact, protesting that he was brought ignorantly upon it.'—*Moy. Cal.* 1591-2.

The Earl of Huntly made an appearance of satisfying the demands of law for the slaughter of Moray, by entering himself in ward in Blackness Castle, as preliminary to his trial; but the king released him after eight days' confinement, and he was not again troubled on that score. It is to be observed, however, that the Bonny Earl's death did not pass without at least an attempt at revenge in the north.

The Clan Chattan or Mackintoshes, and the Grants, were much incensed by the fact, and made great 'stirs' against their superior the Earl of Huntly. The earl sent the Clan Cameron against the one, and a leader called Mackranald against the other, and had great slaughter committed upon both. The Mackintoshes, still indisposed to submit, came in the fall of the year 1592, eight hundred strong, into the Gordon territories of Strathdee and Glenmuick, where they killed four gentlemen of Huntly's vassalage. One of these was the Laird of Brackla, a place near the modern watering-village of Ballater. He was an old man, much given to hospitality, and had received a party of these invaders without any apprehension of their hostile intentions. After a kindly entertainment, they killed the old man in his own hall (November 1)—a circumstance which naturally added much bitterness to the feelings of his friends, as it was considered as the foulest style in which murder could be committed.[1]

The Earl of Huntly was interrupted in an invasion of the Mackintosh estate of Pettie in Inverness-shire, by a report of what was going on in Aberdeenshire. With his uncle, Sir Patrick

[1] It is necessary to distinguish this from the murder of another Laird of Brackla in 1667, on which a ballad has been composed. See Jamieson's *Northern Ballads*.

1591-2. Gordon of Auchindoun, and about thirty-six horsemen, he did not hesitate immediately to ride into Strathdee and attack the Mackintoshes, now passing over a hill called Stapliegate in the Cabrach. After a sharp skirmish, he routed them utterly, killing about sixty. He then caused parties of his people to invade and spoil the Mackintosh and Grant territories; nor did he rest till, by slaughter and pillage, he had completely reduced these clans to his obedience.[1]—*G. H. S.*

It is not unworthy of remark, that the Privy Council Record contains no notice of these outrages in the north, beyond an entry dated November 9, 1592, adverting to 'great cruelties, herships, and disorders recently committit by the lawless broken Highlandmen of the Clan Chattan, Clan Cameron, Clanranald, and others pretending their dependence on the Earls of Huntly and Athole;' which had 'sae wrackit and shaken louss sundry parts of the north country, that great numbers of honest and peaceable folks are murtherit, their houses burnt now in the winter season, their guids spulyit, disponit, and exponit in prey, in far greater rigour nor it was with foreign enemies;' for which reasons a commission was granted to the Earl of Angus to go north and

[1] In a memoir of the family of Grant, written by Mr James Chapman, minister of Cromdale, in 1729, and preserved in the Macfarlane Collections in the Advocates' Library, there is a curious traditionary anecdote, which the writer connects with the murder of the Laird of Brackla, and yet dates in 1540. It is given in the following terms: '[James Laird of Grant, called *Shemus nan Creagh*, or James the Ravager] distinguished himself in assisting the Earl of Huntly, his cousin, against the insults of several enemies, and particularly in revenging the murder of Gordon Baron of Brackla, on Dee water-side, who was murdered by the countrymen there. The revenge went such a length, that above sixscore orphans were left in the desolate country on Deeside, nobody knowing who their parents were. These miserable orphans were, out of pity and commiseration, carried by the Earl of Huntly into his castle, where they were maintained and fed thus. A long trough of wood was made, wherein was put pottage or any other kind of food allowed them; and the young ones, sitting round about the trough, did eat their meat out of it as well as they could. The Laird of Grant visiting the earl, was, for diversion's sake, brought to see the orphans slabbing at the trough; which comical sight so surprised him, that he proposed to carry one-half of them to Balcastle, alleging that, having a hand in destroying their parents, he was bound in justice to take a concern in their preservation and maintenance. Those of them that were brought to Castle-Grant are to this day called *Slioch Namor*—that is, the Posterity of the Trough.' As *Shemus nan Creagh* died in 1553, and the Grants were not engaged on the Earl of Huntly's side on this occasion, but participated with their relatives and allies the Mackintoshes in suffering from his vengeance, it may be presumed that this barbarous tale refers to the date assigned for it by Chapman—namely, a period fully fifty years earlier than the murder of the Laird of Brackla. It has nevertheless been introduced by Sir Walter Scott in his *Tales of a Grandfather*, as applicable to the reign of James VI.; and the reader who turns it up there, may experience some amusement in contrasting its ample and picturesque details with the simple original anecdote as above narrated.

deal with the said earls for the pacification of the country, and, failing this, to raise the well-affected people in arms, and put down the lawless by force. This view of the matter is so inconsistent with the statement of Sir Robert Gordon, above quoted, as to suggest that the Scottish government knew hardly anything of the relations of parties, and had heard only of there being troubles in a certain district. No notice whatever is taken of the sweeping vengeance executed by the Earl of Huntly upon the Mackintoshes and Grants. Certainly, no feature of the time is more remarkable than this freedom and power of the great nobles to do what they considered justice upon their enemies, while the king was unable by any force under his own immediate control to protect himself in his own palace. 1591-2.

We learn from another source, that the Earl of Angus brought matters to a bearing in conformity with the king's direction, by causing 'baith the parties subscryve ane assurance, bot of their awn form.'—*Moy*.

Richard Graham had for some years been noted as a prominent licentiate of the devil's medical college. He professed to despise common witchcraft as a vulgar thing, and would only admit that he consulted spirits. Spottiswoode, speaking of the death of the good Earl of Angus, says: 'In the time of his sickness, when the physicians found his disease not to proceed of any natural cause [it was concluded to be by enchantment], one Richard Graham being brought to give his opinion of it, made offer to cure him, saying, as the manner of these wizards is, "that he had received wrong." But when he [the earl] heard that the man was suspected to use unlawful arts, he would by no means admit him, saying: "That his life was not so dear to him, as, for the continuance of it some years, he would be beholden to any of the devil's instruments; that he held his life of God, and was willing to render the same at His good pleasure, knowing he should change it for a better."'[1] FEB. 28.

It is related that Sir Lewis Bellenden, Lord Justice-clerk, dealt with Graham to raise the devil. Graham having raised him in Sir Lewis's own yard in the Canongate, 'he [Sir Lewis] was thereby so terrified that he took sickness and thereof died.'—*Stag. State*.

[1] The Earl of Angus in this anecdote was a Protestant, and succeeded by the earl noticed in the preceding article, who was of the ancient faith.

1591-2. It was satisfactorily made out that Graham had been the adviser of the witch Barbara Napier and her associates; and we have just seen that the Earl of Bothwell was likewise believed to have consulted him regarding the king's death. This wizard, therefore —'notour and knawn necromancer, ane common abuser of the people'—was apprehended; and on the day noted in the margin, he was 'worried and burnt at the Cross of Edinburgh.' According to Calderwood, 'he stood hard to his former confession touching Bothwell's practice against the king; that Arran, Lord Fairnyear,[1] was an enchanter; that the devil was raised at the Laird of Auchinleck's dwelling-place, and in Sir Lewis Bellenden the Justice-clerk's yard. The bruit [rumour] went that the chancellor [Maitland] had some tables and images about his neck, and that he was sure [safe] so long as he used them so; but Richard Graham deponed no such matter.'

Mar. 7. The presbytery of Edinburgh laboured hard to get the Earl of Huntly and his friends excommunicated. They could not be brought to see that there was any need for the same severity against the Earl of Bothwell and his associates, who had tried to seize the king in his palace by night. James 'grudged' at this, 'and said it would not be weel till noblemen and gentlemen got licence to break ministers' heads.'—*Cal.*

1592. Mar. 31. We have at this date a peculiar proceeding recorded, regarding a dyvour or bankrupt. 'In presence of the provost, bailies, council, and community of the burgh of Edinburgh, Patrick Lindsay, tailor, was sworn in judgment that he was not worth five [. . . .], sworn in judgment, divour and *bare man*. This was because he was reteinit in ward at the instance of John Anderson, burgess of the said burgh, for the sum of eighty pounds, by the space of sax ouks. After[wards], he was brought to the Cross, convoyit with the provost, bailies, and officers; and thereupon, after three *Oyez*'es, the said aith was published by Bartilmo Uchiltree, officer, wha cut the said Patrick's belt in three pieces in presence of the haill people. This form of law was never practised in Edinburgh on the first erection thereof, and therefore I thought necessary to put [it] in memory.'—*Jo. Hist.*

June (?) 'There came from Aberdeen a young woman, called Helen

[1] Fairnyear, the last year: the phrase means, formerly a lord.

Guthry, daughter to John Guthry, saddler, to admonish the king of his duty. She was so disquieted with the sins reigning in the country—swearing, filthy speaking, profanation of the Sabbath, &c.—that she could find no rest till she came to the king. She presented a letter to him when he was going to see his hounds. After he had read a little of it, he fell a laughing that he could scarce stand on his feet, and swore so horribly that the woman could not spare to reprove him. He asked if she was a prophetess. She answered she was a poor simple servant of God, that prayed to make him a servant of God also; that was desirous vice should be punished, and specially murder, which was chiefly craved at his hands; that she could find no rest till she put him in mind of his duty. After the king and courtiers had stormed a while, she was sent to the queen, whom she found more courteous and humane. So great and many were the enormities in the country, through impunity and want of justice, that the minds of simple and poor young women were disquieted, as ye may see; but the king and court had deaf ears to the crying sins.'—*Cal.* 1592.

Half a year had now elapsed since Bothwell's fruitless attempt on Holyroodhouse. The king was living his usual free-and-easy life in his little hunting-seat or palace of Falkland in Fife, when the forfeited lord thought proper to make a new attempt in his peculiar style at a change of administration, or restoration of himself to power and favour. A little after midnight, he suddenly appeared before the royal residence with three hundred men, and tried, but in vain, to obtain entrance. James had been forewarned; and, throwing himself into the tower of the palace, which he had had time to furnish with provisions, he set the assailants at defiance. Bothwell, baffled, and fearing to meet the friends who he knew would speedily rally to the king's assistance, left the place at seven in the morning, carrying off all the horses, in order to check pursuit. JUNE 28.

'Thereafter his majesty came over the water, and made ane oration in the Great Kirk of Edinburgh. Immediately after the fray, Bothwell and his men came over the water, and there were eighteen of them taken in Calder Muir, and in other parts near Calder Muir, lying sleeping for want of rest and enterteenment; and, immediately after their taking, they were all brought to Edinburgh, and [five of them] hangit.

'At the same time [July 1] the Lairds of Niddry and

1592. Samuelston [friends of Bothwell][1] were taken by Lord John Hamilton [lying sleeping in the meadow of Lesmahago], and warded in the Castle of Draphane . . . . Lord Hamilton] came to Edinburgh, thinking to have got grace to them from his majesty. He came down to his majesty's lodgings at the Nether Bow, and going into Mr John Laing's house, where his majesty lodgit, the guard standing above the [Nether Bow] port, with their hagbuts, guns, and other weapons . . . . . seeing my Lord Hamilton, for the honour of his lordship, shot ane volley at my lord. There was ane man [James Sinclair of Earstone] speaking to his lordship, shot through the head; ane other by him shot through the leg; and ane bullet struck the lintel of the gate just above my lord's head where he stood, yet no more harm done. So that, by mere accident, the said Lord Hamilton had [al]most have been slain, and not through any evil will.

'The Lord Hamilton, seeing he could get no grace to the said two gentlemen, sent word to his bastard son Sir John, who convoyit the said two gentlemen away, and went with them himself for their more safety.'—*Bir.*

Early in August, a plan was devised by two courtiers, Wemyss of Logie and the Laird of Burleigh, to bring Bothwell privately into the royal presence at Dalkeith Castle. On this occasion also, the king was forewarned, and Bothwell had to retire without being introduced. Burleigh confessed his fault; but Logie either stood out, or at the utmost admitted that he engaged in the plot for a good end, desiring to learn what was the purpose of the enemy. 'The king said: "That was too much, not making him privy." Logie said: "God forbid I should have told you anything, who can keep nothing close!" The king regretted to the queen that he had none about him who were sure.'—*Cal.* Logie was put into confinement.

'Because the event of this matter had sic a success, it sall also be praised by my pen, as a worthy turn, proceeding from honest, chaste love and charity, whilk should on nae ways be obscurit from the posterity for the guid example: and therefore I have thought guid to insert the same for a perpetual memory.

'Queen Anne, our noble princess, was served with divers gentlewomen of her awn country, and namely with ane called Mrs Margaret Twinstoun, to whom this gentleman, Wemyss of Logie, bure great honest affection, tending to the godly band

[1] Andrew Wauchope of Niddry, and John Hamilton, younger, of Samuelston.

of marriage; the whilk was honestly requited by the said gentlewoman, yea even in his greatest mister [trouble]. For, howsoon she understood the said gentleman to be in distress, and apparently by his confession to be punished to the death; and she, having privilege to lie in the queen's chalmer, that same very night of his accusation, where the king was also reposing that same night, she came furth of the door privily, baith the princes being then at quiet rest, and passed to the chalmer where the said gentleman was put in custody to certain of the guard, and commanded them that immediately he should be brought to the king and queen; whereunto they giving sure credence, obeyed. But howsoon she was come back to the chalmer door, she desired the watches to stay till he should come forth again; and so she closed the door, and convoyed the gentleman to a window, where she ministrat a lang cord unto him to convoy himself down upon; and sae by her guid charitable help he happily escaped by the subtlety of love.'—*H. K. J.* 1592.

'Logie married the gentlewoman after, when he was received into the king's favour again.'—*Cal.*

This incident has been made the subject of a popular ballad.

About this time, Bothwell was understood to be retired to his great estate in Liddesdale, and to be there engaged in a kind of work which is usually the privilege of royalty. 'His majesty was informed that Bothwell had ane that cunyied false cunyie in the house of Row in Liddesdale. . . . . His majesty wrate to the Lord Ochiltree, desiring him to go to the said house, and to bring sic men to his majesty as he fand there, together with all sic instruments as could be there had for cunying, with power to raise the haill country if need were. . . . . The Lord Ochiltree gathered to the number of seven or aucht score horse, all in armour, and rade first to Jedburgh, where they stayit that night, and refreshit himself and his company; and Ferniehirst, his brother-in-law, sent with him three score horse upon the morn at night. [They] rade to the house of the Row at Liddesdale, and there took the twa men out of the house beside the tower, and thereafter strake up the doors of the tower, and brought the irons that prentit the cunyie, with all the instruments, together with ane number of thirty-shilling [half-crown] pieces, whilk were cunyied there, and delivered the same to his majesty in the Abbey. The false cunyier was gone in England, and was not to be had; to seek metal to cunyie more, as was reported.'—*Moy.* Aug. (?)

1592. Aug. On the high ground which skirts the Carse of Gowrie to the north, near the village of Rait, once stood a fortified house called Gaskenhall. Only a bit of broken garden-wall and a few trees now indicate the site. Here lived, at the end of the sixteenth century, Robert Bruce of Clackmannan, chief of the family which had given Scotland a king three centuries before, and described in the grave pages of Douglas's *Baronage* as a most respectable person, 'in high favour with King James VI., who conferred on him the honour of knighthood at the baptism of his son Prince Henry.' Let us see, from the actual doings of this knight, what sort of person he was.

In August 1592, some goods belonging to Bruce, having to pass through Perth, were subjected to payment of custom by the magistrates, who, on payment being refused, seized them. Clackmannan sent a letter of remonstrance, threatening, if his goods were not restored, to make the Perth citizens suffer for it when they chanced to pass his house. This not being attended to, he attacked a party of citizens on their way from Dundee, and despoiled them of their weapons; for in those days a party of quiet burghers passing through twenty miles of even this central and comparatively civilised district of Scotland, could not go unarmed. The only reply the laird got to a message offering the weapons back in exchange for his goods, was a visit from a company of Perth citizens, who destroyed a good deal of his growing corn with their horses. He came out to remonstrate, and an altercation ensuing, he was provoked to strike one of the aggressors with a pistol. He then seized the two chief men of the party, William Inglis and John Balsillie, and took them as prisoners into his house of Gaskenhall.

That same night, a large party of the citizens of Perth, headed by the bailies and council, came out in arms to Gaskenhall, where, upon the morrow, before daylight, they sounded their drum, besieged the laird in his house, and discharged hagbuts and pistols in at the doors and windows, whereby a servant of his was wounded. At last setting fire to the house, they entered at the roof, set free their friends, and seized the laird, whom they 'transportit away with them ane certain space, barefooted and bare-legged, not suffering him to put on his awn claithes.' They likewise 'spulyit and took away with them his haill silver-wark, bedding, claithes, and all the plenishing of his house.'—*P. C. R.*

This affair came before the king, who seems to have taken no step in the case beyond declaring both parties in the wrong, and

ordering the laird and the magistrates into divers prisons, there 1592.
to lie at their own respective costs, until they should be subjected to an assize. A Perth chronicler states: 'They were thereafter agreed upon the town's large charges.' The agreement, however, does not seem to have been effectual, for, on the 28th of April 1593, as John Wilson and John Niven, with other citizens of Perth, were passing the Coble of Rhynd on their way to the market of St Andrews, they were beset by the laird, accompanied with nine horsemen and footmen, all well armed. 'The said John Wilson and John Niven, being baith hurt and wounded in divers parts of their bodies, to the effusion of their blood in great quantity, the said laird and his accomplices maist shamefully tirrit them baith naked, and in maist barbarous and shameful manner scourgit them with horse bridles through the town of Abernethy, as gif they had been thieves or heinous malefactors; [then] left the said John Niven lying there for dead, and took the said John Wilson, naked, as captive and prisoner away with them.'

On the complaint of the magistrates of Perth, among whom was the afterwards famous Earl of Gowrie, acting as provost, the Laird of Clackmannan was charged to appear before the king, on pain of being denounced as a rebel in case of failure.

'The ministry of Edinburgh devised twa purposes, which they Oct.
had baith in head at a time; either thinking to prevail in ane or else in baith, as tending to the glory of God, as they pretended. The ane was to discharge the merchants of Edinburgh from haunting and resorting to Spain; the other was, that nae mercat-day should be halden in Edinburgh for selling of wool and sheep's skins; whereat baith merchants and craftsmen were grieved. . . . . The ministers at nae time proponit thir matters to be reasoned or disputed by the provost of the town and his council, to whom it specially apperteinit; but, as they did, thought it mair expedient to divulgate the matter openly in the kirk, in presence of the haill people, alleging that the merchants could not make voyage to Spain without danger of their sauls, and therefore willit them in the name of God to abstein. . . . . At divers times this was openly required, while at last, finding that the merchants continued in their trade as before, they cried out that unless they wald forbear, they should expreme their names to the people, and therefore cited divers merchants before their session, and there commanded them to abstein. The merchants, seeing this, gave in their complaint to

1592. the king, and tauld how they were discharged [forbidden] by the ministers, but wald disobey thereunto, if his majesty wald grant them liberty to pass, whilk was granted; whereat the ministers were sae grieved, that they boasted [threatened] the merchants with excommunication. But the provost and council interceded, and stayed that purpose, because that to the merchants divers Spanyards were addebted, whilk wald never be repaid unless they went themselves to make count and reckoning with them; and siclike divers of them were awing to creditors there, and in that respect till their counts were perfyted and ended, they could not abstein from travelling. . . . . Sae the ministers had patience for that time, otherwise this matter had turned to a great popular scism.

'. . . . the other conceit had almaist have made a worse end; because it was sae prejudicial to the commonwealth and estate of the haill merchants and craftsmen, to wit, the abolition of the Monday's mercat, whilk was the only special mercat-day of all the week in respect of the rest. The reason that the ministers had for them was, that all men that came to the Monday's mercat did address him to his journey on Sunday, whilk day sould be sanctified and keepit holy; but amang many great infallible reasons, it was funden that the maist part of the mercat folks did never address themselves to journey while Monday morning, and therefore the mercat should not cease; and as to these that came far off, it became the pastors of their parochin to hinder them. Besides all this, that mercat-day was authorised to the town by the princes of ancient time, and therefore it became not a subject to consent to the abolition thereof, unless the matter was moved in presence of the three estates of parliament.'—*H. K. J.* The people in general murmured at these interferences with their secular affairs, well meant as they undoubtedly were. Calderwood speaks bitterly of the satirical rhymes vented on the occasion against the clergy, adding: 'Such has always been the religion of Edinburgh, when they are touched in their particular.' At length, in April 1593, the affair of the market came to a head. 'The shoemakers, who were most interested in that business, hearing that the same was to be put in execution, tumultuously gathering themselves together, came to the ministers' houses, menacing to chase them furth of the town if they did urge that matter any more. After which the motion ceased, the market continuing as before. This did minister great occasions of sport at that time in court, where it was said, "that rascals and souters could obtain at the ministers' hands what the king could not in matters more reasonable."'—*Spot.* 1592.

'Dame Margaret Douglas, sometime Countess of Bothwell, met the king at the Castle-yett of Edinburgh on her knees, having up her hood, crying for Christ's sake that died on the cross, for mercy to her and her spouse, with mony tears piteous to behold. The king putting out his hand to have tane her up, she kissed the back of his hand thrice. Then he passed into the castle, and the lady came down the street. The same day, ere the king came out of the palace, the Lairds of Niddry and Samuelston, with sundry others forfaultit of before, came on their knees in the outward close of the palace, wha were received in favours.'—*Jo. Hist.* Nov. 17.

'Ane proclamation that no man shall receipt the Countess of Bothwell, give her entertainment, or have any commerce or society with her in any case, wha had been so lately received in his majesty's favour before. Behold the changes of court!'—*Bir.* Nov. 23.

A few days before this date, the Earl of Mar was married at Alloa to Mary, the second daughter of the late Duke of Lennox and sister of the Countess of Huntly. The king honoured the marriage with his presence, and spent his Christmas with the newly wedded pair. It is rather surprising to find Mar, who had always been on the ultra-Protestant side, allying himself to a daughter of the papist Lennox; but tradition informs us that the god of love had in this case overcome that of politics—if there be such a deity. There were also some natural obstructions, for the earl was a widower of five-and-thirty, while the bride was little more than a girl. The story is, that his lordship, finding the young lady scornful, became low-spirited to such a degree as to alarm his old school-fellow, the king, for his life. Learning what was the matter, James told him in his characteristic familiar style: 'By ——, ye shanna die, Jock,[1] for ony lass in a' the land!' He then used his influence as virtual guardian of the Lennox family, and soon brought about the match. From this pair have descended some of the most remarkable patriots, lawyers, statesmen, and divines, to which our country has given birth.[2] Dec. 25.

In the midst of the festivities at Alloa, the king was unpleasantly

[1] The king, probably from recollection of some incident of their early school-days, used to recognise the grave earl by the name of *Jock o' Sklaitts.*

[2] The above anecdote was communicated to me by Sir Walter Scott in 1827, immediately

1592. disturbed by intelligence of the capture of George Ker, adverted to in the next article.

In the latter part of this year, the king was nearly on as bad terms with the clergy as ever. They openly reproached him in their pulpits with slackness of justice against the enemies of religion. One maintained that he might very properly be excommunicated, if he resisted their behests. The king told the provost to pull them out of their pulpits when they spoke so against him; but this the provost plainly said he could not do—he preferred God before men. Things were in this ticklish state when George
DEC. 27. Ker was taken with sundry letters from Catholics at home to Catholics abroad, and three blank letters from Huntly, Errol, and Angus, believed to be the foundation of a conspiracy with Spain against the Protestant religion. The brethren met in Mr Robert
1592 3. JAN. 9. Bruce's gallery to devise measures, and a huge deputation went down to Holyroodhouse, to confer with the king. He received them in the great hall, and was at first very angry with them for their thus meeting unauthorisedly, saying, '"he knew not of it till all the wives in the kail-mercat knew of it." Yet in the end, to mitigate them in some measure, he said he liked weel their zeal, for he knew they did it for love of the good cause.'—*Cal.* So began a sort of civil war, which lasted two or three years, and ended in the banishment of the three Catholic nobles, as already related.

Mr Tytler attributes these new troubles to the persecuting spirit of the Presbyterian divines. 'The principle of toleration,' he says, 'divine as it assuredly is in its origin, yet so late in its recognition even amongst the best men, was then utterly unknown to either party, Reformed or Catholic. The permission even of a single case of Catholic worship, however secret; the attendance of a solitary individual at a single mass, in the remotest district of the land, in the most secluded chamber, and where none could come but such as knelt before the altar for conscience' sake, and in all sincerity of soul; such worship and its permission for an hour, was considered an open encouragement of Antichrist and idolatry. To extinguish the mass for ever, to compel its supporters to embrace what the kirk considered to be the purity of presbyterian truth, and this under the penalties of life and limb, or in its

after he had derived it from the Earl of Haddington (Earl Charles), to whom, I suppose, it had come through his predecessors, the descendants of Lord Mar's brother-statesman, Thomas, first Earl of Haddington.

mildest form of treason, banishment and forfeiture, was considered not merely praiseworthy, but a high point of religious duty; and the whole apparatus of the kirk, the whole inquisitorial machinery of detection and persecution, was brought to bear upon the accomplishment of these great ends.' 1592 3.

The king, whether from his natural disposition, or views of policy, was averse to harassing the papists. He one day spoke privately to Lord Hamilton of his unhappy position. '"You see, my lord, how I am used, and have no man in whom I may trust more than in Huntly, &c. If I receive him, the ministers cry out that I am an apostate from the religion; if not, I am left desolate." "If he and the rest be not enemies to the religion," said the Lord Hamilton, "ye may receive them; otherwise not." "I cannot tell," saith the king, "what to make of that; but the ministry hold them for enemies. Always, I would think it good that they enjoyed liberty of conscience." Then the Lord Hamilton crying aloud, said: "Sir, then we are all gone, then we are all gone, then we are all gone! If there were no moe to withstand, I will withstand." When the king perceived his servants to approach, he smiled and said: "My lord, I did this to try your mind."'—*Cal.* Few things could better illustrate the sanctity in which the principle of intolerance was then held, than to find a contemporary historian relating this anecdote as one simply illustrative of the infirm adherence of King James to the presbyterian cause.

The Earl of Errol, one of the exiled Catholic lords, writing to the king from Middleburg in July 1596, speaks of having undergone incessant troubles ever since he professed the Catholic religion, and of having for three or four years past been in daily and extreme peril of his life. He says: 'My late and greatest extremities have proceeded only upon that over-great fervour and onnecessar rigour of the ministry, wha, disdainfully rejecting all reasonable conditions, will force men's consciences, not as yet persuaded, till embrace their opinions in matters of religion.'[1]

Mr John Graham of Hallyards, a judge of the Court of Session, had an unfortunate litigation with Sir James Sandilands, the Tutor of Calder, about some temple-lands which his wife had brought to him. There had been a deed forged in the case, and a notary hanged for it, and a collision between the Court of Session and

[1] *Letters and State Papers of the Reign of James VI.* Abbotsford Club Series. 1838. P. 16.

1592-3. the General Assembly as to jurisdiction, and now Sir James Sandilands had become incensed to a degree of fury against his opponent the judge.

Graham, being charged by the king, for peace' sake, to depart
FEB. 13. from Edinburgh, was passing down Leith Wynd in obedience to the order, attended by three or four score persons for his protection, when Sir James Sandilands, accompanied by his friend the Duke of Lennox, and an armed company, followed hard at his heels. Graham, thinking he was about to be attacked, turned to make resistance. The duke sent to tell him that if he proceeded on his journey, no one would molest him; but the message proved of no use, in consequence of some stray shot from Graham's company. The party of Sandilands immediately made an attack; the other party hastily fled. Graham fell wounded on the street, and was carried into a neighbouring house. A French boy, page to Sir Alexander Stewart, one of Sandilands's friends, seeing his master slain, followed the hapless judge into the house, 'douped a whinger into him,' and so despatched him. Such was the characteristic termination of a lawsuit in 1593.—*Cal.*

It is highly worthy of remark, that, not many months after, Sir James Sandilands was once more peaceably living at court.

1593. Amongst the complications of the affair between Huntly and Moray in February 1592, there were mingled the details of a plot in which Huntly and the Chancellor Maitland were connected with three chieftains of the clan Campbell—Ardkinlas, Lochnell, and Glenurchy—against the life of John Campbell of Calder, who was obnoxious to the latter persons on account of his supreme influence in the affairs of the minor Earl of Argyle. By the exertions of Ardkinlas, a man called MacEllar was procured to undertake the assassination of Calder: and in the same month which saw the tragedy at Dunnibrissle, this wretched man shot Calder with three bullets, through a window, as the victim sat unsuspecting of danger in the house of Knepoch in Lorn.

The youthful earl having threatened vengeance against Ardkinlas, the latter seems to have lost heart; and being extremely desirous of recovering his young chief's regard, he seriously made an endeavour to that effect by means of witchcraft, and was much disappointed when that resource failed him. He subsequently tried to accomplish his purpose by revealing what he knew of another plot in which the same parties were concerned against the earl's life. This, however, is aside from our present subject. It may be sufficient to remark that MacEllar and a higher agent in the person of John Oig Campbell of Cabrachan, a brother of Lochnell, were taken and executed for Calder's death; but owing to various causes, among which the complicity and friendship of Maitland was probably the chief, Ardkinlas continued for a considerable time to keep out of the grasp of the law. 1593.

At the time noted, he sustained an assault of private vengeance which might well make him tremble. A complaint which he entered before the Privy Council sets forth that, having occasion to be at Dumbarton with some friends, including Duncan Campbell, Dean of Brechin, on his way to Edinburgh, whither he was going in obedience to a summons of the king, 'he took purpose to hald forward in his journey that same night after supper, by reason of the troubles whilk are in the country, lippening [trusting] for naething less than ony injury or trouble to have been intended him.' Nevertheless, John Buchanan of Drumfoid, with a party of friends, and 'sundry others, broken men and fugitives, to the number of twenty-four persons, on horse and foot, all bodin in feir of weir, with lang hagbuts, jacks, pistolets, and other weapons invasive,' took up a position in a yard beside the road, with the design of murdering Campbell. 'The said Duncan and ane other of his [Ardkinlas's] servants, being ganging a little before him, and the persons foresaid surely believing that ane of them had been the Laird of Ardkinlas, they dischargit ane dozen of hagbuts at the said twa persons, and shot the said Duncan in the head; and thereafter, coming furth of the yard, finding the said Duncan not to be dead, and still believing he had been the said Laird of Ardkinlas, they shamefully and barbarously mangled and slew him with swords, and cuttit off his head. And then, perceiving themselves to be disappointed, they sharply followit the said laird, shot aucht or nine hagbuts at him, and had not failed likewise to have slain him, were not that by the providence of God he escaped.' MAR. 28.

The next notice we have of affairs connected with the Campbell conspiracies is a curious, though obscure one, regarding what was in the language of that time called a *Day of Law*, held in Edinburgh on the 19th of June (the king's birthday) 1593. There appeared as seekers of justice for Calder's slaughter, the Earl of Argyle (seventeen years of age), the sheriff of Ayr, the Earl of Morton, and some others; as defenders in that cause, Ardkinlas, Glenurchy, and others. The Chancellor Maitland, whose concern was suspected, but did not become clear till our

1593. own time, had his friends assembled also—namely, the Earls of Montrose, Eglintoun, and Glencairn, and Lord Livingstone, 'who all accompanied Lord Hamilton on the streets.' Against them were mustered the Duke of Lennox, the Earl of Mar, Lord Home, and some others, who, favoured with the countenance of the queen, talked of bringing in Lord *Quondam* against the chancellor: by this name they indicated Captain James Stuart, long sunk out of credit and means, but still eager to take any desperate means of recovering his place. To this goodly company it was expected that Lord Maxwell and the Laird of Cessford would soon be added. The affair seemed so threatening, that the king was seriously alarmed, and commanded all to keep their lodgings; after which he 'dealt with the chancellor to entreat them to depart in peace.' Such was a *day of law* in the reign of gentle King James.

It was not till September 1596 that Ardkinlas underwent a trial for the slaughter of the Laird of Calder. The matter having doubtless been arranged beforehand, no pursuers appeared, and he was set at liberty.[1]

June 21. George Smollett, burgess of Dumbarton (an ancestor of the novelist), was denounced rebel for not answering certain charges made against him by the burghs of Glasgow and Renfrew. It was alleged that Smollett, having purchased a letter of the king, used it as a sanction to deeds of violent oppression against the Highland people resorting with merchandise to those towns. 'He not only masterfully reives the goods and bestial, claithing, and other wares, brought by the inhabitants of the Isles and other parts of the Highlands, to the said burghs, by sea and land, but takes, apprehends, and imprisons their persons, and sometimes pursues themselves by way of deid.' It was added that the people of the Highlands were, in consequence, inspired with a deadly hatred of the burghs of Glasgow and Renfrew, and were already committing such reprisals as threatened civil war.—*P. C. R.*

July 7. An act of Privy Council, reciting that 'vile murders have not only been committed within kirks and other places, but even within the burgh of Edinburgh and suburbs thereof, ewest [near] to his hieness' palace, to the great hazard of his awn person,'

[1] Calderwood. *History of James VI.* Pitcairn's *Criminal Trials.* Gregory's *History of the Western Highlands and Isles.*

commands the authorities of the city, the king's guard, the master 1593.
and porter of his palace, to 'search for all hagbuts and pistolets' worn by any persons in the city and king's palace, and convey the wearers to prison, the weapons to be escheat for the benefit of the apprehenders. In the parliament which sat down a few days afterwards, it was enacted: 'Whaever sall happen, at ony time hereafter, to strike, hurt, or slay ony person within his hieness' parliament-house during the time of the halding of the parliament; within the king's inner chalmer, cabinet, or chalmer of presence, the king's majesty for the time being within his palace; or within the Inner Tolbooth the time that the Lords of Session sit for administration of justice; or within the king's privy council-house the time of the council sitting there; or whaever sall happen to strike, hurt, or slay ony person in the presence of his majesty, wherever his hieness sall happen to be for the time; sall incur the pain of treason.' For those who commit the like offences in places and presences of less importance, severe penalties are denounced. Another act aimed at strengthening the hands of the magistrates of Edinburgh in their endeavours to apprehend turbulent persons and rebels, seeing that the weakness of such authorities 'is the original and principal cause wherefra the great confusion and disorder of this land, in all estates, proceeds.'—*S. A.* and *P. C. R.*

The feud between the Lord Maxwell and the Laird of Johnston, which had been stayed by a reconciliation, broke out again afresh in consequence of a foray by William Johnston of Wamphray, usually called, from his reckless, dissipated character, the *Galliard*, in the lands of the Crichtons of Sanquhar and Douglases of Drumlanrig. The Galliard being taken in the fray and hanged, his friends, on being pursued for the recovery of the stolen cattle, stood at bay and fought so desperately that many of their enemies bit the dust. A remarkable scene was consequently presented in JULY 22.
Edinburgh. 'There came certain poor women out of the south country, with fifteen bloody shirts, to compleen to the king that their husbands, sons, and servants, were cruelly murdered by the Laird of Johnston, themselves spoiled, and nothing left them. The poor women, seeing they could get no satisfaction, caused the bloody shirts to be carried by pioneers through the town of Edinburgh, upon Monday, the 23d of July. The people were much moved, and cried out for a vengeance upon the king and council. The king was nothing moved, but against the town of

1593. Edinburgh and the ministry. The court alleged they had procured that spectacle in contempt of the king.'—*Cal.*

JULY 24. Bothwell had now been little heard of for upwards of a twelvemonth, a long interval of quietness for such a politician. The time had at length come for a third attempt to regain favour with the king. 'At eight hours in the morning, the Earl of Bothwell, the Laird of Spott, Mr William Leslie, and Mr John Colville' [' to the number of twa or three hundred men'], 'came into the king's chalmer, weel provided with pistol. It was reported that the said Earl and Mr John were brought in by the Lady Athole, at the back yett of the abbey. This earl and his complices came not this way provided with pistols and drawn swords to harm the king's majesty any ways, but because he could not get presence of his majesty, nor speech of him, for the Homes, who were courtiers with the king, and enemies to the said Earl of Bothwell. Sae they came into his majesty's chalmer, resolving themselves not to be halden back till they should have spoken with him; and sae after they came in, his majesty was coming frae the back-stair, with his breeks in his hand, in ane fear—howbeit he needed not. The foresaid Bothwell and his complices fell upon their knees, and gave their swords upon the ground, and beggit mercy at his majesty; and his majesty being wise, merciful, a noble prince of great pity, not desirous of blood, granted them mercy, and received them in his favour; and at four hours afternoon proclaimed them his free lieges.'

'There was ane great tumult in Edinburgh for this. They come all down in arms, and cried to understand the king's mind, who cried out and said, that he was not captive, but weel, in case that whilk was promised by them should be keepit; and commanded them all to the abbey kirk-yard, to stay there till he called for them. Immediately thereafter, [he] sent for the provost and bailies, and commanded them to dissolve and go homeward; he houpit all should be weel.'—*Moy. Bir.*

For a time the Chancellor Maitland, Lord Home, and other courtiers gave way before the replaced Bothwell. The English ambassador exerted influence in his behalf. The zealous clergy befriended him, not for any virtues he could be said to possess, for he had none, but for that which was a compendium of all virtue, his professing to be for 'the trew religion.' King James was obliged to seem his friend, and to be quite against the Catholic lords. One day, as the king was travelling by Fala, near Soutra

Hill, these nobles came up unexpectedly, threw themselves on their knees before him, and entreated forgiveness and favour. He told them he could do nothing for them unless they satisfied the kirk, and 'he sent back, that same nicht, the Lord Treasurer and the Abbot of Lindores to the ambassador of England and the ministers of Edinburgh, *desiring that they should conceive nae evil opinion of his part for their coming to him.*'—*H. K. J.* Such were the relations of royalty to the priesthood in those days. 1593.

Notwithstanding such powerful support, Bothwell could not long maintain his place at court. We soon find him again at the horn, and passing through a rather picturesque adventure on a mountain-road a few miles to the south of Edinburgh. 'It fortuned Sir Robert Kerr, younger of Cessford, accompanied only with one of his awn servants called Rutherford, to pass out of Edinburgh, homeward to his wife quietly; in the way of plain accident, [he] forgathered with the Earl Bothwell, and ane Gibson with him, beside Humbie on this side of Soutra Hill; where, meeting twa for twa, they fought a long time on horseback . . . . The Laird of Cessford's man was hurt in the cheek, and at length baith the parties so wearied with long fechting, [that] they assented baith to let the others depart and ride away for that time. Cessford came back to Edinburgh, and tauld the king's majesty of that accident.'—*Moy.* Dec. 11.

Aberdeen, a commercial town with a university, bore a singular moral relation to the adjacent Highlands of the Dee, where a wild and lawless population, speaking a different language, and using a different dress, existed. Many were the troubles of the industrious burghers from these rude neighbours, who would sometimes come sweeping down upon their borders like a flight of locusts, and leave nothing of value uneaten or undestroyed. At this time, we find the council of the northern city meeting to consider 'the barbarous cruelty lately exercit by the lawless hielandmen in Birse, Glentanner, and thereabout, not only in the unmerciful murdering of men and bairns, but in the masterful and violent spulying of all the bestial, guids, and gear of a great part of the inhabitants of these bounds . . . . committit near to this burgh, within twenty miles thereto;' for which reason it was ordained that the whole inhabitants should be ready with arms to meet for the defence of the town, and to resist and repress the said hielandmen, as occasion shall be offered.' July 31.

1593. The Crichtons and Douglases, whom the Johnstons had plundered in the summer of this year, having induced Lord Maxwell to take up their cause, and enter with them into bonds of *manrent* for mutual support, it behoved the Laird of Johnston to be stirring. To his aid came the reiving clans of Scott and Graham, and with them he fell upon and cut off a party of the Maxwells. This led to a decisive attempt of Lord Maxwell to bring the Johnstons to subjection; but, though undertaken under sanction of his office as warden of the west marches, it ended in a way very unfortunate for himself.

DEC. 6. 'The Lord Maxwell, being on foot 1500 and horse together, coming to the Lochwood, having special commission of the king to have destroyed the said Lochwood, and banished and destroyed the haill Johnstons, because he [the laird] was ane favourer of the Earl Bothwell in some of his turns—being come over the Water of Annan—the Laird of Johnston, with the Scotts, to the number of 800 or thereby, ombeset the said lord in his way; where, without few or na strakes, the said lord was slain with the Laird Johnston's awn hand [or, as is alleged, by Mr Gideon Murray, being servitor till Scott of Buccleuch[1]]; never ane of his awn folks remained with him (only twenty of his awn household), but all fled through the water; five of the said lord's company slain; and his head and right arm were ta'en with them to the Lochwood, and affixed on the wall thereof. The bruit ran that the said Lord Maxwell was treacherously deserted by his awn company.'—*Jo. Hist.*

Such was the famous clan-battle of *Dryfe's Sands*, the last of any note fought in the southern part of Scotland.

1593-4. JAN. 21. For some time we have heard nothing of Eustachius Roche, *quondam* tacksman-general of the Scottish mines. From this circumstance, and the difficulties he seemed to be labouring under the last time we heard of him, it is little to be doubted that he had found his adventure unprofitable and hopeless, and given it up. Now another comes forward, one really noticeworthy, since he prospered to some extent in his undertaking, and laid the foundation of a property and a work which still exist. This was Thomas Foulis, goldsmith in Edinburgh.

[1] This interlined in the manuscript in a different hand. Another report is, that Lord Maxwell was slain by Willie Johnston, nephew of the *Galliard*, mentioned under July 22, 1593.

The Edinburgh goldsmiths of that day, though only occupying a few small obscure shops stuck between the buttresses of St Giles's Church, comprehended in their number two or three persons of such considerable wealth, as to verge upon a historic importance. Such, for example, was George Heriot, who in 1597 became goldsmith and jeweller to the king, and in time accumulated the fortune which enabled his executors to erect the magnificent hospital bearing his name. Another of the number was Thomas Foulis, who, when in spring 1593 the king had to march an army against the Papist lords in the north, supplied a great part of the funds required for the purpose. What the Bank of England has often in modern times been to the British government, Thomas Foulis, the Edinburgh goldsmith, was in those days to King James —a ready resource when money was urgently required for state purposes. On the 10th of September 1594, the royal debt to Thomas was no less than £14,598; and as a security so far for this sum, the king consigned to him 'twa drinking pieces of gold, weighing in the haill fifteen pund and five unce,' which the consignee was to be at liberty to coin into 'five-pund pieces,' if the debt should not be otherwise paid before the 1st of November next, 'the superplus, gif oney beis,' to be forthcoming for his majesty's use. The value of the gold of these drinking-cups at the present day would be about £950, which shews that the debt in question was expressed in Scottish money. It may be remarked, that on the same day the king consigned another gold drinking-cup, weighing twelve pounds five ounces, in favour of John Arnott, burgess of Edinburgh, who had lent him £6000. It further appears that Thomas Foulis, very soon after, lent the king £12,000 more 'for outredding of sundry his hieness' affairs.' 1593-4.

In consideration of the loans he had had from Thomas Foulis, the king granted him (January 21, 1593–4), a lease of the gold, silver, and lead mines of Crawford Muir and Glengoner for twenty-one years. The Edinburgh tradesman probably had the sagacity to see, in a little time, that there was not, in those districts, a sufficiency of the more precious metals to pay the expense of collecting. We find, however, that in 1597 he was working the really valuable lead deposit of Lanarkshire, as there are acts of council in that year for the protection of his lead-carriers against 'broken men of the borders.'[1]

[1] G. L. Meason's preface to *Discoverie and Historie of the Gold Mynes of Scotland.* Bannatyne Club. 1825.

1593-4. We shall meet Thomas again. Meanwhile, it may be observed that his lead-mines in time passed through his granddaughter into the possession of (her husband) James Hope of Hopetoun, sixth son of the great lawyer, Sir Thomas, and the founder of the noble house of Hopetoun. It has long been one of the best estates in Scotland; and it is certainly curious to trace its origin to the hypocritical military expedition against the Catholic lords, into which King James was forced by his ultra-zealous Presbyterian subjects, when he would have much rather been 'drinking and driving ower in the auld maner' at home.

Whatever became of the gold-diggings in Foulis's hands, we find that, before the expiration of the term of his lease, they were actively worked by another person. An Englishman named Bulmer, with the licence and favour of Queen Elizabeth, and a patent from the king of Scots, set seriously to work in five different moors—namely, Mannoch Muir and Robbart Muir in Nithsdale, the Friar Muir on Glengoner Water, and Crawford Muir in Clydesdale, and Glengaber Water in Henderland, Peeblesshire. 'Upon Glengoner Water he builded a very fair country-house to dwell in; he furnished it fitting for himself and his family; he kept therein great hospitality; he purchased lands and grounds round about it; he kept thereupon many cattle, as horses, kine, sheep, &c. And he brought home a water-course for the washing of and cleansing of gold; by help thereof he got much straggling gold on the skirts of the hills and in the valleys, but none in solid places; which maintained himself then in great pomp, and thereby he kept open house for all comers and goers; as is reported, he feasted all sorts of people that thither came.' A verse upon the lintel of the door of the house in Glengoner has been preserved:

Sir Bevis Bulmer built this bour,
Who levellèd both hill and moor;
Who got great riches and great honour
In Short-cleuch Water and Glengoner.[1]

Bulmer also set regular apparatus at work in Short-cleugh Water and Long-cleugh Braes, in Crawford Muir, and often found considerable quantities of the ore: in the latter place, his people found one piece of six ounces' weight within two feet of the mosses. He also found a considerable quantity in Glengaber, but erected no apparatus there. After a persevering effort,

[1] *Archæologia Scotica*, iv. 404.

he became embarrassed, in consequence, it is affirmed, of prodigal housekeeping, and retired from the adventure no richer than he commenced it. 1593-4.

'. . . . between twa and three hours in the morning, the queen was delivered of ane young prince, within the Castle of Stirling, in his majesty's chalmer there; whilk was a great comfort to the haill people, moving them till great triumph, wantonness, and play, for banefires were set out, and dancing and playing usit, in all parts, as gif the people had been daft for mirth.'—*Moy.* FEB. 19.

The king had scarcely seen his wife out of the perils of childbirth, when he was obliged to come to Edinburgh to take measures against the Earl of Bothwell, who was now breaking out into open rebellion. Fearing to live in Holyroodhouse, which had already been twice broken into by the turbulent lord, he took up his quarters in 'Robert Gourlay's lodging' within the city.

'. . . . being Sunday, his majesty came to Mr Robert Bruce's preaching, [who] said to his majesty, that God wald stir up mae Bothwells nor ane (that was, mae enemies to him nor Bothwell), if he revengit not his, and faucht not God's quarrels and battles on the papists, before he faucht or revenged his awn particular.'—*Bir.* MAR. 13.

The king 'came to the sermon, and there, in presence of the haill people, promised to revenge God's cause, and to banish all the papists; and there requested the haill people to gang with him against Bothwell, wha was in Leith for the time. The same day, the king's majesty rase, and the town of Edinburgh in arms. The Earl of Bothwell, hearing that his majesty was coming down, with the town of Edinburgh, rase with his five hundred horse, and rode up to the Hawk-hill, beside Lesterrick [Restalrig], and there stood till he saw the king and the town of Edinburgh approaching near him. He drew his company away through Duddingston. My Lord Home followed till the Woomet, at whilk place the Earl of Bothwell turned, thinking to have a hit at Home; but Home fled, and he followed; yet by chance little blood. The king's majesty stood himself, seeing the said chase' [at a safe distance, namely, on the Burgh-moor].—*Bir.* 1594. APR. 3.

Within a few days after this affair, the earl, seeing he could not effect his object, retired into England. Soon after, much to the scandal of the preachers, he joined the papist lords. All his plans, however, were frustrated; and early in the next year, he left Scotland, an utterly broken man, never again to give his royal cousin any trouble.

1594. MAY. Kenneth Mackenzie of Kintail was rising to be a wealthy and influential man in the west of Inverness-shire. Beginning as simple chief of the Clan Kenzie, with a moderate estate, he ended as a peer of the realm and the lord of great possessions. A remarkable notice regarding him occurs at this time in the Privy Council Record, and it is the more so, as he had been for some time a member of that body. It is recited that he had, some time before, purchased a commission of justiciary from the king, for a district including the lands of certain neighbours, besides his own, and conferring the power of proceeding against persons accused of treasonable fire-raising. This was declared to have been given on wrong representations, and to be contrary to the laws of the kingdom, and Kenneth was commanded to appear by a certain day before the Council, and meanwhile abstain from acting upon the commission.—*P. C. R.*

As a specimen of how nobles possessing castles acted towards meaner men who had fallen under their displeasure—James, Lord Hay of Yester, was charged before the Privy Council with having, on the day of June previous, gone to the house of Brown of Frosthill, and taken him forth thereof, and carried him to his 'place of Neidpath,' where 'he put him in the pit thereof, and detenes him as captive, he being his majesty's free subject . . . . having committit nae crime nor offence, and the said lord having nae power nor commission to tak him.' The king had granted letters charging Lord Yester to liberate Brown, and that they should both come before him; and this had been of none effect. JULY 4. The matter being now before the Council, and a procurator having appeared for Brown to explain that he was still a prisoner at Neidpath, while Lord Yester made no appearance, officers were charged to go and denounce the latter as a rebel if he should refuse to obey the king's command, Brown having meanwhile given surety to the extent of two hundred pounds that he should be ready to answer any accusation that might be brought against him.—*P. C. R.*

JULY. Robert Logan of Restalrig is one of the darkest characters of this bloody and turbulent time. A few years later, he was plotting with the Ruthvens of Gowrie for an assault upon the king. So early as February 1592–3, he was denounced for trafficking with the turbulent Bothwell. In June of this year, he was again denounced, and for a more serious matter—his sending out two

servants, Jockie Houlden and Peter Craik, to rob travellers on the 1594.
highway, near his house of Fast Castle in Berwickshire. They had attacked Robert Gray, burgess of Edinburgh, as he was passing the Boundrod, near Berwick, and taken from him nine hundred and fifty pounds, besides battering him to the peril of his life.—*P. C. R.* His residence, as is well known, was a fortalice perched on an almost inaccessible crag overhanging the waves of the sea, with black cliffs above, below, and nearly all round—perhaps the most romantically situated house in our ancient kingdom. Here, it is known, Logan had Bothwell for his occasional guest.

In July of this year, Logan entered into a contract with John Napier of Merchiston, proceeding upon the fact of 'diverse auld reports, motives, and appearances, that there should be within the said Robert's dwelling-place of Fast Castle a sowm of money and pose, hid and huirdit up secretly.' John Napier undertook that he 'sall do his utter and exact diligence to search and seek out, and be all craft and ingyne that he dow [can], to tempt, try, and find out the same, and, be the grace of God, either sall find out the same, or than mak sure that nae sic thing has been there.' For this he was to have a third of any money found. He was also to be convoyed back in safety to Edinburgh, unspoiled of his gains.

As Logan was competent to make simple mechanical search for the supposed treasure without the aid of a philosopher, there is much reason to believe that Napier designed to use some pseudo-scientific mode or modes of investigation, such as the divining-rod, or the so-called magic numbers. The affair, therefore, throws a curious light on the state of philosophy even in the minds of the ablest philosophers of that age, the time when Tycho kept an idiot on account of his gift of prophecy, and Kepler perplexed himself with the *Harmonices Mundi.*

It is not known whether Napier did actually journey to the spray-beaten tower of Fast Castle, and there practise his craft and ingyne. Probably he did, and was disappointed in more ways than one, as, two years after, he is found letting a portion of his property to a gentleman on the strict condition that no part of it shall be sub-let to any one of the name of Logan.[1]

'This year, in the Merse, there was a great business about

[1] Napier's *Life of Napier of Merchiston.*

1594. sorcery and the trial of witches, and many was there burnt, as, namely, one Roughhead, and Cuthbert Hume's mother of Dunse, the parson of Dunse's wife, and sundry of Eyemouth and Coldingham; near a dozen moe, and many fugitives, as the old Lady A. Sundry others were delated, and the Ladies of Butt: and Lady B.: the Laird of B.: his sister; one in Liddesdale by virtue of [a] superstitious well, whereat was professed great skill; one Dick's sister, who had her mother hanged before in Waughton. They confessed the death of the whole goods [live-stock] of the country.'—*Pa. And.*

Nov. The disposition to violent and lawless acts at this time is strikingly shewn in the proceedings against Claud and Alexander, two sons of James Hamilton of Livingstone, in Linlithgowshire. Having some ground of offence against David Dundas of Priestinch, they had gone at mid-day with an armed party to his fold, and, there barbarously mutilated and slaughtered a number of his cattle. They and their elder brother, Patrick, also destroyed a mill leased by the same person, and further set fire to his barn-yard at Duddington. Two months afterwards, when John Yellowlees, a messenger, went with two assistants to the Peel of Livingstone, to deliver letters of citation against these young men, the laird, with his wife and four sons, came forth to the gate, and taking him first by the throat, proceeded to beat him unmercifully, and then, with a bended pistol at his breast, and many violent threats, forced him to eat and swallow his four letters, and to promise never to attempt to bring any such documents against them in future; besides which, they struck the two witnesses with swords and pistols, and left them for dead. The family were denounced as rebels.—*Pit.*

1594-5. Jan. 19. A great *tulyie* or street-combat this day took place in Edinburgh. The Earl of Montrose, head of the house of Graham, was of grave years—towards fifty: he was of such a character as to be chosen, a few years afterwards, as chancellor of the kingdom: still later, he became for a time viceroy of Scotland, the king being then in England. Yet this astute noble was so entirely under the sway of the feelings of the age, as to deem it necessary and proper that he should revenge the death of John Graham (see under February 13, 1592-3) upon its author, under circumstances similar to those which attended that slaughter. On its being known that the earl was coming with his son and retinue to Edinburgh, Sandilands was strongly recommended by some of his friends to withdraw from the town, 'because the earl was then over great a party against him. His mind was, notwithstanding, sae undantonit, and unmindful of his former misdeed, finding himself not sae weel accompanied as he wald, he sent for friends, and convokit them to Edinburgh, upon plain purpose rather first to invade the said earl than to be invadit by him, and took the opportunity baith of time and place within Edinburgh, and made a furious onset on the earl [at the Salt Tron in the High Street], with guns and swords in great number.[1] The earl, with his eldest son, defendit manfully, till at last Sir James was dung [driven down] on his back, shot and hurt in divers parts of his body and head, [and] straitly invadit to have been slain out of hand, gif he had not been fortunately succoured by the prowess of a gentleman callit Captain Lockhart. The lord chancellor and Montrose were together at that time; but neither reverence [n]or respect was had unto him at this conflict, the fury was sae great on either side; sae that the chancellor retirit himself with gladness to the College of Justice. The magistrates of the town, with fencible weapons, separatit the parties for that time; and the greatest skaith Sir James gat on his party, for he himself was left for dead, and a cousin-german of his, callit Crawford of Kerse, was slain, and mony hurt: but Sir James convalescit again, and this recompense he obteinit for his arrogancy. On the earl's side was but ane slain, and mony hurt.'—*H. K. J.* 1594 5.

Hercules Stewart was hanged at the Cross in Edinburgh, for his concern in the crimes of his brother the Earl of Bothwell. The people lamented his fate, for 'he was ane simple gentleman, and not ane enterpriser.'—*Moy.* He 'was suddenly cut down and carried up to the Tolbooth to be dressed; but within a little space he began to recover and move somewhat, and might by appearance have lived. The ministers, being advertised hereof, went to the king to procure for his life; but they had already given a new command to strangle him with all speed, so that no man durst speak in the contrary.'—*Pa. And.* FEB. 18.

Commenced 'ane horrible tempest of snaw, whilk lay upon the ground till the 14th of April thereafter.'—*Bir.* MAR. 10.

[1] Another writer represents the Master of Montrose as setting upon Sir James Sandilands.

1595. May 26. 'John Gilchrist, Henderson, and Hutton, all three [were] hangit for making of false writs and pressing to verify the same. Jun. 11. Ane callit Cuming the Monk [was] hangit for making of false writs.'—*Bir.*

July. Two gentlemen of Stirlingshire, one named Bruce, the other Forester, happened to love one woman, about whom they and their respective friends consequently quarrelled. At a meeting held by the parties with a view to composing differences, Bruce was hurt. Then the 'clannit men' of the names of Livingstone and Bruce in the Carse of Falkirk banded themselves together for revenge. A bailie of Stirling, named Forester, who had had no concern in the dispute, was soon after about to journey from Edinburgh to Stirling, when the friends of the deceased 'belaid all the hieways for his return.' Before he had gone many miles, they set upon him, and with sword and gun slew him. The most remarkable part of the affair was what followed. Forester being a special servant of the Earl of Mar, it was resolved that he should be buried with solemnity in Stirling. The corpse was met
July 12. at Linlithgow by the earl and a large party of friends, with displayed banner, and in 'effeir of weir.' On their journey to Stirling, they passed through the lands of Livingstone and Bruce, exhibiting 'a picture of the defunct on a fair canvas, painted with the number of the shots and wounds, to appear the more horrible to the behalders, and this way they completed his burial.'[1]—*H. K. J.*

Another curious circumstance followed. The parties involved in the homicide had a *day of law* appointed for them in Edinburgh, December 20th, and they, in customary style, summoned their respective friends to be present. A great attendance was expected; but the Privy Council, knowing there was deadly feid between a great number of them, 'feirit that, upon the first occasion of their meeting, some great inconvenients sall fall out, to the break of his hieness' peace, and troubling of the guid and quiet estate of the country[!], beside the hindering of justice,' forbade the coming of such persons to Edinburgh under pain of 'deid without favour.'—*P. C. R.*

Aug. 1. Complaint was made to the Town Council of Edinburgh by the corporation of surgeons, against M. Awin, a French surgeon, for

[1] The writer of this curious story speaks of the form of the funeral as rare.

practising his art within the liberties of the city. He was ordered 1595.
to desist, under a penalty, except for certain branches of surgery—namely, cutting for the stone, curing of ruptures, couching of cataracts, curing the pestilence, and diseases of women consequent on childbirth.[1]

The violences of the age extended even to school-boys. The Sep.
'scholars and gentlemen's sons' of the High School of Edinburgh had at this time occasion to complain of some abridgment of their wonted period of vacation, and when they applied to the Town Council for an extension of what they called their 'privilege,' only three days in addition to the restricted number of fourteen were granted. It appears that the master was favourable to their suit, but he was 'borne down and abused by the Council, who never understood well what privilege belonged to that charge. Some of the chief gentlemen's sons resolved to make a mutiny, and one day, the master being on necessary business a mile or two off the town,
they came in the evening with all necessary provision, and entered Sep. 13.
the school, manned the same, took in with them some fencible weapons, with powder and bullet, and renforcit the doors, refusing to let [any] man come there, either master or magistrate, untill their privilege were fairly granted.'—*Pa. And.*

A night passed over. Next morning, 'some men of the town came to these scholars, desiring them to give over, and to come forth upon composition; affirming that they should intercede to obtein them the license of other eight days' playing. But the scholars replied that they were mocked of the first eight days' privilege . . . . they wald either have the residue of the days granted for their pastime, or else they wald not give over. This answer was consulted upon by the magistrates, and notified to the ministers; and the ministers gave their counsel that they should be letten alone, and some men should be depute to attend about the house to keep them from vivres, sae that they should be compelled to render by extremity of hunger.'—*H. K. J.*

A day having passed in this manner, the Council lost patience, and determined to use strong measures. Headed by Bailie John Macmoran, and attended by a posse of officers, they came to the school, which was a long, low building standing on the site of the ancient Blackfriars' monastery. The bailie at first called on the boys in a peaceable manner to open the doors. They refused, and

[1] Council Register in Maitland.

1595. asked for their master, protesting they would acknowledge him at his return, but no other person. 'The bailies began to be angry, and called for a great jeist to prize up the back-door. The scholars bade them beware, and wished them to desist and leave off that violence, or else they vowed to God they should put a pair of bullets through the best of their cheeks. The bailies, believing they durst not shoot, continued still to prize the door, boasting with many threatening words. The scholars perceiving nothing but extremity, one Sinclair the chancellor of Caithness' son, presented a gun from a window, direct opposite to the bailies' faces, boasting them and calling them *buttery carles*. Off goeth the charged gun. [The bullet] pierced John Macmoran through his head, and presently killed him, so that he fell backward straight to the ground, without speech at all.'[1]

'When the scholars heard of this mischance, they were all moved to clamour, and gave over. Certain of them escaped, and the rest were carried to prison by the magistrates in great fury, and escaped weel unslain at that instant. Upon the morn, the said Sinclair was brought to the bar, and was there accused of that slaughter; but he denied the same constantly. Divers honest friends convenit, and assisted him.'[2] The relatives of Macmoran being rich, money-offers were of no avail in the case: life for life was what they sought for. 'Friends threatened death to all the people of Edinburgh (!) if they did the child any harm, saying they were not wise that meddled with the scholars, especially the gentlemen's sons. They should have committed that charge to the master, who knew best the truest remedy without any harm at all.'

Lord Sinclair, as head of the family to which the young culprit belonged, now came forward in his behalf, and, by his intercession, the king wrote to the magistrates, desiring them to delay proceedings. Afterwards, the process was transferred to the Privy Council. Meanwhile, the other youths, seven in number, the chief of whom were a son of Murray of Spainyiedale and a son of Pringle of Whitebank, were kept in confinement upwards of two months, while a debate took place between the magistrates and the friends of the culprits as to a fair assize; it being alleged that one composed of citizens would be partial against the boys. The king commanded that an assize of

[1] Patrick Anderson's History MS. He adds: 'I was at the time by chance an eye-witness myself.'

[2] *Hist. K. Ja. 6.*

gentlemen should be chosen, and, in the end, they, as well as Sinclair, got clear off. 1595.

The culprit became Sir William Sinclair of Mey. He married Catherine Ross of Balnagowan, whom we have seen unpleasantly mixed up in the charges against Lady Foulis, under July 22, 1590.

Bailie Macmoran's House.

'Macmoran,' says Calderwood, 'was the richest merchant in his time, but not gracious to the common people, because he carried victual to Spain, notwithstanding he was often admonished by the ministers to refrain.' It would appear that he had been a servant of the Regent Morton, and afterwards was what is called a messenger, or sheriff's officer.[1] We have also seen that, after the

[1] March 16, 1575-6, John Macmoran, messenger, reported to the Privy Council, that in January last, when using his office in execution of letters upon Patrick M'Kie, burgess of Wigton, he had been set upon by Alexander M'Kie of Myreton and his two brothers, who

1595. fall of Morton, he was reported to have been concerned in secreting the treasures which had been accumulated by his former master.[1] His house, still standing in Riddell's Close in the Lawnmarket, Edinburgh, gives the idea that the style of living of a rich Scottish merchant of that day was far from being mean or despicable.

Sep. 22. 'Among the constancies of the court this year, one was remarkable, that at Glasgow, in September, the king received the Countess of Bothwell into his favour, the 22d day, at night; and on the 3d of December, again proscribed and exiled her, under the pain of death; yet gave her a letter of protection, under his awn hand, within six days thereafter.'—*Bal.*

This inconstancy is partly explained away in the Privy Council Record, where it is stated that the countess abused the privilege of the letter granted to her by going about where she pleased and vaunting of her credit with the king, while in reality it was designed only to serve 'for remaining of herself and her bairns within the place of Mostour, that her friends might sometime have resorted to her without danger to his hieness's laws.'

Oct. James Lord Hay of Yester, brother and successor of the turbulent Master of Yester already introduced to the reader, kept state in Neidpath Castle, with his wife, but as yet unblessed with progeny.[2] His presumptive heir was his second-cousin, Hay of Smithfield, ancestor of the present Sir Adam Hay of Haystoun. In these circumstances, occasion was given for a curious series of proceedings, involving the fighting of a regular passage of arms on a neighbouring plain beside the Tweed—a simple pastoral scene, where few could now dream that any such incident had ever taken place.

Lord Yester had for his page one George Hepburn, brother of the parson of Oldhamstocks in East Lothian. His master-of-the-horse—for such officers were then retained in houses of this rank—was John Brown of Hartree. One day, Brown, in conversation with Hepburn, remarked: 'Your father had good knowledge

cruelly struck and chased him, giving him despiteful words, and threatening him with worse if he ever again came there in a professional capacity. The offenders, failing to appear on call to answer for this outrage, were put to the horn.—*P. C. R.*

[1] See *ante*, p. 143.

[2] Lady Yester in her widowhood founded a church in Edinburgh, which has perpetuated her name. Her ladyship, after the above date, brought Lord Yester two sons, the elder of whom carried on the line of the family, and was the first Earl of Tweeddale.

of physic: I think you should have some also.' 'What mean ye by that?' said Hepburn. 'You might have great advantage by something,' answered Brown. On being further questioned, the latter stated that, seeing Lord Yester had no children, and Hay of Smithfield came next in the entail, it was only necessary to give the former a suitable dose in order to make the latter Lord Yester. 'If you,' continued Brown, 'could give him some poison, you should be nobly rewarded, you and yours.' 'Methinks that were no good physic,' quoth Hepburn drily, and soon after revealed the project to his lord. Brown, on being taxed with it, stood stoutly on his denial. Hepburn as strongly insisted that the proposal had been made to him. For such a case, there was no solution but the *duellium*. 1595.

Due authority being obtained, a regular and public combat was arranged to take place on Edston-haugh, near Neidpath. The two combatants were to fight in their doublets, mounted, with spears and swords. Some of the greatest men of the country took part in the affair, and honoured it with their presence. The Laird of Buccleuch appeared as judge for Brown; Hepburn had, on his part, the Laird of Cessford. The Lords Yester and Newbottle were amongst those officiating. When all was ready, the two combatants rode full tilt against each other with their spears, when Brown missed Hepburn, and was thrown from his horse with his adversary's weapon through his body. Having grazed his thigh in the charge, Hepburn did not immediately follow up his advantage, but suffered Brown to lie unharmed on the ground. 'Fy!' cried one of the judges, 'alight and take amends of thy enemy!' He then advanced on foot with his sword in his hand to Brown, and commanded him to confess the truth. 'Stay,' cried Brown, 'till I draw the broken spear out of my body.' This being done, Brown suddenly drew his sword, and struck at Hepburn, who for some time was content to ward off his strokes, but at last dealt him a backward wipe across the face, when the wretched man, blinded with blood, fell to the ground. The judges then interfered to prevent him from being further punished by Hepburn; but he resolutely refused to make any confession.[1]

About this time and for some time onward, Scotland underwent the pangs of a dearth of extraordinary severity, in consequence of the destruction of the crops by heavy rains in autumn. Birrel

[1] Patrick Anderson's Hist. MS. Genealogy of the Hays of Tweeddale.

1595. speaks of it as a famine, 'the like whereof was never heard tell of in any age before, nor ever read of since the world was made.' 'In this month of October and November,' he adds, 'the wheat and malt at £10 the boll; in March thereafter [1596], the ait meal £10 the boll, the humble corn £7 the boll. In the month of May, the ait meal £20 the boll in Galloway. At this time there came victual out of other parts in sic abundance, that, betwixt the 1st of July and the 10th of August, there came into Leith three score and six ships laden with victual; nevertheless, the rye gave £10, 10s. and £11 the boll. The 2 of September, the rye came down and was sold for £7 the boll, and new ait meal for 7s. and 7s. 6d. the peck. The 29 of October, the ait meal came up again at 10s. the peck. The 15 of July, the ait meal at 13s. 4d. the peck; the pease meal at 11s. the peck.

'In this year, Clement Orr and Robert Lumsden, his grandson, bought before hand from the Earl Marischal, the bear meal overhead for 33s. 4d. the boll.' 'The ministers pronounced the curse of God against them, as grinders of the faces of the poor; which curse too manifestly lighted on them before their deaths.'—*Bal.*

As usual, the buying up and withholding of grain with the prospect of increased prices, was viewed with indignation by all classes of people. The king issued a proclamation in December 1595, attributing much of the misery of his people to 'the avaritious greediness of a great number of persons that has bought and buys victual afore it come off the grund, and that forestalls and keeps the same to a dearth,' and to 'the shameless and indiscreet behaviour of the owners of the same victual, wha refuses to thresh out and bring the same to open markets.' He threatened to put the laws in force against these guilty persons, and have the grain escheat to his majesty's use.

Dec. 23. The king professed to be at this time scandalised at the state of the commonweal, 'altogether disorderit and shaken louss by reason of the deidly feids and controversies standing amangs his subjects of all degrees.' Seeing how murder had consequently become a daily occurrence, he resolved upon a new and vigorous effort to bring the hostile parties to a reconciliation 'by his awn pains and travel to that effect,' so that the country might be the better fitted to resist the common enemy, now threatening invasion. The Privy Council, therefore, ordained letters to be sent charging

the various parties to make their appearance before the king on 1595.
certain days, wherever he might be for the time, each accompanied by a certain number of friends who might assist with their advice, but the whole party in each case 'to keep their lodgings after their coming, while [till] they be specially sent for by his majesty.'

The groups of persons summoned were, Robert Master of Eglintoun, and Patrick Houston of that Ilk; James Earl of Glencairn, and Cunningham of Glengarnock; John Earl of Montrose, and French of Thorniedykes; Hugh Campbell of Loudon, sheriff of Ayr, Sandielands of Calder, Sir James Sandielands of Slamannan, Crawford of Kerse, and Spottiswoode of that Ilk; David Earl of Crawford and Guthrie of that Ilk; Sir Thomas Lyon of Auldbar, knight, and Garden of that Ilk; Alexander Lord Livingston, Sir Alexander Bruce, elder, of Airth, and Archibald Colquhoun of Luss; John Earl of Mar, Alexander Forester of Garden, and Andro M'Farlane of Arrochar; James Lord Borthwick, Preston of Craigmiller, Mr George Lauder of Bass, and Charles Lauder son of umwhile Andro Lauder in Wyndpark; Sir John Edmonston of that Ilk, Maister William Cranston, younger, of that Ilk; George Earl Marischal and Seyton of Meldrum; James Cheyne of Straloch and William King of Barrach; James Tweedie of Drumelzier and Charles Geddes of Rachan. The nobles in every instance were allowed to have sixty, and the commoners twenty-four persons to accompany them to the place of agreement, and all, while attending, to have protection from any process of horning or excommunication which might have been previously passed upon them. Fire and sword was threatened against all neglecting to comply with the summons.

Earnest as the king seems now to have been, and influential as a royal tongue proverbially is, we know for certain that several of the parties now summoned continued afterwards at enmity.

'The king made ane orison before the General Assembly, with 1595-6. MAR. 16
many guid promises and conditions. I pray God he may keep them, be content to receive admonitions [from the clergy], and be collected himself and his haill household, and to lay aside his authority royal and be as ane brother to them, and to see all the kirks in this country weel planted with ministers. There are in Scotland 900 kirks, of the whilk there are 400 without ministers or readers.'—*Bir.*

The admonitions which it was so desirable that the king should

1595-6. receive, were embodied in a paper called *Offences in the King's House,* under the following heads: '1. The reading of the Word, and thanksgiving before and after meat, oft omitted. 2. Week-sermons oft neglected, and he would be admonished not to talk with any in time of divine service. 3. To recommend to him private meditation with God in spirit and in his awn conscience. 4. Banning and swearing is too common in the king's house and court, occasioned by his example. 5. He would have good company about him: Robertland, papists, murderers, profane persons, would be removed from him. 6. The queen's ministry would be reformed. She herself neglects Word and sacrament, is to be admonished for night-waking, balling, &c., also touching her company—and so of her gentlewomen.'—*Row.*

On the other hand, the king demanded of this assembly sundry concessions as to his power over the kirk, and that ministers should not be allowed to meddle with civil affairs or 'to name any man in the pulpit, or so vively to describe him as it shall be equivalent to the very naming of him, except upon the notoriety of a public crime.'

On this occasion the clergy denounced the *common corruption of all estates within this realm;* namely, 'an universal coldness, want of zeal, ignorance, contempt of the Word, ministry, and sacraments, and where knowledge is, yet no sense nor feeling, evidenced by the want of family exercises, prayer, and the Word, and singing of psalms; and if they be, they are profaned and abused, by calling on the cook, steward, or jackman to perform that religious duty . . . . superstition and idolatry entertained, evidenced in keeping of festival-days, fires, pilgrimages, singing of carols at Yule, &c. . . . . swearing, banning, and cursing: profanation of the Sabbath, especially by working in seed-time and harvest, journeying, trysting, gaming, dancing, drinking, fishing, killing, and milling: inferiors not doing duty to superiors, children having pleas of law against their parents, marrying without their consent; superiors not doing duty to inferiors, as not training up their children at schools in virtue and godliness; great and frequent breaches of duty between married persons: great bloodshed, deadly feuds arising thence, and assisting of bloodshedders for eluding of the laws: fornications, adulteries, incests, unlawful marriages and divorcements, allowed by laws and judges . . . . excessive drinking and waughting, gluttony (no doubt the cause of this dearth and famine), gorgeous and vain apparel, filthy speeches and songs: cruel oppressions of poor tenants . . . . idle persons having no lawful callings—as pipers, fiddlers, songsters, sorners, pleasants, strong and sturdy beggars living in harlotry. . . . . Lying, finally, is a rife and common sin.' 1595-6.

1596. APR. 12.

Sir Walter Scott of Branxholm, Laird of Buccleuch, performed an exploit which has been celebrated both in prose and rhyme.

About the end of January, a 'day of truce' was held at a spot called Dayholm of Kershope in Liddesdale, by the deputies of the English warden, Lord Scrope, and the Laird of Buccleuch, keeper of Liddesdale. The Scotch deputy, Scott of Goldielands, had but a small party—not above twenty—among whom, however, was a noted border reiver, William Armstrong of Kinmont, commonly known as *Kinmont Willie*. The English deputy was attended by several hundred followers. It happened that, before the end of the meeting, a report came to the English deputy of some outrages at that moment in the course of being committed by Scottish borderers within the English line. He entered a complaint on the subject, and received assurance that the guilty parties should be as soon as possible rendered up to the vengeance of Lord Scrope.

The day of truce ended peaceably; but, as the English party was retiring along their side of the Liddel, they caught sight of the Scottish reivers, and gave chase. Kinmont Willie was now riding quietly along the Scottish side of the Liddel. Mistaking him for one of the guilty troop, the English pursued him for three or four miles, and taking him prisoner, bore him off to Carlisle Castle.

Probably the Liddesdale thief had incurred more guilt in England than ten lives would have expiated. Yet what was this to Buccleuch? To him the case was simply that of a retainer betrayed while on his master's business and assurance. If the affair had a public or national aspect, it was that of a Scottishman mistreated, to the dishonour of his sovereign and country. Having in vain used remonstrances with Lord Scrope, both by himself and through the king's representations to the English ambassador, he resolved at last, as himself has expressed it, 'to attempt the simple recovery of the prisoner in sae *moderate ane fashion* as was possible to him.'

Buccleuch's moderate proceeding consisted in the assembling of two hundred armed and mounted retainers at the tower of Morton, an hour before sunset of the 12th of April. He had arranged that no head of any house should be of the number, but all

1596. younger brothers, that the consequences might be the less likely to damage his following; but, nevertheless, three lairds had insisted on taking part in the enterprise. Passing silently across the border, they came to Carlisle about the middle of the night. A select party of eighty then made an attempt to scale the walls of the castle; but their ladders proving too short, it was found necessary to break in by force through a postern on the west side. Two dozen men having got in, six were left to guard the passage, while the remaining eighteen passed on to Willie's chamber, broke it up, and released the prisoner. All this was done without encountering any resistance except from a few watchmen, who were easily 'dung on their backs.'[1] As a signal of their success, the party within the castle sounded their trumpet 'mightily.' Hearing this, Buccleuch raised a loud clamour amongst his horsemen on the green. At the same time, the bell of the castle began to sound, a beacon-fire was kindled on the top of the house, the great bell of the cathedral was rung in correspondence, the watch-bell of the Moot-hall joined the throng of sounds, and, to crown all, the drum began to rattle through the streets of the city. 'The people were perturbit from their nocturnal sleep, then undigestit at that untimeous hour, with some cloudy weather and saft rain, whilk are noisome to the delicate persons of England, whaise bodies are given to quietness, rest, and delicate feeding, and consequently desirous of more sleep and repose in bed.' Amidst the uproar, 'the assaulters brought forth their countryman, and convoyit him to the court, where the Lord Scrope's chalmer has a prospect unto, to whom he cried with a loud voice a familiar guid-nicht! and another guid-nicht to his constable Mr Saughell.' The twenty-four men returned with Kinmont Willie to the main body, and the whole party retired without molestation, and re-entered Scotland with the morning light. 'The like of sic ane vassalage,' says the diarist Birrel, with unwonted enthusiasm, 'was never done since the memory of man, no, not in Wallace' days!' Buccleuch himself, with true heroism, treated the matter calmly and even reasoningly. The simple recovery of the prisoner, he said, 'maun necessarily be esteimit lawful, gif the taking and deteining of him be unlawful, as without all question it was.'

The matter was brought before the king in council (May 25) by the English ambassador, who pleaded that Sir Walter Scott should be given up to the queen for punishment. It was on this occasion

[1] Thrown down.

that the border knight defended himself in the terms above quoted. 1596.
Of course his own countrymen sympathised with him in a deed so gallant, and performed from such a motive, and the king could not readily act in a contrary strain. Elizabeth never obtained any satisfaction for the taking of Kinmont Willie.—*Spot. Moy. H. K. J. C. K. S. P. C. R. Bir.*[1]

'.... there came an Englishman to Edinburgh, with a 1596 (?) Apr.
chestain-coloured naig, which he called Marroco..... he made him to do many rare and uncouth tricks, such as never horse was observed to do the like before in this land. This man would borrow from twenty or thirty of the spectators a piece of gold or silver, put all in a purse, and shuffle them together; thereafter he would bid the horse give every gentleman his own piece of money again. He would cause him tell by so many pats with his foot how many shillings the piece of money was worth. He would cause him lie down as dead. He would say to him: "I will sell you to a carter:" then he would seem to die. Then he would say: "Marroco, a gentleman hath borrowed you, and you must ride with a lady of court." Then would he most daintily hackney, amble, and ride a pace, and trot, and play the jade at his command when his master pleased. He would make him take a great draught of water as oft as he liked to command him. By a sign given him, he would beck for the King of Scots and for Queen Elizabeth, and when ye spoke of the King of Spain, would both bite and strike at you—and many other wonderful things. I was a spectator myself in those days. But the report went afterwards that he devoured his master, because he was thought to be a spirit and nought else.'—*Pa. And.*

This was 'the dancing horse' to which Moth alludes in Shakspeare (*Love's Labour Lost*, act I., sc. 2). The actual fate of Banks, the keeper of the animal, was not better than that which vulgar rumour assigned to him. It is almost an incredible, yet apparently well-authenticated fact, that horse and man, after wandering through various countries, were burnt together as magicians at Rome.

At this time, while the country was suffering from famine, there 1596. May.
was a renewing of the Covenant with fasting and humiliation in

[1] For the ballad of *Kinmont Willie*, and many particulars of the affair, see *Minstrelsy of the Scottish Border*.

1596. St Andrews presbytery. 'After this exercise,' says James Melville, one of those chiefly concerned in ordering it, 'we wanted not a remarkable effect.' 'God extraordinarily provided victuals out of all other countries, in sic store and abundance as was never seen in this land before;' without which 'thousands had died for hunger,' 'for,' he goes on to say, 'notwithstanding of the infinite number of bolls of victual that cam hame from other parts, all the harvest quarter of that year, the meal gave aucht, nine, and ten pounds the boll, and the malt eleven and twal, and in the south and west parts many died.'

JUNE 7. Napier, still brooding over the dangers from popery, devised at this time certain inventions which he thought would be useful for defending the country in case of invasion. One was a mirror like that of Archimedes, which should collect the beams of the sun, and reflect them concentratedly in one 'mathematical point,' for the purpose of burning the enemy's ships. Another was a similar mirror to reflect artificial fire. A third was a kind of shot for artillery, not to pass lineally through an enemy's host, destroying only those that stand in its way, but which should 'range abroad within the whole appointed place, and not departing furth of the place till it had executed his [its] whole strength, by destroying those that be within the bounds of the said place.' A fourth, the last, was a closed and fortified carriage to bring harquebussiers into the midst of an enemy—a superfluity, one would think, if there was any hopefulness in the third of the series. 'These inventions, besides devices of sailing under the water, with divers other stratagems for harming of the enemies, by the grace of God and work of expert craftsmen, I hope to perform.'[1] So wrote Napier at the date noted in the margin. Sir Thomas Urquhart describes the third of the devices as calculated to clear a field of four miles' circumference of all living things above a foot in height: by it, he said, the inventor could destroy 30,000 Turks, without the hazard of a single Christian. He adds that proof of its powers was given on a large plain in Scotland, to *the destruction of a great many cattle and sheep*—a particular that may be doubted. 'When he was desired by a friend in his last illness to reveal the contrivance, his answer was that, for the ruin and overthrow of man, there were too many devices already framed, which if he could make to be fewer, he would, with his might,

[1] Napier's *Life of Napier*, 4to, p. 247.

endeavour to do; and that therefore, seeing the malice and rancour rooted in the heart of mankind will not suffer them to diminish, the number of them, by any concert of his, should never be increased.'[1] 1593.

John, Master of Orkney, was tried for the alleged crime of attempting to destroy the life of his brother the Earl of Orkney, first by witchcraft, and secondly by more direct means. The case broke down, and would not be worthy of attention in this place, but for the nature of the means taken to inculpate the accused. It appeared that the alleged witchcraft stood upon the evidence of a confession wrung from a woman called Alison Balfour, residing at Ireland, a village in Orkney, who had been executed for that imaginary crime in December 1594. The counsel for the Master shewed that, when this poor woman made her 'pretended confession,' as it might well be called, she had been kept forty-eight hours in the *cashielaws*—an instrument of torture supposed to have consisted of an iron case for the leg, to which fire was gradually applied, till it became insupportably painful. At the same time, her husband, a man of ninety-one years of age, her eldest son and daughter, were kept likewise under torture, 'the father being in the *lang irons* of fifty stane wecht,' the son fixed in the *boots* with fifty-seven strokes, and the daughter in the *pilniewinks*, that they, 'being sae tormented beside her, might move her to make any confession for their relief.' A like confession had been extorted from Thomas Palpla, to the effect that he had conspired with the Master to poison his brother, 'he being kept in the cashielaws eleven days and eleven nights, twice in the day by the space of fourteen days callit [driven] in the boots, he being naked in the meantime, and scourgit with tows [ropes] in sic sort that they left neither flesh nor hide upon him; in the extremity of whilk torture the said pretended confession had been drawn out of him.' Both of these witnesses had revoked their confessions, Alison Balfour doing so solemnly on the Heading Hill of Kirkwall, when about to submit to death for her own alleged crime, of which she at the same time protested herself to be innocent. These are among the most painful examples we anywhere find of the barbarous legal procedure of our ancestors.—*Pit.* June 24.

One John Dickson, an Englishman, was tried for uttering slanderous speeches against the king, calling him 'ane bastard Aug. 3.

[1] Wood's *Peerage*, quoting Urquhart.

1596. king,' and saying 'he was not worthy to be obeyed.' This it appeared he had done in a drunken anger, when asked to veer his boat out of the way of the king's ordnance. He was adjudged to be hanged.—*Pit.* It is curious on this and some other occasions to find that, while the king got so little practical obedience, and the laws in general were so feebly enforced, such a severe penalty was inflicted on acts of mere disrespect towards majesty.

Aug. 17. The court was at this time unable to keep silence under the pelt of pasquils which it had brought upon itself. We have now a furious edict of Privy Council against the writers and promulgators of 'infamous libels, buiks, ballats, pasquils, and cantels in prose and rhyme,' which have lately been set out, and especially against 'ane maist treasonable letter in form of a *cockalane*,[1] craftily divulgat by certain malicious, seditious, and unquiet spirits, uttering mony shameful and contumelious speeches, full of hatrent and dispite, not only against God, his servants and ministers, but maist unnaturally to the prejudice of the honour, guid fame, and reputation of the king and queen's majesties, not sparing the prince their dearest son, besides their nobility, council, and guid subjects.' The only active redress, however, was to proclaim a reward for the discovery of the offenders.—*P. C. R.*

Nov. 3. Since November 1585, when he was driven from the king's councils, James Stewart of Newton (sometime Earl of Arran) had lived in obscurity in the north.[2] Now that the Chancellor Maitland was dead, he formed a hope that possibly some use might be found for him at court; he therefore came to Edinburgh privately, and had an interview with the king at Holyroodhouse. He received some encouragement; but as nothing could be done for him immediately, and there were many enemies to reconcile, he bethought him of going to live for a while amongst his friends in Ayrshire, trusting erelong to be sent for.

The ex-favourite was travelling by Symington, in the upper ward of Lanarkshire, when some one who knew him gave him warning that he was come into a dangerous neighbourhood, for not far from the way he was about to pass dwelt a leading man of that house of

[1] Cockalane—Fr. *coq-à-l'âne*, defined in the dictionary of the Academy, 'Discours qui n'a point de suite, de liaison, de raison.' Equivalent to the English phrase, a *cock-and-bull story*. The word occurs in at least one English author—Etheridge.

[2] Through his connection with the Lovat family, his wife being the mother of the present Lord Lovat, he was sheltered for some time in a small island in the lake of Bruiach, a few miles from Beaufort Castle.—*Anderson's Hist. Acc. Fraser Family*, p. 90, note.

Douglas which he had mortally offended by his prosecution of the 1596. Regent Morton. This was Sir James Douglas of Parkhead, whose father was a natural brother of the regent: he was now the husband of the heiress of the house of Carlyle of Torthorald, and a man of consideration. Stewart replied disdainfully that he was travelling where he had a right to be, and he would not go out of his way for Parkhead nor any other of the house of Douglas. A mean person who overheard this speech made off and reported it to Douglas, who, on hearing it, rose from table, where he had been dining, and vowed he would have the life of Stewart at all hazards. He immediately mounted, and with three servants rode after his enemy through a valley called the Catslack. When Stewart saw himself pursued, he asked the name of the place, and being told, desired his people to come on with all possible speed, for he had got a response from some soothsayer to beware of that spot. Parkhead speedily overtook him, struck him from his horse, and then mercilessly killed him. Cutting off the head, he caused it to be carried by a servant on the point of a spear, thus verifying another weird saying regarding Stewart, that he should have the highest head in Scotland. His body was left on the spot, to become the prey of dogs and swine.[1]

Thus perished an ex-chancellor of Scotland, one who had been permitted for a time to treat the world as if it had only been made for his own aggrandisement, who had governed a king, struck down a regent, and made the greatest of the old nobility of the country tremble. Violence, insolence, and cruelty had been the ruling principles of his life, and, as Spottiswoode says, 'he was paid home in the end.' No decided effort was made to execute justice upon his slayer;[2] but it will be afterwards found that the Ochiltree Stewarts did not forget his death. (See under July 1608.)

An edict of the king against what he called unlawful convocations Dec. 17. of the clergy, had raised a general uneasiness and excitement, many believing that all independent action of the clergy was struck at. The prosecution of a minister named David Black, who had slandered the king and queen in the pulpit, and refused to submit to a secular tribunal, added to the turmoil. James had further raised a great distrust regarding his fidelity to the Protestant

[1] *Spottiswoode*, iii. 40. Johnston's Hist. Scot. MS. Scott's *Staggering State of Scots Statesmen.*

[2] He was put to the horn, and an edict of Privy Council denounced those who should 'reset' him.

1596. religion by his allowing the exiled papist lords to return to their own country. It was at this crisis that the tumult long known in French fashion as the *Seventeenth of December* took place.

'. . . . being Friday, his majesty being in the Tolbooth sitting in session, and ane convention of ministers being in the New Kirk [a contiguous section of St Giles's Church], and some noblemen being convenit with them, as in special Blantyre and Lindsay, there came in some devilish officious person, and said that the ministers were coming to take his life. Upon the whilk, the Tolbooth doors were steekit, and there arase sic ane crying, "God and the king!" other some crying, "God and the kirk!" that the haill commons of Edinburgh raise in arms, and knew not wherefore always. There was ane honest man, wha was deacon of deacons; his name was John Watt, smith. This John Watt raisit the haill crafts in arms, and came to the Tolbooth, where the entry is to the Chequer-house, and there cried for a sight of his majesty, or else he sould ding up the yett with forehammers, sae that never ane within the Tolbooth sould come out with their life. At length his majesty lookit ower the window, and spake to the commons, wha offerit to die and live with him. Sae his majesty came down after the townsmen were commandit off the gait, and was convoyit by the craftsmen to the abbey of Holyroodhouse.'—*Bir.*

The king either was really exasperated or pretended to be so. Retiring to Linlithgow next day, he sent orders to Edinburgh, discharging the courts of justice from sitting there, commanding one minister to be imprisoned and others to be put to the horn, and citing the magistrates to come and answer for the seditious conduct of their people. Great was the consternation thus produced, insomuch that one Sunday passed without public worship—'the like of which had not been seen before.' On the last day of the year, James returned, to all appearance charged with the most alarming intentions against the city. A proclamation was issued, commanding certain lords and Border chiefs of noted loyalty to occupy certain ports and streets. There consequently arose a rumour 'that the king's majesty should send in Will Kinmont, the common thief, as should spulyie the town of Edinburgh. Upon the whilk, the haill merchants took their haill geir out of their booths and shops, and transportit the same to the strongest house that was in the town, and remainit in the said house with themselves, their servants, and looking for nothing but that they should have all been spulyit. Siclike, the haill craftsmen and commons convenit themselves, their best goods, as it were ten or twelve households in ane, whilk was the strongest house, and might be best keepit from spulying and burning, with hagbut, pistolet, and other sic armour, as might best defend themselves. Judge, gentle reader, gif this be playing! Thir noblemen and gentlemen, keepers of the ports and Hie Gait, being set at the places foresaid, with pike and spear, and other armour, stood keeping the foresaid places appointit, till his majesty came to St Giles's Kirk, Mr David Lindsay making the sermon. His majesty made ane oration or harangue, concerning the sedition of the seditious ministers, as it pleased him to term them.'—*Bir.* 1596.

The affair ended three months after, in a way that supports the opinion of the Laird of Dumbiedykes, that 'it's sad work, but siller will help it.' March 22d, 'the town of Edinburgh was relaxed frae the horn, and received into the king's favour again, and the session ordained to sit down in Edinburgh the 25th of May thereafter.' Next day, 'the king drank in the council-house with the bailies, council, and deacons. The said bailies and council convoyit his majesty to the West Port thereafter. In the meantime of this drinking in the council-house, the bells rang for joy of their agreement; the trumpets sounded, the drums and whistles played, with [as] many other instruments of music as might be played on; and the town of Edinburgh, for the tumult-raising the 17 of December before, was *ordained to pay to his majesty thretty thousand merks Scottish.*'—*Bir.*

John Mure, of Auchindrain, in Ayrshire, was a gentleman of good means and connections, who acted at one time in a judicial capacity as bailie of Carrick, and gave general satisfaction by his judgments. He was son-in-law to the Laird of Bargeny, one of the three chief men of the all-powerful Ayrshire family of Kennedy. Sir Thomas Kennedy of Colzean, another of these great men, was on bad terms with Bargeny. Mure, who might naturally be expected to take his father-in-law's side, was for a time restrained by some practical benefits, in the shape of lands, offered to him by Sir Thomas; but the titles to the lands not being ultimately made good, the Laird of Auchindrain conceived only the more furious hatred against the knight of Colzean. This happened about 1595, and it appears at the same time that Sir Thomas had excited a deadly rage in the bosom of the Earl of Cassillis's next brother, usually called the Master of Cassillis. The Master and Auchindrain, with another called the Laird of Dunduff, easily came to an understanding with each other, and agreed to slay Sir Thomas 1596-7.

1596-7. Kennedy the first opportunity. Such was the manner of conducting a quarrel about land-rights and despiteful words amongst gentlemen in Ayrshire in those days.

JAN. 1. On the evening of the 1st of January, Sir Thomas Kennedy supped with Sir Thomas Nisbet in the house of the latter at Maybole. The Lairds of Auchindrain and Dunduff, with a few servants, lay in wait for him in the yard, and when he came forth to go to his own house to bed, they fired their pistols at him. 'He being safe of any hurt therewith, and perceiving them with their swords most cruelly to pursue his life, ... was forced for his safety to fly; in which chase they did approach him so near, as he had undoubtedly been overta'en and killed, if he had not adventured to run aside and cover himself with the ruins of ane decayed house; whilk, in respect of the darkness of the night, they did not perceive; but still followed to his lodging, and searched all the corners thereof, till the confluence of the people . . . . forced them to retire.'[1]

For this assault, Sir Thomas Kennedy pursued at law the Lairds of Auchindrain and Dunduff, and was so far successful that Dunduff had to retire into England, while 'Colzean gat the house of Auchindrain, and destroyit the . . . . plenishing, and wrackit all the garden. And also they made mony sets [snares] to have gotten [Auchindrain] himself; but God preservit him from their tyranny.'[2] Auchindrain, however, was forced 'to cover malice by show of repentance, and for satisfaction of his by-past offence, and *gage* of his future duty, to offer his eldest son in marriage to Sir Thomas Kennedy's dochter; whilk, by intercession of friends, [was] accepted.'[3]

We shall hear more of this feud hereafter (see under December 11, 1601).

FEB. 17. Under a commission from the king, the provost and bailies of Aberdeen commenced a series of witch-trials of a remarkable kind. The first delinquent, Janet Wishart, spouse of John Lees, stabler—a woman considerably advanced in life—was accused of a great number of *maléfices* perpetrated, during upwards of thirty years, against neighbours, chiefly under a spirit of petty revenge. In the greater number of cases, the victim was described as being seized with an ailment under which he passed through the extremes of

[1] Letter of Sir Thomas Hamilton, king's advocate, Pitcairn, iii. 162.
[2] *History of the Kennedies*, 27.
[3] Letter above cited.

heat and cold, and was afflicted with an insatiable drouth. In 1596-7. several cases the illness had a fatal conclusion. For instance, James Low, stabler, having refused Janet the loan of his kiln and barn, took a *dwining* illness in consequence, 'melting away like ane burning candle,' till he died. John, in his last moments, declared his belief that, if he had lent Janet his kiln and barn, he would still have been a living man. 'By the whilk witchcraft casten upon him, and upon his house, his wife died, his only son [fell] in the same kind of sickness, and his haill geir, surmounting three thousand pounds, are altogether wrackit and away.' It was considered sufficient proof on this point, that sundry persons testified to having heard James lay on Janet the blame of his misfortunes. Another person had been ruined in his means, in consequence of his wife obeying a direction of Janet for the insurance of constant prosperity—namely, taking nine pickles of wheat and a piece of rowan-tree, and putting them in the four nooks of the house. Janet had also caused a dozen fowls belonging to a neighbour to fall from a roost dead at her feet. She raised wind for winnowing some malt in her own house, at a moment of perfect calm, by putting a piece of live coal at each of two doors. She caused a neighbour's cow to give something like venom instead of milk. A Mart ox which she wished to buy, became furious; wherefore she got it at her own price, and on her laying her hands on it, the animal became quiet. There is also a terrible recital of her causing a neighbour to accompany her to the gallows in the Links, where she cut pieces from the various members of a dead culprit, to be used for effecting some of her devilish purposes. This story was only reported by one who had received it from the woman herself, now deceased; but it passed as equally good evidence with the rest. It was alleged that, twenty-two years ago, she had been found sitting in a field of green corn before sun-rising, when, being asked what she was doing, she said: 'I have been peeling the blades of the corn: I find it will be ane dear year; the blade of the corn grows withershins [contrary to the course of the sun]: when it grows sungates about [in the direction of the sun's course], it will be ane cheap year.' One of the last points in the dittay was that, for eight days before her apprehension, 'continually there was sic ane fearful rumbling in thy house, that William Murray, cordiner, believit the house he was into, next to thy house, should have fallen and smoorit him and his haill bairns.' This poor woman appears to have been taken to the stake immediately after her trial.

1596-7. Her son, Thomas Lees, was accused of having aided her in her evil deeds, and being 'ane common witch and sorcerer,' and his trial (February 23) brings out some curious points. He was accused of having been one of a large company of witches and sorcerers who had gone to the Market and Fish Crosses of Aberdeen at midnight of the previous Halloween (All Saints' Eve), 'under the guiding and conduct of the devil . . . . playing before you on his kind of instruments.' The company were all transformed, some as hares, some as cats, some in other likenesses, and all danced about the two crosses and the meal-market a long space of time, Thomas being the leader of the ring. One Catherine Mitchell being somewhat laggard, he beat her to make her go faster; a fact to which Catherine herself now bore witness. A woman with whom Thomas had been too intimate also testified to his having offered to take her to Murrayland and marry her, telling her that by the way, at the foot of a particular mountain, he could raise a spirit able to provide them with all necessaries. This poor fellow was also condemned to the flames. The husband and daughters of Janet Wishart—the latter of whom are taxed as well known to be 'quick gangand devils'—narrowly escaped with banishment from the city.

1597. Helen Fraser, who was tried in April, was accused of many witchcrafts of common kinds, and of some less common. For instance, she had translated a sickness from a man's horse to his cow, and, worse than that, the affection of Andrew Tullideff from his wife to a woman called Margaret Neilson, 'and sae michtily bewitchit him, that he could never be reconceillit with his wife, or remove his affection frae the said harlot.' Another man, Robert Merchant by name, who had been married happily to Christian White for two years, being taken to sow corn for a widow named Isobel Bruce, at the Murihill of Foveran, where Helen Fraser was then living, 'fand his affection violently and extraordinarily drawn away from the said Christian to the said Isobel, ane great luve being betwixt him and the said Christian always theretofore, and nae break of luve or discord falling out or intervening upon either of their parts: whilk thing the country supposit to be brought about by the unlawful travelling of the said Helen'—and was further *testified by Robert himself.* Helen was likewise convicted, and of course burnt.

Isobel Cockie took from cows the power of giving healthful milk, making them give a poisonous stuff instead. She also prevented good milk from 'yirning.' Horses had fallen dead under her touch.

Men against whom she had pronounced evil words took deadly sicknesses in consequence, or suffered a decay in their worldly means. Her house being ruinous, the proprietor, Alexander Anderson, had come in her absence, and was proceeding to mend the roof, when she came home, and finding he had uncovered her pantry, where her valuables lay, she said: 'I shall gar thee forthink it, that thou hast tirrit my house, I being frae hame,' and *glowrit up at him.* Immediately Alexander's speech went from him, and he retired to bed sick, and could get no rest or sleep. Under the threats of his son, she was induced to come and charm this sickness away from him, and 'gave him droggis, that his speech came to him again.'[1] By the confession of the recently burnt Thomas Lees, Isobel Cockie had been second to himself in the infernal dance at the Fish Cross, 'and because the devil playit not so melodiously and weel as thou cravit, thou took his instrument out of his mouth, then took him on the chafts therewith, and playit thyself thereon to the haill company.' Isobel was likewise condemned. 1597.

It would be tedious to enter into the long series of trials which extended over this year in and near Aberdeen; but a few particulars are worth giving. The case of Andrew Man, an aged person, formerly of Tarbrugh, in the parish of Rathven, involves a more imaginative style of warlockry than is common. According to his own confessions—that is to say, the hallucinations which he described—the devil came sixty years ago to his mother's house, in the form of a woman, called the Queen of Elfen, and was delivered of a bairn; at which time, he being a boy, bringing in water, was promised by this distinguished stranger 'that thou should know all things; and should help and cure all sorts of sickness, except *stand-deid,* and that thou should be weel enterteinit, but wald seek thy meat ere thou de'ed, as Thomas Rhymer did.' Thirty-two years before, he had begun a guilty intercourse with this Queen of Elfen, at whose first coming, 'she caused ane of thy cattle die upon ane hillock called the Elf-hillock, but promised to do him good thereafter.' Andrew, according to his own account, could 'cure the falling-sickness, the bairn-bed, and all other sorts of sickness that ever fell to man or beast, except the *stand-deid,* by baptising them, reabling them in the auld corunschbald, and striking of the gudis on the face, with ane fowl in thy hand, and by saying thir

[1] The resemblance of this case to the phenomena of what is called electro-biology will be apparent.

1597. words: "Gif thou will live, live; and gif thou will die, die!" with sundry other orisons, sic as of Sanct John and the three silly brethren, whilk thou can say when thou please, and by giving of black wool and salt as a remeid for all diseases and for causing a man prosper and that his blude should never be drawn.' He had cured several persons by his enchantments, one mode being to put the patient nine times through a hasp of unwatered yarn, and then a cat as many times backward through the same hasp, the effect of which was to translate the sickness from the patient to the cat.

The devil, whom Andrew called Christsonday, and believed to be an angel, was raised by the word *Benedicite*, and laid again by taking a dog under his armpit, casting the same in the devil's mouth, and speaking the word *Maikpeblis*. 'The Queen of Elfen has a grip of all the craft, but Christsonday is the guidman, and has all power under God, and thou kens sundry deid men in their company, and the king that died at Flodden and Thomas Rhymer is there.'

'Upon Rood-day in harvest, in this present year, whilk fell on a Wednesday, thou saw Christsonday come out of the snaw in likeness of a staig [young male horse], and the Queen of Elfen was there, and others with her, riding upon white hackneys.' 'The elves have shapes and claithes like men, and will have fair covered tables, and they are but shadows, but are starker [stronger] nor men, and they have playing and dancing when they please; the queen is very pleasand, and will be auld and young when she pleases; she makes any king whom she pleases. . . . . The elves will make thee appear to be in a fair chalmer, and yet thou will find thyself in a moss on the morn. They will appear to have candles, and licht, and swords, whilk will be nothing else but dead grass and straes.' Andrew denied his guilt, but was nevertheless convicted, and doubtless burnt.

In the dittay against Marjory Mutch, it was alleged that, having an ill-will against William Smith in Tarserhill, she came to his plough and bewitched the oxen, so that 'they instantly ran all wood [mad], brak the pleuch, twa thereof ran over the hills to Deer, and other twa thereof up Ithan side, whilk could never be tane nor apprehendit again.' This woman was said to have destroyed much cattle, laid sickness on many persons, and attended all the witch conventions of the district. In token of her being a witch, there was a spot under her left ear, into which a gentleman had thrust a pin without producing any pain.

Margaret Clark, being sent for by the wife of Nicol Ross, when she was in childbed, 'cast the haill dolours, sickness, and pains 1597. whilk she should have susteinit, upon Andrew Harper, wha, during all the time of her travelling, was exceedingly and marvellously troubled, in ane fury and madness as it were, and could not be halden; and how soon the said gentlewoman was delivered, the pains departed frae the said Andrew.'

It is alleged of Violet Leys, that, her husband, a mariner, being discharged from William Finlay's ship, she and her late mother bewitched the said ship, 'that, since thy husband was put forth of the same, she never made one good voyage, but either the master or merchants at some times through tempest of weather, were forced to cast overboard the greatest part of their lading, or then to perish, men, ship, and geir.' Several of the other culprits are accused of raising and calming the wind at pleasure.[1]

It appears that at this time twenty-two unfortunate men and women, chiefly the latter, suffered in Aberdeen and its neighbourhood. Such a tremendous sacrifice to superstition would in itself be worthy of special notice here; but it becomes the more so from a probability which appears that Shakspeare must have been acquainted with the details of these trials. It will be found that the chief of his company, Lawrence Fletcher, was in Aberdeen with a party of comedians in October 1601. That Shakspeare was of the party is not certain; but there is no fact to militate against the probability that he was. Mr Charles Knight[2] has shewn that in these trials there occur many things which strongly recall passages in the witch-scenes of *Macbeth*—as if those scenes had been written by one who had thoroughly studied the dittays against Janet Wishart and her associates. Nearly all of those women—and it is very much a special feature of this group of cases—had laid heavy disease on those whom they held at ill-will, causing them to suffer fearful pains, and their strength to decay.

> 'He shall live a man forbid:
> Weary seven nights nine times nine,
> He shall dwindle, peak, and pine.'

Such are the dread words of the *Macbeth* hags. We see that the Aberdeen witches had power over the winds; so had those of Macbeth. Banquo says to the weird sisters:

[1] The original documents regarding these trials are given in full in the *Spalding Club Miscellany*, vol. i. Aberdeen. 1841.

[2] *William Shakspere, a Biography.* 1843.

1597. 'If you can look into the seeds of time,
And say which grain will grow, and which will not,
Speak then to me.'

This, it must be acknowledged, is wonderfully like a suggestion to the imagination from such a fact as that of Janet Wishart's vaticinations among the growing corn. The witch-dance at the Fish Cross is much like those under the guidance of Hecate; and Wishart's dealing with the malefactor's corpse at the gallows on the Links, might well furnish a hint for the incantations over the caldron.

'Grease that 's sweaten
From the murderer's gibbet, throw
Into the flame.'

And perhaps even the humble cantrip of Marjory Mutch with William Smith's oxen, might suggest the fine passage descriptive of the conduct of Duncan's horses at his death; when they

'Turned wild in nature, broke their stalls, flung out,
Contending 'gainst obedience, as they would
Make war with mankind.'

'If it be not,' says Mr Knight, in concluding this curious speculation, 'to inquire too curiously, may we not trace one of the most striking passages in *Othello* to the humble source of an Aberdeen superstition?

"That handkerchief
Did an Egyptian to my mother give;
She was a charmer, and could almost read
The thoughts of people: she told her, while she kept it,
'Twould make her amiable, and subdue my father
Entirely to her love."

In the information against Isobell Straquhan, it is alleged that "the said Isobell came to Elspet Mutrey in Wodheid, she being a widow, and asked of her if she had a penny to lend her, and the said Elspet gave her the penny; and the said Isobell took the penny, and bowit [bent] it, and took a clout and a piece red wax, and sewed the clout with a thread, the wax and the penny being within the clout, and gave it to the said Elspet Mutrey, commanding her to use the said clout to hang about her craig [neck], and when she saw the man she loved best, take the clout, with the penny and wax, and stroke her face with it, and she so doing, should attain in to the marriage of that man whom she loved."

The "clout" sewed "with a thread" wants, indeed, the poetical colouring of the "handkerchief" of *Othello*; but still 1597.

"There's magic in the web of it."

More curious in the effects produced is another example of the "prophetic fury" of the "sibyl" Isobell Straquhan. She could not only produce love, but remove hatred: Walter Ronaldson had used to strike his wife, who took consultation with Scudder (*alias* Straquhan), and 'she did take pieces of paper, and sew them thick with thread of divers colours, and did put them in the barn amongst the corn, and from henceforth the said Walter did never strike his wife, neither yet once found fault with her, whatsoever she did. He was subdued "entirely to her love."'

1596-7. Mar. 11.

The duellium seems to have been particularly in vogue at this time. 'There chanced a single combat betwixt James Hepburn of Moreham and one Birnie, a skinner in Edinburgh [at St Leonard's Craigs]. They were both slain [and buried the morning after]. The occasion and quarrel was not thought to be great nor yet necessary. Hepburn alleged and maintained that there was seven sacraments; Birnie would have but two, or else he would fight. The other was content with great protestations that he would defend his belief with the sword; and so, with great earnestness, they yoked, and thus the question was decided.'—*P. And.*

There was a traditionary tale in Edinburgh, which Sir Walter Scott had heard in his youth, and which he narrated to the author of this work in 1824, to the effect that, a gentleman having been foully murdered by a man of formidable repute as a swordsman, his widow brought forward two sons in succession to challenge the murderer to mortal combat, and when these had fallen, did not scruple even to send a third, her youngest and favourite, to avenge the slaughter of the rest; thus imitating, as Sir Walter remarked, the conduct of Don Arias Gonzalo, in sending his three sons in succession to meet Don Diego Ordoñez, when the latter challenged the people of Zamora for sheltering the traitor Vellido—as related in the *Chronicle of the Cid*.[1] The two first youths, like the sons of Don Diego, 'died like good men in their duty;' but the third slew the murderer. The last fight, said Sir Walter, took place on Cramond Island in the Firth of Forth, and since then

[1] *Chronicle of the Cid*, translated by Robert Southey, pp. 75-83.

1596-7. there has been no such combat permitted. Apparently the basis of this story is as follows:

James Carmichael, second son of the Laird of Carmichael, had killed Stephen Bruntfield, captain of Tantallon, in a duel at St Leonard's Craigs, 22d December 1596. Adam Bruntfield, brother of the deceased, 'allegit that James Carmichael had slain his brother by treason, having promisit to meet him hand to hand, and had brought others with him to his slaughter, and therefore was a traitor. The other stood to his denial, and they baith seyit [tried] their moyen [influence] at his majesty's hands for ane license to fecht, whilk with great difficulty was granted by his
MAR. 15. grace.' They met on Barnbougle Sands or Links,[1] in the presence of a great multitude, and with the Duke of Lennox, the Laird of Buccleuch, Sir James Sandilands, and Lord Sinclair, to act as judges. 'The one was clothed in blue taffeta, the other in red sattin.' Carmichael, who was 'as able a like man as was living,' seemed at first to have great advantage over Adam Bruntfield, who was 'but ane young man, and of mean stature;' and at the first encounter he struck Adam on the loin. To the surprise of all, however, Bruntfield 'strikes him in the craig [neck], and syne loups aboon him, and gives him sundry straiks with his dagger, and sae slays him. Adam Bruntfield is convoyit to Edinburgh with great triumph as ane victorious captain; and the other borne in deid.'—*Bir. Pa. And. C. K. Sc.*

1597. MAR. (?) This spring, there was 'sic increase of sawing, that the like has not been heard of before. Ane man of Libberton, callit Douglas, had, of ten pecks of beir sawn thirty-one thrave, and every threif had ane boll of beir and ane peck.'—*Bir.*

APR. 20. 'At this time, one Sir James Mac Oniel [Mac Connel], *alias* Sorley Buie, a great man in Ireland, being here for the time to complain of our chief islesmen, was knighted, and went with his train and dependers to visit the Castle and provision therein, and gave great and noble rewards to the keepers.'—*Pa. And.* 'The 7th of May, he went homeward, and for honour of his *bonalley*[2] the cannons shot out of the Castle of Edinburgh.'—*Bir.* 'This Sir James was ane man of Scottis bluid, albeit his lands lies in Ireland. He was ane braw man of person and behaviour, but

[1] Near Cramond Island.

[2] Fr. *Bon aller*, an entertainment at the commencement of a journey.

had not the Scots tongue, nor nae language but Erse [Irish].' —*C. K. Sc.* 1597.

There was a proclamation 'that no man take upon hand to give out money any dearer nor ten for the hundred [ten per cent. interest], or victual according thereto, under the pain of confiscation of their goods, and punishing of their bodies as usurers.'—*Bir.* JUNE 6.

Died Hugh Rose of Kilravock, at an advanced age. A descendant describes him as 'ane excellent person.' 'He found the fortune [of the family] low, and under great burden, which he not only defrayed, leaving it free to his son, but also acquired the whole lands now holden of the Bishop of Moray. He had seventeen sisters and daughters, all whose portions, mediately or immediately, he paid, though their very portions were a considerable debt. He lived in a very divided factious time, there falling out then great revolutions in church and state; religion changed from popery to protestant, and the queen laid aside, living in exile; yet such was his even, ingenious, prudential carriage, that he wanted not respect from the most eminent of all parties. He had troubles from neighbours, which he prudently carried, and yet knew how discreetly to resent them, as appears, that a debate being betwixt him and two neighbours, he subscribed: "Hucheon Rose of Kilravock, ane honest man, ill guided betwixt them both." This was *ridentem dicere verum.* JUNE 10.

'He was a man that could make good use of his troubles, as appears by his answer to King James, who, being in Kilravock in his progress to the north (in the year 1589, as I suppose), inquired how he could live amongst such ill turbulent neighbours; [he] made this reply: "That they were the best neighbours he could have, for they made him thrice a day go to God upon his knees, when perhaps otherwise he would not have gone once." And at the same time, as I have learned many years ago from old persons, the king was pleased to honour him with the name of Father, and desiring he might be covered.

'As to his person, I have had it from such as knew him, that he was of a tall, and of a square well-compact body, but not corpulent. He was of a venerable grave aspect; his beard white and long in his old age. He died full of days, not so much of sickness as nature being worn out. The night before his death, he went forth to his orchard, and there supped upon a little broth, and then going to his bed, died the next morning, without trouble, muttering

1597. these words in Latin at his expiring: "In manus tuas, Domine, commendo spiritum meum."'[1]

June 26. This was a day of great joy to the friends of the reformed faith, for the Earls of Huntly and Errol had at length been wrought upon to make profession of the true religion, and so be relaxed from the pains of excommunication. Though the pressing nature of the motive was obvious, no dread of insincerity seems ever to have entered the minds of the honest zealots who left these lords no other course for their preservation. The affair took place in the kirk of Aberdeen, and was in several respects noticeable. The evening before, the Earl of Huntly shook hands in token of reconciliation with Lord Forbes and young Irvine of Drum, and signed the articles of the established religion, swearing not to decline therefrom. On the Sunday, which was observed as a fast, on account of the importance of this conversion, the two nobles appeared in the marriage desk or pew in the Old Kirk, where was 'sic a confluence of noblemen, barons, gentlemen, and common people, as that the like was never seen in that kirk.'

To pursue the narrative of an eye-witness: 'The bishop preached, and made a godly and excellent sermon. The sermon being concluded, the earls rises furth of their desk, comes in before the pulpit, make ane open confession of their defection and apostasy, affirms the religion presently confessed to be the only true religion, renounces all papistry, &c., and of new swears never to decline again, but to defend the samen to their life's end. The Earl of Huntly confessed his offence, first to God, next to his majesty, to the kirk and country, for the slaughter of the Earl of Moray. And sae the bishop pronounces openly their sentence of absolution frae the sentence of excommunication. The earls are then received by the haill ministry, being in number twelve or thirteen persons, wha, during all the time of the sermon, sat at the table in the mids' of the kirk, and with them the provost, bailies, and maist part of the council. And after the earls were received by the ministry, then Patrick Murray, commissioner for his majesty, received them in his hieness' name; next the provost, bailies, and council. And sae they were received to the bosom of the kirk. At the samen time, the Laird of Gight, before the pulpit, sat down on his knees, and askit God, his majesty, and the kirk pardon and forgiveness for the receipt of the Earl of Bothwell, for

[1] *Genealogical Deduction of Kilravock Family*, written in 1683-4.

the whilk he was excommunicate; and he was absolved frae the excommunication. This being done, the twa earls, with mony mae gentlemen and barons, all the ministry, communicate together at the table of the Lord.' . . . 1597.

Next day, the Market Cross was solemnly hung with tapestry, and in a small house close by a band of musicians was placed. Four score of the young men of the town, in their best habiliments, with hagbuts, took their station around. There also were placed the magistrates and council, with six maskers. On a table set out in the street were wine, glasses, and sweetmeats. The earls' pacification was then formally proclaimed by Marchmont herald. 'The twa earls sat at the Cross in chairs, with his majesty's commissioner and the ministry. The wand of peace delivered to them by Patrick Murray, he receives them in his majesty's name; next the ministry embraces them, and then the provost, bailies, and magistrates. Hagbuts sounded, that day nor dur could not be heard; wine drunk in abundance; glasses broken; sirfootfeats casten abroad on the causey, gather whaso please! After this the earls and their kin passes to the Tolbooth, with the haill ministry; all are made burgesses of this town, the ministry with the rest. At even, naething but waughting.'[1]

Of course, all was a forced hypocrisy on the part of the two lords, merely to avoid the legal consequences of their excommunication. Most curious it would be to know if there were no misgivings on the subject among the clergy: certainly none appear. Huntly, as might have been expected, quickly relapsed to his popish professions, and was again excommunicated in 1606. Nevertheless, he was some years later accepted once more as a Protestant, and restored to his civil rights.

A deputation of ministers went this summer through the provinces of Aberdeen, Moray, and Ross, to complete as far as possible the planting of them with ministers. The chief of the Clan Mackintosh surprised the deputation by the zeal and cordiality he shewed towards the object. He met them at Inverness, exhibited a plan for settling ministers in his country, and subscribed it in their presence. 'Now,' said he, 'it may be thought I am liberal because nae minister will venture to come amang us. Get me men and sey [try] me. I will find sufficient caution in St Johnston, Dundee, or Aberdeen, for safety of their persons,

[1] Letter of Thomas Mallison, Aberdeen, June 28, 1597. *Spalding Club Misc.*, ii. lx.

1597. obedience to their doctrine and discipline, and guid payment of their stipend.'—*Ja. Mel.* We have seen enough of the leading men of this age in Scotland not to be too much surprised on learning that this was the same Highland chief who had sent out his clan on a wild ravaging expedition in 1592, when the hospitable old baron of Brackla was one of their victims, and who is summed up in the *Historie of King James the Sext,* as 'a man unconstant, false, and double-minded, by the report of all men.'

The Lanarkshire lead-mines, under the care of Thomas Foulis, goldsmith in Edinburgh, and Bewis Bulmer, an Englishman, whom Thomas had assumed as partner, were now beginning to be a source of profit. The lead was transported on the backs of horses to sundry parts of the realm, but the greater part of it to Leith, where it was disposed of for exportation. Just, however, as all the mining difficulties had been overcome, the enterprisers found troubles of a different kind. The broken men of the Borders had heard of this valuable metal passing along the uplands of Clydesdale, and it seemed to them not too hazardous an adventure to cross the hills, and make a dash at such a booty. We therefore
June 14. now hear of the carriers of the lead, servants of Thomas Foulis, being occasionally beset on their way, and robbed by the borderers of 'horses, armour, clothing, and their haill carriage.' Nearer
Oct. 11. neighbours, too, respectable men, burgesses of Lanark and Glasgow, were accused of lawlessly helping themselves to the lead and lead ore, won from the mines in Crawford Muir, not scrupling for this purpose to seize it in its passage to Leith, and dispose of it for their own benefit. Nay, these persons, it was said, had appropriated two horse-load of rye and white bread on its way to the mines, and within six miles of them, thus seriously hindering the progress of the work itself.

The Council issued a threatening proclamation against the first class of spoliators. As the latter set represented themselves as having lawfully purchased the lead in question, an order was issued that they should return or pay for it to Thomas Foulis.—*P. C. R.*

Owing to the fame of Andrew Melville, the university of St Andrews was this year attended by a considerable number of foreign youth, Poles, Danes, Belgians, and Frenchmen: 'whilk crabbit the king mickle,' Andrew being no favourite of his.—*Ja. Mel.*

'Much about this time, there was a great number of witches tried to be in Scotland, as the like was never heard tell of in this realm, specially in Athole, both of men and women. There was in May at ane convention upon a hill in Athole, to the number of twenty-three hundred, and the devil amongst them. A great witch of Balwery told all this, and said she knew them all well enough, and what mark the devil had given severally to every one of them. There was many of them tried by swimming in the water, by binding of their two thumbs and their great toes together, for, being thus casten in the water, they floated ay aboon.'—*Pa. And.* 1597. JUNE.

This 'great witch of Balwery' was one Margaret Aiken, who, being tortured on suspicion, not only confessed her guilt, but, for the saving of her own life, informed upon others, stating that they had a secret mark in their eyes, by which she could at once tell that they were witches. For three or four months, she was carried about the country detecting witches. At Glasgow, owing to the credulity of the minister John Cowper, several old women suffered in consequence of her accusations. In time it was found that she was a deceiver; for the same persons whom one day she declared to be guilty, she would next day, when they appeared before her in different clothes, affirm to be innocent. 'At her trial, she affirmed all to be false that she had confessed, either of herself or others, and persisted in this till her death; which made many forthink their too great forwardness that way, and moved the king to recall the commissions given out against such persons.'—*Spot.*

In November we find the presbytery of Glasgow taking notice of 'divers persons wha traduces and slanders the ministry of the city, as the authors of putting to death the persons lately execute for witchcraft;' and it ordains that any person hereafter uttering this slander 'shall be put in the branks at the judges' will.'[1]

As a natural consequence of the deceptions of Margaret Aiken, there was now in some quarters an apprehension that, in the late proceedings against witches throughout the provinces, some injustice had been done. Some had complained 'that grit danger may ensue to honest and famous persons, gif commissions grantit to particular men beiring particulars [that is, having anger] again' them, sall stand and be authorised.' The king professed to see the reality of this danger, and although it was his purpose to persevere in his efforts to extirpate that 'maist odious and abominable crime,'

[1] *Mait. Club Misc.*, i. 89.

1597. the Council (August 12) revoked all the lately granted commissions, certifying to such as hereafter 'proceeds to the execution of persons to the deid, or melling with their guids or geir, that the same sall be repute slauchter upon forethocht, felony, and spulyie.'

At this time, the enthusiastic section of the church was in a state of discouragement; otherwise the king might not have been able to concede to the representations made to him against witch-commissions. It is too remarkable to be overlooked, that the heat of persecution against these unfortunates was generally in some proportion to the influence of the more zealous clergy, either through their direct agency or through the fear for their reproaches in others.

JULY 23. 'Between eight and nine in the morning, there was an earthquake which made all the north parts of Scotland to tremble; Kintail, Ross, Cromarty, Mar, Breadalbane, &c. A man in St Johnston [Perth] laying compts with his compters, the compts lap off the buird; the man's thighs trembled; one leg went up, and another down.'—*Cal.*

This earthquake happening at the time when King James 'interrupted Mr Robert Wallace and undid the ministry of St Andrews,' James Melville likens it to that which God sent to punish Uzziah, king of Judah, for usurping the priestly office—which rent the Temple of Jerusalem, and caused a beam to hurt the king in the face, the beginning of a leprosy with which he was afflicted. He adds what he calls a *Dix-huitaine* on the subject, concluding in the following strain:

'King James the Saxt, this year thou fast aspires
O'er Christ his kirk to compass thy desires.
Oh, weigh this weel, and here exemple tak;
Lest Christ, wha this year shook thy north-wast parts,
And with eclipsed sun amazed the hearts
For kings to come thee just exemple mak.'

AUG. 6. 'The pest began in Leith' (*Bir.*), and soon 'infected sundry parts about Edinburgh, so that many fled out of the town.'—*Cal.* It raged during this year in England, 17,890 persons being carried off in London alone. A fast was held in Edinburgh on account of this visit of the pestilence, from the 7th of August till the end of harvest, when it ceased. Notwithstanding the scarcity of food from October 1595 down almost to this time, the mortality in Scotland does not appear to have been great—a result probably owing in the main part to the abundant harvest of the present year. 1597.

'Ane trouble betwixt certain servants of the Drummonds and Oliver Young, then one of the bailies of Perth, within the Hie Gait [High Street] of the said burgh; when the greatest number of the pursuers leapt the town's walls, and so few number of them as escapit came to the Tolbooth. The agreement was made in the South Inch, the 1st of September thereafter.'—*Chron. Perth.* Aug. 27.

'The Earl of Cassillis marries Dame Jean Fleming, wha was wife to the last chancellor [Lord Thirlstane], ane very unmeet match, for she was past bairns-bearing, and he was ane young man not past twenty-three years or thereby, and his lands unheired. The king and court mockit the same marriage, and made sonnets in their contempt; and specially his majesty took his pastime of that sport.'—*C. K. Sc.* Nov. 3.

'.... it pleased God to tak the Laird of Bargeny in his mercy; wha was the nobillest man that ever was in that country [Carrick] in his time. He was endued with mony guid virtues. First he fearit God, and was fra the beginning on the right side of religion. He was wise and courteous, and therewith stout and passing kind; and sic ane noble spender in outings with the best-halden house at hame that ever was in the land. He was never behind with na party, and keepit himself ever to the fore with his living. He had ever in his household twenty-four gallant gentlemen, double-horsit, and gallantly clad; with sic ane repair to his house, that it was ane wonder where the same was gotten that he spendit.'—*Ken.* Nov. 7.

While so much lawless violence prevailed throughout the country at large, it was not to be expected that the Borders should be quiet. In truth, the greatest disorders prevailed in that district, particularly in the west, where certain broken clans—Armstrongs, Johnstons, Bells, Batisons, Carlyles, and Irvings—lived in a great measure by robbing and oppressing their neighbours. Occasionally, too, they would make predatory incursions into England, and thereby endanger the peace existing between the two realms. The king was at length roused to make a vigorous effort for the repression of this system of violence. He came at the beginning of this month to Dumfries, 'of resolution not to return therefra till that turn was effectuate, as indeed his majesty did meikle to Nov.

1597. it.'—*Moy.* In the course of four weeks, which he spent in the town, 'he hangit fourteen or fifteen limmers and notorious thieves.' From every branch of the guilty clans, he took one or two of the principal men, 'as pledges that the haill stouths and reifs committed by them, or any of their particular branch, should be redressed, and that they and all theirs should abstene from sic insolency in time coming, under pain of hanging.'[1]

For the reception of such persons in general, there was a *pledge-chalmer*—a sort of honourable jail, we presume—in Dumfries. On this occasion, however, the pledges, thirty-six in number, were distributed over his majesty's houses, where it was ordained they should each pay 13s. 4d. weekly for their maintenance.

The arrangement for the Court of Redress at Dumfries was in characteristic terms. It was to be composed of 'aucht special honest gentlemen of the country, *least suspect, maist neutral and indifferent*, and the best inclined to justice,' with 'twa or three of his majesty's council appointit to be present with them.'—*P. C. R.*

Lord Ochiltree, whom the king appointed as warden of the west Border, 'remainit five or six months at Dumfries, halding courts of redress, and pacifying the country. He hangit and slew three score, with the more notable thieves . . . . and kept the country in great quietness and guid order all this time.'—*Moy.*

There is a small silver toy at Dumfries, in the form of a fusee or musket, which King James is represented as having gifted to the Seven Incorporated Trades in 1598, that it might be the prize of an annual shooting-match. 'The siller gun,' as it is called, has till recent times accordingly been carried by the trades in procession to a shooting-field near the town, whence the victor used to bring it home stuck in his hat. Most probably, it was while spending this month in Dumfries, and not during 1598 (when he certainly did not visit the town), that he conferred this mark of his favour.

Dec. 7. A homicide committed at this time brings out a remarkable illustration of the exclusive rule of master over man which then prevailed. On the first day of the sitting of parliament, Archibald Jardine, servitor and master-stabler to the Earl of Angus, was

[1] He held a privy-council on the 4th November, and occasionally during the month till the 29th, at Dumfries.

slain negligently by Andrew Stalker, goldsmith, at Niddry's Wynd 1597.
head. The said Andrew was apprehendit and put in prison. The young men of the town being all in arms, as they use to be in the time of the parliament, they came to his majesty, and desirit grace for the young man wha had done ane reckless deed. *The king's majesty desirit them to go to my Lord of Angus, the man's master, and satisfy and pacify his wrath, and he should be contentit to grant his life.* James Williamson, being captain to the young men, came to my Lord of Angus, offered him their manreid to be ready to serve him gif he had to do: upon the whilk, he grantit them his life, and sae the said Andrew was releasit out of prison upon the said day at even.'—*Bir.*

'Thomas Foulis conceivit sickness.'—*Bir.* One who knew 1597-8. JAN. 16.
nothing more of Thomas Foulis than what Birrel tells, might be surprised to find the simple fact of his becoming sick entered in this pointed way by the old diarist. As we have already had Thomas several times under our attention, and know him for a great goldsmith, banker, and speculator in mines, we can imagine his indisposition as a public fact of that degree of consequence that a diarist might well think worth chronicling. The truth is, King James had gone deeply into debt towards Thomas for goldsmith work and ready money advanced; his creditors were now pressing him, and he had nothing wherewith to satisfy them. The unhappy man consequently fell into a 'phrensie.' It would appear from one chronicler as if the king had not acted humanely towards his creditor under these circumstances. It is alleged that Thomas's offices were taken from him, and he was obliged to surrender a certain jewel of note, called the H, which he had in pledge from the king[1] for the sum of twelve thousand pounds. But all this is scarcely in harmony with the fact that, in June next, one of the doings of a convention parliament was to arrange 'that the debt awand by his majesty to Thomas Foulis be payit in six years, namely, thirty thousand merks every year.'—*Bir.* Thomas was at the same time made master of the *cunyie-house* (mint).

It appears on the 28th May 1601, that the king owed 'nine score thousand punds money' to Thomas Foulis, goldsmith, Robert Jowsie, merchant-burgess of Edinburgh, and Thomas Acheson, master-cunyier, who were in consequence subject to infinite complaints from their creditors. His majesty professed

[1] Calderwood.

1597-8. 'guid affection and desire to the payment thereof,' and arranged that it should be discharged in the course of eleven years by a preferable power over the receipts of the royal rents. 'His majesty als promittis to give to Thomas, his wife and bairns, during their lifetime successive after others, ane yearly pension of ane thousand punds money.'—*P. C. R.*

In December 1602, a piteous complaint was made before the Privy Council by Andrew Lockhart, regarding the hardship he underwent as a creditor of Thomas Foulis and Robert Jowsie, through the effect of a *supersedere* they had obtained for their debts. He speaks of having been, 'with his wife and aucht bairns,' reduced to misery, through the non-payment of what these men owed him, 'he being ane aigit gentleman, and a brother of ane honourable house.' The Council could not interfere, but engaged that when the present supersedere run out, which it would do erelong, no other should be granted.—*P. C. R.*

FEB. 8. The impunity of numberless murders and other atrocious crimes in this reign is not more remarkable than the severity occasionally exhibited in comparatively trifling cases. For making a false writ in a matter of three hundred merks, five citizens of Edinburgh were condemned to death. Such, likewise, was the issue of the trial of John Moscrop, writer in Edinburgh, for giving himself out as a notary, and subscribing divers papers as such, he not being one. The six men appear to have all been tried on one day, and the end of the affair is chronicled by Birrel: 'John Windieyetts, John Moscrop, Alexander Lowrie, John Halliday, and Captain James Lowrie [were] all hangit at the Cross of Edinburgh for counterfeiting false writs; whilk was great pity to see.'—*Bir.*

FEB. 16. It was now five years since the tragic death of the Earl of Moray, and yet his corpse lay unburied. So also did that of the late Lord Maxwell, killed in a conflict with the Johnstons, in December 1593.

Stigmatising this as an abuse that 'of late has croppin in,' and in order to prevent the example from being followed, the king and Council issued an order to the respective relatives of the two noblemen, that they have the bodies buried in their ordinary places of sepulture within twenty days, under pain of rebellion.—*P. C. R.*

FEB. 25. On this day, being Saturday, occurred an eclipse of the sun, total

at Edinburgh, and probably so throughout the country generally. 1597-8.
No event entirely similar had occurred within the memory of living people in Scotland, and the impression which it was naturally calculated to produce in an age when such things were regarded as prodigies, was aggravated by the critical state in which the favourite Presbyterian institutions were then believed to be placed. Men regarded it as the omen of a dark period for the Kirk of Scotland.[1]

'Betwixt nine and ten forenoon,' says Calderwood, 'began a fearful eclipse, which continued about two hours. The whole face of the sun seemed to be covered and darkened about half a quarter of an hour, in such measure that none could see to read a book. The stars appeared in the firmament. Sea, land, and air was still, and stricken dead as it were. The ravens and fowls flocking together mourned exceedingly in their kind. Great multitudes of paddocks [frogs] ran together, making an uncouth and hideous noise; men and women were astonished, as if the day of judgment had been coming. Some women swooned. The streets of Edinburgh were full of cries. Some men ran off the streets to the kirk to pray.'

'In the session-house or college of justice, no letter nor book could be read nor looked upon for the space of an hour for darkness, and yet in the north-east there appeared two stars. After this, the space of eight days fair weather [which] ensued, was admirable. But the day after, yea Friday and Saturday, there fell out the greatest rain that might be, in such a manner that neither plough nor harrow could gang a long time after.'—*Pa. And.*

'I knew,' says James Melville, 'out of ephemeridis and almanack, the day and hour of it . . . . also, by natural philosophy, the causes. I set myself to mark the proceedings of it in a basin of water mixed with ink, thinking the matter but common. But yet, when it came to the extremity of darkness, and I myself losit all the sun, I was strucken with such fear and astonishment, that I had no refuge but to prostrate [myself] on my knees, and commend myself to God, and cry for mercy.'

'The like fearful darkness was never seen in this land, so far as

[1] '. . . that fearful eclipse of the sun which continued the space of two hours, so fearful that that Saturday is yet called by the people the BLACK SATURDAY; a prognostic, as the times give occasion to interpret, of that darkness which was to fall upon the kirk.'—*Scot's Narration.*

1597-8. we can read in our histories, or understand from tradition. The wise and godliest thought it very prodigious, so that from pulpit and by writ, admonitions were given to the ministers, that the changeable and glittering show of the world go not in betwixt them and Christ, the Sun of Righteousness, and remove the clear light of the gospel from the kirk.'—*Cal.*

A Presbyterian diarist is careful to tell us the 'notable *effects* of this eclipse' in the year following; namely, the death of those famous 'lights of the Kirk of Scotland, Mr Thomas Buchanan, Mr Robert Rollock, David Ferguson, &c.'—*Ja. Mel.*

1598. MAR. '. . . . the Duke of Holstein, the queen's brother, came through England to Edinburgh, and was conveyed the first night to the Palace of Holyroodhouse, where he was received and welcomed very gladly by her majesty, and used every way like a prince. His majesty hasted to Edinburgh to meet with the duke, and at his coming saluted and entertained him . . . . as appertained to his rank. The duke made a progress from Holyroodhouse to the other side of the Forth, the first night to Ravensheugh, Lord Sinclair's house, and from thence to Balcomie, Pittenweem, Anstruther, St Andrews, Dundee, Foulis, Stirling, and Linlithgow, and returned again to Edinburgh. He was honourably received and banqueted all the way. His majesty gave him banquets in Holyroodhouse and Stirling sundry times, and entertained him with pastime, and all other things to his great liking and contentment; likewise he was very largely complimented by their majesties.' That is, they gave him large presents.—*Moy. R.*

May 2. 'The Duke of Holstein got ane banquet in Macmoran's lodging,[1] given by the town of Edinburgh. The king's majesty and the queen being both there, there was great solemnity and merriness at the said banquet.'—*Bir.*

June 3. 'The Duke of Holstein took his leave of the king and queen, and shipped at Leith, having got great propines [gifts]; to wit, a thousand five-pound pieces, a thousand crowns, with a hat and a string valued at twelve thousand pounds, besides other rich chains and jewels.'—*Pa. And.* 'To his bonalley, sixty shot of ordnance shot off the bulwark of Leith.'—*Bir.*

APR. Fynes Moryson, gentleman, who had travelled in most of the

[1] The house of Bailie Macmoran, who was killed by a boy at the High School in 1595. This house still exists (see p. 263), and the room where the duke was banqueted is now used as the Mechanics' Library.

countries of Europe, being at Berwick, felt an earnest desire, 1598.
before returning southwards, to see the king of Scots' court. He therefore entered Scotland, and in one day rode to Edinburgh; after which he proceeded to Falkland, and designed to visit St Andrews and Stirling, but was prevented by unexpected business, which recalled him to England. He tells us little that is remarkable about the localities he visited, but makes some general observations regarding travelling in Scotland, which are not devoid of interest.

'In Scotland,' he says, 'a horse may be hired for two shillings the first day, and eightpence the day till he be brought home; and the horse-letters used to send a footman to bring back the horse. They have no such inns as be in England; but in all places some houses are known where passengers may have meat and lodging; but they have no bushes or signs hung out, and for the horses, they are commonly set up in stables in some out-lane, not in the same house where the passenger lies. And if any man be acquainted with a townsman, he will go freely to his house, for most of them will entertain a stranger for his money. A horseman shall pay for oats and straw (for hay is rare in those parts) some eightpence day and night; and he shall pay no less in summer for grass, whereof they have no great store. Himself at a common table shall pay about sixpence for his supper or dinner, and shall have his bed free; and if he will eat alone in his chamber, he may have meat at a reasonable rate. Some twenty or thirty years ago, the first use of coaches came into Scotland; yea, were they rare even at Edinburgh. At this day, since the kingdoms of England and Scotland were united, many Scots have been promoted by the king's favour both in dignity and estate, and the use of coaches became more frequent, yet nothing so common as in England. But the use of horse-litters hath been very ancient in Scotland, as in England, for sickly men and women of quality.'

He tells that the Scotch eat much colewort and cabbage, and little fresh meat. 'Myself,' he says, 'was at a knight's house, who had many servants to attend him, that brought in his meat with their heads covered with blue caps, the table being more than half furnished with great platters of porridge, each having a little piece of sodden meat. And when the table was served, the servants did sit down with us; but the upper mess [those sitting above the salt-vat], instead of porridge, had a pullet with some prunes in the broth. And I observed no art of cookery or furniture of household stuff, but rather rude neglect of both, though myself and companion, sent from the governor of Berwick about Border

1598. affairs, were entertained after their best manner. . . . . They vulgarly eat hearth-cakes of oats [girdles for toasting the cakes over a fire were subsequently invented at Culross], but in cities have also wheaten bread, which for the most part was bought by courtiers, gentlemen, and the best sort of citizens. . . . . They drink pure wines, not with sugar, as the English; yet at feasts they put comfits in the wine, after the French manner; but they had not our vintners' fraud, to mix the wines. . . . .

'Their bedsteads were then like cupboards in the wall, with doors to be opened and shut at pleasure; so we climbed up to our beds. They used but one sheet, open at the sides and top, but close at the feet, and so doubled [still practised, and a comfortable custom it is]. . . . . When passengers go to bed, their custom was to present them with a sleeping-cup of wine at parting.'

'The husbandmen, the servants, and almost all in the country, did wear coarse cloth made at home, of gray or sky colour [hodden gray], and flat blue caps very broad. The merchants in cities were attired in English or French cloth, of pale colour or mingled black and blue. The gentlemen did wear English cloth, or silk, or light stuffs, little or nothing adorned with silk lace, much less with lace of silver or gold, and all followed at this time the French fashion, especially in court. Gentlewomen married did wear close upper bodies, after the German manner, with large whalebone sleeves, after the French manner, short cloaks like the Germans, French hoods, and large falling bands round their necks. The unmarried of all sorts did go bareheaded, and wear short cloaks, with most close linen sleeves on their arms, like the virgins of Germany. The inferior sort of citizens' wives, and the women of the country, did wear cloaks made of a coarse stuff, of two or three colours in chequer-work, vulgarly called *plodan*.'[1]

MAY. '. . . . Lord Home came to Lauder, [and] asked for William Lauder [bailie of that burgh, commonly called *William at the West Port*], being the man who hurt John Cranston (nicknamed *John with the gilt sword*). [William] fled to the tolbooth, as being the strongest and surest house, for his relief. But the Lord Home caused put fire to the house, and burnt it all. The gentleman remained therein till the roof-tree fell. In end he came desperately out amongst them, and hazard[ed] a shot of a pistol at John Cranston, and hurt him. But [it] being impossible

[1] Fynes Moryson's *Itinerary*, folio, 1617.

to escape with life, they most cruelly without mercy hacked him with swords and whingers all in pieces.'—*Pa. And.* 1598.

Lady Marischal, sister of Lord Home, 'hearing the certainty of the cruel murder of William Lauder, did mightily rejoice thereat, and writ it for good news to sundry of her friends in the country. But within less than twenty-four hours after, the lady took a swelling in her throat, both without and within, after a great laughter, and could not be cured till death seized upon her with great repentance.'[1]—*Pa. And.*

A remission for this barbarous slaughter was granted by the king, in 1606, to the Earl of Home, Hume of Hutton Hall, Thomas Tyrie, tutor of Drumkilbo, John Hume in Kells, and other persons.[2]

It does not appear that any effectual order was taken with the Laird of Johnston for his resistance to the royal authority at Dryfe's Sands and the slaughter of Lord Maxwell (December 6, 1593). His turbulent proceedings at length caused him to be denounced as a rebel. A few days before this event, his portrait was hung, head downwards, on the gibbet at the Cross of Edinburgh, and he declared 'a mansworn man.'—*Bir.* He was restored to his honours in 1600. JUNE 5.

The king gave a letter of patent to Archibald Napier, apparent of Merchiston, for an invention of his, a 'new order of gooding and manuring of field-land with common salt, whereby the same may bring forth in more abundance, both of grass and corn of all sorts, and far cheaper than by the common way of dunging used heretofore in Scotland.' That nothing came of this plan need not be told. JUNE 22.

The Merchiston Napiers must have been a theme of some curiosity and no little remark at this time, seeing that three generations were now living, all of them busy-brained, ingenious, and original-minded persons. First was the laird himself, master-general of the cunyie-house, still in the vigour of life, being not more than sixty-five years of age. Second was John Napier, the fiar or heir, only sixteen years the junior of his father, constantly engaged in puzzling out profound problems in mathematics and prophecies in the Apocalypse. Finally, this grandson of the laird,

[1] For an anecdote of this lady, see under October 1590.

[2] Pitcairn's *Crim. Trials*, iii. 116.

1598. a youth of four-and-twenty, and already, as we see, exhibiting the active intellect of the family.

Archibald became a favourite courtier of James VI. and Charles I., by the latter of whom he was raised to the peerage. He joined the anti-covenanting party, and endured some adversity in his latter days.

The carboniferous formation, as is well known, does not extend in Scotland beyond the Ochils; but in the remote county of Sutherland, on the coast at Brora, there is a patch of oolite, in the lower section of which is a workable bed of coal, between three and four feet thick. John, tenth Earl of Sutherland, had discovered this valuable deposit, but being cut off by poison (anno 1567), he had no opportunity of trying to turn it to advantage. The Sutherland estates were now under the management of a woman of some force of character, and who has by accident a place in our national history—Lady Jean Gordon. Being divorced by Bothwell, in order to admit of his marriage to Queen Mary, she had subsequently married one Earl of Sutherland, and become the mother of another, for whom she was now acting. By this clever countess the coal of Brora was for the first time worked, not merely for its use in domestic purposes, but as a means of establishing a salt-work. Some pans being erected by her 'a little by-west the entry of the river,' there was good salt made there, 'which served not only Sutherland and the neighbouring provinces, but also was transported into England and elsewhere.' This was a good effort, but, like all similar enterprises in that rude age, it met with interruptions. One vigorous renewed effort was made by the countess's son, Earl John, in 1614. It was not, however, till our own time, when the first Duke of Sutherland spent £16,000 on the coal-works, and £2337 on the salt-works, that the original designs of Countess Jean could be said to be fully realised. The works are stated to have given forth twenty thousand tons of coal between the years 1814 and 1826.[1]

JULY 10. '. . . . ane man, some callit him a juggler, playit sic supple tricks upon ane tow, whilk was fastenit betwixt the top of St Giles's Kirk steeple and ane stair beneath the Cross, callit Josia's

[1] Gordon's *Hist. House of Sutherland.* Phillips's *Geology.* *New Stat. Acc. Scot.* H. Miller's *Testimony of the Rocks*, p. 496.

Close head, the like was never seen in this country, as he rade 1598.
down the tow and playit sae mony pavies on it.'—*Bir.*

Practitioners of such dangerous arts were not uncommon in those days. The death, in Edinburgh, of one Kirkaldy, 'who had before danced at the cock of the steeple [St Giles's],' is noted in the history of the civil broils of 1571.[1]

Mr James Melville reports in 1600: 'Being in Falkland, I saw a funambulus, a Frenchman, play strange and incredible proticks upon stented tackle in the palace close before the king, queen, and haill court.' He adds the vulgar surmise of the day: 'This was politickly done, to mitigate the queen and people for Gowrie's slaughter.'

It appears that these diverting vagabonds were well rewarded. The juggler of 1598, called an 'English sporter,' had twenty pounds from the king for the steeple-trick. Two months after, six pounds thirteen shillings and fourpence was ordered to 'David Weir, sporter,' supposed to be the same person. To Peter Bramhill, the French *pavier*—that is, player of pavies—there is a precept from his majesty, ordering him no less a sum than £333, 6s. 8d.[2]—but of course Scottish money.

'This year the wheat was blasted.'—*Chron. Perth.* 'The ait meal sold for 6s. the peck.'—*Bir.*

There was, consequently, towards the end of the year, 'ane extraordinar dearth of all kinds of *pultrie and other vivres,*' throughout the realm, but particularly did this kind of scarcity prevail in Edinburgh, 'where his hieness, his nobility and council, in sundry seasons of the year, make their chief residence.' The king issued a proclamation, fixing a minimum of prices for the said articles, not to be exceeded under certain penalties. This, however, was now found 'likely to become altogether ineffectual, partly through the avaritious greediness of some persons wha forestalls and buys the pultrie in grit, and keeps the same in secret houses, and there sells the same far above the prices exprest in the proclamation,' and partly by the negligence of magistrates, who take no care to punish 'the authors of this disorder.' For these reasons, a more rigorous and menacing proclamation was now made.

A fortnight after, followed an edict of Council against twenty-four poultrymen of Edinburgh (surprising there should have then

[1] *Calderwood*, iii. 76.

[2] Notes to James Melville's *Diary*, Wodrow edition.

1598. been so many in the business), who, it was said, had contravened the late proclamation by forestalling and secretly selling their poultry at high prices, representing the fowls as 'his majesty's awn kain fowls, or that they are bocht by them for his majesty's awn mouth . . . . slanderand his majesty hereby, as if his majesty were the chief cause of the break of the said proclamation.'

It is amusing to observe the apparent astonishment of the king and his councillors on finding how little respect was paid to edicts of this kind, as if it were a most unrighteous and undutiful thing of the people to try to get prices for articles proportionate to the small quantity there was to sell. We must not, however, be too ready to indulge in a smile at the false political economy of the Scottish monarch of 1598, when we remember that a law-made scarcity of *vivres* was kept up in Great Britain till 1846, and observe that at the present day the sovereign of France still dictates the prices at which beef and mutton are to be sold in Paris. At the very time when this notice is penned (September 1856), the newspapers describe the conduct of butchers in Paris as precisely that of the twenty-four poultrymen of Edinburgh in 1599; that is to say, they sell their meat in secret to persons who will give suitable prices.

Considering the scarcity which marked the close of 1598, it is not surprising to find the Chronicle of Perth adverting next year to 'ane great deid among the people.'

DEC. The Privy Council Record at this date gives an anecdote which reads like a tale of patriarchal times—the time when Jacob told his sons to go down into Egypt and buy corn, 'that we may live and not die.'

On some recent occasion of pestilence, Dumfries, being specially and severely afflicted, was, as usual, sequestered from all intercourse and traffic—its markets became altogether decayed, and the inhabitants, in addition to all their other distresses, found themselves 'evil handlit for want of necessar sustentation.' In these circumstances, it seemed good to them to send two of their number, unsuspected of infection, to the country about the Water of Cree in Galloway, to purchase cattle. The two men, James Sharpe and John Mertine, set forth on this quest, and, coming to the burgh of Wigtown, were there well received by the magistrates, who seemed willing to give them Christian help and countenance for their object, on the condition that the cattle were paid for and the burgh of Wigtown satisfied in their customs. Thus sanctioned, the Dumfries emissaries went into the country and bought thirty-eight nolt, which they began to drive towards Dumfries, looking for no interruption or impediment. At Monygaff on the Water of Cree, they were met by a large armed party under the command of Patrick Ahannay, provost of Wigtown, and John Edgar and Archibald Tailfer, bailies, who laid violent hands upon them, and carried them and their cattle to Wigtown. We do not learn what was the motive of this conduct, but may reasonably surmise it was some claim in the way of custom which the Dumfriessians had failed to satisfy. At Wigtown the cattle were detained eight days, getting gradually leaner for want of food, till at last they were 'extreme lean;' and it was not till their owners had paid a hundred merks, that they were allowed to proceed with the beeves to the starving burgh of Dumfries. 1598.

This pitiable affair, which reads so strangely of Dumfries, now the scene of magnificent markets for the transfer of cattle, came under the notice of the Privy Council, and was remitted to the ordinary judges to be settled by them as they might think best.—*P. C. R.*

1598-9. JAN. 19.

Thomas Lorn, residing at Overton of Dyce, was brought before the provost of Aberdeen, accused of 'hearing of spreits, and wavering ofttimes frae his wife, bairns, and family, by the space of seven weeks,' they not knowing 'where he has been during the said space.' He agreed that, if he should ever be found absenting himself in that manner, without giving warning, he should suffer death 'as ane guilty person, dealer with spreits.'—*Ab. C. R.*

1599. JULY 26.

Andrew Melville, of whose courage and zeal for pure presbytery Scottish history is at this time full, presided at a disputation in the theological hall of St Mary's College, St Andrews, where the question was, 'Whether by divining or diabolical force of witches and hags, bodies may be transported or transformed, or souls released for a time from bodies, and whether this transportation or transformation of bodies, or resemblance of a projected corpse, without sense and motion, as if the soul were banished, be a simple lethargy, or a certain evidence of execrable demonomania?'[1]

If the reader be at a loss to conceive how any body of learned men could gravely treat such a question, he may have the fact

[1] See in *Deliciæ Literariæ* (Edin. 1840), the title of the rare tract printed by Waldegrave in 1599, announcing this disputation.

1599. verified to his mind by looking into King James's book on *Demonologie*, where the same matter is fully debated between Philomathes and Epistemon, the two interlocutors in the dialogue of which that treatise consists. In answer to the question of Philomathes, by what means may it be possible for witches to come to those conventions where they worship the devil and receive his orders, Epistemon coolly says: 'One way is natural, which is natural riding, going, or sailing: this may be easily believed. Another way is somewhat more strange . . . . being carried by the force of the spirit which is their conductor, either above the earth or above the sea swiftly, to the place where they meet; which I am persuaded to be likewise possible, in respect that as Habakkuk was carried by the angel in that form to the den where Daniel lay, so think I, the devil will be ready to imitate God as well in that as in other things. . . . The third way is that wherein I think them deluded: for some of them say that, being transported in the likeness of a little beast or fowl, they will come and pierce through whatsoever house or church, though all passages be closed, by whatsoever open the air may enter in at: and some say, that their bodies lying still, as in an ecstasy, their spirits will be ravished out of their bodies and carried to such places; and, for verifying thereof, will give evident tokens, as well by witnesses that have seen their body lying senseless in the meantime, as by naming persons whom-with they met, and giving token what purpose was amongst them, whom otherwise they could not have known; for this form of journeying they affirm to use most, when they are transported from one country to another.'

OCT. The reformed clergy did not at first take a decidedly hostile view of theatricals, and we have seen that even the Regent Moray allowed a play to be represented before him. In March 1574, the General Assembly forbade the playing of 'clerk plays,' and 'comedies and tragedies made of the canonical scriptures' both on Sabbath and work-days; but as to 'comedies, tragedies, and other profane plays not made upon authentic parts of scripture,' they were willing that such might be considered before they be proposed publicly, provided they were to be set forth on work-days only.—*B. U. K.*

Accordingly, it is not surprising that, when a company of comedians came to Perth in June 1589, and applied to the kirk-session for a licence to represent a play, of which they produced a copy, that reverend court expressed itself as follows: '*Perth*,

June 3, 1589.—The minister and elders give licence to play the play, with conditions that no swearing, banning, nor nae scurrility shall be spoken, whilk would be a scandal to our religion, and for an evil example to others. Also, that nothing shall be added to what is in the register of the play itself. If any one who plays shall do in the contrary, he shall be wardit, and make his public repentance.'—*P. K. S. R.* 1599.

These are among the proofs to the general conclusion, that the puritanic strictness for which Scotland has been noted, did not reach its acme during the first age succeeding the Reformation.

Ten years had since elapsed, during which the English drama had passed through a vigorous adolescence, drawing the highest wits of the land into its service. No regular theatre had been set up in Scotland, nor was the time come when one could be supported; but some inclination was manifested by the London acting companies to pay occasional visits to the north, where the mirth-loving king and his court were ready to patronise them. The clergy were by this time disposed to look more sourly on the children of Thespis. An English company did come to Edinburgh about October 1599—possibly the Blackfriars company, to which Shakspeare belonged; but on this point, and as to the question whether Shakspeare was of the party, we have no information. It received a licence from the king to perform.

Roused by 'certain malicious and restless bodies, wha upon every little occasion misconstrue his majesty's haill doings,' the general kirk-session of the city passed an act in direct opposition to the purport of the royal licence, threatening with censure all who should support the comedy; and this they ordered to be read in all pulpits, where, at the same time, the 'unruly and immodest behaviour of the stage-players' became the theme of abundant declamation. The king chose to take up this act as a discharge of his licence, and called the sessions before him, when, after a conference, they professed to be convinced that 'his hieness had not commandit nor allowit ony thing carrying with it ony offence or slander;' and they readily agreed to annul their former act. This was accordingly done next day, 'sae that now not only may Nov. 10.
the comedians freely enjoy the benefit of his majesty's liberty and warrant grantit to them, but all his majesty's subjects, inhabitants within the said burgh, and others whatsomever, may freely at their awn pleasure repair to the said comedies and plays, without ony pain, reproach, censure, or slander to be incurrit by them.'—

1599. *P. C. R.* We learn, however, from Spottiswoode, that this was 'to the great offence of the ministers.'

OCT. The Western Isles being a scene of almost incessant private war and strife, and the crown-rents remaining unpaid, the king became desirous to reduce that part of his dominions to obedience and the arts of peace. It was thought that a plantation of industrious Lowlanders might prove an effectual means of civilising the district. As a preliminary step, an act of parliament was passed (June 1598) for depriving of their lands all who should not shew their titles by a particular day—a most arbitrary measure, which to some extent the turbulent chieftains were justified in resisting. In this manner the islands of Lewis and Harris, the lands of Dunvegan in Skye, and of Glenelg on the mainland, were declared to be at the disposal of the government. It was resolved to proceed, in the first place, with the planting of the Lewis, where there were only two illegitimate sons of the late proprietor to give any opposition.

Accordingly, a set of gentlemen, chiefly belonging to Fife, associated themselves together as adventurers; namely, the Duke of Lennox; Patrick, Commendator of Lindores; William, Commendator of Pittenweem; Sir James Anstruther, younger of that Ilk; Sir James Sandilands of Slamanno; James Learmont of Balcomie; James Spens of Wormiston; John Forret of Fingask; David Home, younger of Wedderburn; and Captain William Murray. By the terms of a contract between these individuals and the government, they were, in consideration of the great expenses to be incurred by them, and the improvements which they were expected to make, freed from any payment of rent for the lands which they were to occupy, for seven years. At the end of that time, an annual grain-rent of one hundred and forty chalders of beir was to commence.[1]

In October 1599, 'the adventurers met altogether in Fife, where they assembled a company of soldiers, and artificers of all sorts, with everything which they thought requisite for a plantation. So, transporting themselves into the Lewis, they began apace to build and erect houses in a proper and convenient place fit for the purpose. In the end, they made up a pretty town, where they encamped. Niel Macleod and Murdo Macleod—now only left in that island of all Rorie Macleod his children—withstood the

[1] Gregory's *History of the Western Highlands and Isles.*

undertakers. Murdo Macleod invaded the Laird of Balcomie, 1599.
whom he apprehended with his ship [near the Orkneys], and killed all his men: so, having detained him six months in captivity within the Lewis, he released him, upon promise of a ransom. But Balcomie died in his return homeward to Fife,[1] after his releasement, whereby Murdo Macleod was disappointed of his ransom.'—*G. H. S.*

The two brothers soon after quarrelled, and Niel took Murdo prisoner. The enterprisers entered into an agreement with him for the delivery of Murdo to themselves, promising him, in requital, a portion of their lands. Niel consequently obtained a pardon at Edinburgh, while Murdo was hanged at St Andrews, confessing that the Lord of Kintail, the ambitious chief of the Mackenzies, had been the instigator of his brother and himself in their opposition to the plantation, the fact being, that Kintail desired to obtain the Lewis himself.

The truth of this appeared when the Lord of Kintail soon after set at liberty Tormod Macleod, legitimate son of the late proprietor, who immediately proceeded to raise a new war against the undertakers. Niel joining him, they attacked the settlement, which they destroyed, killed most of the people, and took the commanders prisoners. These gentlemen were only released eight months after, on a promise that they should abandon the island, and never return; besides which, they undertook to procure a pardon from the king for their conquerors.

Thus ended, for a time, the attempt to plant the Lewis.

Till this time, the new year legally held in Scotland was Dec. 17.
that originally pitched upon by Exiguus when he introduced the Christian era—namely, the 25th of March, or day of the Annunciation. King James, probably looking upon the approaching year 1600 as the beginning of a new century, thought it would be a good occasion for bringing Scotland into a conformity with other countries in respect of New-year's Day. There was therefore

[1] This James Learmont of Balcomie had, nearly twenty years before, fixed on the college-gate at St Andrews a placard offensive to Andrew Melville, who consequently broke out upon him as he sat in church, to this effect: 'Thou Frenchiest, Italianest jolly gentleman, wha has defiled the bed of sae many married [men], and now boasts with thy bastinadoes to defile this kirk and put hands on His servants, thou sall never enjoy the fruits of marriage, by having lawful succession of thy body; and God shall baston thee in His righteous judgments!' 'This,' says James Melville, 'was remembered when the said James lived many years in marriage without child, and taken by the Highlandmen coming out of Lewis, was sicearly bastoned, and sae hardly used, that soon thereafter he died in Orkney.'

1599. passed this day at Holyrood an act of Privy Council, in which it is set forth that 'in all other weel-governit commonwealths and countries, the year begins yearly upon the first of January, commonly called New-year's Day, and that this realm only is different frae all others in the count and reckoning of the years;' for which reason they ordained that, in all time coming, Scotland shall conform to this usage, and that the next first of January shall be the first day of the year of God 1600.

Dec. 27. A singular combat being intended betwixt Alexander Livingstone of Pantaskin and John Kennedy, appeirand of Baltersand, without any warrant from his majesty, the Privy Council denounced and prohibited the encounter as contrary to law, and 'not likely to settle the trouble whereupon the challenge proceeded and procure peace to baith parties.'—*P. C. R.*

On the 1st of April 1600, there was a strong edict for the execution of the laws against single combats, which were said, through slackness of the law, to have become frequent.

During this year 'there were divers incursions in the Highlands and Borders, and sundry slaughters committed in divers parts of the country. Five sundry men were slain in one week within two miles of Edinburgh.'—*Cal.*

Circa 1599. M'Alexander of Drumachryne in Ayrshire had a lease of the teinds of his estate from the Laird of Girvanmains, who in his turn was head-tenant of these teinds from the Earl of Cassillis. 'But this Drumachryne, being ane proud man, wald now be tenant to my lord himself, and his man. [That is, he preferred being *man* or vassal to the earl.] The Laird of Girvanmains came to my lord, and said his lordship "had [done him wrang] in setting of his teinds to his awn man ower his head; and for ony gains he sall reap by that deed, the same sall be but small." My lord answerit and said: "Ye dar not find fault with him; for, an ye do, we knaw whare ye dwell." The other said: "An he bide by that deed, he should repent the same, do for him wha likit!" My lord said: "Ye dar not steir him for your craig [neck]!" and bade him gang to his yett [gate]. The Laird of Girvanmains rides his ways, and thinking that the Laird of Drumachryne wald come after him, he stayit, and his twa servants with him, on a muir called Craigdow, behind ane knowe [knoll], while that he saw him coming. His brother, the Laird of Corseclays, being with him, and Oliver Kennedy of . . . .; but they strake never ane strake in his defence. Girvanmains pursues him, and his twa men with him, callit Gilbert M'Fiddes and William M'Fiddes, ane boy, wha was the spy. They come to them on horseback, and strake him on the head with swords, and slew him. My lord was very far offendit at this deed, and avowit to have ane mends thereof, and causit denounce Girvanmains to the horn; and did all he could to have his life, and wrack him in his geir.'—*Hist. Ken.* Circa 1599.

A less tragical, but equally characteristic affair occurred in the same district about the same period. Let it first be understood that Kennedy of Bargeny and the Earl of Cassillis had long been on hostile terms.

'My lord, having ane decreet against ane servant, of the Laird of Bargeny's, callit John M'Alexander, of the lands of Dangart . . . . wald put the same in execution, and intromit with the haill corns that was upon the grund; and send his household servants, and gart [caused] intromit with some of the corns, and shore ane part thereof. This coming to the Laird of Bargeny's ears, he loups on in Ardstinchar, and rides to the land, and with horse and carts brought the corns that they had shorn with him to Ardstinchar; for, he said: "My lord had nae richt to the corns, albeit he had obteenit decreet against the land." This being on the Saturday, my lord provides with all his force he can, against Monday, to shear the rest of the corns. And the Laird of Bargeny, in the same manner, provides for the same effect. The Laird of Bargeny, [being] the nearest hand, comes first to the grund, and to the number of six hundred men on horse, with twa hundred hagbutters. And my Lord of Ochiltree came also, with the number of ane hunder horse; so that, in all, he was, or [ere] twelve hours, the number of nine hunder men, on foot and horse. My Lord of Cassillis come also, with his haill force that he might mak, to the like number or few mae [more]. But the Laird, being in the house and yards, and he having many basses and hagbuts of found with him, the same was onpossible for my lord to mend himself. But my Lord of Cathcart, being ane nobleman wha had married to his wife ane near kinswoman of my Lord Cassillis, and his son having married the Laird of Bargeny's sister, travelled amang them, and took up the matter in this sort, that the laird should have the haill corns that was on the grund to his servant, and should find caution for the duty of the land, whilk was my lord's; and that my lord should come to the grund of the lands, and, according to his decreet, tak possession of the same, but not to steir the corns; and the Laird of Carleton and the Gudeman of Ardmillan to be

Circa 1599. cautioners for the foresaid duty, and my lord fand caution not to trouble the corns, nor the man in the shearing of them. And [according] to this agreeance, the laird rade his way to Ardstinchar; and my lord came to the land and took possession; and John M'Alexander shore his corns in peace.'—*Hist. Ken.*

1600. Jan. There was a feid of old standing between the Lindsays of Forfarshire and the Lords Glammis; but for some years the parties were put under the restraint of *letters of assurance.* On a particular Sunday, during this month, Sir John Lindsay of Woodhead was passing along the High Street of Edinburgh, 'gangand to the kirk,' when he met Lord Glammis. The noble and gentle, 'for the reverence they bure to his majesty and for observance of the assurance standing betwix them, past by other without provocation of offence or displeasure in word or countenance offerit by ony of them.' As in the case of Montague and Capulet, however, the servants were not always to be restrained by the same feelings as the masters. After they were past, Patrick Johnston, a servant or tenant of Glammis, 'drew his sword, invadit and pursewit the complenar [Lindsay] of his life, and strak and cuttit through the shoulder of his cloak, coat, and doublet, without the allowance of Lord Glammis, and thereby did what in him lay to have begun ane new feid and quarrel betwixt them, whilk wald not have faillit to have fallen out were not Lord Glammis himself and the complenar stayit it.'

Jan. 13. Two days after, Lord Glammis appeared personally before the Privy Council, and 'renouncit Patrick to be his man, tenant, or servant, sae that he sall not be repute, halden, nor esteemit to be his man, tenant, or servant hereafter;' further avouching that 'he sall quarrel nor beir grudge to nane that sall invade or pursue the said Patrick.' The Council at the same time charged Patrick to compeir and answer for 'his late violent and unhonest pursuit and invasion of Sir John Lindsay, *without the consent, knowledge, or allowance of Patrick Lord Glammis,* in whais company he was for the time, doing thereby what in him lay to have brocht on and protinued furder trouble and inconvenients betwixt the said Lord Glammis and the friends of the house of Crawford, to the break of his majesty's peace and disquieting of the country.'—*P. C. R.*

An order to denounce Patrick as rebel for not appearing, was given on the 6th of March.

We receive in this notice a rich illustration of the relation of superior and 'man' in Scotland at the close of the sixteenth

century. Johnston's crime of assault is here touched upon lightly; 1600.
what is pressed, is his committing this assault without the consent of his lord, and endangering a further quarrel between that lord and the assaulted man.

The affair appears to have had a sequel not less remarkable than itself. On Sunday the 6th of August 1601, as Patrick Johnston, designated as tenant of the Halltown of Belhelvies, was leaving the kirk of that parish, in time of the ministration of the sacrament of baptism, accompanied by his wife and two of his children, he was set upon, within two paces of the door, by Lord Glammis and a party of his lordship's relatives and servants, and mercilessly slain with pistols and swords. We can scarcely doubt that this was the same Patrick who had incurred his superior's anger by attacking Sir John Lindsay. A complaint against Lord Glammis and his 'complices' for the act was made before the presbytery of Aberdeen, by 'the wife and aucht fatherless bairns' of the slain man, and by that reverend court an effort was made, but in vain, to bring the matter to an arrangement in their favour. The guilty parties were cited for their crime before the Court of Justiciary in March 1602; but no punishment appears to have followed. Lord Glammis obtained a remission for his concern in Johnston's slaughter, under the great seal. The ancient feudal ideas of Scotland were still too strong to allow of such a case being deemed one of common murder.[1] The fact did not prevent Lord Glammis from receiving advancement in court-favour and elevation in rank. He was made Earl of Kinghorn in 1606. It is also somewhat curious to reflect that to his taste and munificence we owe much of what is grand in the architecture of Glammis Castle.

At this time arrived in Edinburgh the young Earl of Gowrie, and FEB.
his brother, Alexander Ruthven, from Padua, where they had been studying for some years. To all appearance, they were disposed to be peaceable subjects of the king, notwithstanding the hard measure which had been dealt out to their father sixteen years before. When, some months afterwards, they came to so tragical an end, a circumstance, which occurred not long after their arrival in Edinburgh, was remembered, as betraying a state of mind different from what appeared on the surface of their general behaviour.

A certain Colonel Stuart of Houston, who, as commander of the royal guard, had been employed in seizing the late unfortunate Earl

[1] *A. P. R.* Pit. Wood's *Peerage.*

1600. of Gowrie, was still employed at court. One day in June, as the young earl, accompanied with seven or eight of his servants, was passing along the long gallery of the palace, on his way to the king's chamber, he observed Colonel Stuart come forth from an interview with his royal master. To avoid a too close meeting with one so painfully associated with his family history, he stepped aside a little, in order to let Stuart pass by. 'The same being espied by ane of the said earl's servants, going in the rank before him, callit Mr Thomas Kinrosser, [he] said ardently till him: "What, my lord, are you going back for ony man here? Come forward, my lord, bauldly!" Whilk going aside and then coming forward again, being seen by Colonel Stuart, he went in again to the king.

"Sir, it will please your majesty hear ane strange matter, that, for guid service done to your grace, I sould be so evil rewardit as I am. Here comes in the Earl of Gowrie, and I see he minds to begin first at me; but beware next of the best of you all."

Herewith the said earl enterit in his majesty's chalmer, and the colonel went out thereof; but there was nothing of that purpose spoken betwixt his majesty and the earl at that time. But, the colonel's words to the king being reported to the earl, he answered: "*Aquila non captat muscas.*"'—*Jo. Hist.*

Mar. 14. The king, returning from a General Assembly in Edinburgh to his palace of Falkland, crossed the Firth of Forth by the ferry between Leith and Kirkcaldy. The weather was fair at starting, but became foul on the passage, and the mariners were obliged to run their boat upon the sands at Kirkcaldy, where the king was taken out on horseback. 'He exclaimed with execration, that he was ever in danger of his life in going to those assemblies.'—*Cal.*

Apr. 2. '. . . . being the Sabbath-day, Robert Auchmuty, barber, slew James Wauchope at the combat in St Leonard's Hill, and upon the 23d, the said Robert [was] put in ward in the Tolbooth of Edinburgh. In the meantime of his being in ward, he hang ane cloak without the window of the iron house, and another within the window there, and, saying that he was sick, and might not see the light, he had aquafortis continually seething at the iron window, while [till] at the last the iron window was eaten through. Sae, upon a morning, he causit his prentice-boy attend when the town-guard should have dissolvit, at whilk time the boy waited on, and gave his master ane token that the said guard were gone, by the show or wave of his handcurch. The said Robert hung out ane tow whereon he thought to have come down. The said guard spied the wave of the handcurch, and sae the said Robert was disappointit of his intention and device; and sae, on the 10 day, he was beheadit at the Cross, upon ane scaffold.'—*Bir.* 1600.

We possess the rental-sheet of the Marquis of Huntly for this date, and obtain from it a striking idea of the worldly means resting with that noble and potent lord. In the first place, the document extends over fifty-nine pages of print in small quarto, detailing the particulars of money and produce due from each farm on his lordship's various estates—in the lordship of Huntly, the lordship of the Enzie, the lordship of Badenoch, the barony of Fochabers, the lands of Marr, the Cabrach, and Lochaber. The sum of 'silver mail' or money-rent is £3819, besides £636 of teind silver. The 'ferm victual' payable to his lordship was 3816 bolls, besides which there were 55 bolls of custom meal, 436 of multure beir, 108 of custom oats, 83 of custom victual, 167 marts (cattle for slaughter), 483 sheep, 316 lambs, 167 grice (young pigs), 14 swine, 1389 capons, 272 geese, 3231 poultry, 700 chickens, 5284 eggs, 4 stones of candle, 46 stones of brew tallow, 34 leats of peats, 990 ells of custom linen, 94 stones of custom butter, 40 barrels of salmon, 8 bolls of teind victual, 2 stones of cheese, and 30 kids. The large proportion of payment in kind speaks of a country in which there was little industry or commerce beyond what was connected with husbandry and store-farming; but it is easy to see what an amount of power the noble marquis would derive from possessing the means of feeding so many retainers. MAY.

In old times, so wealthy a lord was a kind of kinglet, owning, indeed, the superiority of a sovereign, but at the same time enjoying among minor lords and gentlemen a sway which barely owned a restraint in the royal authority. Men approaching him in influence were glad to form alliances with him, either through the ties of marriage, or by direct *bonds of manred*, in which they mutually agreed to support each other in all causes, against all living or dead, excepting only the king's grace. Of such bonds, the Gordon charter-chest exhibits a grand series, extending from 1444, when James of Forbes 'becomes man till ane honourable and mighty lord, Alexander of Seton of Gordon . . . . again all deadly,' down to 1670, when Alexander Rose of Tillisnaucht, gave George, Marquis of Huntly, an engagement to live peaceably under his protection; being a hundred and seven in all. Even within the last seventeen years, during which the now existing marquis had

1600. been conducting his own affairs, the house had been receiving bonds of manred from a remarkable number of important men in the Highlands. The Earl of Argyle, in 1583, promised to 'concur and take aefald, true, and plain part' with the Gordon, 'in all his honest and guid causes against whatsomever that live or die may, our sovereign lord and his authority alone excepted.' Two years later, Macleod of Lewis receives promise of maintenance on the condition of obedience. At the same time, the chief of the Clan Kenzie, Colin of Kintail, enters into a bond of faithful service, 'contrair all persons.' His lordship received the like engagements from Monro of Foulis, the chieftain Glengarry, Macgregor of Glenstrae, and Drummond of Blair. In 1586, Kenneth Mackenzie of Kintail, Donald Robertson, the heir of Strowan, Donald Gorm of Sleat (progenitor of the present Lord Macdonald), John Grant of Freuchie, and the Lady Menzies of Weem, entered into similar undertakings. In 1587, Rattray of Craighall binds himself, with his dependents, 'to serve the said earl in all his actions and adoes, against all persons, the king's majesty only excepted, and sall neither hear nor see his skaith, but sall make him foreseen therewith, and sall resist the same sae far as in me lies, and that in respect the said earl has given me his band of maintenance.' The remaining bonds before 1593 are from the Earl of Orkney, Menzies of Pitfoddles, Lord Lovat, Menzies of that Ilk, Scott of Abbotshall, the Laird of Melgund, Mackintosh of Dunnachtan, Innes of Innermarky, Lord Spynie, Cameron of Locheil, the Clan Macpherson, sundry barons of Moray, and the Laird of Luss. We may thus see what a formidable person this Earl of Huntly was to the Protestant interest in the year last named, and what a problem it must have been to the pacific King James to give him effectual opposition, however well he had been so inclined.[1]

The Marquis of Huntly chiefly dwelt in an ancient seat called Strathbogie Castle, situated where the rivulet Bogie joins the Doveran, near the village of Huntly, in Banffshire. He had another seat, called the Castle of the Bog or of Bogangicht, on the extensive plain at the embouchure of the Spey, in the same county. The migrations of the family between the two places, and between them and a town-mansion in Aberdeen, are frequently alluded to by the annalist Spalding. In 1602, the marquis rebuilt Strathbogie Castle in a handsome style; and the remains of the house yet attest a grandness of living suitable to the wealth and political

[1] *Gordon Papers, Spalding Club Misc.*, iv. 123–319.

importance of the family. 'A spacious turnpike-stair leads to what has been a very grand hall, and still bears the marks of splendour and magnificence. Its length is about forty-three feet, its breadth twenty-nine, and its height sixteen. There is another grand apartment over this, thirty-seven feet in length, and twenty-nine in breadth. The chimneys of both are highly ornamented with curious sculpture of various figures . . . . . Most of the apartments are still in tolerable preservation, particularly the ceilings, which are ornamented with a great variety of paintings in small divisions, containing many emblematical figures, with verses expressive of some moral sentiment in doggerel rhyme.'[1] 1600.

John Kincaid of Warriston, near Edinburgh, was married to a handsome young woman, named Jean Livingstone, daughter to a man of fortune and influence, the Laird of Dunipace. Owing to alleged maltreatment, the young wife conceived a deadly hatred of her husband. A base-minded nurse was near, to whisper means and ways of revenge, and the lady was induced to tamper with a young man named Robert Weir, a servant of her father, to become the instrument. At an early hour in the morning marginally noted, Weir came to Warriston, and, being admitted by the lady into the gentleman's chamber, there fell upon him with his fists, and soon accomplished his death. While Weir fled, the lady remained at home, along with the nurse. Both were immediately seized, subjected to a summary kind of trial before the magistrates, and condemned to death. July 2.

In the brief interval between the sentence and execution, this unfortunate young creature—she was only twenty-one—was brought, by the discourse of an amiable clergyman, from a state of callous indifference to one of lively sensibility and religious resignation. Her case was reported in a small pamphlet of the day. She stated that, on Weir assaulting her husband, she went to the hall, and waited till the deed was done. She thought she still heard the pitiful cries uttered by her husband while struggling with his murderer. Afterwards, by way of dissembling, she tried to weep; but not a tear could she shed. She could only regard her approaching death as a just expiation of her offence. Her relations, feeling shamed by her guilt and its consequences, made interest to obtain that her execution should be as little public as possible, and it was accordingly arranged that, while the nurse was being burnt on the

[1] *Stat. Acc. Scotland*, xi. 477.

1600. Castle Hill at four in the morning, and thus attracting the attention of any who might be out of their beds, the lady should be conducted to the Girth Cross, at the opposite extremity of the city, and there despatched by the Maiden.

According to the contemporary pamphlet: 'The whole way, as she went to the place of execution, she behaved herself so cheerfully, as if she had been going to her wedding, and not to her death. When she came to the scaffold, and was carried up upon it, she looked up to the Maiden with two longsome looks, for she had never seen it before. This I may say of her, to which all that saw her will bear record, that her only countenance moved [her countenance alone would have excited emotion], although she had not spoken a word. For there appeared such majesty in her countenance and visage, and such a heavenly courage in her gesture, that many said: "That woman is ravished with a higher spirit than man or woman's!"' After reading a short address to the multitude at the four corners of the scaffold, she calmly resigned herself to her fate, uttering expressions of devotion till the descent of the axe cut short her speech.

Weir, being taken four years after, was broken on the wheel (June 26, 1604), a severe death, scarcely ever before inflicted in Scotland.—*Pit. Bir.*

JULY 21. In Edinburgh, this day, 'at nine hours at even, a combat or *tulyie* [was fought] between twa brether of the Dempsters, and ane of them slain by John Wilson. [He], being tane with het bluid, was execute at the flesh-stocks, where he had slain the man the night before.'—*Bir.*

Quick as legal vengeance was in this instance, we have proof of its being of little avail for prevention of like outrages. Alexander Stewart, son of James Stewart of Allanton, had applied for admission to the king at Holyroodhouse, at a time 'when his majesty desirit to be quiet,' and Alexander Lockhart, one of the ushers of the chamber, had accordingly denied him admittance. The young man, conceiving deadly hatred at Lockhart for this,
JULY 25. trained him out of his house unarmed, and there set upon him with sword and bended pistol to take his life. For a wonder, Lockhart escaped with only two wounds in the head. The guilty youth was denounced rebel for not answering for his offence.—*P. C. R.*

JULY. The calamities of dearth, want, and a high mortality continued this year to press upon the people, in almost all parts of the country. 'A sheaf of oat-straw was sold for forty shillings in Edinburgh. There was also a great death of little children; six or seven buried [in Edinburgh] in a day.'—*Cal.* 1600.

In October, the pest was in the town of Findhorn, in consequence of which there was an edict of the Privy Council, charging all the people there and thereabouts to keep at home, lest they should spread the infection.—*P. C. R.* We find the magistrates of Aberdeen in December ordaining a fast 'in respect of the fearful infection of the plague spread abroad in divers parts of Moray.'—*Ab. C. R.*

'The year of God 1600, fourteen whales, of huge bigness, were casten in by the sea, upon the sands under the town of Dornoch in Sutherland. They came in alive, and were slain immediately by the inhabitants, who reaped some commodity thereby. Some of these fishes were ninety feet in length.'—*G. H. S.*

In the midst of a time unmarked by great events, great excitement was caused by the attempt of the Earl of Gowrie and his brother upon the king's liberty or life, at Perth. James Melville notes that 'a little before or hard about the day of this accident, the sea at an instant, about low-water, debordit and ran up aboon the sea-mark, higher nor at any stream-tide, athort all the coast-side of Fife, and at an instant reteired again to almaist low-water, to the great admiration of all, and skaith done to some.' Aug. 5.

While Robert Bruce and some others of the clergy professed to regard the conspiracy with incredulity, the great bulk of the people, going with their loyalty, as often happens, far beyond the merit of its object, manifested all tokens of extreme satisfaction at the king's escape. On the arrival of the news, 'there was sic joy, that the cannons shot, the bells rang, the trumpets sounded, the drums strake. The town rase in arms, with shooting of muskets, casting of fire-works, and banefires set forth; the like was never seen in Scotland, there was sic merriness and dancing all the nicht.'—*Bir.* Aug. 6.

The same day, the state-officers, with some other nobles, went to the Cross, 'and there heard Mr David Lindsay make ane orison, and the haill people sat down on their knees, giving thanks to God for the king's deliverance out of sic ane great danger.'—*Bir.*

A few days later, the king returned from Perth to Edinburgh. 'The town, with the haill suburbs, met him upon the sands of Aug. 11.

1600. Leith in arms, with great joy and shooting of muskets, and shaking of pikes. He went to the kirk of Leith, to Mr David Lindsay's orison. Thereafter, the town of Edinburgh having convenit, and standing at the Hie Gait [High Street], his majesty passed to the Cross, the Cross being hung with tapestry, and went up thereon with his nobles. Mr Patrick Galloway being there, made ane sermon upon the 124 psalm; he declared the haill circumstances of the treason proposed by the Earl of Gowrie and his brother, whilk the king testified by his awn mouth, sitting on the Cross all the time of the sermon.'—*Bir.*

Sep. 11. 'For divers guid respects and considerations,' the king in council ordered that thenceforth the Castle of Stirling, in which his son was kept, should not be accessible to the whole trains of the nobility and gentry at such times as the king himself was not present; but every earl should 'have access with four persons only, every lord with twa persons, every baron with ane person, and every gentleman and other person single, and all, ane and all, without armour, saving their swords.' All except the earls, lords, and barons, to 'lay their swords fra them at the yett.'—*P. C. R.*

Soon after, there was an edict for restricting the number of persons brought to court by noblemen in their trains. An earl was enjoined to bring not 'mony mae' than twelve persons; a lord, eight; and a baron, four. The indefiniteness of the order amusingly marks the want of all stern will in King James.

Sep. 14. This being the Rood Fair-day in Jedburgh, a party of rough borderers, Turnbulls, Davidsons, and others, to the number of twenty, came to the town, armed with hagbuts and pistols, and there presented themselves before the lodging of Sir Andrew Kerr of Ferniehirst, 'forment the market-cross, and after divers brags, insolent behaviour, and menacings, in contempt of him and his servants,' slew his brother, Thomas Kerr, and one of his servants. Eleven persons stood a trial for this act, when it appeared that they were only, *more suo*, executing a horning of the sheriff of Roxburgh against Thomas Kerr. Sir Andrew Kerr and others stood a counter-trial for resisting the execution of the horning. But the only practical result was, that one Andrew Turnbull, brother of Turnbull of Bewly, was beheaded at the Cross of Edinburgh (Dec. 16) for the slaughter of Thomas Kerr.—*Pit.*

Oct. 8. Francis Tennant, a wealthy merchant of Edinburgh, was hanged at the Cross of Edinburgh for uttering pasquils against the king 1600. and 'his maist noble progenitors.' Tennant had been an active friend of the Earl of Bothwell, and when that nobleman was at his last extremity, towards the end of 1594, this merchant-burgess had undertaken to get him delivered up to the king. 'But by the contrair, howsoon he came to Bothwell, he revealit the cause of his coming to him, and shew[ed] what reward he had gotten, and offerit himself with all his guids in Bothwell's will, affirming that he would not betray him for all the gold in the warld.' It was in a ship furnished by Francis Tennant that the forlorn Bothwell escaped to France.

Francis appears to have consequently forfeited his position in his native country. Having now fallen into the king's hands, he was arraigned for writing a calumnious letter against the king, dated at Newcastle, January 17, 1597, addressed to Mr Robert Bruce, the minister, and another to Mr John Davidson, both being under fictitious signatures; and which letters 'he had laid down in the kirk of Edinburgh, to the effect the same might have fallen in the hands of the people, thereby to bring his majesty in contempt, and steir up his people to sedition and disobedience.' King James must have been stung to an unusual degree of wrath by these pasquils, for, after the trial, he sent a warrant to the justice-clerk, ordering for sentence, that Francis Tennant should 'have his tongue cuttit out at the rute,' and then be 'hangit.' Four days later, indeed, he departed from this cruel order, and sent a second warrant, stating that, 'for certain causes moving us, we have thought good to mitigate that sentence, by dispensing with the torturing of the said Francis, other [either] in the boots, or by cutting out of his tongue, and *are content* that ye only pronounce doom agains him to be hangit.'

The baptism of the young prince, subsequently Charles I., took Dec. 23. place this day at Holyroodhouse. The manner in which the king obtained the means of holding any such ceremonial is illustrated by the following letter (printed *literatim*),[1] which he addressed on the occasion to the Laird of Dundas:

'Richt traist friend, we greet you heartily well. The baptism of our dearest son being appointit at Halyrudhouse upon the xxiii day of Decem^{r} instant, wherat some princes of France, strangers, with the specialis of our nobility, being invyted to be present,

[1] Published in the *Scots Magazine*, January 1807.

1600. necessar it is that great provisions, gude cheir, and sic uther things necessary for decorations thairof be providit, whilks cannot be had without the help of sum of our loving subjects, quhairof accounting you one of the specialis, we have thought good to request you effectuously to propyne with vennysons, wyld meit, Brissel fowlis,[1] caponis, with sic other provisions as are maist seasonable at that time and errand. To be sent into Halyrudhouse upon the 22 day of the said moneth of December instant, and herewithall to invyte you to be present at that solemnitie, to take part of your awin gude cheir, as you tender our honour, and the honour of the country; swa we committ you to God. From Lithgow, this 6th of Decem^r. 1600—James R.'

At the close of the century, in the midst of the order of things arranged under the care of the reformed church, we may be said to have arrived at a point where it may be proper to take a general survey of the customs and manners of the people. We are enabled to do this with comparative ease by the copious extracts which have been published from the session-records of Perth, Aberdeen, Glasgow, and Edinburgh, the burgh-records of these cities and other documents.

[SUPERSTITIONS AND SUPERSTITIOUS PRACTICES.]

Of some of the superstitions of the people, particularly that regarding the pretended power of witchcraft, abundant illustrations have been presented in the chronicle of the bypast forty years. It may now be remarked, that, besides the witches of malevolent character, who were objects of dread to the community, there were 'wise women,' who were understood to possess the power of curing diseases generally, and restoring the health of sickly children, by charms and other means. We hear, in 1623, of one Janet at Black Ruthven, near Perth, of whom 'the bruit went that she could help bairns who had gotten ane dint of ill wind.'—*P. K. S. R.* At Ruthven, or Huntingtower, there was a well the water of which was believed to have sanative qualities when used under certain circumstances. In May 1618, two women of humble rank were before the kirk-session of Perth, 'who being asked if they were at the well in the bank of Huntingtower the last Sabbath, if they drank thereof, and what they left at it, answered, that they drank thereof, and that each of them left a prin [pin] thereat; which was

[1] Brazil fowls; that is, turkeys.

found to be a point of idolatry, in putting the well in God's room.' —*P. K. S. R.* They were each fined six shillings, and compelled to make public avowal of their repentance. In August 1623, Janet Jackson was cited before the same court for following a witch's advice in employing the deceased Isobel Haldane 'to go silent to the well of Ruthven, and silent back again with water to wash her bairn.' It was admitted that 'Isobel brought the water and washed the bairn therewith, and put the bairn through a cake made of nine curns of meal gotten from women, married maidens,' which was said to be 'a common practice used for curing bairns of the cake-mark.'

At St Wollok's Kirk, a ruin in the parish of Glass, Aberdeenshire, are two pools by the river's side, amongst high rocks, and known far and wide by the name of St Wollok's Baths, Wollok having been an anchoritic saint who dwelt here in the fifth century, and is reckoned as the first bishop of Aberdeen. These pools, always full of water even in times of the greatest drought, were resorted to so lately as the seventeenth century, if not later, for the bathing of sickly children. Near by was St Wollok's Well, also believed to have a supernatural virtue for the healing of diseases.[1]

It was customary for great numbers of persons to go on a pilgrimage barefooted, on the first of May, to Christie's Well, in Menteith, and there perform certain superstitious ceremonies, 'to the great offence of God and scandal of the true religion.' In May 1624, the Privy Council issued a commission to a number of gentlemen of the district, enjoining them to post themselves at the well and apprehend all such superstitious persons and put them into the Castle of Doune.

At the Bay of Nigg, near Aberdeen, was a well dedicated to St Fiacre, and commonly called St Fittich's Well, which was long held in the greatest veneration for its efficacy in disease. On the 28th of November 1630, Margaret Davidson, a married woman, residing in Aberdeen, was adjudged in an unlaw of five pounds by the kirk-session, 'for directing her nurse with her bairn to St Fiack's Well, and washing her bairn therein for recovery of her health . . . . and for leaving an offering in the well.' The prevalence of this custom is indicated by the decree of the session on the same day, threatening heavy censure and punishment to all who should be 'found going to Sanct Fiack's Well, for seeking health to themselves or bairns.'

[1] Macfarlane's *Genealogical Collections*, Adv. Lib.

This Fiack was a Scottish saint—believed to be a son of Eugenius IV., king of Scotland—and it is curious to be assured, as we are, that 'the name *fiacre* was first given to hackney-coaches, because hired carriages were first made use of for the convenience of pilgrims who went from Paris to visit the shrine of this saint.'[1]

When we consider that sanative effects are attributed in our own time, by a great number of practitioners, to pure water, we may be the more disposed to believe that there was some natural ground for the faith which the simple people of old entertained regarding saints' wells, the saintly connection being assumed of course as indifferent in the case. It is remarkable, moreover, how long this faith continued to be maintained even in its most superstitious form. We are told in the *New Statistical Account of Scotland*, that a well dedicated to the Virgin Mary, at Sigget in Aberdeenshire, continued, till within the memory of living persons, to be resorted to on Pasch Sunday, the votaries always taking care to leave money or some other article beside the venerated lymph on departing. In Easter Ross, there are wells which are still resorted to by some of the more ignorant portion of the rustic classes.

Charms for the healing of sores and gunshot wounds were in great vogue. In May 1631, Laurence Boak and his wife were before the kirk-session of Perth, accused of using such charms, and they admitted that the following was the formula employed for sores:

'Thir sairs are risen through God's wark,
And must be laid through God's help;
The mother Mary, and her dear son,
Lay thir sairs that are begun.'

The chief of fallen spirits was the subject of a strange superstition, which dictated that a piece of every farm should be left untilled for his especial honour. It went by the respectful appellation of the *Goodman's Croft*. In May 1594, the General Assembly had under their attention that such a weird custom was rife in Garioch, Aberdeenshire; and it called for an act of the Estates 'ordaining all persons possessors of the said lands, to cause labour the same, betwixt and a certain day to be appointed thereto; otherwise, in case of disobedience, the said lands to fall into the king's hands, to be disponed to such persons as please his majesty, who will labour the same.'—*Cal.*

So lately as 1651, at a visitation of the kirk of Rhynie in

[1] Butler's *Lives of the Saints.*

Aberdeenshire, it was admitted by Sir William Gordon of Lesmore, that a part of his *mains* or home-farm was given away to the *Goodman*, and used not to be laboured; 'but he had a mind, by the assistance of God, to cause labour the same.'[1]

Some religious practices of the Romish Church continued to be in vogue for many years after the Reformation, notwithstanding all that the Presbyterian kirk could do for their suppression. There had been a custom of pilgrimising, for penitential purposes, to certain holy places, precisely as there still is in the more Catholic districts of Ireland. We may presume that, as in the sister-island, people went barefooted to the sacred spot, walked on bare knees repeatedly round it, repeating prayers, and afterwards formally confessed their sins to the priests who superintended the ceremonial. In these reformed times, the affair would be of course shorn of many of its rites; but certainly the habit of going on pilgrimage was still such as to give great concern to presbyteries and general assemblies. One of the chief places still in vogue was the Chapel of Grace, on the western bank of the Spey, near Fochabers—a mere ruin, but held in great veneration, and resorted to by devout people from all parts of the north of Scotland. Another was the Chapel of the Virgin, at Ordiquhill in Banffshire, where also there was a well believed to possess miraculous virtue. We find the General Assembly which met at Linlithgow in 1608, recommending that, for remedy of the growth of papistry, 'order be taken with the pilgrimages'—specifying these two, and a well in the district of Enzie. Of course Catholics were most disposed to making the pilgrimages. In 1592 Robert Wauchope of Caikmuir, suspected papist, was accused before his presbytery of going yearly *barefooted* in pilgrimage to the Cross of Peebles, and he admitted having been guilty of such proceedings a few years back, but now he had given it up as a 'rite unprofitable and ungodly.' We hear of Lady Aboyne going to the Chapel of Grace every year, being a journey of thirty Scotch miles, the two last of which she always performed on her bare feet.[2] About the time of the National Covenant (1638), what remained of the Chapel of Grace was thrown down, with a view to putting a stop to the practice; but this seems to have been far from an effectual measure. In a work written in 1775, the author says: 'In the north end of the parish [of Dundurcus] stood the Chapel of Grace, and near to it the well of

[1] Extracts from Presbytery Book of Strathbogie (Spald. Club), xxiv.

[2] Father Blackhall's *Narrative*.

that name, to which multitudes from the Western Isles do still resort, and nothing short of violence can restrain their superstition.'[1]

There were even practices of an obviously heathen origin still flourishing in the country. That of kindling fires at Midsummer and on St Peter's Eve seems to have been among the most difficult to eradicate. In July 1608, several inhabitants of Aberdeen were accused before the kirk-session, of having had fires kindled in front of their houses on one of these evenings. Gilbert Keith of Achiries, 'a common banner and swearer,' confessed the fault. Mr Thomas Menzies, bailie, gave an equivocating answer. Others alleged that the fires had been kindled by their servants and children.—*A. K. S. R.*

[HOLIDAYS AND POPULAR PLAYS.]

The observance of Yule (Christmas), Pasch (Easter), and the various saints' days, had been sternly repressed at the Reformation. So were the May-games and other holiday amusements in vogue under the ancient faith. Nevertheless, we still find all of these matters enjoying a sort of twilight life. They assert their vitality by the very efforts made from time to time to extinguish them. Passing over the Robin Hood play and other Edinburgh May-sports, to which repeated reference has been made in the chronicle, we may advert to the corresponding doings at the Fair City of the Tay.

The people of Perth had been in the habit, before the Reformation, of observing Corpus Christi Day (second Thursday after Whitsunday) and St Obert's Day. On the former, it was customary to have a play. After the change of religion, there was a great inclination to keep up these old practices, which the church, however, condemned as 'idolatrous, superstitious, and slanderous.' In 1577, the kirk-session of Perth prosecuted several persons for taking part in the Corpus Christi play. Thomas Thorsails, who had borne the ensenyie or flag, had to submit himself to the discipline of the kirk, and promise 'never to meddle with such things again,' in order that he might have his bairn baptised. A considerable number of persons had to make the like submission that they might be at peace with the session. Nevertheless, on the ensuing 10th of December, being St Obert's Eve, there was a

[1] Shaw's *History of the Province of Moray*, p. 326.

procession as usual; and several citizens were brought to submission, 'in that they superstitiously passed about the town, disguised, in piping and dancing, and torches bearing.' John Fyvie afterwards confessed that on this occasion 'he passed through the town striking the drum, which was one of the common drums of the town, accompanied with certain others—such as John Macbeth, William Jack riding upon ane horse going in men's shoes.'—*P. K. S. R.*

In Aberdeen, December 30, 1574, certain persons were charged before the kirk-session of Aberdeen 'for playing, dancing, and singing of filthy carols on Yule Day [Christmas Day] at even, and on Sunday at even thereafter.'—*A. K. S. R.* January 10, 1575-6, 'the haill deacons of crafts within this burgh are ordained to take trial of their crafts for sitting idle on Yule Day last was.'—*Ibid.* In Perth, January 10, 1596-7, 'William Williamson, baxter, is accused of baking and selling great loaves at Yule, which was slanderous, and cherishing a superstition in the hearts of the ignorant.'—*P. K. S. R.*

[FROLICS AND MASQUERADINGS.]

The sessions appear to have everywhere had great battlings with old-accustomed habits of festival-keeping and merry-making, in which the people indulged, probably without any idea of committing a sin. Some of their habits were connected with superstition, and thus gave double offence.

There was a cave called the Dragon-hole, on the face of the Kinnoul Hill near Perth. It was of difficult access, and old tradition had her stories about it. The common sort of people were accustomed to make a merry procession to the Dragon-hole once a year in May; perhaps they had continued to do so since the days of heathenrie. May 2, 1580, 'because that the assembly of minister and elders understand that the resort to the Dragon-hole, as well by young men as women, with their piping and drums striking before them through this town, had raised no small slander to this congregation,' they therefore ordain that each person guilty of this practice shall pay twenty shillings to the poor, and make public repentance.

Notwithstanding all efforts at repression, cases of excessive conviviality and of questionable frolics are not infrequent in these moral registers. It seems to have been a favourite prank to interchange the dresses of the sexes, and make a parade through the town by night, singing merry songs. At Aberdeen, February 9, 1575–6, Madge Morison is 'decreit to pay 6s. 8d. to the magistrate, and Andrew Caithness is become caution for her repentance-making when she is required, and that for the abusing of herself in claithing of her with men's claiths at the lyke [wake] of George Elmsly's wife.' A month after, in the same place, a group of women, 'tryit presently as dancers in men's claiths, under silence of night, in house and through the town,' are assured that if found hereafter in the same fault, 'they sall be debarrit fra all benefit of the kirk, and openly proclaimit in pulpit.'

At some blithesome bridal which took place in Aberdeen in August 1605, a number of young men and women danced through the town together, 'the young men being clad in women's apparel, whilk is accounted ane abomination (Deut. xxii. 5), and the young women with masks on their faces, thereby passing the bounds of modesty and shamefacedness, whilk aught to be in young women, namely [especially] in a reformed city.' The matter was referred to the provincial assembly, and severe penalties threatened for future instances of the offence.—*A. K. S. R.*

At Perth, in 1609, we find the kirk-session dealing with an ultra-merry company, composed of Andrew Johnston, James Jackson, and David Dickson, and three women, two of whom were the wives of the first two men. They were accused of having gone about the town on the evening of the preceding Tuesday, disguised, and with swords and staves, molesting their neighbours. They stated that they had been supping, and after supper, from mere merriness, had gone about the town, but without molesting anybody. 'It was certainly found that they were disguised; namely, Andrew Johnston's wife having her hair hanging down, and a black hat upon her head; her husband with a sword into his hand; James Jackson having a mutch [woman's cap] upon his head, and a woman's gown; and that they hurt and molested several persons.' The matter was aggravated by the consideration that it was a time of plague, and the offenders were convalescents new come in from the fields, with 'the blotch and boil' still on their persons. A public repentance was decreed to them.—*P. K. S. R.*

The chief element of conviviality among the common people, at this time, and for several generations later, was a light ale which the keepers of taverns made at home; hence *browster-wife* came to be a synonym for a woman keeping a public-house. The fierier and more fatal whisky was, however, not unknown. In the

Aberdeen Kirk-session Register, under March 1606, we have two men brought up for 'abusing themselves last week by extraordinar drinking of aqua-vitie.'

[OBSERVANCE OF SUNDAY.]

The Protestant Church took the observance of Sunday as a Sabbath from the ancient church; and the Presbyterians of Scotland adopted it fully, while rejecting all the other festivals—a fact with which Ninian Winzet did not fail to taunt them as an inconsistency in his *Tractates*, published immediately after the Reformation.[1] Not merely ecclesiastical acts, but several statutes of the realm, were put in effect for the purpose of enforcing the observance of the day as a day of rest and of religious exercises. From the terms of these, however, and from the accounts we have of frequent punishments for their neglect or infraction, it is evident that many years elapsed before the people of Scotland attained to that placid acquiescence in the order for the day which we now see.

The main demands of the new church were for a complete abstinence from work and market-holding, as well as from public amusements, and a regular attendance on the sermons. We have seen some instances of the struggles of the church to induce mercantile people to abandon Sunday-marketing. So late as 1596, it is evident that their wishes were not fully attained, as we find the presbytery of Meigle then complaining to the Privy Council of the obstinate refusal of the people in their district to abandon a Sunday-market.[2] Two years later, the Town Council of Aberdeen was content to ordain that 'nae mercat, either of fish or flesh, shall be on the Sabbath-day *in time of sermon*'—a clear proof that they did not look for a complete suppression of marketing on that day, but

[1] Winzet, remarking how John Knox had put down festival-days as unsanctioned in Scripture, says: 'I misknow not some of you to object the command, charging *sex days to labour, and the sevint to sanctify the Lord*; therefore I desire the doubtsome man to cause his doctor and prophet aforesaid [John Knox], with all the assistance of his best learned scholars, to answer in writ, what Scripture has he, or other authority, by [besides] the consent of the haly kirk universal, to sanctify the Sunday to be the sevint day. And gif he abolishes with us the Saturday, as ceremonial and not requirit in the law of the evangel, what has he by [besides] the consent of God's kirk to sanctify ony day of the seven, and not to labour all the seven days. . . . . Why abolishes he not the Sunday, as he does Yule, Pasch, and the rest, &c.?'—*Tractates*, 1563, reprinted for Maitland Club, 1835.

[2] Privy Council Record.

only its cessation in time of church-service. There are many similar indications that at this early period taverns were allowed to be open, and public amusements permitted, at times of the day apart from 'the sermons.' It is somewhat startling to find the General Assembly itself, in 1579, expressing indifference to marriages being solemnised on Sunday (*B. U. K.*), and only so late as January 1586, discharging 'all marriages to be made on Sundays in the morning in time coming.' Nor is it less surprising to find a kirk-session, so late as 1607, requiring that 'the mill be stayit from grinding on the Sabbath-day, *at least by eight in the morning.*'[1] It clearly appears to have been common in 1609 for tailors, shoemakers, and bakers in Aberdeen, to work till eight or nine every Sunday morning, 'as gif it were ane ouk day.'—*A. K. S. R.*

Breach of the Sunday arrangements was usually punished by fines. In Aberdeen, in 1562, for an elder or deacon of the church to be absent from the preachings, inferred a penalty of 'twa shillings;' for 'others honest persons of the town,' sixpence. November 24, 1575, it is statute that 'all persons being absent fra the preachings on the Sunday, without lawful business, and all persons ganging in the gait or playing in the links [downs], or other places, the times of preaching or prayers on the Sunday, and all persons making mercat merchandise on Sunday within the town . . . . sall be secluded fra all benefit of the kirk unto the time they satisfy the kirk in their repentance, and [the] magistrate by ane pecunial fine.' Notwithstanding this statute, we find the Town Council in 1588 referring to the fact, that a great number of the inhabitants of the burgh keep away from church both on Sundays and week-days, and give themselves to 'gaming and playing, passing to taverns and ale-houses, using the trade of merchandise and handy labour in time of sermon on the week-day;' for which reason it is ordained that all shall attend the sermons on Sunday, 'afore and after noon;' as also every Tuesday and Thursday 'afore noon,' under certain penalties—a householder or his wife, 13s. 4d.; a craftsman, 6s. 8d.; 'and in case ony merchand or burgess of guild be found within his merchand booth after the ringing of the third bell to the sermon on the week-day, to pay 6s. 8d.' These ordinances were acted upon. November 28, 1602, 'the wife of James Bannerman, for working on the Sabbath-day, [is] unlawit in 6s. 8d.' 'The same day, the session ordains that nae baxters within this burgh work, nor bake any baken meat, in time coming, on the

[1] Extracts from Reg. Kirk-session of Rothiemay, Spal. Club.

Sabbath-day.' Four Aberdeen citizens were, January 16, 1603, 'unlawit, ilk ane of them, in 3s. 4d., for their absence fra the sermons on Sunday last, confessit by themselves.'—*Ab. C. R.* Soon after we find a bailie and two elders appointed to go through the town in time of sermon, and searching any house they pleased, note the names of all they found at home; likewise to watch the ferry-boat, and note the names of 'sic as gangs to Downie, that they may be punishit.'—*A. K. S. R.*

At Perth, January 8, 1582–3, 'it was ordained that an elder of every quarter shall pass through the same every Sunday in time of preaching before noon, their time about, and note them that are found in taverns, baxters' booths, or on the gaits, and delate them to the Assembly, that every one of them that is absent from the kirk may be poinded for twenty shillings, according to the act of parliament.' Soon after, a married woman named Hunter was fined three pounds for her absence from church during the bygone year, and other three pounds for her absence during the time of fasting. In September 1585, tavern-keepers were subjected to a heavy fine for selling wine and ale in time of sermon. In 1587, the Sunday penalties were extended to the Thursday sermon. February 21, 1591–2, John Pitscottie, younger of Luncarty, and several other persons, 'confessed that on the Sunday of the fast, in the time of preaching in the afternoon, they were playing at foot-ball in the Meadow Inch of the Muirton, and that the same was an offence; therefore they were ordained on Sunday next to make their repentance.'

In the same town, January 29, 1592–3, 'the Lady Innernytie being called, and accused for absenting herself and the rest of her family from the hearing of the word on Sabbath, compears and confesses that she does it not, neither in contempt of the word nor of the minister, but only by reason of her sickness, and promises when she shall be well in health, to repair more frequently to the kirk and hearing of the word.' This lady was the wife of Elphinstone of Innernytie, a judge of the Court of Session, and a Catholic. It is therefore probable that her submission was hypocritical. July 31, 1598, 'Andrew Robertson, chirurgeon, being accused of breaking the Sabbath-day by polling and razing of the Laird of   , declared he did it quietly at the request of the gentleman, without outgoing.' He was ordained to make repentance, and warned for the future. It will be understood that under the designation of chirurgeon both surgery and the functions of the barber were embraced.

The Perth kirk-session also exerted itself to prevent Highland reapers from sauntering on the streets on Sunday, waiting to be hired (August 1593); and they took strong measures to put an end to the practice of cadgers departing from the Saturday market on Sunday morning (March 1599). Four persons were rebuked in November of this last year for 'playing at golf on the North Inch in the time of the preaching after noon on the Sabbath'—a sport which would not now be indulged in on Sunday in any part of Scotland. April 13, 1601, 'George Murray [was] accused for suffering of ale to be sold in time of preaching on the Sabbath in his house. [He] answered that he was in the kirk himself, and his wife also; but his servant came, and brought his wife out of the kirk to ane daughter of Tullibardine's [Murray of Tullibardine—the family since become Dukes of Athole], to give her some clothes which she had of hers in custody, and in the mean time caused fill drink to the said gentlewoman and her servants with her.' Murray was dismissed with an admonition.

By a stern act of the Aberdeen town-council, passed in 1598, a severe tariff of fines was ordained for various ranks of people on their staying away from Sunday and week-day services in the churches, every husband to be answerable for his wife, and every master for his servants. A burgess of guild or his wife was to pay 13s. 4d. for absence from church on Sunday. 'Likewise, following the example of other weel-reformit congregations of this realm, [the council] statutes and ordains that the wives of all burgesses of guild, and of the maist honest and substantious craftsmen of this burgh, sall sit in the midst and body of the kirk in time of sermon, and not in the side-ailes, nor behind pillars, to the effect that they may mair easily see and hear the deliverer and preacher of the word; and siclike ordains, that the women of the ranks aforesaid sall repair to the kirk, every ane of them having a cloak, as the maist comely and decent outer garment, and not with plaids, as has been frequently used; and that every ane of them likewise sall have stules, sae mony as may commodiously have the same, according to the decent form observed in all reformit burghs and congregations of this realm.'—*Ab. C. R.*

While it is thus apparent that observance during time of sermon and attendance thereupon were the principal objects held in view, it clearly appears that the day, in its totality, was then a different thing from what it now is. It was, as in Norway still, held to commence at sunset of Saturday, and to terminate on Sunday at sunset, or at six o'clock. As illustrations of this fact, two curious notices may be cited. In May 1594, the presbytery of Glasgow is found forbidding a piper to play his pipes on Sunday 'frae the sun rising till the sun going-to.'[1] When a fast was ordained in Edinburgh, in December 1574, on account of impending pestilence, it was to commence 'on Saturday next at aucht hours at even, and sae to continue while [until] Sunday at six hours at even.'[2] An act of the presbytery of Glasgow, January 1, 1635, ordered that the Sabbath be from 12 on Saturday night to 12 on Sunday night;[3] a clear proof that there was previously a different arrangement.

Another curious fact, indicative of a progress in the ideas of the reformed kirk as to Sabbath-keeping, is that there were 'play-Sundays' till the end of the sixteenth century. The presbytery of Aberdeen ordered in 1599 that 'there be nae play-Sundays hereafter, under all hiest pain.'—*A. P. R.*

In April 1600, in obedience to an ordinance of the General Assembly, it was arranged at Aberdeen—and of course a similar arrangement would be made in other places—that 'on Thursday, ilk ouk [every week], the masters of households, their wives, bairns, and servants should compeir, ilk ane within their awn parish kirk, to their awn minister, to be instructit by them in the grunds of religion and heads of catechism, and to give, as they should be demanded, ane proof and trial of their profiting in the said heads.'

After this arrangement had been made, the religious observances of the citizen occupied a considerable share of his time. He was bound under penalties to be twice in church on Sunday, to make Monday a 'pastime-day, for eschewing of the profanation of the Sabbath-day,' to give Tuesday forenoon to a service in the parish church, to do the same on Thursday forenoon, and on that day also to attend a catechetical meeting with his family. Three forenoons each week remained for his business and ordinary affairs. Notwithstanding this liberal amount of external observance, the General Assembly appointed, in 1601, 'a general humiliation for the sins of the land and contempt of the gospel, to be kept the two last Sabbaths of June and all the week intervening.'

[1] See extracts from their Register, Maitland Club Miscellany, i. 67.
[2] *Extracts from Register of General Kirk of Edinburgh*, same book, p. 111.
[3] Niel's edition of Zachary Boyd's poems (1855), p. xli.

[LICENTIOUS CONDUCT.]

Licentious conduct was from the first an object of severe observation to the reformed church, and many sharp measures were taken and harsh punishments inflicted for its repression.

In 1562, the kirk-session of Aberdeen ordained as its punishment, for the first offence, exposure before the congregation; for the second, carting and ducking; for the third, banishment from the town. A subsequent act of parliament imposed still severer punishment—'That is to say, for the first fault, as weel the man as the woman sall pay the sowm of forty pounds, or than [else] he and she sall be imprisoned for the space of aucht days, their food to be breid and small drink, and thereafter present[ed] to the mercat-place of the town or parochin, barehead[ed], and there stand fastened, that they may not remove, for the space of twa hours.' To this punishment some additions were made for a second offence, as cold water for food, and a shaving of the head. A third inferred ducking and banishment.

At Aberdeen, in 1591, in a case where a marriage relationship existed, the punishment inferred the depth of horror with which the offence was on that account regarded, the man being ordained to be banished from the town, but first to be set up at the cross on three several market-days, bound to the pillar by a pair of branks, and having a paper-crown on his head inscribed with his crime; also to stand on three several Sundays at the kirk-door, in haircloth, barelegged and barefooted, while the people are assembling; after which to be exposed in like guise at the pillar of repentance during the whole time of worship.[1]

November 20, 1582, the kirk-session of Perth ordains John Ronaldson, having offenders of this class in his custody, 'to put every one of them in a sundry house in time coming, to give them bread and small drink, to let none of them come to the nether window [probably a window where they could see or converse with the people passing on the street]; and when they come to the cross-head, that they shall be fast locked in the irons two hours, their kurchies [caps] off their heads, and their faces bare, without ane plaid or any other covering.'

A stool or seat was raised in a conspicuous situation in each

[1] *Extracts from the Council Registers of Aberdeen*, p. 71.

church, where penitents under this as well as other offences had to sit during service, and afterwards bear the rebuke of the minister. Many entries in the session records shew the difficulty there had always been in getting penitents, while in this situation, to remain unmuffled or uncovered. The only correction that seems to have been available was to ordain that such a sitting went for nothing. The Aberdeen session, August 1608, ordain that, 'because, in times past, most part of women that come to the pillar to make their public repentance, sat thereon with their plaids about their head, coming down over their faces the haill time of their sitting on the stool, so that almaist nane of the congregation could see their faces, or knaw what they were, whereby they made nae account of their coming to the stool, but misregarded the same altogether'—the officer should thenceforth take the plaid away from each penitent 'before her upganging to the pillar.' The Perth session, in August 1599, had to take sharp measures with Margaret Marr, because being exalted to the seat of repentance, 'she sat in the back side with her face covered, and being desired by John Jack, officiar, to sit on the fore side, and uncover her face that she might be seen, she uttered words against him in a bitter manner, and extended her voice in such sort that she was heard through all the kirk in time of sermon, and so behaved herself uncomely in the presence of strangers, to the great slander of this congregation.' In very gross cases, a paper-crown was added to the external marks of infamy inflicted on delinquents.

As a specimen of the interference with private life to which the clergy were led in their anxiety to suppress licentiousness—the kirk-session of Perth (1586–7) would not suffer two unmarried sisters to continue to live together in one house, but ordained them to go to service, 'or where they may be best entertained without slander,' under pain of imprisonment and banishment from the town.

A custom obtained in those days of entering into conjugal life on the strength simply of a contract of marriage. It was called *hand-fasting.* The ceremony of marriage might take place afterwards or not, as the parties pleased. This the reformed clergy denounced as immoral, and they set themselves to correct it. The Aberdeen session, December 10, 1562, ordained, 'Because sundry and many within this town are hand-fast, as they call it, and made promise of marriage a long space bygane, some seven year, some sax year, some langer, some shorter, and as yet will not marry and complete that honourable band, nother for fear of God nor love of their party'—that 'all sic persons as has promised marriage faithfully complete the samen betwixt this and Fasteren's Even next to come;' penalty left blank. Such parties are also ordained in the meantime to live as single persons. April 12, 1568, the same session ordained that 'neither the minister nor reader be present at contracts of marriage-making, as they call their hand-fastings, nor make nae sic band.'

The kirk-session records of the period must be held as revealing on the whole a very low state of morals, particularly among the humbler classes of the people.

[ECCLESIASTICAL DISCIPLINE IN OTHER MATTERS.]

Ecclesiastical discipline took upon it in those days to interfere with many matters in which it would be set at defiance in our day. It was part of the earnestness of the general religious feeling, while as yet no one had ventured to think that there are points which may best be left to the private consciousness, or which, at least, it can serve no good end to make matter of public regulation.

Of the sharp dealing of the Presbyterian preachers and their courts with avowed Catholics, we have already seen abundant illustrations, and more will yet be presented. Having become satisfied that the Catholic religion was a system of damnable error, our ancestors acted logically on the conviction, and thought no measure, however forcible or severe, misapplied, if it could save the people of that persuasion from the unavoidable consequences, and prevent the evil from spreading. To purge the land of papists and idolaters was therefore an object held constantly in view by the church-courts.

The slightest suspicion of being papistically inclined was sure to bring any one to trouble. One David Calderwood in Glasgow being found in possession of a copy of Archbishop Hamilton's popish catechism, the presbytery sent a minister 'to try and find of the said David's religion.' Another citizen of Glasgow was taken to task, on a charge of having, in the way of his profession as a painter, painted crucifixes in sundry houses. A Lady Livingston being suspected of unsoundness in the faith, in order 'that she may be won to God,' a deputation was sent by the presbytery to confer with her, 'anent the heads of religion,' and she was summoned under pain of excommunication. The same reverend body, hearing of one James Fleming, an Irishman, sent 'to inquire of him his religion.' On the 5th of June 1599, they are found taking measures for discovering Irishmen in their bounds, and ascertaining 'wha are papists and pernicious to others they haunt amang.'

That to receive a Catholic priest into one's house was a serious matter in those days, there is abundant evidence, some of which will be found in the sequel. But even to receive or keep company with an excommunicated papist, inferred severe pains; and in the Perth kirk-session register there are several instances of these being inflicted. For example, Gabriel Mercer was, in 1595, ordered to make public declaration from his seat in church of his offence in entertaining for three days Elphinstone of Innernytie, an excommunicated papist. The same order was given in 1610 in the case of Alexander Crichton of Perth, 'who was convicted on his own confession of haunting and frequenting the company of Robert Crichton, excommunicate papist, eating and drinking with him in taverns, and walking on the street.'—*P. K. S. R.*

In 1598, we find the presbytery of Glasgow concerning itself about a young man who had passed his father without lifting his bonnet. He was judged 'a stubborn and disobedient son to his father.' About 1574, the kirk-session of Edinburgh was occupied for some days in considering the case of Niel Laing, accused of making a pompous convoy and superfluous banqueting at the marriage of Margaret Danielston, 'to the great slander of the kirk,' which had forbid such doings.

The absence of external appearances of joy in Scotland, in contrast with the frequent holidayings and merry-makings of the continent, has been much remarked upon. We find in the records of ecclesiastical discipline clear traces of the process by which this distinction was brought about. To the puritan kirk of the sixteenth and seventeenth centuries every outward demonstration of natural good spirits was a sort of sin, to be as far as possible repressed. To make marriages sober and quiet was one special object. It was customary in humble life for a young couple, on being wedded, to receive miscellaneous company, and hold a kind of ball, each person contributing towards the expenses, with something over for the benefit of the young pair. Such a custom has been kept up almost to our own time, but much shorn of its original spirit. In the latter years of the sixteenth century, it was customary for the party to go to the Market-cross, and dance round it. At Stirling, October 30, 1600, the kirk-session, finding 'there has been great dancing and vanity publicly at the Cross usit by married persons and their company on their marriage-day,' took measures to put a stop to the practice. It ordained 'that nane be married till ten pounds be consigned, for the better security that there be nae mair ta'en for ane bridal lawing than five shillings according to order,' 'with certification, gif the order of the bridal lawing be broken, the said ten pounds sall be confiscat.'[1]

In like manner the kirk-session of Cambusnethan, in September 1649, ordained 'that there suld be no pipers at bridals, and who ever suld have a piper playing at their bridal, sall lose their consigned money.' And in June next year, the same reverend body decreed that men and women 'guilty of promiscuous dancing,' should stand in a public place and confess their fault.[2]

The power of the kirk to enforce its discipline and maintain conformity, was a formidable one, resting ultimately on their sentence of excommunication, of which the following contemporary description may be given: '. . . . whasoever incurs the danger thereof is given over in thir days by the ministers, in presence of the haill people assembled at the kirk, in the hands of Satan, as not worthy of Christian society, and therefore made odious to all men, that they should eschew his company, and refuse him all kind of hospitality; and the person thus continuing in refusal by the space of a haill year, his goods are decerned to appertain to the king, sae lang as the disobedient lives.'[3]—*H. K. J.*

No unprejudiced person can doubt that the Presbyterian clergy of this age were in general correct in their own deportment, and sincerely anxious to promote virtue among the people; but it is also evident to us, under our superior lights, that they carried their discipline to a pitch at once irreconcilable with the natural rights of mankind, and calculated to have effects different from what were intended. It dived too much into the details of private life, was too inconsiderate of human infirmity, was extremely cruel, and altogether erred in trusting too much to force and too little to moral suasion. Even the innocent playfulness of the human heart seems to have been viewed by these stern moralists as an evil thing, or at least a thing leaning to the side of vice. On the injurious tendency of any system which equally makes a crime out of some peculiarity of opinion, or indifferent action, and of an actual infraction of the rights of our fellow-creatures, it were needless to insist.

[1] *Maitland Club Misc.*, i. 135. [2] *Ibid.* p. 431.

[3] '. . . . in that church excommunication is so terrible, that few will have any manner of conversation with one excommunicated; and the generality of the people, when they see a man whom their ministers declare to be excluded from heaven, are easily induced to think him unworthy to live on earth.'—*Ed. Phillips's Cont. of Baker's Chronicle*, 1670, p. 617.

[CUSTOMS.]

In the Council Register of Aberdeen, we obtain many notices of the customs of the burgh, most of which were probably common to other towns.

It seems to have been the practice of the whole people to assemble, but only at command of the council, in order to deliberate together upon any matter of importance, and make such arrangements as were required for the general weal. For this purpose, they were summoned by the bellman, who went through 'the haill rews of the town' ringing his bell, of which he had to make oath in order to render legal what was ordained by the meeting.

In 1574, it was ordained at such a meeting that John Cowpar should 'pass every day in the morning at four hours, and every nicht at eight hours, through all the rews of the town, playing upon the Almany whistle [German flute?], with ane servant with him playing on the tabroun, whereby the craftsmen their servants and all others laborious folks, being warnit and excitat, may pass to their labours and frae their labours in due and convenient time.'

In 1576, it is 'statute with consent of the haill town, that every brother of guild, merchant, and craftsman, shall have in all time coming ane halbert, Danish axe, and javelin within his booth.' The wearing of plaids by the citizens was at the same time strictly forbidden, also the use of blue bonnets—for what reason does not clearly appear. The town's landmarks were ridden every year. The keeping of swine within the town is (1578) forbidden, on penalty of having the animals taken and slain.

December 5, 1582, the town-council of Aberdeen ratified a contract with John Kay, lorimer, 'anent the mending of the town's three knocks [clocks], and buying fra him of the new knock, for payment to the said John of twa hundred merks.' December 17, 1595, the council, considering that 'the twa common knocks of this burgh—namely, the kirk knock and the tolbooth knock—sin Martinmass last, has been evil handlit and rulit, and has not gane induring the said space, feed Thomas Gordon, gunmaker, to rule the said twa knocks, and to cause them gang and strike the hours richtly baith night and day.' The employment of a lorimer and a gunmaker in this business seems to imply, that a clockmaker or watchmaker was not yet one of the trades of Aberdeen.

By an old custom, the boys of the grammar-school of Aberdeen had at Christmas taken possession of the school, to the exclusion of their masters and all authority, and a vacation of about a fortnight took place. In 1580 and 1581, the magistrates are found exerting themselves to enforce certain statutes by which this assumed privilege of the boys had been abrogated and discharged; and they agreed that to make up for the vacation, there should be three holidays at the beginning of each quarter, making twelve in all for the year. From this and other facts, it appears that the long vacation now customary in summer or autumn in Scottish schools, was then unknown.

The school disorder at Yule is again spoken of in 1604 as very violent, the boys 'keeping and halding the same against their masters with swords, guns, pistols, and other weapons, spulying and taking of puir folks' geir, sic as geese, fowls, peats, and other vivres, during the halding thereof.' It is ordered that, to avoid such disorders in future, no boy from without the town shall be admitted without a caution for his good-behaviour.

The Aberdeen magistrates, on hearing (February 22, 1593-4) how the burghs of Edinburgh, Perth, Dundee, and Montrose had celebrated the birth of a son and heir to the king 'by bigging of fires, praising and thanking God for the benefit, by singing of psalms through the haill streets and rews of the towns, drinking of wine at the crosses thereof, and otherwise liberally bestowing of spiceries,' ordained that it should be similarly observed in their burgh on *Sunday* next, the 24th instant, immediately after the afternoon sermon. It was ordered that there should be 'ane table covered at the Cross, for the magistrates and baith the councils, with twa boyns[1] of English beer . . . . the wine to be drunken in sic a reasonable quantity as the dean of guild sall devise, four dozen buists[2] of scorchets,[3] confeits, and confections, to be casten among the people, with glasses to be broken.'

June 7, 1596, a number of persons are cited as contravening the ancient statutes ordaining that 'all burgesses of guild and freemen of free regal burghs sall dwell, mak their residence and remaining, with their wives, bairns, servants, households, and family, hauld stob and stake,[4] fire and flet,[5] within the burgh where they are

[1] Tubs. [2] Boxes. [3] Supposed to be a kind of sweetmeats.

[4] To hold stob and stake in a place, is an old periphrasis for making it one's permanent residence.

[5] The flet was the inside of a house.

free, scot, lot, watch, walk, and ward.' In the event of their not conforming to the rule by an appointed day, they are assured that they shall lose their privileges.

A prayer appointed (1598) to be said before the election of the magistrates of Aberdeen is not unworthy of preservation, as a trait of the feelings of such communities in that age: 'Eternal and ever-hearing God, who has created mankind to society, in the whilk thou that is the God of order and hates confusion, has appointed some to rule and govern, and others to be governed, and for this cause has set down in thy word the notes and marks of sic as thou hast appointed to bear government; likeas of thy great mercy thou has gathered us to be ane of the famous and honourable burghs of this kingdom, and has reservit to us this liberty, yearly to cheise our council and magistrates; we beseech thee, for thy Christ's sake, seeing we are presently assembled for that purpose, be present in the midst of us, furnish us with spiritual wisdom, and direct our hearts in sic sort, that, all corrupt affections being removed, we may cheise baith to be council and magistrates, for the year to come, of our brethren fearing God, men of knawledge, haters of avarice, and *men of courage and action*, that all our proceedings herein may tend to thy glory, to the weel of the haill inhabitants of this burgh, and we may have a good testimony of conscience before thee. . . . .'

In the Aberdeen council records, frequent allusions are made to 'a custom observit in this burgh heretofore in all ages,' of giving an entertainment to strangers of distinction on their arriving in the town. Being informed, December 13, 1598, that the Duke of Lennox and the Earl of Huntly are to be in the town this night, the council 'ordains the said twa noblemen, in signification of the town's guid will and favour, to be remembered with the wine and spicery at their here-coming.' The articles ordered are, 'ane dozen buists of scorchets, confeits, and confections, together with six quarts of wine, thereof three quarts of the best wine, to wit, Hullock and wine tent, and three quarts of other wine.' The Earl of Huntly got another similar entertainment, March 28, 1599, on coming to Aberdeen, 'for halding of justice-courts on shooters and havers of pistols.'

A comical regulation regarding public worship occurs in the Perth kirk-session record under 1616. The session ordained 'John Tenender, session-officer, to have his red staff in the kirk on the Sabbath-days, therewith to wauken sleepers, and to remove greeting bairns furth of the kirk.' Acts of session referring to the practice of the bringing of dogs into church, by which worship was much disturbed, are also frequent.

The hours for meals were in those days of a primitive description. King Henry, Lord Darnley, dined at two o'clock. This was, however, comparatively a late hour. In 1589, King James, then living in William Fowler's house in Edinburgh, went out to the hunting in the morning, 'trysting to come in to his dinner about ane afternoon.'—*Moy.* In 1607, the wooden bridge of Perth was carried away by a flood 'betwixt twelve and ane, on ane Sunday, *in time of dinner*.' Queen Mary was sitting at supper between five and six in the afternoon, when Riccio was reft from her side and slaughtered. And Agnes Sampson, the noted witch, appointed certain persons to meet her in the garden at Edmondstone, 'after supper, betwixt five and sax at even.' The reader will remember that it was after supper, and probably some conviviality following upon it, that King James (May 1587) led forth his nobility in procession to the Cross of Edinburgh, and delighted the citizens with the spectacle of so many reconciled enemies.

[TRAITS OF MANNERS.]

The Aberdeen council, in 1592, 'considering the wicked and ungodly use croppen in and ower frequently usit amang all sorts of people, in blaspheming of God's holy name, and swearing of horrible and execrable aiths,' ordained the same to be punished by fine. To make this the more effectual, masters were ordained to exact the fines from their servants, and deduct them from wages; husbands to do the same from their wives, keeping a box in which to put the money, and punish their children for the like offence with 'palmers' [an instrument for inflicting lashes on the open hand]—'according to the custom of other weel-reformed towns and congregations.' In 1604, the presbytery of Aberdeen enforced this effort of the magistracy by an edict, ordering that, for the repression of oaths and blasphemous language, the master of every house should keep a 'palmer,' and therewith punish all offenders who have no money to pay fines.—*A. P. R.*

In February 1592-3, the Aberdeen council, when expecting a visit of the king, ordained that 'there sall be propynit to his majesty's house . . . . ane puncheon of auld Bourdeaux wine, gif it may be had for money, and, gif not, ane last of the best and finest ale that may be gotten within this burgh, together with . . . four pund wecht of pepper, half pund of maces, four unces of saffron, half pund of cannel, fourteen pund of sucker, twa dozen buists of confeits, ane dozen buists of sucker-almonds, twa dozen buists of confections, and ane chalder of coals.'

The king informed the council of Aberdeen in a letter, June 1596, that he understood 'that the inhabitants and others resorting to this burgh, cease not openly to wear forbidden weapons, to the great contempt of his hieness' authority and laws.' He demands, and the council agrees, that strict order shall be taken to put down this custom, agreeably to acts of parliament.

The council records of Aberdeen do not bear traces of such frequent street-conflicts as prevailed in Edinburgh during this period. Such troubles were not, however, unknown. We find, for example, one citizen now and then drawing his whinger upon another, and either commencing a fight, or frightening away his adversary. In November 1598, a quarrel having taken place between a gentleman named Gordon, brother of Gordon of Cairnbarrow, and one Caldwell, a dependent and servant of Keith of Benholm, the magistrates immediately feared a disturbance in which Keith's chief, the Earl Marischal, would as a matter of course be involved, and hearing that the parties were 'convocating their friends on either side to come to the cawsey and trouble the town, and to invade others,' they ordered that 'the haill neighbours of this burgh, merchants and craftsmen, should . . . . compear in their arms, and specially in lang weapons . . . . for staying of trouble to be betwixt the said parties . . . . and that the town be warnit to that effect by the officers in particular, bell or drum, as sall be thought expedient in general.'

Popery, not infidelity, was the bugbear of those days; but heterodox opinions were not altogether unknown. The public notice taken of them was of a kind which might be expected in an age of sincere faith, unacquainted with reactions or with refined policy. At Aberdeen, one Mr William Murdo was apprehended by the magistrates, 6th January 1592, as 'a maintainer of errors, and blasphemer against the ancient prophets and Christ's apostles, ane wha damns the haill Auld Testament except the ten commandments, and the New Testament except the Lord's Prayer; an open railer against the ministry and truth preached'—who 'can not be sufferit in ane republic.' He was ordained to be banished from the burgh, with a threat of having his cheeks branded and ears cropped if he should come back.—*Ab. C. R.*

There are many entries in the Council Record of Aberdeen, shewing that the burgal authorities took upon them to inquire into cases of reckless and disorderly life, and cases where regular communicating at the Lord's table was neglected. In 1599, one John Hutcheon, a flesher, was threatened with banishment on these accounts.

The kirk-sessions were rigorous in punishing slander and scolding. That of Aberdeen made a statute, in 1562, ordaining a fine for slander, 'and gif the injurious person be simple and of puir degree, he sall ask forgiveness before the congregation of God and the party, and say: "*Tongue, ye lied,*" for the first fault, for the second sall be put in the cockstool, and for the third fault sall be banished the town.' The same body ordained at the same time that 'all common scolds, flyters, and bards be banished the town, and not to be suffered to remain therein for nae request;' bards being strolling rhymers, who were felt in those days as an oppression much the same as sturdy beggars.

At the Perth kirk-session, August 4, 1578, 'Catherine Yester and John Denite were poinded each in half a merk for flyting, while John Tod, for slandering, was ordained to pay a like sum, and stand in the irons two hours, besides asking Margaret Cunningham forgiveness.' In May 1579, Thomas Malcolm was fined and imprisoned for 'having called Thomas Brown *loon carle.*' In August of the same year, it was ordained that such as were convicted of flyting, and not willing 'to pass to the Cross-head [that is, to be exposed on the Cross], according to the act passed before, should pay half a merk money to the poor, besides that other half-merk mentioned in the act of before.' Subsequently the session gave up this leniency, and finally returned to it again. 'Money,' it has been remarked, 'must have been of great value at that time, when so small a sum was proposed as the price of exemption from a most shameful punishment.'

April 25, 1586, the kirk-session of Perth has this minute: 'Forasmeikle as John Macwalter and Alison Brice his spouse have been sundry and divers times called before the assembly for troubling their neighbours, and especially for backbiting and slandering of Robert Dun and his wife, and of Malcolm Ferguson and his wife, and presently are convicted of the crimes laid to their charge by Robert Dun and Malcolm Ferguson; therefore it is ordained, first, that the said John Macwalter and his wife be put in ward until the time repentance be found in them for their slanderous life; secondly, they shall come to the place where they made the offence, and there on their knees crave pardon of the offence committed, at the persons whom they have offended; thirdly, they shall pay a sufficient penalty to the poor, according to the act made against flyters; lastly, if they ever be found in word or deed hereafter to offend any neighbour, *the bare accusation shall be a sufficient plea of conviction*, that so the act made against flyters be extended against them, and finally to be banished the town for ever.'

November 2, 1589, the act against slandering was put in force at Perth, on an occasion where we should have little expected it. 'Forasmeikle as this day was assigned to certain honest neighbours of Tirsappie[1] to be present, and of their conscience to declare if it was true that Guddal, spouse to Richard Watson, was ane witch, as John Watson then alleged, or what evil likelihood they saw in her—Walter Watson, John Cowing, George Scott, James Scott, being inquired severally, as they would answer to God, what they knew, altogether agreed in one without contradiction, that they saw never such things into her whereby they might suspect her of the same, but that she was ane honest poor woman, who wrought honestly for her living, without whose help her husband, Richard Watson, would have been dead, who was ane old aged man: therefore the minister and elders ordain the act of slander to be put in execution against the said John Watson and Helen Watson his daughter.'

[TRAITS OF THE PUBLIC ECONOMY.]

At Aberdeen, in a time of scarcity in 1579, the transportation of victual by sea to other parts of the realm was forbidden. In 1583, it was forbidden to take any sums of money from merchants in other towns 'to buy wares and salmon, against the common weal.' The exportation of sheep-skins to Flanders was at this time prohibited, Edinburgh, Perth, and Dundee having done the like. In 1584, a severe fine is imposed on all who should buy grain on its way to market, 'whilk is the occasion of great dearth, and the cause that the poor commons of this burgh are misservit.' A statute aiming at the same object was passed in 1598, because such enormities could no longer be sustained 'without the imminent peril and wrack of this commonwealth.'

[1] A neighbouring hamlet.

In September 1584, when the pest raged in divers parts of the realm, the Aberdeen authorities ordered a port to be built on the bridge of Dee, and other ports to be built at entrances to the town, in order to check the entrance of persons who might bring the infection. In May of the ensuing year, the danger becoming more extreme, the magistrates erected gibbets, 'ane at the mercat-cross, ane other at the brig of Dee, and the third at the haven mouth, that in case ony infectit person arrive or repair by sea or land to this burgh, or in case ony indweller of this burgh receive, house, or harbour, or give meat or drink to the infectit person or persons, the man to be hangit, and the woman to be drownit.' Frequent notices occur in the Aberdeen Council Records of precautions adopted on similar occasions: yet it is remarkable, that in an act of council on the subject in 1603, it is mentioned that 'it has pleasit the guidness of God of his infinite mercy to withhald the said plague frae this burgh thir fifty-five years bygane.'

October 8, 1593, the magistrates of Aberdeen found it necessary to take order with 'a great number of idle persons, not having land nor masters, neither yet using ony lawful merchandise, craft, nor occupation, fleeing as appears frae their awn dwelling, by reason of some unlawful causes and odious crimes whereof they are culpable, whilk are very contagious enemies to the common weal of this burgh.' The town was ordered to be cleared of them, and their future harbourage by the inhabitants was forbidden.

In those days, and for a long time subsequently, there was no regular post for the transmission of letters in Scotland. When there was pressing or important business calling for a transmission of letters to a distance, a special messenger had to be despatched with them at a considerable expense. The city of Aberdeen seems to have kept a particular officer, called the Common Post, for this duty; and in September 1595, this individual, named 'Alexander Taylor, alias *Checkum*,' was ordered by the magistrates a livery of blue, with the town's arms on his left arm. Other persons were occasionally employed, and the town's disbursements on this ground continue to occupy a prominent place in its accounts down to 1650, if not later.

In 1574, a general assembly of the inhabitants agreed to weekly collections for the native poor, according to a roll formerly made with their own consents, 'except they wha pleases to augment their promise.' It was at the same time decreed that beggars not native should be removed, while those born in the town should wear 'the town's taiken on their outer garment, whereby they may be known.' In 1587, the council, 'having consideration of the misorder and tumult of the puir folks sitting at the kirk-door begging almous, plucking and pulling honest men's gowns, cloaks, and abulyment,' ordained the repression of the nuisance. Eight years thereafter, January 23, 1595-6, there was another public meeting, at which it was agreed to arrange the poor in four classes —'babes, decayed persons householders, lame and impotent persons, and sic as were auld and decrepit.' Individuals agreed to take each man 'ane babe' into his own house, and a quarterly collection for the rest was agreed to; begging to be suppressed.

September 2, 1596, the council took into consideration a petition of 'Maister Quentin Prestoun, professor of physic, craving at them the liberty and benefit, in respect of his debility, being somewhat stricken in age, and sae not able to accomplish the duty without ane coadjutor, to entertain ane apothecar and his apothecary-shop, for the better furnishing of this burgh and of the country, of all sorts of physical and chirurgical medicaments.' The request was granted during the will of the council.

April 6, 1599, four fleshers in Aberdeen were fined for contravening the acts of parliament which forbade that 'ony flesh should be slain or eaten frae the first day of March *inclusive* to the first day of May *exclusive*.'

Among the violences of the age, what would now be called agrarian outrages were very common. Sometimes it was a pretender to proprietorship who came in to trouble the tenants of the landlord in possession; sometimes a tenant was the object of wrathful jealousy among persons of his own class. Of the former order of troubles we have an example at this time, in a charge brought before the Privy Council (February 19, 1601) against David Hamilton, younger, of Bothwell-haugh, 'servant to the Laird of Innerwick.' It was for the turning out of his wife from Woodhouselee, that Hamilton of Bothwell-haugh murdered the Good Regent. We now see his representative breaking other laws on account of the same lands.[1] Sir James Bellenden of Broughton, 1601. FEB.

[1] January 12, 1591-2, the king repossessed David Hamilton of Bothwell-haugh, Isobel Sinclair and Alison Sinclair, heretrices-portioners of the lands of Woodhouselee, of 'their lands, houses, tacks, steadings, and possessions, wherefra they were dispossest upon occasion of the late troubles.'—*P. C. R.*

1601. who was landlord *de facto*, complains against David Hamilton, that, with a company 'bodin and furnist in feir of weir,' he had come, on the 10th of February instant, to the tenants of the lands of Woodhouselee, 'where they were in peaceable and quiet maner at their plews,' and there assailed them with furious speeches, 'threatening to have their lives gif they insistit in manuring and lawboring of the said lands,' and actually compelled them through fear to give up their work. As David failed to appear and answer this charge, letters were ordered to denounce him as a rebel.

Before a month elapsed, the Council had under its attention a still more violent affair, forming a specimen of the second class of outrages. The complainer here is Patrick Monypenny of Pilrig—an estate with an old manor-house situated between Edinburgh and Leith. Patrick states that he was of mind to have set that part of his lands of Pilrig, called the Round-haugh, to Harry Robertson and Andrew Alis, to his utility and profit. But on a certain day not specified, David Duff, indweller in Leith, came to these persons, and uttered furious menaces against them in the event of their occupying these lands, so that they had departed from their purpose of occupying them. Duff, accompanied with two men named Matheson, had also, on the 2d March instant, attacked the servants of Monypenny, as they were labouring the lands in question, with similar speeches, threatening their lives if they persisted in working there; and at night, they, or some persons hounded out by them, had come and broken their plough, and thrown it into the river. 'John Matheson, after the breaking of the complenar's plew, come to John Porteous's house, his tenant, and bad him gang now betwix the plew stilts, and see how she wald gang while [till] the morn.' To this was added a threat to break his head if he should ever say that Duff had broken his plough. 'Likeas the said David sinsyne come to the complenar's lands, being tilled, and trampit and cast the tilled furs down, thus committing manifest oppression upon the complainant.' In this case, the accused persons were assoilzied, but only, it would appear, by hard swearing in their own cause.

APR. 15. 'The king's majesty came to Perth, and was made burgess at the mercat-cross. There was ane puncheon of wine set there, and all drucken out. He receivit the banquet frae the town, and subscribit the guild book with his awn hand—"JACOBUS REX: PARCERE SUBJECTIS, ET DEBELLARE SUPERBOS."'—*Chron. Perth.*

John Watt, Deacon of the deacons in Edinburgh, or he would have latterly been called Convener of the Trades, was shot dead on the Burgh-moor. This was the same gallant official who raised the trades for the protection of the king at the celebrated tumult of the 17th December 1596. One Alexander Slummon, a by-stander, was tried for the murder, but found innocent. We are told by Calderwood that Watt, having offered to invade the person of the minister, Robert Bruce, was well liked by the king, who accordingly was *exact* in regard to Slummon's trial. The historian also relates that 'the judgment threatened against this man by Mr Robert Bruce came to pass.' Such threatenings or prognostications of judgments are of course very likely to bring their own fulfilment. 1601. APR. 17.

'Sundry Jesuits, seminary priests, and trafficking papists, enemies to God's truth and all Christian government,' were stated to be at this time 'daily creeping within the country,' with the design, 'by their godless practices, not only to disturb the estate of the true religion, but also his hieness' awn estate, and the common quietness of the realm.'—*P. C. R.* APR. 24.

William Barclay, a new-made advocate, brother of Sir Patrick Barclay of Tollie, was tried in Edinburgh for the crime of being present at 'twa messes whilk were said by Mr Alex. M'Whirrie, ane Jesuit priest, within Andro Napier's dwelling-house in Edinburgh,' aggravated by perjury, he having some time before sworn and subscribed before the presbytery of Edinburgh, that he was of the religion presently professed within the realm. The culprit was declared infamous, and banished from the country, 'never to return to the same, unless, by satisfaction of the kirk, he obtain our special licence to that effect.'—*Pit. Cal.*

A week later, Malcolm Laing and Henry Gibson, servants of the Marquis of Huntly, confessing their having been present 'at the late mass within the burgh of Edinburgh,' were adjudged by the Council to banishment for life. At the same time, two female servants of the marchioness having made similar confession, the Council, 'seeing their remaining with the said *marquesse* may procure a forder sclander to the kirk,' ordained that her ladyship should remove them from her company, and no more receive them, under pain of rebellion.

'. . . . Archibald Cornwall, town-officer, hangit at the Cross, and hung on the gibbet twenty-four hours; and the cause wherefore he APR. 27.

1601 was hangit—He being an unmerciful greedy creature, he poindit ane honest man's house, and among the rest, he poindit the king and queen's pictures; and when he came to the Cross to comprise the same, he hung them up upon twa nails on the same gallows to be comprisit; and they being seen, word gaed to the king and queen, whereupon he was apprehendit and hangit.'—*Bir.*

Cornwall sustained a regular trial before a jury, eight of whom were tailors. The dittay bears that 'in treasonable contempt and disdain of his majesty, he stood up upon ane furm or buird, beside the gibbet, and called [drove] ane nail therein, as heich as he could reach it, and lifted up his hieness' portraitor foresaid, and held the same upon the gibbet, pressing to have hung the same thereon, and to have left it there, as an ignominious spectacle to the haill world, gif he had not been stayed by the just indignation of the haill people, menacing to stane him dead, and pulling him perforce frae the gibbet.'

The punishment goes so monstrously beyond the apparent offence, that one is led to suspect something which does not appear. The 'honest man' whose goods were taken might be a known friend of the king, while Cornwall was known to be the reverse. It was perhaps inferred that the 'unmerciful greedy creature' was only too ready to embrace the opportunity of holding up the king to contempt. These remarks are only meant to suggest motives, not to justify the severity of the punishment.

The gibbet on which the portrait had been hung—as something rendered horrible by that profanity—was 'taken down and burnt with fire.'

James Wood, *fiar*—that is, heir—of Bonnington, in Forfarshire, was a Catholic, and received excommunication on that account a few years before. He had at the same time had quarrels with his father regarding questions of property. In March of the present year, he again drew observation upon himself by coming to Edinburgh and attending the mass in Andrew Napier's house. It was further alleged of him that he had harboured a seminary priest. On the 16th of March, accompanied by his brother-in-law, William Wood of Latoun, by two blacksmiths named Daw, and some other persons, he broke into his father's house, and took therefrom certain legal papers belonging to the Lady Usen, besides a quantity of clothes, napery, and blankets. The circumstances connected with this act, did we know them, would probably extenuate the criminality. The father made no movement to prosecute his son. He was, however, tried along with Wood of Latoun before an assize in Edinburgh; when both were found guilty, and condemned to be hanged. Wood of Latoun obtained a remission, and great interest was made for the principal culprit by the Catholic nobles, Huntly, Errol, and Home. James might have listened favourably, and been content, as in Kincaid's case, with a good fine payable 'to us and our treasurer;' but 'the ministers were instant with the king, to have a proof of his sincerity:' so says Calderwood, without telling us whether it was his sincerity against papists or his sincerity against malefactors in general that was meant. The young man regarded himself, by admission of the same author, as suffering for the Catholic religion—though, perhaps, he only meant that, but for his being a papist, his actual guilt would not have been punished so severely. He was beheaded at the Cross at six o'clock in the morning, 'ever looking for pardon to the last gasp.'—*Pit. Cal. Bir.* 1601. APR. 27.

The General Assembly arranged that certain ministers should go to the Catholic nobles, Huntly, Errol, Angus, Home, and Herries, and plant themselves in their families for the purpose of converting them from their errors. These ministers were to labour at all times for this object by preaching, reading, and expounding, and by purging the said houses of profane and scandalous persons. They were also to catechise their families twice a day, 'till they attain some good reasonable measure of knowledge.'—*Row.* MAY.

It fully appears that this arrangement was carried into effect. We find in 1604 that Lord Gordon, the eldest son of the Marquis of Huntly, and the Master of Caithness, eldest son of the Earl of Caithness, were being brought up together, under the care of two pedagogues, Thomas Gordon and John Sinclair, who were compelled to declare themselves adherents of the reformed faith, and examined as to the nature of the religious instructions which they imparted. John Sinclair admitted that, in France, he had gone to mass, but only for the purpose of seeing the king there. The mass itself he professed to 'abhor and detest frae his heart.' The two pedagogues stated that they instructed the two young nobles in grammar and oratory, and on Sunday trained them by a little catechism, besides reading and expounding of the New Testament.—*A. P. R.*

In 1609, to insure that the sons of noblemen sent abroad under preceptors, should not be liable to have their religious convictions

1601. perverted, it was enacted by parliament that no preceptor could lawfully undertake such a duty without a licence from the bishop of his diocese.

JUNE. An effort was made at this time by the burghs to introduce a cloth-manufacture into Scotland. Seven Flemings were engaged to settle in the country, in order to set the work agoing, six of them being for says, and the seventh for broadcloth. When the men came, expecting to be immediately set to work in Edinburgh, a delay arose while it was debated whether they should not be dispersed among the principal towns, in order to diffuse their instructions as widely as possible. We find the strangers on the 28th of July, complaining to the Privy Council that they were neither entertained nor set to work, and that it was proposed to sunder them, 'whilk wald be a grit hinder to the perfection of the wark.'

The Council decreed that 'the haill strangers brought hame for this errand sall be halden together within the burgh of Edinburgh, and put to work conform to the conditions past betwix the said strangers and the commissioners wha dealt with them.' Meanwhile, till they should begin their work, the Council ordained 'the bailies of Edinburgh to entertene them in meat and drink,' though this should be paid back to them by the other burghs, and the strangers were at the same time to be allowed to undertake any other work for their own benefit.—*P. C. R.*

On the 11th of September, the burghs had done nothing to 'effectuat the claith working,' and the Council declared that unless they should have made a beginning by Michaelmas, the royal privilege would be withdrawn.

AUG. The bare, half-moorish uplands of Buchan, in Aberdeenshire, are varied, on the course of the river Ythan, by a deep woody dell, on the edge of which is perched an ancient baronial castle, named Gight. Here dwelt a branch of the noble house of Huntly—the GORDONS OF GIGHT—noted in modern literary history by reason of the heiress, in whom the line ended, having thrown herself and her family property into the arms of a certain spendthrift named Byron, by whom she became the mother of one who flourished as the most noted poet of his day.[1] The old castellated house

[1] Miss Gordon having married Mr Byron without any 'settlement,' her property was seized by his creditors, and sold for £18,500, while she and her son, the future poet, were left to penury.

in which these lairds lived, and the moderate estate which gave them subsistence, have for seventy years been part of the possessions of the Earl of Aberdeen, for whose visitors the ruined walls and the wildering dell are now merely matters of holiday interest.[1] At the time of which we are speaking, the Laird of Gight was a personage of some local importance, a baron of the house of Gordon, a noted supporter of the marquis in all his enterprises; above all, a man deeply offensive to the government of his day, on account of his obstinate adherence to popery. 1601.

The kirk had levelled its artillery at George Gordon, the young laird, for a long time in vain; he had always hitherto contrived to put them off with fair promises. Now at length the presbytery of Aberdeen met in a stern mood, and appeared as if it would be trifled with no longer. Gordon, feeling that his means of resistance were failing, wrote a pleading letter to the reverend court, telling how he was deadly diseased, and unable to leave the country, but was willing, if agreeable to them, to confine himself within a mile of his own house, 'and receipt nane wha is excommunicat (my bedfellow excepted);' or he would go into confinement anywhere else, and confer with Protestant clergymen as soon as his sickness would permit. 'I persuade myself,' he adds, 'you will nocht be hasty in pronouncing the sentence of excommunication against me, for I knaw undoubtedly that sentence will prejudge my warldly estate, and will be ane great motive to you in the kirk of Scotland to crave my blude.' He concludes: 'If it shall please his majesty and your wisdoms of the Kirk of Scotland sae to tak my blude for my profession, whilk is Catholic Roman, I will maist willingly offer it; and, gif sae be, God grant me constancy to abide the same.' This letter proved unsatisfactory to the court, seeing it 'made nae offer that micht move them to stay from the excommunication.' Therefore, the court in one voice concluded that, unless Gordon came forward in eight days with sufficient surety for either subscribing or departing, he should be excommunicated without further delay.

While thus appearing as willing to be martyrs for religious principle, the Gight Gordons were no better in secular morality than many of the Presbyterian leaders of the past age. Indeed, they appear to have been men of fully as wild and passionate temper as their descendant, the mother of the poet. Having, for

[1] The name has been changed to Formartin—a proceeding against which every person interested in the verity of history, not to speak of considerations of taste, must protest.

1601. some reason which does not appear, a spite at Magnus Mowat of Balquhollie, the laird and two of his younger sons had, in June this year, gone with a large armed and mounted company to his lands, and destroyed all the growing crops. Following upon this, they conceived mortal wrath against Alexander Copeland and Ralph Ainslie, inhabitants of the village of Turriff, probably in consequence of some circumstances in connection with the above outrage. On the 18th of July, John Gordon, the second son, came to Turriff with a friend and a servant, and, attacking these men with deadly weapons, wounded the latter past hope of his life. The minister came out and interfered in behalf of peace, promising that the whole inhabitants should be answerable for any injury the men had done. But though the Gordons left the village for the time, they returned in greater strength at midnight—and on this occasion both the laird and his eldest son were present—broke into the house of William Duffus, and bringing him forth to the street 'sark-allane,' there had nearly taken his life by firing at him a charge of small-shot.

Alexander Chalmer, messenger, went on the 27th of September to deliver letters to the Laird of Gight and others, commanding them to appear and answer for these frightful outrages. He was returning quietly from the house, 'lippening for nae harm or pursuit,' when he found himself followed by a number of armed servants, and was presently seized and dragged before the laird. The ferocious baron clapped a pistol to the man's breast, and seemed of intent to shoot him, when some one mercifully put aside the weapon. 'He then harlit him within his hall, took the copy of the said letters, whilk he supposed to have been the principal letters, and cast them in a dish of broe [broth], and forcit the officer to sup and swallow them,' holding a dagger at the heart all the time. Afterwards, the laird, being informed that the principal letters were yet extant, 'came to the officer in a new rage and fury, rave the principal letters out of his sleeve, rave them in pieces, and cast them in the fire.'

When King James was at Brechin in the latter part of October, the Laird of Gight failing to appear to answer for these outrages, a horning was launched against him. At the same time, the young laird was accused of having reset John Hamilton, a notorious trafficking Jesuit, and was commanded to enter himself in ward in Montrose on that account. Surety was given that he would do so. A few days later, the Privy Council took into consideration the Turriff outrages, and commissioned the Earl of Errol to raise a body of men in arms to proceed against the Gordons and their abettors, but not till the 15th of November. How the matter ended, does not appear; but for further matters concerning the Gight Gordons, see under date 20th January 1607. 1601.

Among the many men of name pursuing lawless and violent courses, one of the most noted was George Meldrum, younger, of Dumbreck. In 1599, he set upon his brother Andrew at the Milltown of Dumbreck, and wounded him grievously, after which he carried him away, and detained him as a prisoner for several weeks. In the ensuing year, he had committed a similar attack upon Andrew Meldrum of Auchquharties, conveying him as a malefactor from Aberdeenshire to the house of one Fyfe, on the Burgh-moor of Edinburgh, where he was kept several days, and till he contrived to make his escape. Law and private vengeance were alike devoid of terror to this young bravo, who seems never to have had any difficulty in procuring associates to assist him in his outrageous proceedings. SEP. or OCT.

About the time here noted, he entered upon an enterprise partaking of the romantic, and which has actually been the subject of ballad celebration, though under a mistake as to his name and condition in life. Mr Alexander Gibson, one of the clerks of Session, and who subsequently was eminent as a judge under the designation of Lord Durie, was, for some reason which does not appear, honoured with the malice of young Dumbreck. Possibly, there was some legal case pending or concluded in which Gibson stood opposed to the interests of the brigand. However it was, Gibson was living quietly at St Andrews—he being a landed gentleman of Fife—when Meldrum, tracking him by a spy, learned one day that he was riding with a friend and a servant on the water-side opposite Dundee. Accompanied by a suitable party, consisting of two Jardines, a Johnston—border thieves, probably—one called John Kerr, son to the Tutor of Graden, and Alexander Bartilmo, with two foot-boys, all armed with sword, hagbuts, and pistols, he set upon Mr Gibson and his friend in a furious manner, compelling them to surrender to him as prisoners; after which he robbed them of their purses, containing about three hundred merks in gold and silver, and hurried them southward to the ferry of Kinghorn. There, having liberated the friend and servant, he conducted Mr Gibson across the Firth of Forth, probably using some means, such as muffling of the face, to

1601. prevent his prisoner from being recognised. At least, we can scarcely suppose that, even in that turbulent age, it would have been possible otherwise to conduct so important and well-known a man as an involuntary prisoner to the house of William Kay in Leith, and thence past the palace of Holyroodhouse through the whole county of Edinburgh, and thence again to Melrose, for such was the course they took. Before entering Melrose, Meldrum divided the money they had taken between himself and his accomplices, each getting about twenty merks. He then conducted Mr Gibson across the Border, landing him in the castle of Harbottle, which appears to have then been the residence of one George Ratcliff; and here the stolen lawyer was kept in strict durance for eight days.[1] We may here adopt something of the traditionary story, as preserved by Sir Walter Scott: 'He was imprisoned and solitary; receiving his food through an aperture in the wall, and never hearing the sound of a human voice save when a shepherd called his dog by the name of *Batty*, and when a female domestic called upon *Madge*, the cat. These, he concluded, were invocations of spirits, for he held himself to be in the dungeon of a sorcerer.'[2]

How Mr Gibson was liberated, we do not learn. During his absence, his wife and children mourned him as dead.[3] George Meldrum contrived, in November 1603, to gain forcible possession of his brother Andrew's house of Dumbreck; and there he hoped to set law at defiance. The case, however, was too clamant to allow of his escaping in this manner. A party of his majesty's guard being sent to Aberdeen for his capture, the citizens added a force

[1] Pitcairn's *Criminal Trials*, ii. 429. See also vol. iii. 409.

[2] See the ballad of Christie's Will, with the notes, in the *Minstrelsy of the Scottish Border*, iii. 151. This ballad was composed by the editor on the traditionary story, in which the Earl of Traquair is introduced as a litigant for whose benefit the capture of the judge was made, the object being to prevent an adverse judgment in the Court of Session.

[3] Alexander Gibson of Durie, commonly called Lord Durie, and author of a well-known work called *Durie's Practicks*, died June 10, 1644. The story of his kidnapping was related a century after, as follows: 'Some party in a considerable action before the Session, finding that the Lord Durie could not be persuaded to find his plea good, fell upon a stratagem to prevent the influence and weight which his lordship might have to his prejudice, by causing some strong masked men kidnap him, in the links of Leith, at his diversion on a Saturday afternoon, and transport him to some blind and obscure room in the country, where he was detained captive, without the benefit of daylight, a matter of three months (though otherwise civilly and well entertained); during which time his lady and children went in mourning for him as dead. But after the cause aforesaid was decided, the Lord Durie was carried back by incognitos, and dropt in the same place where he had been taken up.'—Forbes's *Journal of the Session*, Edin. 1714.

of sixteen men, with a commander, and then a regular siege was established round the den of the outlaw. Being compelled to submit, he was carried to Edinburgh; and subjected to a trial, which ended in his having the head struck from his body at the Cross, January 12, 1604. 1601.

At this time, Aberdeen was visited by a company of players, who bore the title of the 'king's servants,' and had come 'recommended by his majesty's special letter.' They performed 'comedies and stage-plays,' according to the somewhat awkward report of the town-council record, where it is stated that the provost, bailies, and council ordained a present to them of thirty-two merks, equal to about 35s. 6d. sterling. On the 22d of October, thirteen days after the ordinance for this gift, the council conferred the freedom of the burgh—the highest mark of honour they had it in their power to bestow—upon a batch of strangers, among whom were Sir Francis Hospital, a French nobleman, and several Scottish gentlemen of rank and importance; among whom, also, was 'Lawrence Fletcher, comedian to his majesty,' being apparently the chief of the histrionic company then performing in the city. Oct.

This fact has an extrinsic interest, on account of Fletcher being known to have belonged to the company of players in London which included the immortal Shakspeare. About eighteen months after this time, May 1603, immediately after James VI. arrived in London to take possession of the English throne, he granted a patent in favour of the players acting at the Globe Theatre, 'Pro Laurentio Fletcher, Gulielmo Shakspeare, et aliis,' and which licenses the performances of 'Lawrence Fletcher, William Shakspeare, Richard Burbage, Augustine Phillips, John Hemings, Henry Condel, William Sly, Robert Armin, Richard Cowley, and the rest of their associates.' It has therefore been judged as not unlikely that Shakspeare was present on this occasion in Aberdeen, as one of the company of 'the king's servants' headed by Fletcher—a probability which Mr Charles Knight has shewn to be not inconsistent with other facts known regarding Shakspeare's movements and proceedings about the time, and to be favoured by many passages in the subsequently written tragedy of *Macbeth*, which argue a more correct and intimate knowledge of Scotland than is usually possessed by individuals who have not visited it.[1]

[1] *Book of Bon Accord* (Aberdeen, 1839), p. 246. Knight's *William Shakspere, a Biography*, p. 443.

1601. Nov. 20. The presbytery of Aberdeen was occupied with the case of Walter Ronaldson of Kirktown of Dyce, a man who was 'a diligent hearer of the word, and communicat with the sacrament of the Lord's Table.' Walter was brought before the reverend court for 'familiarity with a spirit.' He confessed that, twenty-seven years before, 'there came to his door a spirit, and called upon him, "Wattie, Wattie!" and therefrae removed, and thereafter came to him every year twa times sin-syne, but [he] saw naething.' At Michaelmas in the by-past year, 'it came where the deponer was in his bed sleeping, and it sat down anent the bed upon a kist, and callit upon him, saying "Wattie, Wattie!" and then he wakened and saw the form of it, whilk was like ane little body, having a shaven beard, clad in white linen like a sark, and it said to Walter: "Thou art under wrack—gang to the weachman's house in Stanivoid, and there thou shall find baith silver and gold with vessel."' Walter proceeded to say that, in compliance with this direction, he went with some friends and spades to Stanivoid in order to search. He himself was 'poustless' [unable to act]; but his friends searched, and found nothing. He expressed his belief, nevertheless, that 'there is gold there, gif it was weel sought.' Walter was remitted to his parish minister, 'to try forder of him.'—*A. P. R.*

Nov. 24. The pest was declared to have at this time broken out in the town of Crail in Fife, and in the parishes of Eglesham, Eastwood, and Pollock in Renfrewshire. Orders for secluding the population of those places were, as usual, issued.—*P. C. R.*

On the 21st of December, the pest was understood to have entered Glasgow. The inhabitants of that city were therefore forbidden to visit Edinburgh.

On the 26th of January 1602, it is stated that the infected families of Crail, being put forth upon the neighbouring moor, and there being no provision for 'the entertening of the puir and indigent creatures,' they had wandered throughout the country in quest of food, and thus endangered the spread of the disease. The sheriff of Fife was ordered to see provision made for these people, and to take measures for punishing those who had wandered.

On the 4th of February, the pestilence was in Edinburgh, and the Court of Session was obliged in consequence to rise. Birrel notes: 'The 19 of February, John Archibald with his family were taken out to the Burrow-muir, being infectit with the pest.' Probably others immediately followed. This circumstance brings before us the celebrated John Napier, younger of Merchiston, who, on the 11th of March, complained to the Privy Council that the magistrates having ploughed up and turned to profitable service the place where they used formerly to lodge people infected with the pest, had on this occasion planted the sick in certain yards or parks of his at the Scheens, without any permission being asked. The magistrates did not come forward to defend themselves; nevertheless, the Council, considering the urgency of the demands of the public service, ordained that the lands in question should be left in the hands of the magistrates till next Candlemas, on terms to be agreed upon. 1601.

On the 16th of March, the pest still increasing in Edinburgh, the king took thought of Dunfermline, 'being the ordinar residence of the queen, his dearest spouse, and of their majesties' bairns,' and ordained that, for its preservation from the contagion, the passage by the Queensferry should be stopped. He himself seems to have at the same time gone north to Brechin, where we find the Privy Council held for some weeks.

The 20th of May was 'ane solemn day of fasting and thanksgiving for his merciful deliverance of the pest.'—*Bir.*

Owing to the influence of the noble family of Maxwell, popery had a great harbourage in the town of Dumfries. At this time denunciations were launched against sundry gentlemen connected with the place—William, Lord Herries; John, Master of Herries; Walter Herries of Knockshinnan, Edward Maxwell of the Hills, John Herries in Braco, Robert Herries in Killiloch, Adam Corsan, John Corsan, Robert Carran, John Horner, Matthew Forsyth, John Gibson, Robert Ka, Patrick Ka, Mr John Maxwell, and upwards of a dozen more, charging them with contravening sundry 'guid and loveable acts of parliament and secret council' against saying and hearing of mass, and entertaining priests. Mr John Hamilton, and Mr William Brown, sometime commendator of New Abbey, had been kept amongst them, and they had heard these men say mass, and allowed them to baptise some children, to the displeasure of God, and contempt of the king and his laws. For these reasons they were summoned to appear and answer, under pain of rebellion.—*P. C. R.* Nov. 26.

On the 24th of December, sixteen of the men who had been summoned, including Lord Herries, appeared. For some others a certification was presented, that they were prevented by infirmity from travelling. Those who appeared were asked to declare upon

1601. their oath what they knew about the matters in the charge; and on their refusing to do so, they were ordained to be kept in ward in Edinburgh till they should be tried for their alleged offence. The others were again summoned.

These, on the 14th of January, the day appointed for their appearing, failed to appear, and were denounced as rebels.

Dec. 11. Great hatred and strife had now lasted for some years between the Earl of Cassillis[1] and Sir Thomas Kennedy of Colzean, on the one side, and the Laird of Bargeny, the Laird of Blairwhan, the Laird of Girvanmains, and some other Carrick gentlemen, on the other. The crafty Laird of Auchindrain, though professedly reconciled to Sir Thomas Kennedy,[2] was mainly on the side of Bargeny, who was his brother-in-law. It is believed that he employed himself to inflate Bargeny, who was but a youth, with ambitious designs, making him believe that he could easily put himself on a level with the Earl of Cassillis. The king made an effort to reconcile the parties, but it had no permanent effect. For some time these Carrick chieftains were chiefly busied in devising plots against each other's lives. On one occasion, the earl, having been induced to accept the hospitality of the Laird of Blairwhan, was apprised that certain of his unfriends, along with Blairwhan, intended to murder him in his bed; he therefore left the house by a back-door, and made his way by night to Maybole. On another occasion, with the consent of Bargeny, the Laird of Benand, with some associates, lay in ambush in the kiln of Daljarrock, in which they had made holes for their hagbuts, designing to shoot Lord Cassillis as he passed that way. Receiving timely warning, he escaped the danger by going his journey by another road.

On the 6th of December 1601, the Laird of Bargeny had occasion to go to Ayr on business. Along with him rode his brother and the Laird of Benand—the two leaders in the affair of the kiln—and ten or twelve other horsemen. Passing within a quarter of a mile of Cassillis Castle, and not stopping to pay their respects to the earl, they violated one of the most sacred of the social laws then existing. Lord Cassillis could interpret it into nothing but the grossest insult. He was the more enraged, knowing that Bargeny's two principal companions had lately lain in wait for his life. He immediately took measures for gathering

[1] John, fifth Earl of Cassillis, son of the lord who roasted Allan Stewart in Dunure Castle; see pp. 65–67.

[2] See under January 1, 1596–7.

his friends about him, and sent spies to Ayr to apprise him of all Bargeny's movements. 1601.

After spending four or five days in Ayr, Bargeny proposed to return to his own house, much against the advice of his friends, who feared dangers by the way. Setting out with a company of about eighty on horseback, in the midst of a dense snow-storm, he made a halt at the Bridge of Doon—that place since made so famous from another cause—and there addressed his people, protesting that he sought no quarrel with Lord Cassillis, but expressing his hope that, if attacked, they would stand around him, and do their duty as became men of honour. They all assured him that they would die in his defence. He then divided his train into two parties, and riding on, at the Lady Cross met the earl, who came out of Maybole with fully two hundred men. 'Being all ready to meet, the ane on the Teind knowe, and the other on the next, within the shot of ane musket, they began to flyte [use despiteful language towards each other]. Patrick Rippet [of the earl's party], cryit: "Laird of Benand! Laird of Benand! Laird of Benand! This is I, Patrick Rippet, that took thy [hagbut]. Come down here in the holm, and break ane tree for thy love's sake!" But the other gave nae answer, albeit he had given the laird stiff council to ride forward before.'

The Laird of Bargeny, anxious still to avoid fighting if possible, led off his men along the side of a bog; but the Cassillis party came by the other side, and met him at the bottom. He then made a dash forward across a ditch, with Mure of Auchindrain, his page, and three other gentlemen, but, not being supported by any others, found himself outnumbered by the enemy. A brief conflict took place, in which the laird and his friends did some damage to the opposite party; but it was all in vain. Auchindrain was wounded, the page was killed, one of his friends unhorsed, and another sore hurt. He himself, though but one of his friends remained, was not daunted, but rode rapidly into the ranks of the enemy, calling: 'Where is my lord himself? Let him now keep promise and break ane tree!' He was instantly set upon by a host of the earl's friends, who strake at him with swords, and bore him back by sheer force. At that moment, one John Dick, who had formerly received benefits at his hands, thrust a lance through his throat and stopped his breath. The poor gentleman was then borne off by his horse towards such of his party as still stood their ground, and fell at their feet. The skirmish being now at an end, they were allowed to conduct him away from the field, taking him

1601. first to a barn at a place called Dingham, then to Maybole, and finally to Ayr, where he soon after died, being but twenty-five years of age, leaving a widow and two children to bewail his bloody end. 'He was,' says the contemporary historian of the Kennedies, 'the brawest man that was to be gotten in ony land; of hich stature and weel made; his hair black, but of ane comely face; the brawest horseman, and the ae-best of mony at all pastimes . . . . gif he had [had] time to [have] had experience to his wit, he had been by his marrows [superior to all his mates].'

The procedure consequent on this sad tragedy is very notable. The Countess of Cassillis—a lady much the senior of her husband, the widow of the late Chancellor Maitland, and of course well acquainted with all the principal people around the king—rode immediately to court, to intercede for James's favour towards her lord. With the help of the Laird of Colzean, she contrived to obtain an act of Council, making the earl's part in the late conflict 'good service to the king'—the pretext being that, in the opposite party, was Thomas Kennedy, Bargeny's brother, a denounced rebel. '*The ten thousand merks given to the treasurer was what did the turn.*'[1] The earl was able afterwards to reimburse himself by causing all the gentlemen who had been with Bargeny to come to him and purchase remissions for their concern in the death of one of his followers, slain in the skirmish.

'The Lady Bargeny rade to Edinburgh, and made her complent to the king and queen, but was little better, or least but heard; for she was compellit to buy the ward of her son, and to give thirteen thousand merks for the same.' It is alleged that she afterwards used all the means she could to take the life of Lord Cassillis, in revenge for her husband's death. An ambush was laid for him at Monkton, but getting timely warning, he waited for an increase to his retinue, by which he overawed the intending assassins. Lady Bargeny died in 1605, on her way home from London, whither she had gone to consult Dr Martin for 'the eittik' [that is, hectic, meaning a pulmonary consumption]. Her body was met at Sanquhar by 'the haill friends of the house,' and by them brought ceremonially to Ayr, and placed beside her

[1] Such is the account of a partial contemporary. In the Privy Council Record, it is stated that the conflict was provoked by Bargeny, and that his party were fully armed for the purpose with muskets, hagbuts, and pistolets, while Cassillis's attendants wore only their swords. Cassillis's defence, on the ground of his having commissions giving him authority over his district, was sustained.

deceased husband in the church. She had, however, erected a 1601.
sumptuous tomb to her lord in the church of Ballantrae, and to this the two bodies were transferred with great state, 'the *honours* and all the rest being preparit very honourably.' By this is meant, a procession bearing the escutcheon, pencil of honour, sword, helmet, corslet, &c., of the deceased. 'The day being come, there was of noblemen the Earls of Eglinton, Abercorn, and Winton, with the Lords Semple, Cathcart, Loudoun, and Ochiltree, the Lairds of Bombie, Blairwhan, and Gairland [Garthland], with ane great number whilk I will not mint [attempt] to express; his honours being borne by the Guidman of Ardmillan, the Guidman of Kirkhill, with sundry mae of the friends; his sister's son, Young Auchindrain, bearing the *Banner of Revenge,* whereon was paintit his portraiture, with all his wounds, with his son sitting at his knees, and this ditty written betwixt his hands: "JUDGE AND REVENGE MY CAUSE, O LORD!" And sae, conveyit to Ayr, bure all very honourably, to the number of ane thousand horse, of gentlemen, and laid in the foresaid tomb.'—*Hist. Ken.*

It is scarcely necessary to remark the amount of local means here indicated by a funeral train of a *thousand mounted gentlemen.* The Banner of Revenge seems to have been an imitation of that carried in the streets of Edinburgh in June 1567, to inflame the popular mind against Queen Mary.

The winter of 1601–2 is described by Birrel as of unheard-of 1602.
severity and duration. It lasted from the 1st of November to the 1st of May. In February was a ten-days' snow-fall.[1] The Earl of
Sutherland was at this time travelling with his ordinary train from FEB. 13.
Golspie through the glen of Loth, on his way to Killeirnan. The ground being already deeply covered with snow, the party found themselves in a hard plight, when a fresh storm burst upon them, driving thick snow full in their faces. The like was not seen for many years after. 'Some of the company being thirsty, drank *aquavitæ,* which by chance happened to be there. This made them afterwards so feeble, that they were not able to endure against the storm.' This is an observation in conformity with a statement of Sir John Franklin respecting his men when travelling in the frozen regions. Spirituous liquor, according to him, did no one any good. The earl, being strong, made his way through the snow,

[1] Birrel, by an evident mistake, places this in 1601.

1602. and such of his company as kept close together near him were safe. 'Some were dispersed by the extremity of the tempest; some were carried home upon their fellows' shoulders, and recovered afterwards.' Several others, including the earl's *harper*, were found dead in the snow next morning.—*G. H. S.*

FEB. 14. James and George Vallam, sons of David Vallam of Woodwrae, were hanged in Edinburgh for stouthrief. The dittay reveals some of the practices of the age. These two men had, in June 1596, attacked two cadgers or carriers at the Cot-town of Melgum in Forfarshire, as they were 'driving seven packs of merchant geir on seven horses towards Brechin, to the fair thereof,' and did 'thiftously and masterfully convey the same away with them, together with the said cadgers, to the mouth of Glenmoy, and disponed upon a grit part of the said merchant geir at their pleasure.' The circumstances are precisely what might occur at the present day in Spain.—*Pit.*

FEB. 26. After such a variety of examples of violence in the south and west provinces, where a comparative civilisation prevailed, it may be curious to see an example of the outrages occasionally committed in the north. On this day, if we are to believe the statement of the suffering party, the house of Moy, belonging to John Campbell, commissary of Inverness, was attacked, despoiled, and utterly destroyed by a party under command of Alexander M'Ranald of Glengarach. They came 'to the number of three score persons,[1] all thieves, broken men, and sorners of clans, bodin and furnist with bows, habershons, twa-handit swords, and other weapons invasive, and with hagbuts and pistolets.' Reaching Moy 'upon fair day-licht,' they 'divided their company in twa several companies, ane whereof remainit about the complenar's house and biggings, where they treasonably and awfully raisit fire, burnt and

[1] The names of the party, as given in the Privy Council Record, are curious as a sample of Highland nomenclature of the day. These were Donald Glas M'Rannald, and Ronald M'Rannald, brothers of the aforesaid Alexander; Allaster M'Ean Vich Innes, John, Angus, Donald, and Ronald, his sons; Gorie M'Allaster Vich Gorie, and Allaster his brother; John Dow M'Connell Vich Rannald, Allan and Angus his brothers; Gillespich M'Ean Vich Connell, William and Angus his brothers; William M'Connell Vich Gorie, and Angus his brother; John M'Ean Vich Finlay Roy, and Ewen M'Finlay Roy his brother; John Dow Vich Connell Vich Finlay; John M'Innes Vich Connachie, and Paul M'Connachie Vich Innes his son; Farquhar Dow M'Connell Vich Farquhar, Allaster Dow his brother; Gilliecallum M'Farquhar Vich Connell Vich Farquhar, son to the said Farquhar; Donald M'Innes Vich Ean Dowie; Gillespich M'Innes his brother, &c.

destroyit his haill house, onsets, and biggings; consisting of ane 1602.
hall, twa chalmers, ane kitchen, ane stable, and ane barn, and some other office-houses; together with his haill corns being in the barn and barn-yard, extending to twa grit stacks of aits, ane stack of wheat, and ane grit stack of beir, after they had spulyit, reft, and intromittit with his haill insicht plenishing.'

The other company 'past to the house of umwhile James Buchan, the complenar's tenant, where they first spulyit his house, guids, and geir, and then treasonably raisit fire therein. . . . . They took James Buchan, Patrick Buchan his son, and Robert Anderson his servant, and having cuttit off their legs and arms, and otherwise dismemberit them at their pleasure, they cast them quick in the fire and burnt them. . . . . In their departing, they reft and away-took with them twenty oxen and three score sheep pertening to the complenar, and wrackit and herryit his haill puir tenants. The like of whilk barbarous cruelty committit sae fer within the in-country has sendil been heard of.'

All that could be immediately done in this frightful case was to denounce the guilty parties as rebels for not appearing to answer Campbell's complaint. Soon after, we find the Privy Council expressing its grief that the broken men of the Highlands, 'not content with the robbery and reif whilk they were accustomed to commit upon the borders of the country, have tane the bauldness in troops to repair in fair day-licht within the heart of the in-country and to the ports of Elgin, whilk was the maist peaceable and obedient part of the haill land, and there to herry and sorn at their pleasure.' The gentlemen of Morayshire were summoned to advise with his majesty, as to the best means of restraining this insolence.—*P. C. R.*

There is afterwards (June 28), a complaint by Campbell of Moy as to the favour and entertainment which Dunbar of Westfield, sheriff of Moray, had given to the men by whom his estate was despoiled. It was even alleged that the Dunbars had brought the broken men into the country. This group of men accordingly had some trouble about this business, but not any of serious consequence. We do not find that any of the actual perpetrators of the outrage at Moy ever suffered for it.

Thomas Musgrave, Captain of Bewcastle, being accused before APR. 3.
the Privy Council of England, of sundry breaches of duty, particularly of having made Bewcastle a den of thieves, and open to the Scots at their pleasure, challenged the accuser, one Lancelot

1602. Carleton, to the trial by combat on Canonbie Holm, 'before England and Scotland,' on Thursday in Easter-week, being the 8th of April 1602, betwixt nine o'clock and one of the same day. It was agreed that they should fight on foot, armed with jack, steel-cap, plait sleeves, plait breeches, plait socks, two baslaerd swords,[1] with blades a yard and half a quarter long, and two Scotch dirks at their girdles. Two gentlemen were to view the field, and see that the agreement as to arms and weapons was strictly observed; and the field being so viewed, the gentlemen were to ride to the rest of the company, leaving the combatants only two boys to hold their horses. The result is not known.[2]

MAY 11. Sir Thomas Kennedy of Colzean was this day murdered in the immediate neighbourhood of the town of Ayr. 'He was ane very potentous man, and very wise. He had buildit ane proper house in the Cove [the mansion superseded by the present Colzean Castle], with very brave yards; and, by ane moyen and other, had conquest ane guid living.' We have seen, under January 1, 1596–7, an attempt upon the life of this gentleman at Maybole, by Mure of Auchindrain, who subsequently was reconciled to him, and, for the confirmation of amity, caused his son to be married to Sir Thomas's daughter. It nevertheless became in time apparent that Mure was the prime mover of this atrocious murder, the circumstances of which are thus related by the king's advocate, Sir Thomas Hamilton.

Sir Thomas Kennedy, 'being only intentive on his own *adoes*, whilk did require his resort to Edinburgh, there to consult with his lawyers in his weehty business, he send his servant to Maybole, to seek Auchindrain and advertise him of his purpose; with direction, if he missed him there, that he sould certify him by letter of his intended journey; to the effect Auchindrain might, upon the next day, meet him upon the way at [the Duppil, a place near Ayr], and inform him of anything he wald wish him to do for him in Edinburgh, seeing it was but ane travel for him to do his friend's business and his own. This servant of Colzean's, missing Auchindrain in Maybole, desired Mr Robert Mure, schoolmaster at Maybole, to write ane letter of that substance to Auchindrain; who did so, and sent it by ane boy of his school, called William Dalrymple; who, finding Auchindrain at his house of Auchindrain, with his cousin Walter Mure of Cloncaird, ane deadly enemy to the Earl of

[1] Poniard swords. [2] Nicolson and Burn's *Hist. Westmoreland*, i. 595.

Cassillis; so soon as he [Auchindrain] fand himself certified of Colzean's purpose and diet, he dismissed the boy, commanding him to return back in haste, carrying the letter with him; directing him further to shaw to his master and Colzean's man that he had not fand him at his house. . . . . Immediately thereafter, [he] resolved with his cousin Cloncaird, that this occasion of revenge of Bargeny's slaughter by Colzean's murder was not to be unslipped. . . . . After some deliberation, [he] concluded upon the choice of the actors and manner of the execution, making advertisement thereof, as weel by letter to Thomas Kennedy of Drumurchy . . . . as by message to Cloncaird. . . . . The said Thomas Kennedy, Walter Mure of Cloncaird, and four or five servants with them, weel armed and horsed, convoying themselves near the way appointed by Colzean's letter for his meeting with Auchindrain, did lie await for Colzean's by-coming; who, being in full security of his dangerless estate, riding upon ane pacing nag, and having with him ane servant only, they suddenly surprised him, and with their pistols and swords gave him ane number of deadly wounds; and, not content to have so barbarously and traitorously bereft him of his life, spoiled him of ane thousand merks of gold, being in his purse, ane number of gold buttons upon his coat, and some rings and other jewels.' 1602.

'He being slain, his man Lancelot brings him with him to the Greenan, and there gets ane horse litter, and takes him to Maybole, where there was great dule made for him.'—*Hist. Ken.*

Sir Thomas Hamilton proceeds to narrate that, while the actual murderers were first outlawed and afterwards forefaulted, Auchindrain fell under strong suspicion of having been the deviser of the deed. He, 'being summoned to underlie the law, did boldly compear, and, seeing that the pursuers, for want of sufficient evidence, were not then to adventure his trial, fearing that he might be cleansed and so perpetually freed of that crime . . . . he seemed grieved thereat, as bragging exceedingly of his innocency, whereof he had given proof, by offering himself to trial of law—[he now proposed] if there were any man of Colzean's kindred or friendship, who wald advow him any ways participant of the device or execution of that murder, he wald readily offer himself in that quarrel to the trial of combat to the death. . . . . So, wanting ane party, [he] was dismissed, more free in the persuasion of most part of such as were present, than in his own conscience.'

The reader must be referred onward to July 1611 for the remainder of the history of this extraordinary criminal. Here,

1602. however, may be introduced the remarkable fact, that the Earl of Cassillis made an attempt to obtain a private revenge on Auchindrain for the murder of his uncle Colzean. The earl had long been on bad terms with his brother Hugh, whom we have seen as the guilty associate of Auchindrain. Now, he made up all past quarrels with Hugh, and granted him a bond, September 4, 1602, stating: 'Howsoon our brother, Hugh Kennedy of Brownston, with his complices, *takes the Laird of Auchindrain's life*, we sall mak guid and thankful payment to him and them of the sum of twelve hundred merks yearly, together with corn to six horses, [until] we receive them in household with ourself, beginning the first payment immediately after their committing of the said deed. Attour [moreover], howsoon we receive them in household, we shall pay to the twa serving gentlemen the fees, yearly, as our awn household servants. And hereto we oblige us, *upon our honour*.'[1]

Oct. 8. A proclamation issued by the king at Dumfries, gives some idea of the social state of the middle marches, and of the arrangements required for the execution of justice amongst the rude and turbulent people of that district, while as yet the government had no standing force at its command. 'Forsamickle,' it proceeds, 'as the king's Majesty has causit proclaim and appoint justice-courts to be halden within the burghs of Peblis and Jedburgh upon the fifteen and twenty-sex day of October instant, for punishing and trying be order of justice the monyfauld enormities and insolencies whilk has been sae frequent and common thir years bygane within the middle marches, Like as his Majesty, accompaniet with a nowmer of his council, intends to be present at the said courts, and to hald hand to the due execution of justice, Wherefore necessity it is that his Majesty be weel and substantially accompaniet with a force of his guid subjects, Therefore ordains letters to be direct, charging all and sundry his Majesty's lieges and subjects betwixt saxty and saxteen years, and others fencible persons, as well dwelling to burgh as to land, regality and royalty, within the bounds of the sheriffdoms of Peblis, Selkirk, and Roxburgh, that they ilk ane of them weel bodin in feir of weir in their substantious and weirlike manner address themselves to meet his Majesty at the days and places following;

[1] See this singular document in Pitcairn's *Crim. Trials*, iii. 622; also in *Maitland Club Misc.*, i. p. 141, where a fac-simile of it is presented.

That is to say, the saids inhabitants within the sheriffdoms of Selkirk and Peblis to meet his Majesty at Peblis the said fifteen day of October instant, and the saids inhabitants within the sheriffdom of Roxburgh to meet his Majesty at Jedburgh upon the twenty-five day of the same month, provided to remain and attend upon his Majesty the space of fifteen days after their coming to the said burghs under the pain of tinsel of life, lands, and guids.'—*P. C. R.* 1602.

From some expressions in this proclamation, it seems likely to have been written by the king himself.

He did make a progress by Peebles and Jedburgh, and executed justice upon a number of luckless Elliots and Armstrongs.

A quarrel at this time took place between two chiefs of the North Highlands, Kenneth Mackenzie of Kintail and Macdonald of Glengarry. It were not easy to arrive at a just understanding of the case, or of the degrees of blame to which the several parties were liable; but it is not necessary. Enough that there was blood between these fierce paladins of the north, and that, however the right stood, the affair boded ill for Glengarry, seeing that he had to contend with an enemy crafty and able far beyond his class, and one who, by these means, was generally able to keep on good terms with the heads of administration in Edinburgh.

According to an unprinted memoir of the Clan Mackenzie—Glengarry and his son Angus, who had recently attained perfect age, took advantage of the temporary absence of Kintail in France to make a charge against the latter before the Privy Council; and Mackenzie was summoned at the pier of Leith to 'compear' before a certain day, under pain of forfeiture. This 'moved Mr John Mackenzie of Tollie, parson of Dingwall, to travel to France, and bring his chief against the day of compearance. He came to Edinburgh only the night before, and having advised with his friends, he kept the diet unexpectedly before the Council. In the meantime, Alister M'Gorrie and Ronald M'Rorie [Glengarry men] made another onset to the Brae of Kissearn, and killed a gentleman of the family of Davachmaluach, called Donald M'Kinnich Vich Allister, sleeping in his bed; whose bloody shirt Mr John Mackenzie presented that day at Edinburgh. Glengarry could prove nothing against Mackenzie done in his time; but Mr John proved Glengarry to have been the instruments of this murder. Likewise he proved him to be a worshipper of the *Coan*, which image was afterwards brought to Edinburgh, and

1602. burnt at the Cross. Also he gave in against him that he was an extortioner and oppressor, sorning on his own commons and the commons of others, and that he still lived in adultery. Which moved Glengarry to steal from the place of justice, and to take to the hills, whereupon he was proclaimed rebel, and Mackenzie got the laws against him.'

Glengarry's son having invaded Kintail, and done some mischief there, Mackenzie raised a force of seven hundred men, and retaliated by spoiling the district of Morar. Then the Macdonalds came in thirty-seven boats to Loch Broom, and counter-retaliated. Here Alister M'Gorrie, one of their party, was killed, and his party beat back to sea. Indeed, the whole expedition failed. Soon after, however, while Mackenzie was absent in Mull, the Macdonalds came once more to his country, at Loch Carron, and committed great devastations. Their leader, Glengarry's son, not only carried off all the cows he could find, but slew all the people that fell in his way, even the women and children. He was overtaken, however, by a fearful retribution.

'Advertisement was sent to Kintail and Lochalsh, who gathered as fast as they could; but he [Glengarry's son, Angus] had his boats laden before they came. After they gave him a flight of arrows, he took the sea, and they wanting boats, could not follow; but part of them went afoot to the Kyle; others made straight to Ellandonan, where they got a ten-oared boat and a four-oared boat. Mackenzie's lady carried to them arrows and ammunition with her own hand. They rowed to the Kyle boldly, having no chieftain, but ilk ane striving who would act more for his mistress's credit, and for the country's defence. They came to the Kyle [a narrow strait] after the night had fallen. When they spied the first of Glengarry's boats, they resolved to let her pass without challenge. He followed next himself in his long-boat of thirty-two oars, loaded with men and spoil, which, when they perceived, they rowed calmly to meet him; and he challenging them, and asking who they were, they answered: "We are all Clan Vich Allister," giving them balls and arrows alike; at which they took alarm. The clouds overshadowing the moon, made a dark shadow on the sea; so they thought it had been shore, and got all to the fore-end of the boat, which made the boat to sink. When the Mackenzies saw their boat sink, they sent their little boat ashore, lest any should make their escape to land, and *the Kintail men had the killing of them like selchies* [seals]. At last they killed Glengarry's son and all those that were in that great boat with him. The rest, when they heard the alarm, retired to Strathardle, and left their boats; from whence they went afoot, and took boats from the Isles to Morer. When they knew their chieftain was dead, with the best of his company, they gathered all together to ane isle, where the Lord Kintail came timeously the next morning in the sight of the Isles. . . . . 1602.

'When Mackenzie came to the Kyle, he spied a number of dead corpses which the rage of the sea had casten ashore, which made him to think, seeing his enemy together a little while before, that it was his own men that were killed there. He had in his company two of Glengarry's natives, who had quat Glengarry and submitted to him, and who were acquaint with both the country people [both clans or sets of people in the district] . . . . whom he desired to go ashore and see who they were that were dead. No sooner were they ashore but he espied them strike their hands upon their breasts, making great lamentation. "Praised be God!" said Kintail, "it is not for my countrymen you make such great lamentation. I am confident that God hath been favourable to my countrymen in giving them a pleasant victory." When Robert [one of the Glengarry men] returned to the boat, Kintail asked: "What news?" "My lord," saith he, "good news for your lordship; there is many a brave fellow of your enemies dead in yonder place; not so much as one of your countrymen amongst them." Immediately they sailed away to Ellandonan, where Kintail's men were no sooner landed but he met his countrymen returning from the burial of young Glengarry, whom they buried *in the very door of the Kirk of Kintail, as testimony that they might trample over his body whenever they went to church.*'[1]

Next year, Glengarry and some of his friends were indicted for slaughter in the Mackenzie country; and not long after, his lands of Lochalsh and castle of Strome had passed to the possession of the chief of Kintail.

In a *Catalogue of the Scots Nobility and Officers of the Estate*, by John Colville, written between 1600 and 1603, several of the Highland or rather Hebridean chiefs are described, as 'The Lord of the Isles, callit Makrenald; ane Irish [Celtic] and barbar—The Lord of Kintyre, callit Makoneill; Irish and barbar—The Lord of the Lewis, callit Makgloyid; Irish and barbar—The Lord of Makklen, callit Makklen; Irish, a child of good expectation.'

[1] Hist. Clan Mackenzie, MS. in possession of John W. Mackenzie, Esq.

1602. The chief personage of the preceding notice is thus introduced: 'The Lord of Makkenzie, callit Makkenzie; Irish; a protestant *and verey politique.*'

Nov. 1. At Perth—'Henry Balnaves and William Jack made their repentance in their awn seats on Sabbath afternoon, for making libel against Mr William Couper, minister, and Henry Elder, clerk—

> As King David was ane sair sanct to the crown,
> So is Mr William Couper and the clerk to this poor town.

Ane act of council against them, that nane of them should bear office or get honourable place in the town thereafter.'—*Chron. Perth.*

Dec. 1. It had become a practice for persons who had revengeful feelings towards their neighbours to obtain petards from the continent, and employ them for the destruction of those against whom they had an ill-will. The king now issued a proclamation against 'sic detestable and unworthy crimes, without example in any other kingdom,' whereby 'na man of whatsomever rank and calling can assure his awn safety and preservation within his awn house and iron yetts.' He ordered all who have any 'pittartis' to surrender them at the next burgh immediately, and forbade any more being brought home by sea, or made or mended within the country.—*P. C. R.*

It seems not unworthy of observation, that by his familiarity with this explosive practice in his own country, as well as by the recollection of his father's fate at the Kirk of Field, James might be in some measure prepared to smell out the gunpowder treason, as he did a few years later.

1603. Jan. 3. 'John Haitly of Mellerstanes [was] slain at the Salt Tron [in Edinburgh] by William Home, his guid-father.'—*Bir.*

We have no account of what led to this dreadful kind of homicide; but, five years after (April 28, 1608), we find that the king had exerted himself to reconcile the friends of the parties, and they were ordered by the Privy Council to come forward on a particular day, and *chop hands* on the subject.—*P. C. R.*

Jan. 30. 'Francis Mowbray brak ward out of the [Edinburgh] Castle, and he fell owir the wall, and brak his craig [neck]. Thereafter, he was trailit to the gallows, and hangit; and thereafter he was quarterit, and his head and four quarters put on the four ports.' 1603.

In this brief manner Birrel narrates the sad end of a sprightly and gallant, though intemperate spirit. Francis Mowbray was a son of Sir John Mowbray of Barnbougle, an ancient house long since gone down to nothing. Francis himself was the friend and companion of the Earl of Buccleuch, the hero of the attack on Carlisle Castle in 1596. He had taken part in that exploit, but soon after got into trouble, in consequence of a quarrel with one William Schaw, whom he struck through with a rapier, and killed. Worse than this, he was a Catholic, and engaged himself actively in some of those underhand political practices which at length came to a head in the Gunpowder Treason. He spent some time in a most suspicious place—the Infant's Court at Brussels.

An Italian fencer named Daniel, residing in London, denounced Mowbray to Elizabeth's government as having undertaken to kill the king of Scots. Mowbray denied the accusation, and offered the combat. The two being sent down to Edinburgh, it was arranged that they should fight hand to hand in the great close of Holyroodhouse; but before the appointed day arrived, notice came from England that some witnesses had come forward who could prove the treason. On the 29th of January, Mowbray was confronted with the two witnesses, who, however, were considered as 'of light account,' being men of bankrupt fortunes, who had from that cause left their country. Mowbray still stood stoutly to his denial, uttering this adjuration before the king: 'If ever I thought evil, or intended evil against my prince, God, that marketh the secrets of all hearts, make me fall at my enemies' feet—make me a spectacle to all Edinburgh, and cast my soul in hell for ever!' The two were placed in several apartments in Edinburgh Castle, the Italian occupying a room immediately above Mowbray.

At eight o'clock in the evening of the 30th of January, being Sunday, Francis Mowbray was found dying at the foot of the Castle rock. It was stated that he had sewed his blankets together, and let himself down over the wall; but the line being too short, he fell, and mortally injured himself. The unfortunate man died in the course of the night. An attempt was made by some friends to raise a report that he had been thrown over the window; but this was believed by few, and really is not very credible. The authorities shewed no hesitation about the matter; but, concluding

1603. on the guilt of the deceased, had his body dragged backwards through the streets to the bar of the Court of Justiciary, where sentence was duly passed against him. The corpse was then dealt with as Birrel relates. The superstitious remarked the verification of the fearful words of the deceased—that he might fall at his enemies' feet, and become a spectacle to all Edinburgh. —*Pit. Cal. Spot. Notes to Russell's edition of Spottiswoode*, 1851.

This year was published in Edinburgh a comedy, entitled *Philotus*, which we must consider as a curiosity in its way, since it is the first known effort of the Scottish muse in that department of literature.[1] It is founded on a story which we find under the name of *Philotus and Emilia* in a volume by Barnaby Riche, originally published in 1581,[2] being, in plain terms, a somewhat licentious Italian novel. The Scotch comedy is in rhymed verse, and entirely in the characteristic Scotch manner of that age; but not a shadow of plausible conjecture has yet been indulged in regarding the possible author.[3]

The main series of incidents involves the fate of a young woman, Emilia, who is solicited to become the second wife of Philotus, an old and rich man. A *Macrell*, or go-between, is employed to bring her to his wishes, and addresses her in a long speech, which incidentally illustrates the life of a fine lady of that age:

'Ye neither mell with lad nor loon,
But with the best in all this toun;
His wife may ay sit foremost doun,
  At either buird or bink,
Gang foremost in at door or yett,
And ay the first guid-day wald get,
With all men honourit and weel-tret,
  As ony heart wald think.

See what a woman's mind may meese,[4]
And hear what honour, wealth, and ease,
Ye may get with him, an ye please
  To do as I devise:

[1] This Scottish *Philotus* is to be distinguished from the *Philotas* of Daniel, for which see Collier's *Annals of the Stage*, iii. 350.

[2] *Riche his Farewell to Militaire Profession*, &c. Another of the tales in the same volume is dramatised by Shakspeare in *Twelfth Night*.

[3] See Mr J. W. Mackenzie's edition of *Philotus*, presented to the Bannatyne Club in 1835.

[4] Calm, gratify.

Your fire sall first be burning clear, 1603.
Your maidens then sall have your geir[1]
Put in guid order and effeir,[2]
Ilk morning or[3] you rise.

And say: 'Lo, mistress, here your muils;[4]
Put on your wyliecoat or it cuils;
Lo, here ane of your velvet stuils,
Whereon ye sall sit doun:
Then twasome come to kame your hair,
Put on your head-geir soft and fair;
Tak there your glass—see all be clair;
And sae gaes on your goun.

Then tak, to stanch your morning drouth,
Ane cup of Malvoisie, for your mouth;
For fume cast succar in a fouth,[5]
Together with a toast.
Three garden gowps[6] tak of the air,
And bid your page in haste prepare,
For your disjune, some dainty fair,
And care not for nae cost.

Ane pair of plovers piping het,
Ane partrick and ane quailie get,
Ane cup of sack, sweet and weel set,
May for ane breakfast gain.[7]
Your cater he may care for syne
Some delicate, again' you dine;
Your cook to season all sae fine,
Then does employ his pain.

To see your servants may you gang,
And look your maidens all amang,
And, gif there ony wark be wrang,
Then bitterly them blame:
Then may ye have baith quoifs and kells,[8]
Hich candie ruffs, and barlet bells,
All for your wearing and nought els,
Made in your house at hame.

And now when all thir warks are done,
For your refreshing after noon,
Gar bring into your chamber soon,
Some dainty dish of meat;
Ane cup or twa with Muscadel,
Some other licht thing therewithal—
For raisins or for capers call,
Gif that ye please to eat.

[1] Apparel. [2] Condition. [3] Ere. [4] Slippers.
[5] A quantity. [6] Mouthfuls. [7] Serve. [8] Cauls.

1603.

Till supper time then may ye chuse,
Into your garden to repose,
Or merrily to tak ane gloze,[1]
Or tak ane book and read on;
Syne to your supper are ye brought,
Till fare, full far that has been sought,
And dainty dishes dearly bought,
That ladies love to feed on.

The organs then, into your hall,
With shalm and timbrel sound they sall,
The viol and the lute withal,
To gar your meat digest:
The supper done, then up ye rise,
To gang ane while, as is the guise[2]—
By ye have roamit ane alley thrice,
It is a mile almaist.

Then ye may to your chalmer gang,
Beguile the nicht, gif it be lang,
With talk, and merry mows[3] amang,
To elevate the spleen.
For your collation tak ane taste,
Some little licht thing till digest,
At nicht use Rhen'sh wine ay almaist
For it is cauld and clean.

And for your back I dare be bold,
That ye sall wear even as ye wold,
With double garnishings of gold,
And crape above your hair.
Your velvet hat, your hood of state,
Your missle[4] when ye gang the gait,
Frae sun and wind, baith air and late,
To keep that face sae fair.

Of Paris wark, wrought by the lave,[5]
Your fine half-cheinyies ye sall have;
For to decore, ane carkat[6] crave,
That comely collar-bane.
Your great gold cheinyie for your neck,
Be bowsome to the carle, and beck,
For he has gold eneuch, what-reck?
It will stand on nane.

And for your gouns, ay the new guise
Ye with your tailors may devise,
To have them loose with plaits and plies,
Or claspit close behind:

[1] A warm at the fire. [2] Custom. [3] Jests.
[4] Mask. [5] Above the rest. [6] Necklace.

The stuff, my heart, ye need not hain, 1603.
Pan velvet raised, figurit or plain,
Silk, satin, damask, or grograin,
The finest ye can find.

Your claiths on colours cuttit out,
And all pasmented[1] round about,
My blessing on that seemly snout,
Sae weel, I trow, sall set them!
Your shanks[2] of silk, your velvet shoon,
Your broidered wyliecoat aboon,
As ye devise, all sall be done,
Uncraipit, when ye get them.

Your tablet, by your halse[3] that hings,
Gold bracelets, and all other things,
And all your fingers full of rings,
With pearls and precious stanes,
Ye sall have ay while ye cry ho,
Rickles[4] of gold and jewels too,
What reck to tak the bogle-go,
My bonny bird, for anes.'

This is the date of an outbreak of private warfare which throws all contemporary events of the same kind into the shade. FEB. 9.

In pursuance of a quarrel of some standing between the Clan Gregor and Colquhoun, Laird of Luss, the former came in force to the banks of Loch Lomond. The parties met in Glenfruin, and the Colquhouns, out-manœuvred by the enemy, were overthrown. The Macgregors, besides killing a number of persons, variously stated at three score and four score, in the battle, are alleged to have murdered a number of prisoners (amongst whom, by the way, was Tobias Smollett, bailie of Dumbarton, very likely an ancestor of the novelist, his namesake), and also some poor unarmed people. The whole slaughter is set down at 140 persons. Besides all this, they carried off 600 cattle, 800 sheep and goats, fourteen score of horse and mares, 'with the haill plenishing, gudes and geir, of the four-score-pound land of Luss, burning and destroying everything else.' It has been alleged that they killed the laird after taking him prisoner, and murdered a number of school-boys from the college or school of Dumbarton; but these would appear to be groundless charges. Such as their guilt was, it proved the commencement of a long course of oppression and misery endured

[1] Decorated with lace.
[2] Stockings.
[3] Throat.
[4] Heaps.

1603. by this clan. According to a contemporary writer, a mournful procession came to Edinburgh, bearing eleven score of bloody shirts, to excite the indignation of the king against the Macgregors. There being no friend of the Macgregors present to plead their cause, letters of intercommuning were immediately issued against them.

The feeling of a state-officer of these days regarding the unruly population of the north, comes strongly out in a letter of the President Lord Fyvie, written to the king a few weeks after he had gone to London. 'Your majesty will understand by your Council's letters the estate and proceedings with the Macgregors. *Gif all the great Highland clans war at the like point, I wald think it ane great ease and weel to this commonwealth, and to your majesty's guid subjects here.*'[1]

It was arranged soon after that a large number of the Clan Gregor should be deported from the country, but whither does not appear. The Privy Council requested the king to allow a ship to be sent for them, 'seeing all these wha are to depart, in whilk number the laird himself is ane, are . . . . unable of themselves aither to defray their charges, furnish themselves of victuals, or pay their fraught.'

[1] *Letters and State Papers of the Reign of James VI.*, p. 47.

Witch seated on the Moon.—From a Sculpture in Elgin Cathedral.

REIGN OF JAMES VI.: 1603-1625.

The death of Elizabeth, March 24, 1603, opened the way for King James to the English throne. He left Scotland on the 5th of April, after taking a tender farewell of his Scottish subjects, and promising to revisit them once every three years. He did not allow one year to elapse without making an effort to accomplish a union between England and Scotland; but it ended in the comparatively narrow result of establishing that the *postnati*—that is, Scotsmen born after the king's accession to the English crown—should be regarded as naturalised in both countries.

James, thoroughly believing that no puritan could be a loyal subject, continued to be anxious for the reduction of the Scottish Church under the royal supremacy and a hierarchy. The personal influence he acquired as king of England enabled him in some degree to accomplish this object, though all but wholly against the inclinations of the clergy and people.

The more zealous Presbyterian clergy had made up their minds, in a General Assembly now to be held at Aberdeen, to 'call in question all the conclusions taken in former assemblies for the episcopal government.'[1] The king, hearing of their design, caused his commissioner, Sir Alexander Straiton of Laurieston, to forbid the meeting. About twenty bold spirits, nevertheless, assembled (July 1605); and when Sir Alexander ordered them to dissolve, they did not obey till they had asserted their independence by appointing another day of meeting. When called soon after before the Privy Council, thirteen came in the king's mercy; but eight stood out for the independence of their church, and were sent to various prisons.

Six of the recusant clergymen were tried at Linlithgow (January 1606) for high treason, and found guilty. After their condemnation, they were remanded to various prisons to await his majesty's pleasure. (See November 6, 1606.)

At a parliament held in Perth (July 1606), under the king's favourite minister, George Home, Earl of Dunbar, bishops were introduced, and the king's prerogative confirmed in ample style. The Scottish statesmen and councillors were full of servility to the king. James caused several of the more zealous Presbyterian clergy, including the venerable but still energetic Andrew Melville, and his nephew James, to be brought to a conference in London, hoping to prevail upon them to cease their opposition;

[1] Spottiswoode.

but it ended in the one being banished for an epigram, and the other being confined for life to the town of Berwick. In 1610, the king's supremacy was acknowledged by the General Assembly, and consecrated bishops were settled in authority over dioceses. A court of High Commission, with immense power over clergy, schools, colleges, and people was also introduced. Regal influence, gold, cajolery, and a judicious deliberation, effected the *appearance* of an episcopal reformation, while the great bulk of the people endured with a silent protest what they could not resist.

At the same time, the new strength of the crown, as administered under the able chancellor, Seton, Earl of Dunfermline, and Thomas, Earl of Melrose (subsequently of Haddington), caused such an obedience to the laws throughout Scotland as had never before been known. The attempt at a plantation of the island of Lewis, with a view to the civilisation of the Hebrides, was renewed under these favouring circumstances, but altogether without success.

The king's sole visit to his native kingdom took place in 1617, as to some extent detailed in the chronicle. His chief design was to advance the desired reformation of the national religion, by paving the way for an introduction of some of the English ceremonies. These were—kneeling at the eucharist, private administration of baptism to weak children, private administration of the communion to dying Christians, the confirmation of children, and the observance of Christmas and Easter. Protestant churches of most respectable character make no objection to these rites and forms; but among the Scottish people of that day they were viewed with great dislike. From a subservient General Assembly (1618), the Five Articles of Perth, as they were called, received a reluctant assent, and three years after they were confirmed by parliament.

While these struggles were going on between Presbyterianism and Episcopacy, the adherents of both systems cordially concurred in the persecution of the Catholics. Nobles and gentlemen of that persuasion were unblushingly called upon either to embrace Protestantism or submit to forfeiture of property and country. Priests were severely punished; one hanged. Shewing severity to the Papists was one of the principal means used by the king to conciliate the Presbyterians to his prelatic innovations.

Beyond inducing a few ministers to accept the mitre, and obtaining a hollow conformity from persons in authority, James made no progress in converting the Scotch to episcopacy, excepting in Aberdeenshire and some other northern provinces. The people refused to kneel at the communion, or have baptism and the eucharist administered in private. The holidays were disregarded. Withdrawing from the churches, the people began to meet in conventicles or in private houses for worship after their own manner. The established church sank into the character of 'an institution.'

The English reign of James VI. was, nevertheless, in secular respects, a comparatively serene and happy time in Scotland. Peace blessed the land. For the first time, the law was everywhere enforced with tolerable vigour; some practical improvements were introduced. Even the Highlands began during this period to shew some approach to order.

James died March 27, 1625, in his fifty-ninth year, after a nominal reign over Scotland of little less than fifty-eight years.

Intelligence of the death of Elizabeth—the event took place at 1603.
an early hour on the morning of Thursday the 24th March—was brought to King James by Robert Carey, a young aspirant of the English court, who, making a rapid journey on horseback, reached Holyroodhouse on Saturday evening after the king had retired to Mar. 26.
rest. This was probably the most rapid transit from London to Edinburgh previous to the days of railways. The son of the governor of Berwick came next day and delivered the keys of that town to the Scottish monarch. On the ensuing Sunday, James appeared in his ordinary seat in St Giles's Kirk, attended by a Apr. 3.
number of the English nobility; and after service, made an *orison* or harangue to the people, promising to defend the faith, and to 'visit his people and guid subjects in Scotland every three years.' On the 5th of April, 'his majesty took journey to Berwick; at whilk time there was great lamentation and mourning amang the commons for the loss of the daily sight of their blessit prince. At this time, all the haill commons of Scotland that had rede or understanding were daily speaking and exponing of Thomas the Rhymer his prophecy, and of other prophecies whilk were prophecied in auld times; as namely it was prophecied in Henry the 8 days—HEMPE is begun, God give it long to last; Frae Hempe begun, England may tak rest. To make it that it may be understood, H for Henry, E for England, M for Mary, P for Philip, king of Spain, that marryit with Queen Mary, and E for worthy good Queen Elizabeth: sae it is come that England may tak rest; for there is no more England, but Great Britain. Siclike it was spoken in Scots—Ane French wife shall bear a son shall brook all Britain by the sea. For it is true that King James 6 his mother was ane French wife, in respect she was marryit to the

1608. Prince of France, wha was so stylit. . . . . It was likewise writ in another prophecy:

> [*Post Jacobum, Jacobus Jacobum, Jacobus quoque quintus;*
> *At Sextus Jacobus regno regnabit utroque.*]'—*Bir.*

Now-a-days, it would be 'all the people that had *not* rede or understanding' that would be speaking of prophecies in relation to public events. At that time, however, as has been stated before, metrical and other prophecies, commonly attributed to Thomas the Rhymer, a sage who lived at the end of the thirteenth century, were in great vogue. In this year, Robert Waldegrave printed a *brochure* containing a collection of these metrical predictions, ascribed to Merlin, Bede, Waldhave, Thomas Rymour, and others. In this volume may be found the prediction of Hempe, but in a different form, and the two others quoted by Birrel. The reader may turn back to January 1, 1561–2, for an account of Waldegrave's book of prophecies, and some remarks on that special prediction regarding the son of the French wife, which was now called so particularly into notice.

MAY 28. 'The queen and prince came from Stirling [to Edinburgh]. There were sundry English ladies and gentlewomen come to give her the convoy.' On the 30th, 'her majesty and the prince came to St Giles Kirk, weel convoyit with coaches, herself and the prince in her awn coach, whilk came with her out of Denmark, and the English gentlewomen in the rest of the coaches. They heard ane guid sermon in the kirk, and thereafter rade hame to Halyroodhouse.'—*Bir.*

JUNE. The pestilence, which had for some time been raging in England, is noted as now affecting the south of Scotland, and continuing till the ensuing February.—*Chron. Perth.*

JULY 21. James Reid, a noted sorcerer and charmer, was strangled and burnt on the Castle Hill of Edinburgh for his alleged practice of healing by the black art. 'Whilk craft,' says his dittay, 'he learnt frae the devil, his master, in Binnie Craigs and Corstorphin Craigs, where he met with him and consulted with him to learn the said craft; wha gave him three pennies at ane time, and a piece creish[1] out of his bag at ane other time; he having appeared to the said James diverse times, whiles in the likeness of a man, whiles in

[1] Grease.

the likeness of a horse . . . . whilk likewise learned him to tak south-rinning water to cure the said diseases.' It was alleged that James had cured Sarah Borthwick of a grievous ailment by 'casting a certain quantity of wheat and salt about her bed.' He had tried to destroy the crops of David Libberton, a baker, by directing an enchanted piece of raw flesh to be put under his mill-door, and casting nine stones upon his lands. Nay, he had done what he could to destroy David himself, by making a picture of him in wax, and turning it before a fire. The authorities made short work of so grievous an offender by sending him direct from judgment to execution.'—*Pit.* 1603.

Campbell of Ardkinlas, set on by the Earl of Argyle, exerted himself to capture Macgregor of Glenstrae, who for some months had been under ban of the government on account of the slaughterous conflict of Glenfruin. He called Macgregor to a banquet in his house, which stands within a loch, and there made no scruple to lay hold of the unfortunate chieftain. Being immediately after put into a boat, under a guard of five men, to be conducted to the Earl of Argyle, Macgregor contrived to get his hands loose, struck down the guardsman nearest him, and leaping into the water, swam to land unharmed. OCT. 2.

Some time after, the Earl of Argyle sent a message to Macgregor, desiring him to come and confer with him, under promise to let him go free if they should not come to an agreement. 'Upon the whilk, the Laird Macgregor came to him, and at his coming was weel received by the earl, wha shew him that he was commanded by the king to bring him in, but he had no doubt but his majesty wald, at his request, pardon his offence, and he should with all diligence send twa gentlemen to England with him. . . . . Upon the whilk fair promises, he was content, and came with the Earl of Argyle to Edinburgh' (January 9, 1604), 'with eighteen mae of his friends.'[1]

The sad remainder of the transaction is narrated by the diarist Birrel, with a slight difference of statement as to the agreement on which the surrender had taken place. Macgregor 'was convoyit to Berwick by the guard, conform to the earl's promise; for he promised to put him out of Scots grund. Sae he keepit ane Hieland-man's promise, in respect he sent the guard to convoy him out of Scots grund; but they were not directed to part with him, but to

[1] MS. Hist. of Scotland, quoted by Pitcairn.

1603. fetch him back again. The 18 of January, he came at even again to Edinburgh, and upon the 20 day, he was hangit at the Cross, and eleven mae of his friends and name, upon ane gallows; himself being chief, he was hangit his awn height above the rest of his friends.'

A confession of Macgregor has been printed by Mr Pitcairn. It might rather be called a justification, the whole blame being thrown upon Argyle, whose crafty policy it fully exposes. It is alleged that, after instigating Ardkinlas to take Macgregor, the earl endeavoured to induce Macgregor to undertake the murder of Ardkinlas, besides that of the Laird of Ardencaple. 'I never granted thereto, through the whilk he did envy me greatumly' [that is, bore me a great grudge]. His whole object, Macgregor says, was 'to put down innocent men, to cause poor bairns and infants beg, and poor women to perish for hunger, when they are herried of their geir.'

Even in that barbarous age, when executions were lamentably frequent, the spectacle of twelve men hanging on one gallows, one of them a chieftain of ancient lineage, must have been an impressive one. 'A young man, called James Hope, beholding the execution, fell down, and power was taken from half of his body. When he was carried to a house, he cried that one of the Highlandmen had shot him with an arrow. He died upon the Sabbath-day after.'—*Cal.*

The subsequent persecution of the Macgregors, persevered in by the government during many years, belongs to history. Its severity 'obliged multitudes of them to abandon their habitations; and they retired to such places as they thought would afford them security and protection. The better sort made the best bargains they could with their enemies, and gave up their estates and possessions for small compositions. By these transmigrations, they came, in the end, to be scattered through all parts of the kingdom, where their posterity are still to be found under different names, and even many of them have lost the very memory of their original. . . . They are still pretty numerous in the Highlands . . . . many are found in other parts of the kingdom, who are possessed of opulent fortunes; and some of that race have since made a considerable figure, both in civil and military government, though covered under borrowed names.'—*Memoir of Sir Ewen Cameron, by Drummond of Balhadies, about* 1737.

Nov. 20. It was found at Aberdeen, that, great numbers of people resorting thither at Whitsunday and Martinmas 'for their leesome affairs, some to receive in their debts, others to uplift and give out siller on profit,' quarrels were extremely apt to fall out amongst them, on account of old 'feids standing unreconcilit.' Hence, it sometimes happened that this commercial city became a scene of wide-spread tumult, the strangers dividing into hostile parties and fighting with each other, in defiance of all that the magistrates could do to make them desist. Nay, 'the magistrates and neighbours of this burgh, standing betwixt the said parties, for redding and staunching the said tumults, has been divers and sundry times in great danger and peril, and some of them hurt and woundit, not being of power to resist the said parties.' 1603.

For these reasons, the town-council, at this date, passed a strict act for the preservation of the peace, but probably with very little immediate effect.

1604. APR.

'Ane servant woman of Mr John Hall, minister, died in his awn house, alleged to be the pest, as God forbid: yet he and his house was clengit.'—*Bir.* The fear of pestilence, here so strikingly expressed, was too well founded. The disease spread in May, and increased in the heat of July. The people fled from the town, and we find that one William Kerr, a blacksmith, thought it a good opportunity for helping himself to property not his own, and was hanged in December for having opened the doors of several of the empty houses.—*Bir.*

JUNE 15.

'The men of Black Ruthven and Huntingtower cuist turfs on our burgh moor at command of the comptroller, Sir David Murray, captain of his majesty's guard, and our provost for the time. The town rase aught hundred men in arms, and put them off. Angus Cairdney died of the apoplexy there. No ma harm, but great appearance of skaith.'—*Chron. Perth.*

It is remarkable to find that Perth could then send out 800 armed men. This, however, was not the utmost strength of the Fair City; for in the ensuing month, when a parliament was held there, 'the town mustered fourteen hundred men in arms and guid equipage.'—*Chron. Perth.*

Patrick, Earl of Orkney, paid a visit to the Earl of Sutherland at Dornoch, where he spent some time, 'honourably enterteened with comedies, and all other sports and recreations that Earl John could make him.'—*G. H. S.*

1604. James Melville notes in his *Diary* the appearance of a brilliant star which shone out this year 'aboon Edinburgh, hard by the sun,' in the middle of the day; 'prognosticating, undoubtedly, strange alterations and changes in the world; namely, under our climate.'

This notice most probably refers to a star, of the same kind with that mentioned in 1572, and nearly as brilliant, which is described as having appeared in the east foot of Serpentarius, in October of this year.

SEP. 10. 'The general master of the cunyie-house took shipping to London, for the defence of the Scotch cunyie before the Council of England. Wha defendit the same to the uttermost; and the wit and knawledge of the general was wondered at by the Englishmen. The said general and master came hame the 10 of December.'—*Bir.*

That the general master of the cunyie-house should have shewed so much wit and knowledge on this occasion, will not excite much surprise in the reader, when it is made known that he was Napier of Merchiston, father of the great philosopher.—*Bal.*

DEC. 7. 'Ane hour before the sun rose, the moon shining clear two days before the change, in a calm and pleasant morning, there was at ane instant seen great inflammations of fire-flaughts in the eastern hemisphere, and suddenly thereafter there was heard ane crack, as of a great cannon, and sensibly marked a great globe or bullet, fiery coloured, with a mighty whistling noise, flying from the north-east to the south-west, whilk left behind it a blue train and draught in the air, most like ane serpent in mony faulds and linkit wimples; the head whereof breathing out flames and smoke, as it wald directly invade the moon, and swallow her up; but immediately the sun, rising fair and pleasant, abolished all. The crack was heard of all, within as without the house; and sic as were without at the time, or hastily ran out to see, did very sensibly see and mark the rest above rehearsed. Here was a subject for poets and prophets to play upon. . . . .'—*Ja. Mel.*

1605. JAN. 19. 'James Young, player at cards and dice, was slain in the kirk [St Giles] by ane boy of sixteen years of age, called Lawrence Man. This Lawrence was beheaded on the Castle Hill, the last day of Januar.'—*Bir.*

MAY 2. A curious case was considered by the Privy Council. James Blackadder of Tulliallan had been charged by Sir Michael Balfour

of Burleigh, to address himself to Perth, and there buy from him 1605.
and his factor John Jamieson three stands of horsemen's arms, under pain of rebellion if he failed to do so before a particular day. James represented to the lords that long before Sir Michael had brought home these arms, he had provided himself otherwise with 'twa good corslets of proof for his awn person, besides a number of jacks for his servants, with certain muskets, hagbuts, pikes, spears, and all other sort of arms sufficient for aucht persons,' although not bound by his rent to provide arms for more than two. He wholly resisted the demand of Sir Michael, inferring an outlay of sixty pounds, on the ground that his estate did not extend beyond twenty-four chalders of victual, out of which he had diverse sums of interest to pay—inferring that he was not liable to have more than one stand of horsemen's arms. The lords decreed that James was in the right, and that Sir Michael's proceedings against him should cease.—*P. C. R.*

'Ane combat or tulyie [was] foughten at the Salt Tron of JUNE 17.
Edinburgh, betwixt the Laird of Ogle [Edzell], younger, and his complices, and the young Laird of Pitarrow, Wishart. The faught lasted frae 9 hours till 11 at night, twa hours. There were sundry hurt on both sides, and ane Guthrie slain, which was Pitarrow's man, ane very pretty young man. The 18th, they were accusit before the Council, and wardit.'—*Bir.*

The Lairds of Edzell and Pitarrow were committed to ward, for not having confined their sons, as the chancellor had commanded. Edzell, foreseeing troubles to himself and his son from the death of Guthrie, sent a surgeon to examine the corpse, with a view to establishing that the young man had not died of the wounds he received in the tulyie, but had been 'smoored in the throng.'

Edzell was in his way a remarkable man. Possessing a degree of taste uncommon in that age, he had built for himself at Edzell on the Esk in Forfarshire, a mansion of singular elegance, possessing in particular a screen-wall, ornamented with allegorical figures, the remains of which even at this day excite the surprise of the passing traveller. His latter days were clouded by the consequences of the violent passions of his eldest son, one of the principals in the above combat. We shall presently hear more of both him and his son.

A man called Alister Mac William Mor, a servant of Hugh Mackay of Far, happening to go into Caithness on some business,

1605. was there entrapped by emissaries of the Earl of Caithness, who bore him a grudge for his conduct in a former feud. The earl caused Alister to be beheaded before his eyes next day. The subsequent proceedings are curious. Mackay prosecuted Lord Caithness before the Justiciary Court at Edinburgh; but the Marquis of Huntly brought them together at Elgin; and 'the Earl of Caithness acknowledged his offence before the friends there present; whereupon they were finally agreed, and all past injuries were again forgiven by either party.' Not a word of the general claim of justice on behalf of the public!—*G. H. S.*

JULY. At the end of this month, the pest broke out in Edinburgh, Leith, St Andrews, and other parts of the kingdom. Among the first houses infected in Edinburgh was that of the Chancellor Dunfermline. James Melville, looking to the recent proceedings of this statesman against the more zealous ministers, considered him as overtaken by 'the penalty pronounced by Joshua upon the building up of Jericho. . . . . His eldest and only son died, and a young damosel his niece, so that he was compelled to dissolve his family, and go with his wife alone, as in hermitage, with great fear of the death of his daughter also, on whom the boils brake forth. This was marked and talked of by the people.'

The Fife adventurers who had been obliged to leave the Lewis in 1601 on a promise never to return, made a new attempt at this time to complete their unhappy undertaking. Attended with considerable forces, led partly by one William Mac Williams, chieftain of the Clan Gunn, they landed in the island, and 'sent a message unto Tormod Macleod, shewing that if he would yield unto them, in name and behalf of the king [now a more formidable name than it had been], they should transport him safely to London, where his majesty then was; and being arrived there, they would not only obtein his pardon, but also suffer him, without let or hindrance, to deal by his friends for his majesty's favour, and for some means whereby he might live. Whereunto Tormod Macleod condescended, and would not adventure the hazard of his fortune against so great forces as he perceived ready there to assail him. This did Tormod Macleod against the opinion and advice of his brother, Niel Macleod, who stood out and would not yield.

'So the adventurers sent Tormod Macleod to London, where he caused his majesty to be rightly informed of the case; how the Lewis was his just inheritance; how his majesty was sinistrously informed by the undertakers, who had abused his majesty in making him believe that the same was at his disposition, whereupon proceeded much unnecessary trouble and great bloodshed; and thereupon he humbly entreated his majesty to do him justice, and to restore him to his own. The adventurers, understanding that his majesty began to hearken to the complaint of Tormod Macleod, used all their credit at court to cross him. In end, they prevailed so far—some of them being the king's domestic servants—that they procured him to be taken and sent home prisoner into Scotland, where he remained captive at Edinburgh, until the month of March 1615 years, that the king gave him liberty to pass into Holland, to Maurice, Prince of Orange, where Tormod ended his days.'—*G. H. S.* 1605.

Tormod being thus put out of the way, 'the enterprise of the Lewis was again set on foot by Robert Lumsden of Airdrie and Sir George Hay of Netherliffe, to whom some of the first undertakers had made over their right. In August they took journey thither, and by the assistance of Mackay Mackenzie and Donald Gorm, forced the inhabitants to remove forth of the isle, and give surety not to return.

'Airdrie and his copartners, thinking all made sure, returned south about Martinmas, leaving some companies to maintain their possession, which they made good all that winter, though now and then they were assaulted by the islesmen. In the spring, Airdrie went back, taking with him fresh provision, and fell to building and manuring the lands. But this continued not long; for, money failing, the workmen went away, and the companies diminishing daily, the islesmen made a new invasion about the end of harvest, and by continual incursions so outwearied the new possessors, as they gave over their enterprise, and were contented for a little sum of money to make away their rights to the Laird of Mackenzie [Mackenzie of Kintail]. This turned to the ruin of divers of the undertakers, who were exhausted in means before they took the enterprise in hand, and had not the power which was required in a business of that importance.'—*Spot.*

It will be found that there was a third attempt to plant the Lewis. See under 1609.

Mr Gilbert Brown, called Abbot of New Abbey, had for many years escaped the law while exercising his functions as a priest in the neighbourhood of Dumfries. The Presbyterian historians stigmatise him as 'a famous excommunicat, forfaulted, perverting AUG.

1605. papist,' who 'kept in ignorance almost the haill south-west parts of Scotland,' and was 'continually occupied in practising against the religion.' He was now taken prisoner by Lord Cranston, 'not without peril from the country people, who rose to rescue him out of his hands.' He was brought to Blackness, where, for a night, he was the fellow-prisoner of the recusant Presbyterian brethren. It is to be feared that community of misfortune did not bring the two parties into any greater harmony or charity with each other than they had hitherto been. When the government thus 'took order' with a papist priest, the only feeling of the zealous people on the other side was a jealous curiosity to see whether it was in earnest or not. The government, on its part, felt that it was on its good behaviour, and dreaded to be too lenient. Abbot Brown, being taken to Edinburgh Castle, was for some time entertained with an unpopular degree of mildness and liberality, his food being furnished at the king's expense, and his friends being allowed to see him, while the Presbyterian captives were obliged to live at their own charges. Finally, the 'excommunicat papist' was allowed to quit the country with all his priestly furnishings, not without some suspicion of having been allowed to say mass in private before his departure.—*Cal.*

It is probable that this leniency was found to have been attended with the effect of exciting a troublesome degree of suspicion against the government, for another 'priest, who had been a certain time in ward in the Tolbooth of Edinburgh, was (September 27, 1607) brought down on the mercat-day to the Mercat Cross, with all his mess clothes upon him, wherewith he was taken, with his chalice in his hand. He stayed at the Cross from ten hours till twelve. Then all his mess clothes and chalice were burned in a fire beside the Cross, and himself carried back to ward.'—*Cal.*

Oct. 3. The Privy Council, sitting at Perth, dealt with a complaint from Mr Alexander Ireland, minister of Kincleven, against Sir John Crichton of Innernytie, who has already been introduced to our notice as a professor of the ancient faith. It appeared that the minister had had to adopt measures of discipline with Sir John 'for halding of profane plays on the Sabbath-day, resetting of seminary priests, and divers other offences condemned by the word of God.' The knight, rebelling against an authority which he bore in no reverence, had resented the interference with his personal freedom by going with an armed party to Ireland's house and committing sundry outrages, even to the beating of his wife, though she was not far from her confinement. Owing to an imperfection of the record, the end of the affair is unknown.—*P. C. R.* 1605.

On the evening of this day, when the Gunpowder Plot was to have taken effect, a high wind produced some effects in the north of Scotland, which seemed in harmony with that wild affair. 'All the inner stone pillars of the north side of the cathedral church at Dornoch (lacking the roof before), were blown from the very roots and foundation, quite and clean over the outer walls of the church; which walls did remain nevertheless standing, to the great astonishment of all such as have seen the same. These great winds did even then prognosticate and foreshew some great treason to be at hand; and as the devil was busy then to trouble the air, so was he busy, by these his firebrands, to trouble the estate of Great Britain.'—*G. H. S.* Nov. 5.

The Privy Council issued sundry proclamations 'anent the Poulder Treason,' one for the apprehension of Percy, the prime conspirator. There was a general joy in Scotland at the detection of the plot. In Aberdeen, the people repaired to the church to give formal thanks for the deliverance of the royal family and nobility. Bonfires were lighted on the public ways, and the people went about for an afternoon, singing psalms of thankfulness. The magistrates and others had also a public banquet at the market-cross, where glasses were 'drunk and cassen,' in token of their rejoicing for the said merciful delivery.—*Ab. C. R.*

1606. Jan. 21.

The Earl of Errol wrote from Perth to the king, promising, in compliance with a command just received, to be 'careful to provide ane tercel[1] to the hawk of Foulsheuch,' and to be 'answerable to your majesty for the same, in case the auld tercel be dead.' Foulsheuch is a sea-cliff about four miles south of Stonehaven, 200 feet in height, where so lately as 1808 a family of hawks, of uncommonly large size, continued to build. James's love of what old Gervase Markham calls the 'most princely and serious delight' of hawking, caused him to keep up a constant correspondence with friends in Scotland for the supply of the needful birds, and of this the earl's letter is a specimen. His lordship goes on with laudable particularity: 'Your majesty's mongrel falcon, whilk I have, sould have been at your hieness lang or now [ere now], but that as my falconer

[1] The tercel is the male hawk (*Falco peregrinus*), so called because one-third the size of the female.

1606. was ready to tak his journey, she contracted ane disease, wherewith he durst not adventure to travel her, in respect of the great frosts and storms. I will be answerable to your majesty that she has been in nae ways stressed, but as weel treated as any hawk could be. Naither shall your majesty suspect that I have reteinit her for my awn plesure, whilk I sall never compare in the greatest thing whatsoever with your majesty's meanest contentment, nor am I able as yet, even at this present, to travel upon the fields for any game. Albeit, how soon it sall be possible that the hawk may in any sort be travellit, she sall be at your majesty with all diligence. She had the same sickness the last year, in this same season, and was not free of it till near March.'[1]

So keenly interested was James respecting the tercel of Foulsheuch, that he had written to the Earl of Mar regarding it; and this nobleman replied on the same date with Lord Errol, assuring the king that he will see after it carefully. 'I cannot as yet,' he says, 'certify your majesty whether he be alive or not, but, within few days, I think, I sall go near to get the certainty that may be had of so oncertain a matter.'

There is extant a characteristic letter written by James at Perth in March 1597, to Fraser of Philorth, regarding a bird of sport. 'Hearing that ye have ane gyre-falcon, whilk is esteemed the best hawk in all that country, and meetest for us that have sae guid liking of that pastime, we have therefore taken occasion effectuously to requeest and desire you, *seeing hawks are but gifting geir*, and nae otherwise to be accounted betwix us and you, being sae well acquainted, that of courtesy ye will bestow on us that goshawk, and send her here to us with this bearer, our servant, whom we have on this errand directed to bring and carry her tenderly. Wherein, as he sall report our hearty and special thanks, sae sall ye find us ready to requite your courtesy and good-will with nae less pleasure in any the like gates [ways] as occasion sall present.'

MAR. 29 and 30. The equinoctial gale of this year is described by a contemporary chronicler as of extreme violence. He says, with regard to the two days marginally noted: 'The wind was so extraordinary tempestuous and violent, that it caused great shipwreck in Scotland, England, France, and the Netherlands. It blew trees by the roots, ruined whole villages, and caused the sea and many rivers so

[1] *Letters and Papers of the Reign of King James VI.*, p. 76.

to overflow their wonted limits and bounds, that many people and chattels were drowned and perished.'—*Bal.* 1606.

An outbreak of touchiness on heraldic matters, which recently took place in Scotland, excited some surprise amongst English statesmen and others. It is certain, however, that wherever two nations are associated under one monarchy, the smaller usually manifests no small amount of jealousy regarding its national flag and every other thing which marks its distinction and may have been associated with the national history. The government of Sweden is at this day under constant anxiety regarding the rampant lion and battle-axe of the Norwegian flag, lest on any occasion due honour should not be paid to it, and feelings of international hostility be thereby engendered.

When the Scottish king added England and Ireland to his dominions, his native subjects manifested the utmost jealousy regarding their heraldic ensigns; and some troubles in consequence arose between them and their English neighbours, especially at sea. We find that at this time, 'for composing of some difference between his subjects of North and South Britain travelling by seas, anent the bearing of their flags, and for avoiding all such contentions hereafter,' the king issued a proclamation, ordaining 'the ships of both nations to carry on their main-tops the flags of St Andrew and St George interlaced, and those of North Britain in their stern that of St Andrew, and those of South Britain that of St George.'—*Bal.* APR. 12.

In an early and rude state of society, bankruptcy is always looked on with harshness, and punished cruelly; and perhaps it is really then less excusable than it becomes when commerce is more advanced, and the returns of transactions can less certainly be calculated on. Even Venice in old times had its stone of shame for bankrupts. Well, then, might Edinburgh have one in 1606. At the date noted in the margin, the Privy Council ordered the magistrates of that city to erect 'ane pillory of hewen stone near the Mercat Cross; upon the head thereof ane seat to be made, whereupon in time coming sall be set all *dyvours*,[1] wha sall sit thereon ane mercat-day, from ten hours in the morning till ane hour after dinner.'[2] The unfortunates were obliged to wear a yellow bonnet on these occasions, and for ever after—the livery of slavery MAY 17.

[1] Bankrupts. [2] Maitland's *History of Edinburgh*.

1606. in the middle ages, and of which we have a relic in the under-clothes of the Christ's Hospital boys in London.

An act of the Lords of Session in 1688 is more particular regarding the indignities to be visited upon dyvours. It 'ordains the magistrates of the burgh (where the debtor is incarcerated), before his liberation out of prison, to cause him take on, and wear upon his head, a bonnet, partly of a brown, and partly of a yellow colour, with uppermost hose, or stockings, on his legs, half-brown and half-yellow coloured, conform to a pattern delivered to the magistrates of Edinburgh, to be keeped in their Tolbooth; and that they cause take the dyvour to the Mercat Cross, betwixt ten and eleven o'clock in the fore noon, with the foresaid habit, where he is to sit upon the dyvour-stone, the space of ane hour, and then to be dismissed; and ordains the dyvour to wear the said habit in all time thereafter; and in case he be found either wanting or disguising the samen, he shall lose the benefit of his bonorum.'[1]

JULY 1. A parliament met at Perth, chiefly with a view to reinstating the bishops in those revenues which alone could make them efficient in their office. They themselves appeared for the first time during many years in a style calculated to impress the senses of the people. The king had taken care that they, as well as the nobility, should wear ceremonial dresses.[2] In the 'riding' or equestrian procession to the parliament house, they took their place immediately after the earls, 'all in silk and velvet foot-mantles, by pairs, two and two, and St Andrews, the great Metropolitan, alone by himself, and ane of the ministers of no small quality, named Arthur Futhie, with his cap at his knee, walkit at his stirrup along the street.' 'This was called the *Red Parliament*, whilk in old prophecies was talked many years ago sould be keepit in St Johnston, because all the noblemen and officers of estate came riding thereto and sat therein, with red gowns and hoods, after the manner of England, for ane new solemnity; whilk many did interpret a token of the red fire of God's wrath to be kindled both upon kirk and country.'—*Ja. Mel.*

At this parliament appeared two western nobles between whose families there had long subsisted great enmity—namely, the Earls

[1] *Acts of Sederunt*, p. 161.

[2] The Privy Council in the previous April had passed an act, 'that the haill marquisses and earls of this kingdom sall leave off their former resolution anent the wearing of velvet robes in time of parliament,' and 'that they sall provide themselves with robes of red scarlet cloth again the next session, &c.'—*Maitland Club Misc.*, i. 147.

of Eglintoun and Glencairn. Notwithstanding the known anxiety of the king for an oblivion of all such 'deidly feids,' the two earls and their respective attendants came to a collision on the street. 'It lasted fra seven till ten hours at night, with great skaith,' one man of the Glencairn party being slain outright. It was not without great exertion on the part of the citizens that the tumult was quelled. 1606.

This feud, which was of early origin, acquired fresh stimulus from the murder of the Earl of Eglintoun by Cunningham of Robertland in 1586, the Earl of Glencairn, as head of the Cunninghams, being held as in some degree answerable for, and bound to protect, the actual assassin. The affair now involved the Lord Semple and other men of consequence in the west, and it took no small pains on the part of the king and his Scottish ministers to get it composed.

The reconciliation of the Earl of Glencairn with Lord Semple took place in a formal and public manner, at the command of the Privy Council, nearly three years afterwards (May 22, 1609). The scene of this important transaction was the Green of Glasgow. On the occasion, 'for eschewing of all inconvenients of trouble whilk may happen (whilk God forbid!),' the town-council arranged that the provost with one of the bailies and whole council should go to the place, attended by forty citizens in arms, while the other two bailies, each attended by sixty of the citizens with 'lang weapons and swords,' should 'accompany and convoy the said noblemen, with their friends, in and out, in making their reconciliation.'—*M. of G.*

Glasgow—now a city of 400,000 inhabitants, and the scene of a marvellous concentration of the industrial energies of the nineteenth century—how curious to look in upon it in 1606! when it was only a small burgh and university town, containing perhaps 5000 inhabitants at the utmost, some of them merchants (that is, shopkeepers), others craftsmen—not such folk, however, as would now be found carrying on trade and the useful arts in a burgh of the same size, but men accustomed to the use of arms, and the exercise of the violent passions which call arms into use—not inspired with the independent political ideas of our time, but trained to look up to the great landlords of their neighbourhood as leaders to be in all things followed: in short, a small burgal community, retaining a strong tinge of the old feudal system. JULY.

The city was at this time the scene of 'a very great trouble and JULY 5.

1606. commotion,' arising from a change which had been made in the system of municipal election. The change seems to have been effected in legal and proper manner by Sir George Elphinstone, the provost; but it was odious to a neighbouring knight, Sir Matthew Stewart of Minto, whose ancient local influence it threatened to subvert. He accordingly wrought upon the 'crafts' of the burgh, till he induced them to believe that the new system was a gross tyranny to their order. They consequently held a meeting in the house of a citizen—an act unlawful, without the sanction of the magistrates—ostensibly to get up a petition, but in reality armed for action with swords, targes, and other abulyiements. Climbing up to the platform of the Market Cross, they proclaimed their remonstrance against the new arrangements, in the sight of the magistrates, who sat in their council-house close by. It was believed that the object of the insurgents was to provoke the magistrates to come out and interfere with their proceedings; which might have been made a pretence for involving them in a murderous quarrel. But 'God furnished the magistrates with patience to abide all their indignities.' They even so far deferred to the popular party, as to appoint a day when they might meet and argue out their differences.

According to the provost and magistrates, in a complaint which they sent to the Privy Council, this peaceful measure did not suit the views of Sir Matthew Stewart and his friends. Accordingly, 'knawing that, upon the twenty-three day of the month, whilk was the day preceding the appointit time of meeting, Sir George was to go to the archery, they made choice of that time and occasion, to work their turn.' Sir Walter Stewart, son of Sir Matthew, with John and Alexander Stewarts, 'lay in wait for him and his company, wha were but five in number, without ony kind of armour, saufing their bows; and perceiving them, about seven hours at even, come up the Dry-gate, of purpose to have passed to the *Castle butts,* and there to have endit their game, and James Forrat, ane of Sir George's company, going to his awn house with his bow disbendit in his hand, to have fetchit some Bute arrows; Sir Walter thought meet to mak the first onset upon him, and thereby to draw Sir George back.' The assault upon Forrat having caused a great cry to arise, Sir George returned through the Castle port to learn what was the matter, when, meeting young Minto in the act of pursuing the unarmed man, he remonstrated first in gentle words, and then in language more emphatic, finally commanding him in the king's name to desist and go home. Hereupon

a party of forty, all armed with steel bonnets, secrets, plait sleeves, 1606.
'lang staffs,' and other weapons, issued from the wynd-head, where they had been concealed, and, joining with young Minto, drove Sir George and his small party of friends back to the Castle port, where they were happily relieved from present danger. Being thus disappointed of their purpose, the rioters retired to the wynd-head, and presently sent off one of their number down the High Gait to rouse the other citizens. This man, James Braidwood, ran along crying, 'Arm you! arm you! They are yokit!' whereupon a great number of the seditious faction, including Sir Matthew Stewart of Minto himself, assembled in arms, and joining the other party at the wynd-head, came in full force, and in the most furious manner to the Castle, where, but for the interposition of the Earl of Wigton and two other privy-councillors, who were present, they would certainly have slain their provost. 'Seeing they could not win towards Sir George with lang staffs and weapons, they despitefully cast stanes at him.' Then, refusing to obey the commands of the privy-councillors to go peaceably home, 'they past tumultuously down the gait to the Barras Yett, far beneath the Cross, and come up the gait again with three hundred persons, with drawn swords in their hands, some of the rascal multitude crying: "I sall have this buith, and thou sall have that buith!" and of new assailit the Castle port, with full purpose by force to have enterit within the same.' It was alleged that, but for the courageous resistance of the three noble privy-councillors, they would have accomplished the destruction of Sir George Elphinstone on this occasion. As it was, they laid violent hands on three several magistrates who came to his help, altogether 'committing manifest insolency and insurrection within the said city, to the great trouble and inquietation thereof, and ane evil example to others to do the like hereafter.'

Such was the Elphinstone story regarding this tumult. It was, however, met by a counter-complaint from young Minto, to the following effect. He was, he said, 'coming down the Rotton Raw, in peaceable and quiet maner to his awn lodging, accompanit only with twa servants,' when 'he perceivit Sir George Elphinstone with nine or ten persons in his company, coming up the Dry Gait.' Although he was in the straight way for his lodging, 'yet in respect of some dryness between Sir George and him, he left that gait, and past ane other way, of purpose to have eschewit all occasion of trouble and unquietness betwixt them.' Here, however, 'James Forrat, ane of Sir George's company, cast him directly in the complainer's way, and pressit to have stayit his passage.' When

1606. young Minto 'soberly found fault with him,' Forrat 'immediately bendit his bow, and had not failed to have shot and slain him, were not ane in company with the complainer cuttit the bow-string.' Whereupon, according to the recital, Sir George Elphinstone and his servants fell upon young Minto and his servants in the most violent manner with their swords, and would certainly have slain them, if they had not by God's providence escaped.—*P. C. R.*

We learn from another source, that, after all, 'the skaith was not great; only ane man callit Thomas Cloggy died, without ony wound, and sundry hurt with staves.'[1]

The government authorities must have felt puzzled by this local squabble, and hardly known how to apportion punishment amongst the parties. The Minto knights were ordered into ward in Dumbarton Castle, and Sir George Elphinstone in the castle of Glasgow, till his majesty's pleasure should be known. The Privy Council afterwards absolved young Minto from the charge of being the aggressor in the conflict of the 23d July; but the two knights and their principal supporters were confined for some time in Linlithgow, on account of the general 'insolency' of which they had been guilty.

There is something affecting in the history of the families concerned in this tumult. A mural tablet in Glasgow cathedral commemorated the names of six or eight Stewarts of Minto in succession, 'knights created under the banner,' and men of great sway in the district. But when M'Ure wrote his *History of Glasgow* in 1736, the family was 'mouldered so quite away, that the heir in our time was reduced to a state of penury little short of beggary.' A memorandum of Paton, the antiquary, queried, 'If true that the last of the family was a poor boy sent into Edinburgh barefooted with a letter to Stewart of Coltness, who [being] promising, was recommended to the Duke of Hamilton, got some education, and afterwards went abroad to Darien, where he died.' Sir George Elphinstone, who had been the familiar servant and friend of King James, acquired a great estate at Glasgow, and after this time rose to be Lord Justice-clerk, nevertheless 'died so poor, that his corpse was arrested by his creditors, and his friends buried him privately in his own chapel adjoining his house.' His family went out in the second generation.

[1] Letter of the three privy-councillors, in *Letters and State Papers of the Reign of James VI.*, p. 84.

While the attention of the people was absorbed by the matter of the bishops and their robes and renewed dignity, the consequences of the continual neglect of those natural conditions on which their physical health depended were about to be once more and most severely felt. The *pest* broke out and spread over the more populous districts with frightful rapidity. 'It raged so extremely in all the corners of the kingdom, that neither burgh nor land in any part was free. The burghs of Ayr and Stirling were almost desolate; and all the judicatories of the land were deserted.'—*Bal.* It was not till the middle of winter that it sensibly declined. 1606. Aug.

The chancellor wrote to the king in October, that scarcely any part of the country was free of the scourge. 'This calamity,' he says, 'hinders all meetings of Council, and all public functions for ministration of justice and maintenance of good rule and government, except sic as we tak at starts, with some few, at Edinburgh, or in sic other place for a day, to keep some countenance of order.'

The unconforming clergy now imprisoned at Blackness wrote a petition for mercy to the king (August 23), in which they describe the state of the country under its present affliction. They speak of 'the destroying angel hewing down day and night continually, in sic a number in some of our congregations, that the like thereof has not been heard many years before.' They add: 'What is most lamentable, they live and die comfortless under the fearful judgment, filling the heaven and the earth with their sighs, sobs, and cries of their distressed souls, for being deprived not only of all outward comforts (whilk were great also), but also of all inward consolation, through the want of the ordinary means of their peace and life, to wit, the preaching of the word of our ministry.'[1]

We have a remarkable trait of the treatment of the pest in outlying districts, in a bond granted on this occasion by some Aberdeenshire gentlemen to the burgh of Dundee for five hundred merks, as requital for their sending two professional *clengers* from their town to the valley of the Dee, that they might deal with an infection which had fallen forth in the house of Mr Thomas Burnet, minister of Strathauchan, and in the house of John Burnet of Slowy—two places divided by the river, but both on the line of the great road leading from the south to the north of Scotland. The country gentlemen, on hearing of the infection in their district, had been obliged to convene and devise measures for meeting the calamity.

[1] Melville's *Diary*, p. 648.

1606. Their first step was to send for two *clengers* a hundred miles off to come with all speed, although at a high cost, which the gentlemen, as we see, were obliged to pay in behalf of themselves and neighbours.[1]

Another trait of the public economy regarding this pestilence occurs in the record of the Privy Council. It was represented to that august body on the 2d of September, that 'certain lodges' had been 'biggit by James Lawrieston and David and George Hamiltons, upon the common muir of Gogar, for the ease and relief of certain their tenants, infectit with the pest;' but Thomas Majoribanks, portioner of Ratho, and other persons had cast down these lodges, apparently on the plea that the erecting of them was an intrusion on their property. The Council found that the muir was common property, and ordered the lodges to be rebuilt by those who had originally set them up, on the part of the muir nearest to their own grounds, 'where they may have the best commodity of water,' the other party being at the same time forbidden to interfere under heavy penalties.—*P. C. R.*

Sep. 4. The Chancellor Dunfermline intimated to the king the pitiful case of the inhabitants of Dumbarton, their town being unable to defend themselves against 'the surges and inundations of the sea, which is likely to destroy and tak away their haill town, and cannot be repulsit by nae moyen their poor ability and fortunes are able to furnish.' Those who were appointed to inquire into the matter now reported that it would require at least thirty thousand pounds Scots to make a proper bulwark. It was proposed to defray this charge by a tax on the country.[2]

Sep. 'George, Earl of Dunbar, his majesty's commissioner for ordering the Borders, took such a course with the broken men and sorners [there], that, in two justiciary-courts halden by him, he condemned and caused hang above a hundred and forty of the nimblest and most powerful thieves in all the Borders . . . . and fully reduced the other inhabitants there to the obedience of his majesty's laws.' —*Bal.* The chancellor told the king next month that the Borders were now 'satled, far by onything that ever has been done there before.'[3]

[1] These particulars are derived from a fragment of the deed entered into by the gentlemen for payment of the money.

[2] *Letters, &c., of the Reign of James VI.*

[3] Ibid., p. 89.

It was declared a few months later (November 20), that one of the principal difficulties experienced by the emissaries of government in executing justice on the Borders lay in the strength of the houses in which the 'thieves and limmers' dwelt or took refuge, and particularly the 'iron yetts' with which these houses were furnished. The Privy Council therefore ordained that all iron yetts in houses belonging to persons below the rank of barons, should be 'removit and turnit in plew irons or sic other necessar wark as to the awners sall seem expedient.'—*P. C. R.* 1606.

These iron gates, of which many specimens still survive in ancient country-houses in Scotland, are composed grill-wise, the bars curiously interlacing with each other, and generally with huge staples and padlocks. Such a gate, made in 1568 for Kilravock Castle, Nairnshire, by George Robertson, smith in Elgin, weighed thirty-four stone three pounds, and cost '£34, 3s. 9d. usual money, together with three bolls meal, ane stane butter, and ane stane cheese.'[1]

The six clergymen who had been tried for treason, on account of their refusal to break up the General Assembly at Aberdeen, and who had been condemned to banishment, were sent forth of the kingdom at Leith, after a long confinement in Blackness Castle. The punishment, it may be remarked, would have been remitted if they would have acknowledged their alleged offence and come in the king's will. Nov. 7.

'The 6 of November, about four afternoon, they were desired to come to the boat whilk was prepared for them by the water-bailie of Leith and Edinburgh; who, obeying, came, accompanied with some of their dearest friends and wives, to the pier, where there was a good number of people waiting on, to tak the guid-night at them, and to see them; but after their coming thither, Mr John Welch conceived a prayer, whilk bred great motion in the hearts of all the hearers. Prayers ended, they took guid-night of their friends, wives, and many other weel-wishers who were present, [and] entered into the boat, where they remained a guid space waiting on the skipper.' The skipper not being ready to weigh that night, 'they were desired by the water-bailie either to go aboard and lie in the ship that night, or else to go to their lodging, and be ready at the next call.

'They, by God's special providence, chused to go to their

[1] *Geneal. Deduction of Fam. of Rose of Kilravock*, Spald. Club, p. 249.

1606. lodging; for that night came on a great storm, [so] that the ship was forced to save herself in Kinghorn road all that night. They were called again by two hours in the morning, who, obeying, came to the shore and pier, accompanied as the night before, no small concourse of people being with them, beyond expectation, so early to see them boat. Prayer conceived as before by Mr John Welch, they embarked, giving many exhortations to all to hold fast the truth of the doctrine whilk they had delivered; for the whilk they doubted nothing to lay down their lives, let be to suffer banishment; adding thereto, that whilk they suffered was the great joy of their conscience. In the meantime, the mariners hasted them away . . . . they departed out of our sight, making us hear the comfortable joy whilk they had in God, in singing a psalm.'[1]

While Protestant clergymen of the puritan type were thus suffering, and evoking by their fortitude the deserved sympathy and admiration of large masses of their countrymen, they were so far from being alone in martyrdom, that suffering was inflicted upon another class of religionists, if not at their dictation, at least with their full approval. The Earl of Angus, one of the three Catholic lords whose correspondence with Spain caused so much trouble sixteen years before, had since lived at home in quietness and obedience. It was not many months after the embarkation of the six Presbyterian ministers at Leith, that we find his lordship pleading that, to avoid imprisonment for his religion, he might be allowed to go into exile—thus calling for the punishment inflicted upon the six clergymen, as a kind of relief from the more severe penalties demanded against him by the party to which these clergymen belonged. In a letter to the king, August 10, 1608, adverting to the fact of the General Assembly having given forth an act for his immediate excommunication, he says: 'What grief and sorrow this brings to my heart, God knows; because my greatest care has ever been, and sall be, that I might end my days (whilk, I am persuaded, will not be many) at peace with God, and in your majesty's obedience. . . . . The permission whilk of grace only I crave (gif it please not your hieness to ease me with a better) is either to depart this country . . . . with surety not to return, or else that it wald please your majesty to confine me in ane of mine awn houses, and so mony miles about the same, where I am glad to live as

[1] Letter in James Melville's *Diary*, Wodrow Club ed., p. 671.

ane private subject, and never to meddle me with public affairs, but by your majesty's direction.' 1606.

The earl was compelled to leave his country, and he died at Paris three years after, aged fifty-seven. In his epitaph, he is made to say—'jussus, religionis causâ, patriâ excedere aut in custodiam pergere, vitæ quietiori turbinibus averruncandis delegeram Galliam, caram alteram Scotis patriam.'

The utter unconsciousness of the persecuted Presbyterians of there being any harm in visiting the papists with the like severities might almost provoke a smile. While the six ministers lay in expectation of banishment, their brethren detained in England received a visit from Law, Bishop of Orkney. The conversation turned on the present state of the church in Scotland, and the bishop endeavoured to convince them that the royal policy was right, as the same Linlithgow convention which had condemned the six recusant ministers had 'taken strait order with the papists.' Seeing they appeared to have no great faith in that demonstration, the bishop endeavoured to reassure them. '*They shall call me a false knave*,' said he, '*and never to be believed again, if the papists be not sae handled as they never were in Scotland*.'[1]

The Privy Council had some time ago issued a proclamation, Dec. 23. forbidding what was called the *backing of pairties to the bar*—that is, each party in a lawsuit coming into court with a number of friends and favourers behind him, with a view to exercising some influence over the course of justice. Finding that the former denouncement of 'this indecent and unseemly custom' had not been attended with any effect, partly through the public being unacquainted with it, and partly through the negligence of the officers of the law, the Council now renewed their proclamation, with assurance that their orders would in future be strictly acted upon. The reader will find that the practice continued in force some years later.—*P. C. R.*

At this time, Gordon of Gight, Forbes of Corsindae, and some 1607. Jan. 20. others, formed themselves into what they called the Society of the Boys—much after the manner perhaps of the White Boys of Ireland, in more recent times. They bound themselves by oath to consider all quarrels as common amongst them, and

[1] Melville's *Diary*, p. 688.

1606. are accused of having committed 'open and avowed reifs, herships, and other enormities, in all parts where they be maisters and commanders.' All this appears from a letter of the Privy Council, of date January 20, 1607, to the Marquis of Huntly, commanding him to take order for their suppression, 'as your lordship wald eschew that hard censure and construction which his majesty maun mak of your behaviour in this point.'

It will be remembered that Gight was a Catholic, and the probability is that this fraternity of the Boys was simply a desperate effort on his part and that of his co-religionists to repel, as far as they could, the persecutions to which they were subjected.

However this might be, we soon after (April 2) find the Council engaged in trying to bring George Gordon of Gight to justice for sundry popish practices of which he was alleged to have been guilty. It was charged against him that, at the burial of his mother, Isobel Ochterlony, on a particular day in the year 1604, he had caused his tenant, David Wilson, to 'carry ane crucifix upon ane speir immediately before the corpse;' in like manner, at the burial of the late William Gordon of Gight in 1605, he had caused George Crawford, his servant, to 'bear ane crucifix upon ane speir the haill way before the body;' he being personally present on both occasions: 'whereby, as he has offendit God, slanderit his kirk and haly ministry, sae he has committit a very great contempt against his majesty, and has violate his hieness' laws and acts of parliament.' The laird and his two dependents having failed to appear on several former occasions, the officers of justice were now directed to go to them, and command them to enter as prisoners in Edinburgh Castle within fifteen days, on pain of rebellion.—*P. C. R.*

The immediate results of these measures do not appear. Seven years after (February 1614), we learn that the Lairds of Gight and Newton, both Gordons, and both Catholics, were sentenced by the Privy Council to perpetual banishment, and 'never to set foot in Scotland under pain of death, unless they submit themselves to the orders of the church;' that is, embrace the Protestant faith as professed in Scotland.

However it was as to their faith, the Gight Gordons are found in their usual place in Aberdeenshire only two years after this time. See under December 1615.

APR. The pest broke out again in Dundee, Perth, and other parts of the country.—*Ab. C. R.*

The Privy Council refer to 'a very ancient and lovable custom,' of giving a blue gown, purse, and as many Scotch shillings as agreed with the years of the king's age, to as many 'auld puir men' as likewise agreed with the king's years; and seeing it to be 'very necessary and expedient that the said custom should be continuit,' they give orders accordingly.—*P. C. R.* 1607. JUNE 2.

The 'auld puir men' so favoured were called the King's Bedesmen, and were privileged to go about the country as beggars, notwithstanding any general enactments that might exist against mendicancy. Their blue cloak bore a pewter badge which assured them of this right. They were expected to requite the king's bounty by their prayers; and, doubtless, as they had such an interest in the increase of his years, their intercessions for his prolonged life must have been sincere. The distribution of their cloaks and purses used to take place on the king's birthday, at the end of the Tolbooth of Edinburgh, till a time not long gone by.

A sad account is given of the country of Athole. This province, 'whilk of auld was maist quiet and peaceable, and inhabit be a number of civil and answerable gentlemen, professed and avowed enemies to thieves, robbers, and oppressors,' is described as having 'now become very louss and broken,' 'ane ordinary resett for the thieves and broken men of the north and south Hielands;' moreover, a great number of the native people, 'sic as John Dow M'Gillicallum and his complices,' shaking off all fear of God and reverence for his majesty and the laws, 'are become maist insolent, committing wild and detestable murders, open reifs, privy stouthrie, barbarous houghing and goring of oxen, and other enormities,' without hinderance or challenge. JUNE 30.

The Privy Council ordered the immediate reappointment of a guard or watch for the country, such as was customary. James Gordon of Lesmoir undertook to apprehend John Dow and his brother Allaster; and when many attempts had failed, 'in end lichtit upon the limmers.' 'After a lang and het combat, and the slauchter of four or five of the principals of them, the said Allaster was apprehendit, and John, being very evil hurt, by the darkness of the night escaped.' Allaster, who had many murders on his head, was brought to Edinburgh, and laid in irons in the Tolbooth, notwithstanding many offers from his friends for his liberation. He was in due time tried and executed.—*P. C. R.* AUG.

David, Master of Crawford, was noted as a wicked and lawless

1607. man. In the course of his violent proceedings in the district where he possessed influence—Forfarshire—he had slaughtered (October 25, 1605) Sir Walter Lyndsay of Balgavies. This brought out the violent feelings of the young Laird of Edzell, whom we have already seen engaged in matters of blood. Young Edzell and his brother determined to avenge the slaughter of their uncle, Sir Walter, upon the Master of Crawford, who was also their near relation.

JULY 5. One summer evening, between nine and ten o'clock, the Master of Crawford was walking up the High Street of Edinburgh, accompanied by his uncle, Alexander, Lord Spynie, and Sir James Douglas of Drumlanrig. Lord Spynie was a popular character, a favourite courtier of King James, and uncle to both the Master of Crawford and young Edzell. Knowing the revengeful design of the latter person, he had been endeavouring to bring about a peace between him and the Master; but his well-meant efforts were destined only to result in his own death. At this very time young Edzell was lying in wait with eight armed men to attack the Master. The three gentlemen approach, and are in a moment beset by the ambushed party; sword-strokes and pistol-shots are exchanged; the Master and Drumlanrig are severely wounded, and Lord Spynie receives mortal hurt. Young Edzell then withdrew his party.

Drumlanrig recovered from his wounds with difficulty; Lord Spynie died of his in eleven days. Thus the innocent alone suffered from this attempt at 'wild justice;' the very kind of event which wild justice is most apt to bring about, and for which it is chiefly to be condemned.

Young Edzell fled, with the dismal pain upon his conscience of having caused the violent death of his own uncle, whom he had ever regarded with affection. To escape justice, he was compelled to retire to the remotest parts of his paternal property in the Braes of Angus. Meanwhile, his father suffered great harassment from the law on his account, and was soon brought down in sorrow to the grave. It cost the son a good estate and ten thousand merks to settle matters ultimately with the heirs of Lord Spynie.[1]

JULY. A tragical event, which now occurred at Dornoch in Sutherland, is related in a characteristic manner by Sir Robert Gordon.

'About the year 1585, there came into Sutherland one called Mr

[1] Pitcairn. *Lives of the Lyndsays. Lands of the Lyndsays.*

William Pape, a reasonable good scholar, and of a quick and ready wit. This man was first admitted to be schoolmaster in the town of Dornoch; then he was appointed to be resident minister in that same place; and withal he came to be chanter of Caithness. In progress of time, by his virtue and diligence, he became wealthy, and of good account in the county of Sutherland. His two brethren, Charles and Thomas, perceiving his good success, came also thither out of Ross, where they were born, thinking to settle their fortunes with their elder brother. Thomas Pape was made chancellor of Caithness, and minister at Rogart. Charles Pape was a public notary, and a messenger-at-arms; who, being of an affable and merry conversation, did so behave himself that he procured the love of his master, the Earl of Sutherland, and the good liking of all his countrymen, so that in the end he was made sheriff-clerk of Sutherland. These three brethren married in Sutherland, and anchored their fortunes in that country; but as wealth and prosperity often beget pride, so doth pride bring with it a certain contempt of others. These brethren, dwelling for the most part in Dornoch, being both provident and wealthy, thought by progress of time to purchase and buy the most part of the tenements of that town, and drive the ancient and natural inhabitants from their possessions; which the townsmen in end perceiving, they grudged in their hearts, though they could take no just exceptions thereat, seeing that these brethren did purchase the same with their money; yet they concluded with themselves to utter their hatred and revenge when occasion should serve. So at last, upon a particular quarrel which began between one of these brethren, and one of the inhabitants of the town, their ruin thus followed: 1607.

'Every man being departed from the town of Dornoch unto this convention at Strathullie [to resist an invasion of the Earl of Caithness], except William Moray, a bowyer, and some few others, who were also ready to go away the next morning. Mr William and Mr Thomas Pape, with some others of the ministry, had a meeting at Dornoch concerning some of the church affairs. After they had dissolved their meeting, they went to breakfast to an inn or victualling-house of the town. As they were at breakfast, one John Macphail entered the house and asked some drink for his money, which the mistress of the house refused to give him, thereby to be rid of his company, because she knew him to be a brawling fellow. John Macphail, taking this refusal in evil part, reproved the woman, and spoke somewhat stubbornly to the ministers, who began to excuse her; whereupon Thomas Pape did

1607. threaten him, and he again did thrust into Thomas's arm an arrow with a broad-forked head, which then he held in his hand. So being parted and set asunder at that time, Mr William and his brother Thomas came the same evening into the churchyard, with their swords about them; which John Macphail perceiving, and taking it as a provocation, he went with all diligence and acquainted his nephew, Hutcheon Macphail, and his brother-in-law, William Moray the bowyer, therewith; who being glad to find this occasion whereby to revenge their old grudge against these brethren, they hastened forth, and meeting with them in the churchyard, they fell a quarrelling, and from quarrelling to fighting. Charles Pape had been all that day abroad; and at his return, understanding in what case his brethren were, he came in a preposterous haste to the fatal place of his end and ruin. They fought a little while; in the end, Charles hurt William Moray in the face, and thereupon William Moray killed him. Mr William and Thomas were both extremely wounded by John Macphail and his nephew Hutcheon, and were lying in that place for dead persons, without hope of recovery; but they recovered afterwards beyond expectation. The offenders escaped, because there was none in the town to apprehend them (except such as favoured them), the inhabitants being all gone to the assembly at Strathullie. John Macphail and his nephew Hutcheon have both since ended their days in Holland. William Moray yet lives (reserved, as I should suppose, to a greater judgment). Mr William Pape and his brother Thomas thereupon left the county of Sutherland, and settled themselves in Ross, where Thomas now dwelleth. Mr William died in the town of Nigg, where he was planted minister. Thus did these brethren begin and end in this country; which I have declared at length to shew us thereby that man in full prosperity should never think too much of himself, nor contemn others, upon whom it hath not pleased God to bestow such measure of gifts and benefits.'—*G. H. S.*

Aug. 5. A parliamentary enactment had appointed the 5th of August to be kept as a holiday, on account of the king's escape from the Gowrie treason. On this occasion, the day 'was solemnly kept in Edinburgh. The king's scoll [health] was drunk by the duke his commissioner, and some other noblemen, at the Cross of Edinburgh, which was covered for the greater solemnity. Bacchus was set up, and much wine drunk, and sweetmeats cast about; much vanity and pastime, beside ringing of bells, and setting on of balefires. *The pest brake up soon after.*'—*Cal.*

The death of the late Lord Maxwell in the battle of Dryfe's Sands left a feeling of deadly bitterness in his son's mind against the name of Johnston. A series of turbulent proceedings, marking the untamable spirit of the young lord, ended in his being warded in the Castle of Edinburgh, where he had for a fellow-prisoner a Hebridean magnate of similar character and history—Sir James M'Connel or Macdonald. 1607.

'Seeing not how he was to be relieved, he devises with Sir James M'Connel and Robert Maxwell of Dinwoodie, what way he and they might escape. So, he calls ane great number of the keepers of the Castle into his chalmer, where he drinks them all fou.' Pretending to act a sort of play, he asked them for their swords as part of the performance; and having thus armed himself and his two companions, he passed out with them, locking the door behind him. The three passed to the inner gate, where a servant stood in the way, holding the porter in parley. The latter, an old man, tried to make resistance. 'False knave,' cried Maxwell, 'open the yett, or I shall hew thee in blads' [pieces]. He did strike the man in the arm, and likewise wounded another keeper in the hand. Then he and Sir James 'passed to the west castle-wall that goes to the West Port of Edinburgh,' and climbing over it, leaped down, and disappeared amongst the suburbs. Robert Maxwell, however, was locked in and detained. The insular chieftain, who had irons upon him, was seized in an attempt to conceal himself in a dunghill, while Lord Maxwell escaped on a horse which had been kept in readiness for him. 'The king was very far offended, and made proclamation that nane should reset him under the pain of death.'[1] Dec. 4.

'A vehement frost continued from Martinmas till the 20th of February. The sea froze so far as it ebbed, and sundry went into ships upon ice and played at the *chamiare* a mile within the sea-mark. Sundry passed over the Forth a mile above Alloa and Airth, to the great admiration of aged men, who had never seen the like in their days.'—*Cal.* Nov.

The keenness and duration of this frost was marked by the rare occurrence of a complete freezing of the Thames at London, where accordingly a fair was held upon the ice. In Scotland, rivers and springs were stopped; the young trees were killed, and birds and beasts perished in great numbers. Men, travelling on their affairs,

[1] See depositions of witnesses, &c., in Pitcairn, iii. 47.

1607. suffered numbness and lassitude to a desperate degree. Their very joints were frozen; and unless they could readily reach a shelter, their danger was very great. In the following spring, the fruit-trees shewed less growth than usual; and in many places the want of singing-birds was remarked.—*Jo. Hist.*

1608. 'The Lord Maxwell, being proclaimed traitor after the breaking out of ward in the Castle of Edinburgh, and thereupon driven to great straits, sent to the Laird of Johnston, craved a meeting, pretending he would now be heartily reconciled with him, and not for the fashion, as he was before at the king's pleasure, because he perceived he did not trouble him now, being an outlaw, as
Apr. 6. he looked for. They meet at the place appointed, Maxwell and one with him, Johnston and another with him; and Sir Robert Maxwell of Spotts (near cousin to the Lord Maxwell, and brother-in-law to the Laird of Johnston), who was employed by Maxwell to draw on the tryst. They meet on horseback, and salute each other heartily in outward show, and went apart to confer together. While Johnston and Maxwell are conferring apart, Maxwell's second began to quarrel Johnston's second, [and] shot a pistolet at him, whereupon he fell. Johnston, hearing the shot, cried "Treason!" and, riding from Maxwell to the two gentlemen, to understand what the matter meant, Maxwell shooteth him behind the back. So Johnston fell, and died of the shot. Soon after, proclamation was made at the Cross of Edinburgh, that none, under pain of death, transport or carry away the Lord Maxwell out of the country, in ship or craer, seeing the king and Council was to take order with him, for the traitorous murdering of the Laird of Johnston and his other offences.'—*Cal.*

'The fact was detested by all honest men, and the gentleman's misfortune sore lamented; for he was a man full of wisdom and courage, and every way well inclined, and to have been by his too much confidence in this sort treacherously cut off, was a thing most pitiful. Maxwell, ashamed of that he had done, forsook the country, and had his estate forfeited.'—*Spot.*

Horse-racing was early practised as a popular amusement in Scotland. In 1552, there was an arrangement for an annual horse-race at Haddington, the prize being, as usual, a silver bell. Early in the reign of James VI., there were races at both Peebles and Dumfries. The Peebles race was accustomed to take place on Beltane-day, the 1st of May; it was the chief surviving part of the

festivities which had from an early period distinguished the day 1608.
and place, and which were celebrated in the old poem of *Peebles to the Play*.

The great difficulty attending such popular festivals arose from the tendency of the people to mark them with bloodshed. Men assembled there from different parts of the country, each having of course his peculiar enmities, and the object of similar enmities in his turn; and when they met and had somewhat inflamed themselves with liquor, it was scarcely avoidable that mutual provocations should be given, leading to conflicts with deadly weapons. So great reason was there now for fearing a sanguinary scene at
Peebles, that the Lords of Council thought proper to issue a APR. 28.
proclamation forbidding the race to take place.[1]—*P. C. R.*

This day commenced an unfortunate adventure of the king for MAY 8.
obtaining silver in certain mines at Hilderstone in the county of Linlithgow. Some years before, a collier, named Sandy Maund, wandering about the burn-sides in that district, chanced to pick up a stone containing veins of a clear metal, which proved to be silver. A gentleman of Linlithgow, to whom he shewed it, recommended him to go to Leadhills, and submit it to Sir Bevis Bulmer, who was engaged in gold-seeking there. The consequence was, that a search was made at Hilderstone for silver, and, some very hopeful masses of ore being found, a commission was appointed by the king, with the consent of Sir Thomas Hamilton, his majesty's advocate, the proprietor of the ground, for making a search for silver ore, with a view to trying it at the mint. In January 1608, thirty-eight barrels of ore, weighing in all 20,224 pounds, were won, packed, and sent to the Tower of London. It is said that this ore gave about twenty-four ounces of silver to every hundredweight,

[1] 28th April 1608. 'Forsameikle as the Lords of Secret Council are informit that there is ane horse-race appointit to be at Peblis the day of May nextocome, whereunto grit numbers of people of all qualities and ranks, intends to repair, betwixt whom there being quarrels, private grudges, and miscontentment, it is to be feirit that at their meeting upon fields, some troubles and inconvenients sall fall out amangs them, to the break of his Majesty's peace and disquieting of the country without remeed be providit; Therefore the Lords of Secret Council has dischargit, and be the tenor hereof discharges, the said horse-race, and ordains that the same sall be nawise halden nor keepit this year; for whilk purpose ordains letters to be direct, to command, charge, and inhibit all and sundry his Majesty's lieges and subjects by open proclamation at the mercat-cross of Peblis and other places needful, that nane of them presume nor tak upon them to convene and assemble themselves to the said race this present year, but to suffer that meeting and action to depart and cease, as they and ilk ane of them will answer upon the contrary at their heichest peril,' &c.

1608. while some gave double this quantity. Samuel Atkinson, who was engaged in working the mine, tells that on some days he won as much silver as was worth £100. The shaft, indeed, received the name of *God's Blessing*, as expressive of its fertile character. The whole results appearing favourable, the king's cupidity was excited, and he easily fell into the proposal of his astute councillor, Hamilton, to become the purchaser of *God's Blessing* for the sum of £5000, and work it at the public expense. Bulmer, created a knight, was its governor. There were 'drawers up of metal, drawers up of water, and lavers up of water to the pumps under the ground, shedders and washers, washers with the sieve, dressers and washers with the buddle, and washers with the canvas, quarriers, shoolmen,' and many other workers of different kinds. A mill for melting and fining the metal was established at Leith.[1] Another fining-mill and a stamp-mill, with warehouses, were built on the water running out of Linlithgow loch. Some Brunswick miners were brought to give the benefit of their skill. All, however, was of no avail. From the time of the transference of the mine into royal hands, it did no more good. After a persevering effort of two years and a half, the king gave up the adventure, with a loss of a considerable sum of money.

The same mine was granted, in 1613, to Sir William Alexander, Thomas Foulis, and Paulo Pinto, a Portuguese, to be wrought by them on the condition of their paying a tenth of the refined ore to the crown. What success attended this adventure is not known.

The scene of the mining operations is still traceable in a hollow place to the east of Cairn-apple Hill, four miles south of Linlithgow. A neighbouring excavation for limestone is named from it the *Silver-mine Quarry*: such is the only local memorial of the affair now existing.[2]

MAY 31. Margaret Hertsyde had entered the service of the queen in a humble capacity in Scotland, and accompanying her majesty to England, was there considerably advanced, and received from the queen many marks of favour. Enriched with the royal liberality, she returned to her native country as a great lady, attended by her husband, John Buchanan, who had been a servant

[1] This was probably at the place called Silver Mills, on the Water of Leith; now involved in the suburbs of Edinburgh.

[2] Atkinson's *Discoverie of Gold Mynes in Scotland* (Bann. Club), 1825. *Chron. Kings of Scotland.*

of the king. The pair attracted an invidious attention by the high airs they gave themselves, affecting by the purchase of land to become persons of quality, appearing in a carriage drawn by white horses, and apparently wholly forgetful of their humble origin. It was therefore with no great regret that the public learned that Margaret was apprehended, on suspicion of having taken jewellery from her royal mistress, to the value of upwards of £400 sterling. The unfortunate woman confessed her guilt to the queen ; but on her being brought to trial at Linlithgow, some technical difficulties arose as to how far a person could be considered guilty of theft who had only withheld unaccounted for certain articles of which she had been in trust. A direct conviction could not therefore be recorded. In these circumstances, by an irregularity which marks the character of the age, the king interfered with an order that Margaret Hertsyde be declared infamous and banished to Orkney. She was also adjudged to pay £400 sterling to the commissioner upon her majesty's dotarial estate of Dunfermline. A grave historian of that day moralises upon the case as a sad example of the mutability of fortune. 1608.

In 1619, 'her doom having been humbly and with great patience embraced and underlain by her, and her behaviour continually sin syne having been very dutiful,' Margaret so far succeeded in obtaining the king's grace as to have the reproach of infamy removed.—*Pit. Jo. Hist.*

By slow and safe steps, King James was constantly working for the subjection of Scottish ecclesiastical matters to an episcopal model. At this time, his favourite Scottish minister, the Earl of Dunbar, came down from London, accompanied by two eminent English divines, Dr Abbot (subsequently Archbishop of Canterbury) and Dr Higgins, while a third, named Maxy, came by sea. JUNE.

On the approach of the earl and his clerical associates, 'the noblemen, barons, and councillors that were in Edinburgh went out to accompany him into the town. So he entered in Edinburgh with a great train. The chancellor, then provost, the bailies, and many of the citizens, met him at the Nether Bow Port. It was spoken broadly that no small sums of money were sent down with him to be distributed among the ministers and sundry others. The English doctors seemed to have no other direction but to persuade the Scots that there was no substantial difference in JULY 1.

1608. religion betwixt the two realms, but only in things indifferent concerning government and ceremonies.'—*Cal.*

JULY 5. Dundee is described as suffering under 'the contagious sickness of the pest, and a great many of the houses are infectit therewith, and greater infection like to ensue in respect of the few number of magistrates within the same, and the little care and regard had of the government thereof, ane of the said magistrates being departit this life, and ane other of them visited with disease and infirmity, and not able to undergo sae great pains and travels in his person and otherwise as is requisite at sae necessar a time.' For these reasons, the Privy Council appointed three citizens to act as assistant-magistrates.—*P. C. R.*

JULY 13. We hear at this time of one of the last attempts to settle a dispute by regular combat; and it is the more remarkable, as several persons were concerned on each side. On the one part stood 'the Lord Sinclair, David Seton of Parbroth, and John Sinclair elder and John Sinclair younger, sons to the said Lord Sinclair;' on the other were George Martin of Cardone and his three sons. A mutual challenge had passed between the parties, 'with special designation of time, place, form, and manner of the combat,' and the rencontre would have, to all appearance, taken place, had not some neighbours interfered to prevent it. The parties were summoned before the Privy Council, to answer for their conduct.

Martin and his sons were denounced as rebels for not appearing (July 21).—*P. C. R.*

The slaughter of Captain James Stewart by Sir James Douglas of Parkhead, in 1596, had not been allowed to pass unnoticed by the Ochiltree family, to which the murdered man belonged. At that time, however, a man of rank was not to be punished as a malefactor in Scotland. His offence was expiated by an assythment, or the king interposed to reconcile the friends of the deceased to the culprit and his friends, as if the affair had been merely an unfortunate quarrel. For years there stood a variance between the Ochiltree Stewarts and the murderer of their relation, and from time to time they had to come under heavy sureties to keep the peace towards each other, Lord Ochiltree and Sir James Douglas (now called Lord Torthorald) in £5000 each; and the brothers and nephews of Stewart in lesser sums. This arrangement had been last renewed on the 30th of May, to endure for a year. All seemed composed—a General Assembly was sitting in Edinburgh—no one seems to have been apprehensive of any immediate quarrel or trouble, when a terrible incident suddenly fell out. 1608.

Lord Torthorald was walking one morning, between six and seven o'clock, in the High Street, below the Cross, unaccompanied by any friend or servant, dreading no harm, when William Stewart, nephew of the man he had slain twelve years before, observing him, was unable to restrain the rancorous feeling of the moment, and pulling out a short sword he carried, stabbed him in the back, so that he fell to the ground and instantly died. July 14.

William Stewart escaped, and we hear no more of him. The Privy Council, horror-struck at the outrage, had two meetings on the same day to consider what should be done. At the first, before noon, they ordered that the Earl of Morton, James commendator of Melrose, Sir George and Sir Archibald Douglas, his uncles, —— Douglas now of Torthorald, William Douglas, apparent of Drumlanrig, Archibald Douglas of Tofts, and Sir James Dundas of Arniston—all friends of the deceased, and presumably eager to revenge his slaughter—should be confined to their lodgings. Lord Ochiltree, on whom the Douglases might be apt to vent their fury, was likewise commanded to keep within doors. At the second meeting, after noon, they gave an order for the apprehension of the culprit.

There is a remarkable connection of murders recalled by this shocking transaction. Not only do we ascend to Torthorald's slaughter of Stewart in 1596, and Stewart's deadly prosecution of Morton to the scaffold in 1581; but William Stewart was the son of the Sir William Stewart who was slain by the Earl of Bothwell in Blackfriars' Wynd in 1588. This, however, is the last open murder of one gentleman by another which we have to record as taking place on a street in Edinburgh.

Lord Torthorald lies buried under a carved slab in Holyrood Chapel, where the guide reads his name daily to hundreds of visitors, few of whom know what a series of tragic circumstances in old Scottish history lies concentered in the body of him who sleeps below.

The progress of persecution against the Catholics may be traced all through this period by the equal progress of the king's measures for introducing the episcopal system into the church. A

1608. General Assembly, which met at Linlithgow in December 1606, was brought by court influence to give a consent to the principle of permanent moderators for presbyteries—a necessary step to the assumption of entire power over dioceses by the bishops. They sent the act to court, with a petition for fresh securities against the Catholic nobles of the north, and their ladies. James affected to listen to their desires, and promised well, but does not seem to have taken any decisive steps till he found that the act for constant moderators, as interpreted by him, met considerable
JULY. resistance. He then called another General Assembly, mainly for the purpose of taking 'strait order' with the adherents of the proscribed faith.

This reverend body professed to consider the country as in unexampled danger from popery. It is found complaining that Jesuit and seminary priests were allowed to traffic within the land, that papistical books were brought from abroad, and that persons in authority often shewed favour to traffickers and excommunicated papists, 'such as the abbot of New Abbey and other mass priests, demitted, as is thought, out of ward, not without reward [bribery], and without all warrant of his majesty, and presently tolerated in this country without pursuit.' Amongst some objects petitioned for from the king, were—that papists of rank be imprisoned, and only Protestants have access to them; that orders be given for down-casting of the Laird of Gight's chapel, and the house of John Cheyne in Kissilmonth, who receipted all Jesuits and seminary priests; and that order be taken with the pilgrimages—namely, to the Chapel called Ordiquhill, and the Chapel of Grace, and to a well in the bounds of Enzie upon the south side of Spey.

The most important of their actual measures bore reference to the Marquis of Huntly, and the Earls of Angus and Errol, who were considered as the prime supports of popery in the northern section of the kingdom. Huntly we have seen (June 1597) received formally and publicly into the Presbyterian Church, with all appearances of sincerity on his part, while the truth was that he only gave a lip-obedience in order to save his estates and place in the country, of which otherwise he would have been deprived. The hollowness of his professions was soon after sufficiently apparent, for he built a popish chapel in his house, and he continued, as before, to 'reset' priests. The Presbyterian tutors imposed on his family may be presumed to have made little progress in their work, as his children all grew up Catholics. Processes had been raised against him in the church-courts for 'relapse in popery;' and though the king had tried to screen him from the vengeance he had incurred, it was ineffectual. It was now necessary for James, if he would make way with his episcopal innovations, that he should give proof of sincerity in Protestantism, by leaving his old friend and councillor to the mercy of the General Assembly. 1608.

Accordingly, the business being ripe for instantly proceeding, the moderator—being the same Bishop Law who had promised such a sore 'handling' of the Catholics to James Melville and his friends in London (see under November 7, 1606)—pronounced the sentence of excommunication 'after a very solemn manner;' while the Earl of Dunbar, the king's commissioner, promised that, 'forty days being expired from the pronouncing of the sentence, the civil sword should strike without mercy or favour to him or his; and although some of his friends should come and buy his escheat, it should be refused.'—*Cal.* Arrangements were made for taking the same measures with Errol and Angus, Dunbar promising the like severity with them.

While the Assembly continued sitting, a gentleman came on behalf of the Marquis of Huntly, pleading for a little extension of time 'till he had perfyter resolution,' shewing that he was not *opiniâtre*, as had appeared from his 'yielding to have conference,' and from his 'going to the kirk;' he entreated to be heard for himself before final condemnation. But the petition was set aside as frivolous, and because he had failed to fulfil his promise given by solemn bond a month ago to communicate before a certain day.—*Cal.*

The plague broke out in Perth, and continued till the ensuing May, 'wherein deit young and auld five hundred persons.'—*Chron. Perth.* AUG. 29.

It was reported to the Privy Council that a quarrel had arisen between John Napier of Merchiston, and the sons and daughters of the late Sir Archibald Napier of Edinbellie, regarding the right to the teind sheaves of the lands of Merchiston for the crop of the present year. 'Baith the said parties,' says the record, '*intends to convocate their kin, and sic as will do for them in arms*, for leading [home-bringing], and withstanding of leading, of the said teinds; whereupon further inconvenients are like to fall out.' To prevent breach of the peace, William Napier of Wrightshouses, a neutral person, was ordered to collect the teind sheaves of Merchiston, and account to the Council.—*P. C. R.* 'Whilk order,' says John SEP. 1.

1608. Napier, 'is guid eneuch for me, and little to their contentment;' that is, to the contentment of his Edinbellie relatives.[1]

This, it must be owned, is a new light in which to view the inventor of the logarithms. It is, however, worthy of observation, that a dispute between other parties on the same grounds is described in precisely similar terms, and the same arrangement made to preserve the peace.

SEP. 'In the beginning of September, the Duke of Wirtemberg, a prince in Germany, a young man of comely behaviour, accompanied with twenty-four in train, came to see the country. He was convoyed from place to place by noblemen, by the king's direction, and weel enterteened. His train were all clothed in black.'—*Cal.*

The duke was a great friend and ally of the king, who, soon after his accession, sent Lord Spencer with a splendid ambassage to Stuttgart, to invest his serene highness with the Order of the Garter.

The records of Privy Council are still full of instances of assaults made by men of rank and others with deadly weapons upon persons against whom they bore hatred. It would be wearisome to enumerate even those which occur throughout a single year. It is to be remembered there were famous acts of parliament against going armed defensively or offensively; yet in every case we find the guilty parties set about their vengeful proceedings in steel bonnets, gauntlets, and plait-sleeves, and with swords and pistolets.

As an example—one Gavin Thomson, burgess of Peebles, was held at hatred by Charles Pringle, another burgess; we do not learn for what cause. One day in September 1608, as Gavin was walking in sober and quiet manner along the High Street of the burgh, Charles Pringle, accompanied by nine or ten persons, all armed with lances and whingers, set upon and 'cruelly hurt and wounded the said Gavin upon the left hand, drave him perforce back, and housit him within the dwelling-place and lock-fast yetts of Isobel Anderson; and were it not by the providence of God, that the Person and Minister of Peebles, accompanied with some others weel-affected persons to the peace of the said town, and knawing the said Gavin his innocency, come forth to the redding,[2]

[1] Napier's *Life of John Napier*.

[2] Literally, the separation; in larger sense, the restoration of order.

they had not failit, as they had begun, with great jeists, trees, and fore-hammers, to have surprised and strucken up the yetts and doors of the said dwelling-house, and within the same to have unmercifully slain and murdered the said Gavin.' 1608.

For several subsequent months, Pringle and his associates had lain in wait at divers times to kill Gavin, so that he had been prevented from attending kirk or market, or going about the business of his farm. At length, on the 2d of December, as he was walking peaceably on the street, they attacked him again, armed as before. 'Being informit that he had come furth of his house, they first bostit and menaced him aff the hie street, and he retiring himself hame again in quietness, they all followit and pursewit him with drawn swords,' when one of the party, Alexander Dalmahoy, 'by his sword, with ane great stane of aucht pund wecht in his hand, hurt the said Gavin his thie-bone.' The assailants 'hurt and woundit William Murray of Romanno and divers other gentlemen redders, and in end fiercely pursewit Gavin and housit him within the dwelling-house of the close yetts of William Elliot, and cryit for jeists and fore-hammers, and had not failit to have strucken up the doors and yetts thereof, and to have slain the said Gavin within the same, were not timous relief come at hand.'

The active parties in this wickedness were denounced rebels by the Council.—*P. C. R.*

William Turnbull of Airdrie lived in Edinburgh, having in his family a daughter, Elizabeth, eleven years of age. He admitted to his house, and often civilly entertained Robert Napier son of William of Wrightshouses—a gentleman who has just been under our notice. On the 4th of October, Turnbull complained to the Privy Council that, on the 29th of September, Robert Napier had by craft and violence taken away his daughter, under cloud of night, and now keeps her in some obscure place, refusing to render and deliver her up to her father. The Council caused Robert Napier to be denounced as a rebel for this fact. OCT.

The abduction of women, of which some examples were formerly given, was still an offence of frequent occurrence. On the subsequent 8th of December, there is a complaint before the Council from Margaret Stewart, widow, that as she was walking home from her booth to her dwelling-house in Edinburgh, between seven and eight o'clock in the evening of the 5th of the same month, accompanied by her orphan grandchild, Katherine Weir, fourteen years of age, a young citizen, named William Geddes,

1608. had beset her with six men armed like himself with swords, gauntlets, steel bonnets, and plait-sleeves, and violently took the child from her, 'without pity of her manifold exclamations and crying.' Geddes was likewise denounced rebel.

Nov. 8. 'There was an earthquake at nine hours at night, sensible enough at St Andrews, Cupar, Edinburgh, Glasgow, Dundee, but more sensible at Dumbarton; for there the people were so affrayed, that they ran to the kirk, together with their minister, to cry to God, for they looked presently for destruction. It was thought the extraordinar drouth in the summer and winter before was the cause of it.'—*Cal.*

At Perth, this earthquake shook the east end of the Tolbooth, insomuch that 'many stones fell aff it.'—*Chron. Perth.*

At Aberdeen, where the shock excited great alarm, the kirk-session met, and accepting the earthquake as 'a document that God is angry against the land, and against this city in particular, for the manifold sins of the people,' appointed a solemn fast to be held on the ensuing day, and 'the covenant to be renewed by the haill people with God, by halding up of their hands publicly before God in his sanctuary, and promising by his grace to forbear in time coming from their sins.' There was one particular sin which was thought to have had a great concern in bringing about the earthquake—namely, the salmon-fishing practised on the Dee on Sunday. Accordingly, the proprietors of the salmon-fishings were called before the session, and rebuked. 'Some,' says the session record, 'promist absolutely to forbear, both by himselfs and their servands in time coming; other promised to forbear, upon the condition subscryvant; and some plainly refusit anyway to forbear.'[1]

Dec. 1. 'The Earl of Mar declared to the [Privy] Council that some women were ta'en in Broughton, as witches, and being put to ane assize, and convict, albeit they persevered constant in their denial to the end, yet they were burnt quick [alive], after sic ane cruel manner, that some of them deit in despair, renuncand and

[1] The fishing of salmon in the river Dee on Sunday was a custom of some antiquity, as it had been expressly warranted by a bull of Pope Nicolas V. in 1451. The privilege was limited to the Sundays of those five months of the year in which salmon most abound; and the first salmon taken each Sunday was to belong to the parish church. The bull recites that both by the canon and the common law, the right of prosecuting the herring-fishing on Sunday was conceded to all the faithful.—*Reg. Epis. Aber.* (Spalding Club).

blasphemand, and others, half burnt, brak out of the fire, and was cast in quick in it again, while [till] they were burnt to the deid.'[1] 1608.

1609. Jan. 5.

'. . . . the wind did blow so boisterously, that the like was not heard in the memory of man. Houses in burgh and land were thrown down with the violence of it; trees rooted up, corn-stacks and hay-stacks blown away. Some men passing over bridges were driven over violently and killed. The wind continued vehement many days and weeks, even till mid-March, howbeit not in the same measure that it blowed this day.'—*Cal.*

The book entitled *Regiam Majestatem*, containing the ancient laws of Scotland, seems to have been printed by a contribution from the burghs. In April this year, we find the magistrates of Glasgow charged to make payment of £100 on this account. In September, the learned author, Sir John Skene, had some difficulty with his printer, Thomas Finlayson, of importance enough to come under the attention of the Privy Council. It was alleged that Thomas, after *perfyting* the Scottish volume, 'upon some frivole consait and apprehension of his own, without ony warrant of law or pretence of reason,' maliciously refused to deliver the volume to Sir John, 'but shifts and delays him fra time to time with foolish and impertinent excuses, to Sir John's heavy hurt and prejudice.' The Lords of Council ordered Thomas to deliver the book to its author within eight days, on pain of being denounced rebel; and 'whereas there is some little difference and question betwixt the said parties *anent their comptis*,' a committee was appointed 'to sort the same, and put them to ane rest.'—*P. C. R.*

The severities called for by the General Assembly against the papist nobles and others, had been, to appearance, backed up by the royal power. The Marquis of Huntly was actually in prison at Stirling as an excommunicated rebel. The king probably felt this a high price for the soothing of Presbyterian scruples regarding episcopacy; but it had so far been paid. He contemplated having the observance of Christmas brought in at the end of the year; and it was therefore advisable to shew a little further earnestness in the right direction. May.

[1] *Earl of Haddington's Notes, quoted by Pitcairn*, iii. 597. It may be worthy of remark, that no notice of such shocking transactions occurs in the Privy Council Record at this time.

1609. By the activity of Spottiswoode, archbishop of Glasgow, John Hamilton, a zealous trafficking priest, was apprehended—an act the more important that this culprit was uncle to the king's advocate. Another priest, named Paterson, was taken with all his vestments, while celebrating mass in a house in the Canongate in Edinburgh before an audience of thirty persons. These must, of course, have been gratifying proofs of the royal zeal, albeit Calderwood cannot repress a bitter remark as to the 'tolerable entertainment' allowed to the prisoners (the allowance made in another case for an incarcerated priest, and probably in these also, was a merk—1s. 1⅓d. sterling—*per diem*), while ministers incarcerated for opposition to the king's episcopal innovations 'were left to their shifts.'

About the same time, the archbishop went with a party to the town of New Abbey, in the stewartry of Kirkcudbright, and there broke into the house of Mr Gilbert Brown, former abbot of New Abbey, 'and having found a great number of popish books, copes, chalices, pictures, images, and such other popish trash, he most worthily and dutifully as became both a prelate and a councillor, on a mercat-day, at a great confluence of people in the hie street of the burgh of Dumfries, did burn all those copes, vestments, and chalices,' delivering up the books to Maxwell of Kirkconnel, to be afterwards dealt with. The Privy Council (June 13, 1609) allowed this to be good service on the part of the archbishop, and granted him a gift of the books left unburnt.—*P. C. R.*

In the parliament held a few days after the last date, several acts were passed against popery—one ordaining that pedagogues sent abroad with the sons of noblemen and others, should be duly licensed by a bishop; another that the young persons so sent abroad should remain at places where 'the religion' is professed, and 'where there is no cruel inquisition;' a third for confiscating the property of papists to the king's use; a fourth was meant to deprive Catholics of all benefit from the legal system of the country. The more severe class of Presbyterians looked on, with no inclination to object to these measures, but only with a disbelief in the sincerity of the government which had brought them forward. They had begun to see that it was 'to grace the bishops, and procure them greater credit and authority in the country,' that popery was thus dealt with.—*Cal.*

JULY. We have seen that, so lately as September 1606, the Borders were reduced to obedience by a moral medicine of considerable sharpness, administered by the Earl of Dunbar; that is to say, one

hundred and forty thieves had been hanged. We now find that the 1609.
effect was only temporary, for it had become necessary for the earl to go once more to Dumfries to hold a justice-court. On this occasion, he was equally severe with such offenders as were in custody, causing many to be hanged.—*Cal.* The Chancellor Dunfermline wrote to the king that Lord Dunbar 'has had special care to repress, baith in the in-country and on the Borders, the insolence of all the proud bangsters, oppressors, and nembroths [Nimrods], but [without] regard or respect to ony of them; has purgit the Borders of all the chiefest malefactors, robbers, and brigands as were wont to reign and triumph there, as clean, and by as great wisdom and policy, as Hercules sometime is written to have purged Augeas, the king of Elide, his escuries; and by the cutting aff . . . . the Laird of Tynwald, Maxwell, sundry Douglases, Johnstons, Jardines, Armstrangs, Beatisons, and sic others, *magni nominis luces*, in that broken parts, has rendered all those ways and passages betwixt your majesty's kingdoms of Scotland and England, as free and peaceable, as Phœbus in auld times made free and open the ways to his awn oracle in Delphos, and to his Pythic plays and ceremonies, by the destruction of Phorbas and his Phlegians, all thieves, voleurs, bandsters, and throat-cutters. These parts are now, I can assure your majesty, as lawful, as peaceable, and as quiet, as any part in any civil kingdom of Christianity.'[1]

This was too happy a consummation to be quite realised. We find, not long after, a representation going up to the king from the well-disposed people of the Borders, shewing that matters were become as bad as ever. It is a curious document, full of Latin quotations. The thieves, it says, are like the beasts of the field, according to the words of Cicero in his oration for Cluentius; *quæ, fame dominante, ad eum locum ubi aliquando pastæ sunt, revertuntur.* Lord Dunbar being now gone with his justice-courts, they are returned to their old evil courses, and there is nothing which they will not attempt. 'Wild incests, adulteries, convocations of lieges, shooting and wearing of hagbuts, pistolets, and lances, daily bloodsheds, oppression, and disobedience in civil matters, neither are nor has been punished . . . . there is no more account made of going to the horn, than to the ale-house.' Lord Scone and his guard are of no use, for they favour their friends. 'If diligent search were made . . . . there would be found ane grit number of idle people, without any calling, industry, or lawful means to live

[1] *Letters and State Papers of the Reign of James VI.*

1609. by, except it be upon the blood of the poorest and most obedient sort.'

The final attempt to plant the Lewis took place this year, under the care of only two adventurers, Sir George Hay (subsequently chancellor of Scotland) and Sir James Spens of Wormiston. The Lord of Kintail had in the interval made an unsuccessful attempt to obtain a grant of the island.

The two undertakers went to the island with a force which they considered sufficient to meet the opposition of the pertinacious Niel Macleod. 'The Lord of Kintail did privately and underhand assist Niel Macleod, and sent his brother, Rorie Mackenzie, openly with some men to aid the undertakers by virtue of the king's commission. He promised great friendship to the adventurers, and sent unto them a supply of victuals in a ship from Ross. In the meantime he sendeth quietly to Niel Macleod, desiring him to take the ship by the way, that the adventurers, trusting to these victuals, and being disappointed, might thereby be constrained to abandon the island, which fell out accordingly; for Sir George Hay and Sir James Spens failing to apprehend Niel, and lacking victuals for their army, they wearied of the bargain, and dismissed all the neighbouring forces. Sir George Hay and Wormiston retired into Fife, leaving some of their men in the island to keep the fort, until they should send unto them supply of men and victuals. Whereupon Niel Macleod, assisted by his nephew . . . . and some other of the Lewis men, invaded the undertakers' camp, burnt the fort, apprehended the men which were left behind them in the island, and sent them home safely into Fife, since which time they never returned again into the island.'—*G. H. S.*

The Lord of Kintail afterwards obtained possession of the isle of Lewis, and Niel, thoroughly circumvented by the Clan Kenzie, was driven for refuge with a small company to a fortified rock called Berissay. 'The Clan Kenzie then gathered together the wives and children of those that were in Berissay, and such as, by way of affinity or consanguinity, within the island, did appertein to Niel and his followers, and placed them all upon a rock within the sea, where they might be heard and seen from Berissay. They vowed and protested that they would suffer the sea to overwhelm them the next flood, if Niel did not presently surrender the fort; which pitiful spectacle did so move Niel Macleod and his company to compassion, that immediately they yielded the rock and left the Lewis; whereupon the women and children were rescued and rendered.'—*G. H. S.*

This unfortunate insular chief, falling into the hands of his enemies, was taken to Edinburgh, and there executed in April 1613. 1609.

There was a Presbyterian prejudice against burying in churches, and the *blame of kirk-burial* had not only been a subject for the pamphleteer, but the legislature. Nevertheless, John Schaw of Sornbeg in Ayrshire, on the death of his wife, resolved to inhume her corpse in his parish kirk of Galston, in spite of all the minister and session could say or do to the contrary. Accompanied by his brother and his 'bailie,' and attended by a numerous party, 'all bodin in feir of weir,' he came to the church, broke up the door with fore-hammers, and dug a grave, in which he deposited his spouse. He was afterwards glad to make public repentance for this fact, and pay twenty pounds to the box-master of the kirk, besides which the Privy Council ordained him to appear again as a penitent, and solemnly promise never again to attempt to bury any corpse within the church.'—*P. C. R.* AUG.

Notwithstanding Lord Ochiltree's protestations of innocence regarding the assassination of Lord Torthorald, the relatives of the latter continued to bear a deadly grudge at him, and seemed likely to wreak it out in some wild manner. This came to the knowledge of the king, who felt himself called upon to interfere. The Privy Council, in obedience to the royal letters, had the parties summoned before them. William Lord Douglas and James Lord Torthorald appeared before them that day, and undertook, before the 20th of September, that 'they sall owther pursue the said Lord Ochiltree criminally before his majesty's justice in the Tolbooth of Edinburgh, for airt, part, rede, and counsel, of the slaughter of umwhile Lord Torthorald, or then that they sould reconceil themselves with the said Lord Ochiltree, and be agreit with him.'—*P. C. R.* AUG. 10.

Under favour of the king, a number of strangers had been introduced into the country to practise the making of cloths of various kinds. A colony of them was settled in the Canongate, Edinburgh, headed by one John Sutherland and a Fleming named Joan Van Headen, and 'are daily exercised in their art of making, dressing, and litting of stuffis, and gives great licht and knowledge of their calling to the country people.' These industrious and inoffensive men, notwithstanding the letters of the king, investing them with various privileges, were now much molested by the magistrates of the Canongate, with a view to

1609. Oct. 26. forcing them to become burgesses and freemen there in the regular way. On an appeal to the Privy Council, their exemption was affirmed.

From London, where the pest had long been, a ship had lately come to Leith, and was now lying at the west side of the bulwark there, prepared to discharge her cargo. The case looked the more alarming, as several of the mariners had died of plague during

Nov. 7. the voyage. The Lords of Council immediately issued orders that the vessel should be taken to Inchkeith, where her cargo should be taken out and handled, cleansed, and dressed, the inhabitants affording all facilities for that purpose, 'with such houses and other necessaries as are in the said inch.'—*P. C. R.*

The time was approaching when, in accordance with a recent act, the Egyptians were to depart from Scotland, under pain of being liable thereafter to be killed by any one without challenge of law. In anticipation of this dread time, one of the nation, named Moses Faw, appeared before the authorities of the kingdom, and pleaded for permission to remain under protection of the laws, on the ground that he had wholly withdrawn himself and his family from that infamous society, and was willing to give surety for his

Nov. 9. future good behaviour. The desired permission was extended to him on that condition.—*P. C. R.*

Dec. 25. Having of late shewn some zeal against popery, King James thought he might now effect one little change essential to episcopacy, without more than enough of outcry from the earnest Presbyterians. By his order, sent by Chancellor Seton, it was arranged that Christmas-day should henceforth be solemnly held in Scotland. The Court of Session accordingly rose for that day, and till the 8th of January ensuing. 'This,' says Calderwood, 'was the first Christmass vacance of the session keepit since the Reformation. The ministers threatened that the men who devised that novelty for their own advancement, might receive at God's hand their reward to their overthrow, for troubling the people of God with beggarly ceremonies long since abolished with popery. Christmass was not so weel keepit by feasting and abstinence from work in Edinburgh these thretty years before, *an evil example to the rest of the country.*'

1610. Jan. 'About the end of Januar, the Scotch Secretar, Sir Alexander

Hay, came from court with sundry directions, and among the rest, for the habit of the senators of the College of Justice [which the Chancellor had told the king was now, since the departure of the court to England, '*the special spunk of light and fondament of your majesty's estate, and only ornament of this land*'],[1] advocates, clerks, and scribes; which was proclaimed in the beginning of Februar—viz., that the senators should wear a purple robe or gown in judgment and in the streets, when they were to meet or were dissolved; that advocates, clerks, and scribes should wear black gowns in the judgment-hall and in the streets . . . . the provost and bailies of burghs and their councillors should wear black when they sat in council and judgment; that ministers should wear black clothes, and in the pulpit black gowns; that bishops and doctors of divinity should wear black cassikins syde to [long enough to reach] their knee, black gowns above, and a black crape about their neck. . . . . On the 15th of Februar, the Lords of the Session and the bishops put on their gowns and came down from the chancellor's lodging, with their robes, to the Tolbooth [the court-house—a section of St Giles's Church]. All the robes, except the chancellor's, were of London cloth, purple coloured, with the fashion of an heckled cloak from the shoulders to the middle, with a long syde hood on the back, the gown and hood lined with red sattin. The people flocked together to behold them. The bishops were ordeened to have their gowns with lumbard sleeves, according to the form of England, with tippets and crapes about their craigs [necks]; which was performed.'—*Cal.* 1610.

On the 20th of June, the lord provost of Edinburgh exhibited in his council 'twa gowns, the ane red, the other black claith linit in the breists with sable furring, sent to his lordship by the king's majesty for to be worn by him, and to be patterns of the gowns to be worn by the provost and bailies, and sic of the council and town as are appointed thereto by his majesty.'[2]

Alexander Kirkpatrick, younger of Closeburn, being in the Tolbooth of Edinburgh for the slaughter of James Carmichael, son to John Carmichael of Spothe, the Lady Amisfield, wife of a neighbour, came to the prison, and entered into conference with the keeper in his private apartments. At her persuasion, the man allowed 'Young Closeburn' to come to speak with her; and she FEB. 27.

[1] *Letters and State Papers of the Reign of James VI.*, p. 56.
[2] *Mait. Club Misc.*, i. 158.

1610. then executed her design of exchanging clothes with him, and so allowing him to escape. The lady was warded in the Castle; but what ultimately became of her does not appear.—*Pit.*

JUNE. A General Assembly was held at Glasgow, so constituted and managed by royal authority that the king at length accomplished one grand portion of his ecclesiastical scheme for Scotland, in being acknowledged as the head of the kirk. Three English divines, chaplains to the king, Dr Christopher Hampton, Dr Phineas Hodson, and Dr George Meriton, were present to use their influence in reconciling the country to 'a more comely and peaceable government in our kirk than was presently.' But for the absence of the six banished ministers, and the confinement of zealous, fiery, fearless Andrew Melville in the Tower, it might not have been possible to carry this measure. The Presbyterian historians also insinuate that bribes were used with the members, whence they take leave to call it *the Golden Assembly.*

'Immediately after this, the Bishops of Glasgow and Brechin took journey to court, to report what was done, and got great thanks frae the king. Galloway followed, who all three abode there till the month of November, at what time . . . . by a special commission from the king to the Bishop of London to that effect, the Archbishop of Glasgow and the other two were solemnly ordained, inaugurat, and consecrated, with anointing of oil and other ceremonies, according to the English fashion.' [The ceremony, which took place in the chapel at London House, was celebrated by a banquet, at which 'gifts were bestowed, and gloves were distributed, in token of the solemnisation of the marriage between the bishops and their kirks.'—*Cal.*] The three new prelates, 'thereafter [January 23, 1611] returning to Scotland, did to the Archbishop of St Andrews, in St Andrews, as they were done withal at Lambeth, as near as they could possibly imitate; and thereafter the two archbishops consecrated the rest, and the new entrant bishops as they were nominat by the king . . . . first quietly, as being ashamed of the foolish guises in it, but afterward more and more solemnly, as their estate grew.'—*Row.* 'All of them [the whole thirteen] deserted their flocks, and usurped thereafter jurisdiction over the ministers and people of their dioceses.'—*Cal.*

At the same time the king established in Scotland a court of High Commission, by which the new hierarchy acquired great power over the people.

'The king was so earnest upon the creating of bishops, that he cared not what it cost him. . . . . In buying in their benefices out of the hands of the noblemen that had them, in buying votes at Assemblies, in defraying of all their other charges, and promoving of all their adoes and business, as coming to, and going from, and living at court prelate-like; that is, sumptuously and gorgeously in apparel, house, diet, attendants, etc., [he] did employ (by the confession of such as were best acquainted with, and were actors in, these businesses) above the sum of £300,000 sterling money, one huge thing indeed; but sin lying heavy on the throne, crying aloud for wrath on him and his posterity, is infinitely sadder nor £300,000 sterling!'—*Row*. 1610.

The Marquis of Huntly, and other papists of rank, had meanwhile been suffering considerably in order to dispose the Presbyterian opposition to yield to the king's wishes. But now there was no longer any immediate occasion for severity. The marquis, professing to be once more thoroughly Protestant, was relieved from excommunication, and allowed to return to his palace in the north. With Errol there was greater difficulty. The king, through the Earl of Dunbar, had promised that he should lose his lands. He had, what Huntly happily wanted, a painfully tender conscience. One day, he was brought to promise that he would subscribe; but that very night he fell into such a trouble of mind as to have been on the point of killing himself. 'Early next morning, the Archbishop of Glasgow being called, he confessed his dissimulation with many tears, and, beseeching them that were present to bear witness of his remorse, was hardly brought to any settling all that day.' By some treacherous excuse, lenity was extended to Errol also. Such was the way in which the king performed his engagements on this solemn subject. 'The turn being done,' says Calderwood, 'promises were not keepit.'

An act was passed by the Privy Council in favour of Anthony Aurego, Anthony Soubouga, and Fabiano Fantone, allowing them to live in the country, and practise their 'trade and industry of making hecks and other machines for taking of rottons and mice.' —*P. C. R.* July 3.

Piracy was at this time a flourishing trade, and the Scottish and Irish seas were a favourite walk of its practitioners. Vessels of various countries besides Scotland, were pursued by these marauders and mercilessly plundered, their crews seized, tortured, and sometimes slaughtered, or else set ashore on desolate coasts, that they July 27.

1610. might not be readily able to take measures of redress. The Long Island, on the west coast of Ireland, appears to have served as a regular station for pirate ships; they also haunted much the Western Isles of Scotland. In 1609, a piratical crew, headed by two captains named Perkins and Randell, started from the Long Island in a vessel of 200 tons, named the *Iron Prize*, attended by a nimble pinnace of about half that burden; and for some months they roamed about the northern seas, picking up whatever small-craft came in their way. They even had the audacity to shew themselves at the mouth of the Firth of Forth. The attention of the Privy Council being called to their proceedings, three vessels were fitted out in a warlike manner at Leith, and sent in quest of the pirates. Perkins and Randell had meanwhile come to Orkney to refit. They 'landed at the castle, and came to the town thereof,' where they 'behaved themselves maist barbarously, being ever drunk, and fechting amang themselves, and giving over themselves to all manner of vice and villany.' Three of them attacked a small vessel belonging to the Earl of Orkney, lying on the shore, and were taken prisoners in the attempt by the earl's brother, James Stewart. A day or two after this event, the three government ships made their appearance, and immediately a great part of the piratical company made off in the pinnace. A pursuit proving vain, the government ships returned and attacked the *Iron Prize*; and after a desperate conflict, in which they had two men killed and sundry wounded, they succeeded in capturing the whole remaining crew, amounting to nearly thirty men, who, with those previously taken, were brought to Leith and tried (July 26). Being found guilty, twenty-seven of these wretched men, including the two captains, were hung upon a gibbet next day at the pier of Leith. Three were reserved in the hope of their giving useful information.

The Chancellor Dunfermline, who took the lead in this severe administration of the law, tells the king in a letter written on the day of the execution: 'This company of pirates did enterteen one whom they did call their Person [parson] for saying of prayers to them twice a day, who belike either wearied of his cure, or foreseeing the destruction of his flock, had forsaken them in Orkney, and, privily convoying himself over land, was at length deprehendit in the burgh of Dundee.' As he confessed and gave evidence against the rest, besides bringing some of them to confession, he was reserved for the king's pleasure, and probably let off.—*Pit.* *C. K. Sc.*

There was at this time 'a great visitation of the young children [of Aberdeen] with the plague of the pocks.' There were also 'continual weets,' which threatened to destroy the crops and cause a famine. The cause being 'the sins of the land,' a public fast and humiliation was ordered in Aberdeen, 'that God may be met with tears and repentance.'—*A. K. S. R.* 1610. Aug. 12.

'The Archbishop of St Andrews [Gladstanes], reposing in his bed in time of the afternoon sermon, the Sabbath after his diocesan synod in St Andrews, was wakened, and all the kirk and town with him, with a cry of blood and murder. For his sister son [Walter Anderson], master of his household, with a throw of his dagger, killed his cook [Robert Green], while as he was busy in dressing the lord-bishop's supper. The dagger light[ed] just under the left pap of the cook, who fell down dead immediately.'—*Cal.* Oct. 21.

The young man was committed to prison; but, 'the poor man's friends being satisfied with a piece of money, none being to pursue the murder, he was by moyen [influence] cleansed by a white assize (as they call it) and let go free.'—*Row.* This trial took place before the regality court of St Andrews. On the ensuing 17th January, letters were raised by the king's advocate against the assize, but with what result does not appear. —*P. C. R.*

'. . . . before the going to of the sun, there were seen by twelve or thretteen husbandmen, great companies of men in three battles, joining together and fighting the space of an hour, on certain lands perteening to my Lord Livingston and the Laird of Carse. The honest men were examined in the presence of divers noblemen, barons, and gentlemen, and affirmed constantly that they saw such appearance.'—*Cal.* Nov. 1.

We have now the first hint at public conveyances in Scotland in a letter of the king, encouraging Henry Anderson of Trailsund to bring a number of coaches and wagons with horses into Scotland, and licensing him and his heirs for fifteen years 'to have and use coaches and wagons, ane or mae, as he shall think expedient, for transporting of his hieness lieges betwixt the burgh of Edinburgh and town of Leith . . . . providing that he be ready at all times for serving of his majesty's lieges, and that he tak not aboon the sum of twa shillings Scots money for transporting of every person betwixt the said twa towns at ony time.' Dec. 23.

1610. Dec. 24. A patent was granted for the establishment of a glass-manufacture in Scotland. The business was commenced at Wemyss, in Fife, and, about ten years after, we find it, to all appearance, going on prosperously. 'Braid glass'—that is, glass for windows—was made, measuring three quarters of a Scots ell and a nail in length, while the breadth at the head was an ell wanting half a nail, and at the bottom half an ell wanting half a nail. It was declared to be equal in quality to Danskine glass. The glasses for drinking and other uses not being of such excellence, it was arranged that some specimens of English glass should be bought in London and established in Edinburgh Castle, to serve as patterns for the Scotch glass in point of quality. For the encouragement of the native manufacture, and to keep money within the country, the importation of foreign glass was (March 6, 1621) prohibited.—*P. C. R.*

1611. Mar. The Veitches and Tweedies of the upper part of Peeblesshire had long been at issue,[1] and peace was only kept between them by means of mutual assurances given to the Privy Council. The king heard of the case, and was the more concerned about it, because he believed he had, by his personal exertions, so entirely suppressed what he called *the auld and detestable monster of deidly feid* in Scotland, that 'we do hardly think there be any one feid except this in all that kingdom unreconciled.' As to these belligerent men of the Tweed, 'the wrongs and mischiefs done by either of, as we understand, to others' [each other], is 'in such a proportion of compensation, as neither party can either boast of advantage, or otherwise think himself too much behind.' He now ordered his Scottish Council, 'that you call before you the principals of either surname, and then take such course for removing of the feid, and reconceiling, as you have been accustomed to do in the like cases'—that is, force them into bonds of amity, if they would not go of their own accord.—*P. C. R.*

May 10. It was found necessary to put some restraint upon the number of poor Scotch people who repaired to the English court in hope of bettering their circumstances. The evil is spoken of as a 'frequent and daily resort of great numbers of idle persons, men and women, of base sort and condition, and without ony certain trade, calling, or dependence, going from hence to court, by sea and land.' It was said to be 'very unpleasant and offensive to the king's majesty,

[1] See under June 1590.

in so far as he is daily importuned with their suits and begging, and his royal court almost filled with them, they being, in the opinion and conceit of all behalders, bot idle rascals and poor miserable bodies;' the country, moreover, 'is heavily disgracit, and mony slanderous imputations given out against the same, as gif there were no persons of guid rank, comeliness, nor credit within the same.' The Council, therefore, deemed it necessary to cause an order to be proclaimed in all the burghs and seaports, forbidding masters of vessels to carry any people to England without first giving up their names, and declaring their errands and business to the Lords, under heavy penalties.—*P. C. R.* 1611.

A number of the king's Scottish courtiers had, as is well known, accompanied or followed him into England, and obtained shares of his good-fortune. Sir George Home, now Earl of Dunbar; Sir John Ramsay, created Earl of Haddington; Sir James Hay, ultimately made Earl of Carlisle; and recently, Mr Robert Ker, who became the king's especial favourite, and was made Earl of Somerset, are notable examples. The English, regarding the Scottish courtiers with natural jealousy, called them 'beggarly Scots,' of which they complained to the king, who is said to have jocosely replied: 'Content yourselves; I will shortly make the English as beggarly as you, and so end that controversy.' On one occasion, this jealousy broke out with some violence at a race at Croydon, in consequence of a Scotsman named Ramsay striking the Earl of Montgomery with his riding-switch. 'The English,' says the scandal-mongering Osborne, 'did, upon this accident, draw together, to make it a national quarrel; so far as Mr John Pinchbeck, a maimed man, having but the perfect use of two fingers, rode about with his dagger in his hand, crying: "Let us break our fast with them here, and dine with the rest in London!" But Herbert, not offering to strike again, there was nothing lost but the reputation of a gentleman.'[1] A ballad of the day described the metamorphosis which Scotchmen were understood to have undergone after their migration into England:

'Bonny Scot, we all witness can,
That England hath made thee a gentleman.

Thy blue bonnet, when thou came hither,
Could scarce keep out the wind and weather
But now it is turned to a hat and a feather;
Thy bonnet is blown, the devil knows whither.

[1] Osborne's *Traditional Memoirs—Secret Hist. Court James I.* Vol. i., p. 219.

1611.

> Thy shoes on thy feet, when thou camest from plough,
> Were made of the hide of an old Scots cow;
> But now they are turned to a rare Spanish leather,
> And decked with roses altogether.
>
> Thy sword at thy back was a great black blade,
> With a great basket-hilt of iron made;
> But now a long rapier doth hang at thy side,
> And huffingly doth this bonny Scot ride.'[1] &c.

Even Osborne acknowledges that the ordinary conceptions as to the enrichment of the Scots courtiers were exaggerated. He says: 'If many Scots got much, it was not more with one hand than they spent with the other;' and he explains how Cecil, Earl of Salisbury, the king's English treasurer, 'had a trick to get the kernel, and leave the Scots but the shell, and yet cast all the envy on them. He would make them buy books of fee-farms, some £100 per annum, some 100 marks; and he would compound with them for £1000 . . . . then would he fill up this book with such prime land as should be worth £10,000 or £20,000, which was easy for him, being treasurer, so to do. . . . . Salisbury by this means enriched himself infinitely.' The case is a significant one. The experience by the Scots, a simple rustic people, of the superior mercantile sharpness of the English, on coming into business relations with them, is probably the main cause of that dry cautious manner which the English censure in them as a national characteristic.

JULY 11. From an act of the Privy Council of this date, we get a curious idea of the customs of the age regarding legal suits. It was declared that one of the chief causes of 'the frequent and unlawful convocations, and the uncomely backing of noblemen and pairties upon the streets of Edinburgh,' was the fact that 'noblemen, prelates, and councillors repairing to this burgh, do ordinarily walk on the streets upon foot, whereby all persons of their friendship and dependence, and who otherwise has occasion to solicit them in their actions and causes, do attend and await upon them, and without modesty or discretion, importunes and fashes them with untimely solicitations and impertinent discourses, and sometimes by their foolish insolence and misbehaviour gives occasion of great misrule and unquietness within this burgh.'

The remedy ordered was as curious as the evil itself. It was,

[1] Printed in full in Ritson's *Country Chorister*.

that noblemen, prelates, and councillors, when they come to the 1611. council, or are abroad in the town on their private affairs, should, as became their rank, 'ride on horseback with footmantles or in coaches'—thus freeing themselves of that flocking of suitors which so much beset them when they appeared on foot.—*P. C. R.*

This day, John Mure of Auchindrain, James Mure, his son, JULY 17. and James Bannatyne of Chapeldonald, were brought to trial in Edinburgh for sundry crimes of a singularly atrocious character. The first of these personages has been before us on two former occasions—namely, under January 1, 1596-7, and May 11, 1602; to which reference may be made for an introduction to what is now to be related.

Auchindrain, it appears, felt that the boy William Dalrymple, who had carried the letter making the appointment for a meeting with Colzean, was a living evidence of his having been the deviser of the slaughter of that gentleman. He got the lad into his hands, and kept him for a time in his house; then, on his wearying of confinement, sent him to a friend in the Isle of Arran; thence, on his wearying of being 'in a barbarous country among rude people,' he had him brought back to his own house, and, as soon as possible, despatched him with a friend to become a soldier in Lord Buccleuch's regiment, serving under Maurice Prince of Orange. Dalrymple had not been long in the Low Countries, when he tired of being a soldier, and came back to Scotland. Once more he was at large in Ayrshire, and a source of uneasiness to Mure of Auchindrain. It was now necessary to take more decisive measures. Mure and his son (September 1607) sent a servant to the young man to take him to the house of James Bannatyne of Chapeldonald, and arranging to join them on the way, 'held divers purposes, speeches, and conferences with him, tried of him the estate of the Low Countries and sundry other matters,' and finally placed him as a guest in Chapeldonald House, under the name of William Montgomery.

According to appointment, at *ten o'clock of the evening of next day,* James Bannatyne came with Dalrymple to meet the two Mures on the sands near Girvan. There, the elder Mure explained to Bannatyne the cause of his fears regarding the young man, telling him 'he saw no remeed but to redd Dalrymple furth of this life, since he could not otherwise be kept out of his way. Whereunto Bannatyne making answer, that it was ane cruel purpose to murder the poor innocent youth, specially seeing they

1611. might send him to Ireland, to be safely kept there . . . . . Auchindrain seemed to incline somewhat to that expedient; and, in the uncertainty of his resolution, turning toward the part where his son stood, of purpose, as appeared, to consult with him, young Auchindrain perceived them no sooner near, but, thereby assuring himself of their assistance, in the execution of that whilk his father and he had concluded, he did violently invade Dalrymple, rushed him to the ground, and never left him till, helped by his father, with his hands and knees he had strangled him.'

The horrid deed being accomplished, the Mures, *with spades they had brought*, tried to bury Dalrymple in the sand; but, finding the hole always fill up with water, they were at length obliged to carry the body into the sea, going in as far as they could wade, and hoping that an outgoing wind would carry it to the coast of Ireland. Five nights after, it was thrown back upon the beach at the very scene of the murder, and was soon found by the country people. The Earl of Cassillis heard of it, and caused an account of the discovery to be published throughout the district. By the mother and sister of Dalrymple, it was at once pronounced to be his corpse, and suspicion instantly alighted upon the Mures. A relative, advised with about the rumour, said it could not be safe for them to brave the law in the teeth of so much prejudice; neither, supposing they absconded under such a suspicion, could their friends stand up for them. The only expedient was to make an excuse for going out of the way—assault, for instance, Hugh Kennedy of Garriehorn, a servant of the Earl of Cassillis, a man against whom they had many 'probable quarrels.' The Mures actually adopted this expedient, setting upon Garriehorn in the town of Ayr, and only failing to slay him by reason of the vigour of his defence. The earl then saw that it was necessary to take strong measures against enemies capable of such doings, and he accordingly had them summoned both for Dalrymple's murder and for the assault of Garriehorn. They allowed themselves to be put to the horn—that is, denounced as rebels for not appearing—but loudly professed that, if freed on the score of the assault, they would stand their trial for the murder, alleging their entire innocence of that transaction. The king was now made acquainted with the case, and, by his orders, Auchindrain the elder was seized, and thrown into the Tolbooth in Edinburgh. The two culprits nevertheless continued to feel confidence in the want of proof against them, believing that, if Bannatyne were out of the way, it would be impossible to bring the fact home to them. The younger Mure, still at large, accordingly dealt with Bannatyne to 1611. induce him to go to Ireland. It is a wonder he did not at once send his friend to a more distant bourn. When Bannatyne was gone, young Mure came boldly forward to take his trial, somewhat to the embarrassment of the officers of justice. However, by the suggestion of his majesty, he was not allowed to depart till he should have suffered the torture, with a view to making him confess. To the admiration of all, he bore this treatment with unflinching fortitude, and confessed nothing.

Public sentiment now rose in favour of the Mures as persecuted men, and the Privy Council was inclined to let them off; and would have done so, had not the king continued firm in his belief of their guilt, and ordered them to be detained. Some years passed on, and proof seemed still past hope, when the Earl of Abercorn contrived to find out Bannatyne in Ireland, and caused him to be brought over to his own house in Paisley. There, Bannatyne gave a full account of the murder, but claimed, as fulfilment of a condition, that he should be allowed his freedom. The earl told him he had had no such understanding of the matter; but, to take away all ground of complaint, he would liberate him for the meantime, but at the end of ten days make every possible effort to take him unconditionally, whether dead or alive. At this Bannatyne hesitated; he knew that already the Mures had been laying plots to get him cut off in Ireland—now, between their vengeance and the extreme persecution threatened by Lord Abercorn, he could see no chance for safety. He therefore avowed his inclination to make a full confession before a court of law, and trust to his majesty's clemency.

On being confronted with Bannatyne, the Mures appeared as obstinate in their protestations of innocence as ever, contradicting everything he said, and denouncing him as a tool of their enemies. They were, nevertheless, brought to trial, along with Bannatyne, on the day noted in the margin—found guilty, and condemned to be beheaded at the Cross of Edinburgh, with forfeiture of all they possessed to his majesty's use. So ended this extraordinary tissue of crimes, old Auchindrain being at the time about eighty years of age.[1]

Macleod of Raasay had been proprietor of the lands of Gairloch Aug.

[1] A large collection of documents illustrative of this case will be found in Pitcairn's *Criminal Trials*, iii. 124–199. The story has been made the subject of a play, under the name of the *Ayrshire Tragedy*, by Sir Walter Scott.

1611. on the mainland of Ross-shire. He had the misfortune to live in the same time with Kenneth Mackenzie of Kintail, who has already been described as a man much too clever for his neighbours. Lord Kintail—for he had recently been made a peer—had a wadset or bond over a third of Gairloch, and by proper use of this legal footing in the estate, joined to neglect of legal defences by the insular chieftain, was in the way of becoming proprietor of the whole. While Raasay, however, neglected law, he had no reluctance to use the sword: so a hot feud subsisted between him and the crafty Mackenzie. The latter had already pursued the Macleods out of Gairloch with fire and sword.

Under the date noted in the margin, Lord Kintail hired a ship, that his son Murdo Mackenzie might go to Skye with a proper following, in order to apprehend one John Holmogh MacRorie, a duniwassal of Raasay,[1] who had given him some trouble in the Gairloch. The vessel, with whatever design it set out, soon changed its course, and arrived opposite Macleod's castle in the isle of Raasay—the same place where Johnson and Boswell afterwards found such an elegant scene of Highland hospitality. MacGillie-callum—such is the Highland appellative of the Laird of Raasay—seeing the vessel, went out to it with twelve of his followers, to buy some wine. 'When Murdo Mackenzie did see them coming, he, with all his train, lest they should be seen, went to the lower rooms of the ship, leaving the mariners only above the decks. The Laird of Raasay entered; and, having spoken the mariners, he departed, with a resolution to return quickly. Murdo Mackenzie, understanding that they were gone, came out of the lower rooms; and perceiving them coming again, he resolved to conceal himself no longer. The Laird of Raasay desired his brother Murdo to follow him into the ship with more company in another galley, that they might carry to the shore some wine which he had bought from the mariners; so returning to the ship, and finding Murdo Mackenzie there beyond his expectation, he consulteth with his men, and thereupon resolveth to take him prisoner, in pledge of his cousin John MacAllan MacRorie, whom the Laird of Gairloch detained in captivity.'—*G. H. S.*

The History of the Mackenzie family (MS.) says that Raasay, on coming the second time into the vessel, fell to drinking with Murdo Mackenzie in loving terms. 'Four of Murdo's men, fearing

[1] The superior men of a Highland clan were called the duniwassa's.

the worst, kept themselves fresh [sober] . . . . Raasay, sitting on the right hand of Murdo, said to him: "Murdo, thou art my prisoner!" Murdo, hearing this, starts, and, taking Raasay by the middle, threw him upon the deck, and said he scorned to be his prisoner. With that a fellow of Raasay's strake him with a dirk. He, finding himself wounded, drew back to draw his sword, [so] that he went overboard. He, thinking to swim to the coast of Scousarie, was drowned by the small boats that were coming from Raasay. His men, seeing him killed, resolved to sell their lives at the best rate they could. The four men that kept themselves fresh, fought so manfully in their own defence, and in revenge of their master, that they killed the Laird of Raasay and Gilliecallum More, the author of this mischief, his two sons, with all the rest that came to the vessel with Raasay. Tulloch's son, with six of Murdo's company, were killed as they were coming above deck from the place where they lay drunk. The four [sober] men . . . . were all pitifully hurt. When they were drawing the anchor, the fourth man, called Hector Oig M'Echin Vich Kinnich, ane active young gentleman, was shot with a chance bullet from the boats. The other three, cutting the tow of the anchor, did sail away with the dead corpses of both parties.' 1611.

'Thus,' says Sir Robert Gordon in conclusion to this murderous story, 'hath the Laird of Gairloch obtained *peaceable* possession of that land.'

'Sir James Lawson of Humbie, riding in Balhelvie Sands, where many other gentlemen were passing their time, sank down in a part of the sands and perished. He was found again on the morn, but his horse was never seen.'—*Cal.* SEP. 24.

It had been customary for the Scottish universities to receive students who had, through misbehaviour, become fugitives from other seats of learning; and now, as a natural consequence, it was found that the native youth at the university of Edinburgh, presuming on impunity for any improprieties they might commit, or a resource in case of punishment being attempted, 'has ta'en and takes the bauldness to misknow the principal and regents, and to debord in all kind of uncomely behaviour and insolencies, no wise seemly in the persons of students and scholars.' The Privy Council therefore issued a strict order forbidding the reception of fugitive students into the universities.—*P. C. R.* OCT. 25.

1611 Nov. 4. The Privy Council was at this time obliged to renew former acts against *Night-walkers* of the city of Edinburgh—namely, idle and debauched persons who went about the streets during the night, in the indulgence of wild humours, and sometimes committing heinous crimes. If it be borne in mind that there was at that time no system of lighting for the streets of the city, but that after twilight all was sunk in Cimmerian darkness, saving for the occasional light of the moon and stars, the reader will be the better able to appreciate the state of things revealed by this public act.

Reference is made to 'sundry idle and deboshit persons, partly strangers, who, debording in all kind of excess, riot, and drunkenness . . . . commit sundry enormities upon his majesty's peaceable and guid subjects, not sparing the ordinar officers of the burgh, who are appointit to watch the streets of the same—of whom lately some has been cruelly and unmercifully slain, and others left for deid.' The Council ordered that no persons of any estate whatsoever presume hereafter to remain on the streets 'after the ringing of the ten-hour bell at night.' The magistrates were also ordained to appoint some persons to guard the streets, and apprehend all whom they might find there after the hour stated.—*P. C. R.*

1612. In this year there happened a strife between the Earl of Caithness on the one side, and Sir Robert Gordon of Gordonston and Donald Mackay on the other, highly illustrative of a state of things when law had only asserted a partial predominancy over barbarism.

One Arthur Smith, a native of Banff, had been in trouble for coining so long ago as 1599, when his man actually suffered death for that crime. He himself contrived to escape justice, by making a lock of peculiarly fine device, by which he gained favour with the king. Entering into the service of the Earl of Caithness, he lived for seven or eight years, working diligently, in a recess called the Gote, under Castle Sinclair, on the rocky coast of that northern district. If we are to believe Sir Robert Gordon, the enemy of the Earl of Caithness, there was a secret passage from his lordship's bedroom into the Gote, where Smith was often heard working by night, and at last Caithness, Sutherland, and Orkney were found full of false coin, both silver and gold. On Sir Robert's representation of the case, a commission was given to him by the Privy Council to apprehend Smith and bring him to Edinburgh.

While the execution of this was pending, one William MacAngus MacRorie, a noted freebooter, was committed to Castle Sinclair, and there bound in fetters. Contriving to shift off his

irons, William got to the walls of the castle, and jumping from 1612.
them down into the sea which dashes on the rocks at a great depth below, swam safely ashore, and escaped into Strathnaver. There an attempt was made by the Sinclairs to seize him; but he eluded them, and they only could lay hold of one Angus Herriach, whom they believed to have assisted the culprit in making his escape. This man being taken to Castle Sinclair without warrant, and there confined, Mackay was brought into the field to rescue his man —for so Angus was—and Caithness was forced to give him up.

The coiner Smith was living quietly in the town of Thurso, MAY.
under the protection of the Earl of Caithness, when a party of Gordons and Mackays came to execute the commission for apprehending him. They had seized the fellow, with a quantity of false money he had about him, and were making off, when a set of Sinclairs, headed by the earl's nephew, John Sinclair of Stirkoke, came to the rescue with a backing of town's-people, and a deadly conflict took place in the streets. Stirkoke was slain, his brother severely wounded, and the rescuing party beat back. During the tumult, Smith was coolly put to death, lest he should by any chance escape. The invading party were then allowed to retire without further molestation. 'The Earl of Caithness was exceedingly grieved for the slaughter of his nephew, and was *much more vexed* that such a disgraceful contempt, as he thought, should have been offered to him in the heart of his own country, and in his chief town; the like whereof had not been enterprised against him or his predecessors.'

The strife is now transferred in partially legal form to Edinburgh, where the parties had counter-actions against each other before the Privy Council. Why the word *partially* is here used, will appear from Sir Robert Gordon's account of the procedure. 'Both parties did come to Edinburgh at the appointed day, where they did assemble all their friends. There were with the Earl of Caithness and his son Berriedale, the Lord Gray, the Laird of Roslin, the Laird of Cowdenknowes (the earl's sister's son), the Lairds of Murkle and Greenland (the earl's two brethren); these were the chief men of their company. There were with Sir Robert Gordon and Donald Mackay, the Earl of Winton and his brother the Earl of Eglintoun, with all their followers; the Earl of Linlithgow, with the Livingstones; the Lord Elphinstone, with his friends; the Lord Forbes, with his friends; Sir John Stewart, captain of Dumbarton (the Duke of Lennox's bastard son); the Lord Balfour; the Laird of Lairg Mackay in Galloway; the Laird of Foulis, with

1612. the Monroes; the Laird of Duffus; divers of the surname of Gordon . . . . with sundry other gentlemen of name too long to set down. The Earl of Caithness was much grieved that neither the Earl of Sutherland in person, nor Hutcheon Mackay, were present. It galled him to the heart to be thus overmatched, as he said, by seconds and children; for so it pleased him to call his adversaries. Thus, both parties went weel accompanied to the council-house from their lodgings; but few were suffered to go in when the parties were called before the Council.'

All of these friends had, of course, come to see justice done to their respective principals—that is, to outbrave each other in forcing a favourable decision as far as possible. What followed is equally characteristic. While the Council was endeavouring to exact security from the several parties for their keeping the peace, both sent off private friends to the king to give him a favourable impression of their cases. 'The king, in his wisdom, considering how much this controversy might hinder and endamage the peace and quietness of his realm in the parts where they did live, happening between persons powerful in their own countries, and strong in parties and alliances, did write thrice very effectually to the Privy Council, *to take up this matter from the rigour of law and justice unto the decision and mediation of friends.*' The Council acted accordingly, but not without great difficulty. While the matter was pending, Lord Gordon, son of the Marquis of Huntly, happened to come to Edinburgh from court; and his friends, having access to him, were believed by the Earl of Caithness to have given him a favourable view of their case

JUNE. against himself. 'So, late in the evening, the Lord Gordon coming from his own lodging, accompanied with Sir Alexander Gordon and sundry others of the Sutherland men, met the Earl of Caithness and his company upon the High Street, between the Cross and the Tron. At the first sight, they fell to jostling and talking; then to drawing of swords. Friends assembled speedily on all hands. Sir Robert Gordon and Mackay, with the rest of the company, came presently to them; but the Earl of Caithness, after some blows, given and received, perceiving that he could not make his part good, left the street, and retired to his lodging; and if the darkness of the night had not favoured him, he had not escaped so. The Lord Gordon, taking this broil very highly, was not satisfied that the Earl of Caithness had given him place, and departed; but, moreover, he, with all his company, crossed thrice the Earl of Caithness his lodging, thereby

to provoke him to come forth; but perceiving no appearance 1612.
thereof, he retired himself to his own lodging. The next day, the Earl of Caithness and the Lord Gordon were called before the Lords of the Privy Council, and reconciled in their presence.'

It was not till several years later that these troubles came to an end.

Proceeding upon the principle that the smallest trait of industrial MAR. 23
enterprise forms an interesting variety on the too ample details of barbarism here calling to be recorded, I remark with pleasure a letter of the king of this date, agreeing to the proposal lately brought before him by a Fleming—namely, to set up a work for the making of 'brinston, vitreall, and allome,' in Scotland, on condition that he received a privilege excluding rivalry for the space of thirteen years. About the same time, one Archibald Campbell obtained a privilege to induce him 'to bring in strangers to make red herrings.' In June 1613, he petitioned that the king would grant him, by way of pension for his further encouragement, the fourteen lasts of herrings yearly paid to his majesty by the Earl of Argyle, 'as the duty of the tack of the assize of herrings of those parts set to him,' being of the value of £38 yearly.—*M. S. P.*

Some of the principal Border gentlemen—Scott of Harden, MAR. 29.
Scott of Tushielaw, Scott of Stirkfield, Gladstones of Cocklaw, Elliot of Falnash, and others—had a meeting at Jedburgh, with a view to making a final and decisive effort for stopping that system of blood and robbery by which the land had been so long harassed, even to the causing of several valuable lands to be left altogether desolate. They entered into a sort of bond, declaring their abhorrence of all the ordinary violences, and agreeing thenceforth to shew no countenance to any lawless persons, but to stand firm with the government in putting them down. Even where the culprits were their own dependents or tenants, they were to take part in bringing them to justice, and, if they fled, were to deprive them of their 'tacks and steedings,' and 'put in other persons to occupy the same.' Should any fail to act in this way, or to pursue culprits to justice, they agreed that a share of guilt should lie with that person. This bond seems to have been executed with the concurrence of the state-officers, and more especially under encouragement from the king, who, they say, had shewn his

1612. anxiety every way 'for the suppressing of that infamous byke[1] of lawless limmers.'[2]

MAR. APR. The Presbyterian historian of this period notes, that 'in the months of March and April fell forth prodigious works and rare accidents. A cow brought forth fourteen great dog-whelps, instead of calves. Another, after the calving, became stark mad, so that the owner was forced to slay her. A dead bairn was found in her belly. A third brought forth a calf with two heads. One of the Earl of Argyle's servants being sick, vomited two toads and a serpent, and so convalesced; but after[wards] vomited a number of little toads. A man beside Glasgow murdered both his father and mother. A young man going at the plough near Kirkliston, killeth his own son accidentally with the throwing of a stone, goeth home and hangeth himself. His wife, lately delivered of a child, running out of the house to seek her husband, a sow had eaten her child.'—*Cal.* It is curious thus to see what a former age was capable of believing. The circumstances here related regarding the first two cows are now known to be impossibilities; and no such relation, accordingly, could move one step beyond the mouths of the vulgar with whom it originated. Yet it found a place in the work of a learned church historian of the seventeenth century.

JUNE. There was at this time an 'extraordinary drowth, whilk is likely to burn up and destroy the corns and fruits of the ground.' On this account, a fast was ordered at Aberdeen.—*A. K. S. R.* In September, and for some months after, there are notices of 'great dearth of victual,' doubtless the consequence of this drouth. 'The victual at ten pound the boll.'—*Chron. Perth.*

JULY 28. Gregor Beg Macgregor, and nine others of his unhappy clan, were tried for sundry acts of robbery, oppression, and murder; and being all found guilty, were sentenced to be hanged on the Burgh-moor of Edinburgh.—*Pit.* The relics of the broken Clan Gregor lived at this time a wild predaceous life on the borders of the lowlands of Perthshire—a fearful problem to the authorities of the country, from the king downward. One called Robin Abroch, from the nativity of his father (Lochaber), stood prominently out as a clever chief of banditti, being reported, says Sir Thomas Hamilton, king's advocate, as 'the most bluidy

[1] Hive. [2] Notes to *Border Minstrelsy*, i. clxxvi.

murderer and oppressor of all that damned race, and most terrible to all the honest men of the country.'[1] In a memoir of the contemporary Earl of Perth occurs an anecdote of Robin, which, though somewhat obscure, speaks precisely of the style of events which modern times have seen in the Abruzzi and the fastnesses of the Apennines. The incident seems to have occurred in 1611. 1612.

'In the meantime, some dozen of the Clan Gregor came within the *laigh* of the country—Robin Abroch, Patrick M'Inchater, and Gregor Gair, being chiefs. This Abroch sent to my chamberlain, David Drummond, desiring to speak to him. After conference, Robin Abroch, for reasons known to himself, alleging his comrades and followers were to betray him, was contented to take the advantage, and let them fall into the hands of justice. The plot was cunningly contrived, and six of that number were killed on the ground where I, with certain friends, was present; three were taken, and one escaped, by Robin and his man. This execution raised great speeches in the country, and made many acknowledge that these troubles were put to ane end, wherewith King James himself was well pleased for the time.'[2] We nevertheless find the king's advocate soon after desiring of the king that, for the sake of public peace, he would withdraw a certain measure of protection he had extended to Robin, and replace him under the same restrictions as had been prescribed to the rest of his clan.

In this year, a large body of troops was levied in Scotland in a clandestine manner for the service of the king of Sweden, in his unsuccessful war with Christian IV. of Denmark. As the king of Great Britain was brother-in-law of the latter monarch, this illegal levying of troops was an act of the greater presumption. The Privy Council fulminated edicts against the proceedings as most obnoxious to the king,[3] but without effect. One George Sinclair—a natural brother of the Earl of Caithness, and who, if we are to believe Sir Robert Gordon (an enemy), had stained himself by a participation in the treacherous rendition of Lord Maxwell—sailed with nine hundred men, whom he had raised in the extreme north.

The successful course of the king of Denmark's arms had at this

[1] Melrose State Papers.

[2] *Spal. Club Misc.*, ii. 396. For something more regarding Robin Abroch, see under October 26, 1624.

[3] Privy Council Record.

1612. time closed up the ordinary and most ready access to Sweden at Gottenburg, and along the adjacent coast. A Colonel Munckhaven, in bringing a large levy of mercenaries from the Netherlands in the spring of 1612, had consequently been obliged to take the riskful step of passing through Norway, then a portion of the dominions of the Danish monarch. The greater part of his soldiery entered the Trondiem Fiord, landed at Stordalen, and proceeded through the mountainous regions of Jempteland towards Stockholm, where they arrived in time to save it from the threats of the Danish fleet.[1]

Colonel Sinclair resolved to take a similar course; but he was less fortunate. Landing in Romsdalen, he was proceeding across Gulbrandsdalen, and had entered a narrow pass at Kringelen, utterly unsuspicious of the presence of an enemy, when he fell into a dire ambuscade formed by the peasantry. Even when aware that a hostile party had assembled, he was craftily beguiled on by the appearance of a handful of rustic marksmen on the opposite side of the river, whose irregular firing he despised, till his column had arrived at the most difficult part of the pass. The boors then appeared amongst the rocks above him, in front and in rear, closing up every channel of egress. Sinclair fell early in the conflict. The most of his party were either cut off by the marksmen, or dashed to pieces by huge rocks tumbled down from above. Of the nine hundred, but sixty were spared. These were taken as prisoners to the houses of various boors, who, however, soon tired of keeping them. It is stated that the wretched Scots were brought together one day in a large meadow, and there murdered in cold blood. Only one escaped.

The Norwegians celebrated this affair in a vaunting ballad, and, strange to say, still look back upon the destruction of Sinclair's party as a glorious achievement. In the pass of Kringelen, there is a tablet bearing an inscription to the following purport: 'Here lies Colonel Sinclair, who, with nine hundred Scotsmen, was dashed to pieces like clay-pots by three hundred boors of Lessöe, Vaage, and Froen. Berdon Segelstadt of Ringeböe was the leader of the boors.' In a peasant's house near by were shewn to me, in 1849, a few relics of the poor Caithness-men—a matchlock or two, a broadsword, a couple of powder-flasks, and the wooden part of a drum.

1613. After the treacherous slaughter of the Laird of Johnston in 1608,

[1] Von Buch's *Travels through Norway.*

Lord Maxwell was so hotly prosecuted by the state-officers, as to 1613.
be compelled to leave his country. His *Good-night,* a pathetic ballad, in which he takes leave of his lady and friends, is printed in the *Border Minstrelsy:* afterwards, he returned to Scotland, but could not shew himself in public. A succession of skulking adventures ended in his being treacherously given up to justice by his relative, the Earl of Caithness; and he was, without loss of time, beheaded at the Cross of Edinburgh—the sole noble victim to justice out of many of his order who, during the preceding thirty years, had deserved such a fate.

When informed by the magistrates of the city that they had got orders for his execution, he professed submission to the will of God and the king, but declined the attendance of any ministers, as he adhered to the ancient religion. 'It being foreseen by the bailies and others that gif he sould at his death enter in any discourse of that subject before the people, it might breed offence and sclander, he was desirit, and yielded to bind himself by promise, to forbear at his death all mention of his particular opinion of religion, except the profession of Christianity; which he sinsyne repented, as he declared to the bailies, when they were
bringing him to the scaffold.' On the scaffold, the unfortunate May 21.
noble expressed his hope that the king would restore the family inheritance to his brother. He likewise 'asked forgiveness of the Laird of Johnston, his mother, grandmother, and friends, acknowledging the wrong and harm done to them, with protestation that it was without dishonour for the worldly part of it. . . . . Then he retired himself near the block, and made his prayers to God; which being ended, he took leave of his friends and of the bailies of the town, and, suffering his eyes to be covered with ane handkerchief, offered his head to the axe.'[1]

Thus at length ended the feud between the Johnstons and Maxwells, after, as has been remarked, causing the deaths of two chiefs of each house.

Edward Lord Bruce of Kinloss lost his life in a duel fought Aug.
near Bergen-op-zoom with Sir Edward Sackville, afterwards Earl of Dorset. They were gay young men, living a life of pleasure in London, and in good friendship with each other, when some occurrence, arising out of their pleasures, divided them in an irremediable quarrel. Clarendon states that on Sackville's part

[1] Denmylne MSS., apud Pitcairn, iii. 52.

1613. the cause was 'unwarrantable.' Lord Kinloss, in his challenge, reveals to us that they had shaken hands after the first offence, but with this remarkable expression on his own part, that he reserved the heart for a truer reconciliation. Afterwards, in France, Kinloss learned that Sackville spoke injuriously of him, and immediately wrote to propose a hostile meeting. 'Be master,' he said, 'of your own weapons and time; the place wheresoever I will wait on you. By doing this, you will shorten revenge, and clear the idle opinion the world hath of both our worths.'

Sackville received this letter at his father-in-law's house, in Derbyshire, and he lost no time in establishing himself, with his friend, Sir John Heidon, at Tergoso, in Zealand, where he wrote to Lord Kinloss, that he would wait for his arrival. The other immediately proceeded thither, accompanied by an English gentleman named Crawford, who was to act as his second; also by a surgeon and a servant. They met, accompanied by their respective friends, at a spot near Bergen-op-Zoom, 'where but a village divides the States' territories from the archduke's . . . . to the end that, having ended, he that could, might presently exempt himself from the justice of the country by retiring into the dominion not offended.'

In the preliminary arrangements, some humane articles were agreed upon, probably by the influence of the seconds; but, if we are to believe Sir Edward Sackville, Lord Kinloss, in choosing his adversary's weapon, expressed some blood-thirsty sentiments, that gave him reason to hope for little mercy if he should be the vanquished party. Being on his part incensed by these unworthy expressions, he, though heavy with a recent dinner, hurried on the combat. To follow his remarkable narrative:[1]

'I being verily mad with anger [that] the Lord Bruce should thirst after my life with a kind of assuredness, seeing I had come so far and heedlessly to give him leave to regain his lost reputation, bade him alight, which with all willingness he quickly granted; and there, in a meadow ankle-deep in water at the least, bidding farewell to our doublets, in our shirts began to charge each other; having afore commanded our surgeons to withdraw themselves a pretty distance from us, conjuring them besides, as they respected our favours or their own safeties, not to stir, but suffer us to execute our pleasures; we being fully resolved (God forgive us!)

[1] This narrative, as well as the letters of challenge, is printed entire in the *Guardian*, Nos. 129 and 133.

to despatch each other by what means we could. I made a thrust 1613. at my enemy, but was short, and in drawing back my arm, I received a great wound thereon, which I interpreted as a reward for my short-shooting; but, in revenge, I pressed in to him, though I then missed him also, and then received a wound in my right pap, which passed level through my body, and almost to my back. And there we wrestled for the two greatest and dearest prizes we could ever expect trial for—honour and life; in which struggling, my hand, having but an ordinary glove on it, lost one of her servants, though the meanest, which hung by a skin. . . . . At last, breathless, yet keeping our holds, there passed on both sides propositions of quitting each other's swords; but when amity was dead, confidence could not live, and who should quit first, was the question; which on neither part either would perform, and restriving again afresh, with a kick and a wrench together, I freed my long captivated weapon; which incontinently levying at his throat, being master still of his, I demanded if he would ask his life, or yield his sword; both which, though in that imminent danger, he bravely denied to do. Myself being wounded, and feeling loss of blood, having three conduits running on me, which began to make me faint, and he courageously persisting not to accord to either of my propositions, through remembrance of his former bloody desire, and feeling of my present state, I struck at his heart, but with his avoiding missed my aim, yet passed through the body, and drawing out my sword, repassed it again through another place, when he cried: "O, I am slain!" seconding his speech with all the force he had to cast me; but being too weak, after I had defended his assault, I easily became master of him, laying him on his back, when, being upon him, I redemanded if he would request his life; but it seemed he prized it not at so dear a rate to be beholden for it, bravely replying, "he scorned it." Which answer of his was so noble and worthy, as I protest I could not find in my heart to offer him any more violence; only keeping him down, until at length his surgeon, afar off, cried out, "he would immediately die if his wounds were not stopped." Whereupon, I asked if he desired his surgeon should come, which he accepted of; and so being drawn away, I never offered to take his sword, accounting it inhuman to rob a dead man, for so I held him to be. This thus ended, I retired to my surgeon, in whose arms, after I had remained a while for want of blood, I lost my sight, and withal, as I then thought, my life also. But strong water and his diligence quickly recovered me, when I escaped a

1613. great danger. For my lord's surgeon, when nobody dreamt of it, came full at me with his lord's sword; and had not mine, with my sword, interposed himself, I had been slain by those base hands; although my Lord Bruce, weltering in his blood, and past all expectation of life, comformable to all his former carriage, which was undoubtedly noble, cried out: "Rascal, hold thy hand!"'

Thus miserably, a victim of passion, died a young nobleman who might otherwise have lived a long and useful life. Being childless, his title and estates went to his next brother, Thomas. Through what means it came about, we cannot tell, but possibly it might be in consequence of some recollection of a well-known circumstance in the history of a former great man of his family, King Robert Bruce, the heart of Edward Lord Kinloss was enclosed in a silver case, brought to Scotland, and deposited in the abbey-church of Culross, near the family seat. The tale of the *Silver Heart* had faded into a family tradition of a very obscure character, when, in 1808, this sad relic was discovered, bearing on the exterior the name of the unfortunate duellist, and containing what was believed to be the remains of a human heart. It was again deposited in its original place, with an inscription calculated to make the matter clear to posterity. The Bruce motto, FUIMUS, is also seen on the wall,

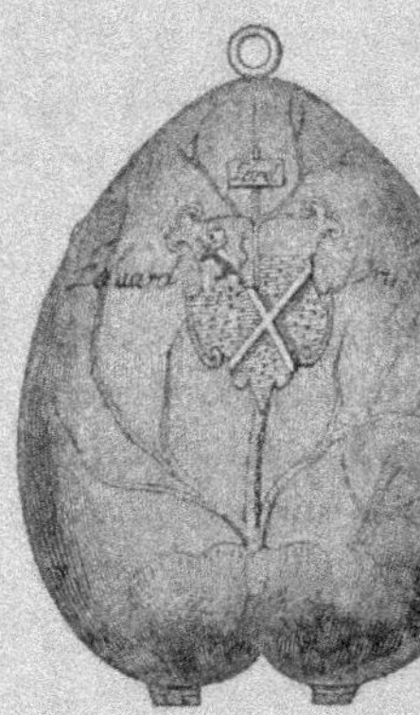

Silver Heart in Culross Abbey-church.

conveying to the visitor an indescribable feeling of melancholy, as he reflects on the stormy passion which once swelled the organ now resting within, and the wild details of that deadly quarrel of days long gone by.

'The unfortunate Lord Bruce saw distinctly the figure or

impression of a mort-head, on the looking-glass in his chamber, that very morning he set out for the fatal place of rendezvous, where he lost his life in a duel; and asked of some that stood by him if they observed that strange appearance: which they answered in the negative. His remains were interred at Bergen-op-Zoom, over which a monument was erected, with the emblem of a looking-glass impressed with a mort-head, to perpetuate the surprising representation which seemed to indicate his approaching untimely end. I had this narration from a field-officer, whose honour and candour is beyond suspicion, as he had it from General Stuart in the Dutch service. The monument stood entire for a long time, until it was partly defaced when that strong place was reduced by the weakness or treachery of Cronstrom, the governor.'—*Theophilus Insulanus's Treatise on the Second-Sight.* 1763. 1613.

Robert Philip, a priest, returned from Rome in the summer of this year, and performed mass in sundry places in a clandestine manner, but with the proper dresses, utensils, and observances. One James Stewart, living at the Nether Bow Port in Edinburgh, commonly called *James of Jerusalem*—a noted papist and resetter of seminary priests—was accustomed to have this condemned ceremonial performed in his house, in presence of a small company. Both men were now tried for these offences; and two days after, SEP. 11. a third, John Logan, portioner of Restalrig, was also put to an assize, for being one of the audience at Stewart's house. One cannot, in these days of tolerance, read without a strange sense of uncouthness, the solemn expressions of horror employed in the dittays of the king's advocate against the offenders, being precisely the same expressions which were used against heinous offences of a more tangible nature. Philip and Stewart were condemned to banishment,[1] and Logan, in as far as he expressed penitence and shewed that he had since conformed to the kirk, and even borne office in the session, was let off with a fine of one thousand pounds!

Robert Erskine, brother of the lately deceased Laird of Dun, DEC. 1. in Forfarshire, was put upon trial for an offence that recalls the tale of the Babes in the Wood. To open the succession to himself, he formed the resolution to put away his two nephews,

[1] In March 1615, James Stewart is once more, and very solemnly, condemned by the Privy Council to exile, in consequence of fresh offences of the same kind.

1613. John and Alexander Erskine, minors, and for this purpose consulted with his three sisters, Isobel, Annas, and Helen. These women, readily entering into his views, attempted to bribe a servant to engage a witch for the purpose of destroying the two boys; but the man's virtue was proof to the temptation. Annas and Helen then made a journey across the Cairnamount to a place called the Muir-alehouse, where dwelt a noted witch called Janet Irving. From her they came back, bearing certain deadly herbs fitted for their purpose, and gave these to their brother. He, doubtful of the efficacy of the herbs, went himself to the witch, to get full assurance on that point; and, finding reason to believe that they could destroy the two boys, lost no time in making an infusion of them in ale, which he administered to his victims in the house of their mother at Montrose. The effect was not immediate; but it inflicted the most horrible torments upon the poor youths, one of whom, after *dwining* for three years, died, uttering, just before death, these affecting words: 'Wo is me! that ever I had right of succession to ony lands or living, for, gif I had been born some poor cotter's son, I had not been sae demeaned [treated], nor sic wicked practices had been plotted against me for my lands!' The other remained without hope of recovery at the time of the trial.

Robert Erskine was found guilty and condemned to be beheaded. His sisters were tried June 22, 1614, for their share of the guilt, and also condemned to death, which two of them suffered. Helen alone, as being less guilty and more penitent than the rest, had her sentence commuted to banishment. The case must have been felt as deeply afflicting by the friends of the Presbyterian cause, as these wretched victims of the mean passion of avarice were the great-grandchildren of the venerated reformer, John Erskine of Dun.—*Pit.*

1613 (?) One John Stercovius, a Pole, had come into Scotland in the dress of his country, which exciting much vulgar attention, he was hooted at on the streets, and treated altogether so ill, that he was forced to make an abrupt retreat. The poor man, returning full of wounded feelings to his own country, published a *Legend of Reproaches* against the Scottish nation—'ane infamous book against all estates of persons in this kingdom.'—*P. C. R.* It will now be scarcely believed, in Scotland or elsewhere, that King James, hearing of this libel, employed Patrick Gordon, a foreign agent—himself a man of letters—to raise a prosecution against

Stercovius in his own country, and had the power to cause the unhappy libeller to be beheaded for his offence! The affair cost six thousand merks, and a convention of burghs was called (December 3, 1613), to consider means of raising this sum by taxation. This mode of raising the money having failed, the king made an effort to obtain aid for the payment of the money from the English resident in the town of Danzig—with what result does not appear. It is a notable circumstance, that while James was on the whole a mild administrator of justice, he was unrelenting towards satirists, and the grossest judicial cruelties of his reign are against men who had been in one way or another contumelious towards himself. 1613 (?)

One of the king's large ships-of-war, which had lain in the Roads of Leith for six weeks, and was about to set sail on her return to England, met her destruction 'about the twelfth hour of the day,' through the mad humour of an Englishman, who, while the captain and some of his officers were on shore, laid trains of powder throughout the vessel, notwithstanding that his own son was on board, along with about sixty other men. 'The ship and her whole provision were burnt; only the bottom and some of the munition were safe. Twenty-four of the men were burnt or perished in the sea; the rest were mutilated and lamed, notwithstanding of all the help that could be made. The fire made the ordnance to shoot, so that none durst come near to help.'—*Cal.* 1613. DEC. 10.

'The sixty-three men that escaped were shipped and transported to London.'—*Bal.*

The Privy Council of Scotland had this day under their consideration a subject which must have sent their minds back to the associations of an earlier and more romantic age. That custom among the people of the Scottish Border, of going into Cheviot to hunt, which had led to the dismal tragedy narrated in the well-known ballad of *Chevy Chase*, was, it seems, still kept up. What was once the border of either country being now the middle of both in their so far united condition, the king felt the propriety of putting down a custom so apt to lead to bad blood between his English and Scottish subjects; and accordingly, his council now ordered that the inhabitants of Roxburgh and Selkirk shires, of Liddesdale and Annandale, should cease their ancient practice of going into Tynedale, Redesdale, the fells of Cheviot and Kidland, DEC. 16.

1613. for hunting and the cutting of wood, under pain of confiscation of their worldly goods.—*P. C. R.*

1614. Jan. 18. Hugh Weir of Cloburn, a boy of fourteen years, had been taken out of the town of Edinburgh from his mother's friends, and carried over to Ireland, and there married to the daughter of the Laird of Corehouse. He 'was, by Sir James Hamilton's means, apprehended in Ireland, and sent back to Scotland, and presented to the Council. He was imprisoned in the Tolbooth, in a room next the Laird of Blackwood, by whose means the boy was taken away and sent into Ireland.'—*Bal.*

Mar. 3. (Tuesday) at 'half an hour to sax in the morning, ane earthquake had in divers places.' 'On Thursday thereafter, ane other earthquake at 12 hours in the night, had baith in land and burgh.' —*Chron. Perth.*

Aug. 12. Theophilus Howard, Lord Walden (afterwards Earl of Suffolk), made a short journey of pleasure in Scotland; and as the details give some idea of the means there were in the country of entertaining a stranger of distinction, they may be worth noting. His lordship was received by the Earl of Home into Dunglass House, in Berwickshire, and 'used very honourably.' He dined next day with his brother-in-law, Sir James Home of Cowdenknowes, at Broxmouth House, near Dunbar. Advancing thence towards Edinburgh, he was met by the secretary of state, Sir Thomas Hamilton of Binning, accompanied by a number of gentlemen of the country, all of whom had waited for him the preceding night at Musselburgh Links, but were disappointed of his coming forward. He was by them convoyed to the Canongate, and lodged in John Killoch's house. Next morning, he proceeded to the Castle, and 'viewed the site, fortification, and natural strength thereof.' Having dined, he rode from Edinburgh with the Lord Chancellor to Dunfermline, where he was entertained with all kindness and respect till Monday, the 16th. He then went to Culross, to see Sir George Bruce's coal-works, which were one of the wonders of the age; 'where, having received the best entertainment they could make him, my Lord Chancellor took leave of him, and left him to be convoyed by my Lord Erskine to Stirling, where he could not be persuaded to stay above one night. The next day, he saw the park of Stirling, dined in the Castle, and raid that night towards Falkland.' On the way, Lord

Erskine transferred him to the care of Lord Scone, who, assisted 1614.
by many gentlemen of Fife, took him to his house in Falkland.' There, doubtless to the great distress of Lord Scone, no entreaties could prevail upon Lord Walden to stay longer than a night, 'to receive that entertainment which he wald gladly have made langer to him.' So, 'after the sight of the park and palace, having dined, his lordship and my Lord of Scone came to Burntisland, where he had ready and speedy passage; but the wind being very loud, he was exceeding sick at sea.' Landing at Leith, the distinguished company was received for refreshment into the house of a rich and prominent person of that day, Bernard Lindsay, whom we shall see erelong entertaining Ben Jonson in the same place. Here the secretary again took up the stranger, and convoyed him once more to John Killoch's in the Canongate, 'whither the bailies of Edinburgh came to him, and invited him to supper the next day, but could not induce him by any entreaty to stay.' Having dismissed them, he went to see the palace of Holyrood. Next day, the 19th of August, he left Edinburgh, and rode with the secretary to Seton, 'where he was received by the Countess of Winton and her children, and used with all due respect.' After taking a sight of the house, which was of princely elegance, with beautiful gardens, Lord Walden proceeded to Broxmouth, and there spent the night.

'In all his journey through this country,' says the contemporary writer, 'great and loving respect has been borne to him by all honest men, whereof he has proven most worthy; for he has esteemed all things to the uttermost of their worth, and in his courteous discretion has favourably excused all oversights and defects. . . . . Every honest man here wishes him happiness in all his other journeys and enterprises, for the honourable, wise, and humane behaviour he has used amang them.'[1]

In this year, a small volume was printed and published by Andro Hart of Edinburgh, under the title of *Mirifici Logarithmorum Canonis Descriptio*, &c., *Auctore et Inventore Joanne Napero, Barone Merchistonii, Scoto.* This was a remarkable event in the midst of so many traits of barbarism, bigotry, and ignorance; for in Napier's volume was presented a mode of calculation forming an essential pre-requisite to the solution of all the great problems involving numbers which have since been brought before mankind.

[1] From a paper in Balfour's MSS., printed in *Bannatyne Miscellany*, vol. iii.

1614. John Napier is believed to have been engaged in the elaboration of his Logarithms for fully twenty years, while at the same time giving some of his time to such inventions as burning-glasses for the destruction of fleets, to theological discussions, and the occult sciences. The tall, antique tower of Merchiston, in which he lived and pursued his studies, still exists at the head of the Burgh-moor of Edinburgh.

Napier's little book was published in an English translation by Henry Briggs of Oxford, the greatest mathematician of his day in England. The admiration of Briggs for the person of Napier was testified in the summer of 1615 by his paying a visit to Scotland, in order to see him. Of this rencontre there is a curious and interesting account preserved by William Lilly in his *Life and Times*. 'I will acquaint you,' says he, 'with one memorable story related unto me by John Marr, an excellent mathematician and geometrician, whom I conceive you remember. He was a servant to King James I. and Charles I. When Merchiston first published his Logarithms, Mr Briggs, then reader of the astronomy lectures at Gresham College in London, was so surprised with admiration of them, that he could have no quietness in himself until he had seen that noble person whose only invention they were. He acquaints John Marr therewith, who went in[to] Scotland before Mr Briggs, purposely to be there when these two so learned persons should meet. Mr Briggs appoints a certain day when to meet at Edinburgh; but failing thereof, Merchiston was fearful he would not come. It happened one day, as John Marr and Lord Napier were speaking of Mr Briggs, "Oh! John," saith Merchiston, "Mr Briggs will not come now." At the very instant, one knocks at the gate. John Marr hasted down, and it proved to be Mr Briggs, to his great contentment. He brings Mr Briggs into my lord's chamber, where almost one quarter of an hour was spent, each beholding other with admiration, before one word was spoken. At last Mr Briggs began: "My lord, I have undertaken this long journey purposely to see your person, and to know by what engine of wit or ingenuity you came first to think of this most excellent help unto astronomy—namely, the Logarithms; but, my lord, being by you found out, I wonder nobody else found it out before, when, now being known, it appears so easy." He was nobly entertained by the Lord Napier; and every summer after that, during the laird's being alive, this venerable man went purposely to Scotland to visit him.'

As Napier (whom Lilly erroneously calls lord) died in April

1617, Mr Briggs could not have made more than one other summer pilgrimage to Merchiston. 1614.

Died John M'Birnie, minister of St Nicolas' Church, Aberdeen—a typical example of the more zealous and self-denying of the Presbyterian clergy of that age. A similar one of the next age says of M'Birnie: 'I heard Lady Culross say: "He was a godly, zealous, and painful preacher; and that he used always, when he rode, to have two Bibles hanging at a leather girdle about his middle, the one original, the other English; as also, a little sand-glass in a brazen case: and being alone, he read, or meditated, or prayed; and if any company were with him, he would read or speak from the Word to them." . . . . When he died, he called his wife, and told her he had no outward means to leave her, or his only daughter, but that he had got good assurance that the Lord would provide for them; and accordingly, the day he was buried, the magistrates of the town came to the house, after the burial, and brought two subscribed papers, one of a competent maintenance to his wife during her life, another of a provision for his daughter.'[1]

The latter part of the winter 1614–15 was of such severity as to 1615.
be attended with several remarkable circumstances which were long remembered. In February, the Tay was frozen over so strongly as to admit of passage for both horse and man. 'Upon Fasten's E'en [February 21], there was twa puncheons of Bourdeaux wine carriet, *sting and ling*,[2] on men's shoulders, on the ice, at the mids of the North Inch, the weight of the puncheon and the bearers, estimate to three score twelve stane weight.' This state of things, however, was inconvenient for the ferrymen, 'being thereby prejudgit of their commodity.' So they, 'in the night-time, brak the ice at the entry, and stayit the passage.'—*Chron. Perth.*

An enormous fall of snow took place early in March, so as to stop all communication throughout the country. On its third day, many men and horse perished in vain attempts to travel. The accumulation of snow was beyond all that any man remembered.

[1] Some Observations of Mr John Livingstone, MS. Adv. Lib. 'It appears from the council registers of Aberdeen, that the corporation voluntarily gave a thousand merks for the support of M'Birnie's widow and children.'—*Notes to Coll. Hist. Aber. and Banff*, Spal. Club.

[2] *Sting* is a Scotch word for a pole, and the phrase *sting and ling* is believed to express simply the method of carrying practised by draymen.

1615. 'In some places, men devised snow-ploughs to clear the ground, and fodder the cattle.'—*Bal.* The snow fell to such a depth, and endured so long upon the ground, that, according to Sir Robert Gordon, 'most part of all the horse, nolt, and sheep of the kingdom did perish, but chiefly in the north.'[1]

The Privy Council, viewing the 'universal death, destruction, and wrack of the beasts and goods throughout all parts of the country,' apprehended that, without some extraordinary care, there would not be enough of lambs left to replenish the farms with sheep for future use. They accordingly interfered with a decree forbidding the use of lamb for a certain time. Nevertheless, so early as the 26th of April, it was ascertained that there were undutiful subjects, who, 'preferring their own private contentment and their inordinate appetite, and the delicate feeding of their bellies, to the reverence and obedience of the law,' continued to use lamb, only purchasing it in secret places, as if no such prohibition had ever been uttered. It was therefore become necessary that severe punishment should be threatened for this offence. The threats launched forth on this occasion were found next year to have been of some effect in preserving the remnant of the lamb stock; and, to complete the restoration of the stock, a new decree to the like effect was then made (March 14, 1616).

JAN. The king and his English council having, with the usual short-sighted policy of the age, decreed that no goods should be imported into or exported out of England, except in English vessels, the burghs of Scotland were not slow to perceive that the interests of their country would be deeply injured thereby, as other states would of course establish similar restrictions, 'and if so, there is naething to be expected but decay and wrack to our shipping, insaemickle as the best ships of Scotland are continually employed in the service of Frenchmen, not only within the dominions of France, but also within the bounds of Spain, Italy, and Barbary, where their trade lies, whilk is ane chief cause of the increase of the number of Scots ships and of their maintenance, whereas by the contrary, the half of the number of

[1] This unheard-of snow-fall was equally notable in the south. When the thaw came, it caused an unexampled flood in the Ouse of Yorkshire, which lasted ten days, carrying away a great number of bridges. 'After this storm followed such fair and dry weather, that in April the ground was as dusty as in any time of summer. The drought continued till the 20th of August, and made such a scarcity of hay, beans, and barley, that the former was sold at York for 30s. and 40s. a wainload.'—*History of York*, 1785, i. 256.

ships whilk are presently in Scotland will serve for our awn 1615.
privat trade and negotiation.'

The king of France did in reality revenge the selfish policy of England by issuing a similar order in favour of French shipping, the first consequence of which was that an English vessel and a Dutch one, lading in Normandy, were obliged to disburden themselves and come empty home. 'Ane Scottish bark perteining to Andrew Allan, whilk that same time was lading with French merchandise,' would have been subjected to the same inconvenience, if the master had not pretended to an immunity in favour of his country, through its ancient alliance with France, 'inviolably kept these 800 years bypast.' The Scots factors in France entered a complaint before the parliament of Paris, reminding it of that ancient alliance, and pleading that the French had ever had liberty of trade in all Scottish ports; shewing, indeed, that Scotland was not comprised in the edict of the English monarch and his council. The parliament accordingly decreed that the Scotch should remain in the enjoyment of freedom of trade within France, as heretofore.

The attention of the king being necessarily called to the interests of Scotland in this matter, he was found obstinate in favour of the general principle of the English order in council. 'Natural reason,' he said, 'teaches us that Scotland, being part of an isle, cannot be mainteined or preserved without shipping, and shipping cannot be mainteined without employment; and the very law of nature teacheth every sort of corporation, kingdom, or country, first to set their own vessels on work, before they employ any stranger.'[1] He was willing, however, to relax in particular cases. James argues logically, but he had not sagacity to anticipate the doctrines of Adam Smith.

This day saw the extraordinary sight of a Scottish earl, cousin- FEB. 6.
german to the king, led out to a scaffold in the High Street of Edinburgh, and there beheaded. The sufferer was Patrick Earl of Orkney, whose father was a natural son of King James V. Forty years earlier, this man would have stood his ground against the law: now, it was too strong for him, and he fell before it.

Earl Patrick appears to have been a man of grand and ambitious views, and his dream of life was to make himself a sort of independent prince in the remote group of islands where lay his estate. The sketch given of his style of living there by a

[1] *Letters and Papers of the Reign of James VI.*, pp. 243, 317. *Balfour's Annals*, ii. 58.

1615. contemporary writer is striking: 'He had a princely and royal revenue; and indeed behavit himself with sic sovereignty, and, gif I durst say the plain verity, rather tyrannically, by the shadow of Danish laws, different and more rigorous nor [than] the municipal or criminal laws of the rest of Scotland; whereby no man of rent or purse might enjoy his property in Orkney, without his special favour, and the same dear bought. . . . Fitchit and forgit faults was so devisit against many of them, that they were compellit by imprisonment and small rewaird to resign their heritable titles to him; and gif he had a stieve purse and no rent, then was some crime devisit against him, whereby he was compellit [to give up] either half or haill thereof, gif not life and all beside. And his pomp was so great there [in Kirkwall], as he never went from his castle to the kirk, nor abroad otherwise, without the convoy of fifty musketeers and other gentlemen of convoy and guard. And siclike, before dinner and supper, there were three trumpeters that soundit still till the meat of the first service was set at table, and siclike at the second service; and consequently, after the grace. He had also his ships directit to the sea, to intercept pirates, and collect tribute of uncouth [foreign] fishers, that came yearly to these seas. Whereby he made sic collection of great guns and other weapons for weir [war] as no house, palace, nor castle, yea all in Scotland were not furnished with the like.'

The doings of this insular potentate at length attracted the attention of the law, and he was summoned in 1610 to answer for various acts of the nature of a usurpation of the royal authority during the preceding twenty years. It appears from this summons, that he made laws of his own, and prosecuted divers gentlemen for disobeying them. He had forced some of these persons into a Bond of Manrent, obliging themselves to maintain his cause against whatsoever persons, and that they should never know of any 'skaith' threatening him but they would reveal it within twenty-four hours. He had imprisoned sundry persons in irons and stocks sundry days and weeks, and compelled many of the poorer class 'to work for him all manner of work and labour by sea and land, in rowing and sailing his ships and boats, working in the stane quarry . . . . loading his boats with stane and lime . . . . bigging his park dykes, and all other sorts of servile and painful labour, without either meat, drink, or hire.' While forbidding the people generally to sell any of the produce of their lands without his licence, he imposed on them grievous taxations. In short, he had acted the baronial tyrant in the extremest form of the character.

The earl was now a prisoner in Edinburgh Castle, and there could have been no difficulty in convicting and punishing him. The king, however, felt mercifully towards his cousin; and after several briefer postponements, the case was hung up, and the earl conveyed, for the safer custody of his person, to Dumbarton Castle. It is believed that King James was even willing to have come to a compromise with the culprit, granting him the lucrative keepership of some one of the royal palaces, on condition of his renouncing all claim to Orkney. The earl refused to temporise, and continued to entertain the secret resolution to regain, if possible, his island sovereignty, and there set all law at defiance. 1615.

He had a natural son, Robert, a fitting instrument for his designs. Under his instructions, this youth proceeded to Orkney in 1614, and there assembling a company, took possession of the castle of Kirkwall, at the same time fortifying the church and steeple. Voluntarily or by compulsion, a great number of the islanders signed a bond, engaging to support him; and it was soon understood that Orkney was in rebellion against the crown. The Privy Council met to consider what should be done. The Earl of Caithness was now in Edinburgh, attempting to obtain remission for offences of his own, one of which consisted in his waging war in the preceding year against the Earl of Sutherland. It readily occurred to his wily mind, that, for a culprit like himself, nothing could be so good as to offer to help the government to punish the crimes of others. It was, moreover, rather a pleasure than a duty to carry war into Orkney. His offered services were accepted, and he quickly sailed with a strong military party for Kirkwall. He found the fortress strong, the country people generally in favour of the rebels, and great deficiency of provision for his troops. He nevertheless beleaguered the castle for about a month, during which time some damage was done by ordnance on both sides. At length, by adroit dealing with one Patrick Halcro, the chief associate of Robert Stuart, he brought about a surrender of the house and all it contained (September 29, 1614), with a condition for the saving of Halcro's life, but for no favour to any other.

Robert Stuart was brought to trial in Edinburgh, and condemned to death. He was a youth of only twenty-two, 'of a tall stature and comely countenance;' and it is to be remembered in his favour, that he withstood all the persuasions of the Earl of Caithness to give up Kirkwall Castle, foreseeing that he should be tortured into revealing his father's guilt; he only surrendered on

1615. Jan. 6. finding that Halcro was going to betray him. He died penitent, with five of his company.

The doom of the earl, the prime mover of the rebellion, followed. He 'took the sentence impatiently.' An attempt was made to excite the king to spare the royal blood, but without effect. 'The ministers, finding him so ignorant that he could scarce rehearse the Lord's Prayer, entreated the Council to delay his execution some few days, till he were better informed, and received the Lord's Supper. . . . . So he communicate on the Lord's day, the 5th of February, and was beheaded at the market-cross of Edinburgh upon Monday the 6th of February; when Sir Robert Ker, the Earl of Rochester, was decourted. The king laid the blame of his death upon him [Rochester], but late, as his custom was, when matters was past remedy.'—*Cal. G. H. S. Pit.*

An entry in the session record of Perth, under September 1632, forms a curious and striking pendant to the history of this unfortunate branch of the Stuart family. 'Disbursed at the command of the ministers to ane young man called Stewart, son to umwhile the Earl of Orkney, seven shillings.'

Feb. 28. This day, John Ogilvie, a Jesuit, was hanged in Glasgow, being the first priest who had suffered in that way in Scotland since the execution of the Archbishop of St Andrews at Stirling in 1571.[1]

Ogilvie was a Scotsman of good family, who had lived for twenty-one years in a Jesuit college at Gratz. He came to Scotland in the autumn of 1613, and spent some time amongst the Catholics in the north, then went to London, and finally came back to Scotland in June 1614. For three months he lived skulkingly in Glasgow, occasionally performing mass, but was at length apprehended in October, along with thirteen or fourteen persons who had been present at those ceremonies. The latter were thrown into Dumbarton Castle, and only liberated on payment of large fines. Ogilvie himself was subjected to examination and trial. The only account he would give of himself was that he came to Scotland at the command of his superiors, 'to save souls.' To induce further confession, he was put on low diet and kept from sleep for several

[1] Catholic historians note the martyrdom of one of their faith, which took place amidst the more immediate tumults of the Reformation. His name was Black, and he is described as a Dominican monk of Aberdeen, respectable both for piety and learning. Being taken to Edinburgh to dispute with Willox and other apostles of the Reformation, the populace cut short the argument by stoning him to death on the streets, January 7, 1562.—*Dempster. D. Camerarius.*

nights in succession; and being thus made 'light in the head,' 1615.
he 'began to discover certain particulars, but, howsoon he was permitted to take any rest, he denied all, and was as obstinate in denying as at first.'

The king, who was tolerant of the religion of the papists, as apart from their anarchical doctrines regarding papal supremacy, told his Council to let Ogilvie go unharmed into banishment, if he was but a Jesuit who had said mass, and only to deal severely with him if he had been a practiser of sedition, or refused to take the oath of allegiance. They soon found from his answers to certain questions that he was a bold and decided adherent of the doctrines of his order, holding that the pope was superior to the king, and might excommunicate him, and not clearly denying that the subjects might thus be absolved from their allegiance to their sovereign, and even slay him. He denied that he had been guilty of any real crime, saying that acts of parliament were but the dicta of partial men. The king's authority came from predecessors who had acknowledged the supremacy of the pope: 'if he will be to me as his predecessors were to mine, I will acknowledge him,' not otherwise. In declining the king's authority in such matters, he did no more than the best of the Presbyterian clergy did—a course in which they would persevere if they were wise. 'I have done no offence,' said he, 'neither will I beg mercy. If I were even now forth of the kingdom, I should return. If all the hairs in my head were priests, they should all come into the kingdom.'

The one chance which Ogilvie had in the tolerant spirit of the king was thus closed. The zealous Presbyterians had of course nothing to say in arrest of judgment. According to their historian, the bishops felt it to be necessary that they should do something decided against the papists '*for honesty's sake*'—that is, some unmistakably sound and good thing on the right side, such as the hanging of a Jesuit clearly was—lest they should appear more inclined to persecute the ministers of the true, than those of a false religion. Accordingly, John Spottiswoode, archbishop of Glasgow, was all along the most conspicuous man in the prosecution of the unfortunate Jesuit. The trial took place in the Town-hall of Glasgow, before a commission composed of the magistrates and a number of noblemen, and condemnation was followed in *three hours* by execution.

'He continued a while upon his knees at prayer, with a cold devotion; and when the hour of execution approached, his hands being tied by the executioner, his spirits were perceived much to

1615. fail him. In going towards the scaffold, the throng of people was great, and he seemed much amazed; and when he was up, Master Robert Scott and Mr William Struthers, ministers, very gravely and Christianly exhorted him to a humble acknowledgment of his offence, and if anything troubled his mind, to disburden his conscience. In matters of religion, they said, they would not then enter, but prayed him to resolve and settle his mind, and seek mercy and grace from God through Jesus Christ, in whom only salvation is to be found. Ogilvie answered that "he was prepared and resolved." Once he said that he died for religion, but uttered this so weakly as scarce to be heard by them that stood by on the scaffold. Then addressing himself to execution, he kneeled at the ladder-foot, and prayed. Master Robert Scott, in that while, declaring to the people, that his suffering was not for any matter of religion, but for heinous treason against his majesty, which he prayed God to forgive him. Ogilvie, hearing this, said: "He doeth me wrong." One called John Abercrombie, a man of little wit, replied: "No matter, John, the more wrongs the better." This man was seen to attend him carefully, and was ever heard asking of Ogilvie some token before his death; for which, and other business he made with him, he was put off the scaffold.

'Ogilvie, ending his prayer, arose to go up the ladder; but strength and courage, to the admiration of those who had seen him before, did quite forsake him. He trembled and shaked, saying he would fall, and could hardly be helped up on the top of the ladder. He kissed the hangman, and said: "Maria, Mater gratiae, ora pro me; Omnes Angeli, orate pro me; Omnes Sancti, Sanctaeque, orate pro me!" but with so low a voice that they which stood at the ladder-foot had some difficulty to hear him.

'The executioner willed him to commend his soul to God, pronouncing these words unto him: "Say, John, Lord have mercy on me, Lord receive my soul!" which he did, with such feebleness of voice, that scarce could he be heard. Then he was turned off, and hung till he was dead.'[1]

This hanging would of course have procured some popularity for the king and bishops, if it had proceeded from the right motive. But the people saw that no gratitude was really due. 'Some,' says Calderwood, 'interpreted this execution to have proceeded rather of a care to bless the king's government, than of *any sincere hatred of the popish religion*. Some [alleged] that it was

[1] *True Relation of the Proceedings against John Ogilvie*, 1615: reprinted in Pitcairn.

done to be a terror to the sincerer sort of the ministry, not to decline the king's authority in ony cause whatever.' 1615.

There was believed to be at this time an unusual number of Jesuits and seminary priests in Scotland, 'pressing by all means possible to subvert the true religion.' The kirk launched a fast at them, and ordered a general celebration of 'the holie communion' for discovery of all recusants. In Aberdeen, the elders subsequently reported three men and two women as having been absent on this occasion. Such persons were proceeded against, so as to force them, if possible, into conformity, in which case each person was expected to come forward publicly, and declare, 'for the peace of my own conscience,' I do, 'by my own free choice and voluntary consent, renounce all the errors and superstitions of popery,' and profess, 'in the true simplicity of my heart,' that 'I shall own and maintain all the doctrines of the true Reformed Protestant Religion, and shall adhere to the whole worship and discipline thereof to my life's end.'[1] In the present case, four persons remained recusant, and actually were excommunicated in the ensuing January; thus, in fact, losing all privileges as subjects of the realm. MAR.

On the 14th of August, three citizens of Edinburgh, named Sinclair, Wilkie, and Cruikshanks, all men in respectable circumstances, were tried for the crime of entertaining in their houses three Jesuits or trafficking priests, including the unfortunate John Ogilvie. Sinclair confessed to having reset Mr James Moffat in the preceding October, but said he did it 'only upon simplicity.' The three men were condemned to be executed as traitors; and, as if to shew the certainty of their doom, a special order from the king was read in court for proceeding to both sentence and execution. The zealous multitude were accordingly in full hope of the punishment being inflicted; but there was no earnestness in the government in these proceedings. Let Calderwood tell the remainder of the tale. 'The day following [the trial], betwixt four and five in the afternoon, they were brought furth with their hands bound, to the scaffold set up beside the cross and a gallows in it, according to the custom of execution. While a great multitude of people were going to see the execution, there was a warrant presented to the magistrates of Edinburgh to stay the execution. So they were

[1] See the entire form of abjuration in *Selections from the Records of the Kirk Session, Presbytery, and Synod of Aberdeen.* Spalding Club. 1846.

1615. turned back again to their wards. The people thought this form of dealing *rather mockery than punishment.'*

The sentence was commuted by the king's order to banishment from Edinburgh for Cruikshanks, and for the other two to banishment from the king's dominions, both during his royal pleasure.—*Pit. Cal.*

A little trait of the domestic circumstances of Catholics of rank at this time is worthy of notice. The Earl of Errol, as a recusant papist, was only enabled to remain in his country on condition that he should not pass beyond a small circle around his own castle in Aberdeenshire. Being embarrassed by debt, and troubled by his creditors, he found himself constrained to take some legal steps 'for the provision of his mony young children, and settling of some good course for the estate of his house.' It was necessary that he should be allowed to break temporarily through the obligation under which he lay to live within a certain space round his house. He therefore got a formal licence (November 9, 1615), 'to repair to Edinburgh, and there to remain in some lodging, *not kything ony way in daylight upon the heich street,* for ten days after the 20th of November.'—*P. C. R.*

APR. On the Saturday before Pasch Sunday, 'ane extraordinar riot' took place in the usually quiet little burgh of Burntisland. The gentleman who acted as chamberlain of the queen in the management of her dotarial estate of Dunfermline, was called upon, in the course of his duty, to send 'precepts of warning to remove' to Burntisland, 'according to common order.' No immediate steps of a strong character were meditated; it was merely a form of law. The inhabitants, led, as afterwards appeared, by their pastor, Mr William Watson, conceived a violent anger at the proceeding, and determined to give it an active resistance. When the officer and his witness came to the cross for the execution of his office, he was assailed by 'a multitude of women, above ane hundred, of the bangster Amazon kind'—so states the grave chancellor, Earl of Dunfermline—and 'maist uncourteously dung [driven] off his feet, and his witness with him, they all hurt and bloodit, all his letters and precepts reft frae him, riven and cast away, and sae staned and chased out of the town.' The magistrates are alleged to have looked on without interference; nay, 'the bailie's awn wife' was 'the principal leader of this tumultuary army of Amazons;' so that there was no room to doubt that the male inhabitants were the instigators of the riot.

Some sharp measures were taken for the punishment of the rioters, and the chancellor besought the king to send off Mr Watson to some quieter part of the country, and ordain Burntisland 'to be provided with some minister of mair calm port, to rule and circumscde sic het humours as may be in that people.'—*M. S. P.* 1615.

Accordingly, on the 14th of December, the Council decreed that Mr William Watson should 'transport himself out of the burgh of Burntisland' before the 10th of January next, and thereafter 'on nae wise repair to the said burgh, [nor] within aucht miles of the same, and on nae wise entertein ony intelligence with the inhabitants of Burntisland in ony matter concerning the government of that town.'—*P. C. R.* The king sent a warrant from Newmarket for this being carried into effect.

'Amang the mony abuses whilk the iniquity of the time and private respect of filthy lucre and gain has produced within the commonwealth'—thus gravely commences an act of the Privy Council—'there is of late discoverit a most unlawful and pernicious tred of *transporting of eggs furth of the kingdom.*' 'Certain avaritious and godless persons, void of modesty and discretion, preferring their awn private commodity to the commonweal, has gone and goes athort the country and buys the haill eggs that they can get, barrels the same, and transports them at their pleasure.' As an unavoidable consequence, 'there has been a great scarcity of eggs this while bygane,' and any that are to be had have 'risen to such extraordiuar and heich prices as are not to be sufferit in a weel-governit commonwealth.' 'Moreover,' proceeds this sage document, 'if this unlawful tred be sufferit to be of ony langer continuance, it will fall out that in a very short time *there will no eggs nor poultry be funden within the country.*' Apr. 26.

The Council was therefore prompted to order letters to be directed to all merchants and owners of vessels, forbidding them to carry eggs out of the country, on pain of heavy fines and such further punishment as the Council might see fit to decree.—*P. C. R.*

John Brand, student of philosophy, son of a former minister of Holyrood parish, was tried for the murder of a young man named William King, by stabbing him with a knife 'upon St Leonard's Craigs, beside the park-dyke.' He was sentenced to be beheaded at the Cross.—*Pit.* May 30.

1615. July. 'About this time certain bare and idle gentlemen lay in wait upon passengers by the ways about Edinburgh, and in parts of East Lothian, and would needs have money from them. The common people called them *Whilliwha's*.'[1]—*Cal.*

Francis Hay, son of the late George Hay of Ardletham, and cousin-german to the Earl of Errol, was on terms of the most friendly intimacy with Adam Gordon, brother of Gordon of Gight. One day, when living familiarly together, a quarrel took place between them, followed by a single combat, in which Adam Gordon had the advantage, taking Hay's sword from him, but instantly restoring it. Hay not being able to digest the affront, challenged Gordon some time after to renew the fight. Gordon, if we can believe a historian of the same name, 'desired him to forbeir, seeing there was enough done already for any quarrel that was amongst them. Whereupon Francis came to Adam's dwelling-place on horseback, with a pair of pistols at his girdle, and finds Adam walking about the fields, with his sword about him. Francis flies from his horse, and desires Adam to do him reason. So they go to it. Then again it was Adam his good hap to overcome Francis, and grants him his life; but as Adam was returning home, Francis, disdaining to be thus twice overthrown, shoots Adam behind his back with a pistol, and slays him.'

Gordon of Gight, resolved to revenge his brother's death, came to the house of William Hay of Logyruif, and there, without any
Dec. 18. warrant, seized Francis Hay, whom he immediately brought along to Aberdeen, and imprisoned in his own lodging, called the *Bonnie Wife's Inn*, in the Gallowgate, where he kept him for forty-eight hours, excluding all his friends from seeing him. The sheriff-depute of Aberdeen was also a Gordon, and, of course, felt as a clansman regarding the late transaction. He therefore consented to preside at an irregular trial, to which Hay was forthwith subjected. At this trial, no one was allowed to appear for the alleged culprit. An advocate, who offered to come and act as his counsel, was told that if he did so, he should scarcely be down stairs till twenty whingers were put into him. Francis, in short, was condemned to lose his head, and next morning was actually led out to a solitary place, and there butchered by the swords of his enemies. In this wild way did the passions of men work themselves out in the north of Scotland, at the time when Bacon

[1] This term is usually applied to an insinuating, wheedling fellow of swindling propensities.

and Grotius were writing, when Drummond sang and Napier geometrised. 1615.

The Earl of Errol now came into the field, grievously offended because his relative had undergone law *without his being consulted.* The Gordons were summoned to answer for the irregularity of their proceedings at Edinburgh. This, again, drew forth their chief, the Marquis of Huntly, both to defend his own sheriffship, and to maintain his kinsmen. 'Huntly and Errol did appear at Edinburgh, with all their friends on either side; so that the whole kingdom was divided in two factions, ready to fall together by the ears.' The king himself now interfered, with a request that all proceedings should be suspended till he should come to Scotland. Accordingly, upwards of a year after, on his visiting his native kingdom, he brought the parties together, and persuaded them to be reconciled to each other, dismissing the offenders with only nominal punishments. 'So was this controversy settled and taken away; yet it was not quite extinguished till 1627, that Viscount Melgum, the Marquis of Huntly's third son, married —— Hay, the Earl of Errol's daughter.'—*Pit. G. H. S.*

Adam French of Thornydykes, 'ane young bairn scarce past fourteen years of age,' was attending school at Haddington, under the guardianship of Sir John Home of North Berwick, 'donator to the gift of his ward and marriage,' when a plot was laid for making that gift of non-effect by his maternal uncle, William Home of Hardiesmill, in connection with John Cranston of Moriston and Sir Patrick Chirnside of East Nisbet. Under divers pretences, the boy was inveigled away from the house where he resided, and taken to Rimmelton Law in the Merse, the house of John Cranston, whence he was next removed to East Nisbet, and introduced to a daughter of the laird, who was destined to become his wife. A proclamation of bans being made in hasty style, the young pair were straightway carried to Berwick, and there married. Nov.

At the urgency of Sir John Home, the three persons concerned in the abduction, together with one Moffat, a servant, were tried before the supreme court (November 8, 1616), on the charge of ravishing and taking away Adam French. It was shewn in defence, that Adam, being fully fourteen years of age, was competent to contract marriage of his own freewill—the marriage was regular—he himself was satisfied with what had been done, and was ready to declare that he considered the accused parties as his friends. There was much discussion between the king's

1616. advocate and the counsel of the accused on points of law; and, finally, the case was remitted to the sheriff of Berwickshire, the parties giving surety that they would not, in the meantime, fall foul of each other.—*Pit.*

Just about this time, an heiress of the same age as Adam French was the victim of similar selfishness on the part of her 'friends.' A narrative laid before the Privy Council represented Helen Graham, daughter of the deceased Sir John Graham of Knockdolian, as having been left by her father in the hands of persons in whom he had confidence, and with 'a reasonable provision.' Now that she was approaching her majority, being 'about the hinder end of the fourteen year of her age,' 'there has fallen out some contestation betwixt them and others of her friends anent the keeping of her person, and she has been coupit fra hand to hand betwixt them, and twice exhibite before the lords of the secret council.' In this contestation, 'there is no regard had by ony of them to her will, but all of them, seeking their awn advantage, do what in them lies to procure her wrack and undoing.' At her last exhibition before the Council, she had been committed to the care of John Muirhead of Brydonhill, who, being no relation to her, had no just pretension to the care of her person nor to the management of her estate. It was now apparent that John had 'made merchandise of her,' for, 'against all modesty and good conscience,' he had agreed and colluded with James Muirhead of Lawhope 'for bestowing her in marriage upon Arthur Muirhead, his bastard son, who has no means, moyen, nor provision whatsoever;' and she had been carried to the house of this James Muirhead, and thence by Arthur 'transported agaitward toward the realm of England, there to have causit some priest marry her upon him.' To all appearance, this project would have been accomplished, but for the interference of certain justices by the way. The complainer had, however, been carried back to John Muirhead's house, and was now 'deteinit as a prisoner by him, secludit and debarrit fra access, conference, and advice with ony person who professes her guid will.' She demanded to be restored to liberty, and to have the free choice of her own curators; 'for gif she be deteinit under the power of thir persons, who, without ony affection to herself, do only respect her estate and geir, she will be miserably undone and wracked.'

John Muirhead appeared in answer to a summons, and succeeded in freeing himself from blame regarding Helen Graham's abduction; while Arthur Muirhead was denounced rebel for non-appearance. John, who is described as 'ane gentleman of ane honest and upright disposition,' professed to be animated by the best wishes towards Helen, being 'mindit, with the advice of the Earl of Montrose, her chief, and others her friends, to provide and foresee the best occasion for her weal.' The lords appointed that Helen should remain with him till she should choose curators; and they at the same time indicated a few gentlemen, including John Muirhead, whom they thought suitable for the trust. 1615.

A few years earlier (June 1612), Mistress Isobel Montgomery, daughter of the deceased Robert Master of Eglintoun, was represented as being kept in durance by Hugh Lord Loudon and Mistress Margaret Montgomery, sister of Isobel, while they endeavoured to compel her to make 'such disposition to the lands, guids, and geir appertaining to her, as to them sall seem expedient.' The accused parties, being summoned to appear and bring Isobel before the lords, answered that the complainer was too sickly to travel; to test which allegation, a medical man was despatched to her residence, charged with the duty of reporting on her condition before a certain day.—*P. C. R.*

DEC. 15. The Privy Council recommended to the charity of the public the case of Andrew Robertson, John Cowie, John Dauling, James Pratt, and some others, formerly mariners of Leith, who, being lately on the coast of Barbary, had fought a bloody skirmish with the merciless Turks, by whom they were led into captivity, and presented for sale in Algiers. James Fraser, a resident in Algiers, had been moved with pity to redeem these poor men by an advance of £140, which they undertook to repay at a certain time. They, however, being in such poverty as to be unable to reimburse Fraser, were now throwing themselves upon the compassion of the public. On the recommendation of the Privy Council, there were collections made for them in churches.

Captivity among the Moors of Northern Africa was no uncommon fate with Scottish mariners of that age. In 1625, there was a church collection 'for the relief of some folks of Queensferry and Kinghorn, deteinit under slavery by the Turks at Sallee.' In 1618, John Harrison sent to King James an account of his unsuccessful attempts to obtain the liberation of certain British subjects detained under Muley Sidan, Emperor of Morocco. Muley seems to have been inaccessible to all pleadings but those which came in the form of money.[1] A collection was made, August 1621, in all the parish

[1] See papers on these subjects in *Spottiswoode Miscellany*, vols. i. and ii.

1615. churches in Scotland, and amounted to a large sum, 'for the relief of the Scots prisoners in Tunis and Algiers.'—*Bal.*

1616. Jan. 27. 'About five afternoon, there was a great fiery star, in the form of a dragon with a tail, running through the firmament, and in the running giving great light and spouting fire, which continued a pretty space before it vanished. Others describe it thus: that the night being fair and frosty, there arose a great fiery light in the south-west, after the setting of the sun, and ran to the north-east, having at the end thereof, as it were, the shape of the moon; and when it vanished out of sight, there were two great cracks heard, as if they had been thunder-claps. There followed a great calmness and frost for eight or ten days; but the month following was bitter and stormy weather.'—*Cal.*

Feb. 20. This day three men were tried for an extraordinary and most atrocious crime.

Sir James Douglas of Drumlanrig (ancestor of the Dukes of Queensberry) had become possessed of the lands of Howpaslot in Roxburghshire, much to the chagrin of the widow of a former proprietor. On a certain day in April 1615, Lady Howpaslot, as she was called, along with her friend, Jean Scott of Satchells, had a meeting at the Cross of Hawick with a man called George Scott, a cordiner of that town, commonly called *Marion's Geordie;* when a course of conduct was resolved upon for the purpose of defeating the design of Drumlanrig to *stock* or *plenish* the lands. The interest of the cordiner in this object does not appear; neither does that of three other men, who entered into an agreement to assist him in his plan—namely, Walter and Ingram Scott, and another Scott described by his nickname of *the Suckler*. A few days after the Hawick meeting, George Scott, accompanied by William Scott of Satchells, 'mussalit' (disguised), proceeded under cloud of night to Elrig-burn-foot, where the Suckler joined them. Then all three went forward to Birnie Cleuch, where they met Walter and Ingram Scott, 'having plaids and blue bonnets.' Here, however, the Suckler deserted the party. The other men passed on to a cleuch or hollow on the lands of Howpaslot, where a flock of sheep were lying at rest. There they fell upon the poor animals with swords, 'bendit staffs,' and other weapons, killing about forty outright, and leaving twenty more wounded and mutilated on the ground.

On the day noted in the margin, George, Walter, and Ingram

Scott, and John Scott the Suckler, were tried for this horrible crime, when the last being accepted as a witness for the crown, the other three were condemned to death. The Suckler suffered for sheep-stealing next year.—*Pit.* 1616.

The numberless feuds standing between gentlemen-neighbours throughout the country, were usually dealt with in one simple way. The parties were summoned to appear personally before the Council, and give assurances for keeping the peace towards each other for a certain time. When the time had nearly expired, the parties were again charged to appear and give renewal of the assurances. Thus things went on from one period to another, while any hatred remained between the parties. At the date noted, Harie Wood of Bonnytoun and Francis Ogilvy of Newgrange were summoned to appear and renew the former standing assurances; and meanwhile the Council ordered them 'to observe our sovereign lord's peace, and to keep good rule and quietness in the country, and that they nor nane of them invade or pursue ane another, for whatsomever deed, cause, or occasion, otherwise nor by order of law, and inflict ather of them, under the pain of three thousand merks.' It is evident, from the Record of the Privy Council, that sanguinary quarrels amongst the upper classes, though not lessened in number, were not in general carried to such ferocious extremes as formerly. In April of this year, we find an aged statesman congratulating the king on the great improvement which he noted in the social state of Scotland. The person alluded to is Sir Robert Melville, the friend and servant of Mary, and who had been a grown man at the time of Pinkie field. Now advanced to near the ninetieth year of his age, this venerable person had lately been created a peer under the title of Lord Melville. He thus writes to the king: 'All the said years [namely, in his younger days], we was destitute of the true religion, our country being full of barbarity, deadly feids, and oppressions. Since the time your majesty took the management of the affairs of your princely dominions in your awn hand, all your hieness's countries has been peaceable and quiet; and specially this country, where the true religion flourishes, and justice [is] sae weel ministrat by your election of faithful officiars, as I may be bauld to affirm that no country is in ane mair happy estate, and has better occasion to be thankful to God and faithful to your majesty.'[1] JUNE 4.

[1] *Letters and State Papers of the Reign of James VI.*, p. 293.

1616. June 11. Stephen Atkinson, an Englishman, heretofore noticed as concerned in various mining adventures, was this day licensed by the Privy Council to search for gold, and 'the Saxeer, the Calumeer, and the Salyncer stanes,' in Crawford Muir, on the condition of his bringing all the gold to be coined at the Scottish mint, and giving a tenth of the product to the king.

It is not likely that much, if anything at all, was done by Atkinson in consequence, as in 1621 another similar licence to one Dr Hendlie speaks of the Crawford gold-field as having been lying for some years neglected.

June 13. A book called *God and the King*, 'shewing that his sacred majesty being immediately under God within his dominions, doth rightly and lawfully claim whatsoever is required by the aith of allegiance,' was now proclaimed as a book of instruction for youth in schools and universities, 'whereby, in their tender years, the truth of that doctrine may be bred and settled in them, and they thereby may be the better armed and prepared to withstand any persuasion that in their riper years may be offered and usit towards them for corrupting of them in their duty and allegiance.' —*P. C. R.*

June 30. This day, being Sunday, Sir Robert Crichton of Cluny went to attend morning-service at St Cuthbert's Kirk, near Edinburgh, and had sat there a considerable time quietly, when he observed a boy belonging to the Earl of Tullibardine come to the door and look in. As the earl had before this time 'sought both his land and life,' he judged the boy to be a spy, and apprehended that some evil was designed to him. He therefore rose to go out, hoping peaceably to convey himself beyond the earl's reach; but no sooner had he done so, than three men of the king's guard—all, be it remarked, bearing the name of *Murray*, being that of the earl—rose from a seat behind, and shewed a warrant for taking him. By their own confession, they had come to church for the purpose of lying in wait to take Sir Robert, though intending not to meddle with him till the end of the service. They now told him that they were willing to wait for him till the dismissal of the people, keeping him meanwhile in a chamber adjoining to the church, whereas if he went forth by himself he might get skaith, as there were several of the earl's 'folk' in the kirkyard. Sir Robert, however, disdained to submit to this ignominious treatment; so he and his son, drawing their swords, prepared to offer resistance. Of course, a tumult took place in the church, 'to the scandal of religion, and the great grief of the haill parochiners and others convenit at the sermon.' 1616.

The three guardsmen were ordered, for this offensive affair, to appear in the place of repentance in the church, and crave forgiveness of God and the people, while Sir Robert was committed to ward in the Tolbooth.—*P. C. R.*

A few years later (December 18, 1623), we find the Council issuing a strict order against the using of captions in churches.

Mr Peter Blackburn, bishop of Aberdeen, departed this life, after he had lain a long time little better than benumbed. He was little of a zealot on the Episcopal side, and studying to please the Presbyterians, made himself ungracious to both parties. Calderwood alleges, 'He was more mindful of a purse and 500 merks in it, which he kept in his bosom, than anything else.' JUNE.

Commissioners from a number of the burghs met to deliberate on a proposal of the king for working up, within the country, the whole wool produced in it, 'in stuffs, plaids, and kerseys.' They expressed themselves as content that the exportation of wool should be prohibited, in order that a trial should be made; but they could undertake no burden in the matter 'anent the home-bringing of strangers,' or for assurance that his majesty's ends would be attained. A prohibition for the exporting of wool was soon after issued.—*P. C. R.* JULY 11.

A few months after the above date, we find a curious reference to wool in the Privy Council Record. The document states, that 'in some remote and uncivil places of this kingdom' an old and barbarous custom was still kept up of *plucking the wool from sheep instead of clipping it.* The king, hearing of the practice, wrote a letter to his Council, denouncing it as one not to be suffered; telling them it had already been reformed in Ireland, under penalty of a groat on every sheep so used, and was 'far less to be endured in you.' The Council immediately (March 17, 1617) passed an act in the same tenor, and further stating that many sheep died in consequence of this cruel treatment—concluding with a threat of severe fines on such as should hereafter continue the practice.—*P. C. R.*

It is remarkable that in the Faröe Islands there is, to this day, no other way of taking the wool from sheep than that which was then only kept up in remote parts of Scotland.

1616. July 19. John Faa, James Faa, his son, Moses Baillie, and Helen Brown, were tried as Egyptians lingering in the country, contrary to a statute which had banished their tribe forth of the realm on pain of death. In respect no caution could be found by them to assure their leaving the country, they were sentenced to be hanged on the Burgh-moor. It is not known that this sentence was carried into execution; but neither is there anything known to make such severity unlikely.

In 1624, six Faas, and two other men of the gipsy tribe, were tried for the same offence of not voluntarily transporting themselves, and these men were executed. A number of their women and children were mercifully allowed to go free, on condition that they should immediately depart from the kingdom.—*Pit.*

Sep. 16. '. . . . there arose such a swelling in the sea at Leith, that the like was not seen before for a hundred years. The water came in with violence beside the bulwark, in a place called the Timber Holf [Howf], where the timber lay, and carried some of the timber and many lasts of herrings lying there, to the sea; brake in sundry low houses and cellars, and filled them with water. The like flowing was in Dunbar, Musselburgh, and other parts of the sea-coast. The people took this extraordinary tide to be a forewarning of some evil to come.'—*Cal.*

The Chronicle of Perth notes for this year 'great poverty of towns and great dearth;' probably a consequence of the stormy spring and adust summer of the preceding year.

Oct. Preparations began to be made for the reception and entertainment of the king, who was expected to visit the country next year. Considerable repairs and improvements were made upon the palaces of Holyrood and Falkland. A proclamation was made that 'beasts be fed in every place, that there might be abundance of flesh when the king came to the country.' The Privy Council issued orders for the inhabitants to prepare clean lodgings for the king's friends and attendants, and took order to have the streets purified.

The chancellor's circular to the burghs ordering them to arrange with their butchers for the furnishing of 'fed beef' against his majesty's 'here-coming,' met an amusing response in the case of one little town—Wester Anstruther—which would appear to have been most unworthily endowed with burgal privileges. 'Our toun,' says this response, 'is ane very mean toun, yea of all the burghts of this realm the meanest; *nather is there ane flesher in our toun,* nor any other person that is accustomit with feeding of beef, *we being all seafaring men and fishers.*' Nevertheless, the two bailies inform his lordship that they had 'dealt with some honest men of our neighbours to feed beef, and has enjoinit them to have in readiness the number of four fed nolt against the time of his majesty's here-coming; whilk may be lookit for in our toun.' Easter Anstruther, which has always been a better sort of town, was equally unacquainted with 'that trade of the feeding of beef;' but the bailie, nevertheless, had 'taken such order that there sall be in readiness to that diet twelve oxen of the best we can get for money.' The response of Dysart was a frank promise to have in readiness 'ten or twelve sufficient and weel-fed beefs upon competent and reasonable prices, and sall feed and keep them *sae lang as we may possibly get sufficient food for them,* according to the season, *not doubting of your lordship's satisfaction in case of our losses.*'—*An. Scot.* 1616.

One of the most notable preparations was the fitting up of a chapel-royal at Holyrood—not in the Abbey-Church, which then served as the parish kirk of the Canongate, but in a private room in the palace. An organ of the value of £400 was sent down from London to aid in the service. There were also timber statues of the twelve apostles and four evangelists, well carved and gilt, for the decoration of the chapel; but 'the people murmured, fearing great alterations in religion, whereupon the bishops dissuaded the king from setting them up in the chapel.'—*Cal.*

We have a curious trait of the feeling of the people about the refitting of the chapel at Holyrood in certain entries found at this time in the Privy Council Record. In July, an agreement had been made with Nicolas Stone, of London, for repairing the chapel; and next month the Council became engaged in an altercation with James Paton, George Coline, and others, slaters in St Andrews, who, doubtless under religious scruples, refused to undertake any conditions of service at the said work, though promised good and thankful payment for their labours. Application had consequently been made to the provost of St Andrews, requesting that he would command these his citizens to do the work proposed to them; but he made answer in a style worthy of the name he bore—John Knox —'disdainfully alleging that it was not the custom of the country to press ony man to work;' 'wherethrough his majesty's warks are hinderit, and by their [evil example] others may take occasion to leave his majesty's service.' The Privy Council ordered letters to

1615. be sent to the parties, charging them to appear and answer for their conduct; and when the day came, and they failed to make their appearance, they were put to the horn as rebels.—*P. C. R.*

An act of Privy Council against beggars, March 5, 1616, describes Edinburgh as infested with them—'strang and idle vagabonds'—'having their resets in some parts of the Cowgate, the Canongate, Potterrow, West Port, Pleasance, [and] Leith Wynd, where they ordinarily convene every night, and pass their time in all kind of riot and filthy lechery, to the offence and displeasure of God.' By day, they are said to present themselves in great companies on the principal streets. Numbers of them 'lie all day on the causey of the Canongate, and with shameful exclamations and crying, not only extorts almous, but by their other misbehaviour fashes and wearies as weel his majesty's nobility and councillors, as others his majesty's subjects repairing to this burgh; sae that hardly ony man of whatsomever quality can walk upon the streets, nor yet stand and confer upon the streets, nor under stairs, but they are impeshit by numbers of beggars.' The Council therefore ordered the magistrates of Edinburgh and Canongate to get these wretched people expelled from their respective bounds, and suffer them no longer to seek alms on the streets. In like manner, they commanded that 'the Laird of Innerleith and his bailies cause their streets and vennels to be kept free of beggars;'[1] as also, that 'Mr Patrick Bannatyne and Mr Umphra Bleenseillis remove the haill beggars out of their houses at the foot of Leith Wynd, and suffer nane to have residence, beild, or reset there.' All this under threat of pecunial fines.

DEC. In anticipation of the king's visit, it now became necessary to repeat the above orders, because 'it is like enough that when his majesty comes to this country next summer, they will follow his court, to the great discredit and disgrace of the country.'

Nothing less, perhaps, than the strong language used by the Privy Council could make us fully aware of what we are spared of unpleasant sights and rencontres by a good poor-law. In those days, the wretched and the insane went freely about the highways and thoroughfares, a constant source of annoyance, disgust, and even terror. Only we of our day who saw Ireland before 1840 can form any idea of what the country was in this respect in the seventeenth century.

[1] The suburb called Portsburgh was under the jurisdiction of Tours, Laird of Inverleith.

The Privy Council this day ordained that there should be a school in every parish in the kingdom, for the advancement of the true religion, and the training of children 'in civility, godliness, knowledge, and learning.' The school was in each case to be established, and a fit person appointed to teach the same, upon the expenses of the parishioners, at the sight and advice of the bishop of the diocese. Another act on the same day ordained regular catechising of children, and their being brought before the bishop for confirmation, under considerable penalties. 1616. Dec. 10.

The above order for the plantation of schools was not vigorously carried out, and in 1626, King Charles I. is found making an effort to remedy the defect.[1]

'The new market-cross of Edinburgh was founded by the community of the said town, and within three months after was completed.' 'Also at this time there was great preparations making for the coming of King James into Scotland, baith in all his majesty's palaces, castles, and abbeys, and especially in his castle of Edinburgh, whereof the new fore wark, with the great hall thereof, and many other rooms therein, was biggit to his majesty's great expenses by Sir Gideon Murray of Elibank, knight, his majesty's treasurer-depute.'—*Jo. Hist.* 1617. Feb.

'The king entered into Scotland, accompanied with the Duke of Lennox, the Earls of Arundel, Southampton, Pembroke, Montgomery, and Buckingham, Bishops of Ely, Lincoln, and Winchester, and sundry barons, deans, and gentlemen. He stayed in Dunglass two nights, and a night in Seaton. On Friday, the 16th, he came to Leith, and about four afternoon, out of Leith to the West Port of Edinburgh, where he made his entry on horseback, that he might the better be seen by the people; whereas before he rode in the coach all the way. The provost, bailies, and council, and a number of citizens arrayed in gowns [of plain velvet], and others standing with speat staves,[2] received him at the port.' The provost, William Nisbet, and the town-clerk, John Hay,[3] having severally harangued him, five hundred double angels in a silver double-gilt basin, were presented to him—'wha, with ane mild May 13.

[1] See documents in *Maitland Club Misc.*, ii. 26.

[2] Sharp-pointed staves.

[3] 'Who thereafter wrote himself Sir John Hay of Landes, knight, one altogether corrupt, full of wickedness and villainy, and a sworn enemy to the peace of his country.'—*Sir James Balfour's Annals.*

1617. and gracious countenance, receivit them with their propyne.' 'The cannons of the Castle were shot. He was convoyed first to the great kirk, where the Bishop of St Andrews had a flattering sermon upon the 21st Psalm, and thanked God for his prosperous journey. He knighted the provost. . . . . When he came to the palace of Holyroodhouse, the professors and students of the College of Edinburgh presented to him some poems made to his praise, and in sign of welcome.'—*Cal.*

MAY 17. '. . . . the English service was begun in the Chapel-royal, with the singing of choristers, surplices, and playing on organs.'—*Cal.* Amid the general feeling of satisfaction at seeing their native prince amongst them once more, this exemplification of ceremonial worship was allowed by the people to pass without tumult, yet not without serious discontents and apprehensions. The bishops were so fearful of the popular spirit, that they endeavoured to dissuade the king, but without success. The common people in Edinburgh, as we are told by a native historian, considered the service in the chapel as 'staining and polluting the house of religion by the dregs of popery. The more prudent, indeed, judged it but reasonable that the king should enjoy his own form of worship in his own chapel; but then followed a rumour, that the religious vestments and altars were to be forcibly introduced into all the churches, and the purity of religion, so long established in Scotland, for ever defiled. And it required the utmost efforts of the magistrates to restrain the inflamed passions of the common people.'[1]

Having to meet his parliament a few weeks after, the king went to Falkland to hunt. But the park of his Fife palace did not content him. Carnegie, Lord Kinnaird, son of a favourite minister of old, and himself a friend of the king, dwelt in state in a noble castle overlooking the embouchure of the South Esk in Forfarshire, with an extensive muir full of game close by—Muirthrewmont or Muirromon (as the country people call it). James gladly rode thither,[2] for the sake of the abundant sport. The house of Kinnaird was furnished on the occasion for various pleasures, and deficient in no sort of enjoyment.[3] Two poets of temporary and local fame came with courtly Latin strains suitable to the occasion.[4] His majesty tarried ten days in the district, and then came to Dundee,

[1] Translated from Johnston's *Historia Rerum Britannicarum*, *apud* Secret Hist. of Court of Ja. I., ii. 30.

[2] *Chronicle of Perth.* [3] Johnston's *Hist. Rer. Brit.*, p. 519. [4] See *Muses' Welcome.*

which welcomed him with poem and with speech. Returning to 1617.
Edinburgh, he set himself to drive his ends with the clergy, who were now less able or disposed to resist his innovations than they had been twenty years before. At his command, several of the Scottish councillors and bishops received the communion in the English manner in the Chapel-royal, and William Summers, one June 8.
of the ministers of Edinburgh, officiated there, 'observing the English form in his prayer and behaviour.' 'On the 15th June, some noblemen and bishops who had not communicat before, communicat kneeling, yet not half of the noblemen that were required. The ministers of Edinburgh, in the meantime, were silent; neither dissuaded the king privately, nor opened their mouth in public against this innovation, or bad example.'—*Cal.*

On the 19th of June, the king formally visited the Castle of Edinburgh, in order to celebrate his fifty-first birthday on the natal spot. Andrew Kerr, a boy of nine years of age, welcomed him at the gate in 'ane Hebrew speech.' At the banquet in the great hall, the English and Scottish nobility and the magistracy of Edinburgh met in the utmost amity and satisfaction. By the desire of the king, who wished to advance his native country in the eyes of the English, the wives and children of the Scottish nobility appeared in their finest dresses, shining with jewels, and were treated with great distinction. The feast was not over till nine at night; and after its conclusion, the Castle rang with a chorus of the ladies' voices and a band of instruments. On the return of the royal party to the Palace, a great multitude assembled there to see 'pastimes with firework.'[1]

On the 26th, 'there was a timber house erected on the back of the Great Kirk of Edinburgh [south side], which was decored with tapestry, where the town prepared a banquet for the king and the nobility. The day following, sundry knights and gentlemen of good note were banqueted in the same house, and made burgesses. They danced about the Cross with sound of trumpets and other instruments; throwed glasses of wine from the Cross upon the people standing about, and ended with the king's scoll [health.]'—*Cal.*

This day is dated from Leith a satire upon Scotland, heretofore June 20.
usually attributed to Sir Anthony Weldon, but upon doubtful evidence. It was entitled, *A Perfect Description of the People and Country of Scotland*, and was printed with the signature JOHNE E.

[1] Johnston's *Hist. Rer. Brit.*, p. 519. Calderwood.

1617. It seems the splenetic effusion of some Cockney who had been tempted to follow the king's train into Scotland, and had found himself a smaller man there than he expected.

In the air, the soil, and the natural productions of Scotland, this railer can find nothing goodly or agreeable. The thistle, he says, is the fairest flower in their garden. Hay is a word unknown. 'Corn is reasonable plenty at this time; for, since they heard of the king's coming, it hath been as unlawful for the common people to eat wheat, as it was of old for any but the priests to eat the show-bread. . . . . They would persuade the footmen that oaten cakes would make them well-winded; and the children of the chapel they have brought to eat of them for the maintenance of their voices. . . . . They persuade the trumpeters that fasting is guid for men of their quality; for emptiness, they say, causeth wind, and wind causeth a trumpet sound sweetly.[1] . . . .

'They christen without the cross, marry without a ring, receive the sacrament without reverence, die without repentance, and bury without divine service. They keep no holidays, nor acknowledge any saint but St Andrew, who, they say, got that honour by presenting Christ with ane oaten cake after his forty days' fast. . . . . They hold their noses if you speak of bear-bating, and stop their ears if you speak of play. . . . . I am verily persuaded if [the] angels at the last day should come down in their white garments, they would run away, and cry: "The children of the chapel are come again to torment us!" . . . . For the graven images in the new beautified chapel, they threaten to pull them down after his departure, and make of them a burnt-offering to appease the indignation they imagine is conceived against them in the breast of the Almighty for suffering such idolatry to enter their kingdom. The organs, I think, will find mercy, because they say there is some affinity between them and their bagpipes.[2] The shipper that brought the singing-men with their papistical vestments, complains that he hath been much troubled with a strange singing in his head ever since they came aboard his ship; for remedy whereof the pastor of the parish hath persuaded him to sell the profaned vessel, and distribute the money among the faithful brethren.'

[1] We can here see the original of Scott's exquisite picture of Caleb Balderstone endeavouring to convince a messenger that cold water was better for his stomach in the morning than ale or brandy.

[2] The organ was no new instrument at Holyrood. There is an entry in the lord-treasurer's book, under February 8, 1557–8, of £36 'to David Melville, indweller in Leith, for *ane pair of organs* to the Chapel in the Palace of Holyroodhouse.'

Our scribbler speaks of the women as huge-boned monsters, 1617.
whereof the upper class are 'kept like lions in iron grates. The merchants' wives are likewise prisoners, but not in such strongholds. They have wooden cages [meaning the timber galleries in front of the houses], through which, peeping to catch the air, we are almost choked with the sight of them. . . . . To draw you down from the citizen's wife to the country gentlewomen, and so convey you to the common dames, were to bring you from Newgate to Bridewell.'

In an answer to this satire, a strong defence is entered on the subject of victuals and other materials of conviviality. 'Except meat should have rained down from heaven, it could not be imagined more cheap, more plentiful. Ane of those twelve pies that were sold for a penny, might have stopped your mouth for his quarrel. . . . . What else would you have had? You know there were some subjects that kept open butteries and cellars from morning till night. . . . . The man is angry that all the taps were not pulled out, that every guid fellow might swim in sack and claret.'[1]

The king commenced a second excursion in his native dominions, June 20.
by Stirling, Perth, St Andrews—thence back to Stirling, where he received a deputation of Edinburgh professors, who disputed before him in the Chapel-royal of the Castle, in the presence of the English and Scottish nobility and many learned men. Here the July 19.
British Solomon was quite in his element. The first question discussed 'by the learned doctors was, "Ought sheriffs and other inferior magistrates to be hereditary?"—a question at this time agitated in the national senate, where it was the earnest wish of King James that it should be decided in the negative. As might have been expected, the oppugners of the question soon got the advantage; for the weighty arguments of royalty were thrown into that scale.

'The king was highly delighted with their success; and turning to the Marquis of Hamilton (hereditary sheriff of Clydesdale), who stood behind his chair, said: "James, you see your cause is lost, and all that can be said for it is clearly answered and refuted."

'The second thesis was On the Nature of Local Motion. The opposition to this was very great, and the respondent produced

[1] See the satire and answer in *Abbotsford Miscellany*, i. 297.

1617. numerous arguments from Aristotle in support of his thesis, which occasioned the king to say: "These men know the mind of Aristotle as well as he did himself when alive."

'The third thesis was Concerning the Origin of Fountains or Springs. The king was so well pleased with this controversy, that, although the three-quarters of an hour allotted for the disputation were expired, he caused them to proceed, sometimes speaking for and against both respondent and opponent, seldom letting an argument on either side pass without proper remarks.

'The disputations being over, the king withdrew to supper; after which he sent for the disputants, whose names were John Adamson, James Fairlie, Patrick Sands, Andrew Young, James Reid, and William King, before whom he learnedly discoursed on the several subjects controverted by them, and then began to comment on their several names, and said: "These gentlemen, by their names, were destined for the acts they had in hand this day;" and proceeded as followeth:

"Adam was the father of all, and Adam's son had the first part of this act. The defender is justly called Fairlie;[1] his thesis had some fairlies in it, and he sustained them very fairly, and with many fair lies given to the oppugners. And why should not Mr Sands be the first to enter the sands? But now I clearly see that all sands are not barren, for certainly he hath shewn a fertile wit. Mr Young is very old in Aristotle. Mr Reid need not be red with blushing for his acting this day. Mr King disputed very kingly, and of a kingly purpose, concerning the royal supremacy of reason above anger and all passions. I am so well satisfied," added his majesty, "with this day's exercise, that I will be godfather to the College of Edinburgh, and have it called *the College of King James*, for, after its founding, it stopped sundry years in my minority. After I came to knowledge, I held to it, and caused it to be established; and although I see many look upon it with an evil eye, yet I will have them know that, having given it my name, I have espoused its quarrel, and at a proper time will give it a royal god-bairn gift to enlarge its revenues." The king being told that there was one in company his majesty had taken no notice of—namely, Henry Charteris, principal of the College, who, though a man of great learning, yet, by his innate bashfulness, was rendered unfit to speak in such an august assembly —his majesty answered: "His name agrees well with his nature;

[1] *Ferly* is the Scotch for *wonder*.

for charters contain much matter, yet say nothing; and, though 1617.
they say nothing, yet they put great things into men's mouths."

'The king having signified that he would be pleased to see his remarks on the professors' names versified, it was accordingly done as follows:

'As Adam was the first man, whence all beginning tak,
So Adamson was president, and first man in this act.
The thesis Fairlie did defend, which, though they lies contein,
Yet were fair lies, and he the same right fairlie did maintein.
The field first entered Mr Sands, and there he made me see
That not all sands are barren sands, but that some fertile be.
Then Mr Young most subtilie the thesis did impugn,
And kythed[1] old in Aristotle, although his name be Young.
To him succeeded Mr Reid, who, though Reid be his name,
Needs neither for his dispute blush, nor of his speech think shame.
Last entered Mr King the lists, and dispute like a king,
How reason, reigning like a king, should anger under bring.
To their deserved praise have I thus played upon their names,
And will their college hence be called *The College of King James*.'[2]

In the course of his excursion, the king had a hunt in the neighbourhood of Dunfermline. At this time, the coal-works at Culross, on the shore of the Firth of Forth, were conducted with great activity under their enterprising proprietor, Sir George Bruce. James invited his company to dine with him at a *collier's house*, referring to an elegant mansion which Sir George had built for his accommodation in the town of Culross. They proceeded in the first place to examine the coal-works, which were then wrought a considerable way under the sea, issuing at some distance from shore in a little island or moat, where the product of the mines was put directly on board vessels to be transported to various places. The king and his courtiers, unaware of this peculiar arrangement, were conducted along the mine till they reached the sea-shaft, and here being drawn up, found themselves suddenly surrounded by the waves. James, always apprehensive of attempts on his life, was excited to great alarm by this unexpected situation, and called out 'Treason!' His courteous host reassured him by pointing to an elegant pinnace moored by the moat to carry him ashore, in the event of his not wishing to return by the mine. Doubtless the affair added a little zest to the banquet which the party immediately after partook of in the hospitable mansion of Bruce.[3]

[1] Shewed. [2] Abridged from the *Muses' Welcome*.
[3] The above is a traditional story related in Forsyth's *Beauties of Scotland*.

1617. The king pursued his progress by Glasgow, Paisley, Hamilton, and Dumfries, passing across the Border to Carlisle on the 5th of August, amidst the general regrets of his subjects. It was remarkable how much peace and good feeling prevailed amongst the people during the royal visit. The Chancellor Dunfermline, in afterwards summing up the whole affair to the king, said: 'In all the time of your majesty's remaining in this kingdom, in sae great companies, and sae many noblemen and great personages of twa nations convened, never ane action, word, or appearance of any discord, variance, or offence betwix any of the nations with other, for whatsomever cause. I doubt gif ever the like has been seen, at sic occasion of so frequent a meeting of men, strangers, and unknown to each other.'—*M. S. P.*

It may be worth mentioning, that by warrant signed at Hitchinbroke, October 23, 1618, the king gave to Sir Gideon Murray of Elibank 'a gilt basin which was given to us by our burgh of Edinburgh, with their propine of money, at our first entry of the said burgh, at our last being in our said kingdom; together with two gilt cups, one of them in form of a salmon, presented to us by our burgh of Glasgow; and another gilt cup which was given us by the town of Carlisle; together with some remanent of musk and ambergrise, which was unspent at our being there; and, lastly, ane large iron chest, which did sometime belong to the late Earl of Gowrie.'—*An. Scot.*

1618. Feb. The king's attention was drawn to two abuses in the police of the city of Edinburgh. Notwithstanding the warning given by a fire in 1584, it was still customary for baxters and browsters to keep stocks of heather and whins in the very heart of the city, to the great hazard of adjacent buildings; and individuals disposed to build houses within the city were in some instances prevented by a fear of the risk to which they would be thus exposed. The other evil complained of was less dangerous, but more offensive. Candlemakers and butchers were allowed to pursue their callings within the town, to the great disgust of 'civil and honest neighbours, and of the nobility and country people that comes there for their private adoes.' Indeed, 'it hath oftentimes fallen out, that in mony streets and vennels of the said burgh, the filth of slaughtered guids is in such abundance exposed to the view of the people, and the closes and streets sae filled therewith, as there can no passage be had through the same.' A proclamation was launched against these abuses.—*P. C. R.*

On the 4th of March 1619, the Privy Council sent an order 1613.
to the magistrates of Edinburgh, demanding that they should take order for keeping the streets of the town clean, and describing the existing state of things in these terms: It 'is now become so filthy and unclean, and the streets, vennels, wynds, and closes thereof so overlaid and coverit with middings, and with the filth of man and beast, as [that] the noble, councillors, servitors, and others his majesty's subjects wha are lodgit within the said burgh, can not have ane clean and free passage and entry to their lodgings; wherethrough their lodgings have become so loathsome unto them, as they are resolved rather to make choice of lodgings in the Canongate and Leith, or some other parts about the town, nor [than] to abide the sight of this shameful uncleanliness and filthiness; whilk is so universal and in such abundance through all parts of this burgh, as in the heat of summer it corrupts the air, and gives great occasion of sickness; and, furder, this shameful and beastly filthiness is most detestable and odious in the sight of strangers, who, beholding the same, are constrained with reason to give out mony disgraceful speeches agains' this burgh, calling it a puddle of filth and uncleanness, the like whereof is not to be seen in no part of the world.' The plan of police proposed by the Council is for each inhabitant to 'keep the streets fornent their awn bounds clean, as is done in other civil, handsome, and weel-governed cities.' No idea of a cleaning department of police.

Considering how closely Edinburgh was built, and that its numberless narrow alleys were kept in the state which is described, it is not at all surprising that the pest so frequently broke out within its bounds. We learn from the above edict that the natural connection of decaying organic matter with pestilential disease, was not then unknown; the fact was admitted, but neglected. At this time, the attention of the public in Scotland was concentrated on questions regarding religious observances—many of them of little substantial consequence—while these real life-and-death matters were wholly overlooked.

It is rather remarkable, that so early as 1527, there appears to have been a general arrangement for cleaning the city of Edinburgh at stated times, and with a profit to the corporation. In that year, there is an entry as follows in the Council Record of the city: 'The gait-dichting, and duties thereof, is set this year to come, with the aventure of deid and weir, to Alexander Pennicuik, for the soum of £20, to be dicht and clengit sufficiently

1618. ilk 8 days anes, with a dozen of servants.' Pennicuik is enjoined to 'tak nae mair duties for the dichting thereof, except and allenarly of fish, flesh, salt, and victuals.'[1]

MAY 13. The king having proposed that 'the most notorious and lewd persons' in the middle shires (Borders) might be 'sent to Virginia, or some other remote parts,' the councillors answered that it was not necessary, because the country was now reduced to 'obedience and quietness;' and it might even prove detrimental, seeing that many who were 'in danger of the laws for auld feids,' but had latterly been at peace, might, if they heard of such a design, 'mak choice rather to loup out and become fugitives, nor to underly the hazard and fear of that matter.'

Notwithstanding the peace and obedience described as now existing, scarcely two years had elapsed when we find evidences that the king's proposal was found to be rational and of promise. In April 1620, 'a hundred and twenty of the broken men of the Borders were apprehended by the landlords and wardens of the Middle Marches, at the command of the Privy Council, and sent to the Bohemian wars, with Colonel Andrew Gray.'[2]—*Bal.*

JUNE 2. The Privy Council issued a commission to certain gentlemen in Irvine, to try two persons of that burgh accused of witchcraft. In the recital on which the commission proceeds, it is set forth —'that John Stewart, vagabond, and Margaret Barclay, spouse to Archibald Deane, burgess of Irvine, were lately apprehendit upon most probable and clear presumption of their practising of witchcraft agains John Deane, burgess of Irvine, and procuring thereby the destruction of the said John, and the drowning and perishing of the ship called the *Gift of God*, of Irvine, and of the haill persons and goods being thereintill: likeas the said John Stewart, upon examination, has clearly and *pounktallie* confessit the said devilish practices, and the said Margaret, foolishly presuming by her denial to eschew trial and punishment, doeth most obdurately deny the truth of that matter, notwithstanding that the said John constantly avows the same upon her,' &c.[3]

[1] Printed in the *Scots Magazine*, January 1806, from a MS. volume of excerpts of the Edinburgh city records in the Advocates' Library.

[2] This Colonel Gray, who is stated to have been a rank papist, embarked at Leith, about the end of May 1620, with a party of fifteen hundred men for the service of the king of Bohemia.—*Cal.*

[3] Act of Secret Council, quoted in *Blackwood's Magazine*, i. 498.

It appears that Margaret Barclay had conceived and expressed violent hatred of her brother-in-law, John Deane, and his wife, in consequence of their raising or propagating a scandal against her. John Deane's ship having been lost at Padstow, on the English coast, and John Stewart, a *spaeman,* having spoken of this fact before it was known by ordinary means, a suspicion arose that the latter had been concerned in some sorcery by which the vessel had suffered. On his being taken up, a confession was extorted from him, that he had taught magical arts to Margaret Barclay, by which she had brought about the loss of the vessel; and he narrated a ridiculous scene of enchantment as having occurred on the shore, with the devil present in the form of a lady's lapdog, Margaret Barclay being the principal actor. Margaret was then apprehended, as also one Isobel Tosh, whom Stewart described as an assistant at the evil deed. Margaret's servant-girl, a child of eight years of age, and Isobel Tosh, were, apparently through terror, induced to make admissions supporting Stewart's statement. A most tragical series of incidents followed. Isobel Tosh, trying to escape from prison, fell and hurt herself so much that she died in a few days. Stewart hanged himself in prison. Margaret Barclay, tortured by the laying of weights upon her limbs, confessed what was laid to her charge; and though she denied all when relieved, yet was she condemned and executed, finally returning to an acknowledgment of guilt, which can only be attributed to hallucination. Throughout all this affair—to all appearance consisting of a series of forced accusations and confessions, till reason at length gave way in the principal party—the Earl of Eglintoun, so noted afterwards as a Covenanter, took part along with the commissioners; while the assistant parish clergyman, Mr David Dickson, and several other ministers, most of them noted in the annals of the time as men of extraordinary piety, assisted in working on the religious feelings of the accused to induce confession. It does not seem ever to have occurred to any of these well-meaning persons, lay or clerical, that a worthy duty in the case would have been to inquire into the facts, and judge by collating them, whether there was any ground whatever for the accusation.[1] 1618.

The Privy Council was informed of 'an abuse lately taken up by a number of young boys and pages, servants to noblemen, barons, JUNE 11.

[1] See the case of Margaret Barclay at greater length in Scott's *Demonology*, p. 307.

1618. and gentlemen.' It was represented that these persons, 'whenever they fund ony boy newly enterit in service, or pagerie, as they term it, lay hands upon him, and impose upon him [the payment of] some certain pieces of gold, to be spent in drinking, riot, and excess, for receiving of him in their society and brotherheid.' It was further alleged that, 'if ony of thir new enterit boys refuse to condescend to them in this point, they do then shamefully misuse them, awaiting all occasions to harm and disgrace them;' so that many open disturbances were the consequence. The Council issued a proclamation against these practices, threatening heavy punishment to all who might be guilty of the like in future.—*P. C. R.*

JUNE 20. 'At twa afternoon, David Toshach of Monyvaird, younger, [was] slain in the south gate of Perth by Lawrence Bruce, younger of Cultmalindy, his brother, and divers others their associates; the twa that was with Monyvaird, ane deadly hurt, but died not; the other [David Malloch], his right hand clean stricken fra him. This done in a moment of time. All the committers thereof eschewit out of the town, before any of the townsmen heard of ony such thing.'[1]

No one seems to have immediately suffered for this outrage; but, four years after, the Privy Council informed the king that Cultmalindy, besides banishing his two sons and a servant, had offered a thousand crowns by way of assythment to the friends of the slaughtered man, and £2000 to the two men who had been mutilated. 'This feid,' it is added, 'has altogether undone auld Cultmalindy; for his estate is exhausted and wracked, and he is become very waik of his judgment and understanding, by the grief that thir troubles has brought upon him; whilk were the occasion of his wife's death, and of the exile and banishment of his sons and friends, now by the space of four years; in the whilk exile twa of his friends of good rank and quality has departed this life.'—*Pit.*

Mr Pitcairn quotes a local proverb as having apparently taken its rise with reference to the misfortune of one of Monyvaird's servants:

'Hands aff's fair-play:
Davie Malloch says nay.'

It was rather a bitter jest for David. This person, from the locality, may be presumed to have been an ancestor, or near

[1] Fleming's MS., Adv. Lib., quoted in Pitcairn, iii. 443.

collateral relation, of David Malloch, subsequently called Mallet, the poet. 1618.

The king's declaration regarding sports on the Sunday and other holidays came to Edinburgh. It commenced with a judicious allusion to the abundance of papists in Lancashire. He had there found, too, the people complaining that they were prevented from indulging in their ancient sports. One effect of this must be that they would think papistry a better religion, since it allowed of sports. Another inconvenience is, 'that this prohibition barreth the common and meaner people from using such exercises as may make their bodies more able for war, when we or our successors shall have occasion to use them, and, in place thereof, sets up filthy tipplings and drunkenness, and breeds a number of idle and discontented speeches in their ale-houses; for when shall the common people have leave to exercise, if not upon the Sundays and holidays, seeing they must apply their labour, and win their living in other days.' The king therefore willed that no lawful recreation be barred to the people—'such as dancing, either men or women; archery for men, leaping, vaulting . . . . nor from having of May-games, Whitsun-ales, and Morris-dances, and the setting up of May-poles;' seeing, however, that no one was allowed so to indulge who had not previously attended service in church. JUNE.

When James Somerville of Drum was at school at the village of Dalserf in Lanarkshire, about 1608, it was customary 'to solemnise the first Sunday of May with dancing about a May-pole, firing of pieces, and all manner of revelling then in use.' His grandson tells an anecdote *apropos:* 'There being at that time few or no merchants in this petty village, to furnish necessaries for the scholars' sports, this youth resolves to furnish himself elsewhere, that so he may appear with the bravest. In order to this, by break of day, he rises and goes to Hamilton, and there bestows all the money that for a long time before he had gotten from his friends, or had otherwise purchased, upon ribbons of divers colours, a new hat and gloves. But in nothing he bestowed his money more liberally than upon gunpowder, a great quantity whereof he buys for his own use, and to supply the wants of his comrades. Thus furnished with these commodities, but with ane empty purse, he returns to Dalserf by seven o'clock (having travelled that Sabbath morning above eight miles), puts on his . . . . clothes and new hat, flying with ribbons of all colours; in this equipage, with his little fusee upon his shoulder, he marches to the churchyard where

1618. the May-pole was set up, and the solemnity of that day was to be kept. There first at the foot-ball he equalled any that played; but for handling of his piece in charging and discharging, he was so ready, that he far surpassed all his fellow-scholars, and became a teacher of that art to them before the thirteenth year of his own age. . . . . The day's sport being over, he had the applause of all the spectators, the kindness of his condisciples, and the favour of the whole inhabitants of that little village.'—*Mem. Som.*

In June 1625, the presbytery of Lanark exercised discipline upon John Baillie, William Baillie, John Hirshaw, John and Thomas Prentices, and Robert Watt, a piper, 'profaners of the Sabbath in fetching hame a May-pole, and dancing about the same, on Pasch Sunday.'—*R. P. L.*

It is manifest from the church-registers of that time, that the universal external observance of the Sunday as a Sabbath, for which Scotland has long been remarkable, was not yet established. In August 1628, the minister of Carstairs regretted to the presbytery of Lanark the breach of the Sabbath 'by the insolent behaviour of men and women in foot-balling, dancing, and barley-breaks.' About the same time, two tailors were libelled before the same court for working on Sunday. Such things could not have happened a few years later, or at any time since.

JULY. A mysterious affair occupied the attention of the state-officers. While the servants of one Kennedy, a notary, residing in Galloway, were 'filling muck in beir-seed time,' they had found a withered human hand amongst some dung. No person having lately been murdered or missed in the country, it was impossible to tell whence this severed member had come or to whom it had belonged. Kennedy, who had lately come to the house, professed to know nothing of the matter. It seemed to him that the hand had been there many years. This affair might have passed over with little notice, if it had not been followed up by a series of marvellous occurrences. As his wife was sitting with some gossips at supper in her husband's absence, some blood was observed upon the candlestick, and afterwards some more matter resembling gore was found on the threshold of the cellar door. It was also stated that, as Kennedy was walking one day with the minister, near the parish church, some drops of blood were seen upon the grass. All these things being reported to the authorities in Edinburgh, they gave orders for Kennedy's apprehension, and he was accordingly brought thither, and kept six weeks in the Tolbooth. When examined, he could assign no cause for the above facts, but 1618. 'complained that his cattle and horses had died in great number, and that his wife had long been vexed with extraordinary sickness; all which he ascribed to witchcraft used against them.' It being impossible to bring anything home against the man, he was dismissed.—*M. S. P.*

That eccentric genius, John Taylor, the Thames waterman, commonly called the WATER-POET, set out from his native London on the 14th of July, on a journey to Scotland—'because,' says he, 'I would be an eye-witness of divers things which I had heard of that country.' He called it a Pennyless Pilgrimage, because he intended to attempt making his way without any funds of his own, and entirely by the use of what he might get from friends by the way. Having traversed the intermediate distance on horseback in about a month, he entered Scotland by the western AUG. 11. border, walking, while a guide rode with his baggage on a gelding. Somewhat to his surprise, he observed no remarkable change on the face of nature.

> 'There I saw sky above, and earth below,
> And as in England, there the sun did shew;
> The hills with sheep replete, with corn the dale,
> And many a cottage yielded good Scotch ale.'

As he passed along Annandale, he counted eleven hundred neat at as good grass as ever man did mow. At Moffat, where he arrived much wearied by his walk from Carlisle, he 'found good ordinary country entertainment; my fare and my lodging was sweet and good, and might have served a far better man than myself.' He travelled next day twenty-one miles to a sorry village called Blyth, in Peeblesshire, where his lodging was less agreeable. Next again, passing through a fertile country for corn and cattle, he entered Edinburgh.

A gentleman named Mr John Maxwell, whom he casually encountered, conducted him to see the Castle, which he deemed impregnable, and where he noted the extraordinary piece of antique ordnance which still exists there under the name of Mons Meg. 'I crept into it, lying on my back, and I am sure there was room enough and to spare for a greater than myself.' He describes the principal street of the city as the fairest and goodliest he had ever seen, 'the buildings on each side of the way being all of squared stone, five, six, and seven stories high.' 'I found

1618. entertainment beyond my expectation or merit, and there had fish, flesh, bread, and fruit in such variety, that I think I may without offence call it superfluity. The worst was,' he adds waggishly, 'that wine and ale were so scarce, and the people there such misers of it, that every night before I went to bed, if any man had asked me a civil question, all the wit in my head could not have made him a sober answer.'

At Leith, he met a bountiful friend in Bernard Lindsay, one of the grooms of his majesty's bed-chamber, and was informed that 'within the compass of one year, there was shipped away from that port fourscore thousand bolls of wheat, oats, and barley, into Spain, France, and other foreign parts, and every boll contains the measure of four English bushels . . . . besides some hath been shipped away from St Andrews, Dundee, Aberdeen, Dysart, Kirkcaldy, Kinghorn, Burntisland, Dunbar, and other portable towns.'

In good time, Taylor commenced a progress through the country, entertained everywhere by hospitable gentlemen, who probably considered his witty conversation ample recompense. At Dunfermline, he viewed with pleasure the palace and remains of the abbacy, and the surrounding gardens, orchards, and meadows. Then he went to visit at Culross the enterprising coal-proprietor, Sir George Bruce, who entertained him hospitably and sent three of his men to guide him over the works. The imagination of the Water-poet was greatly excited by the singular mine which Sir George had here formed, partly within the sea-mark. 'At low-water, the sea being ebbed away, and a great part of the sand bare—upon this same sand, mixed with rocks and crags, did the master of this great work build a circular frame of stone, very thick, strong, and joined together with bituminous matter, so high withal that the sea at the highest flood, or the greatest rage of storm or tempest, can neither dissolve the stones so well compacted in the building, nor yet overflow the height of it. Within this round frame, he did set workmen to dig . . . . they did dig forty foot down right into and through a rock. At last they found that which they expected, which was sea-coal. They, following the vein of the mine, did dig forward still; so that in the space of eight-and-twenty or nine-and-twenty years, they have digged more than an English mile, under the sea, [so] that when men are at work below, a hundred of the greatest ships in Britain may sail over their heads. Besides, the mine is most artificially cut like an arch or vault, all that great length, with many nooks and by-ways; and it is so made that a man may walk upright in most places.' 1618

> 'All I saw was pleasure mixed with profit,
> Which proved it to be no tormenting Tophet;
> For in this honest, worthy, harmless hall,
> There ne'er did any damnèd devil dwell.'

'The sea at certain places doth leak or soak into the mine, which by the industry of Sir George Bruce is conveyed to one well near the land, where he hath a device like a horse-mill, with three great horses and a great chain of iron, going downward many fathoms, with thirty-six buckets attached to the chain, of the which eighteen go down still to be filled, and eighteen ascend still to be emptied, which do empty themselves without any man's labour into a trough that conveys the water into the sea again. . . . . Besides, he doth make every week ninety or a hundred tons of salt, which doth serve most part of Scotland; some he sends into England, and very much into Germany.'

The pennyless pilgrim proceeded to Stirling, of whose castle and palace he speaks in terms of high admiration; stating, moreover, that at his host Mr John Archibald's, his only difficulty was for 'room to contain half the good cheer that he might have had.' Advancing to St Johnston (Perth), he lodged at an inn kept by one Patrick Pitcairn. It was his design to visit Sir William Murray of Abercairny; but he here learned that that gentleman had left home on a hunting excursion. It was suggested that he might overtake him at Brechin; but on reaching that city, he found that Sir William had left it four days before.

Taylor now made a journey such as few Englishmen had any experience of in that age. Proceeding along Glen Esk, and passing by a road which lay over a lofty precipice, he lodged the first night at a poor cot on the Laird of Edzell's land, where nothing but Erse was spoken, and where he suffered somewhat from vermin—the only place, however, in Scotland where he met any such troubles. With immense difficulty, he next day crossed Mount Skene by an uneven stony way, full of bogs, quagmires, and long heath, 'where a dog with three legs would outrun a horse with four,' and came in the evening to Braemar. This he describes as a large county, full of lofty mountains, compared with which English hills are but 'as a liver or a gizzard below a capon's wing.' 'There I saw Benawne [Ben Aven], with a furred mist upon his snowy head, instead of a night-cap.'

1618. He here found his friend, Sir William Murray, engaged in Highland sports, along with the Earl of Mar, the Earl of Enzie (afterwards second Marquis of Huntly), the Earl of Buchan, and Lord Erskine, accompanied by their countesses, and a hundred other knights and squires, with their followers, 'all in general in one habit, as if Lycurgus had been there.' 'For once in the year, which is the whole month of August, and sometimes part of September, many of the nobility and gentry of the kingdom, for their pleasure, come into these Highland countries to hunt, where they conform to the habit of the Highlandmen, who for the most part speak nothing but Irish. . . . . Their habit is shoes with but one sole apiece; stockings which they call short hose, made of a warm stuff of divers colours, which they call tartan: as for breeches, many of them, nor their forefathers, never wore any, but a jerkin of the same stuff that their hose is of, their garters being bands or wreaths of hay or straw, with a plaid about their shoulders, which is a mantle of divers colours, [of] much finer and lighter stuff than their hose; with flat blue caps on their heads, a handkerchief knit with two knots about their neck; and thus they are attired. . . . . Their weapons are long bows and forked arrows, swords and targets, harquebusses, muskets, durks, and Lochaber axes. With these arms, I found many of them armed for the hunting. As for their attire, any man of what degree soever that comes amongst them, must not disdain to wear it; for if they do, they will disdain to hunt, or willingly to bring in their dogs; but if men be kind to them, and be in their habit, then they are conquered with kindness, and the sport will be plentiful. This was the reason that I found so many noblemen and gentlemen in those shapes.'

Taylor allowed himself to be invested by the Earl of Mar in Highland attire, and then accompanied the party for twelve days into a wilderness devoid of corn and human habitations—probably the district around the skirts of Ben Muicdhui. He found temporary lodges called *lonchards*, designed for the use of the sportsmen, and he himself received a kind of accommodation in that of Lord Erskine. The kitchen, he tells us, was 'always on the side of a bank, many kettles and pots boiling, and many spits turning and winding, with great variety of cheer, as venison—baked, sodden, roast, and stewed beef—mutton, goats, kid, hares, fresh salmon, pigeons, hens, capons, chickens, partridge, moorcoots, heath-cocks, cappercailzies, and termagants; good ale,

sack, white and claret, tent (or Alicant), with most potent 1618.
aquavitæ.' Thus a company of about fourteen hundred persons was most amply fed.

'The manner of the hunting is this: five or six hundred men rise early in the morning, and disperse themselves divers ways, and seven, eight, or ten miles compass, they bring or chase in the deer in many herds (two, three, or four hundred in a herd), to such or such a place, as the noblemen shall appoint them. Then, when day is come, the lords and gentlemen of their companies ride or go to the said places, sometimes wading up to the middle, through burns and rivers; and then they, being come to the place, lie down on the ground, till those foresaid scouts, who are called the Tinchel-men, bring down the deer. . . . . After we had stayed there three hours or thereabouts, we might perceive the deer appear on the hills round about us (their heads making a show like a wood), which, being followed close by the Tinchel, are chased down into the valley where we lay. Then, all the valley on each side being waylaid with a hundred couple of strong Irish greyhounds, they are let loose, as occasion serves, upon the herd of deer, [so] that with dogs, guns, arrows, durks, and daggers, in the space of two hours, fourscore fat deer were slain, which after are disposed, some one way and some another, twenty or thirty miles, and more than enough left for us to make merry withal at our rendezvous.'

After spending some days in this manner in the Brae of Mar, the party, attended by Taylor, went into Badenoch, and renewed the sport there for three or four days, concluding with a brief visit to Ruthven Castle. This grand old fortress—anciently the stronghold of the Cumins, lords of Badenoch—seated on an alluvial promontory jutting into the haugh beside the Spey, occupying an area of a hundred and twenty yards long, and consisting of two great towers surrounded by a fortified wall with an iron gate and portcullis,[1] was now the property of the Gordon family. Here, says Taylor, 'my Lord of Enzie and his noble countess (being daughter to the Earl of Argyle) did give us most noble welcome for three days.' 'From thence we went to a place called Ballo[ch] Castle, a fair and stately house, a worthy gentleman being the owner of it, called the Laird of Grant.[2] . . . . Our cheer was more than sufficient, and yet much less than they could afford us. There stayed there four days four

[1] *Survey of Moray*, p. 208.

[2] Now called Castle-Grant.

1618. earls, one lord, divers knights and gentlemen, and their servants, footmen, and horses; and every meal four long tables furnished with all varieties; our first and second course being threescore dishes at one board; and after that always a banquet; and there, if I had not forsworn wine till I came to Edinburgh, I think I had there drank my last.'

The Water-poet was afterwards four days at Tarnaway, entertained in the same hospitable manner by the Earl and Countess of Moray. He speaks of Morayland as the pleasantest and most plentiful country in Scotland, 'being plain land, that a coach may be driven more than four-and-thirty miles one way in it, alongst the sea-coast.' He spent a few days with the Marquis of Huntly at the Bog, 'where our entertainment was, like himself, free, bountiful, and honourable,' and then returned by the Cairn-a-mount to Edinburgh.

Here he was again in the midst of plentiful good cheer and good company for eight days, while recovering from certain bruises he had got at the Highland hunting. In Leith, at the house of Mr John Stuart, he found his 'long approved and assured good friend, Mr Benjamin Jonson,' who gave him a piece of gold of the value of twenty-two shillings, to drink his health in England. 'So with a friendly farewell, I left him as well as I hope never to see him in a worse estate; for he is among noblemen and gentlemen that know his true worth and their own honours, where with much respective love he is worthily entertained.'

In short, Taylor, in his progress through Scotland, seems to have been everywhere feasted sumptuously, and supplied liberally with money. So much of a virtue comparatively rare in England, and so much plenty in a country which his own people were accustomed to think of as the birthplace of famine, seems to have greatly astonished him. The wonder comes to a climax at Cockburnspath, near his exit from Scotland, where he was handsomely entertained at an inn by Master William Arnot and his wife, the owners thereof. 'I must explain,' he says, 'their bountiful entertainment of guests, which is this:

'Suppose ten, fifteen, or twenty men and horses come to lodge at their house. The men shall have flesh, tame and wild fowl, fish, with all variety of good cheer, good lodging, and welcome, and the horses shall want neither hay nor provender; and at the morning at their departure the reckoning is just nothing. This is this worthy gentleman's use, his chief delight being to give strangers entertainment *gratis!* And I am sure that in Scotland, beyond Edinburgh, I have been at houses like castles for building; 1618. the master of the house's beaver being his blue bonnet, one that will wear no other shirts but of the flax that grows on his own ground, and of his wife's, daughters', or servants' spinning; that hath his stockings, hose, and jerkin of the wool of his own sheep's backs; that never by his pride of apparel caused mercer, draper, silk-man, embroiderer, or haberdasher, to break and turn bankrupt; and yet this plain home-spun fellow keeps and maintains thirty, forty, fifty servants, or perhaps more, every day relieving three or four score poor people at his gate; and besides all this, can give noble entertainment for four days together to five or six earls and lords, besides knights, gentlemen, and their followers, if they be three or four hundred men and horse of them, where they shall not only feed but feast, and not feast but banquet; this is a man that desires to know nothing so much as his duty to God and his king, whose greatest cares are to practise the works of piety, charity, and hospitality. He never studies the consuming art of fashionless fashions; he never tries his strength to bear four or five hundred acres on his back at once; his legs are always at liberty, not being fettered with golden garters and manacled with artificial roses. . . . . Many of these worthy housekeepers there are in Scotland. . . . .

'There th' Almighty doth his blessings heap,
In such abundant food for beasts and men,
That I ne'er saw more plenty or more cheap.' [1]

In the summer of this year, Scotland received a visit from the famous Ben Jonson. The burly laureate walked all the way, notwithstanding a previous hint from Lord Bacon, that 'he loved not to see Poesy go on other feet than poetical Dactylus and Spondæus.' Among the motives for a journey then undertaken by few Englishmen, might be curiosity regarding a country from which he knew that his family was derived, his grandfather having been one of the Johnstons of Annandale. He had many friends, too, particularly among the connections of the Lennox family, whom he might be glad to see at their own houses. Indeed, his biographer, Gifford, expressly says he had received from some of these friends an invitation to spend some time amongst them in the north. In September, he was found by Taylor the water-poet, residing with one Mr John Stuart in Leith; and Taylor speaks of

[1] *Works of John Taylor, the Water-poet.* London, folio, 1630.

1618. him generally as being then 'among noblemen and gentlemen who knew his true worth and their own honours, where with much respective love he is entertained.'

Among those with whom he had amicable intercourse, was William Drummond, the poet, then in the prime of life, and living as a bachelor in his romantic mansion of Hawthornden, on the Esk, seven miles from Edinburgh. It is probable that Drummond and Jonson had met before in London, and indulged together in the 'wit-combats' at the Mermaid and similar scenes. Indeed, there is a prevalent belief in Scotland that it was mainly to see Drummond at Hawthornden that Jonson came so far from home. The story is, that the pilgrim came first to Hawthornden, and was received by Drummond with wonted ceremony, under the Covine Tree—that is, company tree—which still stands on the lawn in front of the house, when their greetings very appropriately took the form of a couplet:

D. Welcome, welcome, royal Ben!
J. Thank ye, thank ye, Hawthornden—

the laureate having already learned to address a Scottish laird by what Scott calls 'his territorial appellation.' Be this as it may, we have no authentic notice of any intercourse between the two poets till the commencement of the ensuing year, when they undoubtedly spent a considerable time together, as it was then that they had those *Conversations,* which, being noted down by Drummond, and published many years after in his *Works,* have furnished so much food for modern controversy. These memoranda partly relate facts regarding Jonson himself, but chiefly report his opinions of his poetical contemporaries, which are generally of a censorious character. Added to them, however, is Drummond's report on Jonson himself, in these terms: 'Ben Jonson was a great lover and praiser of himself, a contemner and scorner of others, given rather to lose a friend than a jest; jealous of every word and action of those about him, especially after drink, which is one of the elements in which he lived; a dissembler of the parts which reign in him; a bragger of some good that he wanted; thinketh nothing well done but what either he himself or some of his friends have said or done. He is passionately kind and angry, careless either to gain or keep; vindictive, but if he be well answered, at himself; interprets best sayings and deeds often to the worst. He was for any religion, as being versed in both; oppressed with fancy, which hath overmastered his reason, a general disease in many poets,' &c. Drummond has been severely blamed for stating so much, even privately, regarding a man whom he treated with all the external marks of friendship; but the censure seems scarcely just. It is not necessarily to be supposed that he was the less sensible of the merits of Jonson, that he also observed his being marked by that vanity, impulsiveness, and irritability which have been remarked in so many poets. Neither may he have loved him the less—possibly he only loved him the more—because of his faults. As to the act of taking such notes, some allowance may be made for a man of literary tastes, living at a distance from the centre of the world of letters, in an age when there were no periodicals to prattle about literary celebrities, or an opportunity occurring of hearing a famous poet talk of his poetical brethren, and of seeing that eminent person revealing his own character. 1618.

A letter written by Drummond to Jonson in this very month, and probably only a few days after their conversation, has been preserved:[1]

'TO HIS WORTHY FRIEND, MR BENJAMIN JONSON.

'SIR—Here you have that epigram you desired, with another of the like argument. If there be any other thing in this country (unto which my power can reach), command it; there is nothing I wish more than to be in the calendar of them who love you. I have heard from court that the late masque was not so much approved of the king as in former times, and that your absence was regretted—such applause hath true worth, even of those who otherwise are not for it. Thus, to the next occasion taking my leave, I remain

Your loving friend,

WILLIAM DRUMMOND.

January 17, 1619.'

From a consideration of the whole circumstances, it is most likely that Jonson had spent some time in autumn with his Lennox friends, and thus been introduced to the romantic beauties of Loch Lomond, and perhaps also to the romantic sports indulged in by the gentry of its neighbourhood. Certain it is, from Drummond's report of his conversations, that he designed 'to write a Fisher or Pastoral Play, and make the stage of it on the Lomond Lake.' And after he had returned to London, Drummond sent him 'a

[1] See *Drummond's Works*, folio, Edinburgh, 1711, p. 234.

1618. description of Loch Lomond, with a map of Inch Merinoch,' which, he says, 'may by your book be made most famous.' It is possible, however, that this description of Loch Lomond and map of Inch Merinoch—one of the many isles in the lake—may have been intended for a prose work, which he also contemplated writing—namely, his 'Foot Pilgrimage' to Scotland, which, with a feeling very natural in one who found so much to admire where so little had been known, he spoke of entitling *A Discovery*. Unfortunately, this work, as well as a poem in which he called Edinburgh

'The Heart of Scotland, Britain's other eye,'

has not been preserved to us. We can readily see that the work contemplated must have been of a general character, for Jonson wrote to Drummond (London, May 10, 1619), not merely for 'some things concerning the Loch of Lomond,' but for copies of 'the inscriptions at Pinkie,' referring probably to the Roman antiquities which had been found in Queen Mary's time at Inveresk, and also bids him 'urge Mr James Scott,' and send 'what else you can procure for me with all speed.' The king, he adds, was 'pleased to hear of the purpose of my book.' How much to be regretted that we have not the Scotland of that day delineated by so vigorous a pen as that of the author of *Sejanus!*

The last visit Jonson paid in Scotland was to Drummond at Hawthornden in the month of April, just before his return to London, which, as we see, he had reached before the 10th of May. He lived with Drummond on that occasion three weeks, enjoying, doubtless, the vernal beauties of that romantic spot, as well as the converse of his friend, and the more substantial hospitalities for which, if Drummond be right, he had only too keen a relish. Their parting—which, by Scottish use and wont, would be under the Covine Tree, when royal Ben set out on foot as before to return to London—who but wishes he could picture as it really was! Jonson's letter of the 10th May, written soon after his arrival in London, and breathing of the feelings which his excursion had excited, may aptly conclude this notice:

'TO MY WORTHY, HONOURED, AND BELOVED FRIEND,
MR W. DRUMMOND.

'MOST LOVING AND BELOVED SIR—against which titles I should most knowingly offend, if I made you not some account of myself to come even with your friendship—I am arrived safely, with a most Catholic welcome, and my reports not unacceptable to his majesty. He professed, thank God, some joy to see me, and is pleased to hear of the purpose of my book; to which I most earnestly solicit you for your promise of the inscriptions at Pinkie, some things concerning the Loch of Lomond, touching the government of Edinburgh, to urge Mr James Scott, and what else you can procure for me with all speed. Though these requests be full of trouble, I hope they shall neither burthen nor weary such a friendship, whose commands to me I shall ever interpret a pleasure. News we have none here, but what is making against the queen's funeral, whereof I have somewhat in hand, that shall look upon you with the next. Salute the beloved Fentons, the Nisbets, the Scotts, the Livingstones, and all the honest and honoured names with you, especially Mr James Wroth, your sister, &c. And if you forget yourself, you believe not in 1618

Your most true friend and lover,

BEN JONSON.[1]

LONDON, *May* 10, 1619.'

At the very time when Ben Jonson and John Taylor had the pleasant experiences of the Highlands which are above described and adverted to, sundry parts of that province of Scotland were the scene of lawless violences, which these English poets could not have heard of without horror. M'Ronald of Gargarach,[2] 'with a band of lawless limmers his assisters and accomplices,' went about 'committing murders, slaughters, treasonable fire-raisings, and other insolencies, in all parts where they had any mastery or command.' It was necessary to give his rival and antagonist, Sir Lachlan MacIntosh, a commission 'to pursue him to the deid with fire and sword.' At the same time, several men of the Clan Campbell, taking advantage of the absence of their chief, the Earl of Argyle, 'has lately broken louss, and goes athort the country, in companies, sorning [upon] and oppressing his majesty's guid subjects, in all parts where they may be masters.' The earl, it appeared, had nominated none in his absence 'to have the charge and burden to retein his clan and country under obedience.' To supply this defect, the Council (July 9, 1618) summoned the chief men of the name—the Lairds of Glenurchy, Caddell, Lawers, Auchinbreck, and Glenlyon—to give information about the delinquents, and surety for the future peace of the country.

[1] Gifford's edition of *Jonson's Works*. London, 1816, vol. I., p. cccxxxii.

[2] He seems to have been the same with Macdonald of Keppoch.

1618. Contemporaneously with these outrages, were others of the like nature committed by 'a number of vagabonds and broken men of the Clan Donochie (Robertsons),' particularly in the lands of Simon Lord Fraser of Lovat.—*P. C. R.*

It may be remarked that the Earl of Argyle had gone abroad, either from dissatisfaction with the rewards assigned him for his putting down of the Macgregors and MacConnel of Kintyre,[1] or because of troubles on account of his debts.[2] To the surprise of his countrymen, he entered the service of Philip III. against the people of the Low Countries, and, by the persuasion of his wife, joined the Church of Rome. The poet Craig thus satirised him:

'Now, Earl of Guile and Lord Forlorn, thou goes,
Quitting thy prince to serve his Spanish foes:
No faith in plaids, no trust in Highland trews,
Chameleon-like, they change so many hues.'

The king felt as indignant as any, and on the 4th of February 1619, the Privy Council had this 'shameful defection' under its notice. It was alleged that the apostate earl not only goes openly to mass, but has associated with 'auld M'Ranald' and sundry other exiled rebels. Sundry charges against him having been slighted, the Council now 'do repute him as a traitor,' and ordain him to be pursued as such. The earl, who, before leaving his country, had handed over his estates to his son, did not return till he was enabled to do so by the grace of Charles I. in 1638.

Aug. 20. Thomas Ross, a man of good family, formerly minister of Cargill, in Perthshire, had gone to Oxford to study; but in a moment of partial lunacy—for the act can be accounted for in no other way—he wrote a libel on the Scottish nation, and affixed it to the door of St Mary's Church. It spoke in scurrilous terms of the people of Scotland, excepting only the king and a few others, and counselled that the king should banish all Scots from his court. James took the matter in high dudgeon, and had Ross sent down to Scotland, with strict orders to bring him to condign punishment. He was accordingly tried at the date marginally noted, for an act of which the design was assumed to be to have stirred up the people of England 'to the cruel, barbarous, and unmerciful murdering, massacring, and assassine of the haill Scots people, as well noblemen and councillors as others, attendants

[1] *Johnstoni Hist.*, p 529. [2] Scot's *Stag. State of Scots Statesmen.*

about his highness's royal person in court.' The unfortunate satirist professed penitence, and craved mercy, averring that he had been *inops mentis* at the time of his committing the act. Nothing could avail to save him. His right hand was first struck off, and then he was beheaded and quartered, his head being fixed on a prick at the Nether Bow Port, and his hand at the West Port. —*Pit.* 1618.

Mr John Guthrie, minister of Perth, 'on ane Sunday after the afternoon's sermon, married the Master of Sanquhar with Sir Robert Swift's daughter, ane English knight in Yorkshire. Neither of the parties exceeded thirteen years of age.'—*Chron. Perth.* Aug. 29.

'About the midst of November, there appeared a prodigious comet in the morning, in the north-east, broad, and stretching with a large tail towards the north-west. It appeared fine and clear some few days in the beginning, and after became more dim and obscure, and vanished away at last in the north. This comet by appearance portended the wars of Germany, which began not long after, and continueth yet to this hour.'—*Cal.* Nov. 18.

Dr Bembridge, 'a very profound and learned mathematician,' obliged the king with an account of this comet. He told him it was as far above the moon as the moon is above the earth, and not less than 2,300,000 English miles! Rushworth speaks of it as followed by, first, the Bohemian wars, then the German and Swedish, &c. 'Dr Bembridge observed it to be vertical to London, and to pass over it in the morning; so it gave England and Scotland in their civil wars a sad wipe with its tail.'—*Foun. Hist. Ob.*

This notable comet was observed in Silesia, Rome, and Ispahan. From Skipton's observations, Halley afterwards computed its orbit. It passed its perihelion on the 8th of November, at little more than a third of the earth's distance from the sun. On the 9th of December, its tail was 70° in length, being, according to Kepler, the longest that had been seen for a hundred and fifty years.

This comet is also remarkable as the only one, besides another in 1607, which was observable by the naked eye in the first half of the seventeenth century; whereas in other spaces of time of the same extent, as many as thirteen have been detected. The comet of 1607, which is the same with that seen in 1682, 1759, and 1835, and usually known as Halley's comet, is not mentioned by any of our contemporary chroniclers as having been visible in Scottish skies.

1618. Dec. 25. Christmas was observed in Edinburgh at the command of the king, and two churches opened for service; but the attendance was scant. 'The Great Kirk was not half filled, notwithstanding the provost, bailies, and council's travels. . . . The dogs were playing in the flure of the Little Kirk, for rarity of people, and these were of the meaner sort. . . . Mr Patrick [Galloway] denounced judgments . . . . famine of the word, deafness, blindness, lameness, inability to come to the kirk to hear and see, to fall upon those who came not to his Christmas sermon.'—*Cal.*

A few weeks afterwards, Richard Lawson, James Cathkin, and John Mean, merchants, were obliged to appear before the Court of High Commission, accused of 'not coming to the kirk on Christmas-day, for opening of their booth-doors, walking before them in time of sermon, dissuading others from going to the kirk, and reasoning against preaching on that day. They answered they did nothing of contempt; they reasoned to receive instruction, and to try what warrant others had. They were dismissed, with an admonition to be modest in their speeches and behaviour in time coming.'—*Cal.*

On Christmas-day 1621, there was service in the Old Kirk in St Giles, which the magistrates and state officials attended; but no other church was open, and Calderwood informs us that 'one hundred and six booth-doors or thereby stood open'—a proof of the general disregard of the festival.

Patrick Anderson, doctor of physic, and who is usually said to have been physician to Charles I., published a tract on the 'Cold spring of Kinghorn,' its admirable properties for the cure of sundry diseases. He took care to draw a distinction between the simply natural efficacy of this well and 'the superstitious mud-earth wells of Menteith, or our Lady Well of Strathern, and our Lady Well of Ruthven, with a number of others in this country, all tapestried about with old rags, as certain signs and sacraments, wherewith they arle the devil.'[1] He further assured the public that the 'clear and delicate cauld water' of this spring, being drunk in great quantity, 'is never for all that felt in the belly.' Modern physiologists, it may be remarked, admit the rapid absorption of saline waters by the stomach; and the drinking of nine tumblers before breakfast is at this day not uncommon at Airthry.

[1] Earnest-money is arles in Scotland.

Dr Patrick Anderson was the inventor of a pill of aloetic character, which long had a great celebrity in Scotland, and is still in such repute that an agency-office for its sale may be found in both Edinburgh and London. He is the more entitled to some notice here, as our work has been somewhat indebted to a History of Scotland by him, to be found in manuscript in the Advocates' Library. 1618.

At this time, one Thomas Milne was a maker of virginals in Aberdeen—a calling, however, 'but lately put in practice in the burgh.' The trade must have been tolerably encouraged, as John Davidson, who had served an apprenticeship under Milne, now proposed to set up for himself. On his exhibiting a pair of virginals of his own making as his 'master-stick' before the Council, they gave him the freedom of the burgh without a fee, which he was too poor to pay.—*Ab. C. R.*

Died, 'Mr William Cowper, Bishop of Galloway, a very holy and good [man], if he had not been corrupted with superior powers and warldly cares of a bishopric and other such things. He was buried at the south door of the new kirk callit the South Kirk, in the Greyfriars' Yard, or common burial-place of Edinburgh, whilk kirk was newly completed, and at the funeral sermon consecrated by Mr John Spottiswoode, archbishop of Sanctandrews.'—*Jo. H.* 1619. Feb. 15.

Cowper was an eloquent and able man, and had been conspicuous for his zeal against bishops, 'appearing to all men to hate very much that lordly dignity in a kirkman, comparing them and their godless followers to snuffs of candles, whilk not only is destitute of light, but also casts out a filthy flewrish stink in man's noses.' To a former friend, who had accepted a bishopric, he wrote a despiteful letter, telling him he had fallen away and apostatised, and while he still loved himself, he hated his way. Afterwards, 'perceiving the courses of the bishops daily going forward, and being a proud ambitious man, glorying in his gifts, he began first privately to be social and homely with the bishops, and then, after the Golden Assembly at Glasgow in 1610, perceiving that the bishops had gotten all their intent, he also embraced a bishopric, and (1612) was created Bishop of Galloway.'

Feeling that his conduct had been inconsistent, Cowper wrote an apology, which mainly came to this, that he had got more light than he had before. 'One answered merrily: "It is true; for now

1619. he has upon his table two great candles, whereas before he had but one small candle—other more light I know none."'

In the end, he announced from the pulpit, he would give full satisfaction to all who would come and confer with him. 'Upon whilk invitation, so many came to him, both in the fields and in his own house, that he was wearied with them.' [According to the Chronicle of Perth—'The wives of Edinburgh came in to him, and shewed to him his awn books against friers' books.'] One person went so far as to charge him with apostasy, and call upon him to prepare an answer shortly to the Judge of all the world. It would appear from what followed that the bishop was by this time out of health. 'Within a day or two after, being at his pastime [golf?] in the Links of Leith, he was terrified with a vision, or an apprehension; for he said to his playfellows, after he had in an affrighted and commoved way cast away his play-instruments: "I vow to be about with these two men, who have now come upon me with drawn swords!" When his playfellows replied: "My lord, it is a dream: we saw no such thing," he was silent, went home trembling, took bed instantly, and died.'—*Row.*

MAR. 23. It had been a custom of the congregations in Edinburgh to hold a meeting on the Tuesday before the administration of the communion. 'If anything was amiss in the lives, doctrines, or any part of the office of their pastors, every man had liberty to shew wherein they were offended; and if anything was found amiss, the pastors promised to amend it. If they had anything likewise to object against the congregation, it was likewise heard, and amendment was promised. If there was any variance among neighbours, pains were taken to make reconciliation, that so both pastors and people might communicate in love at the banquet of love.' On the present occasion, the affair had much the character of a modern public meeting, and the people stood boldly up to their pastors, arguing against the innovations of worship now about to be introduced, particularly kneeling at the sacrament.—*Cal.*

'At various times in the year 1621, there were private meetings of ministers and other good Christians in Edinburgh, setting apart days for fasting, praying, and humiliation, crying to God for help in such a needful time; whilk exercises, joined with handling of Scripture, resolving of questions, clearing doubts, and tossing of cases of conscience, were very comfortable. . . . Thir meetings the bishops and their followers, enemies still to the power of godliness and life of religion, hated to the death; and sundry ministers of

Edinburgh inveighed against them, under the name of unlawful conventicles, candle-light congregations (because sometimes they continued their exercises for a great part of the night), persecuting them with odious names of Puritans, Separatists, Brownists, &c.' —*Row.* 1619.

One of the Edinburgh clergy 'sent to Nicolas Balfour, daughter of umwhile Mr James Balfour, minister of Edinburgh, to advertise her that she was to be banished the town, for entertaining such meetings in her house; and reviled her despitefully, when she came to confer with him.'—*Cal.*

This day, being Easter Sunday, the communion was administered in the Edinburgh churches for the first time after it had been arranged that the people should kneel on receiving the elements. There being a general disrelish for this new form, the people left the town in great numbers to communicate at country churches where the order was not yet appointed. Of those who attended in town, few willingly knelt besides government officials and pauper dependents on the church contributions. 'Some were dashed and kneeled, but with shedding of tears for grief.' In some churches throughout the country, certain persons told the ministers: 'The dangers, if any be, light upon your soul, not on ours!' Some departed, 'beseeking God to judge between them and the minister.' 'It is not to be passed over, how that when John Lauder, minister at Cockburnspath, was reaching the bread to one kneeling, a black dog started up to snatch it out of his hand.'—*Cal.* MAR. 28.

On next Easter Sunday, the like disinclination to kneeling was shewn. In the College Kirk, where sixteen hundred people communicated, only about twenty kneeled, and it was thought that none would have done so, 'if they had not brought the poor out of the hospital, to begin, and give a good example.' These, 'being aged, poor, and ignorant persons, durst not refuse;' yet even of them, some, 'when they were kneeling, knocked on their breasts and lifted up their hands and eyes.'

While the officers of the government and many others joined cordially in the new arrangements, the bulk of the people revolted from them. Whenever they heard of a church in the country where they might be allowed to communicate sitting, they resorted to it in great numbers; 'whereupon the auditory of the kirks of Edinburgh became rare and thin.'

On Easter Sunday, 1622, at the communion in the Old Kirk, Edinburgh, 'among all the two hundred and fifty [communicants]

1619. there was not a man of honest countenance but the President, Sir William Oliphant, the Advocate, Sir Henry Wardlaw, the Provost, the Dean of Guild, Dame Dick, the Master of Works' wife, and two bailies, who communicate not: plaids, gray cloaks, and blue bonnets made the greatest show.'

At the same time, 'many of the profaner sort were drawn out upon the sixth of May, to May-games in Gilmerton and Roslin; so profanity began to accompany superstition and idolatry, as it had done in former times. Upon the first of May, the weavers in Paul's Work, English and Dutch, set up a high May-pole, with their garlands and bells hanging at them, whereat was great concourse of people.'—*Cal.*

APR. 2. John Maxwell of Garrarie—'ane landed gentleman, in the rank of ane baron, worth three thousand merks of yearly rent, and above'—was, with his son, George Maxwell, tried for the crime of treason. Garrarie had, in a crafty manner, possessed himself of the estate and whole worldly means of John M'Kie of Glashock, who thus became a miserable dependent upon him, almost constantly living in his house. At length, tiring of the company, and probably also of the complaints of the unfortunate Glashock, Garrarie and his son resolved to be rid of him. On the 8th of July 1618, when Glashock was coming by night to the place of Garrarie, the two Maxwells, attended by an armed band of servants, fell upon him, tied his hands and feet, strangled him, and flung his body into a peat-moss.

The accused protested their innocence, and it was necessary twice to postpone proceedings against them, apparently for lack of evidence. Another remarkable circumstance was, that no fewer than seventeen gentlemen of the district incurred fines by failing to appear as jurymen. Notwithstanding these and other impediments, justice asserted its claims, and Garrarie and his son had their heads stricken off at the Cross of Edinburgh, with forfeiture of lands and goods.—*Pit.*

The period at which we have now arrived, being one of internal peace, is distinguished as the time when the practice of several of the useful arts was first introduced into Scotland. Sir George Hay, the Clerk Registrar—ancestor of the Earls of Kinnoul—a man of talent and intelligence, had set up, at the village of Wemyss, in Fife, a small glasswork, being the first known to have existed amongst us. An ironwork, of what nature we are not informed, was also originated by Sir George.

The Privy Council informed the king that Sir George Hay had enterprisingly set up works for iron and glass, which for some years he supported at high charges, in hopes of being remunerated by profits. 'But now he has found, by experience, that all the country dispatch of his glass in ane haill year will not uphold his glassworks the space of ane month.' It was entreated that the king would allow of Sir George's glass being sold unrestrainedly in England, and at the same time restrict the exportation of coal into that country. By such means he admitted he had a hope of thriving.—*M. S. P.* 1619. July 22.

It would appear that the native manufacture, after all, prospered; for in February 1621, the Privy Council appointed a commission, including Sir George Hay, to meet and confer anent the glassworks, to examine and try the glass, and see that measures were taken for the full supply of the country, so as to save the introduction of foreign glass.

The commission soon after reported that the glassworks at Wemyss were going on satisfactorily. The cradles or cases contained fifteen wisps, each wisp having three tables, three-quarters of a Scots ell and a nail in depth. The glass was fully as good as Danskine glass, though they could wish it to be 'thicker and tewcher.' Being less sure of the character of the drinking-glasses produced, they recommended patterns of English glass of that kind to be established in Edinburgh Castle, for trying the sufficiency of Scots glass in all time coming. On the strength of this report, the Council granted the desired monopoly as against foreign glassmakers, on certain conditions, one of which was, that the price of 'braid glass' should not exceed 'twelve punds the cradle.'—*P. C. R.*

Before this time, soap was imported into Scotland from foreign countries, chiefly from Flanders. It was estimated that the entire quantity brought in was about a hundred and twenty lasts. The king now gave a patent to Mr Nathaniel Uddart for the manufacture of soap within the country, and Mr Nathaniel accordingly raised a goodly work at Leith, furnishing it with all matters pertaining to the business. Before he had been at work two years (June 21, 1621), he petitioned the Privy Council that foreign soap should be prohibited, professing to be able himself to furnish all that was required for the use of the country people, and thus save money from being sent out of the country—a piece of false political economy much in favour, as we have seen, in those Oct. 20.

1619. days. The Privy Council, after taking some pains to ascertain the character of 'Mr Nathaniel his soap,' and becoming convinced that he could furnish the quantity needful, granted the prohibition requested, but not without fixing down the native manufacturer at a maximum price. This was decreed to be £24 per barrel for 'green soap,' and £32 per barrel for 'white soap,' each barrel to contain sixteen stone.

If we are right in considering the stone at 17·39 pounds avoirdupois, and the last as containing twelve barrels, the estimated amount of regularly manufactured soap annually used in Scotland at that time might be approximately 400,880 pounds. In 1845, taking its consumption of the same article as one-seventh of that of Great Britain, Scotland consumed about *twenty-seven million pounds!*

Matters had not proceeded upon the footing of protection for above two years, when complaints became rife as to the inconveniences sustained by the lieges. The merchants of Edinburgh felt it as a grievance that their traffic for soap with the Low Countries was interrupted. They also complained of the quality of the article produced at Leith. The merchants of Dumfries and other distant ports groaned at being obliged to carry soap a long land-journey from Leith, when they could have it brought by ships direct to their doors. In short, it was not to be borne.

The Lords of Council took pains to inform themselves of the whole matter. They also had a letter from the king testifying his 'dislike of this and others the like restraints, as being a mean to overthrow traffic and to destroy commerce.' Being now satisfied that Uddart's privilege was 'hurtful to the commonweal,' and that 'the subjects has not been so commodiously furnist with the soap made by the said Mr Nathaniel as formerly they were with foreign soap,' they decreed (July 1623) that the restraint should terminate in a year, or sooner, if he should produce an inferior or dearer article.—*P. C. R.*

1620. MAR. 30. While the struggle was going on between the Episcopalian and Presbyterian principles, there was a small group of Edinburgh citizens, including the booksellers Cathkin and Lawson, who took a lead in opposing the new practices, and standing up against the dictates of the High Commission. Deeply impressed with evangelical doctrine, and viewing all ceremonies as tending to the corruption of pure religion, they were disposed to venture a good way in the course they entered upon. Their wranglings in the

kirk-session against ministers of the court fashion, and their earnest 1620.
private exercises, were fully known to the king; but he bore with them till they began to lend countenance and active help to the few refractory ministers who fell under the ban of the bishops. He then, at the date noted, ordered them to be removed as 'evil weeds' from Edinburgh—William Rig, merchant, and James Cathkin, bookseller, to Caithness; Richard Lawson, to Aberdeen; Robert Meiklejohn, skinner, to Dunkeld; John Mean, to Wigton in Galloway; and Thomas Inglis, skinner, to Montrose. This was a great stretch of power in a country professedly under regular laws; and even the state-officers felt it to be so. After some dealings, in the course of which the clergy were eager to negative a suspicion of their having sent the names of the men to the king, the archbishop of St Andrews said he would intercede for them, and meanwhile stayed further proceedings. In the end, the offence of the Edinburgh patriots was passed over for this occasion.—*Cal.*

The Edinburgh pulpits were at this time filled with men wholly devoted to the Episcopalian system, and such of the people as were strenuous for the Presbyterian model, had to act not merely without clerical leaders, but in despite of clerical opposition. As a specimen of the spirit of these metropolitan clergy—'Mr William Struthers (January 9, 1619) made a sermon in the Little East Kirk, whilk, by all the holy divines in Scotland, was judged rather to have been a discourse of hateful passion nor a sermon of a charitable divine or loving theologue. For the most part of his haill discourse consisted in calling Christ's flock of Edinburgh a pack of cruel people, seeking the overthrow of their ministry; calling them also the authors of the *Seventeenth of December*.[1] . . . . He also alleged the doings of the good town of that day till be in all histories a foul blot to them for ever. He alleged the people were bund to follow him and the rest of his brethren the ministers, and to do all things that they bade them do, calling the ministers the heid, and the people the tail, and whatever the ministers as the heid spak, it was good and savoury, and whatever the tail or the people spak was unsavoury, adding thereto that the language of the tail was deir of the hearing. . . . . This sermon made me and all the hearers thereof tremble for fear to behold fit untruth spoken in the chair of verity. . . . .'—*Jo. H.*

It has been seen that horse-racing was, from an early time, MAY 3.

[1] See under December 17, 1596.

1620. practised as a public amusement at various places in Scotland. One of these, not formerly noticed, was Paisley. A silver bell of four ounce weight was made in 1608 to serve as a prize for the Paisley race: such was in those days the accustomed prize at a race, giving rise to the proverbial expression—'He bore off the bell.' It may be remarked, however, that the winner of a silver bell at a race did not obtain it as permanent property, but only for a year's keeping, as is customary with the silver arrows and silver clubs now played for by archery and golfing societies.

At the date noted, the Town Council of Paisley, under the guidance of their provost, the Earl of Abercorn, arranged that their annual horse-race should be run on the 6th of May, 'to be start at the gray stane called St Cormel's Stane, and frae that richt east to the little house at the causeyend of Renfrew, and frae that the king's highway to the Wall-neuk of Paisley; and what horse first comes over the score at . . . . Renfrew, sall have ane double angel; and the horse and master thereof that first comes over the score at the Wall-neuk of Paisley, sall have the said bell with the said burgh's arms thereon, for that year, together with the rest of the gold that sall be given with the said bell . . . . except ane double angel that sall be given to the second horse and his master that comes next over the score to the foremost. . . .' The horses and their owners to gather at Paisley in good time before the race, and the riders to be weighed at the Tron of the burgh. It was also arranged that there should be 'an aftershot race . . . . frae ane score at the slates of Ellerslie to ane other score at the causey-head of the burgh of Paisley, by horse of the price of ane hundred merks . . . . for ane furnished saddle, whilk sall be presented by the said bailies of Paisley present and to come at the score of the said causey-head.'[1]

Patrick Anderson, a native of Ross-shire, and nephew of the celebrated Bishop Lesly, had risen by learning and talent to be head of the Scots College at Rome. This situation he left in order to add his exertions to those which a number of his co-religionists were making, at the hazard of their lives, for the recovery of Scotland from what they called the Calvinistic heresy. Dempster speaks of him as 'moribus innocens ac fide integer,' and tells us he had no superior in mathematics and theology. Such as he was, he threw himself into this mission with a zeal and gallantry which no

[1] *Maitland Miscellany*, p. 195.

generous opponent could now dispute, but which was regarded in the Scotland of his own day as only a diabolic mania for the turning of living souls to death and perdition. 1620.

Poor Patrick had not practised long, when he was apprehended with his mass-clothes, books, and papers, and committed to prison as a trafficking Romish priest. He owned to the fact of his having performed mass sundry times, but would not tell in whose houses. In the ensuing October, a brother-missionary, an Irishman, named Edmund Cana, was apprehended, along with a younger brother, 'who carried his mass-clothes, a portable altar, a flagon of wine, and other requisites necessar for the mass.'—*Cal.* MAY 18.

Possibly, King James had heard of the merits of Father Anderson as a man of learning, and felt some sympathy for him; perhaps the French ambassador made friendly intercession in his behalf. However it was, after the Father had suffered nine months' imprisonment, the king came to the resolution to shew him some mercy. At his command, the Privy Council liberated the Father from prison, with a suit of good clothes, and some money in his pocket, on condition that he should leave Scotland, and return no more; otherwise, he would be liable to capital punishment. It was enjoined upon the provost and bailies of Edinburgh that they should 'try and speir out some ship bown from the port of Leith towards France or Flanders; and when the ship is ready to lowse, that they tak the said Patrick Anderson furth of their Tolbooth, carry him to the ship, and deliver him to the skipper, and see him put aboard of the ship; and that they give a strait command and direction to the skipper that the said Anderson be not sufferit to come ashore again till their arrival at their port in France or Flanders, where they sall put him a-land, and sall report a certificate from the magistrates of the town or port where they land, that the said Anderson was set ashore there.'[1]—*P. C. R.*

The Catholic Church was at this time anxiously set upon the recovery of Scotland; and many were they who devoted themselves to the work. We are now disposed to wonder, not merely how so many men were induced to risk their lives in this mission, but how they should have expected to produce conversions in a field so inveterately Protestant. There were, however, some encouraging precedents. It was but recently that St Francis of Sales had brought thousands of the Swiss Calvinists back to the bosom of

[1] Father Anderson was afterwards the author of a book entitled *The Ground of the Catholique and Roman Religion*, 1623, 4to.

1620. the church. He and his cousin, Lewis de Sales, entered a Protestant canton in September 1594, amidst the tears and remonstrances of their friends, who believed their task impracticable, as well as dangerous. In the course of a very few years, says Alban Butler, 'his patience, zeal, and eminent virtue wrought upon the most obdurate, and insensibly wore away their prejudices. It is incredible what fatigues and hardships he underwent in this mission; with what devotion and tears he daily recommended the work of God; with what invincible courage he braved the greatest dangers; with what meekness and patience he bore all manner of affronts and calumnies. In 1596, he celebrated mass on Christmas-day in the church of St Hippolytus at Thonon, and had then made seven or eight hundred converts. In 1598, the public exercise of the Catholic religion was restored, and Calvinism banished by the duke's orders, over all Chablais and the two bailiwicks of Terni and Guillard.' At the same time, 'his extraordinary sweetness, in conjunction with his eminent piety, reclaimed as many vicious Catholics as it converted heretics. The Calvinists ascribe principally to his meekness the wonderful conversions he made amongst them. They were certainly the most obstinate of people at that time near Geneva; yet St Francis converted no fewer than seventy-two thousand of them.'[1] Such success in the great stronghold of Calvinism might well engender hopes regarding Scotland, whose determined adherence to the reformed faith had not then been so much tried as we now know it to have been.

JUNE. The tanning of leather may be said to have been introduced into Scotland at this time. About a dozen tanners from Durham, Morpeth, and Chester-le-Street, were brought in, under royal patronage, in order 'to instruct the tanners and barkers of the kingdom in the true and perfect form of tanning.' They were invested with certain privileges, and distributed to various parts of the kingdom. It was hoped through this means that much money, which was usually spent on foreign leather, would now be kept within the kingdom.

Unfortunately for the success of this reformation, a tax was put upon the leather—four shillings Scots per hide for the first twenty-one years, and thereafter one penny. The consequence was a grievous discontent among the cordwainers, who everywhere did what in them lay to thwart his majesty's design. 'To steir the

[1] *Lives of the Saints*, i. 358.

people up to exclaim against it, they have very extraordinarily raised the prices of boots and shoon, to twenty shillings or thereby the pair of boots, and six shillings or thereby the pair of shoon, more nor was paid before;' thus oppressing the whole country, and particularly the poorer sort of people, besides slandering the king and his Council. In January 1622, the Privy Council dealt with a complaint that many of the tanners throughout the country, disregarding the obvious benefit to themselves and the commonwealth from the new modes, continued the old practice of letting their leather remain but a short time in the pots, and then bringing it to market in a raw state. By way of a stimulus to these persons, a certain number of them were proclaimed rebels. 1620.

At this time, the Earl of Sutherland being a minor, and the family resources much reduced, the inhabitants of the district 'did shew themselves exceeding loving and thankful to their Master and superior; for not only did they give a general contribution —every one according to his estate and ability—for defraying of his sister's portion, who was now to be married to the Laird of Pitfoddels, but also they yielded a voluntary yearly support to the earl and his two brothers' fitter maintenance at the university for the space of five years. . . . . So much did they value and regard the education and good-breeding of him who was to govern and command them, knowing how much it doth concern every state and country to have weel-bred and wise superiors; which good-will and course of theirs was exceedingly weel thought of by the Earl of Sutherland and his greatest friends.'—*G. H. S.* Oct.

We find it noted that in this year a pearl was found in the burn of Kellie, a tributary of the Ythan, Aberdeenshire, so large and beautiful that it was esteemed the best that had at any time been found in Scotland. Sir Thomas Menzies, provost of Aberdeen, obtaining this precious jewel, went to London to present it to the king, who, in requital, 'gave him twelve or fourteen chalder of victual about Dunfermline, and the custom of merchant goods in Aberdeen during his life.'[1] It has been reported that this pearl was inserted in the apex of the crown of Scotland.

Apparently this circumstance called the king's attention to the old repute of certain Scottish rivers for the production of pearls. In January 1621, we find the Privy Council adverting to the fact,

[1] *Succinct Survey of Aberdeen*, 1685.

1620. that the seeking for pearls had for many years been left to interlopers, who pursued their vocation at unseasonable times, and thus damaged the fishery, to the hurt of his majesty's interest, he having an undoubted right to all pearls, as he had to all precious metals found in his dominions. Being now inclined to take up pearl-seeking on his own account, he issued a proclamation for the preservation of 'the waters wherein the pearls do breed;' and, took measures to have the fishery conducted on a regular plan 'no pearls to be socht or taken but at such times and seasons of the year when they are at their chief perfection both of colour and quality, whilk will be in the months of July and August yearly.' The Privy Council commissioned three gentlemen to protect the rivers, and 'nominat expert and skilful men to fish for pearls at convenient seasons;' one gentleman for the rivers of Sutherland, another for those of Ross, and another (Mr Patrick Maitland of Auchincroch) for the waters Ythan and Don. The gentleman just named was further made commissioner 'for receiving to his majesty's use, of the haill pearls that sall be gotten in the waters within the bounds above written, and who will give reasonable prices for the same; the best of the whilk pearls for bigness and colour he sall reserve to his majesty's awn use.'

Patrick Maitland gave up his commission in July 1622, and it was then conferred on Robert Buchan, merchant in Aberdeen, who was reputed to be skilful in fishing for pearls, and 'hath not only taken divers of good value, but hath found some to be in divers waters where none were expected.'—*P. C. R.*

Among the acts of the first parliament of Charles I. was one for the 'discharge of Robert Buchan's patent of the pearl and other monopolies.' Since then, there has occasionally been successful fishing for pearls in this river; it is said that 'about the middle of the last century, a gentleman in Aberdeen got £100 for a lot of pearls found in the Ythan.' The mouth of the river has a great muscle and cockle fishery, and is accordingly the haunt of an extraordinary variety and quantity of sea-fowl. In summer, when the water is low, school-boys often amuse themselves by going in search of pearls, feeling with their toes for the shell, which is distinguished by its curved shape, and griping it when found with a kind of forceps at the end of a long stick.[1]

1621. Feb. 6. The church historian Calderwood notes the occurrence of three

[1] *New Stat. Acc. of Scotland*—Aberdeenshire, *passim*. *Beauties of Scotland*, iv. 190.

fires in Edinburgh in one day as being regarded by the people as 'foretokenings of some mischief.' 'About the same time,' he adds, 'there came in a great whale at Montrose; which was also apprehendit to be a forerunner of some trouble.' 1621.

On a complaint that coal had risen to eight shillings the load, the Privy Council had interfered in the usual rash manner, and dictated a certain maximum price to be exacted for the article; namely, seven shillings the load—that is, horse-load; for coal was borne at this time, and for a long time after, on horseback. Certain coal-proprietors—Alexander, Master of Elphinstone; Samuel Johnston of Elphinstone; Sir James Richardson of Smeaton; Robert Richardson of Pencaitland; Jonet Lawson, Lady Fawside; and David Preston of Whitehill—now petitioned, setting forth that the cost of mining coal had greatly risen of late years, and that the dearth of the article to the public was much owing to the base fellows who act as carriers of coals. It was represented that some of the proprietors of 'coal-heughs' were £10,000, and some even £20,000 out of pocket. The Master of Elphinstone's coal of Little Fawside had been on fire for several years; another mine of the same owner had caused an outlay of £8000. The Smeaton pits had been so unproductive for some years as scarcely to supply the laird's house. The coal of Elphinstone had proved for nine years barren, and 20,000 merks had been sunk upon it, being more than it promised ever to repay. The coal of Mickle Fawside had undone the late laird's estate, and 'made him to sell ane part of his auld heritage:' what with fire on the one hand and water on the other, it was a hopeless case. As for the coal of Pencaitland, it was wasted and decayed, past hope of recovery, but at such extraordinary charges as it was not worth having bestowed upon it. The basis of the evils complained of lay with the coal-carriers, who dealt fraudulently with the public. Had the particulars been rightly known, the lords, it was assumed, would never have given a decreet against the complainers, 'who are gentlemen of grit charge and burden,' overlooking the faults of those base fellows who carry coals. MAR. 1.

The lords appointed a commission to inquire into the matter, and report what prices they thought ought to be fixed for this necessary article. In consequence of a report soon after given in by this commission, it was ordained that the price of coal at 'the hill' should be 7s. 8d. (7⅔d. sterling) per load; and it was at the same time agreed that a measure for the load and a charge for carriage should afterwards be appointed.—*P. C. R.*

1621. On the 23d April 1623, an act of Privy Council was passed in favour of Samuel Johnston, laird of Elphinstone, in consideration of his having super-expended 20,000 merks on his coal-heughs, 'to his great hurt and apparent wrack.' It was stated that he had entertained forty families of men, wives, and children at the work, whose weekly charges exceeded two hundred merks. His coal would be lost, and these work-people thrown on the world, if some remedy were not provided, as he could no longer strive with the adverse circumstances in which he was placed. On the other hand, if the work could be held forward, and got into proper order, it might be 'a gangand coal' for a hundred years to come.

The Council, in consideration of the losses sustained by the laird, and to save so many poor people from being thrown out of employment, granted him what he asked as a remedy—namely, a licence to export coal for seven years.

It follows from the laird's statement that the average weekly gains of a collier's family reached five merks, or about 5s. 6d. sterling.

MAY 12. A small private war between the Lairds of Drumlanrig and Cashogle came to a bearing this day at the Moss of Knockonie. This moss belonged to David Douglas, brother to Drumlanrig; but Cashogle had always been allowed to raise peats from it for his winter fuel. The two lairds having fallen into a coldness, Cashogle would not ask this any longer as a favour, but determined to take it as a right. Twice his servants were interrupted in their operations; so he himself came one day to the moss, with his son Robert and thirty-six men or thereby, armed with swords, hagbuts, lances, corn-forks, and staves. Hereupon, the Laird of Mousewald, a brother of the proprietor of the moss (who was absent), sent a friend to remonstrate, and to urge upon Cashogle the propriety of his asking the peats 'out of love,' instead of taking them in contempt. The Cashogle party returned only contemptuous answers, 'declaring they sould cast their peats there, wha wald, wha wald not.' Some further remonstrances being ineffectual, Drumlanrig himself, accompanied with friends and servants, came upon the scene, shewing that he had the royal authority to command Cashogle to desist. But even this reference failed to induce submission. At length, the Laird of Mousewald, losing temper, exclaimed: 'Ye are ower pert to disobey the king's majesty's charge—quickly pack you and begone.'

'Immediately, ane of Cashogle's servants, with ane great kent

[staff], strak Captain Johnston behind his back, twa great straiks 1621.
upon the head, whilk made him fall dead to the grund with great loss of blood. Then Robert Douglas [son of Cashogle] presentit ane bended hagbut within three ells to the Laird of Drumlanrig's breast, whilk at the pleasure of God misgave. Immediately thereafter, Robert of new morsit the hagbut, and presented her again to him, whilk shot and missed him at the pleasure of God. Robert Dalyell, natural son to the Laird of Dalyell, was struck through the body with ane lance, who cried that he was slain; and some twa or three men was strucken through their clothes with lances, sae that the haill company thought that they had been killed, and then thought it was time for them to begin to defend themselves; whereupon Robert Douglas and three or four of his folk being hurt, was put to flight, and in flying, the said Robert fell, where the Laird of Drumlanrig chancit to be nearest him; wha, notwithstanding the former offer Robert made to him with the hagbut, not only spared to strike him with his awn hands, but likewise discouraged all the rest under pain of their lives to steir him.' One of the Cashogle party was slain.

Such an occurrence as this in the south of Scotland, and amongst men of rank and property, shews strikingly that the wild blood of the country was yet by no means quieted. There was a mutual prosecution between the parties; but they contrived to make up the quarrel between themselves out of court, and, private satisfaction being, as usual, deemed enough, the law interfered no further.[1]

Amongst other symptoms of advancing civilisation proper to this period, was an effort towards the correction of unauthorised medical practice. 'Persons without knowledge of the science of medicine' were everywhere practising, 'to the great and evident hazard of the lives and healths of many of our subjects;' so declared the king. Drugs were also sold by ignorant persons. Another document refers to the judicatories of the kingdom for an account of 'the frequent murders committed by quacks, women, gardeners, and others.' The king, desiring to put a check on these evils, ordered the parliament to frame an act for the erection of a College of Aug. 2.
Physicians in Edinburgh, to be composed of seven doctors and professors of medicine, who should be incorporated, and without

[1] *Letters of Reign of James VI.* Pitcairn.

1621. whose warrant no one should practise medicine in or near the city; three of their number to have the duty of superintending the sale of drugs. From various causes, this good design did not take practical effect till a later age.—*An. Scot.*

MAY. 'About this time there was a great earthquake in the town of Montrose and thereabouts, to the great terror of the inhabitants, so that many fled out of the town. Some was slain with the thunder there.'—*Cal.*

Some foreign vessels trading for coal and salt having been shipwrecked, during the severe storms of the past winter, on the 'blind craigs' (that is, concealed rocks) in the Firth of Forth, it was proposed, by the enterprising coal and salt proprietor, Sir George Bruce, that he should be allowed to erect beacons at those dangerous spots, and reimburse himself by a small tax on the foreign vessels frequenting the Firth during the ensuing year. Hearing of this proposal, the other coal-proprietors in Fife and the Lothians felt that they were much concerned, seeing that 'no stranger-ships come that way but either for coal or salt,' and they considered that 'the payment of this duty wald carry with it a very great reproach and scandal to the country, as if such a small piece of work in the most eminent river in the kingdom could not be gotten done without the contribution and help of strangers.'
JUNE. For these reasons, they themselves undertook to set up the required beacons.—*M. S. P.*

This movement may be regarded as another mark of the enlightened attention now beginning to be paid to things in which the material interests of the people were concerned. How far the proposal of Sir George Bruce was carried out we do not learn; but the probability is that he did not allow his plan to fall asleep. It bears out our view of the spirit beginning to manifest itself in Scotland, that the royal burghs, a few years later (September 1631), contemplated having lights erected on the Isle of May in the mouth of the Firth of Forth, and on 'the Skairheids' (*P. C. R.*), and soon after one was actually put upon the May, being the first known to have been formed in connection with the Scottish coasts, and for generations a solitary example on those of the island generally. A Fife laird, Alexander Cunningham of Barns—a relative, it would appear, of the wife of the poet Drummond—had the merit of establishing this useful protection for shipping. Obtaining the proper authority from

Charles I., he, in 1635, erected on the isle 'a tower forty feet high, vaulted to the top, and covered with flag-stones, whereon all the year over,' says Sir Robert Sibbald, writing in the reign of Charles II., 'there burns in the night-time a fire of coals for a light; for which the masters of ships are obliged to pay for each ton two shillings [twopence sterling]. This sheweth light,' he adds, 'to all the ships coming out of the Firths of Forth and Tay, and to all places between St Abb's Head and Redcastle near Montrose.' 1621.

Through a natural antagonism, we may suppose, between the powers of darkness and the interest here concerned, the architect of the May light-tower was drowned on his return from the isle in a storm believed to have been raised by witches, who were in consequence burnt.[1] The fire was duly kept burning by the successors of Cunningham till the erection of a regular light-house on modern principles by the Commissioners of Northern Lights. It required three hundred and eighty tons of *Wemyss coal* annually, that kind being selected on account of the clearness of its flame. In 1790, the tack or lease of this privileged light, with its tax of three-halfpence a ton on Scottish, and threepence on foreign shipping, rose from £280 to £960, and in 1800 it was let at £1500, 'a striking proof,' as Mr Adamson justly remarks, 'of the increase of the trade of this country' during the period.

This was a day of great concern and sorrow to the earnest Aug 4. Presbyterians of Scotland, as on it the parliament sitting at Edinburgh ratified the Five Articles introducing Episcopalian fashions into the church. At the moment when the commissioner, the Marquis of Hamilton, rose to apply the sceptre to the bills, thus giving them symbolically the royal assent, a flash of lightning burst into the house, followed by a second and a third, and these by loud thunder. A heavy darkness ensued. The discharge of rain was so great, that the ceremonial return to Holyroodhouse could not be effected, and all rushed home in confusion. The people, affected by these signs and wonders, called the day *Black Saturday*.

The weather had been bad during the whole summer, and the harvest was likely to be late and meagre. A Presbyterian historian, after relating what happened at the ratification of the Five Articles, adds: 'That very day made the greatest alteration of prices of victual within eight days, that ever was heard of in so short a space

[1] Adamson's Notes to Sibbald's *Hist. Fife*.

1621. in Scotland, except the *ill-windy Bartle-day* in anno 159-.'—*Row.* It appears that wheat rose to £12 per boll, and the price might have been higher but for the coming in of foreign grain. The autumn was distinguished by heavy rains, carrying away the crops of extensive haughs or meadows. And of such as were preserved, scarcely any was 'won'—that is, secured—before Hallowmass. The wetness of the season was also unfavourable to the winning of peat-fuel. 'Never was greater fear of famine, nor scarcity of seed to sow the ground. Every person was careful to ease himself of such persons as he might spare, and to live as retiredly as possibly he might. Pitiful was the lamentation not only of vaiging beggars, but also of honest persons.'—*Cal.*

AUG. 28. 'Because there was a new brood and generation of the Clan Gregor risen up, who are begun to go in troops and companies about the country, armed with offensive weapons, there was a proclamation published that none who carry the name of Macgregor shall wear any armour, but ane pointless knife to eat their meat with, under the pain of death.'—*Bal.*

The *Chronicle of Perth* notes the holding of a justice court there, May 10, 1624, by the chancellor Sir George Hay, 'where many compeirit and were clengit by assize; only three hangit—*Macgregors!*' A few months later, the same authority tells us of 'Robert Abroch, ane Macgregor, ane great limmer,[1] wha had been ance or twice forgiven and remitted by his majesty, for his oppression, upon hope of amendment, yet continued still in his knaveries; after there was mickle searching made for him in the Highlands, and all his friends chargit to apprehend [him], [he] came to Perth this day, being Tuesday, ane preaching-day, after sermon, and fell down on his knees, and ane tow about his neck, and offerit his sword by the point to the Chancellor of Scotland, wha refusit to accept of it, and commanded the bailies to ward him; like as they instantly warded him, and put baith his feet on the gaud,[2] where he remainit.'—*Chron. Perth.*

'This year, Sir William Alexander of Menstrie undertook a plantation in a part of America, which was then called New Scotland [Nova Scotia], where he intended to send a colony. Sir Robert Gordon, Tutor of Sutherland, joined himself in this

[1] See under July 28, 1612.

[2] A fixed bar of iron, with fetters attached by movable rings.

enterprise, and did indent and contract with Sir William to send thither some men out of Sutherland, weel provided with corns, cattle, weapons, and other provision fit and sufficient for that journey, who should have a good portion of that country allotted them to inhabit. The Earl Marischal of Scotland, the Earl of Melrose, the Earl of Nithsdale, the Viscount of Dupplin, Sir Robert Gordon of Lochinvar, Sir Alexander Gordon of Cluny, James Gordon of Lesmoir, with divers other nobles and gentlemen, were likewise partners in this plantation. And for further advancement of this plantation, his majesty concluded to make heritable knights-baronets in Old Scotland; which honour should be bestowed upon the choicest undertakers of that enterprise, and upon such as were of best quality for vertue, birth, and means among the gentry.'—*G. H. S.* 1621.

This day, Friday, commenced a remarkable flood in the Tay, which lasted for three or four days, and caused extensive destruction. The beautiful bridge, newly completed across the river at Perth, was swept away, excepting one arch only. In the middle of the second night, the water had risen so high, that the people living in low houses near the Castle Gavel Port in Perth, were obliged to remove to higher houses. The town was so environed with water, that no one could enter or leave it for several days. Children were let down from upper windows into boats, in order to be carried to places presumably safer. Household stuff and provisions were destroyed. The rain was accompanied by a violent wind from the east, which would somewhat help to maintain the waters of the river at a high elevation. The water flowed in the High Street and the Speygate 'like mill-sluices;' and one Charles Rollock became a distinguished public benefactor by going about in a boat through those streets, and rescuing people who were in danger of drowning—a service for which he afterwards received a double angel in recompense. Oct. 12.

The people were thrown into a state of extreme consternation, looking for nothing but the entire destruction of their fair city. 'Whereupon Mr John Malcolm, minister, powerfully endued with God's spirit, caused ring the preaching-bell on Sunday at seven hours in the morning, and the haill inhabitants came to the kirk. And there he exhorted them to repent of their sins, which had provoked the said judgment of God to come upon the city; assuring them that if they were truly penitent therefor, and would avow to God to amend their lives in time coming, God would avert

1621. his judgment, and give them deliverance. Whose powerful exhortations moved the people to cry to God with tears, clamours, and cries, and to hold up their hands to God, [promising that they would] amend their lives, and every one of them to abstain from their domestic sins. The like humiliation of men and women has not been seen within Perth before. Fasting, preaching, and praying continued all that week. . . . . The waters began somewhat to decrease after noon on Sunday; but after daylight passed, there arose a greater tempest of wind and rain than at any time before, which so affrighted the people that night, that they looked for nothing but [that] the waters should have arisen to greater height [than] they were before. Notwithstanding thereof, miraculously, through the mercy of God, by [past] all men's expectation, the waters greatly in the meantime decreased, which in the morning moved the people in the kirk and all other places to give hearty thanks to God for his mercy toward them.'[1]

One of the remarks current among the more serious class of people on this occasion, was that the inundation was sent as a judgment on Perth, on account of the five Episcopalian articles passed there by the General Assembly three years before, though how this vengeance should have fallen on the innocent people living in the place of that assembly, and not upon the churchmen who passed the articles, or rather the majority of them as apart from the minority, it is not easy to reconcile to a sense of either Divine wisdom or Divine justice. It chances that Perth is built on the meadow or *haugh* close to a river—namely, what is properly its flood-course; a kind of situation where no human habitations should ever be built. It is of course more or less inundated at every considerable flood, and thus exposed to no small inconvenience, as well as damage. These evils may be considered as the natural punishment inflicted on the people for the solecism against nature which they have committed. It may be safely presumed that, while their town stands there, it will be liable to such disasters as that here described, whether general assemblies reform upwards or downwards within its walls, and in whatever spirit the inhabitants may regard their consequent sufferings. They are, however, not alone in this respect, as, unfortunately, the low banks of rivers are the seats of many towns and parts of towns in all parts of the world.

It is remarkable that, though there had been a bridge across the

[1] Session Register of Perth.

Tay at Perth so early as the beginning of the thirteenth century, the structure now destroyed was not replaced till the erection of the present beautiful fabric in 1771, the intercourse during the intermediate hundred and fifty years being maintained by ferry-boats. 1621.

The Record of Privy Council at this time gives an example of the conduct of a north-country gentleman under ban of the law. George Meldrum of Haltoun had been put to the horn and denounced rebel for some failure of duty towards James Crichton of Frendraught and other persons; and it became necessary for the Marquis of Huntly, as sheriff of Aberdeen, to send a force for the capture of his person. James Gordon of Knockespock and George Gordon of Gowie went with a band for this purpose. Nov. 1

At their approach, Meldrum was out in the fields; but he no sooner saw them, than, surmising their design, he fled to his house, closed the gates, and prepared to stand a siege. They, anxious to vindicate the royal authority, beleaguered the house, resolved not to leave it till they should have reduced the occupant to his majesty's obedience. They had lain about the place forty-eight hours, when John Innes of Crombie, hearing of what was going on, came to them in the utmost possible haste, mounted on his best horse, declaring to them his desire to deal with George for the purpose of inducing him to submit. 'He entreated the deputies that, with their allowance, he might go and confer with the said George thereanent; whereunto they very gladly yielded, seeing they sought nought but obedience. . . . . The Laird of Crombie in the meantime seemed very busy in going and coming to and frae the said George, feeding the deputies with false conceits and hopes, and sometimes with vain promises that he himself wald be cautioner for the said George, for the satisfaction of all his creditors . . . . and so, under this false pretext, having abused the . . . . deputies their sincere and upright meaning making them to believe all that he spak, and sae to be so much the more careless of looking to the house, he then brought the said George out of the house, set him upon his best horse, and put him away, to the great contempt and mocking of justice.' For this conduct, the Laird of Crombie was denounced as a rebel.

Margaret Wallace, the wife of John Dinning, a clothier in Glasgow, was tried before the Court of Justiciary in Edinburgh, for sundry acts of witchcraft, and as a common practiser of that nefarious art. She was reported to have been a friend and 1622. Mar. 20.

1622. confederate of one Christian Graham, a notorious witch of the same city, who was tried, condemned, and burnt in the preceding year. There is something singular in Mrs Dinning's case, for some of the acts of criminality urged against her were cures for which no other than a humane motive was or could be imputed. The case is also curious on account of the remarkable resemblance of some of the means or modes of cure to the proceedings of the modern mesmeric hospital.

It was alleged of Margaret, that she had been a witch for eight or nine years. It was evident that she looked up to Christian Graham as her preceptress and superior. About four years before the time of her trial, being in the house of one Vallance, in Glasgow, she had taken a sudden fit of sickness, and sent for Graham, who came immediately to her relief. Taking Margaret tenderly in her arms, and kissing her, Graham said: 'Nothing shall ail my dear bird;' then led her down stairs, and conducted her to her own house, where she completely recovered. The two women coming back to Vallance's house, found a little child of his, named Margaret, at the bottom of the stair, and it was alleged that they threw the sickness upon her. The child was found by her mother crying dismally; and all that night she lay in horrible pain, with pitiful screeches, shouts, and cries, apparently deprived of the power of her body. Margaret Wallace, coming next day to see the child, 'declarit it was the sudden trance or disease that she had ta'en the day before, and willed the bairn's mother to send for Christian Graham to cure her and relieve her thereof.' The mother 'having absolutely refused sae to do, saying she wald commit her bairn to God, and not mell with the devil or ony of his instruments, Margaret Wallace maist blasphemously answered again, that "Christian Graham could do as mickle in curing of that disease, as gif God himself wald come out of heaven and cure her—and, albeit the deid-strake were laid on, she could tak it aff again—and without her help there could be nae remeed to the bairn!" Thereafter, without the mother's knowledge, Christian Graham was brought in by Margaret Wallace to the bairn; at whase coming, Margaret lifted up the bairn's head, and Christian took her by the shackle-bane [wrist], and brought the bairn forth of her bed where she was lying in great pain before; and thereafter, setting her down upon ane stool, with some crosses and signs made upon her, and by uttering of divers words, restored her to her health.'

It is quite evident here that Margaret was honourably candid, as against herself, in the view she took of the cause of the child's ailment, and her subsequent conduct in trying to restore the child's health, was creditable to her feelings. In another point of her dittay, however, feelings of a different kind came out. 1622.

It was alleged that Margaret had conceived a deadly hatred against Cuthbert Greig, a cooper, because of certain opprobrious speeches he had uttered against Christian Graham. 'She avowed that she should make Cuthbert, within few days thereafter, not of ability to work or win himself ane cake of bread.' According to this devilish threat, Cuthbert was soon after 'visit and troublit with ane strange, unnatural, and unknawn disease,' attended by continual sweating for fifteen days together, till in the end he was reduced to the utmost degree of weakness. It appeared that the man's friends endeavoured to induce Margaret to interfere for his recovery; but she long persisted in refusing. At length, coming to his house, 'she, to manifest her skill for his help, took him by the shackle-bane with the ane hand, and laid her other hand upon his breast, and, without ony word-speaking, save only by moving of her lips, passed frae him at that instant.' Returning next morning, 'she took him by the arm and bade him rise, wha at that time and fifteen days before, was not able to lift his legs without help.' 'She, having urged him to rise, and taking him by the hand, brought him out of his bed, and led him butt the house' [into the outer apartment], where he 'walkit up and down the floor, without help or support of ony.' From that time, it is stated, he quickly recovered from his illness. Here, too, it must be owned, Margaret came ultimately to act a humane part.

Another child having an uncouth sickness, Wallace associated with Graham in a practice for her cure. They went under cloud of night 'to the yard of James Finlay, burgess of Glasgow, where they remained the space of ane hour together practising sorcery and witchcraft, for curing of the bairn by unlawful means,' and 'that same night the sickness was ta'en aff the bairn and she convalesced thereof.' For this, the two practitioners got a goose and a pint of wine. On another occasion, Wallace was alleged to have inflicted deadly sickness on a child, and allowed her to die.

Margaret had good counsel at her trial, and a stout defence was made; but all in vain. She was sentenced to be *worried at a stake and burnt* on the Castle Hill.—*Pit.*

A Dunkirk ship, belonging to the king of Spain, came up to Leith pursued by two Dutch waughters, but both were quickly driven out of the Firth of Forth by a west wind. A few days MAY 22.

1622. thereafter, the same vessels came back to Leith, 'where they had ane great fecht, frae twelve at night till four in the morning, and many men slain.'[1] The magistrates of Edinburgh interfered to prevent further hostilities, and the three vessels lay there inactive for half a year, the Dunkirker not being able to get away for fear of the superior metal of her enemies. At length, the king ordered that the Dunkirker should be allowed to go out, without being followed by the waughters for a couple of tides. On the 4th of May 1623, this vessel left the harbour accordingly, but it ran upon the Mussel-scap, 'within two pair of butt-lengths to the Bulwark,' and thus in due time became liable to the attack of the waughters. While these were playing their guns upon her, the authorities in the city, knowing well the king's favour for Spain, whose Infanta his son was at this time courting, mustered forces and cannon, and came hastily to the rescue. Finding that the Dutch had boarded her, and put up the Prince of Orange's colours, they sent men on board to put up the flag of the king of Great Britain. The people shewed themselves ill affected to the object. 'Some few went down, with their swords, and their cloaks about them. The president, chiding the provost and bailies, said: "I always said to his majesty that Edinburgh was but a nest of traitors. I shall write to his majesty of this your rebellion." It was answered: . . . . "Edinburgh is not bound to serve in such a service without their burgh roods."' An effort was made to secure the vessel within the harbour—'it was sport to see the lords and their gentlemen hailing St Ambrose with a rope into the harbourie. But they laboured in vain, for the water began to fall.' The end of the business was, that, one night, the Dutch, after respectfully removing the guard and flag, set the vessel on fire, and having destroyed it, set sail for their own seas.[2]

MAY 29. 'The Landgrave of Hesse's eldest son, of the second marriage, came to Edinburgh. His lodging and entertainment was not looked to with that respect that became.'[3]—*Cal.*

JUNE 3. '. . . . there was a fiery dragon, both great and long, appeared to come from the south to the north, spouting fire from her, half an hour after the going to of the sun.'—*Cal.*

This was a wretched summer. A fast was ordered at Aberdeen,

[1] *Chronicle of Perth*, 23.

[2] Calderwood.

[3] Philip, second son of the Landgrave of Hesse, came to the English court April 6, 1622, on a negotiation from his father.—*Nichols's Progresses of King James I.*, iii. 759, 763.

July 21st, on account of 'the felt wrath of God by this present plague of dearth and famine, and the continuance thereof threatened by thir tempestuous storms and inundations of weets likely to rot the fruits on the ground.'—*A. K. S. R.* 1622.

The usual consequence is recorded: 'About the harvest, and after, there was such ane universal sickness in all the country as the like has not been heard of—but specially in this burgh, that no family in all the city was free of this visitation. There was also great mortality among the poor.'—*Chron. Perth.*

An act of Privy Council of this date aims at a restriction of the importation of wine into the Western Islands—'with the insatiable desire whereof the said islanders are so far possest, that when there arrives ony ship or other vessel there with wines, they spend both days and nights in their excess of drinking, sae lang as there is any of the wine left; sae that, being overcome with drink, there falls out mony inconvenients amangs them, to the break of his majesty's peace.'[1] JULY.

The Privy Council had the subject of that 'infective weed callit tobacco' under their attention. The king had formerly, upon good reasons of policy, forbidden its importation into the country; but this decree had been sadly evaded, insomuch that 'the country was ever universally filled with tobacco, and public and common merchandise made of the same.' Then his majesty had tried the restraining effect of a duty (20s. Scots, or 1s. 8d. English per pound); but the tobacco-merchants had learned the trick of smuggling, and it was not likely they would let it lie unfruitful when they could thereby save the payment of a tax. It had now, accordingly, become necessary to impose a new restraint; and the importation was again prohibited, under pain of the goods being confiscated to his majesty's use.—*P. C. R.* JULY 30.

An act of the Privy Council in the subsequent November explained that the king did not mean by this restraint 'to deprive his loving subjects of the orderly sale and moderate use of tobacco,' but only to prevent the abuse or excessive use of the herb. It was no part of his design to interfere with the patent which had been granted [November 7, 1616] to the late Captain William Murray, giving him the sole privilege of importing tobacco for the space of twenty-one years. He therefore now ordered proclamations to be

[1] Gregory's *History of the Western Highlands and Isles of Scotland*, 1836, p. 405.

1622. issued, to the effect that the prohibition only held good against such as did not possess a licence under favour of Murray's patent. —*P. C. R.* In the ensuing March, it was arranged that importers of tobacco should pay Murray's representatives a duty of twenty shillings Scots per pound.

In 1624, the widow and daughter of Captain Murray resigned their relative's patent into the hands of commissioners, for his majesty's use, on their becoming bound to pay twenty thousand pounds Scots (£1666, 13s. 4d.) at three half-years terms.[1]

The prejudice of King James against tobacco was a strong feeling, partaking much of the character of antipathy. He published anonymously, and afterwards acknowledged the quaint pamphlet, *A Counterblast to Tobacco*, in which he argues against the use of the herb as a physical as well as moral corruption. Baker's *Chronicle* states that the expedition of Sir Francis Drake, on its return in 1585[6], passed by Virginia, 'a colony which Sir Walter Raleigh had there planted;' 'from whence Drake brings home with him Ralph Lane, who was the first that brought tobacco into England, which the Indians take against crudities of the stomach.' This does not comport with the ordinary notion entertained in England, which uniformly represents Raleigh as the first introducer of the Nicotian herb. Lane became a despised man on account of his pusillanimity in giving up the colony; and there seems all reason to believe that to him King James alludes in the following passage from the *Counterblast*: 'It is not so long,' says he, 'since the first entry of this abuse amongst us here, as this present age cannot well remember both the first author and the form of the first introduction of it amongst us. It was neither brought in by king, great conqueror, nor learned doctor of physic. With the report of a great discovery for a conquest, some two or three savage men were brought in, together with a savage custom. But the pity is, the poor barbarous men died, but that vile barbarous custom is yet alive, yea, in fresh vigour; so as it seems a miracle to me how a custom, springing from so vile a ground, and *brought in by a father so generally hated*, should be welcomed upon so slender a warrant.'

If a tradition existing in 1667 is to be believed, King James was fain on one occasion to get over his antipathy to tobacco; but, to be sure, the compelling cause was a powerful one. 'The smoke of it' [tobacco], says a writer of that date, 'is one of the wholesomest

[1] *Archæologia Scotica*, i. 43.

scents that is, against all contagious airs, for it o'ermasters all 1622.
other smells, as King James, they say, found true, when being once hunting, *a shower of rain drove him into a pigsty for shelter*, where he caused a pipefull to be taken on purpose.'[1]

A trafficking Jesuit, named George Mortimer, had lately been detected in the house of one Haddow, in Glasgow, and he and Haddow were both taken into custody. The king lost no time in
ordering a court of justice to be held in Glasgow for the trying of MAY 18.
Haddow and his wife for the crime of resetting Jesuits, certifying that, if found guilty, they should be banished the kingdom—as the impunity of the offence 'might hearten that wicked and pernicious sort of people more bauldly to go on in perverting good subjects in religion, and withdrawing them from their dutiful obedience to us.' He at the same time wrote to the principal ecclesiastical authorities, desiring them to consult about the best means of checking the present 'new growth of popery,' that 'thereby the world may see that we strike with the sword of justice equally against the papist and puritan, that thereby no just imputation may be laid upon our proceedings as a cause of the increase of popery.'

In September, we learn that Mortimer lay a prisoner at Glasgow, 'so heavily diseased, as it is feared he shall hardly if ever escape.' The king—'because we do not desire the lives of ony of that sort of people, if we may be secured from ony harm which they micht do by the perversion of ony of our guid subjects in their duty to God and us'—was now pleased to order that he should be committed to some ship sailing to a foreign port, 'with certification to him, that gif at ony time hereafter he shall return, it will be capital unto him.'—*P. C. R.*

This and some other instances of lenity towards Romish clergymen were ill looked on by the zealous Presbyterians, and there arose a *fama* to the king's prejudice. On the 30th of October, he wrote from Hitchinbrooke to his Scottish councillors, in great indignation at a report which had gone abroad, in consequence of some late circumstances, to the effect that he intended to '*tolerate or grant liberty of conscience!*' 'The foolish apprehension thereof' had 'given occasion both to papist and puritan to tak heart and grow insolent, the one vainly boasting of the said pretendit liberty, and the other with a seeming fear thereof.' 'God knows,' says the king solemnly, 'that what proceedit in that course concerning

[1] *Virtues of the Indian Perfume Tobacco*, 1667. *An. Scot.*, i. 82.

1622. the papists here was without ony such intention.' It was 'groundit upon good reasons of state, in the deep and mystery whereof every man is not to dive nor wyde.' His conscience and his works alike bore witness of his constancy in the right course. So he 'could not but marvel how ony of our subjects can be possest with *so unjust ane opinion of us.*' The Council was enjoined immediately to consult with the Archbishop of St Andrews as to the best measures for the 'curbing of insolent papists and disconform preachers.' In case any of the former had shewn themselves in consequence of the pretended liberty, they were to be severely punished, as an example and terror to others. The Council, acknowledging his majesty's 'most religious and upright disposition towards the suppression of popery,' communicated accordingly with the archbishop, requesting him to have a care to give his majesty satisfaction.—*P. C. R.*

George Earl Marischal, a noble of great wealth and influence, who has already been under our notice,[1] was now approaching the end of his earthly pilgrimage. After his death, his countess, who had hastily re-married, was accused of having been concerned, along with the gentleman whom she took for her second husband —Sir Alexander Strachan of Thornton, knight—in stealing
Oct. forth of his lordship's house of Benholm a green coffer belonging to him, containing money and other valuables, besides the furniture of the house, and a bag containing evidents of property. James Keith of Benholm was accused of having a share in the same crime.

The case is worthy of notice, chiefly on account of the list of articles contained in the coffer—evidencing as they do a degree of wealth which few will be prepared to find belonging to a Scottish nobleman of that age. There were—'of Portugal ducats and other species of foreign gold to the avail of twenty thousand pounds or thereby; thretty-sax dozen of gold buttons; ane rich jewel all set with diamonts, whilk the earl resavit as ane gift given to him the time he was ambassador in Denmark, worth sax thousand merks; the Queen of Denmark's picture in gold, set about with rich diamonts, estimat to five thousand merks; ane jasp stane for steming of bluid,[2] estimat to five hundred French crowns; ane chenyie of equal pearl, wherein was four hundred

[1] See under October 1590.

[2] Stones supposed to possess medicinal virtues were then not uncommon.

pearls great and small; twa chenyies of gold, of twenty-four unce 1622.
wecht; ane other jewel of diamonts set in gold worth three thousand merks; ane great pair of bracelets, all set with diamonts, price thereof five hundred crowns; the other pair of gold bracelets, at sax hundred pounds the pair; ane turcas ring worth ten French crowns; ane diamont set in ane ring, price twenty-eight French crowns; with ane number of other small rings set with diamonts and other rich stanes in gold, worth three hundred French crowns; mair sixteen thousand merks of silver and gold ready-cunyit, whilk was within the said green coffer; together with the haill tapestry, silver-work, bedding, and other guids, geir, and plenishing, being within the said place.'—*Pit.*

The king, in a letter to the Chancellor Hay, dated 22d August 1624, alludes to a recommendation he had formerly sent, that this injury to his esteemed councillor the Earl Marischal should be inquired into, and adds: 'Whereas we are informed that, in a later letter under our hand, we have shewn to you that it was not our pleasure nor meaning in ony former letters to hurt the said Lady Marischal or ony other person, these are now expressly to mak it known to you, that we nather gave direction to insert any sic clause in our letters, nather, at the putting of our hand to the samen, did tak heed thereto, nor never meant ony sic favour to her who hath so ill deserved of one for whose sake we were only to respect her.' And then he added a command to proceed with the case against the peccant lady.—*An. Scot.*

1623. JAN.
'Lord Colville took journey to France, to crave the re-establishment of the Scots Guard and Company of Scottish Men at Arms, according to their first institution and the French king's promise often made to that effect.'—*Bal.*

The Scots Guard of the French king was an old institution, and for a long time past the command had passed from generation to generation of the Sieurs D'Aubigné (Earls and Dukes of Lennox). Louis XIII. readily agreed to the proposed revival of the corps, and designed to confer the command on Ludovick, Duke of Richmond and Lennox, the favourite councillor of King James. It chanced, however, that the duke was suddenly cut off by apoplexy (February 1624), 'beloved and lamented' beyond all remembered example, 'because he was naturally inclined to do good without distinction of persons.'—*G. H. S.* The honour was therefore transferred to his nephew, Lord Gordon, son of the Marquis of Huntly.

1625. In July 1625, Lord Gordon made his first muster of the corps on the Links of Leith, in presence of several officers deputed by the French king for that purpose. These gentlemen had been conducted to Edinburgh by Sir Robert Gordon, Tutor of Sutherland; they were there entertained in the handsomest manner by the Lord Gordon and other nobles, 'and sent home again to their master, the French king, in great satisfaction and content.' Lord Gordon's younger brother, Lord Melgum, was his lieutenant, and the first gentleman of the company was Sir William Gordon, son of George Gordon of Kindroch, a branch of the family of Pitlurg.—*G. H. S.*

JUNE 20. '. . . . the king's picture in the hall of the palace of Linlithgow fell . . . . and brake in pieces. The like befell the king of France's picture, in that same place, six weeks before his death.' —*Cal.*

Such incidents were then invariably noted with superstitious awe. Aubrey tells us that on the first day of the sitting of the Long Parliament, the picture of Archbishop Laud fell in his closet, by the breaking of the string.[1]

George, Earl of Caithness, was one of the most unruly spirits of his age. The almost uncontrolled power which he possessed in his own remote country, was generally employed by him in advancing base and selfish purposes, and half his life was passed in a state of outlawry. Sometimes he is found at war with the Sutherland family, sometimes with his neighbours the Mackays of Strathnaver. One year, he is proclaimed a rebel; the next, he is found honoured with a royal commission against some other rebel. (See the account of the case of the Earl of Orkney in 1615.) He was overwhelmed with debt, yet did not regard it much. His son, Lord Berriedale, having become responsible for him, lay five years in the Tolbooth of Edinburgh, as a prisoner to the earl's creditors, while Caithness himself passed a pleasant life in his sea-cliff fortalices of Girnigo and Aikergill, in the far north. There must have been something plausible about this singular noble. Notwithstanding all the injuries he had inflicted on the Sutherland family, and the badness of his general character, he contrived, in 1619, to patch up a reconciliation with Sir Robert Gordon, a most respectable man, a friend and servant of the king,

[1] *Miscellanies*, p. 39.

and who represented the interests of that great family. He had 1623. on that occasion visited Sir Robert in Sutherland, and Sir Robert in his turn spent several days with the earl at Girnigo. The truce, however, was not of long continuance, for the Earl of Caithness's outrages were incessant. It was felt by the Privy Council as a scandal to the country, that such a hardy rebel against the ordinary authorities of the land should exist, and they looked about for the means of putting him down. The usual expedient of the age was resorted to—namely, to employ some other great man against him—thus accomplishing by a kind of private war what ought to have been the business of a force of their own. Sir Robert was the man they pitched upon.

Behold, then, this courtier of St James's and Newmarket, leaving those scenes in the south where he was accustomed to meet Bacon and (not many years ago) Shakspeare, and coming down to the land of Mackays, Guns, and Sinclairs, in order to conduct an army against one of those rude grandees who could even trouble a king. He had a strange associate in the enterprise; Lord Berriedale had been liberated from prison, on a paction with the creditors, that he might do what he could to bring his heartless father within the grasp of the law.

Sir Robert's forces were the Clan Sutherland and their friends, a selection of the most active and hardy, and all well armed. Assembling in Strathullie, and having been properly arranged and Sep. 3. officered, they lost no time in setting forth to cross the Ord. A company of the Clan Gun went before to clear the ground and prevent surprise. Before they had advanced far into Caithness, they learned that the earl, unable to withstand so great a force, had deserted the country, and taken refuge in Orkney, intending to go thence to Norway. At Latheron, James Sinclair of Murkle, Sir William Sinclair of Mey, the Laird of Forss, and some other Caithness magnates, came to yield their obedience and offer their assistance. Sir Robert received them with great civility, but 'gave small trust to some of them; neither suffered he any of the inhabitants to come in or go out of the army after the setting of the sun until sunrising.'

Passing Wick, he conducted his troops to Girnigo, a castle so strongly placed on the verge of a lofty cliff overhanging the sea, that there might have been some difficulty in taking it. The keys, however, were at once rendered up, and so the army took quiet possession of the fortress. They went forward, and, in like manner took Aikergill and Keiss, two forts which the earl had

1623. abandoned in succession. Meanwhile, Sir Robert had spies throughout all Caithness to report to him about the dispositions of the people. They were said to be quiet, but angry that any of the House of Sutherland should be charged with such a commission against their lord.

Learning that Lady Caithness, who was his cousin-german, had removed to a house a few miles distant, Gordon went to pay his respects to her. She pleaded for her husband, on the ground that he was not attempting any resistance; but Sir Robert left her no hopes of his being speedily pardoned. He proceeded with deliberation to settle Lord Berriedale in possession of the country and its fortresses, and made various other arrangements for its benefit; after which he returned in triumph to Dunrobin, and dismissed his men. 'Thus you see how the Earl of Caithness, having attained to the top of fortune's wheel, and to the height of his desires, by his service in Orkney, did by his own misdemeanours, and wicked actions, fall into this extremity, which a man of his life and conversation could not escape. Neither could the Earl of Orkney's example, which was recent before his eyes, divert him from the course which brought him to this misery. A notable example to posterity.'—*G. H. S.*

During the earlier half of this year, Scotland suffered under a famine of extreme severity. There was a vast increase to the usually inordinate number of beggars, in consequence of many of the poorer class of tenants throwing their farms in the hands of their landlords, and wandering forth in search of food. And it is remarked that the condition of these new mendicants was the most miserable of all, 'because they, being for the most part ashamed to beg, underlies all the extremities wherethrough the pinching of their bellies may affect them; whereas, by the contrair, strong and sturdy beggars, by their importunity and crying, and sometimes by extorting of almous, are in some measure relieved.'

JUNE 14. The administrators of the state are found in alarm that, unless something be done to enable the poor to tide over till the new harvest should be realised in September, 'numbers of them will betake themselves to live by stowth or [ere] they will starve through hunger, whilk will not only produce a foul imputation agains the whole land, but the wrath and anger of God will be wakened.' At the date noted, therefore, the Privy Council took measures for bringing the principal men together in their respective county towns to arrange for a taxation according to means and substance, in order to procure victual for the poor. A hundred merks for every thousand pounds of substance was the rate recommended. 1623.

In July, the famine 'increased daily, till at last many, both in burgh and land, died of hunger. Many poor came to Edinburgh for succour, of which number some died in the streets.' A fast was held on account of the calamity; 'the sermons began every day in the week at seven hours, and ended at nine. Immediately after the fast was ended, that same night, 7th of July, there was such a fire in the heaven, with thunder and fire-flaught, that the hearers and beholders thought verily that the day of judgment was come.'—*Cal.*

'There was this harvest-time ane great mortality . . . . ten or twelve died ordinarily every day [in Perth] from midsummer to Michaelmas' [September 29].—*Chron. Perth.*

It was probably to this famine that a story told by Wodrow refers. While the poor people were dying in great numbers in the fields, 'some people passing by saw a young child about seven years old, lying and dying by a dike-side—which could not but move their pity, though they could give it no relief. They observed the child to get up to its feet, and looking up cheerfully towards heaven, clapping its hands, making a tripping and dancing motion with its feet, they heard it cry: "O! Lamb's days for evermore! O! Lamb's days for evermore! I see heaven! Lamb's days for evermore!" And with that it presently fell down and died. I had this from my mother, who had it from her mother, and that it was told as a certain truth.'—*W. A.*

Bessie Smith, of Lesmahago, appeared before the presbytery of Lanark, and confessed sundry dealings with unlawful arts. She had 'charmed the heart-fevers.' The patients, kneeling under her direction, asked their health 'for God's sake, for Sanct Spirit, for Sanct Aikit, for the nine maidens that died in the boortree in the Ladywell Bank—This charm to be buik and beil to me, God grant that sae be.' She also 'appointed them the wayburn leaf, to be eaten nine mornings.'—*R. P. L.* JULY 10.

While the Egyptians were everywhere a proscribed race, and often the victims of an indiscriminate severity, there was one spot where mercy and even kindness seems to have been extended to them. This was Roslin. Sir William Sinclair of Roslin, Lord Justice-general under Queen Mary, riding home one day from JULY 15

1623. Edinburgh, found a poor Egyptian about to be hanged on the gibbet at the Burgh-moor, and brought him off unharmed. In remembrance of this kindness, 'the whole body of gipsies were accustomed to gather in the stanks [marshes] of Roslin every year, where they acted several plays during the months of May and June.' So tells us the quaint Father Hay, a connection of the Roslin family; and he adds: 'There are two towers which were allowed them for their residence, the one called Robin Hood, the other Little John.'

At the time noted, the Privy Council had their attention called to this Patmos of the outlawed race. They remark that, while the laws enjoined all persons in authority to execute to the deid the counterfeit thieves and limmers, the Egyptians,' it was nevertheless reported that a number of them were now within the bounds of Roslin, 'where they have a peaceable receipt and abode as if they were lawful subjects, committing stowths and reifs in all parts where they may find the occasion.' The Council, therefore, issued an order to the sheriff of the district, who happened to be Sinclair younger of Roslin himself, commanding him 'to pass, search, seek, hunt, follow, and pursue the said vagabond thieves and limmers,' and bring them to the Tolbooth of Edinburgh for due punishment.—*P. C. R.*

An order for the execution of a number of Egyptians was actually issued on the ensuing 27th of January.

Aug. 1. One Thomas Grieve was tried in Edinburgh for carrying on a species of medical practice by witchcraft. He was accused of having cured many people of heavy sickness and grievous diseases, by various magical arts; as, for instance, the making of signs and crosses upon them, the washing of their shirts in south-running streams, and the uttering of unknown words. He took sickness off a woman near Leslie, in Fife, and put it upon a cow, 'whilk thereafter ran wood [mad] and died.' He cured William Kirk's bairn in Tullibole, of the *morbus caducus*, 'by straiking back the hair of his head,' and wrapping the child in an anointed cloth, by that means putting him asleep. To cure diseased cattle, he sprinkled a byre with enchanted water. He passed various patients through a hasp of yarn three several times, and then threw the hasp into a fire, where it burned *blue;* thus the people were cured. He was alleged to have cured William Cousin's wife by manifest sorcery, 'causing her husband heat the coulter of his plough, and cool the same in water brought from Holywell of Hillside, thereafter making certain conjurations, crosses, and signs upon the water,' which he caused the patient to drink. One of the items in the dittay was, 'curing James Mudie, his wife and children, of the fever; in curing his wife, by causing ane great fire to be put on, and ane hole to be made in the north side of the house, and ane quick hen to be put furth thereat, at three several times, and ta'en in at the house-door withershins [contrary to the course of the sun]; thereafter taking the hen, and putting it under the sick woman's oxter or arm, and therefra carrying it to the fire, where it was halden doun and burnt quick therein.' 1623.

The assize, having read the depositions of sundry parish ministers, and being 'ripely advised,' sentenced Thomas to be strangled at a stake and burnt.—*Pit.*

'. . . . about nine hours at night, there appeared like a rainbow in the west, the moon shining clearly in the east, with some rain in the meantime, whereat many wondered.'—*Cal.* Nov. 30.

1624. Jan.

From Martinmas of the preceding year to the end of January in the present, there was a hard continuous frost, which, after a slight thaw, was resumed, and lasted till the 23d of February. During this time, 'eleven carts, with twenty-one puncheons of wine, came over upon the ice from Dundee here.'—*Chron. Perth.*

'About the midst of Januar, four gentlemen of good credit, having gone out of Stirling some two miles or thereby, to pass their time, heard sensibly like the shots of many muskets, and after that, taking better heed, like the beating upon drums, and playing upon piffers and the sound of trumpets; and last of all, the shot of great cannons; so that for fear they went back again to the town, and reported what they had heard.'—*Cal.*

The Town Council of Aberdeen had occasion to consider an abuse which had lately crept into their burgh, in the form of 'costly banqueting at the baptising of bairns,' and the 'convocating of great numbers of people thereto.' It is mentioned that, on these occasions, there were 'all sorts of succours [sugars], confections, spiceries, and dessert, brought from foreign parts, beside great superfluity of venison, and wild meat of all sorts . . . . and withal, extraordinary drinking and scolling [health-drinking] . . . . to the slander of the town, in sic a calamitous time, when God is visiting the whole land with dearth and famine, and mony poor Feb. 18.

1624. anes [are] dying and starving at dykes and under stairs for cauld and hunger.'

The Council ordained that hereafter no person of whatever degree should have 'mae than four gossips and four cummers at the maist' at their baptisms, that not more than six women be invited 'to convoy the bairn to and frae the kirk,' and that twelve should be the utmost amount of company present 'at the dinner, supper, or afternoon's drink.' All extravagances at table were at the same time strictly forbidden.

MAY 25. The wappinshaw was a periodical muster of the irregular armed force of the country; it got its name from the more immediate purpose of the assembly—namely, an exhibition of weapons. At Dunfermline, on this day, while a wappinshaw was going on, 'William Anderson, son till John Anderson, bailiff of the said town, and Charles Richeson, his servant, being shooting a shot with some of their friends in a certain place of the town, [a little piece of the lunt flieth upon a thack-house, which easily kindled. The fire increased with the violency of the wind[1]], and did flie from house to house, and sometimes wald flie over ane house without doing it any harm, but wald burn the next house, till the great admiration of all men; so that this fire burnt so meikle of the town, that, excepted the abbey and the kirk thereof, the tenth part were not free of it. This, by the judgment of all the beholders, was thought till have been some divinity, or some witchcraft, rather nor this foresaid accidental fire.'—*Jo. H.*

'The fire began at twelve hours, and burnt the whole town, some few sclate houses excepted, before four afternoon; goods and geir within houses, malt and victual in kilns and barns, were consumed.' —*Cal.*

The town of Dunfermline consisted at this time of 120 houses, containing 287 families.—*Bal.*

There was a collection in the parish churches for 'the support of the town of Dunfermline, burnt with fire' (*R. P. L.*); and, in June 1625, King Charles I. ordered £500 sterling to be added to the fund for the relief of the poorer class of sufferers.—*P. C. R.*

MAY. The Clan Chattan or MacIntosh, seated in the centre of Inverness-shire, were dependents of the Earls of Moray. None had entered more heartily into the revenge of the Bonny Earl's

[1] Calderwood.

death against the Marquis of Huntly, and for this service they had obtained certain lands from the Moray family. Now, that the Earl of Moray was reconciled with Huntly, he did not see any occasion longer to patronise or favour the MacIntoshes; so he attempted to remove them from the lands formerly conferred upon them. 'This the Clan Chattan could hardly endure,' says Sir Robert Gordon: about Whitsuntide, assembling five hundred men under their infant chief's uncle, Lachlan MacIntosh [afterwards, by the by, a stout loyalist in the Civil War], 'they keepit the fields in their Highland weed upon foot, with swords, bows, arrows, targets, hagbuts, pistols, and other Highland arms, and first began to rob and spulyie the earl's tenants (who laboured their possessions) of their haill goods, geir, insight plenishing [household furniture], horse, nolt, sheep, corns, and cattle, and left them nothing that they could get within their bounds; syne fell in sorning throughout Moray, Stratherrick, Urquhart, Ross, Sutherland, Brae of Mar, and divers other parts, taking their meat and food perforce where they could not get it willingly, frae friends as well as frae their foes, yet still kept themselves from shedding of innocent blood.' 1624.

The Earl of Moray first brought a band of Monteith Highlanders against these marauders; but the expedition seems to have failed. Another enterprise of the same kind was no more successful. It was not till he went to London, and procured a power of lieutenancy in the north from the king, that he brought the MacIntoshes to subjection. The affair had a very characteristic ending. 'Some slight loons [poor fellows], followers of the Clan Chattan, were execute; but the principal outbreakers and malefactors were spared and never troubled.' Further, the 'honest men' who had disobeyed the order for refusing all supply to the MacIntoshes, being put to trial, the odd scene was presented of the criminals standing as witnesses against them; and while these culprits obtained pardon, their humane resetters 'were soundly fined in as great sums as their estates might bear, and some above their estates were fined, and every one warded within the Tolbooth of Elgin, till the last mite was paid.'—*Spal.* 'The fines were granted by his majesty to the Earl of Moray, as the fines for resetting the Clan Gregor were given to the Earl of Argyle; but these fines did not much advantage either of these two earls.' —*G. H. S.*

Dissent from the 'comely order' of church matters was still JUNE 10.

1624. making itself apparent. We hear at this time of many people in Edinburgh holding private meetings for religious exercises, in contempt of the ordinary services of their regular pastors in the parish churches. 'Like as they have assumed to these their seditious conventicles the name of Congregations, and done what in them lies falsely to impress on the hearts of his majesty's people a persuasion that his majesty persecutes the sincere professors of true religion, and introduces corruption in the church-government.' Considering how such practices 'brought forth damnable sects of Anabaptists, Families of Love, Brownists, Arminians, Illuminati, and mony such pests, enemies to religion, authority, and peace, and occasions the murder of millions of people,' the Privy Council thought proper to issue a proclamation, strictly forbidding all such meetings.

The Council had at the same time before them a set of Edinburgh citizens, partly the same as those whom the king had proposed to banish a few years before[1]—namely, William Rig of Aitherny, one of the bailies, John Hamilton, apothecary, John Mean, merchant, and John Dickson, 'flesher'—who had again come into collision with the ecclesiastical authorities. At the usual congregational meeting before the celebration of the communion, Rig—'puffed up,' says Spottiswoode, 'by a conceit of his own abilities'—took it upon him to challenge Dr Forbes 'for sundry points of doctrine delivered by him in his sermons.' Dr Forbes was a man of remarkable learning and dignity of character, for which reasons he was in time appointed bishop of Edinburgh by Charles I. It did not seem to him proper that he should be liable to the censure of a lay citizen, and he therefore declined to listen to the bailie. Rig then openly threatened the clergy, 'that, unless they returned to the old form of administering the holy communion, the whole people would forsake them;' and in this he was supported by his friends Mean, Hamilton, and Dickson. The Council took the affair up as an attempt to produce a schism in the church and a violation of the law. They answered, however —if we are to believe one of their own party—'so wisely, punctually, and modestly, that the Council admired them.' They were, nevertheless, to satisfy the king, sent to various prisons, as guilty of a misdemeanour. They 'remained there, till by great dealing, pains, and moyen, they were relieved again.'—*Row.*

William Rig and John Mean appear, from the report of their

[1] See under March 30, 1620.

contemporary and friend, Mr John Livingstone, to have been earnest Christians of the evangelical type. Rig was 'much exercised in spirit, and of great experience in the ways of God. I have been several times with him in private meetings, and observed that when he prayed, he began with bitter and heavy complaints and confession beyond any. He spent his income chiefly on pious uses.' Mean 'used both summer and winter to rise about three o'clock in the morning, and always, as he put on his clothes, he used to sing some part of a psalm, and then went to his closet, where he was employed in religious exercises till six. By that time, the rest of his family being got up, he worshipped with them, and then went to his shop. He was so much master of the Scripture, [that] though he had been half sleeping, he could have corrected readers if they miscalled or wrong cited ony scripture.'[1] 1624.

During the time when the king was pressing on the innovations in the church, dissentients of this kind were rising everywhere throughout the southern districts of Scotland, many of them lairds, a few of them nobles, but most of them belonging to the middle classes of society. Of the lairds, Livingstone enumerates Halhill (Fife), Crosshill (Lanarkshire), Cunningham-head, Cessnock, and Rowallan (Ayrshire). There was also a number of ladies, some of them of noble birth, who embraced and strongly held fast the evangelical views. Such were Margaret Countess of Wigton, Anne Marchioness of Hamilton, the Countess of Eglintoun, and Lady Loudon. For the time, these people, as well as the more earnest of the clergy, were kept silent under the frown of an imperious government, or made themselves but little heard; but the fire burned not the less intensely for being covered up; and when the time for resistance came, it was ready to break forth with the greater violence that it had been so long suppressed.

Almost as a matter of course, while these Presbyterian recusants were in hands, the state authorities took some order with papistry. John Gordon of Craig in Aberdeenshire had attracted their notice as 'an excommunicat trafficking papist,' who, not content with blaspheming the truth and its preachers himself, did all that he could to 'withhold his people from coming to the kirk, boasting [threatening] some, and persuading others;' thus, it is alleged, 'he steirs up mony not weel satled in their religion to imitate him in his contemptuous and

[1] *Life of John Livingstone*, Glasgow, 1754, p. 89.

1624. lawless proceedings, and in effect has cassen that pairt of the JULY 1. country lowss.' The Council now charged Gordon to appear and answer for his offences. They likewise despatched an order to the magistrates of Aberdeen, for the routing up of a set of Catholics who for some time had been allowed to live peaceably there, commanding that they be taken and warded till further orders.—*P. C. R.* The government could calculate with tolerable security on the feeling of the great bulk of the people, that by thus striking a blow at popery, they would be allowed without much remonstrance to deal that severity towards puritanism which would frighten it from a troublesome opposition to the now semi-episcopalian establishment.

John Gordon of Craig was obliged for the time to leave the kingdom; but somehow the king was always forgiving to papists, and we accordingly find that in January 1625, having made submission and promised good behaviour in future, this 'excommunicat trafficking papist' was allowed to return to Scotland (*P. C. R.*), but not ultimately to rest there, as will hereafter be seen.

JULY 21. A Border thief, described as Adie Usher in Birkinhaugh, servant of Robert Elliot of Redheugh, was condemned and hanged at Edinburgh for sundry acts of cattle-stealing. In most of his proceedings he had been accompanied by his son, Willie Usher, a mere boy, who was also presented for trial, but spared on account of his youth.—*Pit.* After Willie Usher had spent some months in the Thieves' Hole in Edinburgh, the Lords of the Privy Council received a complaint from him, 'heavily regretting his hard estate and condition by his detention, thir mony owks bygane, miserably in ward in the Thieves' Hole of Edinburgh, without possibility or mean to entertein himself, he being a young innocent boy not past the age of fourteen years, and his umwhile father having underlain his punishment and sufferit death for the crime laid to the said Willie's charge.' The Lords consequently ordered the magistrates 'to attend the commodity of some ship going to the Low Countries,' and see Willie set aboard thereof, 'and mak intimation to the said Willie that if at ony time hereafter he sall return without licence, it sall be capital unto him.'—*P. C. R.*

The master of Adie Usher seems to have been under suspicion of a concern in his delinquencies. In November, when about to fly from the city on account of infection, the Privy Council entered an order in the case of Lady Jean Stewart, whose husband, Robert

Elliot of Redheugh, had been for some time a prisoner in the Tolbooth of Edinburgh. She had represented 'the utter distress, misery, and want whereunto she and her poor children are reduced, having contracted great debts and impandit her abulyiements and clothes for enterteinment of her husband in ward—and she is brocht to that pitch of necessity, that she has nowther means to live nor credit to afford him ony further supply.' The Council ordered her a hundred merks for past charges, and granted her the sum of 'threttein shillings and four pennies' during pleasure—apparently meaning a daily allowance of 1s. 1⅓d. sterling.—*P. C. R.* 1624.

Poland is described as in this age swarming with Scotch pedlers. Its port, Dantzig, contained a number of settled merchants of a respectable order, some of whom were seen from time to time returning to their native country with considerable realised wealth. Formerly, the Scotch merchants at Dantzig, having a kind of rule and governance among themselves, lived in such a way as to secure the esteem of the people of the country. But latterly, 'discipline being dissolved, the most part of them use such a dissolute form of living, that they are odious to the inhabitants, hurtful to themselves, and despised by strangers, to the great ignominy of the whole nation.' There was also a continual immigration of multitudes of miserable, debauched, and weakly people from Scotland, including 'exorbitant numbers of young boys and maids unfit for any service,' reminding us of the overflowings of the Irish population into England, Scotland, and the United States of America in more recent days.[1] During this summer, owing, doubtless, to the pressure of the famine, this scandalous system had been carried to such a height, that the Scotch merchants were threatened with expulsion from the city. In this exigency, they wrote to the king, craving his intercession. Patrick Gordon, who acted as agent for the king in Dantzig, also wrote, apparently, at the same time, shewing how matters stood, and entreating that some order and rule should be established among his countrymen, as they should not otherwise be able much longer to withstand the strength of their enemies.[2] Aug. 30.

The king wrote to the Earl of Mar, requesting him to send Nov. 1.

[1] *Letters of Reign of James VI.*, p. 368.

[2] See the undated letter of Gordon, *Analecta Scot.* ii. 286. Patrick Gordon was the person who had acted for the king in prosecuting poor Stercovius to the gallows for a satire on the Scottish nation. See pp. 448, 449.

1621. into Argyleshire and Glenorchy, for four or five couples of *earth-dogs* (terriers), which he was desirous of obtaining in order to transmit them to France. His majesty further requested 'that ye have a special care that the oldest of them be not passing three years of age, and that ye send them not all in one ship, but some in one ship, and other some in another, lest one ship should miscarry.'[1]

The same Earl of Mar, having to spend the winter of 1631 in Stirling, and designing to amuse himself with fox-hunting, sent a letter to his cousin, the Laird of Glenurchy, entreating the favour of 'a couple of good earth-dogs;' and adding, what shews the importance of the favour, 'I pray you use me as familiarly as I do you, for without ceremony, cousin, you shall not have a friend over whom ye have greater power than over me.' *P. S.*—'What ye send me, let it be good, although it be but one.'

Nov. 2. There is at this time a glimpse of rationality regarding witchcraft in the public authorities, in as far as the Privy Council deemed it right to hesitate about the granting of commissions for the trial of persons charged with that crime. The Council had been troubled by the importunity of persons seeking for such commissions, and at the same time concerned to find that the informations on which the commissions were sought for 'seemed to be very obscure and dark.' As anxious for the truth, and to the intent that neither should the innocent be molested nor the guilty escape, they now arranged that all informations should henceforth pass through the hands of the bishop of the diocese, 'to be seen and considered by him, and such of the ministry as he shall call unto him.'—*P. C. R.*

We have here a revelation of that doubt about the reality of witchcraft which is suspected to have lurked in the minds of all the principal official people throughout the seventeenth century. It was a time of comparative triumph for the established church. The bishops were not particularly in need of popularity. They could afford to be easy with both Romanists and necromancers. It was precisely in such circumstances that we could expect to find the chief administrative body letting slip a doubt as to the soundness of many of the alleged instances of sorcery lately subjected to trial.

Nov. 23. The pest, which had been for some time before in Holland,

[1] *Mait. Club Misc.*, iii. 344.

broke out 'in sundry houses in Edinburgh, to the great terror of the whole town. It began in Paul Hay[1] a merchant's house, a month before, and was not known till now; therefore the more dangerous, because hard to discern the clean from the unclean. Upon the last day of November, the president and other lords of Council and Session, meeting together, resolve to rise, and continue the session till the 8th of Januar.'—*Cal.* 1624.

One consequence of the occurrence of the pest at this time was, that the king's design of enforcing a communion at Christmas, where all the people should kneel, was frustrated. Another result generally satisfactory was a relaxation of the severity against the Edinburgh citizens who were banished and imprisoned for opposing the new ceremonies. William Rig was allowed to leave his prison of Blackness, and remain for fifteen days with his wife at his house of Morton, where she was 'very heavily visite with infirmity and sickness.' Mean, having 'a numerous family and his wife grit with child, and nane to have ane care for order-taking with them, how they sall be providit for and governit in this [time of] danger,' was in like manner permitted to repair to Edinburgh, to see after them, and there remain till the 15th of January. So also John Hamilton was relieved from the Tolbooth to attend on his wife, who chanced to be in the same delicate condition as Mrs Mean. After all, 'the pest raged not; few houses were infected with it; so that it appeared the chief end wherefore the Lord had sent it, was to disappoint the king by scattering the people.'—*Cal.*

Amidst the alarms regarding the pest, people heard of a strange case of personal quarrel and vindictiveness. One William Hamilton, a soldier, son of the deceased William Hamilton, 'called of Inchmachan,' was lately come from the Low Countries, avowing 'a settled purpose and resolution to appeal Captain Harie Bruce to the single combat, or otherwise to watch the opportunity to bereave him of his life.' The Privy Council was obliged to take means for preventing a hostile collision.—*P. C. R.* Dec.

The Privy Council readily apprehended that the prosecution of 'this damnable and cruel intention' would both breed danger to the parties and produce great trouble and controversy among their friends, to the disturbance of his majesty's peace, if timous remeed be not provided. They therefore summoned the parties before them to give assurance of their good behaviour. Dec. 3.

[1] 'Wha had brought money with the infection from Danskein.'—*Chron. Perth.*

1624. Deeming, as was formerly remarked, anything that illustrates the progress of the arts as worthy of notice in this record, though perhaps trifling in itself, we may advert to Mr Alexander Hamilton, brother to the secretary Earl of Melrose, as having now obtained a patent of twenty-one years for a new *cart* invented by him, 'wherein greater weight and burdens may with far less force be drawn, and conveniently carried, than hath been done with ony other kind of cart hitherto known or heretofore used.'[1]

'Sandy Hamilton,' or 'Dear Sandy,' as he was called, was a man of note on account of his skill in some of the useful arts, particularly in those connected with the munitions of war. He practised these arts for some time in Germany, whence he was recalled to England, where the king granted him pensions and allowances to the amount of £800 sterling *per annum*. When the Civil War broke out, he joined his countrymen, and helped to fit out the Covenanting army of 1640 with a species of short but effective gun, which was carried slung between two horses, and the serviceableness of which was proved at the battle of Newburn-ford, when the Scots crossed the Tyne in the face of the enemy and became masters of Newcastle.

In this year we have the latest known notice of a woman of extraordinary attainments who had lived for many years in Edinburgh, practising an art in which she was long after pronounced to have never been excelled. Caligraphy, or the art of beautiful writing, was in greater vogue in the seventeenth century than in our more utilitarian days. Under what circumstances Esther Inglis, a Frenchwoman residing in the Scottish capital, came to give her days to so laborious an art, we do not learn. Neither are we aware how it was that Esther came to live in the Scottish capital. There, however, we find her, so early as 1599, writing one of the little manuscript volumes which have given her celebrity. This book, preserved in the Bodleian Library, is entitled *Les Proverbes de Salomon, escrites en diverses sortes de Lettres, par Esther Anglois, Françoise. A Lislesbourg en Ecosse.* 1599. 'This delicate performance,' says Ballard,[2] 'gains the admiration of all who see it; every chapter is wrote in a different hand; as is the dedication, and some other things at the beginning of the book, which makes near forty several sorts of hands. The

[1] Extract from *Privy Council Record*, *Edin. Mag.*, Oct. 1817.

[2] *Memoirs of Several Ladies of Great Britain*, p. 268.

beginnings and endings of the chapters are adorned with most 1621.
beautiful head and tail pieces, and the margins are elegantly decorated with the pen, in imitation, I suppose, of the beautiful old manuscripts. The book is dedicated to the Earl of Essex, Queen Elizabeth's great favourite. At the beginning are his arms, neatly drawn, with all its quarterings—in number fifty-six. In the fifth leaf is her own picture, done with the pen, in the habit of that time. In her right hand, a pen, the left resting upon a book opened; in one of the leaves of which is written *De l'Eternel le bien: de moi le mal, ou rien.* On the table before her there is likewise a music-book lying open, which perhaps intimates that she had some skill in that art. Under the picture is an epigram in Latin, made by Andrew Melvin; and on the next page another, composed by the same author, which is as follows:

> Æmula naturæ manus exprimit una figuras
> Mille, animans pictis Signa pusilla notis,
> Signa creans animata, polûm spirantia signa:
> Quæ picturata margine limbus obit.
> Mirum opus: at mage mira Manus; mira omnia vincit
> Mens manui moderans, dum manus urget opus.
> ANDRÆUS MELVINUS.

Thus translated into English:

> One hand dame nature's mimic does express
> Her larger figures, to the life, in less.
> In the rich border of her work do stand,
> Afresh created by her curious hand,
> The various signs and planets of the sky,
> Which seem to move and twinkle in our eye.
> Much we the work, much more the hand admire,
> Her fancy guiding this does raise our wonder higher.'

Another of Esther's transcripts was entitled *Historiæ Memorabiles Genesis*, 1600. A copy of the French Psalms, written by her, and presented to Queen Elizabeth, is in the library of Christ Church, Oxford. There is also in the Bodleian a manuscript of hers, entitled *Les Vingts et Six Quatrains de Guy de Faur, Sieur de Pybrac, escrits par Esther Inglis, pour son dernier Adieu, ce* 21 *Jour de Juin* 1617. It seems to have been a gift to the celebrated Dr Hall—subsequently Bishop of Norwich—on parting from him at the time of the king's visit to Scotland. The latest known of Esther's works is a volume preserved in the Royal Library, *Esther Inglis's Fifty Emblems,* dated at Edinburgh 1624.

When the king was at Stirling, Esther's son presented to him

1624. a little book entitled *Sidus Celeste,* and he experienced some of James's good-natured patronage in consequence. In June 1620, Esther is found addressing the king in behalf of this son, who, having completed a school-course, 'would gladly follow theology.' But 'as Dædalus was not able to free himself of his imprisonment in the isle Creta but by the help of wings made of pens and wax, even so my son is not able to free himself of inability to effectuate this his affection, but by the wings of your majesty's letter, composed by pen and wax, through which he may wing his flight happily to some fellowship, either in Cambridge or Oxford, as occasion sall fall out.' If so far favoured by his majesty, 'I may have my tossed mind relieved of the great care I have perpetually for this said youth.'—*An. Scot.*

Ballard states, on the authority of a memorandum of Hearne, the antiquary, that Esther Inglis was married to a Scotsman, named Bartholomew Kello, and had a son, named Samuel Kello, who was educated at Christ Church College, Oxford, and was afterwards minister at Speckshall, in Suffolk.

1625. Mar. 'At this time arose great discontentment betwixt the provost, bailies, and council of Edinburgh, and their ministers, because the ministers had procured the king's letter and direction to the magistrates and council, for augmentation of their yearly stipends. They were not content with twelve hundred merks for every one, beside their house mail [rent], which was more than their predecessors, worthier than they, had, but importunately craved two thousand. The people,' says the zealous Presbyterian historian, 'detested them for their ambition, their avarice, and malice at honest and godly professors. They were well fingerfed in other men's houses, howbeit they had sufficient to maintain them at home.'—*Cal.*

In June 1626, Charles I. enjoined the magistrates to give each of their ministers £100 sterling of yearly stipend, with a free house.—*Bal.*

Mar. 30. The news of the death of King James—which occurred on the 27th of March—reached Edinburgh on the 30th, at the outbreak of a storm of extraordinary violence which raged along the whole coast, destroying much shipping, and throwing down several harbours. 'The water raise above the harbour of Leith, and ran into the houses of the town; yea, the boats and barks within the same floated so above the shore, that some of them were cast away upon the sides of the houses; and great ships therein could not be keepit, with all their anchors and cables, from doing great skaith, ilk ane to ane other, whereof the like was never heard tell of in our days. Sundry mariners, keeping their ships [fra] skaith, were hurt themselves, and in special James Langlands and Robert Dury, two masters of ships, very expert in that art, were baith cast away, working for the relief of their awn ships.'—*Jo. H.* 1625.

'The like harm was done in sundry other parts upon the coast along the Firth, in Saltpreston, Kirkcaldy, Ardross, and other parts. Salt-pans were overthrown, ships and boats broken, coal-heughs beside Culross drowned. The like of this tempest was not seen in our time, nor the like of it heard in this country in any age preceding. It was taken by all men to be a forerunner of some great alteration. And, indeed, the day following—to wit, the last of March—sure report was brought hither from court, that the king departed this life, the Lord's day before, the 27th of March.' —*Cal.*

This was long after remembered as the storm of the *Borrowing Days,* such being a popular appellation for the last three days of March, as expressed in a well-known popular rhyme. It is a proverbial observation of the weather, which seems to be justified by fact, the bad weather being connected with the vernal equinox.

END OF VOL. I.

Edinburgh:
Printed by W. and R. Chambers.

House of Robert Gourlay, a rich Edinburgh Citizen of 1574.
See pages 143 and 255.

CPSIA information can be obtained
at www.ICGtesting.com
Printed in the USA
LVHW111234230223
740172LV00005B/341

9 783382 307141